A CAUSE UNTRUE

David Blacker

Perera - Hussein Publishing House

Published by the Perera-Hussein Publishing House, 2005
ISBN: 955-8897-06-X

First Edition

Cover photograph by Dhammika Dharmawardene.
Cover design by David Blacker.
Printed and bound in Sri Lanka by Samayawardhana

To Recce Group Charlie,
6th Singha Rifles, for taking me there,
and to Antje, for bringing me back.

A CAUSE UNTRUE

David Blacker

A thing is not necessarily true just because a man dies for it.
— Oscar Wilde

Perera - Hussein Publishing House

CONTENTS

FIRE.. 1

SHAPE.. 9

TEETH... 137

SMOKE & DUST..................................... 553

EPILOGUE... 580

GLOSSARY.. 593

FIRE

The heaven shall burn at five and forty degrees,
The fire shall come near the great new city...
— Nostradamus

He missed that first cigarette. Easing back in his seat, Captain Dennis Swanson pushed his aviator glasses up his nose. Just moments earlier he had put his American Airlines Boeing 767 onto its northwest heading before switching to autopilot. He licked his lips and cursed softly, as he had done on every single one of his flights for the last five years.

It was that perfect moment, fifteen minutes into the flight, when the adrenalin of the takeoff had died down and the radio waves were calm. He had quit the smokes five years ago, almost to the day, and never missed them, except for that exact same moment of each flight.

At forty-five, with a wife and two teenaged daughters, and an already well-established paunch to match his thinning blonde hair, Swanson had decided that his pack a day, twenty-year-old habit had to go. Or at least Jenny had decided for him; and Jenny's decisions were something he had long ago come to realize weren't things to go against. He had been between airlines, taking six months off to build their new summer holiday home in California, and it had seemed a good time to do it.

It was, nevertheless, at moments like this that Swanson missed the smoky pain of that first drag. Of course, it would have meant fuck all these days since all flights were non-smoking anyway, and it didn't matter if you were one of the most experienced captains around or not.

Absently he listened to his co-pilot, First Officer Roger Pacini check the weather patterns for any unexpected changes on their scheduled flight path from Boston to Los Angeles. All clear.

Before Swanson could call for coffee, Pacini started off on his usual routine. Swanson knew the man had a subscription to some online joke page or another, and wouldn't be satisfied until he had shared his daily humour fix with someone. If Swanson was to shut his co-pilot up, he knew from experience that the man would target some unfortunate stew, and Swanson would have to listen anyway. Besides, if it was an off-colour story, as it almost invariably was, Swanson knew he'd have a snappy crewmember for the rest of the flight. Sighing inaudibly, he settled down to listen.

"There's this pair of geriatric lovebirds in an old folk's home, see?" started off Pacini. "They're both around ninety, the guy's name is George and the gal's is Sara. Each evening, after supper, George pulls his dick out and places it in Sara's hand. She holds it for about twenty minutes, and they both get their kicks outta this. One evening, George announces that it's all off and that he's dumping Sara for Ethel — one of the other bats in the home. Sara's pissed off and asks George, 'What has she got that I don't?' George replies, 'Parkinson's!'"

Swanson groaned as Pacini gave way to chuckles. An uncle on his father's side had had Parkinson's disease for many years before his death, and there had been very little that was funny about the symptoms. Of course, he reasoned, Pacini had no way of knowing about his uncle, but it was still a rather insensitive anecdote, and he was tempted to tell him so, but didn't. Instead, he reached for the button that would tell the stews he was ready for his first caffeine fix of the flight. Thank God you could still have as much coffee as you could stomach on a single trip.

"D'you realize," he pointed out, "that if we were to lose an engine right now and go straight in, the FAA will soon be listening to that crap on CVR?"

"Shit, Dennis, the engines are perfect, and even if they weren't, I'd look at it as my last will and testament."

The stew, all blonde hair and flashing teeth, walked in with the specially ground first-class coffee, the cockpit filling with her perfume for an instant before the aroma of coffee pouring into the plastic cups slammed welcomingly into Swanson's senses like a dark wall.

"Do you guys wanna have breakfast with the rest of the world back there?" the stew asked, giving Swanson a generous glimpse of her cleavage as she set the coffee down. "I can send Barb up here when she's done with the drinks service."

"Naw, Kathy." Swanson waved a hand as he picked up a cup with the other. "You know I never eat breakfast."

He'd almost said 'honey', but dropped it at the last moment. You couldn't risk any sexual harassment charges in your file these days. He'd known Kathy Roberts for at least a couple of years, and she was fairly easy going, but you never could tell. He remembered wistfully the days when a stew bending over to serve you coffee was an invitation to run your hand up her skirt.

"Bagels, if you got 'em," Pacini cut in with a grin, and Swanson was thankful that he'd got the joke done with.

"Yes, sir, your highness."

Kathy turned away, tossing long hair over her shoulder, but Swanson noticed that she held Pacini's gaze a couple of beats longer than was generally deemed platonic. He wondered momentarily if she was screwing Pacini, but then decided not. Pacini was married and seemingly devoted to his family, but then again. . .

The co-pilot was twelve years younger than Swanson and deeply tanned; a non-smoking fitness freak with a body that was — at least to Swanson — annoyingly trim and muscular. The man's dark hair was kept razored to a barely discernible fuzz that was nevertheless uniformly dense on all parts of his scalp. Wait 'til that bald spot appears, boyo, Swanson smiled inwardly. You'll wish you enjoyed your hair when you'd had it. The thought that Pacini might never have thinning hair was too depressing for the older pilot to even consider.

As Kathy reached for the door, it seemed to Swanson as he craned his neck to eye her firm buttocks, that everything went into slow-motion. It was like his days with the Texas Air National Guard, losing an engine and bringing his Galaxy in on just three, everything going to shit around him, but his mind clear and sharp, his senses taking in everything and his reflexes reacting appropriately. Kathy's hand was on the door when it exploded open, slamming her back against Pacini's seat. A swarthy man in a button-down shirt was into the cockpit in the blink of an eye, moving with heart stopping speed. His right elbow smashed Kathy out of the way with enough force to send her stumbling to her knees, and he reached across with his left hand and grabbed Pacini under the jaw, jerking him back into his seat.

The cockpit doorway seemed to be filling with people, and Swanson saw a second stew — Barbara whatever — shoved in, her face tearful, dark hair falling across her eyes. The snarling, moustachioed man behind the young woman had her twisted up in an arm lock. He held some sort of brightly coloured, plastic-handled knife to her throat, its small square blade glinting dully in the cockpit lights.

A wall of sound seemed to follow them into the cockpit from the cabin area. Screams of fear cut through with the bark of commands. Just before the door slammed shut, Swanson caught a glimpse of a passenger sprawled in the aisle, blood soaking into the carpet beneath him. A dark-haired man in a business suit stood over him, pushing terrified people into seats.

"We have a bomb!" the man roared.

Then, the hijacker holding Barbara — and Swanson was in no doubt that this was what it was, a hijack — kicked the door shut, cutting off the scene. Everything seemed to freeze, with one man holding Barbara, Kathy half crouching, half kneeling in the far corner, and Pacini pinned back in his seat by the hand that gripped him under his chin. Half-turned in his own seat, struggling to rise, Swanson was staring into his co-pilot's bulging eyes as the hijacker cut Pacini's throat with two quick moves, using an identical knife to the one his partner was holding on Barbara.

A bright red fountain of arterial blood splashed forward against the cockpit glass as Pacini gurgled and died, splattering in diminishing spurts across the instrument panel.

With a soft moan, Barbara sagged in the second hijacker's grasp. Her pantyhose darkened as urine flowed down her legs and over her captor's shoes. The man ignored the hot liquid, tightening his hold on the stew.

Leaning across, Pacini's killer ripped Swanson's lip mike and earphones off his head, throwing them to the floor.

This is it, I'm gonna die, Swanson told himself. We're all gonna die. But why, what do they want? No one hijacks domestic flights. This has to be some insane prank. Prank? *Prank?* They just cut Roger's throat, and you're next and then they'll kill Barbara and Kathy and everybody else back there and no one will know why or how we died and who's gonna tellJennythatI'mdeadandthat *wait! WAIT!* I'm the pilot! They won't kill me. Pilots aren't killed by hijackers. Not this early, anyway. They'll want something, they'll wanna go somewhere. They *need* me, man. Calm down, play their game, you're responsible for your crew, your plane.

"Who are you?" Swanson blurted, his voice tight in his throat as he tried to keep himself under control. His eyes kept jumping from the clean-shaven hijacker to Pacini's blood dripping down the glass of the canopy. "What d'you want to—"

"Shutupp!" the man snarled. His eyes danced nervously, but he was totally calm, his hands rock steady. "Do not speak. Do not *move*. Do not do anything that I do not tell you to." The man had a Middle Eastern accent that Swanson immediately recognized. "My men have bombs and knives aboard this plane. Several passengers are already dead. We will blow everything up if you do not follow my instructions. And you will be the next to die." He nodded towards the second hijacker. "My associate and I are both trained pilots, we do not need you. You live only because we wish it."

He moved round till he was standing behind Swanson, his bloody fist resting on the captain's shoulder, the blade of the knife — some sort of box-cutter, Swanson realized — touching his throat.

"Keep the autopilot on. If you touch any of the controls you will die on the spot. If you understand, nod your head, do *not* speak."

Swanson nodded, feeling warm stickiness on his skin.

"You will get up now and remove your co-pilot from his seat. Now!"

Swanson rose shakily and un-strapped Pacini's body, grabbing it as it lolled forward. Holding it under the arms, he struggled to lift the body. He could smell the stink of shit as Pacini's bowels opened.

"Quick! Quick!" The hijacker waved his knife. "Put him on the floor."

Kathy tried to get to her feet as the body was laid in front of her, but the second hijacker's foot lashed out, catching her hard in the ribs. Choking for air she slumped back against the bulkhead.

The smell in the cockpit was now overpowering, a mix of shit, blood, urine, and raw terror. Barbara seemed to be on the verge of collapse, her captor holding her up as she sobbed.

Grabbing Swanson by the collar, the hijacker who had killed Pacini, the one who seemed to be in command, swung the pilot back towards his seat.

"Sit down and strap in."

"Look," Swanson began, "I don't know who you are, but if you tell me where you want to go—"

"Hani," the hijacker snapped to his partner.

Without any hesitation, the second hijacker brought his right arm across the front of Barbara, stabbing the short stubby blade into the left side of her neck. Digging in deep, he dragged it across her throat in a single motion, cutting jugular, carotid, and windpipe in a single swipe. Blood frothed across the cockpit for a second time, and now everything seemed to be covered with it. The hijacker let Barbara's knees buckle, dropping her to the floor next to Pacini. Without batting an eye he then grabbed Kathy by her hair and jerked her in front of him. He held her in the exact way the dead woman had been held moments before. His eyes looked questioningly at his partner.

His gaze calmly on Swanson, the other hijacker raised his hand in restraint. Swanson's mind was now blank, on the edge of insanity; his limbs were shaking so badly he practically collapsed into his seat, his fingers struggling with the harness.

The hijack commander didn't bother gloating. He knew the message had got through. He strapped himself quickly into the co-pilot's seat, ignoring the blood that soaked into his shirt. He slipped the dead man's headphones and mike on.

"Take the plane off autopilot," he told Swanson, "and turn southeast on two four degrees, descending to thirty-thousand feet. I know exactly how it must be done, so no tricks. I think you understand that we have no value for your life, or the lives of your crew. We will carry out our mission regardless."

Swanson wasn't planning any tricks. The fear in his mind was almost overpowering any rational thought process.

As American Airlines Flight 11 swung off course and descended towards New York, the hijacker sitting in the co-pilot's seat calmly told the passengers over the intercom that this was a hijack and that they were to remain calm if they wished to live. The hijackers, they were told, had a very specific mission, and were not interested in killing anyone if that could be avoided.

It was less than five minutes since the men had burst into the cockpit.

Ten minutes later, the hijacker ordered Swanson to drop down to two-thousand feet. This seemed like suicide to the veteran pilot, but he wasn't about to argue or hesitate. Terrorized into submission, he instantly followed orders. Maybe they want me to land at Newark, he wondered. That seemed logical. It was obvious from their altitude that they were headed for a landing, and Newark was the nearest airport. But who'd be dumb enough to hijack a plane to Newark?

Soon they could see New York City on the horizon, and the plane was now at one-thousand five-hundred feet. The hijacker spoke over his shoulder in Arabic to the man holding Kathy, who then dragged her towards the cabin door.

"Dennis!" she screamed, jerking back towards the cockpit. "We'll be OK, just do as they say. Let's just get this baby down on the ground."

The hijacker pushed her through the door, returning to stand behind Swanson's seat. The hijacker in the co-pilot's seat placed his hands on the control column.

"I will take over now," he said. "Release the controls to me and put your hands under your thighs."

Realizing they were not headed for Newark, Swanson nevertheless did as he was told. Looking through the blood-splattered cockpit canopy he could see the steel and glass columns of Lower Manhattan looming ahead, almost level with the 767.

Oh my God, what are they gonna do? There's nowhere to land in New York City, and we're way too low just way too low but they don't care and I can't tell them but what do I do they'll just fucking kill me if I try to say anything and ohshit we're toolow we'regonnagoinandwhat'sthat ahead? Oh God, oh shit, oh fuck, it's the World Trade Centre. And we're too low to make it but oh Jesus he knows that. Oh God, that's the fucking mission—

"You crazy bastards," Swanson screamed as he lunged forward to grab the controls. "What the fuck are you trying to do? You'll kill us all!" He tried to grab the column as the hijacker eased Flight 11 into a dive. The man behind him jerked Swanson back by his hair, and as the blade came round, the captain struggled for every second. "Please please please don't kill me, not yet, we can—"

A hot burning flame opened his throat from ear to ear, and through the spray of blood being pumped out by his own dying heart, Swanson saw the twin towers of the United States' tallest building fill his vision. And in that instant he remembered that tomorrow was Jenny's birthday, September 12th, and he'd forgotten. He'd forgotten to buy her a—

SHAPE

I climbed o'er the crags of Lanka
And gazed on her golden sea,
And out from her ancient places
Her soul came forth to me.
  - Walter Stanley Senior's
    The Call of Lanka

CHAPTER 1

OCTOBER 2001: This was the moment he loved. His body ached from the cramping position he had stubbornly maintained since first light, three hours ago. He knew that there were leeches clinging to his legs beneath the DPM fatigue trousers. What little skin he had exposed between his camouflage net scarf and the ghillie suit hood — that of his fingers, forehead, and left cheek — was swollen with mosquito bites. The reason his right eye wasn't swollen was that it had been glued — except for short minutes of rest — to his rifle scope for the past several hours.

Mosquitoes whined annoyingly in his ears, but his eye didn't leave the scope. Dew soaked through the ghillie suit's camouflaging pattern of dangling strips, but the scope image remained sharp. The ghillie strips had been cut from sacking and dyed green and brown, and it had been part of the sniper's training to painstakingly fashion his own individual pattern. Leaves and small sprigs from the surrounding foliage had also been woven into the ghillie suit the previous evening.

His name was Dayan Premasiri, and he was a corporal in the Sri Lanka Army's 1st Special Forces Regiment. He was enjoying this moment — this perfect moment — as the tropical dawn lit up the land with the speed of a picture on a warming television screen.

However, the arrival of daylight was not the reason Corporal Dayan Premasiri was enjoying this moment. What he enjoyed was the knowledge that his reason for existence was this moment. After two days of walking and hiding and sleeping in the mosquito night, he was here. He and his four-man patrol. He was here, his finger light and dry on the trigger of his rifle, his whole world condensed and concentrated into that circle that was the scope image. The crosshairs bisected the terra checkpoint seven hundred and five yards away.

Without taking his head from the scope, Premasiri knew that his spotter, Sumith, lay ten feet to his right, almost invisible in the brush, scanning the road that ran past the checkpoint. He also knew that somewhere behind him crouched the other two members of his patrol, watching the flanks and rear of the position.

The reason the four-man patrol was here, lying in the Wanni jungles of Sri Lanka's Northern Province and watching a Tiger checkpoint, was the information that Int had passed on to their unit. That information had brought them to this spot the previous day.

The Sri Lankan security forces had been fighting the Liberation Tigers of Tamil Eelam for more than twenty years. The LTTE, a terrorist organization claiming to represent the small sixty-six thousand square-kilometre island's largest minority, the Tamils, was demanding Tamil Eelam, a separate state in the north of the country.

Contrary to American President George Bush's statements claiming that special title for his War on Terror, Sri Lankans recognized the fact that the "first war of the Twenty-First Century" was the Eelam War, just as it had been the last of the Twentieth.

Commonly known as the Tigers — or simply as terras to the security forces — they had grown from a small shotgun-armed guerrilla group to the largest, most sophisticated and capable terrorist organization in the world — dwarfing in many ways the now-infamous Al Qaeda — able to claim as many as twenty-thousand regular troops, its own small-boat "navy", backed by artillery and, very recently, captured armoured vehicles. Along the way, the Tigers had wiped out all other Tamil separatist groups, or driven them into the arms of the government. The remaining smaller Tamil militant organizations had switched sides in order to survive, opting for the "moderate" option.

Funding, both voluntary and extorted, came initially from the huge population of Sri Lankan Tamils overseas, many of whom had been driven out of the country due to persecution by the Sinhalese — the Ireland-sized island's majority ethnic group. In addition, in the early to mid 1980s, much funds and training had come from India, itself with a huge Tamil population in the south of the subcontinent. This however had largely dried up by the late 1980s and early 1990s following fighting between the LTTE and Indian peacekeepers, and the assassination of the Indian Prime Minister, Rajiv Gandhi.

At the beginning of the Twenty-First Century, the Tigers relied, as they had in the 1990s, on the cash generated by their widespread network of smuggling— both goods as well as human — and drug running.

The Sri Lankan security forces, predominantly made up of Sinhalese, were some of the most professional and battle-hardened in the region, though not without their faults; corruption and lack of leadership among the top brass being but a few of the shortcomings.

The fighting itself had varied from small hit-and-run raids by Tigers and Army special operations units, to suicide bomb attacks in the nation's capital Colombo, to full-fledged ground and sea battles involving Israeli-made fast attack boats, Kfir fighter-bombers, and Russian-made main battle tanks. However, almost all the fighting had been confined to the northern and eastern provinces of the country, leaving the rest of the tropical paradise virtually untouched.

The reason this particular Special Forces patrol was in position, was that Military Intelligence — Int to the rest of the Army — had, in August of 2001, discovered a Tiger communications centre south of the strategic, much fought-over town of Mankulam. Rather than using air strikes or commando raids to destroy the complex, Int had decided to eavesdrop on the coded communications in the hope of eventually cracking the codes The transmissions were also being sent in burst mode, obviously not the common or garden variety of radio communications to regular terrorist units in the surrounding jungles. These were going deep into the south to undercover terrorists — recce or suicide units — possibly in Colombo.

Int also knew that dispatch riders brought many messages to the communication centre from one of the Tiger intelligence headquarters, possibly in Mankulam. Popular thinking was that the Tigers, feeling secure in this area deep behind their lines, were only coding the communiqués once they were received at the centre. And so, in October, Corporal Dayan Premasiri's patrol was sent to kill a dispatch rider in the hope of capturing something important. Someone, somewhere, was getting impatient with the code breakers.

Three kilometres away from the comms centre, on the Mankulam road, was a terra checkpoint, consisting of merely a sandbagged position a few metres inside the tree line. Protected from airborne eyes, its occupants stopped all traffic on the road to check for LTTE-issued travel documents.

It was this checkpoint that was the focus of the sniper's gaze. The checkpoint consisted of two sentries and a radio operator, clearly visible through the foliage of the tree line, and Premasiri knew that the sentries would walk out onto the potholed road to stop any vehicles or pedestrians. The road ran right and left across the sniper's field of view. Everyone was required to stop and produce their papers, including dispatch riders. Sixteen hours of daylight reconnaissance had proven this to Dayan.

He would fire the moment the dispatch rider halted. At seven-hundred and five yards — six-hundred and forty-five metres to the half-blind metric world — he couldn't guarantee hitting a moving target first time, not with the slight breeze Dayan could discern blowing from his right. He could feel its touch on his face and the skin of his fingers below the fingerless shooting gloves. The wind had blown steadily from just after dawn, and estimating it as between three and five miles per hour, he had already made the necessary windage adjustments to his 10-power Bausch & Lomb scope. This was not a time for mistakes. One shot, one kill. It was a creed the Sri Lankan snipers lived by.

His second shot would have to take out the radio operator, then whatever opposition was left. Sumith would continue to spot for him.

Twenty minutes of unrelaxing observation later, there was a soft hiss from Sumith.

"Coming."

He spoke in Sinhalese, the island's most widely used language, which had, until recently been Sri Lanka's sole official language — one of the many reasons for Tamil disaffection. Sinhalese belongs to the Indic branch of the Indo-European group of languages, and it differs vastly from Tamil, which is one of the Dravidian languages. The latter, however, heavily influences the vocabulary and structure of the former.

Dayan had already heard the faint snarl of a low-powered motorcycle, though neither that nor Sumith's whisper would have been necessary. After days of waiting for this moment, hours of lying still, only rolling away from the long L-96SM rifle to piss or sleep, Dayan could *feel* the rider approach. He could feel the man's life in his hands like a fluttering moth.

Special Forces, black beret, Dayan murmured to himself, *this is the way we start the day. . .*

He didn't look for the rider, but stayed focused on the checkpoint, knowing the target would ride into his scope.

"Hundred an' fifty yards," Sumith whispered, the spotting scope rock steady on its tripod.

Dayan's concentration was razor-sharp, his finger taking all the slack off the trigger.

"One-twenty. . ."

He could see the scope image blur fractionally with each one of his heartbeats. He would fire at the first target in that crystal moment, between beats.

"Eighty. . ."

Dayan began to exhale, adjusting the rifle as his body sank lower with his deflating chest.

"Sixty. . ."

The Honda scooter coasted into his scope picture, two men on it, the pillion rider carrying a Kalashnikov. The sentries were already on the road, the radio operator behind the sandbags. The scooter stopped short of the crosshairs and Dayan centred them onto the rider's chest.

Boom.

The big 8.6-mm rifle slammed into his shoulder, the recoil and gases erasing the scope image in spite of the muzzle brake. Dayan pulled the bolt back, ejecting the smoking casing before chambering another round. He knew he'd have the crosshairs on the radio operator before the report of the rifle reached the terras.

"Rider down, chest shot," Sumith whispered.

The checkpoint jumped up into his scope as he saw the two sentries drop flat. The radio operator, however, seemed to stand up straighter, like a football fan trying to get a better view of the game. Dayan could still see movement near the fallen scooter.

Boom.

"Radioman down. . . chest shot, I think."

The sentries had disappeared into the roadside brush, but to get into the jungle they'd have to cross a patch of ankle-high weeds several metres wide. The scooter's pillion rider was thrashing around like a landed fish, apparently pinned by the fallen Honda and its rider, but Dayan couldn't see him well enough for a shot. He stayed focused on the sentries.

"Can you get the fucker behind the bike?" he asked Sumith.

Sumith crabbed away from the spotting scope and picked up his G-3SG/1 automatic rifle, gazing through the Schmidt & Bender scope.

"Can't," he said after a moment. "Bike's in the way."

The terra behind the bike continued to struggle and Dayan saw one of the sentries crawl halfway out of the bushes in an attempt to help him.

Boom.

"Terra down, head shot."

The pillion rider had stopped struggling now, and after ten minutes of careful observation, Dayan saw no sign of movement in the bushes by the road.

"Sumith," he said, raising his head from the rifle, "I'm gon' to take Kamal an' go down there. You stay on the scope an' cover us from here. No time to waste. Some bugger might have heard the shots. OK?"

"Fit."

Scooping up the three spent casings and wriggling back into the brush, Dayan slung his sniping rifle and picked up a folding-stock AKSU-74 carbine. He knew there was no point in leaving Sumith the L-96SM as it had been zeroed by him and would affect his shorter partner's aim. He hissed softly through his teeth and a third ghillie-suited figure materialized out of the jungle, carrying a T-56 assault rifle, the Chinese-made version of the AK-47.

"Le'ss go check the road," Dayan instructed quickly. "Tell Banda the scene an' come with me."

Minutes later, the pair were moving quickly through knee-deep water, following an irrigation canal that cut through the paddy fields to the road. The sniper hide had been chosen particularly for this reason; the canal gave easy access to the road and also provided an exfilteration route.

Normally they would have stopped every hundred metres, giving Dayan the chance to scope the road for movement. Now, however, there was no time. Dayan trusted Sumith to cover their approach, even though the range was a bit long for the G-3SG/1. His heart was pounding now, as they moved in, contrasting his icy calm at long-range. This was where the adrenalin started pumping, and controlled aggression was what got you through.

When they were three hundred metres from the road, there were three rapid single shots from the treeline they had left. Dayan recognized the distinctive beat of a Heckler & Koch rifle even as he raised his binoculars to scan the road. But all he could see was a small cloud of dust rising close by the bushes that the remaining sentry had hidden in. Maybe Sumith had spotted the bugger. But had he got him? Fuck it, there was nothing to do but keep going. Int needed the stuff from the rider.

With a hundred and fifty metres to go, there were two more bursts of fire from behind them, and this time the two men were close enough to the road to hear the bullets hit the bike. What the fuck was going on? But they didn't pause now, trusting Sumith to cover them in these the most dangerous moments of the approach.

Fifty metres from the road, they split up, Kamal leaving the canal and cutting diagonally across the paddies, approaching the road fifty metres to the right of where the canal ran under it. He then rolled quickly across the road and into cover on the other side. If someone was waiting on the far side, they'd have expected him to cross under the road, using the culvert the canal flowed through.

Dayan followed the canal to the culvert, but stayed on the near side of the road till Kamal had got into position opposite him. They then moved stealthily along towards the checkpoint, flanking the road.

"There's a bugger dead in the drain here," Kamal whispered across the road as they reached the checkpoint.

"Roger." It was obviously the second sentry, hit by Sumith. "Put a look in the checkpoint while I check the Honda."

"Roger."

Dayan crawled sideways across the road, until he could see the two riders. The one he had hit was still under the scooter, but the pillion rider was a couple of feet away, also dead, hit several times by Sumith in the chest. Dayan could smell burned flesh.

As he pulled the dispatch rider free of the bike, Dayan realized why the pillion rider had been thrashing around like an idiot, drawing fire. The weight of the scooter and the dispatch rider had kept the man pinned beneath the blistering hot exhaust pipe, and Dayan could see where a pink strip of burned meat showed on his bare leg below the tigerstripe fatigue trousers.

Five minutes later, Dayan and Kamal were headed back down the canal to rendezvous with the others. All the dispatch riders possessions had been carefully laid out and photographed, then replaced in his pockets and rucksack. This way, terras finding the ambush site would assume it to have been just one more hit-and-run sniper raid, and not a proper intelligence-gathering mission. There would be no indication that the Army now knew what the rider had been carrying.

They moved to the emergency rendezvous, picked up their sixty-pound rucksacks and immediately began to march southeast. They had to break clear of the net the Tigers would throw around the area to catch them. They marched till dusk and then hid up for the night. Dawn would bring a Huey in to pick them up. The Int might be hot and they couldn't waste time walking out as they would have done on most missions.

As the Bell 212 lifted into the dawn, the patrol lit their first cigarettes in five days, and eased back in the web seats. Dayan inhaled deeply and tried to shield his Bristol from the wind whipping in through the open doors. Below, the dusty green of the jungle stretched like a lumpy pool table to the horizon, torn back in places, like the fur of a great beast, to reveal the geometric-patterned skin of abandoned vegetable and paddy fields. He felt cold and relaxed, floating, as if he was stoned. Days after a clean kill, he would still feel the high.

He noticed Bandara grinning at the Air Force door gunners, enjoying the disgust on their faces. Even the cold blast of air couldn't hide the stink of days in the jungle. At least they hadn't had to shit their trousers, Dayan thought. He had known sniper missions where this had to be done rather than risk moving. Lately, Dayan had tended to rely on pills to control his bowel movements, plugging himself up when out in the field and purging his system when he returned to base. He dreaded to think what his large intestine would be like in a few years.

Sumith had a Walkman plugged in, and Kamal was already napping.

Through the gap between the pilots' seats, Dayan could see a colour photograph of a young woman selotaped to the instrument panel. A wife or girlfriend probably. He himself wished he could remember his wife's face in moments like this, when the rush of relief and weariness hit after a long stressful mission. But long ago, Dayan had found that when he was in the jungle he just couldn't picture her face, no matter how hard he tried, or how much he attempted to memorize her features while in camp. He would have to wait till he was back in his billet, pulling the small pocket-sized album out of its polythene cover.

It was only then her eyes would float out to him, and he'd remember what her long black hair felt like when he touched it, the smell of her skin, the taste of her mouth.

None of the SF troops carried anything personal on the deep recce missions. Nothing the terras could use to kill your family back home. Too many stories of the JVP had drummed the threat into their heads.

Dayan had still been in school during the late 1980s, when the communist insurrection in the south by the *Janatha Vimukthi Peramuna* — the People's Liberation Front — had almost destroyed Sri Lanka. However, he had heard the stories from senior men who had served in those bloody days. Days that had done more to destroy the country's innocence than all the years of the Eelam War. Stories of coming home to find your parents' heads on stakes outside your home, or your wife raped and murdered, breasts cut off and nailed to the front door.

Those had been the years when the gloves came off, when the Sri Lankan security forces had grown out of adolescence. They had learned their lessons well in the south, and the war in the north was now one in which very few prisoners were taken by either side.

Dayan gave up on remembering his wife's face as the chopper descended. In a month he'd be home on leave, and he wouldn't have to remember anything again.

*   *   *

Brigadier Arjuna Devendra walked quickly out of his home in Kotte, one of Colombo's fast-developing suburbs, and crossed the gravel-topped driveway to his official dark green Mazda 323. He tossed his laptop case in before him and settled into the comfortable back seat. His bodyguard was about to slam the door, when Devendra's wife stepped out of the modern two-storey house that was the family home these days.

"Arjuna," she called, "can you somehow pay the *Newsweek* subscription today? Otherwise I have to go into Colombo jus' for that."

The brigadier waved his consent with an irritated grimace. His bodyguard, Sergeant Siriwardene, slid in next to the driver, and the car pulled away. Didn't she know he had a bloody full day today? Why else would he be driving to Army HQ on a Saturday? Oh, well, he'd send the driver at lunchtime.

The Mazda dodged through the heavy morning traffic that had increasingly become a feature of Colombo's main arteries in recent years. Gridlocked streets were something the citizens of Sri Lanka's capital had grown accustomed to, if not comfortable with, along with checkpoints at strategic locations, and permanently closed off streets in the financial district of the Fort.

They got out onto Sri Jayawardenepura Mawatha, which would take them straight into the city, and the traffic began to smoothen out, increasing speed. Fifteen minutes later they were threading their way once more into the chaos of the east Colombo zone of Borella.

As the Mazda inched along past the Kanatte General Cemetery, the city's largest burial grounds, Devendra idly watched the hurrying Saturday-morning mercantile-sector workers rushing for their buses and thanked the stars that he wasn't fighting his way through the usual weekday mess. The city itself — a maze that defied interpretation on a map — had grown inland from the original Portuguese coastal fort, expanding gradually through the

Dutch and British periods. The post-independence era, however, particularly in the 1970s, had seen the city mushroom at an incredible rate as inflation and dissatisfaction sent the traditional farming and fishing communities of the island flocking into Colombo in search of work. With a population of over a million in the city itself, the streets couldn't handle the volume of traffic that seemed to double and triple each year. Plans by the municipal council to widen the main avenues and build parallel arteries moved at a snail's pace while landowners in the areas in question went to court to demand higher compensation. Moves by the government to encourage the population to use public transport were laughed at by automobile owners, a sentiment Devendra could sympathize with as he watched one of the overloaded buses struggle past, heeling over on its suspension, passengers crammed in like sardines and jammed onto the footboard, clinging like monkeys to whatever was at hand. The streets that had been closed off due to security concerns or narrowed to accommodate sandbagged checkpoints didn't help either.

The Mazda moved past the roundabout and onto Buller's Road, moving at a faster pace on the wide avenue, past the Anglican Cathedral and the Bandaranaike Memorial International Conference Hall on one side, and the Chinese Embassy on the other.

It wasn't a beautiful city, the way European cities were beautiful, but it was an interesting and vibrant one. A city of character and contradiction, Devendra decided. The sweeping lawns of the Cathedral and the huge flame-of-the-forest trees that lined the avenue slid across the dark lenses of his sunglasses. The images had replaced the little beggar children he had seen just minutes before, rummaging through an overflowing garbage tip. A city once beautiful but now ravaged, like a woman who still looked attractive from certain angles.

Devendra could have used a Land Rover full of elite troops to clear his way to work each day, since as a brigadier, and Director of Military Intelligence, it was his due. However, even though he knew he was a target high on the LTTE's hit list, Devendra preferred the low-profile approach to the more arrogant and flamboyant attitude of some of his peers. He himself had sat patiently in traffic as a car roared past, escorted front and rear by canvas-topped Land Rovers, the 4x4s packed with white-gloved, maroon-bereted commandos, who waved all civilian traffic out of the way. In fact, many of Devendra's civilian friends and neighbours didn't even know he was *in* the Int, never mind that he was its head. Most thought he worked in Pay and Records. His nondescript features — neither angular nor round — with a neat military moustache below a podgy nose, together with his soft-looking body seemed to project the image of a uniformed bureaucrat rather than a soldier.

Another fact that none of his civilian friends and neighbours knew — and in actuality, few of his compatriots either — was that in addition to having a sharp analytical mind capable of taking in the whole peripheral intelligence picture at a glance, at the age of forty-eight Devendra had a streak of absolute ruthlessness coupled with a farsightedness few of the other intelligence commanders had.

It was these qualities that had made him call an emergency briefing of the Joint Intelligence Committee on this Saturday in October; ten days after Corporal Dayan Premasiri had killed the Tiger dispatch rider, and six weeks after the September 11th terrorist attacks on New York and Washington DC.

This was what they had all been waiting for, he told himself. This was what they *needed*. What *he* needed. The opportunity Devendra had been hoping for since he'd seen the twin towers of the World Trade Centre collapse. Now the Americans understood. Now they knew what it felt like to be kicked in the balls. But it wasn't enough. The American war on 'world terror' seemed to be conveniently confined just to Islamic extremists, and even then, only to those involved with the attacks of September 11th.

Where had the Americans been in 1995 when the Tigers had driven a truck bomb into the Sri Lankan Central Bank in the heart of Colombo's financial district? Where had they been when shoulder-fired rockets were used on the neighbouring Ceylinco Building? The damage to Sri Lanka's economy and tourist industry had been incalculable, the casualties, in a country of twenty million, far greater in proportion than the September 11th attacks.

The world, however, and the Americans in particular, had ignored it, but now they could do so no longer. In his hands he held the weapon that would destroy the LTTE.

The usual weekly Joint Intelligence Committee Briefing was held in the Joint Operations Command building inside the Army HQ complex — commonly called the Galle Face Camp after the grassy esplanade that sprawled opposite it, facing out to sea. Attending the regular briefing would be the committee itself, headed by its chairman, the General Officer Commanding the Joint Operations Command — GOCJOC, or Cock Jock, as he was irreverently called; the Director of Military Intelligence, in this case, Devendra; the head of the Directorate of Internal Intelligence, the country's domestic civilian intelligence network; the chief of the Directorate of Foreign Intelligence — the former's external counterpart; and the Director of Special Forces, under whose control came the SF and Commando Brigades.

In addition to the committee itself, the people normally being briefed would be the members of the National Security Council — the President, the State Minister for Defence, the three commanders of the armed forces, the Inspector General of Police, and the head of the Presidential Security Division.

But today's emergency meeting would consist only of the committee, with the inclusion of the State Minister for Defence. What Devendra possessed would have to be shared with him, because the President was on a state visit to Britain. This was too big for just the military. It would have to involve the top hierarchy of the government.

Major General Sarath Perera, the Director of Special Forces was already in the conference room when Devendra walked in. The general was chatting to Deputy Inspector General Michael Salgado, the Director General of Internal Intelligence, and Deputy Inspector General Jaliya de Silva, the Director General of Foreign Intelligence. General Sujeeva Fernando, the chairman, walked in a minute later, his lean face cheerful, and tea was served and cigarettes lit as they waited for the predictably tardy minister. The cousin of the president, he seemed to stick to the family tradition of avoiding punctuality.

As they waited, Devendra ignored the curious looks and questions of the other committee members on his reason for calling this emergency meeting. They could all wait and be briefed together with the minister. Instead, he tried to gauge what their reactions would be to his news.

General Sujeeva Fernando was a conventional soldier, fifty-eight years old, a former tanker and long-time advocate of armoured warfare as the solution to Sri Lanka's war. His idea of intelligence gathering was of the "I see many footprints going in but none coming out" variety. He would be happy to kick the problem upstairs to the politicians. Slim and over six feet tall, he had a full, but neatly cropped, head of salt-and-pepper hair, and the body — now going to fat — of the national team basketball player he'd once been.

Fortunately, his views were counterbalanced by Major General Sarath Perera and DIG Mike Salgado, both of whom were rabid exponents of unconventional warfare. Both men had commanded special operations units in combat, and were quite aware of what it was like down at the sharp end.

Major General Sarath Perera, a hard, stocky man a couple of years older than Devendra, had US Ranger tabs on his shoulders, and though he didn't have too much Int experience, his command and knowledge of airborne and special forces were probably second to none in the country. No one was exactly sure whether Perera had any grey hairs, because his head was always perfectly shaven of even the tiniest stubble. It was rumoured that even his wife had no idea what colour the hair on his head was due to his habit of rising well before dawn in order to complete his ablutions and be out of the city in time to join one of his elite units for their morning run. In contrast to his shaven head, his thick black eyebrows and moustache seemed to jump out of his face.

DIG Mike Salgado was only forty-two, the youngest man in the room, once a company commander in the crack police paramilitary troops — the Special Task Force — he had later moved on to that unit's intelligence outfit. In addition to special warfare experience, he had served a tour with the now defunct National Intelligence Bureau, as well as two secondments to Military Intelligence. He had the gaunt, muscled face and body of a marathon runner, but his bandido moustache and two-pack a day habit destroyed that image.

Devendra knew that both men would back his plan to the hilt.

The man Devendra couldn't gauge was Jaliya de Silva. The Director General of Foreign Intelligence was a very ambitious man, liable to go with the top brass. However, he also had the reputation of being as ruthless as Devendra himself, and was constantly trying to push the peripheries of the war ever wider. When the old National Intelligence Bureau had been replaced in 2000 by the DII and the DFI, Jaliya de Silva, then Deputy Director General of the NIB, had been hand-picked by the president to head the fledgling DFI. Starting off with four officers and twenty men, he had built up the organization by poaching from the DII's experienced personnel, while simultaneously recruiting former Army Int operatives who were now on civvy street. At the age of fifty-six, he was only surpassed in years by the committee chairman himself, but with the physique of a bodybuilder ten years his junior. In spite of the cigarettes, he was to be seen at the police gym thrice a week. He still had all his hair, which though shot through with silver, was worn neither long nor short, with neatly tended sideburns.

Lionel Adikari, State Minister for Defence, rolled importantly into the room, his bodyguard backing out and closing the door behind him.

"Sorry I'm late, men, traffic, you know." Although his fleshy face smiled round at the others as he sat opposite the chairman, his baggy, hooded eyes betrayed no emotion. "What is all this about, Sujeeva? I was about to leave for Kandy when you called me."

"Well, sir, you know as much as I do," Fernando said, pouring the minister a cup of tea. "But Devendra here called the emergency meeting. Apparently it can't wait till nex' week. So without any more delay, I'll let him take over."

Devendra felt the minister's hooded eyes on him as he opened the laptop computer lying on the table before him. He cleared his throat and got right down to it.

"Gentlemen, two months ago, we began monitoring radio transmissions from a Tiger comms centre somewhere in the Wanni. All transmissions were in code and some were being burst-transmitted, indicating that they were not the usual radio traffic. With triangulation as well as SF deep recce patrols the location of the centre was found out to be southwest of Mankulam. We didn', however knock it out, in the hope of cracking the code. This has not happened to date, and sixteen days ago we decided to find out the type of dispatches being transmitted. *Before* they were encoded. Ten days ago an SF patrol ambushed a dispatch rider *en route* to the comms centre, and copied his dispatches. The documents were left as they were, in the hope of not alerting the Tigers to the leak."

The men around the table were listening keenly. They knew this was unusual, because methods of intelligence gathering on the ground were not usually referred to at these briefings.

"Among the dispatches was a single message earmarked for burst transmission," Devendra went on. "It was a name, date, and flight number. The flight was an Emirates flight from Dubai to Colombo, arriving on October twenty-first — two days ago. The passenger manifesto confirmed there was a man on board with the corresponding name. He was allowed through customs without any extra attention, and both he and the man who picked him up at Katunayake were followed into Colombo by us. His airport of origin was Frankfurt, Germany.

"The next day the two men dropped off a parcel at a pickup point, after which we arrested them. The parcel however wasn't collected — possibly we had been spotted — and so we picked up the parcel, too."

There was pin drop silence in the room, and even Salgado had forgotten his cigarette, which was now burning down to the filter.

"Neither man — both Tamils — has any known LTTE connections. The newcomer's passport shows him to have a residence visa for Germany and a work permit. Apparently an IT specialist. The parcel contained twenty-three passports — most of them foreign. All of them genuine."

Devendra pressed a button recessed into the tabletop, dimming the lights. A click of the laptop's keyboard, and the connected overhead projector threw a PowerPoint slide onto the far wall. "Here's a list of the passport names," he went on. "As you can see, it's a fairly mixed lot. Some Canadian, some Middle Eastern, some Pakistani, some Sri Lankan. But they're almost all Muslim names."

"So what's unusual about this?" the minister asked irritably. Obviously he wasn't happy missing his weekend in the hill country for a list of Muslims. "Don't the Tigers regularly use stolen Muslim identities to get their people out of the country? These passports must have been bought or stolen in Europe."

Sri Lanka's Tamils shared a common language with its Muslims — mostly ethnic Moors and Malays — and that made it relatively simple for Tamils to pose as Muslims, thus avoiding the closer scrutiny afforded the former at airports and other high-security points.

"That's correct, sir," Devendra said patiently, "but wha'ss unusual is the first two names on the list."

"Hani Hanjour and Majed Moqed?" Fernando read, stumbling over the unfamiliar pronunciations.

Simultaneously, Devendra heard Jaliya de Silva draw in his breath in a sharp hiss, and Sarath Perera's eyebrows climbed his forehead. But the other three just looked blank.

"What is it, what does it mean?" Adikari snapped, annoyed not to be in the know.

"What are you saying they have done?"

"You don' think these buggers have—"

"*What* buggers?"

Everyone started to talk at once until General Fernando raised his hand. "Gentlemen, please. Let Devendra finish. Devendra, *will* you get on with it?"

Devendra switched to a new slide, this of a *Newsweek* article dated mid-September. The magazine page showed nineteen faces, US Department of Justice pictures of the September 11th hijackers. Two faces had been circled in red marker ink.

This, gentlemen, is Hani Hanjour and Majed Moqed."

"OK," the minister said, "but I still don' know what you're on about—"

"I think, sir," Fernando said, "what he means is that these chaps are connected to the LTTE somehow."

"What?"

"What we feel," spoke up Devendra, "is that the LTTE in Europe helped some of the hijackers get into North America."

There was silence for several heartbeats, then Salgado said, "Are these genuine passports, but?"

"Positive. We think that the LTTE forged new passports for Hanjour and Moqed, and kept the originals for later use. The LTTE forging capabilities are probably the best in the world. We also know that the Tigers try to use genuine passports as much as possible, particularly in a part of the world where they're not too sensitive. While Muslim names might draw attention in the USA, they would be perfect cover here in Asia."

De Silva spoke up now for the first time. "So you're saying that the passports — the genuine ones — were being brought here to be reused? Surely the terras wouldn't be stupid enough to use the passports of known hijackers?"

"Maybe they were going to use them two years from now, after all this has blown over. With the faces changed, who'd remember the names? Maybe they didn't know these fellows were going to hijack planes. Maybe the Tigers fucked up, who knows? But the point is we now have proof that the Tigers helped Al Qaeda. This is what we need to get the world on our side!"

"But it seems a bit far-fetched to me, still, Devendra," the minister said. "What reason has the LTTE to help Al Qaeda? Their objectives are totally opposite. The Tigers won' want to risk their operations in Canada and the US."

"Mister Minister," Perera stepped in, and Devendra remembered that the special forces major general refused to call any civilian *sir*, "in the early nineties, when the terras got twelve-point-seven-millimetre anti-aircraft guns and later Stingers, we knew, but couldn't prove, that they came from Afghanistan. We also knew that several Tigers had been spotted by the Pakistani ISI in Afghanistan. Probably being trained in anti-aircraft tactics in exchange for training Islamic suicide bombers. So there is roughly a ten-year history between the Tigers and Al Qaeda."

"Correct," Devendra added. "And it's possible that the Tigers weren't told of the chaos these buggers were going to create."

"Yes, yes," the minister raised his hands in exasperation, "but what are we supposed to do with this? Walk into the US Embassy and demand they bomb Jaffna jus' because we found two *thamby*-buggers' passports with the Tigers? This is just not enough, brigadier."

"How 'bout this, then, sir?"

Devendra clicked on a fresh slide. It was a colour photograph, and quite grainy. Obviously taken at long range, it was of two men on the platform of a large European railway station. Hands in the pockets of their windbreakers, they were talking intently. The next slide was a tight close-up. One man was shorter, dark and bearded, obviously a South Asian, the other looked Mediterranean. A third slide showed them walking together to the escalators. A train in the background had the letters DB stencilled on it.

"What am I looking at?" Adikari asked. "Where, and who is this?"

"As you can see in that las' picture, it's in Germany. The DB means *Deutsche Bahn*. It's at the Cologne main station, an' that picture was taken by our Bonn military attaché."

DIG de Silva raised an eyebrow at that. His DFI heads of station were usually responsible for intelligence gathering and surveillance within their respective countries. The military attaché, an armed forces officer, was limited — in theory — to liaison duties with the host nations' military. De Silva knew that invariably, in countries that were hives of LTTE activity, the military attaché was always a soldier and, nine times out of ten, from Int. Nevertheless, he would have to ask the Bonn head of station to pull his socks up.

"The chap on the left is Nawaf Al Hazmi," Devendra brought up another of the *Newsweek* mug shots alongside the close-up of the two men in Cologne, "another of the September eleventh hijackers. The one on the right with the beard is Mahen Ramachandran, a known LTTEer. Works for TEEDOR — the Tamil Eelam Economic Development Organization — one of their cover groups, in Cologne. These shots were taken somewhere in late July."

"What were they talking about?" Brigadier Perera asked.

"Dunno. Our guy couldn' get close enough. But the thing is, this proves that the Tigers were in contact with other Al Qaeda hijackers, maybe all of them. And it wasn't just the LTTE who was in contact with them, but their apparently 'legal humanitarian aid' organizations."

"Well, what d'you suggest we do with this?" Adikari asked. "I doubt that the US will move militarily against the LTTE. They're too busy with Afghanistan, even if they believed this."

"That's true, but what we *can* ask them to do is bring more pressure on Canada and — more importantly these days — European countries, to crack down on the Tamil groups. We know that the Canadian SIS and CIS are watching many of these groups already."

"Is that the recommendation of this committee, gentlemen?"

"At the very least, they should start deporting the buggers," Perera said. "But we should start asking for much more intelligence sharing, as well as US military aid."

"I think we should go as far as to ask for an exchange programme in which Sri Lankan security forces and police could work abroad alongside those countries' forces," DIG Salgado added. "And they could come across here to get some practical experience on what we're actually facing here in Sri Lanka."

"Yes," agreed de Silva," the more international cooperation we get the better. We should follow this US coalition's example and start hitting at their finances as well."

"Sujeeva?" Adikari glanced at the committee chairman.

"Well, sir," Fernando muttered around the cigarette he was lighting, "I think it should be a government decision, but what you have heard just now is definitely a strong recommendation."

"Fine." Adikari leaned back, thinking of the dramatic moment when he would spring news of the intelligence coup on his cousin. "I'll meet with the President as soon as she gets back, and with the foreign minister."

CHAPTER 2

Dayan Premasiri's four-man patrol arrived at the Ratmalana Air Force Base, south of Colombo City on a C-130 transport from Vavuniya. They walked down the ramp of the plane, sniffing at the distinct smell of Colombo: a mixture of tropical foliage, sea, and exhaust fumes. To Dayan, it smelled like home.

He had been born in Dehiwela, a suburb of the city, and had grown up on its streets. Until he joined the Army at nineteen — seven years earlier — he'd never been away from the noise and pollution of Colombo for very long.

The four soldiers walked into the toilets to change into civils. Sri Lankan military personnel were not allowed to wear uniform except on official duties. Any travel on public transport had to be done in civilian clothes. Dayan asked the question as the others were changing.

"Sure your wife won' mind us coming?" Kamal returned, splashing water from a sink onto his face. They were all covered in dust from the war zone in the northeast, and stank of aviation fuel.

"What to mind?" shrugged Dayan. "She'll be jus' happy to see me again. An' it's only for two days, no?"

Kamal Gunatilake, Sumith Liyanage, and JL Bandara, the other three SF men, weren't from Colombo, and would soon be headed off to their respective home towns and villages. However, even though their leave had been cut down from two weeks to ten days, they had decided to spend a couple of days in Colombo together, living it up. To save money, they would all stay with

Dayan and his wife. Dayan's wife, however, was still to learn of this arrangement.

There had been no real explanation for their leave being cut, except the vague warning that an upcoming mission had been brought forward. In ten days, the four men were to report to the SF detachment at Army HQ, Galle Face. This in itself was strange, as for regular mission briefs they would return to Vavuniya, or occasionally for special jobs to the SF headquarters at Maduru Oya on the Eastern Province border.

The four men walked out in jeans and T-shirts onto the airbase road and hitched a ride on an Air Force truck to the main Colombo-Galle coastal road two kilometres away. Once there, they lit cigarettes and stood on the pavement, ogling the women, thousands of whom seemed to walk freely around. They'd forgotten what girls in short skirts or tight jeans looked like. None of them had been back south in four months, some for six.

"Where shall we go?" Sumith asked.

"Chi Chiyong is good," recommended Dayan, referring to a Chinese restaurant in Dehiwela. "Booze is cheap an' the bites are good. We'll put a few an' go home for lunch."

"Yah, but how's the arrack?" cut in Bandara. "I don' wan' to drink some shit that'll fuck me up for the nex' few days."

"Drink shit?" Kamal laughed. "I saw the *good stuff* you were putting in Vavuniya. If you drink the water in the *drains* here it'll be better than that paint thinner you had there."

"Fuck off, that was good Dankotuwa white lightning, you bugger." Bandara spat on the ground and blew smoke at Kamal, the only member of the patrol who didn't smoke. He went on to extol the virtues of the moonshine produced in the town of Dankotuwa just north of Katunayake, famous both for its porcelain as well as its illicit brew. "What d'you Galle buggers know about quality arrow? All y'all know is toddy an' dry fish."

Dayan hailed a trishaw — the motorized three-wheeled taxis that raced through Sri Lankan urban centres — and they all piled in. The open-sided death traps were designed to carry two passengers, or three at a pinch. They squashed themselves in, Bandara sitting on Sumith's lap with his Bata trainers waving in the breeze. The trishaw hurtled off down the road, dodging traffic, stray dogs, cyclists, pedestrians and potholes with equal abandon, while the four soldiers craned their necks to get a glimpse of civilization after months of war.

"*Ado*," Sumith said to Bandara, patting the man's rear, "stop bouncing around. You're making me horny with all these chicks around."

"If you're so desperate," came the return crack, "I can give you my cock to suck if you like."

"Maybe if you have a bath."

*　*　*

The Jameson tasted good on Inspector Ian McEdwards' tongue, and he let the whisky roll around his mouth before swallowing. It was a bit early in the day for the hard stuff, but he was not needed by the boss till tomorrow morning, and it was a relief to be able to relax from the constant vigilance of the twenty-two hour journey from Toronto to Colombo.

The reason McEdwards was standing at his room window on the eighth floor of the Galadari Meridian in Colombo, Jameson-on-the-rocks in hand, was that he was an officer in the Royal Canadian Mounted Police's Special Protection Group. The SPG was tasked with protecting cabinet ministers and other VIPs both at home and abroad. Now, as he swirled the ice in his glass, listening to the cubes tinkle, and watching the long curling breakers of the Indian Ocean sweep in from the Maldive Islands, eight-hundred kilometres west, McEdwards thought of the events that had brought him to Colombo. He and his very own VIP.

While the September 11th attacks in the United States had changed the mindset of the western world, it hadn't really affected everyday Canadian life. Not until the visit, a month ago, to Ottawa, of the US Secretary of State. The heavily built ex-Army general had brought both news and a request that would change life in Toronto drastically.

The American brought evidence that the Arab terrorists had used a global people-smuggling network to enter the USA. The network was run by the LTTE, a Sri Lankan Tamil terrorist group with established branches amongst the large Tamil immigrant population in Toronto, mostly centred in the suburb of Scarborough.

There was circumstantial evidence linking Tamils in Germany and France as well, but what the Americans were so deeply concerned with was a potential pipeline for hostile terrorists that led directly to the US' undefended northern border.

The US State Department was very concerned with Canada's lack of surveillance on — as well as apparent tolerance of — an illegal organization. The LTTE had been outlawed in the USA in 2000, but an Ontario provincial government aware of the large number of votes generated by Canadian Tamils had turned a blind eye to the militants' activities. The US Secretary of State had made it abundantly clear that Canada was expected to crack down on the Tigers as part of its duties in the "War on Terror" now being waged globally in general, but specifically in Afghanistan.

The Secretary of State had found a sympathetic ear in the form of Canadian Minister of Foreign Affairs and International Trade, Donald Fenster. The minister, a former head of the Canadian Security Intelligence Service before he moved into professional politics, had once been the CSIS head of station for Colombo, and held no illusions about the LTTE's murderous trade. Fenster had long campaigned for investigation of the LTTE's activities in Toronto, specifically to do with extortion and money laundering. However, except for some increased surveillance of the Tamil community in general, the strong Tamil lobby in government still held sway, helped by a lot of sympathy within the Immigration and Refugee Board as well as Amnesty International.

Nevertheless, the visit of the US Secretary of State had changed everything. Ministers expounding anti-terrorism theories and Canadian home defence seemed to pop out of Parliament Hill's woodwork. This had enabled Fenster to have a new bill brought before Parliament that if passed, would make mere membership of, or connection with, the LTTE a matter for prosecution. In the meantime the RCMP and the Ontario Provincial Police had begun to crack down heavily on Tamil extortion rackets and drug rings in Scarborough and Toronto.

Tamils found to be engaged in criminal activities had been actively prosecuted and several convicted, while a few who were wanted by the Sri Lankan government had already been extradited.

This had brought out demonstrators from both factions of the Sri Lankan community and there had been violent clashes both in Scarborough and downtown Toronto. The demonstrators protesting human rights violations and persecution of a minority by a racist Ottawa were definitely more articulate and better organized, their leaders experts at civil disobedience. In contrast, the opposition groups were much more home-grown and chaotic, if more colourful.

Toronto city police had had to use tear gas on two occasions to break up violent clashes between factions, and Special Weapons teams were called out when a drive by shooting sprayed the Steels office of Canada Sinhala Friends with automatic rifle fire.

Tear gas floating down Toronto streets and intersections patrolled by shotgun-armed policemen were things Ian McEdwards had never dreamed he would see.

It was the reason he was in Colombo, 2/ic of the SPG team watching Donald Fenster on his official visit to Sri Lanka. The team consisted of four men, headed by a chief inspector, and based in the Galadari. At least McEdwards and the two junior men were, the boss was with the VIP at President's House, down the road.

The reason only the team commander was with Fenster was that the Sri Lankan Presidential Security Division had refused to allow foreigners to carry firearms in the President's residence. So rather than hand over their pistols, the team had opted to base a reaction force at the nearby hotel, while the boss stayed with Fenster — unarmed. McEdwards had traced the route to

President's house on foot, and knew that in the event of an emergency they could be there in three minutes.

McEdwards, however, didn't anticipate an emergency. He had checked out security at President's House and was satisfied. Besides, the PSD — hard looking men with killer eyes — had a reputation for shooting first and asking questions much later, if at all. There was no way a Tiger suicide bomber was going to penetrate the defences.

Donald Fenster was in Sri Lanka to reinforce cooperation between the two countries' governments and to discuss methods to clean out the LTTE. Rumour was that a mutual extradition treaty was in the tubes as well.

This followed a visit to the island two weeks previously by the US Secretary of State, during a tour of South Asia aimed at bolstering support for the war in Afghanistan, in which a huge military aid package had been promised to Sri Lanka.

Fenster would be having dinner with the President that night, and the boss would handle security. So while the other three SPG men were on standby, they could afford to relax that evening. The next day, McEdwards would take over from the boss, and the day after that, Fenster had scheduled a visit to the ancient hill capital of Kandy. The full SPG team would go with him.

Downing his whisky, McEdwards headed for the door. The sun was diving for the horizon in a blaze of glory, and he decided he might as well see something of the city while he had the time. Wearing a batik shirt he had bought in the hotel lobby, he tucked the 9-mm Glock into the waistband of his khaki shorts. A camera slung round his neck and sandals on his feet completed the picture of the typical tourist.

Letting the other two SPG men know where he was going, he took the elevator. He had his cell phone with him, and didn't plan on heading too far.

Crossing the road in front of the Continental, he headed south along the sea wall. About a kilometre away, at the far end of Galle Face Green, he could see the facade of the old Galle

Face Hotel, sea spray softening the face of the old lady as she glared at her modern glass and concrete counterparts. Beyond, he could see the blue-green stretch of the coast curving south to the town of Galle, giving this spot its name.

Five minutes later, he was amongst crowds of chattering locals strolling along the sea wall and playing cricket on the grass. Families clustered around vendors who manned little wheeled stalls that sold everything from roasted peanuts to prawn *vadai* — a spicy ring of fried dough, similar in looks to a doughnut. Groups of young men sat at tables set up on the grass, drinking beer or arrack. Further away, closer to the main road which was still busy with evening traffic, bigger stalls were selling a variety of Indian and Arab bread, plus every kind of roasted or barbecued meat McEdwards could imagine. Stray dogs skulked around and crows watched hungrily. There were a few young couples walking hand-in-hand, but he noticed that most of the young people stayed in groups of their own gender. Knots of teenaged girls, their clothes varying clique to clique, from saris and summer dresses to jeans and miniskirts, walked around giggling and pretending to ignore the gangs of young men who eyeballed them and made passing comments.

The sheer wall of sound and sights and smells was overpowering after the quiet of the hotel. McEdwards, an inch under six feet, with stray-dog blonde hair and fair good looks, was an immediate target for the flock of insistent beggars, young and old, who tugged at his shorts and touched his arms as he walked purposefully on, ignoring them.

They seemed such a vibrant, cheerful people, he thought. Even the beggars just grinned and looked after him as he walked on. What were they doing fighting and killing each other as they had been doing for the past two decades?

He reached the Galle Face Hotel, and inspected the trishaw ranks parked outside. In a pinch he could get back to the Galadari in one of these if he was needed. Ignoring the "Taxi, sir?" from several of the drivers — or were they riders? — he headed into the Galle Face Hotel in search of a drink.

He decided it would be his last of the day. Well, maybe till dinner anyway.

*   *   *

It was 7pm when the four soldiers swayed up to Dayan's home down Station Road in Dehiwela. The plan to be home for lunch had been shelved along with the idea of just a couple of drinks, the three bottles of arrack they had drunk stretching through the afternoon and into the evening.

The patrol had sat on the bar's balcony, drinking Old Reserve and smoking Benson & Hedges, watching the bustle of Colombo, chatting with the ease of men who'd spent countless hours of mind-numbing danger and boredom together. They'd just *watched*, amazed at the variety of colours after the dull green of military dress. The voices and car horns and laughter had rolled over them like refreshing breakers at the beach after the hot silence of the jungle.

It had been a good time until two men at the next table had started talking about the war, discussing the security forces' mistakes with the confidence of armchair generals. *They'd* have done it differently. *They'd* have done this, *they'd* have done that. But *they* had never been there. *They* were here in Colombo drinking cold fucking beer while the boys up there drank dirty water.

The empty arrack bottle Kamal threw had exploded on the neighbouring table, showering its occupants with broken glass and ending the diatribe.

The only reason the bar owner hadn't called the cops was that he had known Dayan for years from the neighbourhood. But they had nevertheless been asked politely to leave.

Sunethra ran into Dayan's arms, burying her face in his neck and hugging him fiercely. She said nothing about the ruined lunch and the smell of alcohol that flowed off him. He held her gently by the ears, grinning into her face as she danced from one foot to the other like a little girl. Sunethra — beautiful eyes, it meant in Sinhalese. Whatever her parents' faults, they had named her well.

"*Kho'madha?*" he asked in Sinhalese, the universal Sri Lankan greeting that could be loosely translated as 'how are you?'.

"OK." she answered. "*Where* on earth were you all this time? I thought the flight was delayed or something."

"Went for a shot."

"All this time? With whom?"

Dayan turned to the doorway, and three grinning faces appeared out of the dark, followed by a wave of alcohol fumes and cigarette smoke. "This is my four-man. They all came back on leave with me an' I tol' them they can stay a couple of days here."

Sunethra's smile faltered a little, but then turned on to high-beam again. Her husband's surprises were well known to her.

"They're all from out-station," Dayan said as if in explanation.

Sunethra raised an eyebrow at him in exasperation before turning to the three men. "Come in, come in."

Introductions were made all around and everyone trooped into the small living room, dumping their bags by the wall, and sinking into the chairs and sofa.

"I suppose y'all will want dinner, no?" Sunethra said with mock severity, as if talking to a bunch of errant schoolboys rather than hardened SF troopers. "Ah'll go an' cook."

"Anything to drink?" Dayan asked hopefully.

"Y'all dowant tea, no?" she said, already headed for the kitchen.

"Actually—"

"I put some beer in the fridge for you."

Dayan followed her into the kitchen and she rounded on him as soon as he entered.

"Why didn't you tell me you were bringing them?" she hissed in a low voice. "Now Ah'll have to cook some more. An' where the hell are they going to sleep?"

"OK, *OK*, Sune," Dayan muttered, putting his hands on her shoulders. "Jus' make some *rotti* or something. An' we'll put some mats on the ground in the hall. The buggers can sleep there."

"I already took five days off from office," she said reproachfully. "I was hoping we could have some time to ourselves. Before you go on your rounds to meet all your friends."

"It'll only be a couple of days. Day after tomorrow they'll go. Then we can do whatever we like." He grabbed four bottles of Lion Lager out of the fridge. "Shall I help you with the cooking?"

"No, no, you go an' drink." She kicked him playfully in the rear and propelled him towards the door. "I know the way you cook!"

After a dinner of string hoppers, beef curry and *pol sambol* everyone got ready to crash. Sunethra insisted on showering first — before all the barbarian soldiers messed up the bathroom, and she vanished from the living room.

Leaving her to it, Dayan unrolled reed mats on the floor and flung bed sheets and pillows at his patrol.

"One of you buggers can sleep on the settee if you want," he said. "Good night." He headed for the bedroom.

"Don' forget which hole to put it into," laughed Sumith.

"After all these months any hole will do," joined in Kamal.

"Fuck off," mumbled Dayan.

He waited till they were busy getting ready for bed, and then tapped softly on the bathroom door.

"Dayan?" he heard her ask over the sound of the shower.

"Who else?"

There was shampoo in her hair as she opened the door just enough for him to squeeze through, and he leaned back against the wall, lighting a cigarette and watching her step back under the shower. The water whipped the shampoo down out of her hair, the white foam sliding down her brown body. Her wet hair was as black as a crow's wing, and had plastered itself to the skin of her shoulders and breasts. The cool water made her dark nipples stand out like rocks across the face of a waterfall.

Her body still had the ability to make him gasp. She was twenty-three, and had married him three years ago. Marriage had done nothing to change the long lean lines of her body, which was still that of the netball player she'd been at school. He could see the tight muscles of her stomach, and below the dark triangle of her pubic hair, the long taut thighs.

She seemed to know he was watching her, and pushing hair and water out of her eyes, she gazed mischievously at him.

"Why don't you throw that bloody fag away an' come here?"

He tossed the cigarette into the toilet bowl — an act that brought an exasperated grimace to her face — and quickly undressed. The shock of the cold water against his sweaty skin made him gasp, but then her warm body was against his, pressing in from knees to lips as she kissed him hotly. She was tall for a Sri Lankan, only a couple of inches shorter than his five feet eight, and his palms ran down the length of her back to the curve of her buttocks. He pulled her crotch against his as her hands glided over him, washing away the sweat and dust of the Northeast.

He closed his eyes, turning his face up to the showerhead, smelling the soap she was using on him. He sucked in a breath, almost choking on water, as her circling palms reached his groin. He had been erect before he even got into the shower, and her touch on his penis was like an electric jolt. With each of her strokes he knew he couldn't take this much longer.

With a cry he spun her around, pushing her forward against the tiled wall. He pushed up between her buttocks, struggling to enter her. His hands cupped her breasts.

"Dayan, wait. . ." she gasped. "The others will hear. Wait till we get into bed—"

"Can't," he muttered, his voice thick in his throat, entering her with a thrust of his hips. "I need you now."

"No, not like this." She pulled free of him, turning to look into his frustrated eyes. "I want it to last when we do it. I've been dreaming of this for *four* months." Still holding him throbbing in her hands, she dropped to her knees. "But how 'bout a compromise?" The tip of her tongue flicked against his cock. "Hmm?"

"Yah, yah. . ." he gasped, tangling his fingers in her hair.

In a single movement she swooped down on the head of his cock, taking it into her mouth, running her tongue along its underside.

Dayan held on for all of three seconds, but the pent up energy of four months of celibacy was just too much for him and he exploded, pulling her head against him as he came, trying to keep his knees from buckling, feeling as if she were drawing the marrow out of his bones.

As Dayan sagged back against the wall, he heard a sound from the door and lazily opened his eyes. A shriek from Sunethra, however, brought him off the wall to see the bathroom door standing ajar. In the doorway stood Kamal and Sumith, eyes popping out, chins dragging at their toes. They both held towels and toothbrushes in their hands.

Realizing he had forgotten to shut the door firmly, Dayan dived across the bathroom, leaving a hysterical Sunethra to find a towel. He stormed through the doorway, still bare-arse naked, slamming the door behind him and glaring at the two members of his patrol.

"What the fuck are you buggers doing?" he howled.

"You never heard of locking the door when putting a jump?" returned Sumith. Both men's eyes were flicking like ping-pong balls from Dayan's dripping face to his now drooping penis.

"Yah," grinned Kamal. "We started to knock on the door an' it jus' opened. But you two were too busy to notice."

"How long were y'all standing there?" Dayan's face was now dark with anger and embarrassment.

"Not long, but enough," chuckled Sumith. "I hope you take a bit longer than that when you're fucking her. Don't you know that bits like to have it inside for more than two seconds?"

Both men were now doubled up, trying to keep their sarongs from falling to the floor as they tried to laugh and talk at the same time. The commotion brought Bandara in from the living room.

"Whassup?" he asked.

"Go an' fucking sleep," growled Dayan. "An' mind your own fucking business! Don't you buggers have any manners?"

"What d'you mean, *us?*" Kamal gasped weakly, tears in his eyes. "You're the one giving us a live blue film."

"*What* live blue film?" Bandara wanted to know, annoyed at being left out of it. "An' why're you walking around with your wee-wee out?"

"Fuck *off!*"

"Don' worry," Sumith said, patting Dayan's bare shoulder. "Your wife is very beautiful, an' we won' tell anybody who isn't in Bravo Squadron, OK?"

Dayan's face had almost reached a shade of purple by now.

"Yah," Kamal assured him, "an' I'll only think of her when I have to give myself a handshake."

Dayan could still hear them laughing in the living room as he went back into the bathroom in an attempt to pacify a tearful Sunethra, who declared she would be leaving early tomorrow morning to her sister's house for two days. When she returned Dayan's three comrades had better be gone.

That night Dayan made love to Sunethra repeatedly, after having assured her several times that the bedroom door was securely locked. The sex in their marriage had always been good, both of them enjoying variety. She made love with an abandon that was similar to her independent personality, something not all Sri Lankan women had.

They had met when she was nineteen, at a carnival in Colombo. He had been on leave, drifting through the city alone, unable to adjust to the civilians around him, drinking. She would say later that it was Dayan's pale brown eyes — unusual but not unique amongst Sri Lankans — that had made her look twice. A month later, Dayan had fucked her for the first time, and a year later they were married.

It was his second marriage. His first, at the age of twenty hadn't lasted much longer than a year. His ex-wife had been from Warakapola, a town in the hills, close to Ambepussa, the regimental home of the Singha Rifles, Dayan's regiment at the time. Coming back on an unexpected weekend pass, he had discovered she was sleeping with someone else. Dayan and a couple of fellow riflemen had beaten the man into a coma. The cops and military police, not taking too kindly to people who cuckolded soldiers had turned a blind eye. Terrified that Dayan would do the same thing to her that he had done to her lover, his wife had fled back to her parents. A month later they were divorced.

His marriage to Sunethra hadn't been that easy either. Her parents were Roman Catholics from Moratuwa, south of Colombo, and hadn't taken too kindly to their eldest daughter marrying a divorced soldier who was, to top it all, a Buddhist. But Sunethra loved her cold-eyed Special Forces trooper, whose gaze seemed to soften only when he looked at her. She married him. Her parents grudgingly came around. The hope of a grandchild was too tempting a prospect to ignore.

However, Dayan knew she wasn't too happy with the job he did. On several occasions she'd mentioned former Special Forces people who were now working in the private security field. She didn't push him too hard; she knew how much the action thrilled him. But looking into her eyes every time he left her at the end of a leave to go back to the Northeast, he could see the unspoken fear in her eyes, her gaze devouring him, trying to remember his every feature in case she never saw him again. Too many SF men returned in sealed coffins, their remains too disfigured for tender civilian stomachs, or sometimes not at all, listed as missing in action.

They lay under the ceiling fan, letting it dry the sweat that the lovemaking had left on their bodies, her hair spread out over the pillows.

"D'you really wan' to go tomorrow?" he asked finally.

"Otherwise?" she snapped. "How can I face that lot after what happened in the bathroom?"

"Mm, OK. But you'll come back day after, no?"

"Yah, yah. Jus' make sure those fine friends are well an' truly gone."

They lay in silence for a while longer, then Dayan rolled over to find a cigarette and she sighed. "You know I hate the smell of those in the bedroom."

"Jus' one," he muttered, finding it and lighting up.

As he lay back and inhaled deeply, she watched the red glow outline his face. "When d'you have to go back?" she asked flatly, her voice emotionless.

"In ten days."

"*What?*" She sat up in bed. "You come back after four months an' tell me you've got only ten days?"

"Orders."

"Orders? Is that all you can say? How can your precious SF do this to you?"

He could hear the tears in her voice, but just shrugged, the irritation rising. "What to do? A job has been brought forward, it seems. Maybe just a course. Who knows?"

As quickly as she had flared up, she calmed down, rolling away from him. She lay quiet, but he knew she was still awake. Women. How could you explain it to them? They never seemed to get it. He had tried to make his ex-wife see it, but it hadn't worked. With Sunethra he hadn't even made the effort.

How do you explain to a woman that this time, this brief string of moments, this period of marital bliss, was just a small part of your life? A bracketed phrase in a sentence that carried all the action and thrill he had ever known. All the excitement and fear he had ever experienced. How did you explain to a woman that the busy beaches of the south could not compare with the lonely sunrise over the Jaffna Lagoon? Or that the excitement of watching a cricket test against India was tame when measured against the rush of adrenalin as you jumped out of a C130 at ten-thousand feet, an eighty-pound ruck strapped to your back? How could you tell her that the colours of the *Vesak* lanterns dotting the streets didn't come close to the hues of Tiger tracer bullets as they reached towards you?

Maybe one day, when the killer instinct had left him, when he was middle-aged and soft-bellied. Maybe then. Not now. Not when he was an NCO in the Special Forces, one of the Fighting Soldiers From the Sky, the Fearless Men Who Fight and Die. Not yet.

He flicked the butt out the window, and saw the glowing end bounce off one of the *anamalu* trees in a shower of sparks.

Airborne, SF, black beret. . . This is the way we end the day. . .

CHAPTER 3

The thirty-two men sitting in the green plastic fibre-glass chairs were dressed in black fatigues and baseball caps, Danner boots on their feet. They were relaxed and confident, chatting softly. The room was warm and comfortable in comparison to the biting November wind of downtown Toronto at dawn.

Lieutenant Jan Conway stretched to ease his back in the hard chair and looked around at the other men. At thirty-eight, ancient for a lieutenant, but promoted from the ranks, he was as fit as anyone in the room, the average age of which was twenty-six, but the chill of Canada's winters were beginning to eat into his bones.

No one was smoking, though a few of the men were looking like they could use a drag. The police Combined Forces Special Enforcement Unit building on Harry Walker Parkway in Newmarket had been declared a no-smoking area, and the rule was rigidly enforced.

Conway and the other men were all members of the Canadian Forces' Joint Task Force 2, based at Kingston, and he knew what the reason for this briefing was. It had to be the Tamils. JTF2 was the Canadian Forces' special operations unit, formed to plug the hole left by the disbanded Airborne Regiment. The unit was also tasked to cover the anti-terrorism role, one that had never been adequately carried out by the Mounties' Emergency Response Teams. There was no reason other than the Tamils that could make the cops call in the military like this. Like other Canadian special operations soldiers, Conway had watched with idle interest the recent police operations against the LTTE in the Greater Toronto area. Most of the busts had been either by the

Immigration Task Force, or in the event of an investigation into drug or extortion rings, by the CFSEU. But the three JTF2 platoons that were based in Ontario had gone to high alert after the last police operation.

During a raid on a building that housed the offices of an employment agency catering largely to Scarborough's Tamils, the cops had run into heavy gunfire. Investigations had revealed that the agency was requiring the families it found jobs for to continue paying a percentage of their salaries. These funds were being funnelled to Europe and the LTTE. What surveillance had failed to show up was that the occupants of the offices possessed at least two M-16A1 automatic rifles. The wall of gunfire had killed one policeman and caused enough confusion for the Tamils to escape.

It looked to Conway, one of the JTF2 platoon leaders, that the cops weren't going to take anymore chances. A second platoon had flown down from Ottawa as backup for Conway's boys, leaving another in the capital as a strategic reserve.

"Morning, folks!" Chief Inspector Alain Watts walked into the room, and Conway noted with satisfaction that he wore dirty blue jeans and a leather jacket. "Kill the lights, will you, Sue."

A WPC at the back of the room dimmed the lights, and Watts tapped the keyboard of a laptop sitting on a desk at the front of the room. A projector threw a colour picture of a busy street onto the whiteboard behind the inspector. On the far side of the street from the photographer was a three-storey building, the ground floor of which seemed to be occupied by a restaurant.

Conway noted that the signage was in English as well as a language that had to be Tamil. All loops and squiggles. "*THE NEW KRISHNA RESTAURANT*", it declared in big green letters, and underneath a smaller line explained that it served "*Indian and Sri Lankan Vegetarian Cuisine*".

"This, gentlemen," said the police officer, "is the focus of our bust. The New Krishna is on Kentin Avenue, off the Kennedy Road in Scarborough. Tamil Town, as it's now being called by its inhabitants. There are more shots of the building available, as well as some architectural plans, so familiarize yourselves with them at the end of the briefing."

The next few pictures showed zoom-ins of the restaurant entrance and the windows on the floors above. "The top floor consists of small apartments rented out to recent Tamil immigrants, but the floor immediately below is taken up with what seems to be office space. Directional equipment picked up the sounds of computer monitors and keyboards as well as voices."

A tap of a button brought up a row of six faces on the board, the names printed beneath the mug shots. "These are the guys we want. We believe that the offices are being used to sell greeting cards online. The cards glorify the Tamil rebellion in Sri Lanka, and are quite popular during Hindu religious festivals. There's one this month called *Deevali* — the Festival of Lights — and so sales are at a high pitch.

"Most of the profits go back to the LTTE, but we also know that some of it is used to run their other rackets here in Toronto — drugs, extortion, forgery — just to name a few. Needless to say, none of it is being taxed, which is the reason for this investigation.

"The two on the right are known LTTEers, and are already wanted for murder in Sri Lanka. They have combat experience over there, so be aware of that. The others we don't know much about, but it should be assumed that at least some of them have firearms experience.

"This brings me to the next subject. Firepower. We know that a lot of automatic weapons are in the possession of these boys, most of them bought in the States and brought across the border. So be ready for that. We don't want a repetition of last week's screw up, which is why you guys have been called in, you know."

Conway hid a smile as he glanced across at the other platoon leader, Lieutenant Mike Collis, a twenty-five-year-old career officer, who rolled his eyes. In spite of public statements about cooperation and teamwork, the Ontario Provincial Police still guarded their turf jealously against their more famous big brother, the Royal Canadian Mounted Police, as well as against the military.

"We've been watching them for four days now. We've got some of our guys in the building across the street, over a grocery store. The Chinese owner's been into something naughty lately. In fact he can't seem to explain to the ITF boys what his brother-in-law is doing in the country without a visa. So we're leaning on him to keep quiet about who he's got upstairs.

"The store backs into an alley that you can use to get some observers in. If you go in as plumbers or as telecom maintenance, there shouldn't be any hassles. I don't want your teams driving by as it's a heavily Asian neighbourhood, and too many white faces will cause suspicion. Your assaulters can move in when we give you control, which will be sometime tomorrow.

"We could hit the sonsofbitches right now, but we need all the perps together at once, which hasn't happened yet. But word is that it'll happen tomorrow. Questions?"

"Yes," said Conway immediately, even though what he had to say wasn't a question. "I'm afraid we'll have to do some drive pasts at some point. We'll have to get eyes on the target in order to come up with an assault plan."

"OK." CI Watts nodded. "But be goddamn discreet about it. Use different vehicles, and come up along Bellefontaine Street rather than Kennedy." He brought up a street map of the immediate area and tapped it.

Lieutenant Mike Collis, the other platoon leader cleared his throat. "Do we take it as given that the Tamils in the area act as lookouts for these guys?"

"Well, it's not like every Tamil in Scarborough is tied to these guys." Watts smiled tightly. "But the LTTE have long tentacles and have put the fear of God into a lot of the immigrants, especially the newer arrivals. It's safer to assume that the locals will give you away, that way there won't be anything unexpected." He looked around at the soldiers. "Anything else?"

"Not right now," Conway said, "but maybe after we see the area. I'd like to put two snipers into the grocery store right now, and carry out a CTR during daylight."

"Fine. One of my guys can give you the grand tour."

*   *   *

On the other side of the world it was already late afternoon, and for the umpteenth time, Ian McEdwards jammed his feet reflexively into the floor well on the passenger side of the dark blue Audi A8, instinctively searching for the brake pedal. With clenched jaw he watched the bus rush towards them at frightening speed. The Audi was on the right side of the road, which in this case was the wrong side — literally, thought McEdwards, because like many former British colonies the Sri Lankans insisted on driving on the left — trying to overtake a battered old Leyland truck as it laboured uphill.

The main Colombo-Kandy "highway" could only accommodate single-lane traffic in most places, and overtaking drivers were forced to pull out into the oncoming lane to do so, something that Sri Lankans did with happy abandon, cheerfully playing chicken with anything from a motorcycle to a container truck.

Just as McEdwards' heart was about to give up on life, the embassy driver casually swung the wheel, cutting off the truck which hooted its indignation, and the oncoming bus thundered past, inches from the Audi's flank.

Glancing over his shoulder, McEdwards noted that the minister was engrossed in the view of Utuwankanda, the hilltop fortress of Saradiel, Sri Lanka's very own Robin Hood, which guarded the road. Fenster was a veteran of the island and was experienced enough to know that looking over one's driver's shoulder was just asking for your life to be shortened by several years.

"Did you know that he was hung by the British, Ian?" the minister asked casually.

"Who sir?" McEdwards managed, hoping Fenster was referring to a particular Sri Lankan driver.

"Saradiel." Fenster pointed to the left of the road. "You can just make out the ruins at the top of the mountain." He sighed. "Sri Lanka seems to revere her failures much more than her successes."

They had just passed through Kegalle, a town only seventy-odd kilometres from Colombo, but they had taken more than an hour to get there on the narrow road, even with their driver's maniacal skills. The land on both sides of the highway was a green sea of paddies, their expanse dotted with scarecrows made of sticks and a few scraps of white cloth. Clay dikes crisscrossed the fields and the occasional water buffalo lay deep in a muddy wallow. The paddy gave way to huge coconut estates in some areas, the trees standing in open ranks like a battalion awaiting inspection, in contrast to the tangled scrub jungle that still clung to the uncultivated areas.

The countryside was mostly flat, broken up by occasional jungle-covered hills, like Utuwankanda, the horizon ahead rising in blue-grey layers as they approached the foothills of the Central Highlands.

McEdwards had the car's overhead sun visor down so that he could use its small vanity mirror to observe the road behind, and now he discreetly adjusted it until he could watch Mrs Fenster. Dressed in a short tan skirt and blouse, she sat next to her husband, seeming to stare out through the front windscreen. However, the dark sunglasses and the honey-blonde bangs of her page boy hair hid her eyes, not revealing if the driver's antics bothered her.

Probably had her morning vodka, decided McEdwards. Patricia Fenster's wild lifestyle and hunger for younger men were well known on the bodyguard circuit. It was just another thing to watch out for. At thirty-six, she was twenty-three years her husband's junior, and had met him soon after his first wife's death, five years earlier.

Fenster himself was in a crisp white cotton shirt and casual khakis, making McEdwards feel overdressed and faintly ridiculous

in his striped tie. As always, the minister's full head of silver hair
was brushed briskly back in stiff waves that made him look several
years younger than he was, in spite of the small bald spot. Tall
and slim at six feet three, he looked after himself, eating right and
exercising regularly, and this contributed to his youthful looks.

The inspector leaned forward, searching in the mirror for
the escort car, as the driver speeded up, racing after a fast-moving
Toyota ahead. Both cars were moving at well beyond the speed
limit, and McEdwards couldn't seem to understand the Sri Lankan
insistence on overtaking anything on the road ahead.

"Not to worry, sir." The driver's round, dark face split into
a grin, noting McEdwards' expression. "I know this road very
well. I drive Mister Shelton many times to Kandy to see the *perahera*."

The little Tamil was the personal driver of James Shelton,
Canadian ambassador to Colombo. The diplomat had lent him to
the minister's entourage, along with the driver of the escort car.

"I read somewhere, Ian," Fenster commented, "that to a
Sri Lankan, the vehicle ahead is not a mere vehicle, but a challenge."

Everyone but Patricia Fenster chuckled, especially the driver.

"What's this *perahera* thing then?" McEdwards asked
the driver.

"Never heard of the Kandy *perahera*, sir? *Aiyo*, famous touris'
attraction, no? It's a Buddhist event, when they parade the holy
tooth relic of Lord Buddha. Massive crowds, and dancers. And
elephants! Many elephants."

"So you have seen this many times?"

"Me, sir? No, only once. I stay in the drivers' quarters at
the hotel. I'm a Hindu. Not so interested in these Buddhist things."

"The tooth is one of the holiest of objects to Buddhists
everywhere," explained Fenster. "It was supposedly rescued from
the Buddha's funeral pyre in 543 BC and smuggled into Sri Lanka
a hundred years later, hidden in the hair of a princess. How about
that for a story, huh? It was always a closely guarded treasure, a
Sinhalese king even going all the way to India to rescue it when it
was stolen by an invading army in the thirteenth century AD. The

Portuguese later seized it and destroyed it in Goa, burning it in public as a heathen idol, though they probably just thought it was a symbol the Sinhalese would rally behind in rebellion." Fenster chuckled. "Of course, the Sinhalese claim it was just a replica that was burned, and that the original — now in Kandy — was hidden by monks."

McEdwards watched the driver out of the corner of his eye, but the man showed no reaction to the minister's story, concentrating on the road.

The Sri Lankan portion of the Canadian embassy staff in Colombo seemed to be almost entirely made up of Tamils, a state of affairs they seemed to studiously guard. The majority of fresh job applicants inevitably were from that community as well, a determined few from the other ethnic groups — Sinhalese, Moors, Malays, and the fast-disappearing Burghers — applying each year, but somehow being blocked or dissuaded by the existing mafia.

They arrived in Kandy by noon, but continued through the crowded town and onto the Mahiyangana Road. Donald Fenster scorned hotels, claiming that the true way to touch the pulse of a nation's people was by living in their homes. He could still lay claim to several affluent and influential Sri Lankan friends from his tenure in the country, and never failed to call on them on the few occasions when he had returned.

Rajan Kumaraswamy was a millionaire textile exporter, a Tamil who held dual Sri Lankan and Canadian citizenship, and he had been delighted to have his old friend Don weekend with him. Sharply conservative and moderate in his politics, especially regarding the Tamil fight for independence, he inevitably found himself defending Tamil militancy against Fenster's virulent anti-terrorist views. The weekend would be an opportunity to renew some of those old debates, which had been frequently waged over a bottle of Glenfiddich at the Colombo Swimming Club.

The Kumaraswamy holiday home or "out-station house" was in Teldeniya, southeast of Kandy, on the banks of the Victoria hydro-catchments project, and as they crossed the Mahaweli River on the outskirts of Kandy, McEdwards watched women washing clothes in the waters below the bridge. They wore brightly printed cotton sarongs wrapped tightly around their breasts and torsos as they slapped clothing against the rocks that broke the fast-moving current. The shiny brown bodies of children flashed in the sunlight as they splashed in the shallows or dived into deeper pools.

When questioned about it by McEdwards, the driver — who was named Baskaran — explained that many of the country's poorer homes did not have running water, not even in the towns and cities, with many families living in poverty. But he said they were still much better off here — "Fresh air, sir, nice vegetables also," — than the slum dwellers of Colombo's shanty towns.

The road followed the Mahaweli, the island's longest river, swooping over the hills, with Baskaran pushing the car on the comparatively open road, trying to make up time. The blast of a horn made McEdwards jump, and the next instant a red Nissan van roared past from behind, full of shirtless young men, clapping and singing. As they swept past, the passengers on the nearside hung out the windows, grinning down at Patricia Fenster's long legs, waving and shouting unintelligibly.

Then they were gone, flashing round a bend in the road ahead, narrowly missing a cyclist who wandered unknowingly along.

"Mad fellows," grumbled Baskaran. "Dunno who taught them to drive."

The view as they breasted the next hill made McEdwards draw in his breath. The road curved down towards a vast expanse of blue-grey water that reflected the hills beyond. The surrounding jungle-clad slopes fell steeply towards the surface of the artificial lake, seemingly devoid of human habitation. A strip of sandy soil divided the water's edge from the green jungle above, a sign that the lake was below its maximum flood level. The branches of dead trees stuck out of the water in places, like the fingers of a skeleton. Portions of the shore were hidden by sweeping coves, tiny inlets and jutting promontories, as confusing as the outline of an amoeba. It was a vista of seemingly untouched beauty, like a glimpse into the Jurassic past. McEdwards almost expected to see huge dinosaurs wading through the shallows.

They raced through the town of Teldeniya and turned away from the Victoria Reservoir, climbing steeply through dense jungle. Here and there small hamlets of lime-daubed houses and shops hugged the road, big-eyed urchins waving mischievously at the cars.

The security guard at the gate of the Kumaraswamy property was just letting them in when the escorting Mazda caught up and followed the Audi in. The house was of two-storey construction and built in the style of a Dutch colonial bungalow.

A short, stocky man was striding across the flagstoned veranda as the cars drew to a halt.

"Don!" he cried, smiling through a big, snow-white moustache that made him look like an Asian Bismarck. The ring of hair that crowned his head was the same colour, contrasting starkly with his dark pate. "How are you, my friend?" He grasped Fenster's hand, looking up at the tall Canadian. "Patricia, so nice to see you again in Sri Lanka," he beamed at Mrs Fenster who actually smiled as she followed her husband up the steps of the veranda.

One of the SPG policemen had walked back down the drive to talk to the gate security, while another went with the cars to make sure they were secure and easily accessible. McEdwards' eyes quickly took in the house and surrounding land as he and the boss were introduced to Rajan Kumaraswamy.

"What is the matter, Don?" the Sri Lankan said in mock horror as he led them into the house. "Since when does a Canadian minister need bodyguards?"

"It's a new world out there, Rajan," Fenster replied as they walked into the split-level living room. "Since September eleventh, we all need to look over our shoulders."

"Yes, yes, I've heard about your government's new plans." Rajan Kumaraswamy's voice was flat, though the side of his mouth curled in distaste as he spoke.

"Well, Rajan, I was hoping we could keep the politics away until evening, at the very least," said Fenster jovially.

Kumaraswamy laughed, leading them through the big room. It was furnished in heavy wood in the style of the Kandyan kingdom, but statues and carvings from Jaffna to Bali dotted the room. Expensive originals hung framed on the walls, ranging from a soft water colour of the cliffs of Dover to a nineteenth century de Ransonnet lithograph of the Beira Lake, both contrasting and complimenting the vibrant hues of Keith Herring and Hundertwasser.

Huge French windows opened onto a terrace beyond, the view from which was even more astounding than the one McEdwards had seen from the road. The Fensters and Kumaraswamy sat at a table in the shade of an awning while the boss stood a discreet distance away. McEdwards walked to the corner of the terrace which overlooked the cool blue depths of a swimming pool on the level below. Looking at the sun flash on the water, McEdwards was aware of the sweat trickling down his spine.

While the VIPs were served Lion beer and lime juice, McEdwards noted with approval that the other two members of the team were already checking the grounds. He would need to get a mental layout of the property after lunch when the minister and wife were happily tucked away for their siesta. Accepting a glass of juice from the servant, he pointed out his men in the garden below, asking that they be taken care of, too.

Beyond the tiled area of the pool, the lawn stretched away in a gentle slope for a hundred metres until it met the jungle which in turn fell away in ridges to the lake. The water lay shimmering between the surrounding hills until, squinting into the glare of the lowering sun, McEdwards could just make out the white expanse of the Victoria Dam at the far end of the valley.

*   *   *

By the next morning everything was in place and Lieutenant Jan Conway sat in the front room above the grocery store on Kentin Avenue. The blinds were pulled down and the room was in almost total darkness. What little light there was came from a computer monitor that showed black and white mug shots of the Tamils who were the targets of the raid. Through the narrow gap between the blinds and the window sills, tripod-mounted binoculars and the dish-shaped directional mikes were trained on the windows across the street.

It was eight in the morning on a Friday, and still totally dark in Scarborough. It was almost -5°C, and a thin layer of dirty snow softened the sidewalks and roofs. The streets between the areas of Underwood and Hillcrest Village were already busy with people hurrying to work and school.

There were very few white faces on the streets, and Conway felt as if he was in a foreign land. The middle-aged were dressed fairly conservatively, but the younger generations, like youth in any western country, opted for tight jeans, baggy shell or cargo pants, and bright jackets with US or Canadian sports logos on them. The smells of Asian cooking drifted on the frosty morning air, and the music that was already blaring from the dozens of shops down Kentin Avenue was everything from American rap to Moroccan *rai* to Hindi and Tamil pop. All the shops, ranging from restaurants to kiosks to appliance stores to sari boutiques had signage in both Tamil and English. Some, like the video rental store at the far end of the block, didn't even bother with English. Conway smirked. He had thought English and French were the official languages of Canada. The store's glass frontage was plastered with garish Tamil and Hindi movie posters portraying macho moustached heroes in bad Beatles haircuts and wild-haired dark-eyed heroines in wet T-shirts or silk and jewellery and little else.

He heard a siren in the distance and stiffened, then relaxed as he realized it was an ambulance, probably headed for the Grace Division Hospital on Birchmount Road.

In addition to Conway, who sat at the binos, two cops from the CFSEU were monitoring the directional receivers and bugging the land telephone line. Both men were second generation Sri Lankan Tamil immigrants and spoke the language fluently.

Conway had wanted a fibre-optic line drilled through the wall of the target building so that they could see more of the interior, but that had proven impossible. There was no way of getting into the building neighbouring the New Krishna Restaurant without raising suspicion.

"Perp number three is getting off the bus on Finch," said CI Alain Watts, standing behind Conway. He was on the radio to one of his men.

Though control had been handed over to Conway and JTF2, a CFSEU man was tailing one of the last Tamils to arrive. Conway wouldn't trigger the assault till all the targets were in the office suite.

"Charlie Team, Target Three is at Finch," Conway said into his lip mike.

"Charlie, roger."

Charlie Team were three JTF2 soldiers parked on Belbrook Road, also off the Kennedy Road, south of Kentin and parallel to it. Once Target 3 turned onto Kentin, they would move north up Kennedy as a cut-off.

"Delta, sitrep," Conway said

All the JTF2 teams were on the same net and could hear everybody else.

"Same-same, Zulu," came the soft reply. Delta Team were the pair of snipers on Bellefontaine Street, north of Kentin, their scopes trained on the rear windows of the building. They would also cover the four men of Alpha Team who would climb the fire escape and assault through the windows.

The front and rear windows of the target building had their curtains drawn, but occasional glimpses front and rear had revealed movement. Recon during the day, the wiretaps, and directional receivers had five targets in the building. Target 3 — one of the men wanted for murder — was *en route*.

"Alpha, sitrep?"

"Alpha in place." They were in a Ford Transit van parked on Bellefontaine.

Echo Team, the two snipers in the room with Conway, had nothing new to report either. They were seeing the same things he was. They would cover Bravo Team, which was downstairs, as they moved across the street into the New Krishna and assaulted up the stairs. The Chinese grocery store owner normally opened for business only at 9am, and so there wasn't the worry of customers getting in the way.

"Bravo, sitrep?"

"Bravo in place."

"Stand by, all teams, stand by."

Conway saw his snipers crouch a little lower, snuggling closer to their G-3SG/1 rifles, and he knew the rest of his platoon would be fine-tuning in a similar fashion. Alpha Team would be huddled against the rear doors of their van, chest to back, rounds chambered, safeties off, waiting for his word that would send them exploding out and up the fire escape. Bravo Team would be doing the same downstairs, hitching flak vests up, making sure Kevlar helmets were secure, ready to race across the street. They would be thinking, rehearsing in their minds everything that could go wrong. What if there's ice on the street? What if diners in the restaurant get in the way? On Belbrook Road, Charlie Team would be switching their car engine on, checking traffic, easing pistols in their holsters.

Charlie Team would get the "go" first, moving up Kennedy once Target 3 had turned onto Kentin. As soon as the Tamil had entered the restaurant and the directional kit had confirmed he was in the upstairs office, Alpha and Bravo Teams would get their "go".

Though the sun wasn't up yet, the darkness had faded enough to make the streetlights look pale and weak.

"Hold it, Jan," Watts snapped, listening to his earpiece. "Perp three has stopped."

"Stand by, all teams, stand by."

"He's buying cigarettes at a kiosk."

"Target Three is stationary on Kennedy. Stand by, all teams."

"He's moving south again," Watts reported. There was a pause of a minute as Watts waited for his man to report.

"Stand by, all teams, standby."

"OK, Jan, perp three is at the corner of Kentin."

"Charlie Team, go!" Conway snapped out. "Charlie Team, go!"

⁂

"Go, go, go!" snarled the Charlie Team leader, a corporal, as he and the man in the back drew their pistols. The driver slammed the Toyota Corolla's automatic transmission into drive and pulled away from the sidewalk with a squeal of tires.

The policeman tailing Target 3 was forty metres behind his man when the Tamil stopped on the curb at the intersection of Kennedy and Kentin.

"My boy's stationary at the corner of Kentin," he reported in a whisper to Watts at the command post. "Lighting a smoke."

"The bastard's stopped on Kennedy!" Watts warned Conway.

"Charlie Team abort!" Conway ordered tersely. "Charlie Team abort! Target Three's still on Kennedy."

"We're *on* goddamn Kennedy!" snapped back Charlie 1.

The cop saw the Tamil look up sharply as the Corolla came screaming through the intersection in a blare of horns, running through the light. Dropping the cigarette he'd just lit, the Tamil started into his jacket pocket.

"Perp three knows the score," he reported. "He's got a phone on him!"

"We're blown," Watts warned.

"Phone ringing in the target building," called out the guy on the directional receiver.

"Shit, he's calling 'em," muttered Watts.

Conway's mind raced, weighing his options. Should he give the go now, with one target out in the open? The alternative was

to wait in the hope that everything would calm down in an hour
or so. But that could leave the operation at the mercy of countless
variables. Some of the targets might decide to leave the building,
or someone might spot an assault team.

"All teams," he went out on the air, "go go go!"

Instantly there was a crash of a door slamming open
downstairs, and Conway saw Bravo Team race across the street in
two pairs, the lead man carrying a shotgun, the others MP-5As.

"Weapons being cocked in there!" came the report from
the directional receiver technician.

People screamed and sheltered behind cubicles as Bravo 3,
in the lead, crashed into the New Krishna Restaurant, trying to
get through and up the stairs before the men above were able to
react. The restaurant was half full of breakfasters, mostly young
university students or manual labourers. A waiter, eyes goggling at
the black-clad soldiers, stood paralysed in their path.

"*Canadian Forces!*" yelled Bravo 3. "Everybody down!"

He jabbed the unresponsive waiter in the stomach with the
muzzle of the Remington pump, doubling him over, pushing him
into a cubicle of diners to get him out of the way of the team.

They were up to the first landing when they heard the crack
of plastic explosives upstairs followed by several bursts of
automatic fire.

Reaching the top of the stairs, Bravo 3 didn't bother trying
the door's lock but put a Brenekr solid slug into it, pumped and
put a second one into the top hinge, the thunder of the Remington
deafening in the stairwell. He stepped aside, slinging the shotgun
and drawing his Glock as Bravo 1 and 2 went piling through the
door, submachine-guns ready. He followed them, leaving Bravo 4
to secure the doorway with his MP-5A.

Conway saw the curtains at the front of the building flutter
in a breeze as Alpha Team used frame charges to blow the rear
windows.

"Target Two armed by the front door," sang out one of
the snipers in the room.

"Do him!"

When the "stand by" had been given, the Echo Team snipers had raised the windows high enough to shoot out of, and now a G-3SG/1 cracked, the muzzle gases causing notepaper on the desk below it to jerk violently.

Bravo 1 broke left into a small reception area immediately beyond the front door, and Bravo 2 broke to the right. The Tamil was crouched by a desk on the far side of the room, a Colt Commando carbine in his hands. The weapon was aimed at the doorway and he was obviously experienced enough to ignore the chaos ensuing from the back room behind him.

Bravo 1 and 2 were still off-balance, orientating themselves with the room, and Bravo 3 was still coming through the door when the window behind the Tamil exploded, the curtain blowing in with a blast of broken glass.

The man with the Commando ducked, hesitating long enough for both Bravo 1 and 2 to put short bursts into him, knocking him back over the flimsy desk.

The door of the back room opened and another Tamil dashed through, skidding to a cartoonish halt as he saw three weapons pointed at him.

"Canadian Forces! Freeze!" screamed Bravo 1. "On the floor!"

The man seemed to be unarmed, and in his late teens. He raised his hands shakily and dropped to his knees on the carpeted floor. Bravo 3 jumped him as the others covered, using his superior bodyweight to pin the man to the ground. Cuffing the guy, he dragged him across the room by the scruff of his neck and threw him down by the stairs where Bravo 4 could cover him.

As suddenly as it had begun, the gunfire and yelling ended, leaving the vacuum that follows close-in fire fights. A shell casing tinkled onto a hard surface, a few splinters of glass fell to the floor. There was equal silence from the next room.

"Bravo, clear," whispered Bravo 1 into his lip mike.

"Alpha, clear," came the reply.

Of the remaining three Tamils in the back room, one had been armed with a revolver, and had been killed, along with one of his companions in the confusion of the crossfire. The third man had been captured. There were no casualties amongst the JTF2 assaulters.

On Kennedy Road, the CFSEU cop saw Target 3 whirl at the sound of automatic fire and come racing towards him, fumbling to put his mobile phone away. The JTF2 Corolla was roaring up the street on the same side in pursuit.

"Perp three's on the run towards me," he snapped out, talking into the mike concealed at his throat, under his roll-necked pullover. He drew a chunky 9-mm SiG as Target 3 dodged through pedestrians.

"Stop! Police!" he roared, pushing panicky people out of the way.

Pedestrians screamed and dived for cover behind fire hydrants and into doorways, clearing the sidewalk as if it was the main street gunfight scene in a cowboy movie.

Target 3 had been looking over his shoulder at the pursuing Corolla as he ran, but now he faced front, eyes jumping across faces until they settled on the cop crouching in his path, pistol levelled, white face twisted in fear and determination.

In one clean movement, without breaking his stride, the terrorist drew a V261 Skorpion machine-pistol from under his jacket and cocked it. Ten metres from the cop, he put a four-round burst into the detective's chest.

The cop tumbled back, his legs tangled under him, dying from the 7.65-mm bullets that had shattered his chest and torn open his lungs. The Tamil abruptly changed direction, and with the short stubby machine-pistol still in his hand, he cut across Kennedy, cars screeching and swerving to avoid him, the crunch of metal and glass punctuating screams and curses. He headed back south on the far side of the road, and the Corolla skidded into a U-turn in an attempt to follow. There was a crash of rending metal as the Corolla was hit by an oncoming Jeep Cherokee; worse, more vehicles piled in, adding to the confusion.

The three men of Charlie Team exploded out of the Corolla's doors and windows, the team leader and back-seat passenger taking off after the terrorist, while the driver ran shakily across the street to the fallen detective.

"Charlie Three," he reported. "Transport immobilized on Kennedy. Man down, I repeat, man down."

"Who's down?" Conway yelled into his mike.

"Come in, Johnny." Watts was trying to raise his man on the net, but was obviously having no joy.

"Tail's down," Charlie 3 reported. "Hit bad. Charlie One and Two are in foot pursuit of Target Three, south along Kennedy."

"*Fuck!*" Watts ripped off his headset and ran for the door.

Conway could hear the thud of rotors. He knew it would be the backup platoon choppering into Huntingdon Hill Heights Park to secure the area. He had called them in as soon as he'd given the "go".

"Zulu, Yankee," they came in on the net. "One minute from LZ."

"Roger that."

"Zulu, Charlie One. We've lost the bastard. We're on the corner of Lovering and Grove Hill."

CHAPTER 4

"Why don't your policemen join us, Don?" Rajan Kumaraswamy waved a lit cigarette at the two Special Protection Group officers standing easily further down the terrace. "I can assure you that you'll be perfectly safe here. Even the bloody local Buddhist priests like me." The Sri Lankan chuckled. "An' *that* is a difficult thing to manage!"

"Well, I'll speak to the chief inspector over there," smiled Donald Fenster, "but I can't promise you anything, Rajan. These guys take their jobs very seriously."

Security had been relaxed considerably since their arrival the previous day, both McEdwards and the team leader realizing that the house and surrounding property were fairly isolated and secure. However, they had still maintained a token effort, taking turns to patrol the perimeter.

It was now 6pm, and as Fenster walked towards his chief bodyguard, he could see the sun touching the hills in the west, turning the sky and the waters of the reservoir into blazing shades of red and orange.

"I think you boys should join us for a drink," Fenster said. "I'm afraid Rajan feels a bit insulted at our lack of trust in his hospitality." He smiled to temper his comment and said, "If you feel you need to, keep a couple of guys at the ends of the terrace."

"OK, Mister Fenster," said the chief inspector, turning to give quick instructions to McEdwards.

The two officers joined the trio at their table, and the two other team members were pulled back from the garden to the terrace, where they leaned over the marble balustrade, sipping beer that the servant brought them.

"Thank you for the invitation, sir," the boss said as they pulled up comfortable rattan armchairs. Chief Inspector Graham Zewelczy was a big man, well over two-hundred pounds, and the chair creaked beneath him. He didn't drink alcohol, but accepted a Bitter Lemon.

"No problem," Kumaraswamy said cheerfully, "I have found that guns don't mean security anyway."

McEdwards savoured his Glenfiddich, and noted that Patricia Fenster was already on her third vodka screwdriver. He had been counting from his vantage point further down the terrace, and he had also seen that, as usual, she didn't join in much of the conversation, preferring the view of the lake. Their host had apologized earlier that Mrs Kumaraswamy could not be there to provide some female conversation, as she was in Los Angeles visiting their son.

"What do you mean?" Zewelczy asked. "About guns and security, I mean?"

"Well, it doesn' help much, no? Don an' I were jus' discussing it now. Look how easily Rajiv Gandhi was assassinated, and our own *dearly* departed President Premadasa."

The tone of sarcasm wasn't lost either on McEdwards or the chief inspector, but neither said anything, and Fenster made no comment either.

"These men were surrounded by armed men," Kumaraswamy went on, "but what good did it do them?"

"But as I said," interjected Fenster, "proper use of intelligence helps the guns."

"India's RAW is one of the best intelligence networks in the region," Kumaraswamy pointed out. "But the Tigers got through. No, I think politics and diplomacy is the bes' way to keep your enemies away, or make them your allies."

"But surely intelligence sharing is a way of making allies, too?" suggested the boss.

"Sharing, yes, meddling, no." Kumaraswamy jabbed his cigarette into the air. "Intelligence sharing is very often a pretext for intelligence gathering in neighbouring countries. And when I mean neighbours, I don't mean only the next-door country, as these days we're all neighbours."

"That's exactly my point, Rajan," Fenster said. "*Now* is the time for us to stand together against terrorism. You've always said that guns aren't the answer to problems. I agree. The world's governments agree—"

"But for how long?" Kumaraswamy cut in. "Once this Bin Laden shit is solved in Afghanistan — *if* it's solved — everyone will be back to the old backstabbing game. The US arming it's so-called 'freedom fighters', Libya and Iraq supporting the 'terrorists'. Look at India, Don. She has spent her years since independence from Britain actively destabilizing the nations around her, so that India remains the economic and political giant of the area. But if they wanted that, they should have done it through peaceful economic means, but no, how did they do it? — By arming guerrilla groups. They armed the Muktabahini against the Pakistanis in what is now Bangladesh. The Tigers in Sri Lanka. Remember the attempted coup in the Maldives in 1988? Well, it seems strange that the Indians had a reaction force ready and waiting. Two battalions were flown into the Maldives the very next day and the rebels — who turned out to be Sri Lankan Tamil mercenaries — surrendered without much of a fight. India still maintains a base in the Maldives, something the buggers didn't have before."

"Are you suggesting the Indians were behind the coup?" Fenster raised an eyebrow.

"Come on, Don, don't play the innocent. You were in Sri Lanka at the time. You know the story. Some obscure Maldivian businessman was made the scapegoat, India claiming that he'd hired former TNA fighters. The Tamil National Army — what a coincidence — was trained by the Indians to replace their own peace-keeping force once the Tigers turned on India. And the only reason India dumped the Tigers was because they'd found an easier way to get their fingers into Sri Lanka. Send peace keepers to fight their own protégés."

"OK, OK," Fenster raised a hand in surrender. "I remember now."

"As if you forgot. Ha!" Kumaraswamy poured himself another Glenfiddich, still talking. "The only people the Indians couldn' screw were the Chinese. *Those* buggers had too much muscle an' didn' give a damn about world opinion. If India had continued arming the Tibetan rebels — like they tried in the fifties — the Chinese would have happily wiped out the lot and then invaded northern India." Kumaraswamy took a sip. "But wait. Now that India is wagging its tail so hard at George Bush, I'm sure they have a plan. Pakistan will never be able to continue its little war in Jammu and Kashmir, not after September eleventh. And US interest in this region is just what India needs to get revenge on China. The Chinks are the only fellows who've put India in its place."

"But don't you think proxy-wars are still better than an outright conventional war?" Zewelczy asked.

"Well, here in Sri Lanka it couldn't have got any bloodier than this," Fenster pointed out before Kumaraswamy could answer. "The guerrilla war in the north has claimed a conservative estimate of sixty thousand deaths. The communist rebellion in the late '80s added something like another thirty thousand."

"Many leaders in this region have paid for their mistakes with their lives," added Kumaraswamy, "learning far too late that terrorists can't be controlled. When Indira Gandhi was the Indian Prime Minister, her government supported both the Muktabahini and the Tamil rebels. In 1984 she was killed by a Sikh terrorist, one of her own bodyguards. Her son, Rajiv, when he became Prime Minister, continued support for the Tigers and other groups. When he dumped them, they killed him in 1991. President Premadasa supplied weapons to the Tigers when he wanted them to drive the Indian Peace Keeping Force out in the late eighties, but in the nineties the tables were turned once more, and the Tigers killed him in 1993."

"So the bottom line is that the world getting together on this is a good thing, eh, Rajan?" Fenster said.

"I repeat, for how long? There is no intelligent defence of the acts of September eleventh, but who will decide in the future who a terrorist is, before he commits another September eleventh? Why call the *Mujahidin* 'freedom fighters' but the Al Qaeda 'terrorists'? Why is a Contra a 'rebel' but a Tiger a 'terrorist'? Yasir Arfat and Martin McGuiness were both terrorists, but one is now Palestine's *de facto* head of state, and the other is Northern Ireland's Minister of Education."

Kumaraswamy sighed, looking out into the now darkening sky. "Violence cannot end it, Don. You know that. You're a politician. It may get attention, but eventually it has to be given up. And the root causes must be addressed. D'you think that bombing them in Afghanistan and throwing them out of Canada will end it?" He looked back at Fenster. "Don, they fight because they suffer. And suffering must be addressed, not bombed."

Fenster smiled in triumph. "But suffering can be addressed only by civilization, Rajan. And civilization must be defended."

"*Civilization?*" Kumaraswamy thumped his heavy whisky glass down on the table. "Where was your civilization when hundreds of Tamils were massacred in 1983? When Tamil families were burnt alive in their homes because Sinhalese shanty dwellers fancied the TV they owned? Where is your civilization *now* when Iraqi children starve because the US hasn't the balls to get rid of Saddam Hussein?" The Sri Lankan glared across the table, moustache bristling.

"It's not *my* civilization, Rajan," Fenster said gently, slightly taken aback by Kumaraswamy's vehemence, having forgotten how forceful these debates had tended to get, even at the Colombo Swimming Club. "It's *ours*. And in order to be diplomatic, we must first survive. When the terrorists are willing to talk once more, we may do so."

"Please excuse my temper, Patricia." Kumaraswamy leaned back in his seat. "It's a subject that I feel strongly about." He refilled his glass with the single malt whisky. "And this particularly fine Scotch—" he glanced at Fenster with a twinkle in his eye — "*civilized* as it is, makes me forget my manners."

Noticing that McEdwards was gazing past him, he quickly changed the subject. "Interesting, isn't it, Mister McEdwards?" he said, turning to face the lights of the Victoria Dam at the far end of the W-shaped reservoir. "One of the few good and intelligent feats of modern Sri Lanka. Though not as spectacular as the tanks built by the ancient Sinhalese kings to irrigate the dry zone. There's another one southeast of here at Randenigala, and a smaller one to the southwest at Maskeliya. Together, they used to provide ninety-five percent of our electricity."

"Sounds like a prime target for the terrorists," noted McEdwards.

"I presume so, from the amount of security in the area. I'm fascinated by photography and wildlife myself, as Don here will remember, and I used to spend hours exploring the lake by boat. But not anymore. The soldiers at the dam won' let anyone closer than two kilometres, especially not a Tamil like me.

"Recently, however, what once seemed like an endless supply of power doesn't seem to be so endless. Deforestation means that the rains aren't falling as heavily in these catchments areas as they once did. This year was especially bad an' the government was resorting to power cuts. You're lucky to have missed the worst of it, since the rains seem to be back. A few weeks ago we were having up to six or seven hours of cuts per day."

"But why rely so heavily on hydro-power?" inquired the boss. "Surely there must be other sources?"

"Afraid not. Sri Lanka has no fossil fuel, an' we're too poor to buy it. What little we do buy provides about fifteen percent of the total. Think anyone will give us nuclear technology?" Kumaraswamy laughed and lit another cigarette. "Coal power plants were proposed a few years ago, first at Mawelle, and then at Norichcholai. Protests about ecological damage by people who were more interested in political — or religious — power rather than any other sort quickly killed that idea."

"You seem to be doing OK here," Fenster commented, gesturing at the lights blazing in the house behind them, and those that lit the terrace and pool.

"Ah, yes, but that's because I have my own little thermal power plant. A diesel-powered generator that lets me have all the little luxuries like satellite TV and air conditioning. Anyone who can afford it does the same. Including the MPs and ministers, who claim it as a government benefit. So it's not surprising that no one's pushing very hard for a solution to the power crisis. Like with the war, too many people are making a profit to give a shit. It's the little man out there on the street who's getting screwed."

He pushed back his chair and rose, waving for the servant. "But this is getting a bit too depressing now, isn't it, Patricia? Why don't we go in for dinner before the mosquitoes arrive?"

*

Late that night, Fenster sat at a small writing desk in his room, checking his email on a laptop. Patricia was already in bed, under the mosquito net, asleep.

Fenster's staff had remained in Colombo to hammer out some of the details of the extradition treaty with the civil servants in the Sri Lankan ministries of Foreign Affairs and Justice, and they had updated their boss on the current situation, which seemed to be moving along smoothly.

What worried Fenster were the reports from his department in Ottawa, informing him of the JTF2 raid in Scarborough that morning. It was now noon in Toronto, eastern standard time, and there had already been violent protests by the Tamil community, and a lot of adverse publicity in the local and foreign electronic media. Running fire fights with automatic weapons between the military and terrorists on the streets of Canada was something that wasn't going down well. Tamil community leaders were blaming the provincial government for using the military in what was claimed to be a high-handed manner, violating proper procedure. More JTF2 raids were planned for the following days, and some parliamentarians were apparently getting cold feet at the prospect of more violence. Fenster was advised to return to Ottawa as soon as possible if he wished to push through the new bill.

Fenster went into *CNN*'s website and checked out their report on the Scarborough raid. The reporter on the streaming video feed made it sound as if he was ducking RPG fire in Kabul, graphically describing the JTF2 assault on the New Krishna Restaurant. The report gave the impression of jackbooted thugs terrorizing innocent diners while using machine-guns and grenades to massacre mere tax evaders.

He shut down the laptop and turned towards the bed. He'd have to cut short his visit to Sri Lanka by several days. But for now he could enjoy this weekend away from the world of politics and diplomacy.

Patricia rolled over as he got under the thin cotton sheet. The air conditioning had been turned down so that the room was just a degree or two cooler than the night air, and the mosquito net made the room misty and ethereal, as if the bed was cocooned from the world.

"Enjoyed your day, honey?" he asked her as she sleepily shook blonde hair out of her eyes.

Patricia had spent most of the day swimming and sunbathing down at the reservoir while Fenster and Kumaraswamy had engaged in a spot of fishing.

"Mm," she mumbled. "I just wish I didn't have to listen to you guys and your politics all the time."

"C'mon, Patty." He propped himself up against the headboard, leafing through some notes he'd made of what he needed to discuss with Sri Lanka's Minister of Trade on Monday. "You know what Rajan's like. He loves it."

"So do you," she pointed out. "Can't you think of anything else to discuss? Here we are on a beautiful tropical island, not having visited the place in years, and all you can discuss is terrorism and corruption."

"Seems to go hand in hand over here," he muttered more to himself. "But tomorrow will be much better," he said to her with a smile. "We'll be visiting the Temple of the Tooth."

"Oh, golly! How nice." She shook her head in exasperation. "And I suppose you and Rajan will go on about the damage done by that Tiger bomb a few years ago. No, thanks. I think I'll stay here and work on my tan."

"Are you sure? Don't you want to look around Kandy?"

"No. I hated it last time. So congested and crowded."

"Yes, the Brits didn't plan to have the town overrun by Japanese cars when they planned it out."

"And can you stop giving me a history lesson on every place we visit, Donald?" She slid down until only her face was above the covers. "I can read *The Lonely Planet* as well as you." She subsided into a few seconds of sullen silence before continuing: "And if you *have* to leave one of those grouchy babysitters of yours with me, make sure it's that Inspector McEdwards. He's at least a little more sociable than the others."

"Well, good night then." He kissed her on the top of her head and went back to his notes.

"It could be," she said, her voice muffled by the pillow. Her hand ran across his thigh, slipping into his pyjama bottoms.

He looked across at her with a raised eyebrow as she began to stroke him, coaxing him to attention in her fist. Patricia's appetites had nothing to do with her mood, he'd learned. Happy or sad, tired or drunk, fucking came first.

Fenster flicked through the papers, trying to ignore her even though he knew it was useless. She refused to be ignored, and his own body knew it and betrayed him. She rolled over on top of him, her breasts crushing the sheets of A4 paper, naked, as she always preferred to be. Her hips ground down against him even before he had put away his notes, impaling herself on him.

She rocked and plunged, her thighs gripping him, hands grasping the headboard, head flung back, tousled blonde hair falling across her closed eyes; off somewhere in that world he knew he could never enter. Skin, it was just skin. That was all a man ever possessed of a woman, all he could ever predict or be guaranteed. Even the inside of the vagina was just skin.

As always, she came in minutes, back arching as she gave a choking cry that was quickly bitten off. Then she'd roll off him and onto her stomach, burying her face in the pillows as he took her from behind, thrusting urgently in the hope of catching up with her, finding that place she always disappeared into on these occasions.

*   *   *

At the end of his ten days leave, Dayan Premasiri walked into Army Headquarters at Galle Face. He walked up Baladaksha Mawatha, the road that ran through the base from the Galle Road to Slave Island, wondering what was in store for him. The fact that they had been asked to report to the Directorate of Special Forces here in Colombo could mean a job in the city or its suburbs, or it might mean a training course.

The base didn't have the look of a typical military complex, with functional offices, barracks and parade ground, the way most people would expect. In the years of peace in the 1970s, Army HQ had been housed in a single colonial-style building on Baladaksha Mawatha, a street that paralleled the western shore of the Beira Lake, between it and the coastal Galle Road. The mansion had been one amongst many that housed wealthy Colombo families, foreign embassies, and some government ministries. However, with the war swelling the ranks of the Army, and forcing HQ to expand as well, the other stately buildings had been gradually acquired. Now the base encompassed the entire street which was probably the neatest and best maintained one in Colombo. The administrative headquarters of many of the Army's fighting arms — the Directorates of Infantry, Armour, Artillery, and Specia

Forces — were based here too, as well as more obscure departments like the Directorates of Sports and of Welfare. Also within the complex was the huge Colombo Military Hospital.

Dayan entered from the Galle Face gate, knowing that it would be less crowded than the other entrance. Most visitors and soldiers returning from leave used the Slave Island gate, through which the huge numbers of families visiting wounded servicemen were also required to enter. The Galle Face entrance was usually frequented by troops in uniform going on or returning from official duties in the city or elsewhere.

Flashing his Army ID and orders under the nose of the bad-tempered Military Police sergeant, he walked in, ignoring the man's demand for a closer look at the orders. The sergeant didn't demand too hard, though. He'd seen the eagle, sword, and arrows of the SF badge on the ID, and knew better than to push his luck too far.

Hefting his bag further up on his shoulder, he walked on, pretending not to notice the disapproving glares of officers as he inspected the rugby goal posts in the distance, sticking up above the sports complex. Dayan was neatly dressed in shirt and jeans, and he had shaved, but his hair was still longer than regulation and flopped over his collar. SF and Commando troops weren't required to shave or wear military haircuts when on missions, and sometimes even in camp the rules weren't too strictly enforced, in spite of the efforts to the contrary of the rest of the Army. "The Long-Haired Devils", the Tigers called them. This tradition resulted in the most outrageous sideburns, bandido moustaches, ponytails, and beards. These didn't mean that SF and Commando troops were undisciplined or sloppy. Far from it. They had proven over the years, when employed correctly, to be the most efficient fighting units in the country. They just didn't bother that much about formalities or unnecessary silliness. If something didn't interfere with your fighting capability, why change it?

In addition, badges and patches and other flashy kit were generally avoided, unless on special parade. In camp, everyone knew who you were and what you'd done. There was no need to advertise it. Flashy berets, shoulder tabs, and qualification patches were for the infantry, or the Americans.

Dayan had met some of the US Special Forces on training courses. They walked around everywhere with their green berets and polished jump boots, para wings, jumpmaster wings, sharpshooter badges and all the other shit covering their chests. He hadn't been impressed.

Dayan had a friend in Delta Group, one of the Commando units, and he'd heard from him that a visiting US A-team had done a friendly competition run against the commandos in their "Killing House" at Ganemulle. The Killing House was a close-quarter battle training site, built so that the walls and partitions could be moved and changed around to form various indoor hostage situations. Each competing team would take turns to set up a scenario through which the opposing team would have to manoeuvre. The winners would be the team that went through the fastest, nailing all the targets and sparing the hostages.

He had heard that the commandos had gone through in almost half the time, using just a four-man patrol, than the Americans had with twelve. Dayan's friend, who had been an observer that day, had also maintained that the Green Berets had been noisy and uncoordinated.

Dayan had once met two British Special Air Service men at sniper school in Diyatalawa in the Central Highlands. They were there as observers, but had done some work on the ranges and given some helpful advice. Dayan had been deeply impressed by the two NCOs. Neither of whom had worn any badges or patches, their heads protected from the sun by faded jungle hats, battered desert boots on their feet. He hadn't even known they were SAS until they'd left. But they'd been deadly accurate on the ranges, and very good at field craft.

Inside the Directorate, Dayan located the briefing room he'd been instructed to report to, and found the rest of his patrol waiting outside.

"How?" he said in greeting. "How was leave?" He sat down next to Sumith.

"OK. Fucked, drank, and slept, what else?" came the reply.

"How's your wife?" asked Kamal, not cracking a smile.

"Go an' fuck your mother."

"He can't," pointed out Bandara, not wanting to be left out, "she's dead. But his sister is good."

"Yah, my sister's beautiful," retorted Kamal, "not like that ugly one you have. Even a dog won' fuck her."

Sumith laughed and turned back to Dayan as the other two continued to debate the merits of each other's families.

"Something sirra is up," he said. "The OC is here."

"Who, Sudhu Loonu?" asked Dayan, surprised.

"No, his father," replied Sumith sarcastically. "Who else is OC Bravo?"

Sudhu loonu was Sinhalese for garlic, and the officer commanding Bravo Squadron, a captain, had a fondness for the pungent bulbs, something that resulted in him trailing a strong odour of it and earning him his nickname. The squadron sergeant major maintained that it was a good thing the captain didn't go out on many recce patrols anymore as the terras would follow the smell of garlic straight to his hide. The OC being here was something unusual in itself. Most briefings would have been by the SSM or the ops officer, with the troop commander present if required.

"Anyway," went on Sumith, "wonder what's up. I met Samarasekara outside, and the bugger said he hoped I had my passport ready." Samarasekara was the squadron operations officer. "Think they're sending us on an overseas course?" Sumith was looking excited.

"Dunno."

None of the others had been overseas, but Dayan had got his jump wings in Pakistan with the Special Service Group, that country's special operations unit. At the time Sri Lanka didn't have the necessary aircraft to do large-scale parachute training, and many soldiers, mostly special operations troops, were jump-qualified in Pakistan, Israel, and South Africa.

"Morning, boys."

The bulk of OC Bravo swung round the corner and came briskly down the corridor. At six feet two, and over two hundred pounds, he looked the movie ideal of the special forces warrior, shaven headed, and with a handlebar moustache. The only thing that spoiled the image was the garlic. The OC wore faded DPMs with only his captain's stars, jump wings, and the jolly-roger SF qualification sleeve patch on them.

"Good morning, boss," they chorused, following him into the briefing room.

The squadron ops officer, Samarasekara, was already in the room, and with him was an Int lieutenant. There was no one else in there. An overhead projector stood in front of a white board, and there was a television set and VCR nearby. They sat down in the front row of seats, and the OC leaned against the wall next to the white board.

"OK," he said without any formalities. "This is a briefing for a mission. For it, you will be detached to Int, and be under their control." His eyes scanned across their faces. They were not being asked to volunteer. "Does anybody have a problem with that?"

The patrol looked at each other. No one was really too happy to go to Int. Working in the squadrons was what they'd trained for, and were experienced in. All the James Bond stuff was too weird. But there was no point telling the OC that, as he already knew what SF troops thought of the Intelligence Corps.

It was probably an extraction job, decided Dayan, to pull some Int team out of a location in the north. But Sumith's comment about passports kept niggling at him.

"This is obviously not a squadron job, no, boss?" he said. "But are there gon' to be other SF fellows involved?"

"Not in your particular mission," the OC answered. "There'll be other SF patrols doing similar jobs, but there'll be no contact."

"Can you tell us what sort of job it is, boss?" pressed Sumith.

"Look." The OC pushed off the wall impatiently. "You'll get all the details in the briefing. If you have a problem with operating under the control of Int, jus' say so, an' we can have a private chat about it. If not, I'll tell you now that it's a civil clothes job, it's outside the country, and it could last as much as six months."

The patrol stared at him. This was something else. No one was going to turn down the chance of doing a combat mission overseas, even if it was an undercover one.

When there were no more questions or comments, the OC turned over the briefing to the Int officer. The lieutenant rose and started straight off, not bothering to introduce himself. They were told that the briefing would take several days, and that they would be billeted in the base for the duration. The Int man then said that he would start off with an outline of the job, and then they could go into the operating procedures.

The lights were dimmed and the overhead projector switched on. The first slide was a map of Germany.

"Gentlemen, this is the country you'll be operating in."

That hit everyone with a jolt. They'd all been expecting India, or at a stretch, Canada. But *Germany?* They didn't even speak English over there, did they?

The next slide was a map of western Germany, bordering Holland and France. The area known as North Rhine-Westphalia. On it, the city of Cologne was highlighted, situated on the Rhine between the industrial city of Düsseldorf and Bonn, the capital of the old West Germany.

Their mission would be to assist Int in the surveillance of certain buildings used by LTTE cover organizations in Cologne, and to keep tabs on individual LTTEers. It was obvious that Int could do this without any SF help, but they were told that it might be necessary to kill some of these individuals or assault and destroy their offices, and specialist troops would be needed. It was thought that the Tigers might start to shift much of their financial and propaganda operations to Europe now that things were hotting up in Canada. They had already begun this in 2000, but recent events were felt to be speeding up matters. If sufficient proof could be obtained, they would be instructed to nip things in the bud.

This was a totally black operation, being undertaken without the knowledge or permission of the German government, and therefore all precautions had to be taken to ensure security. Firstly, dated documents stating that the four men had been court martialled and kicked out of the Army would be produced if any of them were captured by the German police or the LTTE. They were to avoid capture at all costs, and if any of them were killed, the bodies would be destroyed by the remaining SF men. Their families would be told they had been killed in action in the north, the bodies mutilated, and the coffins would be sealed.

The last was a common practice in the Sri Lanka Army. If enough body parts could not be found of a dead soldier to make up a decent corpse, very often the dead man would be replaced by logs, or bodies of enemy troops. Dayan knew of several occasions when Sinhalese families had possibly buried or cremated the body of the terrorist who had killed their own dearly departed loved one.

Each of the four soldiers would hand in his passport — if he possessed one — and be issued a new one that showed him to be a commercial artist or photographer. Their cover was that they were in Germany on a training programme with a local advertising agency. The small ad agency was owned by a former Sri Lankan soldier, and he had agreed to authenticate their cover. As such they could move around the city like tourists or students, their cameras not causing much suspicion.

They would spend the first couple of months familiarizing themselves with the city and its streets, and also getting the hang of driving around it. Prior to departure for Europe, they would do a two-week crash course in German at the Goethe Institute in Colombo. It wouldn't be anywhere near perfect, but they'd know enough of the language to read road signs and obtain basic information.

Their controller would be an Int operative who had been in Germany for several years, and was thoroughly familiar with the country and its workings. The operative would find them accommodation, and when necessary, vehicles. If weaponry or specialist surveillance kit was needed, it would be supplied by the military attaché at the Sri Lankan consulate in Bonn. Weapons and other stuff could be brought in by diplomatic bag, and it would be easier than trying to buy them in Germany.

They were also warned, however, to stay away from the consulate, and especially the DFI crew, maintaining contact only through their controller. They were told that the reason for this was that operational security was at the highest level for this job, which would be kept strictly Army-only.

Dayan and the patrol would plan and carry out the tasks themselves, in the way thought best, but targets and specific tasking would come from their Int controller.

"It's going into winter in Europe, with temperatures expected to average around zero in Cologne," the briefer said. "At night it'll drop even further, and this could continue till March. I believe Corporal Premasiri has some experience in winter warfare, but for the rest of you it'll be a new thing."

The last comment drew a smirk from the ops officer and a glare from the OC. Dayan shrugged and smiled sheepishly. While in Pakistan for jump training, he had managed to wangle himself a spot in a mountain warfare exercise in Jammu and Kashmir, the disputed province India and Pakistan had fought two wars over. Under the cover of the exercise, his SSG patrol had penetrated thirty kilometres across the Line of Control into Indian territory. They had been over five thousand metres up in the Haramosh Range, and it had been bitterly cold. They had been out in the snow for four days, and Dayan thought he was going to die. It had been –40°C at times, so that they'd had to wear goggles and masks constantly to prevent their eyeballs freezing or teeth shattering. The Pakistani mountain veterans with him, however, had just laughed, drinking tea and smoking under their ponchos.

By the time SF HQ in Maduru Oya found out what he was up to and demanded he get out of J&K — threatening to RTU him if he didn't obey — he was already on his way out.

The Int officer told them to draw funds and do their own shopping for cold weather kit in Colombo, as they couldn't wear military issue kit. Odel was the only store that stocked any winter clothing — mostly for European tourists — and they were told to go there. They were also told that if they didn't bring back receipts for their little shopping spree, the money would be coming out of their pay.

Finally, they were told that Dayan would be reinstated to sergeant. A year ago, he'd received his third stripe, after three years in the SF, but it had been short-lived. A month after promotion, he had flown down to Ratmalana with his troop commander and another soldier to pick up some kit from the Colombo harbour. They were to take four SF men — who were returning from leave and would be waiting for a return flight at Ratmalana — with them to the port to help with loading the kit. They had got the stuff and were driving back to the airbase in a Tata 1210 truck when all hell broke loose.

It had been *Vesak*, the biggest Buddhist festival of the year, when the followers of the Buddha celebrated the day of his birth, enlightenment, and death. All three conveniently on the same day, Dayan often supposed, to save time. The celebrations normally went on for several days, and were generally carried out by hanging colourful paper lanterns on everything in sight, and building huge 'pandols'. A pandol was more or less a large comic strip depicting the life of the Buddha, and was as tall as a five-storey building and festooned with lights that whirled and flashed in mesmerising patterns. The people of the cities thronged the streets in their millions, "going to see *Vesak*," as it was called.

On that fateful *Vesak* evening, on the trip back to the airbase, they discovered that the four SF men returning from leave had brought a bottle of arrack along to join in the festivities. At some point of the journey the bottle had been finished, and one of the soldiers bored with the crowds and traffic, decided to liven things up by tossing a white phosphorous grenade into a nearby *dansala*.

The latter is a stall that provides free food — usually rice and curry — to the crowds touring the streets. In the Buddhist philosophy of sin and merit, sin had to be counterbalanced by acts of merit if one did not wish to be reincarnated as a cockroach or a dung beetle or something equally miserable. Therefore, the *dansala* was an act of merit by its owner.

That night, however, the SF soldier sinned greatly; being extremely lucky that no one in the *dansala* was killed or even seriously injured. But the chaos that followed the *whoof!* of the WP burst was incredible. Men with their sarongs on fire leaped out of the stall, and women and children dashed away in panic. Food and drink was thrown to the winds as devotees tried to escape the flames and choking white smoke.

With the police in hot pursuit they'd screamed along through the crowded streets of Colombo, miraculously avoiding an accident and getting as far as the Galle Road before heavy traffic halted them. The police hadn't been sympathetic, and neither had the Military Police. The RSM had been even less sympathetic when he arrived to bail them out of the MP cell the next morning, having had to cut short his weekend pass and leave an absolutely unsympathetic wife behind.

The soldier who had thrown the grenade, and the troop commander had been RTU'd — returned to unit or, in other words, kicked out of the SF — immediately, Dayan was demoted back to corporal.

The Int briefer said that they would break for lunch and in the afternoon would go into the details of target locations, identities, communications and codes, and all the hundreds of little details that such a mission entailed.

As he watched the four men file out, the OC wondered what they were thinking — fearing — about being sent out into a foreign country. Premasiri would be the one to hold them together. A good SF soldier, though a bit too unpredictable. But he supposed they all were, that's why they were in the SF. On the whole, however, he felt the patrols had been chosen well, they would all do their jobs with that incredible determination that always amazed him in the lower ranks. He expected it of officers, supposedly better educated and brought up, but it was these young farm boys, sons of fishermen, or common labourers who often astounded him. True, these days, some of them were as well — if not better — educated than their officers. Premasiri had his O/Levels, if he wasn't mistaken.

But he had seen the bravery a hundred times in his career as a professional soldier. He remembered his first battle, ten years previously — the Siege of Elephant Pass.

The OC had been a young second lieutenant with his parent unit, the 6th Singha Rifles in 1991, when the huge base at Elephant Pass had been attacked by the terras. The base commanded the causeway that ran through it, the only road and rail connection to the Jaffna Peninsula, and the Tigers had been determined to take it. They had used ZSU-23-2 anti-aircraft guns and heavy machine-guns to cut off the base from aerial resupply. Then they had used armoured bulldozers and human-wave attacks to try and overrun the perimeter.

But the riflemen of 6/SR had held out for a month, along with a few other attached units until seaborne reinforcements had fought their way through to them. The regiment had been shattered in the battle, having to be pulled out for rest and replacements, losing almost sixty percent casualties. But the terras had been given a terrible mauling, having as many as five hundred and fifty guerrillas killed, and many more wounded in the siege alone.

The OC remembered seeing Lance Corporal Kularatne charging an attacking bulldozer with a grenade in each hand, ducking through horrendous fire to climb the armoured sides of the vehicle and drop the grenades in, dying in the attempt. The Sri Lankan media had made a national hero of the soldier, and streets and schools were later named after him. The Ministry of Defence didn't release the fact that in the dark and confusion he'd been hit by friendly fire.

He also remembered the lone riflemen running into Tiger machine-gun fire, being cut down in turn, but each time a fresh soldier replacing the dead one in a suicidal attempt to recover the body of their company commander. Just for the corpse of Captain Crazy, OC Charlie. A corpse that could feel nothing, lying there in the sandy soil riddled by machine-gun fire, not knowing the sacrifice of nineteen-year-old soldiers willing to give their lives to ensure their OC went home.

Now, as at similar moments, the captain tried not to be bitter, tried not to be angry at a world that didn't care — didn't even *know* — of the bravery he had seen, of youth laid on the altar of comradeship.

CHAPTER 5

Covering roughly a quarter of the teardrop-shaped island's sixty-six thousand square kilometres, Sri Lanka's Northern Province is the heartland of the Liberation Tigers of Tamil Eelam. Capped at its northern extremity by the Jaffna Peninsula, its southern border twists diagonally through the scrub jungle of the Dry Zone, from the Kokilai Lagoon on the north-eastern coast to the tiny fishing village of Mullikkulam on the north-western coast. The province itself is made up of its four districts — Jaffna, covering both the peninsula and part of the mainland in the north, Mullaitivu on the northeast coast, Vavuniya on the province's southern border, and Mannar spread across the west coast and including the island of of the same name.

To someone looking at a topographical map, however, or peering out of an aircraft, none of the confusing provincial and district borders would be apparent. Looking north, they would see a huge dusty green wedge of land, flanked on the left by the Indian Ocean and on the right by the Bay of Bengal, narrowing into the hazy distance before being cut off from the Jaffna Peninsula by the Jaffna Lagoon. The terrain itself is covered by deceptively open-looking scrub jungle, interspersed in patches by primary jungle. While the primary jungle isn't the triple-canopied soldier's nightmare that covers countries like Borneo and Vietnam, it contrasts sufficiently with the low scrub to fool the casual observer into thinking the land is open and easily passable. On the ground, the scrub presents a dusty, thorny tangle twelve feet high that blocks any vision beyond several metres. What little moisture there is in the land drains away from occasional low and rocky ridges in hundreds of streams and rivers, all but the largest of which are merely wadis during the dry season. Flowing towards both coasts, they occasionally linger in small reservoirs that have been constructed by the ancient Sinhalese and Tamil kings in an attempt to irrigate the land. Years of war mean these reservoirs have fallen into disrepair, ruining any hope of further rice cultivation on a large scale, at least in the foreseeable future. What the dry months haven't destroyed, the jungle has reclaimed, leaving large areas that are overgrown by secondary scrub and elephant grass. The little cultivation that remains in the interior of the Northern Province is of yams, vegetables, and spices that are grown in slash-and-burn clearings.

While the towns of the province are connected by half a dozen so-called highways from which spread out a network of narrow secondary roads and tracks, the most striking feature to the casual observer — and the most important to a military planner — is the A9 highway that splits the province in half like a spinal column. This highway, which leaves the military logistical hub of Vavuniya in the southern portion of the province, is a two-lane black-topped strip that dwindles in places to a dirt track as it runs north through Mankulam, Kilinochchi, and Paranthan before crossing the Jaffna Lagoon on a causeway at Elephant Pass. The main railway line from the south parallels this highway for most of the distance, though a train has not travelled its length in over a decade, and most of the steel rails and wooden sleepers have been pilfered to construct LTTE bunkers. It is the only road and rail link between the southern three-quarters of the country and the city of Jaffna.

Of the three aforementioned towns that lie between Vavuniya and the Jaffna Lagoon, Paranthan and Mankulam — respectively ten and forty kilometres south of the Jaffna Lagoon — are immediately recognizable for their strategic value. Both these towns command highway junctions, a single road forking away from the A9 at each point, eventually intersecting at the coastal district capital of Mullaitivu. Thus, a lopsided triangle is formed, its north-south baseline being the A9 highway, with Mullaitivu its eastern apex.

The hamlet of Mankulam, at the southern end of the triangle's baseline, is the smallest of the three towns, and it is one of the most fought over and blood-soaked in the Eelam Wars. Lying midway between Vavuniya and the Jaffna Peninsula, it is a vital strongpoint controlling both the railway and main highway running north to south.

The nearby village of Kokavil was once held by two platoons of the 2nd (Volunteer) Singha Rifles, encamped in a perimeter that protected the nearby Sri Lanka Broadcasting Corporation transmitting tower. In July 1990, at the beginning of the Second Eelam War, the camp was cut off and overrun by the Tigers. The OC, Lieutenant Aldeniya refused to withdraw and leave his wounded behind, instead calling artillery in on his own position as the leading Tiger units overran the perimeter. The first soldier ever to be awarded the Parama Weera Vibushanaya, the country's highest award for bravery in combat — only four have been award in twenty years of war — his body was never recovered. Incredible mind-numbing bravery in a war that the world largely ignored.

Mankulam and its Army camp was first lost to the LTTE in November 1990 after three days of heavy fighting, during which a third of a battalion of the Gajaba Regiment was killed before the unit fought its way south. The terrorists used child soldiers with explosives strapped to their little bodies as human Bangalore torpedoes, blowing paths through the camp's minefields and perimeter defences.

Mankulam remained largely in Tiger hands for the next eight years, though Air Force bombing reduced it to ruins. In 1997, the security forces launched a massive steamrolling operation that by June the next year had captured all the towns between Vavuniya and Mankulam. In September 1998, Major Manoj Mudannayake's 6th Singha Rifles took Mankulam in two weeks of bloody fighting in which 6/SR's parent unit, the 551st Brigade, lost two hundred and eight men killed and sixty-three missing in action. LTTE resistance was overcome only after repeated bayonet charges by 6/SR rifle companies had broken the resolve of female Tiger units. The Tigers left two hundred and twenty-five of their own dead behind.

By March the next year however, LTTE artillery based at Mullaitivu on the eastern coast had begun hitting at Army bases east of Mankulam. In an attempt to push further north, the security forces were dangerously overstretched.

In November 1999, the Tigers captured the Army bases at Oddusuddan and Nedunkerni, twenty kilometres east of Mankulam in frontal assaults. A few days later LTTE artillery began pounding the divisional headquarters of the 55th and 56th Divisions at Kanakarayankulam. A day later, the Army camp at Olamadu fell, and then later that day, Mankulam.

The 4th Battalion of the Gemunu Watch fought a desparate rearguard action, allowing the other battalions of the 561st Brigade to withdraw to positions north of Vavuniya. The battalion was cut off and surrounded, preparing to fight to the last man, when Bravo Squadron of the 2nd Special Forces was helicoptered in north of Karappukutti and southeast of Mankulam. In a series of deadly hit-and-run raids the squadron convinced the Tigers that they were the spearhead of a fresh offensive. The LTTE eased the pressure on 4/GW long enough for the ragged remnants to withdraw. At this point, the SF squadron split up into troops and patrols, disappearing into the jungle and escaping south.

With the capture by the LTTE of Kilinochchi, further north, the previous year, the terrorists then turned their attention on Elephant Pass, capturing it a year later in what would be the biggest single defeat suffered by the Sri Lankan security forces. So by the beginning of 2001, the terrorists controlled most of the country from Puliyankulam north to the Jaffna Lagoon, effectively cutting the country in two.

*

General Lakmal Jayawardene, head of the Joint Operations Command at the beginning of 2001, and in actuality the commander of the security forces, had looked on the situation with frustration. He was in the last month of his career before taking retirement, and had wanted to leave on a high note. In February he ordered the Airmobile Brigade to start offensive actions on the western flank of the north-south A9 highway in an attempt to secure Sri Lankan government control over this area.

But lack of sufficient helicopters had made it impossible for more than a couple of companies to be airlifted into an area at a time. The Sri Lanka Air Force also hadn't had enough gunships to suppress the horrendous anti-aircraft fire encountered in the area. Heavy day and night strikes by MiG-27 and Kfir fighter-bombers had seemed to make no impression on the triple-A positions. Two battalions of the Airmobile Brigade — the 4th Gajabas and the 1st Singha Rifles — had managed to capture Mundumurippu, but without transport choppers, there hadn't been any real airmobile capability. The operation was called off before the beginning of the Sinhalese and Tamil new year in mid April.

These problems had been further emphasized in June, when the new JOC head, General Sujeeva Perera sent the 56th Division north towards Nedunkerni in an effort to cut Tiger supply lines to units in the Mankulam area. The only answer to the lack of helicopters had seemed to be to use roads to move troops into the area, and reduce dependence on air resupply and air mobility. By August, mechanized infantry and armoured units of the Army had moved up as far as Puttukkulam, south of Mankulam on the A9 highway. However, if they were to move further north to within striking range of Mankulam itself, the flanks would have had to be secured.

This had begun in September with a brigade assault into the area north of Mundumurippu, west of the highway. The Vijayabahu Infantry and Gemunu Watch battalions met with some success in pushing Tiger units out of the area, and General Perera had ordered a further offensive.

In September, the 561st Brigade of the 56th Division had choppered in two companies south of Nedunkerni on the eastern flank. In a three-day battle, troops of the 1st Sri Lanka Light Infantry had taken the town with twenty-three men killed and almost a hundred wounded. The Tigers were clearly willing to fight.

The loss of the town had forced LTTE main force units to pull back from Karappukkutti, falling back on Mankulam to avoid a pincer movement that would cut them off. They had been ordered to make a stand just outside Mankulam, in a series of prepared fortifications marked on Sri Lanka Army maps as Area 12. Located just south of the town, the area was in effect covered in thick jungle, impenetrable to armour, and dotted by clusters of tiny abandoned villages and hamlets, some so small they only consisted of a half-dozen dwellings. In possession of Mankulam for a year, the Tigers had fortified Area 12 with concrete bunkers and interconnecting trenches and tunnels. The highway had been mined and its flanks were covered by recoilless rifles and heavy machine-guns.

In November 2001, the 56th Division was preparing to attack Mankulam, and Area 12 was held by the LTTE's one thousand five hundred-strong Siruththai Puli Commando Regiment. The Siruththai Puli — which meant 'leopard' in Tamil — was one of the toughest Tiger units, consisting almost exclusively of teenaged children, led by men and women from the Black Tigers, the LTTE suicide cadre.

The operation began on November 10th with the 562nd Brigade, consisting of two mechanized battalions — the 1st and 2nd Reconnaissance — and three light infantry battalions — the 7th and 9th Singha Rifles and the 4th Gajabas — attacking north up the road.

Lieutenant Colonel Waruna de Silva's 9/SR was the lead battalion, having been choppered into the jungle west of the highway in two airlifts. The unit landed without any Tiger resistance, four kilometres southwest of Area 12, and began sending recce patrols towards Mankulam. While the trailing battalions moved up in support, de Silva, seeing no sign of the LTTE, sent Bravo Company to take Area 12.

Moving forward at 1615 hours, the riflemen moved through heavy jungle. The lead scouts stalked carefully through the foliage, watching for landmines and booby traps. Everyone was sweating heavily as the scrub jungle kept the hot air close to the ground. As the leading troops reached some abandoned paddy fields and started to cross, the terras struck with RPG and small arms fire. As dusk was approaching, Bravo Company was ordered to set up a night perimeter while air strikes were called in.

Only six men had been wounded, none of them seriously, and the skirmish could not be called heavy. However, an ambush the next morning killed six more riflemen, and it was clear that the outlying Tiger positions had been reached. Revising his plan, Lieutenant Colonel de Silva sent in Charlie Company on the left flank, moving parallel to Bravo, and skirting some open fields that led into Area 12. Alpha Company was sent round to the south of Mankulam — and Area 12 — to the highway. The idea was for all three companies to get into position for an attack on Mankulam at first light on the 13th.

The companies moved in at 0830 on the 12th after intense air and artillery strikes. Then began a long hellish close-quarter battle that would last eight days and shatter 9/SR both mentally and physically. Tiger resistance seemed to harden with each passing day.

Bravo Company was forced to attack across the abandoned paddies which were covered by line after line of bunkers that seemed immune to air and arty strikes. The armour that might have made the difference could not leave the A9 because of the heavy jungle that lay between it and Bravo.

Day after day, the company attacked, assaulting the bunkers with RPGs, recoilless rifles, machine-guns, and flame throwers, being hammered back each time, taking their wounded with them. By the 15th, Bravo Company was exhausted and had to be replaced by Alpha, itself weakened by repeated futile assaults up the A9.

On the 12th, they'd had to cross a tributary of the Manalaru, south of Mankulam. The bridge had been destroyed, and the company spent twenty-four hours under heavy fire in an attempt to cross. Finally, a night crossing had been decided on, but Alpha was ambushed during the crossing itself by terra units that had already reached the near bank. The company was forced to pull back in the dark, carrying its wounded. A casevac Huey coming in at dawn to evacuate the wounded was shot down and three of its four crewmen killed. The company itself had fourteen men killed.

Charlie Company on the left flank was hit even more hard as it pushed toward Mankulam. Here, too, the Tigers had prepared a careful ambush, letting the riflemen approach closer to Area 12 before springing it on the 13th. The company lost five dead and fifty-three wounded in a few minutes, and de Silva was forced to pull them back. Support Company was stripped of its heavy machine-guns, mortars, and recoilless rifles, and sent in to carry on the attack but didn't do very much better, being stopped by a line of bunkers that refused to be destroyed.

Meanwhile, 7/SR, ordered to move in a circle away from the road in an attempt to outflank Area 12 from the southeast, made little headway in the face of scathing Tiger fire.

By the 16th of November, all the attacks had stalled, the riflemen holding stubbornly in place against ferocious LTTE counterattacks. Morale was low, and only the iron discipline of the Singha Rifles stopped the soldiers from breaking and retreating. De Silva's continued demand for progress from his company and platoon commanders came to nothing, with entire sections wiped out for the gain of a few yards.

However 7/SR had, by the 17th, edged closer to Area 12 and on the 18th the weary rifle companies of 9/SR made enough headway for de Silva to feel that one more full-out assault could overrun the Tigers. Heavy rain on the 16th had, however, enabled the LTTE's Kittu Artillery Regiment to move its 105-mm guns down from Kilinochchi and into Mankulam. Hit by heavy arty fire, 9/SR was stopped yet again, and the attack was abandoned.

On the 16th of January, however, Major General Hamad Ali, commanding the 56th Division, had ordered a fresh brigade — the 563rd — to outflank Mankulam in a wider circle to the east, using the 7/SR attack as a screen. By the 19th, the brigade's three assault battalions — the 6th Singha Rifles, the 10th Sri Lanka Light Infantry, and the 8th Vijayabahu Infantry — were taking up blocking positions east of the A9 and northeast of Mankulam. On the 20th, all three battalions, plus 7/SR and 9/SR, attacked, surrounding Mankulam and cutting off the Siruththai Puli from Kilinochchi.

As 6/SR moved in from the northwest, and 8/VIR from the north, 7/SR assaulted Mankulam from the east and dug into a belt of thick jungle — what was to have been the Siruththai Puli's major avenue of retreat now that the A9 was cut. At the same time, de Silva's 9/SR continued their attacks over now familiar ground, gradually clearing out the bunker lines and driving deeper into Area 12.

Tiger fire didn't slacken, even when Support Company sections reached the outskirts of Mankulam and set up a perimeter. But soon Alpha Company sections were also moving in, and together the riflemen were able to clear the town. By dusk the fighting was dying down.

Conventionally, military victory is seen as territory captured from the enemy and secured for use by oneself, and this was certainly true of the battle for Mankulam. Despite the heavy casualties suffered by the Army — they lost a hundred and sixty killed and almost six hundred wounded in ten days — a strategic stepping stone to the recapture of Elephant Pass had been secured. The LTTE had left one thousand two hundred and sixty bodies — over eighty percent of the Siruththai Puli — behind to be counted by the exhausted soldiers. Warfare in the Twenty-First Century, however, and especially the media-driven public perception of it, even in Sri Lanka, is hardly conventional. As news of the battle filtered into the media, controversy began.

The leader of the opposition claimed in parliament that it was a senseless waste of life, and the controversy was compounded when the LTTE released press statements claiming that the hundreds of female and teenaged terrorists killed at Mankulam were innocent civilians, residents of the town. The media, both local and foreign, speculated that the actual numbers of soldiers killed were much higher, and the Tiger casualties much fewer.

Behind the fog of bluster, however, a fact remained that had been voiced neither in parliament nor in the media; and that was that casualties amongst the soldiers could have been possibly halved had a true airmobile capability been available to the security forces.

CHAPTER 6

It was the week before Christmas, but the streets of Barking in London were far from white. A murky sleet was drizzling down, and pedestrians were hurrying along beneath umbrellas or hunched under raincoats. Shop fronts were decorated in tinsel and Christmas trees glittered behind glass.

She shivered in her long trench coat as she hurried east along Victoria Avenue, away from Priory Park. She hated winter in Britain, especially in London. The city, with its old Victorian buildings and grey rain depressed her. She wished it would snow and brighten things up, the way it did in Toronto.

By the time she turned up Katherine Road the rain had stopped, and she began to feel better, though the wind howling down the broader thoroughfare didn't warm her. She had never thought she'd look forward to the heat and humidity of Sri Lanka, but now she longed for the trickle of perspiration down her back. Well, in a few weeks she'd be sweating enough. The monsoon rains would be hitting the island's northeast, but the rain in Sri Lanka would be refreshing, unlike this chill muck.

Glancing quickly up and down the road, she dodged briskly between parked cars and crossed to the Blarney, standing on the corner of Katherine and Heigham. The Blarney was an Irish pub, and had been specifically chosen for this meeting. It wasn't a place frequented by many Asians, and therefore she'd notice any surveillance.

Also, it was less than a hundred and fifty metres from the International Secretariat of Tamil Eelam, further up Katherine Road, and was therefore convenient for the man she was meeting.

She walked into the pub and looked around, hanging her trench coat by the door and taking off her gloves. She kept her woollen watch cap on her head, walking through the early evening drinkers. The place was done in heavy oak, in a traditional Celtic look, with huge old cartwheels hanging from the ceiling and holding the lights. Dart boards were scattered around the walls and a couple of pool tables stood around. Pictures of Dublin and Belfast covered the walls.

It was a split-level room, and she climbed the open steps to the upper level where she'd arranged to meet him. As she climbed, she was aware of the eyes of several male drinkers aimed at her rear. She wasn't a particularly attractive woman — she always considered her nose too broad and flat — but she had a good figure, and the tight black jeans below the thick woollen pullover showed it off well. Now she wished she'd worn something less revealing. She didn't want anyone to remember her too clearly.

He wasn't there yet. She cursed under her breath and found a seat, ordering an Irish coffee. How long did it take to walk a hundred bloody metres?

Unlike most Sri Lankans, Devini Sundaralingam believed in punctuality. The reason she believed in it was because she had seen people die too many times when plans were not carried out at the appointed time.

And she had seen many deaths in her twenty-seven years. She had hoped the amount of Sinhalese blood she'd spilled in the ensuing time would wipe the shrieks of her dying mother out of her nightmares. Her mother had been burned alive in July 1983, when the small family Fiat had been stopped by a mob in Colombo. Her father had braved the swinging clubs and punching fists to carry his two daughters — aged nine and eleven — to safety, shielding them from the cursing Sinhalese with his body. He had staggered fifty yards to a Roman Catholic church, collapsing at the elderly priest's feet. The priest — also a Sinhalese — had hidden them in the church, but not quickly enough to block out the sounds of the mob dousing the Fiat in its own petrol and setting it alight. Devini's mother had screamed and begged, and then as the flames took her, merely screamed, and it had seemed an eternity to her sobbing husband and daughters till her cries mercifully died with her.

But the years since then had merely replaced them with fresh screams, and Devini quickly blocked out her mother, focusing now on the most frequent of her nightmares. The one about the soldier they had crucified close to Elephant Pass. The one, out of all the prisoners she'd seen die, who had refused to scream.

He still walked through her sleeping hours as he had looked that day in 1991, his grey eyes locking onto his executioners. That was what had struck the members of Devini's platoon the most. His eyes. And the crucifix tattooed on his right bicep. He had obviously not been a Sinhalese, or a Buddhist. But they had not found out anything more from him, not even the usual name, number, and rank. He had not said a word, not even when the nails went in. It had been the tattoo that had given Devini's platoon leader the idea of a crucifixion. He had probably been a Burgher, one of those half-cast pariahs who sold their souls to the Sinhalese just for the joy of the kill.

Her thoughts were interrupted by Gunam's arrival. He plonked himself down opposite her and ordered a Finian's. He was the same height as Devini who was tall for a Sri Lankan woman — five feet six — about average for a Sri Lankan man. But unlike her, he was rail thin, and his narrow face was made longer by his pointed goatee.

"Everything OK?" he asked in Tamil.

"What are you asking me for? *I* should ask *you*. And you're late," she pointed out, and then continued speaking without waiting for his excuses. "Is everything ready? Have the cells been given the equipment and instructions?"

"The cells in the UK are all ready to move," he answered. "They're making final adjustments to plans and will go as soon as they're satisfied with the situation."

"They understand that they must wait till Ottawa announces the new bill?"

"Yes, but what if the Canadians keep quiet about it?"

"They can't. Not after all the publicity that's going on. Our lawyers will keep us informed, and once our newspapers and websites carry the item, the international media will have to run it. But the cells *must* wait till it's international news. It must seem to be a reaction to the bill, and not a reason for the bill being passed. A specific date isn't necessary. But it must be coordinated."

"Understood. We will give them an arranged time gap in hours between the news appearing on a predetermined website and the required beginning of the attacks. That'll make sure it'll be coordinated down to an hour or so."

"And the claiming of responsibility. There is no way it can be traced back to us?"

"Not a chance." He shook his head. "It'll be a hack and untraceable. The denial will be by email to the *BBC*, and will originate from an internet cafe in Lewisham."

"Fine," she said, beginning to relax for the first time since the meeting had begun. "We want London to handle the press releases. In the usual way."

"Understood." He sipped at his red ale and watched her. "You're going straight back to Eelam now?"

"France first, then Germany. I'll be home in a week or two. Before the operation begins."

She finished her coffee and put some money down on the rough-hewn table. Getting to her feet, she said, "Finish your beer and then leave. Give me time to get out of the area. Just in case."

As she left the Blarney, Devini didn't see the two Englishmen in the Ford Mondeo, parked a hundred and fifty metres further down Katherine Road. A digital Nikon with a powerful zoom lens was supported on the passenger's side of the dashboard, focusing on her as she crossed the road, the man behind the camera taking several quick shots of her.

*　　*　　*

Terminal 2 at Frankfurt's huge international airport was fairly crowded with human traffic, but still a far cry from the usual organized chaos of its busier sister, Terminal 1. Sandra Koch eyed the big digital sign announcing the arrivals as she walked in. Lufthansa flight LH453 from Dubai had just landed and its passengers were disembarking.

There were no arrivals as yet moving through the sliding doors from customs, so she looked around for a smoking area from which she could see the doors. Finding an ashtray, she lit up a Camel and waited. She hated to smoke while driving, so the two and a half hour journey from Cologne had been made in an irritable mood.

She'd lived in the city for three years, and had chosen it at the suggestion of her Int contact. Sandra Koch had been to Germany numerous times in the past as an Air Lanka stewardess, enjoying the stopovers in Frankfurt or Düsseldorf, seeing the nightlife with the other crewmembers, hitting the nightclubs and enjoying the freedom away from Colombo's social strictures and gossip.

But then, five years ago, her twin brother, a captain in the Sri Lanka Armoured Corps had been killed in action. Sandra had decided that she couldn't live in Sri Lanka anymore, unwilling to face Colombo with the thought that Kevin was gone. She had a cousin in Düsseldorf who was willing to sponsor her immigration application. He owned a small travel agency specializing in cheap tours to Sri Lanka, and he was even willing to give her a job. Sandra made her decision. Already fluent in German — part of her training at Air Lanka — she knew she'd have no problem adjusting to the country.

A month before her departure she had received a call from an Army officer claiming to have served with her brother. He said he was on leave and would like to meet her. Hoping to learn something more of Kevin's life, she had agreed.

It turned out that the officer was serving in Military Intelligence, and over the course of the meeting — he took her out to dinner — he suggested that there might be a way she could avenge Kevin's death.

So began Sandra Koch's work as a low-grade operative for Int. She didn't have to do much, just a few occasional jobs that merely entailed confirming a particular address in Düsseldorf, or attending a Tamil fund-raising rally and reporting the contents of the speeches.

With her Germanic surname and her fair-skinned Burgher looks she blended in well. For administrative purposes she was given the rank of a lieutenant in the Intelligence Corps, and paid a salary accordingly, but her name appeared on no pay or records sheet. The money, like many other operational funds, came out of an Army "classified-budget project".

Three years previously, her Int control at the Sri Lankan consulate in Bonn had asked her to confirm the addresses of several Tamils living in Cologne. He had then suggested she move to the city, as it might be necessary to keep track of these individuals. By then she had been fairly well settled in her adopted country, and had no trouble finding a job in Cologne. The individuals she was asked to keep tabs on changed frequently, some of them leaving Germany unexpectedly, or being deported by the authorities when various criminal histories came to light. Others stayed on in the city, living and working like so many other immigrants, with no trace of any illegal activities.

But in November 2001, she had been told by her control to apply for her vacation leave in December. This would be her most important job since her arrival in the city. She was given several addresses and instructed to confirm that they were being used by the offices of various Tamil political or humanitarian groups. She had been briefed that they were cover organizations for the LTTE, and that a team of Sri Lankans would be arriving to help her in the surveillance operation.

Still smoking, Sandra Koch straightened up now and searched the faces of the passengers beginning to emerge from customs. Soon she spotted them, their faces and descriptions having been memorized earlier.

None of them carried much baggage, and there were no suitcases to be seen, just backpacks or kitbags. They walked casually, though there was an air of weariness about them, no doubt from the long flights and the tedium of the stopover in Dubai. They looked like any tourists would, heads swivelling constantly, scanning the unfamiliar surroundings, a couple of them carrying cameras round their necks. But they walked in a loose formation, as if on patrol.

The first one through the doors was J.L. Bandara, the youngest and shortest of the group. He was only about five feet five, short even for a Sri Lankan, but with a wiry toughness that even the bulky parka he wore could not hide. He had a thin moustache, and his eyes were constantly searching the faces before him, like a lead scout. He wore trainers on his feet and, like the others, jeans and a pullover under his parka.

The two behind him walked together, and Sandra recognized the one on the left as the senior man, Dayan Premasiri. He was slim and broad-shouldered at about five feet eight, with a hard, unshaven face and pale brown eyes that held none of the warmth usually associated with that colour. He seemed to stalk through the terminal in his desert boots as if he owned it, totally at ease, unlike most Asian newcomers to Europe.

This one kills, thought Sandra, butting her smoke quickly.

Next to Premasiri was Kamal Gunatilake, at six feet one and looking like he weighed over two hundred pounds, a giant amongst Sri Lankans. His big, blunt fingers seemed to almost totally encompass the camera slung from his neck as he cupped it. He had a round, cheerful face, smooth as a baby's and just as shiny, his eyes small and bloodshot.

Bringing up the rear was Sumith Liyanage, the group's second-in-command. He was only about an inch or two shorter than Premasiri, but his stockiness made the difference look greater. He had high cheekbones, his face sharp and angular, his body carrying the same easy power as the others.

Sandra Koch pushed away from the ashtray-cum-dustbin she had been leaning against and walked towards the men, who were now searching the faces of the waiting crowd. People, many of them Sri Lankans, were waving and shouting to attract the attention of relatives or friends who were exiting customs.

Dayan ignored the noisy waving throng as he pushed the trolley with the team's luggage. Their Int control was supposed to meet them here, but he couldn't see anyone who looked like they were it. Most of the Sri Lankan women around were obviously either too young, or too old.

"See any likely candidates?" he asked Kamal.

"No," came the grumbled reply. "Why the fuck does Int have to behave like this is *Mission Impossible*? Couldn' they just have shown us a picture of the bit?"

"Because this might become *Mission Impossible* if we don' watch it." Dayan eyed a young woman walking purposefully towards them. "Hang on, this maybe it."

"Shit, I hope so," drooled Kamal.

Eyeing her, Dayan thought at first that she didn't even look Sri Lankan, but then decided that maybe she was. Her tan looked more in the blood than due to the sun. She had long kinky brown hair with blonde highlights tied in a ponytail under her black baseball cap, and she wore a padded nylon jacket that hung open as a concession to the warmer temperatures indoors. Her cargo pants hugged her hips and thighs before falling baggily down to Adidas trainers, and a tight pullover framed her breasts quite comfortably, thank you.

"Mister Premasiri?" she asked quietly, stopping in front of Dayan.

"Yes, ma'am," he answered, pulling his trolley out of the stream of passengers moving past.

"I'm Sandra Koch." She held her hand out to Dayan.

"Dayan," he volunteered, gripping her hand.

"Banda!" Kamal snapped his fingers to get the attention of Bandara, who had walked right past her.

Her hand was cool and dry, and her grip quite firm. As he introduced the others in the patrol, Dayan noted that her eyes were a greenish hazel. He would have to look up the exact name of that shade, he decided.

There had been the usual jokes about the Int control's name, when it was given at the briefing back in Colombo.

"I wonder whether Miss Koch still likes Sri Lankan cocks," Bandara had mused aloud over lunch at the Int mess.

They had first thought the control was a German when the briefer had told them her name. It had then been explained she was a Burgher.

"Ham or cheese?" Kamal had asked, claiming it was the only sort of burger he knew of.

"Dutch," the Int officer had answered without cracking a smile. "Or maybe German. Who knows?"

The Burghers were the descendants of the European colonists who had first come to Sri Lanka in the seventeenth and eighteenth centuries. Strictly speaking the term meant 'townsman', and at the time classified any Dutch residents of the island as such. However, in the British period — which incidentally followed the Portuguese and Dutch — it came to mean any Ceylonese of European descent. Sri Lankan Burgher families jealously guarded their colour, heritage and family names; many of them able to show records tracing ancestors back to the European port cities of Portsmouth, Rotterdam, and Bremerhaven. But in the latter half of the twentieth century, after independence from Britain, many Burghers decided to emigrate back to Europe, or continue on to Australia, rather than learn Sri Lanka's official language of Sinhalese and be culturally swamped by the locals. With their numbers dwindling each successive year, reduced by emigration and intermarriage, the Burghers were a dying race, soon to exist only in the multitude of European names they held.

Introductions done, the four men accompanied Sandra to the elevators that would take them down to the underground car park. Dayan walked alongside her, trying to break the ice by asking a few questions about Frankfurt, and the weather in general. The other three followed, Kamal's eyes fixed on the tight buttocks Sandra's coat failed to cover.

"Your tongue is hanging," Sumith pointed out helpfully.

As they drove northwest along the A3 *autobahn* in Sandra's VW Jetta station wagon, she kept up a running commentary about the countryside they were passing through and the cities and towns they saw along the way.

Dayan, sitting up front with her, tried to concentrate on what she was saying, but most of it just went right through his head. He was tired. Unlike Bandara and Kamal, he had stopped drinking at Dubai, hoping to arrive in Frankfurt in some vague state of alertness, but the combination of ten hours in the air and three hours hanging around in departure lounges had been enough to make his head feel as if it had been buggered by a hippo. His only consolation was that the others looked even worse than he felt.

The landscape on either side of the *autobahn* was grey and gloomy, the trees poking bare skeletal branches up into low clouds. Close to Limburg, it began to snow, and the three in the back looked out excitedly. It was the first snow they'd ever seen.

Sandra smiled at their expressions. "Snow for the first time, no?" she said to Dayan. "What d'you think?"

He told her he'd seen snow once before, but didn't elaborate on where it had been. He tried to take it in. None of them had ever been to Europe before, and he marvelled at the bleak beauty of the countryside. The pale fields faded into the blue-grey distance, or rose into misted ridges. He had expected congestion and industry wherever he looked, pollution on a large scale, but saw none of that. He saw fields on the side of a ridge, planted with what looked like rows of sticks, and asked Sandra what they were.

"Vineyards," she told him. "This area, and especially further west, close to the Rhine, is famous for wine. At the moment there's nothing growing because it's winter, that's why you just see those posts. At other times of the year the posts support the grapevines."

For a while it was almost like being on holiday, the four tourists with their sexy tour guide, but then as they started passing through the suburbs of Cologne, everyone quietened down. They knew they were here on a job, one that could turn deadly at any time, especially as they had very little support.

They started eyeballing the streets, asking questions, memorizing landmarks. Sumith picked up a street map of the city and began scanning it, trying to track their progress.

CHAPTER 7

As she bent to touch the leader's feet, Devini Sundaralingam wondered at how ordinary they were. They were not the feet of a great man, the conqueror who would free the Tamil people. In their stout leather sandals, they were blunt and calloused, the feet of the fisherman and smuggler he'd once been. But as his hands reached down and grasped her by the elbows, drawing her up, she remembered the legend that claimed those feet had once, decades ago, pedalled a bicycle all over southern Sri Lanka, watching the Sinhalese for weaknesses, plotting the places he would strike. It was a myth the leader had never attempted to deny.

Nevertheless, as she now looked into his eyes, she knew why he was the leader, why he was called *Aiyah* — elder brother or father — by the thousands of men and women of the Liberation Tigers of Tamil Eelam that he commanded.

He had a round, soft face, and an infectious smile that pushed up his cheeks and wrinkled his eyes, but at the age of fifty-four, they were cold eyes. Eyes that had seen death for more than thirty years. Eyes that remained dark and empty no matter whether he was laughing with his teenaged son or pouring vitriol during a rally. At first glance, his fleshy features and stocky body gave the impression that he was someone's favourite uncle, but when one looked in his eyes that idea disappeared.

His passion and leadership had developed the LTTE from a gang of bandits that robbed banks and escaped on bicycles, to a sophisticated terrorist network that owned shipping companies in South America and smuggled heroin into Europe. He was personally responsible for the deaths of tens of thousands of

Sri Lankans — Sinhalese and Tamil and Muslim; and was the most wanted man in Sri Lanka and India.

With absolute power over the Tigers and the areas of the country that they controlled, he ruled with an iron fist and brooked no criticism. The LTTE had murdered and terrorized into non-existence all other Tamil political parties in the northeast of the country.

It was the first time, however. Devini Sundaralingam had been this close to the leader, the first time she had ever felt his touch. Now as he led her towards the small dining table, she knew it would be the last. No matter what the outcome of her mission, she would be dead at the end of it.

Like so many Black Tigers before her, who had ended their lives in a fiery flash in the south, hurling their explosive-laden bodies at a Sinhalese political or military leader, she was here to be accorded the final honour, a sign of mutual respect — a personal meal with the leader.

"I have been looking forward to talking to you, Major Sundari."

He addressed her by her LTTE rank and alias. No Tiger used his or her real name, selecting one — or more often having it given to him or her — on the day they joined the organization. Their rightful names were only revealed when they were painted on the wooden boards that served as grave markers.

"I have waited for this moment all my life, *Aiyah*," she replied.

She had travelled all over Europe and North America in a lifetime dedicated to war, seen so many battles that the blood and killing sometimes blurred together in her mind, but he still had the power to awe her.

As they ate a vegetarian dinner of *poori* and curried potatoes, he questioned her about her life and career in the LTTE, and she talked, telling him about herself, knowing all the time that he had already committed her file to memory.

She told him of the death of her mother, and how she had fled to India as a refugee with her elder sister and broken-hearted father. She told him of the squalor and awful poverty of the camp outside Madras, seemingly magnified after the middle-class comfort of Colombo, of a father who could only drink and cry.

She told the leader how the LTTE representatives worked in the camps, the way they recruited young children. She remembered how her father, disgusted with war and Sri Lanka, had married off her elder sister at the age of fourteen to an Indian Tamil, knowing it was the only way to keep her out of the Tigers.

A year later, her father had drunk himself into an early death, only forty years old, and Devini had volunteered for the LTTE. At the age of thirteen she had arrived at a training camp close to the Tamil Nadu port city of Pondicherry. The camp had not been concerned with military training, but just in physical and classroom education — the latter covering mostly Sri Lankan Tamil literature and history.

It was here that Devini had been raped by a Tiger instructor, but she didn't tell the leader this. She knew it was not in her file.

Six months later, in 1988, she had returned to Jaffna, working as a nurse's aide for the LTTE. It had been a bad time for the Tamil terrorists. The Sri Lanka Army was staying in its bases, and military operations against the rebels were being carried out by the Indian Peace-Keeping Force. Devini had thought she would drown in the blood, labouring eight and ten hours a day on horribly wounded Tigers who were brought to the medical post. What she saw each day scarred her young mind even further, but it was still not what she had come back to the island to do. She wanted to do what her heroes were doing, to carry an AK-47 against the murderers of her mother.

When Devini was raped a second time, she was fourteen, and it was by a Sikh unit that overran her medical post. This was in her file. The jawans had taken turns to hold her and other Tiger nurses down while they raped them. All the adults in the camp were executed, but the children were handed over to the Red Cross.

She told the leader how the Red Cross had looked after her for several months, and that when she returned to the LTTE, she had asked to be sent to a fighting unit. After a month of training, when she finally was taught to fire an AK-47, she was assigned to a children's unit. Consisting of kids in their early teens, many of whom were orphans or refugees like her, they were organized into platoons led by adults, usually women.

In 1989, she told the leader, she had killed for the first time, during the ambush of a Ghurkha patrol close to Kilinochchi, shooting a wounded Indian officer as he lay groaning on the jungle track.

A few months later, soon after her fifteenth birthday, she'd got the chance to kill her first Sinhalese. It was a raid against a village in Manalaru, the area stolen from the Tamil people by the Sinhalese government; the area the invaders had renamed Welioya. The government had settled Sinhalese farming communities in this area, families displaced by the Victoria and Randenigala hydro-catchments projects in the Central Highlands, and they were the target of the Tiger raids.

An adult unit had opened fire on the hamlet with RPGs and mortars, setting the thatch alight. Devini and the other children of her unit had been ordered to open fire at any Sinhalese who escaped the burning homes. The entire hamlet was wiped out that night.

In the following years, with the departure of the IPKF, and the return to war with the Sinhalese Army, Devini had got the chance to kill as many Sinhalese as she wished. She had been in the attack on Mankulam in 1990, and it was her first experience with suicide martyrs. She had watched open-mouthed with the other children as a Black Tiger drove a truck full of explosives into the Army camp's gate.

But the next year she was wounded in the siege of Elephant Pass. For weeks the Tigers hurled suicidal but unsuccessful frontal attacks against the iron defence of the Singha Rifles, shattering many of the fiercest LTTE units, including those consisting of children, and losing over five hundred dead.

She did not tell the leader of the burning pain she had felt as she lay on the ground, her right leg riddled with shrapnel, pain not so much from her wound, but from the sight of her squad being destroyed around her.

It had taken her almost a year to recover from her wounds, and she had then volunteered for Black Tiger training. She had been accepted, and after six brutal months joined a reconnaissance squad at the end of it, spending the next three years crawling through the jungle to observe Sinhalese Army units, eventually entering towns and cities in the south to look for weak spots that Tiger suicide bombers could exploit.

By this point, the LTTE had learned from the Elephant Pass disaster, and its assault units were now child squads led by Black Tigers. The units were far more successful. The children, already fanatical and foolhardy, were tempered by the experience and skill of the Black Tigers, and overran a large security forces camp at Pooneryn on the southern coast of the Jaffna Lagoon. But in October 1995, when the units had been used once more against Manalaru, things were different.

The Sinhalese government had spent the previous years redeveloping the area and improving the infrastructure, fortifying the hamlets with an interconnected complex of bases. The LTTE had known the bases were manned by National Guardsmen, second-rate reservists, and were expecting weak resistance. What LTTE intelligence had failed to find out, however, was that the commander of the area — a special operations brigadier named Janaka Perera — had moved in the 1st Special Forces. These crack guerrilla fighters had been used to shore up and re-train the National Guard troops. When the LTTE struck, it had been decimated, with more than three thousand fighters killed, most of them women and children. It was the single worst defeat the Tigers had ever experienced.

Spurred into thinking she could help change things, Devini had volunteered to lead an assault company. She had taken command of the mixed unit in time for the amphibious attack on Mullaitivu in 1996. She was twenty-two years old. The assault in which her unit took part was hugely successful, with the capture of almost fifty million US dollars worth of military equipment and ammunition and the death of hundreds of Sinhalese soldiers and sailors. She had then, she told the leader, decided to use the opportunity to harden some of her less experienced child troops. She had personally supervised the execution of three hundred captured sailors.

By the end of 1997, she told the leader, she had been commanding a battalion of the Siruththai Puli Commandos in the Wanni. Fighting a defensive battle against the Sinhalese, who had been attacking up the A9 highway in a massive clearing operation, her unit had ambushed two companies of the Gajabas. Outnumbered and low on ammo after several days of fighting, the Sinhalese soldiers hadn't been expected to hold out for long. It had been at the height of the northeastern monsoon, and the Air Force had been grounded. Devini's superior, the Siruththai Puli commander had, however, ordered her to not make a final assault, but to wait for reinforcements that would then enable the LTTE to draw more Sinhalese troops into the trap. But Devini's battalion — fighting and on the run for weeks — had been tired and demoralized, and she wanted to give them a boost. The Gajabas had been down to only a few rifle rounds each, and had no more mortar or RPG ammo left when Devini closed the trap.

The remaining two hundred or so Sinhalese, with empty weapons, their company commanders dead, had fixed bayonets and charged in a last ditch attempt to break through the Tiger ring of steel. But Devini had kept her kids back in cover, gunning down the soldiers as they attacked.

Devini had been relieved by her superior for insubordination. She had defended herself at the hearing that followed, but there was no excuse for disobedience, and she now admitted to the leader that her nerves had been in tatters. Because of her record in the past, she hadn't been punished, but sent to the Eastern Province to help recruiting. In 1999, she had been dispatched to Canada to organize the propaganda and fund-raising operations in Scarborough.

In November 2000, the leader himself had picked her to coordinate his own special international operation. At the time it had been planned as a damage-control device something to be held in reserve and used only in the event of an unavoidable turning of world opinion against the Tigers.

Now as the food was cleared away, the leader began to speak. And like so many before her, whose faces lined the walls of this room, she was drawn in by his soft hypnotic voice. This was not a briefing. That had been completed long before she stepped down into this underground bunker. Now he spoke of the movement, and of their commitment to free the Tamil people from oppression. He spoke of their victories and the great sacrifices made.

As he talked, Devini's eyes wandered across the photographs that covered the bunker walls. Dozens of Black Tigers, now dead, their bodies never recovered to be laid beneath the soil of Eelam, but their songs sung by children in the schools, their names forever engraved in the history of the Tamils.

So many young lives. And she wondered whether they had all felt as she did now, at the beginning of their missions. Fiercely proud of a heritage, loyal to the leader unto the very end, but also bitter at a world of opportunity lost to them.

She had seen the young Tamils in Canada and Britain, in their fashionable western clothes, with their fashionable western lives. Partying, falling in love, going to university. They didn't really care about Eelam, and none of them would want to live in it when it came. They didn't care for the thousands who died to make that dream a reality. They just paid their tax to the Tigers and decided that was enough.

Devini had been glad when she was recalled to Eelam. The secular lifestyle away from what they were fighting for sickened her. But still she wondered. What would it have been like to have grown up a normal Tamil girl, to have gone to school, to have fallen in love?

She remembered talking to a Black Tiger called Sudhen in 1996 just before he went south on a mission. He had no qualms in carrying out his role, but she had been puzzled by his bitterness, something she now understood.

"Born in the north, to die in the south," he had told her.

A few months later, he and a comrade had driven an explosive-packed truck into the Central Bank in Colombo, triggering a massive Tiger assault on the city's financial district.

Two nights later, Devini Sundaralingam boarded the small Sea Tiger gunboat at Veddukkadu, northwest of Pooneryn and midway along a twenty-odd-kilometre spit that stuck out into the Jaffna Lagoon. The Thrikka gunboat, armed with a .50-in machine-gun, would carry her on the first leg of the long circuitous journey to her destination.

She was dressed in civilian clothes, but carried an assault rifle, like the other passengers on board, each going on a different mission. None knew another's mission, but Devini understood that some, like her, would be making a trip for which death lay at the end, while for others it could be a mediocre errand. But whatever the mission was, they would all have to make this most dangerous leg of the journey, running the gauntlet of the Sri Lankan and Indian navies in an attempt to get to Tamil Nadu in south India.

The boat's crew of four, the men manning the machine-guns and steering the craft, wore the distinctive tiger stripe camouflage fatigues of the LTTE.

The petrol engine of the bigger and more heavily armed Muraj escort boat roared to life, and then the commander of Devini's boat followed suit, easing away from the jetty. The thunder of the Thrikka's outboards prevented any conversation except shouts, and Devini settled down, staring past the stern and down the coast. Somewhere back there in the darkness lay Pooneryn, one of the biggest defeats for the security forces.

It had guarded the southern end of a ferry service that once linked the A32 coastal highway to the Jaffna Peninsula, the only road alternative to the Elephant Pass causeway. The ferry terminus had been destroyed in the fighting that had swept back and forth over this area, and the barges sunk. Devini couldn't even remember which side had done it.

Until they cleared the mouth of the lagoon, south of Jaffna, they were in maximum danger, and every fifteen minutes the boats would cut their engines and sit there, rocking in the swells, listening for the Navy and talking softly on the radios.

The shallow waters of the Palk Straits that divided Sri Lanka from India covered land that had, millions of years previously, connected the two countries; and the seas at the south-western end of the straits still gave evidence of that prehistoric link. To the west and southwest of the Jaffna Peninsula the waters were dotted with a confusing pattern of small islands — the three largest being Kayts, Punkudutivu, and Delft. Constantly fought over in a sort of amphibious guerrilla war, the islands were variously occupied by both the Sea Tigers and the Sri Lanka Navy, neither side ever totally sure which island was currently occupied by whom. Further south was more open water, stretching away to the gateway of the Gulf of Mannar.

They made it, however, out of the lagoon and into more open water without a contact. Everyone relaxed imperceptibly as they turned southwest, running for the gap between the islands of Punkudutivu in the north and Palaitivu further south. They would circle around the south of the island of Delft before turning northwest for India. This was generally safer than the heavily patrolled waters between the numerous islands west of Jaffna.

Now the breaks for listening were further apart, and the howl of the wind louder, ripping in from Adam's Bridge and the Gulf of Mannar.

Suddenly, south of Punkudutivu, the engines cut to a barely audible idle, and the boat coasted along silently, nosing into the swells. Devini turned to look at the gunboat commander, the night-vision goggles and radio headset making him look like an alien. He was staring intently ahead into the darkness that hid the escort boat from Devini. All she could hear were the waves slapping the hull and the constant wind. Then in the distance she heard something that sounded like thunder, but more regular, like the beat of a huge racing heart.

"Dvora," the commander said to her.

Somewhere ahead in the darkness was a patrolling Navy gunboat. The Israeli-made Dvoras carried no radar, but their 20-mm cannon and 40-mm auto grenade launchers would make mincemeat of the light-skinned Sea Tiger boats. Devini prayed they were too far away to be picked up by PNV sights.

After ten minutes the sound of the Dvora's engines died away, but the Sea Tiger boats sat there for a further twenty minutes before moving on. Devini noticed her fingers were trembling, and jammed them into her armpits. She hated this. She wished she was ashore and able to run into the jungle at the first hint of danger, flatten herself against mother earth. The sea was as cold and unforgiving as the enemy.

They moved off once more and were just swinging west around the tip of Delft when the night exploded into flashes and the hammering roar of automatic cannon. Directly in their path, Devini could see the strobing beat of gun muzzles and huge balls of tracer came floating across the water, their glow lighting up the wave tops before they flashed overhead.

The commander was screaming to the gun crew as he swung the boat south, heeling it over to port in a tight turn. Devini couldn't make out what he was saying, but it sounded like there was more than one of the enemy. She could see tracers crisscrossing on their right as the Muraj returned fire with its three machine-guns. Then there was a sudden orange ball of flame that lit the water, followed by a rolling hollow *boom*. Firelight glowed around the spot where the escort boat must have been, and now green and white flares were shooting up from the horizon. In the flare light Devini thought she could make out a pair of low streamlined shapes in the distance, but she couldn't be sure. The boat was heeling to port and starboard as it zigzagged furiously, and all she could do was hang on to the gunwale and hope that the smashing blows of the waves against the keel wouldn't throw her overboard.

The flares had ruined the NVGs, and the boat commander had discarded his in an attempt to see. His eyes were staring like golf balls into the darkness ahead, trying to spot anymore ambushers.

Devini decided that they had probably run into Navy gunboats returning from a patrol off Rameswaram in the southwest. The Indian island was separated from the Sri Lankan island of Mannar by a mere twenty-eight kilometres of water, and connected by a chain of rocky islets known as Adam's Bridge. The name came from the myth that Adam had once used it to flee to Sri Lanka from the angry Hebrew god. It was also credited with having helped the monkey god Hanuman reach the island in pursuit of Sita, kidnapped by the Lankan demon Ravana.

The area had once been popular with smugglers, and later with the Tigers, who used it as an access route between the countries. It was still heavily patrolled by both navies, and tension had grown with the arrest of Sri Lankan and Indian fishermen, each country accusing the other of poaching.

"Did the others escape?" Devini yelled to the commander, but the man merely shrugged and shook his head.

He cut the outboards and they listened once more. In the distance they could still see flares flickering and the occasional flash of tracers.

"Nothing on the radio," the commander said.

It was a pointed reminder of how deadly this journey was. If the Muraj with its crew of ten was still afloat, its commander would be in contact with them, trying to establish the extent of the ambush.

*   *   *

"If the plane isn' refuelled in ten minutes, I'll be forced to execute a hostage," the tense but steady voice came over the speakers in the control tower.

"Look, you must understand our position," the negotiator was saying. Through the sound-proof glass partition that divided Air from Ground Operations, X-ray could see him standing calmly by a desk, making notes by the light of a desk lamp as he talked. He was wearing civilian clothes — dress trousers, white shirt and dark tie. "We don' have the equipment ready to refuel this model of aircraft. If you can wait for—"

"Ten minutes!" snarled the voice. "I will not exten' the deadline. After that, a hostage will be executed every twenty minutes 'til you refuel us."

The connection went dead, and X-ray saw the negotiator turn to the man beside him and shrug helplessly. The man with the negotiator was dressed identically to X-ray, in black fatigues and boots. X-ray saw him press the button on his throat mike, and instantly his voice crackled in his own earpiece.

"Bugger won' compromise. I know him. Can you go in now?"

X-ray didn't answer immediately, but picked up the handset of the main net.

"Echoes, do you have a shot?" he asked, even though the panel of lights in front of him had told him the answer before the question was asked. He wanted confirmation.

The sniper team commander came up on the net. "Negative, X-ray. My Echo Two has a partial head shot at a Tango in the cockpit, but no guarantee."

X-ray turned back to the glass partition. "Not yet," he answered finally. "The Kfirs can't land on the runway for another fifteen minutes."

X-ray was the Red Team boss, the commander of the hostage rescue unit assigned to the Bandaranaike International Airport, Katunayake. The man standing next to the negotiator was his second-in-command. Cursing, X-ray stared out of the dark control room, lit only by the dim green glow of radio dials and radar screens. Three-hundred metres across the airbase stood the Sri Lankan Airlines Tri-Star in a circle of brilliantly spot lit tarmac. Through binoculars trained on the cockpit windows, he tried to spot any movement. The hijack leader would be in there where he could see around and use the radios. Beyond the airliner were the lights and bustle of the airport, situated next to the Katunayake Air Force Base, north of Colombo.

He turned to the other side of Air Operations, where an Air Force squadron leader sat by a radar operator.

"Can't you get your chaps here any faster, squadron leader?"

"Sorry, captain," the squadron leader shrugged helplessly. "They're still on an air strike over the peninsula. They'll be here as soon as they finish their las' run."

"Nothing to do but wait, then," the Commando officer said to his 2/ic. "Try an' get the leader on the phone an' delay the execution." He saw the other commando go into a huddle with the negotiator as he himself went back onto the main net. "All teams, stan' by, stan' by!"

"They won't answer us," the 2/ic reported back.

Ten minutes later, the radio connection with the hijacked aircraft came to life. "Ten minutes up," said the hijack leader's voice.

There was a single pistol shot, and though they were all expecting it, everyone in the control tower jumped.

"All teams, stan' by, stan' by!"

The business class door behind the cockpit started to open, but the interior of the plane was in darkness. Through his binos, X-ray could see movement.

Though two lights on the small panel before him switched from red to green, X-ray asked the question anyway.

"Echoes," he snapped, "do you have a shot?"

"One confirmed in the door, one partial."

"Stan' by, stan' by!"

There were known to be five hijackers on board, and procedure dictated that at least three of them should be hittable before a sniper strike could be ordered.

A dark figure dropped from the aircraft doorway, landing limply on the tarmac. It didn't roll or bounce, but lay still, its limbs outstretched.

"You have twenty minutes," the hijacker said calmly, "or this will be repeated."

"The Kfirs are on final approach," the squadron leader hissed from the other side of the room.

X-ray tapped a finger against the glass partition to catch the attention of his 2/ic and the negotiator. When they looked up, he nodded vigorously.

"OK, commander," the negotiator said into his handset. "We can now meet your demands. A refuelling bowser has arrived from the airport, and we can start supplying you."

"We'll be watching very carefully, OK? So don't try anything stupid."

"Don' worry, we just wan' this to end peacefully."

"Yah, I fucking bet."

The negotiator raised an eyebrow at his black-clad companion, and from the other side of the partition X-ray saw the commando's eyes crinkle slightly as he grinned.

"Alpha Team, go!" X-ray ordered.

An orange fuel bowser left the hangars on the right of the control tower and drove slowly towards the left side of the Tri-Star. Almost simultaneously the howl of jet engines began to build up in the distance as the pair of Kfir fighter-bombers came in to land.

Through his binos, X-ray could just make out a man crouching in the airliner's doorway, covering the approaching bowser with a pistol.

"Bravo, Charlie, and Delta, stand by!"

As the refuelling began, still covered by the pistol-wielding hijacker, the men in the tower could hear the screaming jet engines growing closer. The Kfirs had landed, and following orders, were taxiing closer to the Tri-Star.

"What's that racket?" came the query from the hijack leader. "What are those jets doing so close?"

"Nothing to do with us—" the negotiator tried to explain.

"Move them away!" the hijacker yelled. "Do you wan' me to start killing the passengers?"

"Look, please listen to me." The negotiator's voice was calm and reasonable. "This is just a normal Air Force patrol returning. I have no control over it."

But the hijacker was nervous. The Tri-Star had been sitting on the tarmac for two days, and in that time no other aircraft had approached it this closely. The negotiator kept talking to him, however, trying to calm him down as the refuelling continued.

"Alpha, how many Tangos in the door?" X-ray asked.

The radio broke squelch once in answer. The driver of the bowser was too close to the hijacker to talk and not rouse suspicion, so he was using this method to communicate. If there had been two terrorists visible he would have broken squelch twice, thrice if there were three and so on.

"All teams, stan' by, stan' by!"

The Kfirs were turning off the runway and into the parking area close to the Tri-Star, moving across its nose from right to left, the pilots braking and opening the throttles, alternately blipping the engines in a deafening roar.

X-ray hoped this would keep the hijackers eyes and not just their ears occupied.

"All teams, stan' by, stan' by. . . Go, go *go!*"

He picked up a starlight scope as the entire airbase and the airport beyond plunged into darkness. Only the runway lights on the far side of the airport remained on.

"You fucked up!" the hijack leader screamed. "We'll kill everybody—"

"No, no! It's just a power failure, we can—"

X-ray saw the cockpit window glass shatter as it was hit by sniper fire, the sound of shots covered by the Kfirs. Almost at the same time he saw the driver of the bowser draw a pistol and shoot the hijacker in the doorway, now silhouetted by the dim light of the cabin interior.

The three black long wheel-base Land Rover Defenders were already moving out of the hangars under cover of the Kfirs' noise when the lights went. But the drivers just kept their feet down, driving blind, having already memorized every inch of ground between the hangars and the Tri-Star.

As the Defenders screamed round in a sweep to approach the airliner on the far side from the control tower, three men clung to the roof of each like monkeys. Like X-ray, they wore black fatigues, but were also kitted out in full chest rigs that carried a range of ammo and equipment, and wore gas masks over Balaclava hoods as well, completing an image designed for psychological impact as well as practicality. Heckler & Koch MP-5A3 submachine-guns were clipped to their chests in order to free their hands, thus helping them scale the sides of the plane.

The Defenders braked smoothly to a halt below each of the three doors on the Tri-Star's right side, their drivers making sure there was no screech of tires that would give them away. The 4x4 Defenders had special racks mounted on the roof to carry the assaulters and the attached ladder. The first two assaulters swung the ladder up into position, even before the vehicle had stopped, and by the time the soft rubber pads bumped against the fuselage the third assaulter was halfway up it.

The Tri-Star crew had already switched the doors to 'manual', and the first commando on the ladder heaved it open, swinging back off the ladder with it to let his team through. By the time the first of the assaulters was through the doorway, the Defender's driver was already swarming up the ladder, too.

Even as Bravo 1 had a foot in the door, Bravo 2 was hurling an E182 stun grenade over his shoulder. Known as a flash-bang or maroon — for its explosion and the colour of its casing respectively — the grenade caused severe disorientation. The assaulters, however, were trained not to flinch at the detonation, and Bravo 1 followed the grenade straight in to make maximum use of it.

He swung left, aiming over the heads of the seated passengers, knowing that Bravo 2 would go right to cover the Economy Class galley. There was no shouting of "Army!" or "Down!" as this was just time wasted in which a trained terrorist would be able to gather his wits and shoot. Bravo 1 trusted in the effects of the flash-bang to keep the heads of the passengers and crew down, aiming through the smoke to put two three-round bursts into the target that stood in the aisle.

There were more bursts of automatic fire from further up the plane, and then over the net came shouts of "Delta clear!" and "Charlie clear!"

Scrambling over seats and crouching passengers, Bravo 1 reached the riddled mannequin and the man lying on the floor next to it.

Kneeling on the man's back, he said "Bravo clear!"

Instantly, Bravo 4, the assaulter who had opened the door, swung into the plane, sliding the door shut after him. He then activated the escape chute mechanism, which automatically popped open the doors and launched the slides. The doors had to be shut in order to make the system work.

Grabbing the passengers — there was only one for each row of seats — the commandos manhandled them to the door with no signs of gentleness or sympathy. There could still be hijackers hidden among the passengers and they would be sorted out by the hostage reception team waiting at the bottom of the chutes.

As the last passenger disappeared out the door, the hijackers lying around the cabin were handcuffed and flung down the slides, the commandos following close behind.

"All assault and sniper teams regroup at the CP," came the command over the net.

Ripping off his gas mask and Balaclava, and sucking in the cool night air, Sergeant Eric Christofelsz, Bravo 1, began jogging towards the Defender. Around him, grinning faces and dishevelled hair popped out as the rest of Bravo Team did the same. Laughing and breathless they all piled into the vehicle and roared off towards the control tower, headlights blazing now as the airbase's lights came on.

Soon they would be scrambling aboard buses for the short journey back to Ganemulle, home of the Sri Lanka Army's Commandos.

For Delta Group of the 1st Commando Regiment, this had been an exercise, part of build-up training for a tour as the Hostage-Rescue Group. At the end of the training they would take over from Alpha Group of the 2nd Commandos, who were currently the HR Group.

The entire exercise had been an in-house job, except for the 'passengers', who had been volunteers from the Air Force base, and the Tri-Star crew, who had been on loan from Sri Lankan Airlines. The 'hijackers' had been members of the Commando Training Group staff, and the negotiator and hostage reception team had been from the regiment's Operations and Intelligence Group.

The Tri-Star was one that had been damaged in the LTTE attack on Katunayake in July 2001, and was deemed non-airworthy. It had been bought by the Ministry of Defence and was constantly used in training.

The exercise was done as realistically as was possible, with the hijackers not told of the assault sequence, and the negotiations unrehearsed. In order that live ammunition could be used, the hijackers were required to wheel mannequins made up as themselves around from place to place in the plane. When the assault went in, they were to lie flat and trust the assaulters to shoot straight. To prevent bullets passing through the mannequins and into a bystander, the mannequins were packed with high-density foam, and special low-velocity rounds were used in the assaulters' submachine-guns.

The plane crew had been briefed to switch the doors to 'manual' as soon as the lights went. In an actual hostage situation, the doors would have to be blown with strip charges.

For the HR tour, the Commando group would be split into two. Blue Team, under the officer commanding, based in Colombo for scenarios within the city, and Red Team, under the group's second-in-command, at Ganemulle for situations at the airport.

Alpha Group of 2/CR had been the HR Group during the airport attack the previous year, and its Red Team had been called out, losing a man but killing the Black Tiger attackers. It had not been a good tour for Alpha Group, as the terrorists had managed to destroy or damage twenty-six aircraft, the bulk of them from the Air Force.

The commandos of Delta Group, 1/CR, were jubilant however, on their ride back to camp, everyone chattering and swapping stories, smoking. After three days of high tension and little sleep, it had been a successful exercise. And though the HR tour meant a high degree of alertness and constant training, it was a break from the war in the north. A chance to bathe regularly and sleep in real beds, to go watch a movie and ogle friendly girls.

Sergeant Eric Christofelsz blew cigarette smoke out of the window and looked around the crowded bus. There was kit jammed in the aisles, weapons and webbing and respirators. Delta's last tour in the north had not been a good one either. They had been engaged in constant recce patrols against the Elephant Pass area, trying to gather intelligence for an upcoming security forces counterattack on the base that had been captured by the Tigers in 1999.

The constant patrolling behind enemy lines had worn Christofelsz's nerves to tatters, and several four-man patrols had simply disappeared close to Tiger positions.

Having so many choppers around had been the only plus point. American cash had brought in a huge fleet of new helicopters, and training had just been completed on a new joint Army-Air Force airmobile division, a novel concept in Sri Lanka.

Being able to call in gunships or air strikes day or night was like having God on your shoulder.

Being the HR Group meant no drinking, however, as each team kept at constant alert, both Red and Blue teams maintaining half their strength at a fifteen-minute alert and the other half at a one-hour alert.

But it still meant no one was shooting at you, Eric Christofelsz decided. Well, not very often anyway. At least that was something. On several occasions HR Groups had been called out, but it had never happened more than once or twice on a tour.

The driver switched on the radio and Kylie Minogue's *Can't Get You Out of My Head* blasted out of the speakers. Commandos in the back of the bus began moving with the heavy beat, copying it with fists, elbows, and knees on the seatbacks and sides of the bus. Everybody was singing along now.

"Lallalla. . . lallallalalla. . . lallalla!"

CHAPTER 8

"Karin Matthews, *BBC*," the young woman said, holding out her mike to the minister. "Minister Allenbrooke, can you tell me your views on today's proceedings, and just how soon the bill will become law."

The journalist had been the first of the lot to get to the minister, but shoes clattered on the patterned marble floor as the others swarmed together. Above the raucous cacophony of shouted questions and the flash of camera lights, the intricately worked sandstone vaults of the Ottawa parliament's Confederation Hall rose imperiously.

"Well, first of all I'd like to say that I'm obviously pleased with the results," Jonathan Allenbrooke, Canada's Minister of Justice said, ignoring the young woman and looking into the lens that her cameraman poked over her shoulder. "This has been something Donald Fenster and I have always felt strongly about. The events of Nine-Eleven have shown us that without international cooperation we cannot fight the menace of terrorism. We have all seen how, as in Afghanistan, allies can strike a blow for freedom, and today's proceedings go to prove that Canada will not stand for lawlessness."

Standing behind Allenbrooke, Fenster smiled to himself. Contrary to the Justice Minister's statement, the man had hardly been an exponent on prosecuting the LTTE. It had taken a lot of lobbying of the Governor General by Fenster and other members of the House of Commons to initiate the bill, as well as finally, some heavy hints from the Prime Minister himself before Allenbrooke had agreed to back it. Fenster also noted with amusement his fellow minister's use of the Americanism to describe the September 11th attacks. How typical, he thought, that such a horrendous event could be turned into a trite numerical formula by the soundbite-loving media. It was fortunate, he concluded, that such jingoism had not existed during the Second World War. He had no doubt that the modern talking heads of television would have referred to the Japanese air raid on Pearl Harbour merely as 7/12.

"The bill was passed eighteen to twelve. . ." the minister was saying.

Not an overwhelming majority, thought Fenster. There had been heavy debate over whether the bill was too cut-and-dry, mostly fuelled by several ministers who were close to the provincial Premier of Ontario, who in turn was being intensely lobbied by both his Minister of Housing and the honourable member for Scarborough. The latter three were quite conscious of the number of votes generated by the Canadian Tamils, and the honourable member in particular seemed quite willing to ride the current crisis into another term. But Fenster was thankful that the Senate had already rubber stamped the bill without too much delay.

". . . As for how soon the law will go into operation, I cannot say just yet, until my department can iron out the details with the Supreme Court. I *will* say, however, that it'll be very soon. Possibly by the end of this month."

Fickle as ever, the attention of the news people now switched to Fenster, who was patiently waiting his turn.

"Can we have your view on the current situation, Mister Fenster," asked the political correspondent of *The Toronto Herald*, "and your feelings on today's parliamentary events?"

Reluctantly, Allenbrooke stepped imperceptibly aside and made way for Fenster, who cleared his throat and stepped forward.

"Well, having seen the evidence presented by the United States on the LTTE's collusion with Al Qaeda, I can only see today's bill as inevitable. As a close friend and ally of the US, as well as a member of NATO, Canada is obliged to clean up its own backyard. I have long advocated stronger policing of immigrant communities — particularly the Tamils — and this is ample proof that it should have been carried out long ago.

"My visit to Sri Lanka last year was very fruitful, and I believe the cooperation between our governments can only lead to better things — both here and in Sri Lanka. The LTTE is very clearly a terrorist organization bent on succeeding at the cost of innocent lives, and we intend to give the Sri Lankan government every support in its fight against them."

"Would this include military aid, Mister Minister?" the BBC woman chipped in.

"I will not rule that out," answered Fenster, "but right now we're seeing the intelligence and financial war as the battlefield in which Ottawa can help Colombo."

"John McAllister, CNN," spoke up another reporter. "Mister Fenster, it is already common knowledge that the United States has given a huge military aid package to Sri Lanka, as well as military personnel to carry out training programmes. Does Canada plan to send military personnel to the island?"

"Well, I think you'll have to ask that of the Minister of Defence," Fenster parried. "I know of no such plans."

"What d'you have to say to critics of this bill," asked the Toronto reporter, "people who claim that it is too vague and quite heavy-handed?"

"I hardly think it is heavy-handed to crack down on criminals," retorted Fenster. "And we're not talking about harassment here. There will be legitimate investigations and where necessary proper prosecution. Many so-called Tamil community-service organizations are nothing but cover groups for the LTTE. They strong-arm their own people, extort and launder money, dodge taxes. The list is endless."

"How exactly will the Justice Department handle Tamils who hold Canadian citizenship?" asked another journalist. "If they're found guilty of offences."

"Canadian citizens will be dealt with according to the laws of this country," chipped in Allenbrooke. "The only portion of this bill that concerns them is 'membership in an illegal terrorist organization' and 'incitement to commit terrorism'. Both of which will now carry a mandatory sentence. Or if they are wanted for capital offences in Sri Lanka. If so, that will be handled under the new extradition treaty. Any non-Canadian citizens found guilty of criminal activity will be either prosecuted, deported to their country of origin, or both, depending on the severity of the charges."

There was a sudden ripple in the crowd of journalists as several more politicians walked into Confederation Hall. There was a surge from the outer ring of reporters as they rushed across to the newcomers.

"It seems as if the sharks are done with us," muttered Allenbrooke, turning to leave. "Coming, Donald?"

"I think I'll stay awhile," Fenster replied, watching the throng of journalists who had now surrounded Steven Wallis, the Ontario Housing Minister, and Diana Gerhardt, the Scarborough MP.

The federal ministers who had opposed the bill had made themselves scarce, as Fenster knew they would have. With the bill passed, they were required to publicly defend it or resign their cabinet posts. It looked like they had left their lobbyists to do the protesting. And, Fenster noted, it seemed as if the Ontario Premier hadn't even bothered to show up.

Diana Gerhardt was already speaking, answering the first of the questions. Steve Wallis hung back, however, letting his female colleague hog the limelight. Fenster knew that the Ontario Housing Minister would come around now that the bill was fact. The man was too professional a politician to let it drag him down. But he would let Gerhardt run with it, guaranteeing both her and the party the Tamil vote.

"Today was a sad day in the proud history of our nation," Gerhardt was saying. "Canada has always been a warm-hearted nation, opening her arms to the world's refugees. But today we have turned our backs on an oppressed people. This Anti-Terrorism Bill is nothing but a sham to extend trade into South Asia."

"But has not the United States supplied evidence linking the LTTE to Al Qaeda?" the *CNN* reporter asked.

"*Evidence?*" queried Gerhardt with raised eyebrows. "I hardly think the *evidence* would stand up in a court of law. But if the USA can bomb Afghanistan why can't we persecute a few immigrants, eh?"

"Do you then disagree with both the USA and Canada outlawing the LTTE, Miss Gerhardt?" Another journalist asked.

"I have no objection whatsoever to terrorists being arrested and prosecuted, but the claims that volunteer organizations in my constituency are connected to the LTTE are preposterous."

Fenster turned to leave at that point, letting the hubbub die out into the distance behind him as he walked through the quiet vaulted corridors. He took out his mobile phone and dialled his driver, telling the man to bring the car around.

The car was already waiting for him when he stepped out of the parliament building, and Ian McEdwards was already walking up from the driveway. It was mid-February and bitterly cold, with the wind whipping in across the Ottawa River, but Fenster stood there for awhile, looking north over the Alexandra Bridge. Below Parliament Hill, the river was grey and misty, the bridge blurring into the smudge of Hull on the Quebec side of the water.

"Everything OK, sir?" Ian McEdwards asked as he reached Fenster. The inspector's breath was a cloud in the frosty air.

"Yeah, Ian, fine." But he continued to look out across the river, pulling his scarf tighter around his neck.

After several minutes of silence, Fenster said, "It's so different, isn't it?"

"What is, sir?"

"Sri Lanka. Different from here, I mean. And no, I don't mean the weather. But the way of thinking. The point of view. So different."

"Think so, sir?" McEdwards said hesitantly. "I've found the regular people aren't that different anywhere on earth."

"I hope so, Ian." Fenster sighed. "I sure hope so. I just wonder how today's decision will affect things over there. And whether we'll really feel the change back here."

He walked down the steps towards the car, and Ian McEdwards quickly followed him.

TEETH

"*I do not welcome venerable gentlemen...
because in their wake, in their footsteps,
springing up like sharp little teeth, are these
dark young men of random destiny and private
passions – destinies and passions that can be
shaped and directed to violent ends.*

- Paul Scott. *Division of the Spoils*

CHAPTER 9

FEBRUARY - MARCH 2002: With a pre-war population of around a hundred and eighteen thousand, the city of Jaffna was, and is, the cultural as well as symbolic capital of the Sri Lankan Tamils, though in the event of a separate state being created out of the Northern and Eastern provinces, its actual capital will most likely be the port city of Trincomalee on the east coast. Nevertheless, Jaffna remains the true heart of Tamil Eelam. Captured from the government in mid 1990, it was for five years just that, a functioning — if besieged — capital, until the security forces' Operation *Riviresa* — Sunbeam — recaptured it from the LTTE in October 1995. The battered but recovering city sits in the southwest corner of a long, ragged, claw-like peninsula that bears its name. Home to three-quarters of a million people until 1983, the peninsula is a dry and dusty land, its soil more sand than earth, and artificial irrigation was needed to enable the extensive cultivation that was carried out in the early 1980s. Its population bombed, shot, and driven out by the war, the irrigation system destroyed by fighting, the peninsula is a sandy hellhole, thorn scrub invading the mango plantations and the salt marshes shimmering in the 40°C heat.

The Jaffna Peninsula is actually more a collection of islands than a peninsula, shaped like a two-fingered and skeletal hand, cut off at the wrist from mother India and clinging to Sri Lanka by a fingernail. The peninsula itself can be divided into four geographical sections, each divided from the other by a maze of small lagoons, salt marshes, and waterways. The most densely populated and most extensively cultivated of these geographical sections is the hand's palm, the land mass that boasts ownership of the city of Jaffna with its Dutch-period star fort — one of the best preserved examples of its kind, before it was dismantled by the LTTE and its stone used to build more modern fortifications. On the northern coast of this piece of land are the Kankasanturai cement factory and the Palaly airbase. To the west and southwest of the palm are the shattered remains of the wrist, a confusing collection of inhospitable islands and islets. Of these, only the six largest — Karaitivu, Kayts, Analativu, Nayinativu, Punkudutivu, and Delft — have ever held permanent populations. The rest, some hardly more than sandbanks, devoid of much vegetation and with the occasional rocky outcropping, were scattered out into the shallow waters of the Palk Straits, like the shattered wrist of a greedily grasping India. To the east of the palm, beyond a jumble of twisted waterways and nearly impassable marshes, are two long narrow spits of land, like bony fingers, that form the other two portions of the Jaffna Peninsula. The narrower, more northern finger, with the towns of Valvettithurai, Nelliadi, and Point Pedro at its northern end, stretches down through the Chundikkulam Bird Sanctuary until it is connected to the mainland at Kariyalavayal by a land bridge less than a kilometre wide. With its open coastline facing the deep waters of the Bay of Bengal, the finger was long seen by the Tigers as a natural spot for an enemy amphibious landing, and therefore was heavily mined by them during the early 1990s. The villages that dot it are ruined and deserted. Below this finger, divided by a splinter of lagoon is the largest, and most barren of the jigsaw pieces that form the peninsula. Hanging like a tick to the underside of this second finger is its largest town, Chavakachcheri, through which runs the A9 highway and the parallel railway line, travelling the length of the finger and connecting Jaffna to the rest of Sri Lanka. Further south, the highway and rail track cross to the mainland via a causeway at the village of Elephant Pass. Once a huge, sprawling security forces base that encompassed both Elephant Pass and the Saltern Siding on the mainland, it had been captured by the LTTE in May 2000. A strategic necessity if the Jaffna Peninsula was to be resupplied overland, the loss of this complex had been a humiliation the Army had endured for almost two long years.

On February 4th 2002, Sri Lanka's Independence Day, the Army's 53rd Division launched an offensive down the A9 highway from Chavakachcheri towards Elephant Pass. There was heavy Tiger resistance, particularly by amphibious Sea Tiger units that crossed the Jaffna Lagoon from Pooneryn on the mainland. But with air and naval patrols in support, the division had, in five days, fought its way to within striking distance of Elephant Pass's northern perimeter.

On February 10th, Major General Parakrama Jayatunge, commander of the 51st Air Assault Division received fresh orders from the Joint Operations Command. This was the word he had long waited for. He was instructed to airlift one of his battalions and an artillery battery into Mulliyan, northeast of Elephant Pass to reinforce reserve units of the 53rd Division and to protect its communications lines along the A9.

The 51st Air Assault was still an experiment for the Sri Lankan high command, a joint Army-Air Force unit directly controlled by the JOC. It had spent the past four months training in airmobile tactics with the American personnel supplied as part of US military aid and hadn't seen much combat since moving up to Palaly on the Jaffna Peninsula at the end of January.

Jayatunge knew that though his men had performed well in the small-unit skirmishes they had been involved in around Palaly and Vasavilan, this would be their — and his — first test in airmobile operations of this scale against an enemy.

A product of both the Kotalawela Defence Academy and of Sandhurst, an infantryman who was a great advocate of airmobility, Jayatunge had once commanded the fledgling Airmobile Brigade. He had been an immediate choice to command the new division.

Sri Lankan Army units are patterned in the British style and unlike American soldiers, have no pride or affection for the brigade or division they serve in. All their fierce loyalty is reserved for their regiments, each with its own traditions, colours, and battle flags. They tend to look on other regiments as inferior to their own, but still not as low as the position the Air Force commands in their collective evaluations. It had taken all of Major General Parakrama Jayatunge's enthusiasm and leadership, along with months of long and careful training, to weld the battalions, squadrons, and all the other attached units together. A master parachutist who had served tours both with the Sri Lankan Special Forces and the US 101st Airborne Division, he had commanded infantry units from platoon to company level before taking over his own beloved 1st Sri Lanka Light Infantry. A respected combat officer, recognized as one of the most capable in the country, he was popular with his troops, both Army and Air Force. But they needed victory. The JOC commander had personally told Jayatunge that a successful operation was needed to silence the critics in parliament who were questioning the high cost of the new division, which had a comparatively large proportion of non-combat troops.

A major portion of the division consisted of Air Force support personnel — mechanics, technicians, armourers, and others who were needed to keep the helicopters flying. The core of pilots were highly experienced and skilled in flying at treetop height at speeds of up to two hundred and seventy kilometres per hour, and they would season the newer flyers who had been churned through flight training to fill out the new division. The infantry and arty battalions were all veteran units of the war. The division's strength was in its speed and immediately available firepower. The basic tactical unit was six Mi-24 Hind Echo gunships armed with rockets and 20-mm cannon, and six UH-1Ns — the old and trusted Hueys — carrying infantrymen.

Good current intelligence would be needed for the operation to be successful. By the 13th of February, Squadron Leader Dhammika Suriyabandara, the division's intelligence officer, handed in an unusually accurate report. It was clear from air and ground recce that the Tigers meant to mount a massive pincer move to outflank the advancing 53rd Division and cut it off from its logistic and support base of Chavakachcheri. Two Tiger brigades were in the area, the Charles Anthony Regiment at Vannankulam on the peninsula east of Elephant Pass, and the Sea Tigers' 2nd Marine Tiger Regiment to the west at Pooneryn, on the mainland. In addition, a third brigade held Elephant Pass itself. The Charles Anthony was thought to be the LTTE strike unit which would move in between Mulliyan and the Jaffna Lagoon and cut the A9 close to Iyakachchi, while the 2nd Marine Tigers — an amphibious unit — would intercept any seaborne force, or make landings to ambush any ground force, trying to relieve the 53rd Division.

Initially the 51st Air Assault acted in a support role to the 53rd Division as it fought to capture the Elephant Pass stronghold. However, the 51st Air Assault's 511th Brigade, with orders to defend Mulliyan, provide arty support, and act as a reserve force, would soon be in action.

On the 14th of February, at 0445 hours the Charles Anthony Regiment cut the A9 highway at two points south of Iyakachchi. A relief column of armoured vehicles set out from Soranpattu, the next town north, but was ambushed by forward units of the 2nd Marine Tigers who had crossed the lagoon the previous night. The 51st Air Assault was called for, and the 511th Brigade responded instantly, getting its choppers into the air in less than fifteen minutes. For the rest of the day, the brigade's Hind gunships hammered at the Tigers, prising open the jaws of the trap so that Hueys could insert two battalions — the 8th and 10th Sri Lanka Light Infantry. The firepower and quick deployment of the brigade eased the pressure on the 53rd Division enabling it to take the northern perimeter of Elephant Pass on the 15th of February.

The Charles Anthony, hurt but still fighting, melted back into the jungle, but the 2nd Marine Tigers were decimated close to Tanmakkeni. Their retreat across the lagoon was cut off by gunships that destroyed most of their boats and hit the Sea Tiger base at Cheddiyakurichchi, on the mainland close to Pooneryn.

Realizing the threat of the new airmobile units, and fearing being cut off from the south, the Tiger brigade holding the Saltern Siding — Elephant Pass' southern perimeter — abandoned it.

It was now clear that a major opportunity for deploying the entire 51st Air Assault was presenting itself. The Tigers were pulling back, licking their wounds, and a quick reaction might keep them off balance. General Sujeeva Perera, head of the JOC, flew up to the front with the commanders of the Army and Air Force, and ordered the 51st Air Assault in pursuit.

It was what Jayatunge had been waiting for. Freed from reinforcement and support duties, the 51st Air Assault could engage in hard-hitting search-and-destroy operations against LTTE units south of Elephant Pass.

It wasn't just the Tigers they would have problems with. Unlike the Jaffna Peninsula, the mainland south of it was covered in thick scrub and thorn jungle. This stretched more or less unbroken all the way south to Anuradhapura, the ancient capital of the Sri Lankan kings. Wherever the jungle gave way to open land the terrain was covered by tall elephant grass that hid huge boulders and anthills that could flip a landing helicopter on its side. In most places an advance unit would have to rappel down from a hovering chopper and use explosives to blow a landing zone for the following transports.

For the next fortnight most of the 511th Brigade was deployed southwest of the Saltern Siding. Much of their operations involved heavy fighting, and most of them were successful. For instance, on the 21st of February, aerial reconnaissance northwest of Paranthan spotted unusual movement close to the Paranthan-Periyaparanthan road, ten kilometres southwest of the Saltern Siding, and called in units of the 511th Brigade. The enemy had no time to get out of the area and one hundred and thirty-five were killed and two captured. Even bigger a victory was the capture of a complete underground field hospital. Large quantities of essential medical supplies, including morphine and antibiotics were also found.

Two days later, 10/SLLI drew blood again, when it executed a perfect ambush on a company of the LTTE's Jayanthan Regiment, moving along a trail north of Paranthan. The infantrymen had to wait in nail-biting anticipation for an hour until the terras moved into the killing zone. They let the Tiger lead scouts walk right through, while the ambushers' rear guard were treated to the unnerving sight of the Tiger flank guards moving past, between them and the strike group. The deafening roar of Claymores signalled the closing of the trap, and then the infantrymen opened up on full automatic for almost three minutes. There was no return fire.

The infantrymen, however, weren't having everything their own way. Their forward operating base came under sustained, almost fanatical attacks from three Tiger companies, and by midnight the perimeter was in danger of being overrun. Now the advantages of air mobility became clear as Alpha Company of 8/SLLI flew in from the Saltern Siding. The first platoon was on the ground and fighting before 0100.

These first sustained battles by units of the 511th Brigade, though small in scale, were ample justification for the formation of the division, decided Jayatunge. Kiowa scout choppers were regularly locating enemy units; then highly mobile SF or Commando patrols were being flown in to track the terras before rifle battalions arrived to pin them down and massive air and ground firepower was used to inflict maximum casualties. The Sri Lankan security forces were learning many lessons in this — for them — new form of warfare through combat experience.

It was at first disconcerting for infantry battalions to get so suicidally close to Tiger units so fast. Several units were practically dropped into the LTTE's laps by Air Force pilots eager to get them in close behind the prepping arty. It was often difficult to organize arty support for units in highly fluid situations, and casevac was delayed because of a shortage of LZ-clearing kit.

The early encounters of the campaign were also remarkable for the successful deployment of large airmobile units at night.

The battle on February 23rd was the first time a defensive perimeter under heavy fire was reinforced in the dark by Sri Lankan air mobile troops flying into an unfamiliar LZ. It was also the first time that large numbers of gunships were used that close to conventional units at night. At times the Hinds had been hitting Tiger positions just twenty-five metres in front of the infantrymen.

The transport pilots had been taught to fly their Hueys low and fast — getting past the Tiger gunners before they could get them in their sights. Fully laden with troops they had to fly low, but there was no way they could move fast.

Dropping at night into a vicious fire fight was every chopper pilot's nightmare. The terras always knew they were coming. Chopper engines were noisy and could be heard several miles away. Over the LZs, the tracers from the enemy .50-in machine-guns would go through anything.

On March 2nd, Hind gunships working in relays cut the A35 highway between Paranthan and Murasumoddai, stopping traffic and therefore quick LTTE reinforcements. The next day, the 511th Brigade was withdrawn from the Paranthan area, and hurled against Murasumoddai, 8/SLLI and the brigade's reserve battalion, the 9th Gajabas, taking it the day after. The brigade's deployment was extremely successful and almost four hundred Tigers were killed and an estimated three hundred and sixty wounded. Equally importantly, it captured over half a million rounds of 7.62-mm ammo, two 82-mm mortars, three 90-mm recoilless rifles, and over a hundred thousand US dollars worth of medical supplies. A T-62 tank captured earlier from the Army by the Tigers was also destroyed in air strikes.

The Tiger units at Paranthan, now outflanked and, as at the Saltern Siding, fearing vertical envelopment, fell back on Kilinochchi, now the last major town in the Northern Province held by the LTTE.

The 512th Brigade, consisting of the 9th and 10th Gemunu Watch, with the 6th Singha Rifles in reserve, flew into Paranthan. By this time Jayatunge's major concern was that the LTTE units west of Paranthan, cut off from support bases in the east by the fall of the town, would be trying to get out of the immediate area by circling south to where they could regroup around Kilinochchi. He ordered Brigadier Shafi Iqbal, the commander of the 512th, to push patrols west and southwest of Paranthan into the Periyaparanthan area. Brigadier Iqbal, well-trained in airmobile operations, started an immediate hunt for the terras. Intelligence reports indicated that the Charles Anthony Regiment of the LTTE, having taken losses in the defence of Elephant Pass had, in two weeks of hard marching, circled around in a wide sweep. It had escaped from the peninsula via the salt marshes of the Chundikkulam Bird Sanctuary, crossing the A35 highway southeast of Murasumoddai. The regiment had then been reinforced and rearmed close to Kilinochchi before finally crossing the A9 highway and moving into the area southwest of Periyaparanthan. Commando deep recce patrols were now reporting that the regiment was reorganizing along the Akkarayan River. This river runs south to north, thirteen kilometres west of the A9 and virtually parallel to it, connecting the Akkarayan Reservoir to the Jaffna Lagoon. It was also believed that a second brigade-sized unit was in the area, plus reinforcements from Pooneryn, twenty-two kilometres west of Elephant Pass and the Saltern Siding. Signal intercepts were giving the impression that the LTTE expected a massive amphibious landing by the security forces somewhere north of Pooneryn, on the spit of land that juts northwest from the Sri Lankan mainland and forms a boom dividing the Jaffna Lagoon from the open sea. Along with this, Int claimed that the Tigers were also preparing to defend against airmobile blocking forces landing at Nallur on the Periyaparanthan-Pooneryn road, and at Chempankundu on the A32 coastal highway that connects Pooneryn to the Mannar District further south. The Charles Anthony and other units were to act as a screen for the Sea Tiger units in the Pooneryn area to withdraw.

On the 7th of March, the 9th Battalion, the Gemunu Watch, commanded by Lieutenant Colonel Saliya Ganegoda, began a sweep southwest of Periyaparanthan in the direction of the Akkarayan River. Arty support, one of the most essential parts of any airmobile operation, was to be supplied by two 120-mm batteries flown in by Mi-17 medium lift choppers into Periyaparanthan.

A landing zone was selected by Ganegoda, eight kilometres southwest of Periyaparanthan, able to take ten Hueys at a time. The spot was named LZ *Monara* — Peacock — after the cap badge of the Gemunu Watch, and would be the place for the opening air assault. The coordination of all arms would be crucial in the early portion of the operation. At 1000 hours a prep bombardment by the 120s began, and was quickly followed by air strikes. Gunships saturated the LZ, ripple-firing half their load of rockets in less than thirty seconds. Bravo Company came in first. On landing, the troops spread out and secured the LZ for Alpha and Charlie Companies, which quickly followed.

By 1300, however, the LTTE had made further reinforcement of the area very dangerous. The LZ was ringed by scrub jungle and elephant grass and dotted with anthills, providing good cover for the terras who were able to pin down the soldiers. Several Hueys carrying the leading elements of Support Company were hit, and though none were shot down, Colonel Ganegoda forbade the rest from landing. The companies on the ground were ordered to pull into a tight defensive perimeter until the next day.

LZ *Monara* was red-hot. Sitting in a pilot's seat, the target of all the surrounding hostile fire, the men who flew the Hueys — some of them instructor pilots from American training teams — took horrendous risks to fly the resupply missions. Once into the LZ, they were desperate for the soldiers to get out of the ships as quickly as possible. Then there was the seemingly endless wait as the wounded were loaded on board. Aircrews considered themselves lucky if they could get away in less than a minute.

At 1415, Ganegoda again tried to get in the heavy crew-served weapons of his Support Company. He wanted them on the ground before sunset.

The first flight of four Hueys came in with the lead elements of the company and was instantly taken under fire. Two ships were disabled and the forward air controller ordered the second flight to abort. The crews of the two downed ships piled into the other two Hueys and they pulled out of the smoke. Two pilots had been wounded — one an American — and a door gunner had been killed.

By mid-afternoon, Ganegoda knew he was in trouble, and his men were fighting for their lives against the Charles Anthony and the LTTE's elite Imran Pandiyan Regiment. It seemed obvious to Brigadier Iqbal at Periyaparanthan that the terras were determined to destroy 9/GW. He prepared to send in reinforcements to strengthen the LZ; Bravo Company of 10/GW arrived at *Monara* by 1800 hours, and night landing facilities were set up.

By now the situation had improved and it was only an isolated platoon of 9/GW's Bravo Company that was a matter for concern. Although reports suggested that it was holding out with morale still high, eight men had been killed, twelve wounded, and only seven were unhurt. The platoon beat off several attacks that night with the help of arty fire. Dawn revealed dozens of LTTE dead around their positions.

Savage close fighting was also going on all along the *Monara* perimeter. A platoon commander in Charlie Company was killed when he took over from one of his dead machine-gunners. He opened up on a Black Tiger suicide squad assaulting the perimeter, killing seven before one charged into the machine-gun position and blew himself up.

Gemunu Watch troops were found dead with their arms locked around dead Tigers, bayonets or knives still buried in each other's bodies.

By 1030 on the 8th of March, air strikes and Hind gunships firing rockets and 20-mm cannon had blasted the Tigers back and away from *Monara*.

Iqbal was now confident that the terras were no longer strong enough to continue attacking *Monara*, and at 1330 pulled out the tired troops of 9/GW and replaced them with the rest of 10/GW. The fresh battalion was then ordered to push after the Charles Anthony Regiment which was pulling back south, up the Akkarayan River. The Imran Pandiyan, badly hurt by the repeated frontal assaults on *Monara* had crossed the river to regroup and maintain its original role as part of the screen for the Pooneryn LTTE units.

At dawn on the 9th, the 6th Singha Rifles was choppered in behind the Charles Anthony, trapping it now between two tributaries of the Akkarayan. During the length of that long day, the two battalions chopped up the Tiger unit in a series of bloody assaults. Gunships continued to smash pockets of hardened resistance while making the waterways impassable. What was left of the Charles Anthony finally dispersed on the night of the 9th, no longer a cohesive fighting unit.

Brigadier Iqbal now realized that 10/GW and 6/SR were in danger of being cut off by Tigers moving west from Kilinochchi, and pulled them back to *Monara*. 6/SR was ordered to hold the LZ until 10/GW was airlifted to Periyaparanthan, and then on the 11th, it too was choppered out.

The two-day battle around LZ *Monara* was the high-point of the operation, and many Tiger bodies littered the battlefield. Bloodstained bandages suggested that far more had been wounded. Colonel Ganegoda's battalion had taken almost two hundred casualties, dead, wounded, and missing, but the LTTE lost many more. Six hundred and forty-six bodies were counted at *Monara*, over five hundred more were believed wounded or killed, and four prisoners were taken. 10/GW took twenty-eight casualties all told, and 6/SR twenty-three, in the pursuit and entrapment of the Charles Anthony Regiment, which left a further four hundred and twelve bodies behind before dispersing.

By the 16th of March the LTTE had abandoned its bases on the Pooneryn-Kalmunai spit and Sri Lanka Navy infantry, spearheaded by Special Boat Squadron troops, began to move ashore.

The 51st Air Assault Division had been in combat for twenty-four days, and had proven that the face of war in Sri Lanka had changed once more. No longer would government troops have to hack their way through the jungle in pursuit of the enemy. Airmobile troops could respond faster to situations and maintain contact with terra units for longer periods of time.

An equally important fact was that the LTTE in the Northern Province was now finding itself squeezed into an increasingly tighter area between Mankulam in the south and Paranthan in the north.

CHAPTER 10

FEBRUARY 19th 2002, 0800 EASTERN STANDARD TIME (1300 GMT): The morning was blistering cold in downtown Toronto, and headlights cut through the light snow and dawn gloom. A wind that cut to the bone was blowing up Yonge Street — the Longest Street in the World — from the waterfront, and office workers scurried along, huddled into coats or grasping tightly to hats.

It wasn't just the weather that discouraged people from lingering on the streets. The announcement by Ottawa nearly a week before of the new Anti-Terrorism Bill, followed by renewed protests, violence, and a rash of police and Forces raids in Scarborough had lent an air of tension and foreboding throughout Toronto. There was an increased police presence at the main railway and metro stations, and patrol cars prowled the streets.

Nevertheless, a few of Toronto's more nonchalant transient workers paused at some of the fast-food stalls that dotted Yonge and Bloor Streets, grabbing a sandwich and a steaming cup of coffee before moving on. The stalls were actually modified mobile homes, one side opening out to reveal a counter that sold everything from fish-and-chips and *bratwurst* to soup and herbal tea. A few of the hardier individuals lingered long enough for a cigarette before entering their non-smoking office blocks.

The faces of the pedestrians and drivers reflected Toronto's colourful multi-ethnic makeup as stocky Koreans and Chinese mixed in with hulking Jamaicans and slim Indians and Sri Lankans, all seemingly in equal proportion to the whites.

The young couple stood huddled together next to Barry's Chip Wagon, their gloved hands holding paper cups of steaming coffee. Though neither of them was smoking, they didn't head off with the rest of the crowd streaming out of the metro station a hundred metres away at the intersection of Yonge and Bloor. To the casual observer, there was nothing unusual about them. An immigrant couple, probably in their first year of marriage, from southern India or Sri Lanka, and from the look of their particularly bulky coats they were feeling acutely the effects of what was possibly their first Canadian winter. The man was of average height for a South Asian, but the woman was much shorter, not much over five feet. They talked little, except in short bursts, and every minute or so they glanced from their wristwatches to the metro entrance.

At 8:15am, the man nodded at the woman, and they headed north along Yonge, tossing their paper cups into a bin as they went. They were holding hands and walking briskly as they reached the entrance to the metro and took the stairs down. Once underground they bought tickets from an automatic dispenser and pushed through the turnstile on to the westbound platform. It was moderately crowded with people who had got off the southbound route and were waiting for their connection; incoming commuters, however, usually outnumbered the outgoing in the mornings at Yonge & Bloor.

The couple were closer to the edge of the platform than most, standing just behind the yellow safety line, but now they split up. Instead of standing together, they placed themselves almost thirty metres apart, and after a nervous exchanged glance, ignored each other. Behind them, the platform began to fill up.

At precisely 8:26am, the train from Scarborough arrived, two minutes late. The doors slid open and passengers poured out, cursing the delay and rushing to make up time. The waiting crowd on the platform moved opposite the doors, the young couple amongst them, waiting for the arriving commuters to disperse so that they could get on.

Five seconds after the doors opened the couple detonated the explosives strapped to themselves under their coats. The thunderous explosions killed almost everyone standing behind them, and blew the carriages off the track and against the far wall of the underground station. Window glass torn into splinters by the blast ripped through the compartments and the people in them. Everyone in the two carriages opposite the couple died, but the radius of the explosions were large enough to encompass the carriages further up and down the line, killing, maiming and trapping many more.

Pedestrians on both Yonge and Bloor Streets stopped in their tracks as the rumble of the bombs reached them through the ground. A plume of grey smoke shot from the metro entrance. Cars screeched to a halt and were hit from behind by other vehicles skidding on the icy street. Traffic piled up, but there wasn't the usual blare of horns. Drivers and passengers stared open-mouthed as dazed, bleeding survivors stumbled from the metro entrance, their clothes and faces blackened and scorched, covered by the dust of collapsed ceilings.

1315 GMT: At the time of the Toronto explosions, the streets in the Broadgate area of the city of London were also busy, but with workers already hurrying back to their offices after a quick lunch and a pint at the local pubs. Though not as bitterly cold and snowy as Toronto, the city of London was its usual wet self, with a light drizzle glossing the streets.

In the driving seat of the white Mitsubishi L200 van, the twenty-something South Asian driver glanced at his wristwatch as he drove past Liverpool Station, heading south on Bishopsgate, worrying about whether the blocking car would still be in place. He slowed behind a red double-decker bus as it stopped to allow pedestrians to cross. Black taxicabs lined the pavement outside the station, its drivers sitting inside to escape the cold and rain as they waited for fares.

As the lights changed, the driver of the van swung it onto Liverpool Street. The road ahead was heavy with traffic and he cursed softly in Tamil. The urge to slam down on the horn as he would have in Colombo was tempting, but he resisted, not wanting to draw attention. He finally got through and onto Wilson Street, heading north once more on the wider avenue. He pulled up in front of the Horse & Crown, but didn't get out, finally giving vent to his frustrations by blipping the horn.

A minute later, a man the same age as the driver, wearing jeans and a leather jacket came trotting out of the pub and scrambled into the passenger seat.

"Everything alright?" the driver asked in Tamil. His own coat collar was turned up, and the woollen watch cap on his head was pulled down to his eyebrows, making him look like a dark little gnome.

"Yes," the newcomer replied. "I left the car last night as planned, and put some more money in the metre an hour back."

With a quick nod, the driver pulled the van back into traffic and continued north. He could smell beer on the other man's breath and shot him a furious glare.

"Couldn't you wait until after the job to put a shot?" he demanded.

The passenger clicked his tongue in exasperation. "I'm fine. And anyway, you were late and I couldn't just stand around and draw attention, no? No one will notice another Paki having a lunchtime pint."

Still muttering to himself, the driver turned into Finsbury Square. The pavements were lined with parked vehicles as they had predicted during the planning stage. Drawing to a halt, he let his passenger out. The man walked quickly over to a Mondeo station wagon that was parked in front of Scotia House and got in. The Mondeo pulled out of the parking space and the van replaced it. The van driver went over to the metre and put in several coins before joining his companion in the car. He glanced again at his watch. He still had an hour and fifteen minutes.

Driving at a moderate pace, the Mondeo continued through Finsbury Square and onto the City Road, turning north and increasing speed. Behind them, the Mitsubishi van sat in front of Scotia House, the head office of the Bank of Nova Scotia, one of the biggest Canadian banks in the city.

An hour and a quarter later, the hundred kilos of C4 packed into the roof and right side panels of the van's windowless rear exploded. The floor of the van and the left side had been armoured, while the roof and right side had been weakened to channel the blast up and outwards towards Scotia House.

The blast blew nearby cars across the street and brought down the entire front facade of the ancient building. A newly added mezzanine floor, weakened by the explosion, collapsed into the lobby and personal banking areas, trapping and killing scores of employees and customers.

*

1430 CENTRAL EUROPEAN TIME (1330 GMT): The annual Frankfurt Trade Expo, which had opened earlier that week at the Festhalle, northeast of the city centre, was a long-standing trade fair, and particularly popular with Third World nations that wanted to showcase their export trade and encourage foreign investment. A large portion of its popularity was the fact that it was much cheaper and more accessible to nations that couldn't afford the flashier trade fairs dominated by western nations.

Unlike organized events in other parts of Europe, German security at the trade fair was tight, and visitors to the Expo were all forced to walk through metal detectors. Armed police personnel in their green and tan uniforms patrolled the trade fair grounds in pairs, and there were more police stationed at key points in the series of interlocking halls that made up the Festhalle. The place had also been swept through with bomb-sniffing dogs prior to the opening.

Removed from the financial centre of Frankfurt am Main — so named for the river that runs through it — the sprawling Festhalle was ringed by a circuit road and stood at the intersection of four major road systems — the B8 running east, Hambürger Allee running northeast, Senckenberganlage running north, and Friedrich-Erbert-Anlage that connected it to the city. Knowing that many terrorism-affected countries were taking part in the Expo — such as Israel, Pakistan, and Sri Lanka — the police were patrolling these roads heavily.

The Sri Lankan trade hall was particularly attractive to visitors, with its colourful displays and a fashion show that showcased the country's textile and fashion industries. Several stalls had different brands of tea and other beverages on show, as well as a sampling of food, along with cafe-style areas where visitors could taste the products. Other stalls displayed rubber products, and some — including Sri Lankan Airlines — were promoting the island's tourism prospects. On a small stage at one end of the hall, several traditional Sri Lankan dance troupes were taking turns to entertain visitors.

In contrast to traditional industries such as these, several stalls showed off fledgling computer and communications industries alongside the more established garment industry, in the hope of tempting European investors. Other stalls advertised the opportunity to take advantage of cheap Sri Lankan labour and real estate.

Sumedha Fernando was sitting behind the information desk of the Mackenzie Holdings stall, easing back in his chair. If he could move a couple of inches to his right, he was sure he'd be able to see the panties of the blonde sitting in the cafe opposite, sipping tea. She was wearing a black mini skirt that reached to mid-thigh when she was standing and now, seated as she was, the skirt kept inching higher up her slim dark-stockinged legs. Fernando had been watching her for ten minutes now.

He finally achieved the right angle and, yes! There it was He could make out the flash of pale skin above the blonde's stocking tops, and the white triangle at the juncture of her thighs. Fernando squirmed in his seat as his erection struggled against his suit trousers.

Fernando and two other Sri Lankans, all three working for Mackenzie Marketing, one of the subsidiary companies in Mackenzie Holdings, were in Frankfurt to run the group's stall. The parent company had its finger in practically every pie in Sri Lanka. Originally a Scottish tea and rubber trading firm during the nineteenth century, Mackenzie Holdings had expanded rapidly in the 1950s into shipping and real estate, and in the 1980s into banking, tourism, hotels, and electronics. It was one of the country's biggest commercial groups now and had been listed in *Asia Today* as one of the region's top one hundred companies.

The Mackenzie Holdings stall was a slick prefab job in blue and grey, the group's corporate colours. Huge back-projection screens covered several of the stall's walls and partitions, showing various aspects of the Mackenzie network. While one screen would show footage of luxurious beach hotels and cultural sites, another would be running a clip on the tea plantations and the process of picking, processing, and export. Headphones that could be clipped into small consoles below the screens were available for visitors wishing to hear the voice of the narrator. A host of PCs were scattered through the stall, their monitors displaying the group's website, and enabling visitors to go online and explore Mackenzie's products, services, and companies in closer detail.

Sumedha Fernando straightened up guiltily as he lifted his gaze from the blonde woman's crotch and found himself looking straight into her blue eyes. He turned away quickly, trying to appear busy with some corporate brochures that lay on the information counter, but his gaze jumped back to the woman as she rose from her table and started to walk towards the Mackenzie stall. He got to his feet, grinning brightly, and moved across to intercept her as she entered the stall. Maybe this was his chance. He'd heard what German women were like, especially blonde ones.

"May I help you?" he said in German, joining her at one of the PC stations.

She turned her icy blue eyes on him. "No, thank you. I am just interested in some of the online facilities your company offers."

"I'll be happy to show you, madam," he offered, reaching for the keyboard.

"I'm quite alright on my own," she replied, and Fernando decided that her voice was as cold as her eyes.

He returned to the information desk, scowling at Dilani Weerasinghe. The only female in the Sri Lankan marketing team, she was now smirking knowingly at him from the other side of the stall where she was attending to some visitors. Fernando contented himself with eyeing the blonde's buttocks as she bent over the PC. Her skirt outlined her assets quite well, and since he could see no betraying panty line he decided she was wearing a thong.

These pleasant thoughts were interrupted by a middle-aged Belgian businessman who wanted information on the tea industry, and Fernando turned away from the blonde.

He had just finished with the Belgian when he saw Dilani hurrying over, obviously agitated.

"Sumedha, check the PCs over here," she said in English. "The ones on that side have all frozen."

Fernando stepped over to the blonde, who was now moving the PC's mouse back and forth over the pad, trying to get the cursor to move. The latter, however, remained frozen, the screen showing the Mackenzie search engine that specialized in searches on Sri Lankan sites.

"What's wrong?" The blonde turned to him, her eyes a fraction softer. "It has crashed."

"Just a small technical problem," he explained, restarting the PC and moving on to the next station. "Dilani," he called over to his associate, "restart all the PCs."

Neither Fernando nor Dilani noted the blonde tug a small Iomega pen drive out of the PC's port and slip its stylish chain over her head. The slim pendant-like drive disappeared into her blouse to nestle in her cleavage, and when Fernando returned she had already disappeared.

He cursed. Frustrated visitors were already leaving the stall, and the PCs would only reload the Windows sky-and-clouds desktop screen before freezing once more. He repeatedly restarted the machines to no avail.

"Call the maintenance fellows," he snapped to Dilani.

They had been given a Frankfurt phone number to call in case they had any software problems during the trade fair. Though Fernando had a working knowledge of computers and online trouble-shooting, he was no expert. The computer set-up had been handled by a Frankfurt company. It was their number that Dilani was now dialling.

In the cellar of a block of flats on Mainzer Landstrasse, close to the Frankfurt central railway station, a man sat wearing a pair of headphones. Next to him, a second man sat at a desk with an Apple iBook open in front of him. The phone number Dilani was punching out appeared on the laptop's screen.

"That's the one," he said in Tamil to the man with the headphones, holding down the shift key and generating a ringing tone. After two rings he released the shift key and hit return.

"Werner Online GmbH, good afternoon," the man with the headset said into his lip mike in German. "Maintenance here. How can we help you?"

A few minutes later, the two men were scrambling into a blue Opel van that was painted with the company name and the Werner Online logo. Swinging onto Friedrich-Ebert-Anlage and driving fast, they were at the Festhalle in under ten minutes. They were stopped at the entrance to the organizer's car park by a pair of police constables.

Recognizing the computer company's logo, the policewoman walked over to the driver's window.

"A network has crashed again," the driver said as he rolled down his window.

"Again?" laughed the policewoman, her face wet with rain. "That's the fourth one today." She looked at the two Asian faces in the van. "I didn't see you here before. Where are the two from the morning?"

"Their shift is over," explained the driver. "We're on 'til midnight." He grimaced.

"Too bad," the cop chatted.

"But the overtime money's good," grinned the driver.

"We'll have to look in the back," she explained.

"OK." The driver got out and walked round to the double doors at the back. "But don't let that big muddy animal in. We've got fragile equipment here."

"Don't worry, he's too busy with the dog."

The bomb-sniffing dog's handler was getting his German shepherd ready, but the policewoman waved him off, still laughing at her own joke.

She glanced perfunctorily into the back, taking in the spare computer monitors in their padding, several towers, boxes of CDs and tools, and jumbles of wire. She waved the van through.

While the driver parked, the other man grabbed a toolbox and entered the Sri Lankan hall. At the Mackenzie Holdings stall, he introduced himself and sat at the server keyboard.

Recognizing a fellow Sri Lankan, Fernando chatted to the technician as he attempted to restart the PC.

"Been working in Germany long?" he asked.

"Four years," the man replied. "Our company usually handles the computer set-up for the Expo. This sort'f stuff always happens. Especially with the Sri Lankan stalls." He laughed. "That's why the boss put me on it. Easier for us Sri Lankans to work together than with these *suddha* buggers, no?"

Fernando nodded, looking around for the blonde and hoping she'd be back.

"Dunno wha'ss wrong," the technician said. "Maybe a virus. You have all your stuff backed up?"

"We've got the entire system on CD," Fernando said.

"OK. Then I'll have to take your server back with me an' have a look at it. We'll give you a replacement for now."

Fernando agreed, and the technician used a mobile phone to call the driver, who wheeled in two Pentium towers on a trolley.

"You reload your stuff onto this one," the technician said, hooking up one of the towers. "I'm leaving the second one as a standby. If the same thing happens again, switch to the second one. Then I won't have to rush out here again. Hopefully by this evening I'll have figured out what's wrong."

The two Tamils waited until Fernando had finished copying the system onto the new server and everything was up and running once more before leaving.

Half an hour later, the twenty kilos of explosives in the spare tower detonated, killing Fernando, Dilani, and nineteen visitors to the Mackenzie Holdings stall. In addition, the explosion demolished the neighbouring stalls, killing and injuring dozens more, mostly Sri Lankans, but also many German visitors.

*

1500 CENTRAL EUROPEAN TIME (1400 GMT): The two young women wore dark jogging suits and windbreakers. White trainers shod their feet and their hair was tucked up into woollen watch caps. They jogged at a moderate pace down Rue Clement Marot, exchanging a few monosyllabic words as they turned onto the broad length of Avenue Montaigne. Mid-afternoon was not a normal time for joggers, but the women were young enough to be university students, dodging class and going for a quick run. The avenue was fairly clear of traffic and stretched ahead of the joggers for half a kilometre until it met Paris' famous Champs-Elysees. The women kept up their pace for a few more metres then, as if on cue, stopped for a break. They used the pavement railing for support as they stretched limbs, their slowing breath clouding the chilly air with condensation.

A few minutes later, a gate fifty metres ahead of the women, set in the wall of a garden bordering the avenue, opened and a big black Mercedes Benz limousine roared out. It was followed by a smaller escort car, and together paused for a break in the traffic before turning towards the joggers. The garden was large and separated the avenue from a grand old mansion, one of the many dotting the embassy area of Paris.

He was right on time, going home early as he did every Tuesday to play squash with his wife. One of the joggers took a mobile phone from the 'bum bag' she carried strapped to her waist, noting as the cars approached, that the escort vehicle was a sign of increased security since the announcement by Ottawa.

"He's on the move," she said into the phone. The two women ignored the cars and resumed their jog.

As the two cars passed the women and approached the intersection they had just left, the lights turned green, and the big Mercedes increased speed as it swept through, heading in the direction of the river and the Place de l'Alma. A small Vespa scooter moving down Rue Clement Marot, however, ran through the red light, leaving a blare of horns and shouted curses behind as it turned onto Avenue Montaigne and followed the limousine and its escort.

A *gendarme* taking a cigarette break close to the intersection tossed aside his smoke and gunned the engine of his patrol bike. He switched on his siren and went screaming after the Vespa.

The scooter rider was dressed from head to toe in black, his helmet and leather riding suit trimmed in red. Thick gloves, knee and shoulder pads, all contributed to give him an insect-like appearance. Hearing the police siren behind him, he glanced in his rear-view mirror, but rather than slowing or moving aside, he increased speed. Ahead he could see that the two cars had been caught by a red light at the Rue du Boccador intersection. Both cars had their right indicator lights on, preparing to turn in the direction of the ambassador's residence.

The rider swung his Vespa up onto the pavement to get around the escort car, sending pedestrians squealing and cursing out of the way as he skirted around a lamppost and turned towards the limousine. Increasing speed even more, he aimed for the rear passenger door. Even as he flicked on the scooter's headlight, arming the bomb, he saw the doors of the escort car burst open. His teeth gritted tight under the black visor of his helmet, he jammed his thumb onto the horn an instant before he slammed into the big Citroen, detonating the explosives in the carrier box over the Vespa's front wheel.

The explosion tore his body in two at the waist and tossed the blackened smoking halves up and over four lanes of traffic to smash into the pavement on the far side of Avenue Montaigne. The blast literally sheared the top of the Mercedes off like the lid of a can, killing the Canadian ambassador to Paris, his driver and bodyguard in one instantaneous flash. Though the bomb wasn't as powerful as the one in Toronto, or the one in London, and killed only half a dozen or so nearby pedestrians, the explosion was still strong enough to also kill the three Special Protection Group policemen who had scrambled out of the escort car, and blow in its windshield, permanently blinding the French driver.

* * *

FEBRUARY 20th: The morning after the spate of attacks in Canada and Europe, an emergency meeting of the Sri Lankan Joint Intelligence Committee was called in Colombo. Unlike the one in October, the previous year, this was called by the new State Minister for Defence himself.

In December the previous year, Sri Lanka's conservative United National Party had won the general elections by a narrow margin. While theoretically, this should not have affected the post of the country's socialist Executive President, long-awaited — and fought-over — constitutional changes were finally pushed through by the new government. The Executive Presidency was abolished more than two decades after it was instituted, the president being largely relegated to ceremonial duties as the titular head of state.

The leader of the UNP — now the Prime Minister — took over as the leader of the nation.

Brigadier Arjuna Devendra had made a concession to the situation and called for a Land Rover escort, drawing the line, however, at just one escort vehicle. The attacks of the previous day could be the forerunner of a national and international crisis, and today's meeting was crucial, and not one that could be delayed by tardiness. The long-wheel base Land Rover Defender rocketed through the early morning school traffic, maroon-bereted commandos, brandishing submachine-guns, leaned out of the back, white-gloved hands waving traffic to the side of the road.

The head of Military Intelligence had been pulled out of bed at 6am by the call from the Ministry of Defence. As he dressed he had watched the night's events on television, flipping from one channel to another to get the views of *CNN*, *BBC*, and *Sky*, the three international news channels available in Sri Lanka.

All three channels stated that a new, unheard of terrorist group, calling itself the Eelam Republican Army, had claimed responsibility for the attacks. The *BBC* was also proclaiming that its London offices had received an email from the LTTE, denying any involvement in the attacks.

As his convoy raced along Galle Road and past the Taj Samudra, Devendra could see a dark green Bell 412 helicopter coming in to land at the Army sports grounds. Punctuality seemed to be one of the trademarks of the new administration. A Hind gunship thundered low across the road, and as the convoy approached the Joint Operations Command compound, Devendra noted the men of the Prime Ministerial Security Division, recognizable in their black trousers and white Mao shirts, lining the pavement.

Even the base's main gate had been taken over by the PMSD, and all traffic had been halted on Galle Road. Devendra knew that even the Slave Island end of the base would be now deserted of all civilians.

Devendra flashed his ID at the PMSD men manning the gate and was allowed to enter. He would have to walk the last hundred metres or so into the JOC, as the PMSD were not letting any vehicles into the area.

As he crossed to the JOC building, he could see the prime ministerial entourage exiting the sports grounds, and he quickened his pace. The Prime Minister himself was not visible, shielded by a cluster of bodyguards.

Devendra was stopped at the conference room door by more PMSD men, his ID checked more carefully this time, and finally he was frisked before being allowed to proceed. Not even the head of the JOC would have been spared this indignity when it came to the security of the Prime Minister. Entering the room, he noted that he was the last member of the Joint Intelligence Committee to arrive. The babble of voices dropped as everybody turned to the door, expecting the Prime Minister. When they saw it was Devendra, the conversations started off once more.

Everybody was present, except for DIG Michael Salgado, head of the Directorate of Internal Intelligence, who was in Trincomalee, the capital of the Eastern Province, and couldn't be contacted in time for the meeting. Devendra also noticed that the Foreign Minister, Harry Rajendran, was also there. Evidently some high-level decisions would be taken at this meeting.

Devendra had barely squeezed into his seat when the double doors were opened once more by two PMSD men. Everyone rose quickly as the hulking dark-suited figure of Deputy Inspector General Dayananda Weerasuriya entered. The head of the PMSD, one of the most feared and powerful men in the country, glared around the room. He then stepped aside to admit the Prime Minister. The State Minister for Defence, John Jayavickrama followed him in.

Dressed in the long white flowing shirt that was part of the national dress and fell to mid-thigh, the Prime Minister drew the line at the white sarong favoured by most Sri Lankan politicians, opting instead for grey trousers. The Prime Minister smiled briefly at everybody and sat at the end of the long table opposite the chairman, General Sujeeva Fernando. He was flanked by John Jayavickrama and Harry Rajendran. With a final glower at the gathering, in which he hadn't been included, DIG Weerasuriya left, shutting the doors.

"Good morning, gentlemen," the Prime Minister said in his high-pitched voice, "even though it isn't. I hope it'll get better." His famously cheerful boyish face and Cupid lips grim and tense.

He paused as a female corporal from the General Service Corps brought in pots of tea and coffee.

"All of you must have heard of what happened yesterday," he said after the corporal had left. "There have been five separate attacks on Canadian and Sri Lankan interests in Canada and Europe, all carried out more or less simultaneously."

"Five?" General Fernando spoke up with a frown. "I thought there were only four."

"At twenty-one hundred Dutch time, a ship was hit by a suicide boat at Rotterdam." The speaker was the DFI boss, DIG Jaliya de Silva.

"Canadian ship?" asked Major General Sarath Perera, the Director of Special Forces.

"Yah. But the cargo was a load of diesel power generators being brought to Colombo. They were to be part of the new thermal energy plant at Sapugaskanda."

Everyone at the table winced unconsciously. The new power plant, established with American aid, would have taken a heavy load off Sri Lanka's strained hydro-electric plants.

"How come this attack was later than the others?" General Fernando wanted to know.

"Jaliya," the Prime Minister cut in, "your DFI people have been in contact with the Canadian and European police, plus Interpol, I believe? Why don't you give us a quick outline of the situation and the investigations."

"Yes, Your Excellency," de Silva said, straightening up. He cleared his throat and shuffled some notes before starting off.

"In Toronto, the RCMP believes that two suicide bombers blew themselves up at the Yonge and Bloor metro station. Eye witnesses claim to have heard only a single explosion, but preliminary investigations indicate that there were two explosions. The bomb site is still being searched by forensics, and they have no idea of the ID of the bombers.

"The Nova Scotia Bank bomb in London was *not* a suicide attack. It was a car bomb, or rather, a van bomb. British Special Branch is looking for the van driver, but the van itself was stolen.

"In Frankfurt, the police seem to have a decent idea of how the bomb got into the Expo. There was apparently tight security, and they're fairly sure it wasn't a suicide bomber. They do know for sure that the explosion was in the Mackenzie Holdings stall. Police at the gate say that a van from a Frankfurt computer company was close to the Sri Lankan hall half an hour before the blast. They had searched the van before it entered the premises but hadn't found anything. They did take down the van number as part of normal procedure. This van, too, was stolen, and the company that it supposedly belonged to denies sending anyone to the trade fair at that particular time. The police at the gate claim that the two men in the van were Asian, but spoke fluent German. They're putting out the descriptions today for a nationwide hunt.

"The assassination of the Canadian ambassador in Paris *was* definitely a suicide bomber. Eye witness accounts make it seem very similar to the killing of Admiral Clancy Fernando in 1995. GIGN has ID'd the bomber from what was left of him. Sri Lankan student on a scholarship at the Sorbonne. They sent us the info and we've already checked here, but he had no link to the Tigers or any other Tamil group. Born in Jaffna, but grew up in Colombo, coming here in the mid '80s. The parents live here in Colombo, and we'll be taking them in for questioning today.

"We have very little info from the Rotterdam blast. That's a hell of a mess. Soon after it was hit by the suicide boat the Canadian ship collided with a Dutch oil tanker before it sank. The

Dutch authorities have a major oil spill to clean up before they can even start looking for pieces of the boat or whoever was in it. Plus the ship went down in one of the main shipping lanes out of Rotterdam, just south of Merwehaven, so it's blocking other ships. The only reason this attack was several hours after the others was possibly because the Canadian ship was a few hours late in leaving. The terrorists must've been watching."

Jaliya de Silva paused to take a sip of tea before continuing. "Within minutes of the Toronto bombing, somebody hacked into the official Canadian government website and left a message on the home page. This apparently new group, the Eelam Liberation Army, is claiming they were responsible, and that more attacks will follow. They also call the Sri Lankan government a terror organization and accuse the Canadian government of helping us murder Tamils. They also call the LTTE traitors to the cause, and say that the torch has now passed to new hands. While the Canadians immediately issued a nationwide alert, the word didn't get across to Europe in time. Even if it had, it would probably have been too late. The London bomb went off just over an hour after the Toronto one, and had probably been placed earlier in the day.

"As soon as the news got on TV, the *BBC* in London got an email from the Tigers claiming innocence, and vowing no involvement in the attacks."

"Why London?" John Jayavickrama asked.

"London was their international headquarters before Britain outlawed them," Devendra explained. "They just went underground, and still operate from there."

"Ottawa is standing on their heads, absolutely worried, they've never faced anything like this before," commented Harry Rajendran, the Foreign Minister.

Grey-headed and soft-spoken, a Tamil himself, the minister was renowned for his poise and eloquence, having done a lot to re-establish a more civilized image of Sri Lanka in the west.

Formerly a member of the socialist Sri Lanka Freedom Party, a
leading component in the governing People's Alliance prior to
December 2001, he had held the portfolio of Foreign Minister
until he resigned and crossed over to the UNP just prior to the
elections. He had been reinstated by the Prime Minister to his
former post.

"Heavy protests are expected today in Scarborough and
Toronto," he continued. "A lot of those killed in the Toronto
bombing were Tamils. This is obviously in response to the
Anti-Terrorism Bill, even though this new group has been subtle
enough to leave it unmentioned. It will be disastrous if Ottawa
decides to put the bill on hold because of this."

"Surely they won't do that?" the Prime Minister said, looking
worried. "It'll look like they're backing down under the threat of
violence. It'll destroy their standing both as a NATO country and
a US ally."

"Right now, they're in a major panic, we don't know what
they'll do," Rajendran replied. "One must remember that this bill
was pushed through their parliament on a very narrow margin. A
lot of people didn't agree with it. And the British Foreign Secretary
has just informed me that a *BBC* reporter managed to interview
an LTTE spokesman soon after the email at an 'undisclosed
location'. The *BBC* will be running the story today, and the gist of
it is that the LTTE claim these attacks are only a result of Canadian
foreign policy. More or less the same line as apologists for the
September eleventh attacks in the US. They say that they find it
difficult to control these rogue elements, especially now that their
infrastructure is being unjustly attacked. The spokesman suggested
that if Ottawa revokes the bill, calls for a ceasefire in Sri Lanka,
and actively takes a part as a third-party mediator, the LTTE
might be able to bring this new group — the ERA — under control,
and even help national police forces to hunt down the perpetrators."

"So the LTTE seem to be asking for the same things as the
ERA, then?" General Sujeeva Fernando asked.

"Seems so."

"What a coincidence," said the Prime Minister. "Do we know if this ERA is just another wing of the Tigers, like the Ellalan Force?"

The Ellalan Force had been a group responsible for a series of bombings in Colombo's five-star hotels in the mid-1990s, an attempt at the time to stall the tourist industry. The group had later turned out to be controlled by the LTTE.

"Well, their *modus operandi* seems to be the same as the Tigers," commented Major General Perera. "No warning of the bombs, several of the attacks suicide ones — something none of the other Tamil terrorist groups have done before — and as usual, the Tigers deny everything. They haven't claimed responsibility for an attack in the last eight or nine years."

"And with the way the situation is going in the north, it's a perfect moment for the terras to try and pull something like this," added Fernando.

"Harry," the Prime Minister turned to his Foreign Minister, "I want you to leave for Ottawa as soon as possible. Tomorrow, or even today if you can. I already phoned the Canadian Premier and gave him my condolences and expressed our absolute commitment to stand together with Canada on this, but you must speak to him in person. You have to convince him that the best thing in both our national interests is to stick to our guns and not give in to terror threats."

The minister nodded, already planning his agenda.

"Jaliya," John Jayavickrama said to the DFI chief, "what links can we establish between the ERA and the LTTE? You have boys in Europe and Canada, no? Any intelligence available?"

"Well, sir," de Silva said, a bit uncomfortable, "my heads of station have been maintaining surveillance on known LTTEers, but there has been no unusual activity."

Arjuna Devendra smiled to himself, knowing full well that the DFI surveillance in Europe was almost nonexistent. They were better at it in Canada and the United States, where they could operate alongside federal agencies.

"Arjuna?" the Defence Minister queried, his cool eyes scanning the brigadier. "Any info from your end?"

A former infantry colonel before going into politics, the silver-haired Jayavickrama wore his trademark poker face. It was rumoured that the only time he had been known to smile was early in his Army career, when he had learned of his mother-in-law's death.

This was the opportunity Devendra had been waiting for, and he spoke up immediately. "My chaps have noticed quite a lot of activity with LTTE cover groups in Europe." Out of the corner of his eye he saw the DFI chief's knuckles drum lightly against the edge of the table, a sign of his growing irritation. "Particularly in Germany, Holland, France, and the UK. But also in several Scandinavian countries and in the Mediterranean. The latter two areas may be the targets for the next wave of attacks."

"But that's assuming there's a connection between the Tigers and this group," the Prime Minister pointed out.

"Yes, Your Excellency," Devendra agreed. "And in Germany we're fairly sure there is a connection. One of our teams tailed a former TEEDOR man, now working for the World Tamil Association, from Cologne to Frankfurt. In Frankfurt he was photographed meeting with a man who fits the police description of one of the occupants of the van at the Expo."

"So let's go to the German police with this," said Jayavickrama. "We can start the same process that was done in Canada: get the Germans to — at long last — start squeezing the Tigers!"

"Just a minute now!" interrupted Rajendran forcefully, and all eyes turned to him. "Revealing to the German authorities that we have been carrying out illegal surveillance operations in their country isn't going to go down well at all. Not with just some photos as supposed proof. We must have more convincing evidence if we're to take this gamble."

"Harry's right," decided the Prime Minister. "We need to gather more evidence or try and stall any future Tiger attacks. In the meantime we need to go full force on the diplomatic and law enforcement fronts. I will be asking our ambassadors in these countries to start speaking to the respective foreign ministries, and Harry will have to do a quick tour of Europe to shore up support on his way back from Canada. In the meantime, Jaliya, I need your heads of station to start extending help to the police forces in these countries in a much more concerted manner. Even if we can't reveal what proof we have yet, we can point them in the right direction."

"Yes, Your Excellency."

He turned back to the Foreign Minister. "Harry, let's get cracking on outlining a press statement as well as a plan on Canadian and European policy." The Prime Minister rose to his feet, and scanned the faces of the others as they sprang up. "You'll have to excuse Harry and myself while you iron out things. Gentlemen."

He turned to leave, and Perera opened the doors for him.

The room relaxed after the Prime Minister had left, and cigarettes were lit and backs stretched.

"Brigadier," Jayavickrama said to Devendra after a few minutes of quiet, "I think you need to tell us just how we can stall the terras."

CHAPTER 11

FEBRUARY 24th 2002: It had snowed the night before, but the humidity of the Rhine ensured that this Monday morning was merely grey and wet. The wind blowing across the open expanse of Cologne's Roncalliplatz made Sandra Koch hunch deeper in her trench coat. She stared in wonder at the hardcore skateboarders who braved the weather to clatter down the steps from the Domplatte and bounce their boards off the handrails.

Walking next to her, Dayan Premasiri ignored the cold, and concentrated on scanning the faces in the square. His sniper training allowed him to get into what he called his 'bubble', focusing all his energies only on the job at hand. It was a skill that had enabled him to lie long hours in the jungle, waiting for his quarry, ignoring the insects that would crawl and sting his body. It had kept his mind off the gnawing hunger in his stomach, and the stink of filth and urine on his clothes. Instinctively now, he glanced up at the huge Dom standing in the centre of the square, scanning the cathedral's heights for the glint of a scope. Then, however, common sense made him ignore it further, and concentrate once more on the faces, looking for Asians, and when he found them, watching for any expression on their faces that would betray more than idle curiosity.

As they walked past the black Gothic cathedral, Dayan remembered watching the *BBC* television series *The World at War* when he was a boy. He could still remember the jerky black-and-white footage of the British thousand-bomber raids during World War II. The city of Cologne, a sea of flame, with only the twin black spires of the Dom standing like a doomed victory sign.

When Dayan had first arrived in Cologne in December, he had been amazed by the city's ancient architecture, its churches, pubs, and museums. He had expected that Allied bombing would have gutted the city the way it had done the Japanese cities, that all he would see would be modern post-war architecture. But seeing the old structures had cheered him up considerably, in spite of the winter chill. It had enforced on his mind the thought that there was a future beyond war. That there might still be hope for his own homeland.

Beyond the cathedral, within sight of the entrance to the city's subway system and main railway station, Dayan and Sandra stopped, leaning against a low wall and lighting up. They were five minutes early, but it was always better to check out the scenario. They stood close, shoulders touching, looking the part of a tourist couple. Dayan took several pictures of the Dom with a cheap camera, then stepped away for a moment and snapped a shot of Sandra as she smiled for him.

As he looked at her face through the viewfinder, Dayan knew that in the two months they had been working together, they had got dangerously close. The surveillance jobs meant sitting together for hours in cars, or apartments, or walking through the streets, holding hands to give the impression of intimacy, and this had in itself begun to breed something of the image they were trying to portray. The patrol and Sandra had been split into two teams of two for surveillance, with one person standing off as a command post. The CP job, the more boring — if comfortable — of the two, had been rotated between them, but Dayan and Sandra had increasingly found themselves paired off on jobs.

He walked back to her and she pressed up close to him, using his body as a shield from the wind. The years in Europe had done nothing to immunize her to the winter chill.

Dayan had never been unfaithful to his wife, at least not on an emotional level. Sure, there had been the times when the need for sexual relief had made him pick up a woman somewhere, but that was all part of being a soldier. Sunethra would understand, he often told himself. But he had never had what he would term an affair, a protracted relationship.

Watching Sandra's lips tighten round the filter of the Camel as she dragged on the smoke, Dayan knew that he could fuck her if he pushed it. But he also knew he wouldn't. Not while the job was on. Maybe if there was a bit of free time before they went back—

His thoughts were interrupted by a nudge from Sandra.

"Here he comes."

Dayan spotted the Sri Lankan stepping off the escalator at the entrance to the *U-Bahn*, the city's subway. He was at least six feet tall, and well built, like a rugby lock, his parka and watch cap making him look even bigger. They walked across to him, Sandra waving to get his attention.

The newcomer kissed Sandra on both cheeks like an old friend, and then was introduced to Dayan. In spite of appearances, this was hardly a social meeting. In the past couple of months, Dayan knew that Sandra had been in regular contact with her control, but this was the first time he himself was meeting Major Sunil Jayawardene. A member of the Bonn military attaché's staff, he was second in authority only to the attaché himself. The reason for Sunil Jayawardene's relatively junior rank was the fact that Sri Lanka only maintained a consulate in that city, with the attaché himself being only a lieutenant colonel. The embassy itself had been moved to Berlin, soon after that city became Germany's capital once more in 1991, and it warranted at least a colonel or brigadier as the military attaché. The major handled all dealings with Sandra, the attaché being considered too high profile a member of the consulate staff to avoid surveillance.

Sunil Jayawardene had insisted that the SF team commander be present at this meeting, so it meant something was on. Maybe this would mean an upgrade in their tasking, Dayan thought as the trio strolled back towards the Hohe Strasse that ran south through Cologne's main shopping area. Maybe this was the order to start hitting back.

The adrenalin rush at the idea of hitting the terras in Europe had slowly waned with the boredom of constant surveillance in the past months. If he had been honest with himself, Dayan would have admitted that he had been relieved at the lack of action. Committing what would be seen as an act of terrorism on European soil, was not something to be taken lightly. He didn't really fancy seeing what the inside of a German prison cell would be like.

The Int major handed over a stack of envelopes to Dayan. They were all addressed to members of his patrol, who were officially supposed to be stationed at Maduru Oya, the Special Forces HQ, on a training course. The letters would be from loved ones who had no idea that their sons, husbands, boyfriends, or brothers were in Europe. The letters would have been passed on to the consulate in Bonn, and the replies would be sent in reverse via the consulate to SFHQ, where they would be censor-checked before being reposted with Sri Lankan stamps and postdates. Scanning the envelopes quickly, Dayan noted that two were for him, both from Sunethra.

"So, anything new for me?" Jayawardene asked in Sinhalese as they walked along the busy street, pausing to look at the shop front displays.

"No special activity as such," Sandra replied in the same language. "Since the Frankfurt attack, we are fairly sure that Kumaradeven is the liaison with this new group. We have dropped the other targets and are concentrating on him. But there has not been much to see. He just goes to work every day, goes to the gym, drinks in his local pub with some of his colleagues, the usual thing. Why? Do we expect another wave of attacks?"

"There's bound to be," Jayawardene said. "As you might have heard in the news, Ottawa has made up its mind to stand firm, and has been making defiant statements against the terras. They're also going to be stepping up operations against both the ERA and the LTTE in Canada. So these bastards are sure to hit again."

"Any hints as to what and where?" Dayan asked.

Jayawardene gave a half smile. He was brilliantly handsome, with almost Negro-dark skin and angular features. Stardom, however was denied him by his tobacco-stained teeth.

"That's what *I* need from *you*," he said. "But we think that the next round may not be bombings. Could be anything. From a sniper hit to an online assault on the stock markets."

They paused in front of a hunting and camping store, and Dayan eyed absently the expensive Italian and English shotguns in the window.

"Colombo wants you to increase surveillance on your targets. Try and get phone taps in. If we can get any hint of a fresh attack, you will have to try and get proper proof of the plans. Or stop it. Colombo doesn't want to go just yet to the German cops, because it will mean blowing your cover. And then the shit could hit the fan. If there is no sign of another attack whatsoever, or if there is an attack that you do not detect in time, you are to hit your target anyway. Even if we cannot prove this ERA-LTTE connection, we need to show the terras that we will not take this sort of nonsense."

The major switched abruptly to English, a common if somewhat confusing trait with most bilingual Sri Lankans. "We don' want anything spectacular, and I don' need to tell you that civilian casualties need to be avoided, no? But make sure the bugger goes down an' that it's obviously not an accident."

"OK," Sandra said. "We'll start with the phone taps. We can bug his office, but his home might be a problem. His wife doesn't work and she's always in the house. Also, he has a cell phone that we can't do anything about."

"Sort it out."

"We'll need some special kit," Dayan said.

"No probs. Here's a joint in Cologne that'll give you what you need." He scribbled on a piece of paper. "Draw whatever cash you need from the bank."

"Also," continued Dayan, "if we need stuff heavier than our pistols, how fast can you get it to us?"

"I already have a few SMGs and AKs stockpiled, but if you need anything special or heavier, give me a couple of days notice an' we'll fly it out."

The night after the meeting with Jayawardene, Bandara broke into the World Tamil Association office on the first floor of a building on Niehler Strasse, in the northern Cologne area of Nippes. He bypassed the cheap burglar alarm system while Dayan and Kamal sat in the car and kept watch. Once inside, he bugged all the phone receivers, and while he was there, made a quick search of the office. He didn't have enough time to make a detailed search, and the only unusual thing he came across were photocopies of several weapons catalogues. The pages all dealt with various shoulder-fired light anti-armour rocket launchers. Bandara had the sense to leave everything as it was and got the hell out of there.

For the next week, the SF men and Sandra — who had by now quit her travel agency job — stepped up surveillance on Douglas Kumaradeven, the target. They planned, discussed, and rejected various options for a hit. They monitored and taped his phone conversations from the WTA office, but turned up nothing important or significant. They were sure he wasn't stupid enough to use his official phone for contact with the Eelam Republican Army, but with no possibility of bugging his home phone or mobile phone, it was all they could do.

Then on the morning of March 4th, which was a Monday, with Dayan and Sandra tailing Kumaradeven from his Bickendorf flat, he did something unusual. They pounced on it as a possible prelude to something new, like his trip to Frankfurt the previous month, days before the Expo bombing. Instead of heading northeast along Innere Kanalstrasse towards Nippes, as he did each morning, Kumaradeven drove straight onto Hohenzollernring and turned south.

The team had been switching cars every couple of days, using rented ones to tail the Tamil and avoid raising his suspicions. On that particular day, Sandra held the blue Opel Vectra back in traffic, far enough to remain inconspicuous, but close enough not to get stuck at an intersection. The target continued south till he reached Barbarossa Platz, southeast of the city centre, then turned east towards the Rhine. They followed him over the Severins Bridge into east Cologne, where he parked close to the river. Sandra drove briskly past him as he walked north towards a pedestrian access stairway to the bridge. As he disappeared up the steps, Dayan told Sandra to drive under the bridge and along Siegburger Strasse — a street that paralleled the river — for another hundred metres before pulling over.

"Co'mon, le'ss see what the bugger's up to." Dayan got out of the car and beckoned Sandra over onto his side of the vehicle.

He pushed her gently back against the car and pressed his body up against her. Through their jackets he could feel her breasts pushing into his chest. Her eyes widened, but Dayan grinned and pulled out a small pair of binoculars.

"Put your arms round me," he instructed, and as she did, he raised the binos to his eyes, keeping his cheek pressed close to hers. Through the binos he could see Kumaradeven walking along the northern or downstream side of the bridge.

"What's he doing?" Sandra asked, and Dayan could feel her breath tickle his ear.

"Dunno. Just walking." He watched Kumaradeven walk to the centre of the bridge and lean over the rail. "Bugger has a camera with a big bloody zoom on it, and he's taking shots."

Dayan lowered the binos and looked downstream, trying to figure out what the Tiger was snapping. A long pier ran parallel to the far bank, a protective arm that seemed to enclose some sort of marina. A similar, but narrower one ran along the near bank as well, and the two were part of the Severins Bridge's supports. There were several buildings on the far pier, including some sort of low steel and glass structure at the very end that looked like an oversized and elaborate greenhouse.

"What the hell is that?" Dayan pointed out the building to Sandra.

She squirmed around to look over the Vectra's roof. Dayan was conscious of her curved buttocks against his crotch, and stepped back a fraction, feeling the beginnings of an erection.

"That's the Chocolate Museum," she supplied.

"They have museums for *chocolate* in this country?" he asked incredulously.

She laughed, and he scanned further downstream, looking for anything else that could be the subject of Kumaradeven's camera. All he could see was another bridge, the Deutzer Brücke, in the distance. Sandra had left the Vectra's engine running for a quick getaway, and through the half open window he could hear a song on the radio. *Which bone in her body should I break first. . .* Lambretta with *Bimbo*.

By now, Kumaradeven was on his way back, and they ducked into the car, grateful for its cocooning warmth. March had brought slightly warmer weather with the advent of spring, but it still wasn't more than a few degrees above zero.

> *Now she's sleeping in my bed*
> *God, I wish that she was dead. . .*

The Tamil drove back across the Rhine, and Dayan and Sandra let him get ahead and out of sight, figuring he'd be heading for the WTA office. Dayan warned Sumith and Kamal, who were already in Nippes, to keep an eye open for him. Ten minutes later, they confirmed his arrival.

* * *

MARCH 13th: The ice on Ottawa's Rideau Canal had thinned with the promise of approaching spring, and the World's Longest Skating Rink was empty of skaters. Condensation puffed over Donald Fenster's shoulder in the early evening chill. The marginally warmer weather had brought out a few other hardcore joggers like him, but largely the footpaths on both sides of the canal seemed to be more frequented by casual pedestrians or people walking their dogs.

Inspector Ian McEdwards was matching Fenster stride for stride, but holding station ten metres behind as they passed the University of Ottawa on their left. Five hundred metres beyond the university, the canal doglegged sharply away to the southwest, and Fenster slowed to a fast walk, as he always did, before stopping for his customary stretch break. McEdwards caught up and started to stretch his thigh muscles.

The SPG officer was extremely fit, hard muscles packed onto his frame, and with lungs that could go on forever. Fenster's usual kilometre or two hardly made McEdwards break a sweat.

Fenster was dressed in a red track outfit and white trainers, but McEdwards wore an old gangsta hoody over even older Army fatigue trousers, and tattered grey trainers. A bum bag fitted snugly against his belly.

For a few more minutes, as he flexed his ankles and calves, the minister held his silence before finally speaking.

"Things are looking good, Ian."

"What things, sir?"

The policeman had found that the minister frequently used his stretching session as an opportunity to sound him out. It seemed as if Fenster was looking for an opinion beyond the cloistered views of Parliament Hill.

"This new ERA group hasn't responded to our announcements and raids for three weeks now," replied Fenster.

Following the wave of bombings three weeks previously, and the subsequent visit of Sri Lanka's foreign minister, Ottawa had announced that it would not be intimidated or terrorized. The announcement had been followed by the Supreme Court of Canada giving, as a preliminary to the Anti-Terrorism Bill passing into law, the nod to increased police surveillance and raids on suspected Tamil militant links in Scarborough and Toronto. It hadn't gone down well with the LTTE, or naturally, with the incumbent

MP for Scarborough. Both had made their protests vociferous, and the Tamil protest groups had renewed their marches, occasionally bringing downtown Toronto to a standstill as they clashed with riot police. However, the anticipated second wave of strikes by the ERA hadn't happened in spite of the Canadian Security Intelligence Service's predictions and the Forces' demands to be more involved in the anti-terror effort. Sri Lankan DFI agents had been working closely with the CSIS, the CCIS, the RCMP, and the Ontario provincial police, and Sri Lanka's Foreign Minister HarryRajendran had hinted that his country's intelligence operatives in Europe were doing their best to crack this new terrorist organization.

The wave of attacks, especially the Toronto metro bombing, had shocked Canada deeply. Not even the September 11th attacks on New York and Washington DC had brought terrorism so close to home. There had been serious debates in the Commons as to whether Ottawa should really take sides in Sri Lanka's ethnic war. There had been vocal recommendations that Canada should act the role of a neutral mediator, much as Norway had attempted to do in the past, but use its influence in the United States to force both warring parties to the negotiation table.

Finally, it had been the weight of the United States that had swung the balance, hinting that the current situation in Sri Lanka made a ceasefire just what the LTTE needed. A time to regroup, rearm, and build up their forces. A visit by the Canadian Prime Minister to the White House had reinforced Washington's request, and stronger opinions by politicians, such as Fenster himself, had made sure Ottawa stood her ground.

Security coverage of Canadian VIPs and Canadian interests, both foreign and domestic, had been substantially increased. Ottawa was confident that the second wave of expected attacks could be prevented.

"It doesn't look like there's going to be a second wave of attacks, does it?" Fenster continued. "The ERA probably realized that they were only reinforcing our resolve."

"Think Ottawa can stand another wave of successful attacks, sir?" McEdwards asked with a grin.

"I'd like to think we can defend ourselves from the next wave. Besides, if the attacks were coming, I'd think it would have happened in the week following our 'screw-you' announcement. The ERA would need to be seen as responding to Ottawa's decision."

"Maybe they're just waiting for us to relax, sir," suggested McEdwards.

Throughout the kilometre-long run and while they were chatting, McEdwards' eyes had never ceased their scanning of the surroundings. He had managed to get the minister to change his usual jogging schedule, making sure the man never ran the same location too regularly or left the department at the same time. McEdwards tensed now as a car slowed on Colonel By Drive, above them and to their left. He relaxed as the car moved off. A glance over his shoulder confirmed that two fit-looking joggers were doing callisthenics by the side of Queen Elizabeth Driveway, on the far side of the canal. The minister's protection team had been beefed up to six men and two women since the ERA attacks. Donald Fenster was considered a prime target.

"Whatever happens, Ian," Fenster went on, "the Sri Lankan situation needs to be resolved. Both over there and in Toronto simultaneously. I don't think one would happen without the other."

He recalled his words to McEdwards that day on the steps of Parliament Hill. He had wondered aloud what effects the passing of the Anti-Terrorism Bill would bring to Canada. Now, he just hoped he had seen the most drastic of them.

Well, he said to himself, as he started to retrace his path over the kilometre back to the Rideau Centre car park, if you pray for rain you have to expect mud.

It was almost 7pm by the time McEdwards finished his shift and left the minister's official residence on Sussex Drive, heading back south into Byward Market. The good thing about the larger protection team was that it meant shorter shifts. The job entailed an almost nonexistent private life at the best of times, and Martina had been getting particularly antsy about it lately. His fiancée had known what to expect when she had started dating a cop, but his transfer to the SPG hadn't gone down well. McEdwards decided that now was the time to try and make it up to her.

He had met Martina Hiver two years previously, when he was on the Toronto CID murder squad. Born in Montreal, she had been one of the prosecution attorneys on a case McEdwards' squad had brought to court. He had just split up with his girlfriend of three years, mostly because of his drinking, and Martina's soft Quebecois accent never failed to turn him on, even as he sat in the witness box. They had hit it off well, and a year later had been engaged. Martina was a year older than him, and very much into her law career, but had plans to give it up and start a family as soon as he was ready to settle down. She had even moved to Ottawa to be near him. The fact that he spent six days a week babysitting a politician wasn't what appealed to her as good husband material.

Byward Market was winding down for the day as McEdwards turned his Toyota Corolla onto Cumberland Street. A fairly busy area during the day, it calmed down later, except for the nightlife areas between Dalhousie Street and Sussex Drive.

He drove into the underground garage and parked, pausing at his letterbox before taking the elevator up to his flat. Martina would be off work by now, and a shower and a quick call to her could mean an interesting evening. She loved middle-eastern food, and if he was lucky, McEdwards could still get them a table at Shwarma Place.

He leafed through his mail as he rode the lift up to his fifth-floor apartment. The usual bills; and except for a postcard from his brother on holiday in Bali, the only thing that caught his attention was a buff A4-sized envelope. A glance at it showed him that it had been hand-delivered, his name and address written in neat block letters on the front.

McEdwards sniffed the envelope cautiously as he let himself into his flat. The previous year's anthrax attacks in the States had made everyone overcautious. What the hell. Who would want to poison him?

Heading for the phone to call Martina, he tore open the envelope. Two large-format colour photographs fell to the carpet. As he bent to retrieve them, his breath choked in his throat. The pictures weren't of the best quality, somewhat over-exposed, but their contents were clear. As he picked them up, his mind flashed back to that afternoon in Sri Lanka, the previous year.

Looking down now into those frozen and staring eyes, he remembered the day Donald Fenster and their host, Rajan Kumaraswamy, had left for the Temple of the Tooth in Kandy, along with the rest of the SPG team. McEdwards had stayed behind at the Teldeniya mansion to mind Patricia Fenster.

Soon after the others left, Mrs Fenster had descended into the swimming pool where she lolled against its side, eyes hidden by her dark sunglasses. Nevertheless, McEdwards had had the strange but not uncomfortable idea that she was watching him. When she had climbed out of the water to retrieve a cocktail from a nearby table, her wet bikini clung to every crevice of her taut body, the breeze raising her nipples through the thin fabric.

Pushing her sunglasses up her head, she had declared that she was bored, that she would be pleased if Mr McEdwards — could she call him Ian? — would join her for a swim. It had been a warm and humid day, and McEdwards had been already sweating. Against his better judgement, he had changed into swimming trunks and entered the pool, leaving his loaded pistol on the tiled edge, under a shirt and within reach.

For the next hour she had chatted pleasantly to him, more than the sentence or two they had exchanged in the past, and she had taken every opportunity to rub her body up against his. A hand had rested lightly against his chest as she reached over for her drink, a leg had brushed his as she passed by, or her buttocks had pressed fleetingly against his groin as she had turned to swim a length of the pool. Soon he had been struggling in vain to hide a throbbing erection.

They had had lunch by the pool, being served chicken *biriyani* by Rajan Kumaraswamy's politely distant manservant, Patricia Fenster's eyes seeming to burn his skin. After lunch, she had announced she was going to her room for a nap, and with a meaningful glance, had left. He had sat by the pool, sipping a glass of lime juice, willing himself to be disciplined. Mrs Fenster's predatory appetites were well documented, but she had never shown the slightest interest in McEdwards before.

Ten minutes later, when he had convinced himself that it was just his imagination, he heard her call his name.

"Ian!" He had looked up to see her leaning over her balcony, dressed in a bathrobe. "Bring me a bottle of wine, will you? I can't seem to find that servant anywhere."

Knowing that he was being a fool, McEdwards had risen and gone into the house. He had known that if she wanted the servant, the man was where he always had been, in the kitchen.

She had opened the room door for him, still in her bathrobe, and taken the bottle from him. McEdwards still recalled her words as he had stood in the doorway.

"Just the way I like it," she had said, examining the bottle of South African wine. "Cold and white."

She had brandished two glasses and invited him in. Things had moved rapidly from that moment on. She had been naked under the robe, and they were barely into their first glass when she had boldly reached for his towel, tugging it away and stroking his stiffening penis through the thin swimming trunks. They had tumbled across the bed, the wine growing warm as they fucked repeatedly, their cries floating through the open balcony door, their sweat mingling.

McEdwards' heart pounded now as he stared at the photographs. They were both overhead shots of the double bed, taken from what had to have been a secret opening in the ceiling, the blurred arc of the ceiling fan softening their bodies in the afternoon sun that streamed through from the balcony. In the first picture, Patricia lay sprawled across the crumpled sheets, her head thrown back and eyes closed, mouth open in ecstasy. Her arms squeezed her breasts together and her fingers tangled in the hair on McEdwards' head, which was buried between her thighs. Thighs, which lay languidly apart, knees, bent, and as he looked at the image he could still taste the salty musk of her skin on his tongue. In the second photograph, McEdwards himself lay on his back while Patricia rode him, hair falling wildly across her upturned face. Her eyes seemed to stare up at the camera lens, face distorted by her orgasm, but still recognizable as the wife of Canada's Minister of Foreign Affairs and International Trade. Worse still, was the fact that McEdwards own likeness was quite clear, his blonde hair falling across a sweaty forehead. Even the small Superman 'S' he had had tattooed on his left pectoral as a teenager was visible.

There was nothing else in the envelope, and turning the photographs over, he saw that there was writing on one of them. In the same block capitals used to address the envelope it said, *IF YOU WISH THESE PICTURES TO REMAIN PRIVATE, BE AT THE BAR OF THE MANX PUB TONIGHT AT 10PM.* There was nothing more.

McEdwards felt a wave of bile rise in his chest and just made it to the toilet before the vomit spewed out of him.

Donald Fenster shivered as he stepped out of the shower, pulling his thick bathrobe tighter around him. He turned up the heating and combed his hair, examining himself in the mirror and wondering whether the bald patch at the crown of his head had expanded any further. Behind him, the central heating clicked lethargically. He wished these ancient houses were easier to heat. At least it didn't still rely on fireplaces as his last official residence had done, when he had been head of the CSIS.

Patricia was curled up on the sofa with a vodka screwdriver in her hand, watching TV as he crossed to his study. He paused to kiss her quickly, and she turned up her face to him with a tight smile.

"Tough day?" she asked.

"Oh, no worse than usual, honey," Fenster replied, deciding to pour himself a whisky before checking his email. Choosing a Glenlivet single malt, he asked, "What about you?"

"Well, the usual damn troubles at the club, Don." Patricia then unleashed an involved tale of her day's activities as Fenster sipped at his drink. She was on the committees of various high-society Ottawa clubs, and her life seemed to be an endless round of political infighting that occasionally rivalled his own.

He wasn't really listening, except to note that her narration was more rapid and strained than usual. She had never been a very relaxed or laidback person, but over the past week or so she seemed to exude an increased air of tension. He finally turned for his study as Patricia's tale lost momentum, but a question from her stopped him in the doorway.

"Don, are you planning on visiting Sri Lanka anytime soon?"

Fenster turned back to look at her. "No, of course not. Just our official visit to Sydney next Monday. Why?"

"Oh, no reason." She was already concentrating on the TV again. "Just thought another visit there might be nice."

"I hardly think I'll have much time off for a few more months, hon," he said, as he entered his study, but she didn't reply.

By 9:45 that night, McEdwards was on his second double Glenfiddich. The small pub, close to the Ritz, had an arty decor and was popular for its single malt whiskies and its range of microbrewery beer. Soft country music played in the background, and he scanned the room for the blackmailer who was to meet him. And there was no doubt that it was blackmail. It wasn't the sort of thing that could be a joke.

Sitting at the bar, a riot of thoughts crowded McEdwards' head. Who had taken the photographs? It could have only been Rajan Kumaraswamy's servant. He wondered whether the Tamil billionaire knew of his employee's activities. And what did the blackmailer want? McEdwards wondered if the servant himself would arrive to make his demands. Or was he in tow with someone else? And what could McEdwards offer a blackmailer? A RCMP inspector didn't exactly make a fortune. And what if he refused to cooperate? Would the blackmailer make the pictures public? It would mean the end of his career. A cop involved with the wife of the man he was protecting. Of course, it had happened before, and he remembered that on both occasions he had heard of, the bodyguard in question had been severely dealt with, his chances in the force ruined. And McEdwards pictured Donald Fenster's face as he saw the pictures, realized that his wife had been romping in bed with a man he had trusted his life to, a man he had considered, if not a friend, then a confidant. And then there was Martina to consider. If this were to come out. . . Oh, God. McEdwards felt another wave of nausea begin to rise and took a burning swallow of whisky.

His miserable thoughts were interrupted as the bartender leaned across to him.

"Ian McEdwards? Call for you." The man held out a phone receiver to him.

McEdwards grabbed the phone. "Hello?" he blurted.

"Mister McEdwards, I trust you've taken time to examine the interesting photographs we delivered to you today." The voice had a faint American accent. "Do you wish us to make them public?"

"No, of course not." McEdwards cupped his hand over his mouth and the voice piece, trying not to sound as if he was pleading. "What do you want?" He looked up to see if the bartender was listening, but the man had moved off, serving a customer further down the bar.

"I'm so glad you're a reasonable man, Mister McEdwards," the caller said. "We want you off Donald Fenster's bodyguard team with immediate effect."

"What? Why? That's impossible."

McEdwards hadn't been expecting a phone call. He had counted on the blackmailer being there in person, of being able to bargain, argue, threaten even, if it was necessary. Now he was stalling for time, trying to gather his thoughts.

"What and why are not questions to consider, Mister McEdwards." The voice was calm, faintly amused. "And as for impossibilities, I don't want to hear what is impossible. I know just what is possible. And it is highly possible that those photographs will find their way into the Ottawa tabloid press. Still think a transfer is impossible?"

"OK, OK," said McEdwards. This was not a demand he had been expecting. He had expected extortion, a demand of money, favours. Who the fuck was this man? "Let's say it's possible, but it'll take time. Transfers within the RCMP take time."

"We don't have time, Mister McEdwards. Make up an excuse. Say your mother in Edmonton is ill, dying, that you have to go to her." McEdwards sucked in air and the caller chuckled. "You see, we know a lot about you, inspector." There was a pause, then the voice continued, all trace of humour gone. "It needn't be a permanent transfer. Take a few weeks off, when you return to Ottawa you can rejoin Fenster's team. There is a Canadian Airlines flight to Edmonton at thirteen twenty-two hours tomorrow, Thursday the fourteenth, Mister McEdwards, be on it. If you're not, I'm sure you'll find the weekend papers most interesting. Good night, inspector."

"Wait!" McEdwards almost shouted into the phone. "If I do as you say, will you hand over the negatives? What guarantee do I have of that?"

He heard the caller laugh softly. "Think this is the movies, inspector? There are no deals. If you are on that plane tomorrow, you'll never hear from me or see those pictures again. That is my only guarantee. Unless, of course, you want to check the weekend papers."

With a sinking heart McEdwards realized the line was dead. He handed the receiver to the bartender, mind racing. Who were these people? Why did they want him off the team? On Monday, Donald Fenster was leaving for an Asia-Pacific trade summit in Sydney. Patricia was accompanying him. Was there going to be an assassination attempt? But what use was getting him off the team to them? Someone would replace him, someone just as good, or better even.

But the fact began to dawn on McEdwards that this was no ordinary blackmail. This was a matter of national security. He had taken an oath to Queen and country. How could he simply slip away and pretend it had never happened. He was duty bound to report this.

But the thought of Martina's face as she opened the weekend papers, the thought of the damage that would be done to his career, made him pick up his mobile phone to call the boss and ask for emergency compassionate leave.

CHAPTER 12

THURSDAY MARCH 14th: For the first week and a half of the month, Douglas Kumaradeven visited the Severins Bridge at least once a day, sometimes twice, even on the weekend, and always at different times. He invariably took photographs, but did nothing else. Various members of the team had stood at the same spot and tried to figure out what he was shooting, but no apparent target was visible.

"Maybe they're going to hit that other bridge — the Deutzer Brücke — with rockets," suggested Bandara, when they were all sitting around the team's flat in Bayenthal.

"Don' be stupid," said Kamal. "It's too far away. An' what good will it do to hit a bridge with an RPG?"

"If they wanted to drop the bridge they'd use charges on the bridge itself," pointed out Sumith.

"And why should they anyway?" pondered Sandra aloud. "So far they've only hit Canadian or Sri Lankan targets, no?"

"Maybe we should bump the bugger off now," commented Kamal. "That way, whatever the terras are planning, it won' work."

"Yah, but maybe it's already on the cards," argued Dayan, "and this is only a CTR. We could hit him now, and the attack might still go in. I say we wait. He's bound to make contact with the ERA."

"*If* this is a real attack," said Sumith. "Maybe he's just into photography."

"Well, where has he been all these bloody months, then?" asked Bandara. "He never took snaps before. Was he hibernating or what?"

"*Hibernating?*" grinned Kamal. "Didn' knowyou knew such big words, Banda."

"I know more," returned Bandara. "Sodomy, and fornication. And you can go an' do both to yourself."

Everyone laughed, and Dayan raised a hand. "OK, OK. So the decision is whether we hit him now or wait."

"I say we should just do it now an' get it over with," stated Kamal. "If the attack goes in anyway, we'll just look for more Tigers to kill."

Sumith agreed with him. "We don't have enough coverage of the bugger to risk waiting. He might give the OK to the assault team an' we won't even know."

Both Bandara and Sandra thought they should wait, while trying to step up surveillance. The final decision would now be Dayan's.

"So we wait, then," he said. "But we need to tap his home phone. We can't do without that. It'll be worth the risk."

That night, Dayan and Kamal broke into Kumaradeven's apartment block, and entered the cellar. Working as fast as they could, the two men tapped into the Tamil's phone line. A call by Sandra on her mobile phone to Kumaradeven's number confirmed that they'd got it right. As soon as Mrs Kumaradeven's sleepy voice was heard, Sandra hung up.

Lacking all the equipment needed for a professional wiretap job, it meant that the Sri Lankans had to station a closed van with their listening post in it a couple of streets away, and hope that no one phoned the cops to report a suspicious vehicle. They would have to take turns manning the wiretap.

Two evenings later, they got lucky.

·:·

SATURDAY MARCH 16th: At 10:20pm, Sumith was sitting in the back of the van, headphones on, reading a magazine by torchlight when the call came in.

Sumith switched on the tape as Mrs Kumaradeven answered the phone. A man's voice, speaking in German, asked for Douglas. As the Tiger came on the line, the caller switched to Tamil, talking too quickly for Sumith to get it all, but he did pick up the word Trier.

Listening to the tape an hour later, the others deciphered the rapid-fire Tamil into an understandable conversation in which the caller was arranging to meet Kumaradeven the next afternoon in the city of Trier, close to the Luxembourg border.

"That's it, then," said Dayan. "We tail him to Trier tomorrow. We'll use two cars. Sumith and Banda together, me an' Sandra. Kamal, you're staying in Cologne to keep an eye on the WTA office."

Driving through unfamiliar territory always needed a team of two per car. One to drive and watch the target, the other to map read.

         ✳

SUNDAY MARCH 17th: "Blue Team, there's a petrol shed and rest area two klicks ahead," Dayan said into his throat mike. "Target is moving into the right-hand lane. He might be pulling in there, so get set to stick with him."

"Roger, Red."

Dayan and Sandra were driving a dark green Golf GTI, and had just passed Blankenheim, more or less halfway from Cologne to Trier. They were on the A1 *autobahn*, and Sandra estimated another hour and a quarter till they reached the old Roman city. In his rear-view mirror, Dayan could see the black Ford Focus that Kumaradeven owned, two hundred metres behind. He was definitely slowing, anticipating the turnoff.

Dayan knew, but couldn't see, that the blue VW Passat with Sumith and Bandara would be a kilometre behind the target. The idea was that the trailing car stayed out of sight, but was kept informed of the target's moves by the lead car. If Kumaradeven was suspicious, he'd be watching his tail, not the vehicles ahead. If the lead car couldn't stay with the target, due to the target turning off the road or stopping, they'd circle around and get back on his tail while the trail car moved up and maintained contact. Once the former lead car had closed to a kilometre of the target, the original trail car would take the lead position, maintaining constant contact with the target.

With four hundred metres to the turnoff, Dayan saw the Ford's right indicator come on.

"OK, Blue, he's turning off for sure," he said.

"Roger, Red", said Sumith, who was driving the Passat. "I could do with a fag break."

"We need to circle around," Dayan said to Sandra, who was hunched over in the passenger seat, a map spread over her knees.

"Take the next turnoff. It's the Mülheim one. We can circle round through Blankenheim an' back onto the *autobahn*."

*

Sumith topped off the Passat's tank at the shed while he waited for Bandara. When he got back to the car after paying for the petrol, he found Bandara back. Two cans of Coke from the drinks dispenser outside the neighbouring restaurant were sitting on the Passat's roof.

"What's the bugger doing?" Sumith asked, grabbing a can.

"Saw him going in to put a piss," Bandara said as they pulled away from the pumps. "I'm a bit pisstight myself."

"Tie a knot in your dick," muttered Sumith, parking where they could watch the exit. "We'll be there soon."

"Bullshit," wailed Bandara, watching Sumith sadistically gurgle his Coke. "That'll take more than an hour. "I'll jus' put a pump against that tree and come."

Sumith lit up a cigarette and watched the exit. Bandara had barely stepped behind his tree when the black Ford Focus with Kumaradeven smoking behind the wheel shot past.

Tossing his cigarette aside, Sumith started the Passat's engine. "Oi!" he shouted to Bandara. "Our boy's off. Come on!" But Bandara didn't appear. "Come on, you cunt! We'll lose him."

Bandara trotted round the tree, still zipping up as he approached. He dived into the car and Sumith pulled away.

"If we lose the bugger, Ah'll kick your arse all the way to Trier."

"So how to stop once I started? You thought it's like a fucking tap or something?"

"Red, we're mobile again."

"Roger that. We're back on the A1, three klicks behind you."

For another hour, the cars switched positions frequently as they headed south, neither car staying in contact with the target long enough to give themselves away. Ideally, Dayan would have preferred three cars, but they just didn't have the resources. However, knowing Kumaradeven's destination made it easier, and they could afford to stay loose. Dayan would tighten up on the target when they were approaching the outskirts of Trier. It would be the crucial moment. Though they knew the meeting was arranged for Trier, they had no idea where it would be. That had probably been established earlier.

Dayan and Sandra were the trail car as they passed the Schweich turnoff and Sumith came up on the net.

"Blue turning onto the A602. Target is following."

"Rog."

The A602 *autobahn* would take them west and straight into Trier. Fifteen minutes later, Dayan and Sandra were following the long curve south along the bank of the Mosel that formed the city's western boundary. They now needed to turn east if they were to head into the city centre, but the target was giving no sign of changing direction. He was heading south.

"Tighten up, Red," Sumith said. "Target's bound to do a left soon, and if he does it quick we'll lose him."

"Roger." Dayan began to drive more aggressively, using the small Golf's fast pickup speed to crowd the cars ahead and force them to give way. He ignored the irritated looks he got from German drivers, as he leapfrogged up the column of traffic, trying to get a glimpse of the Ford Focus. Next to him, Sandra was still watching the map, giving him a running commentary on each upcoming side road, and where it led, trying to paint a mental map for him.

"Red, target's gone left," snapped Sumith before Dayan was in sight of the Focus, "down. . ." Sumith was hesitating, obviously unable to see the street name.

"*Where*, Blue?"

"Kaiserstrasse, Red." It was Bandara. "Target's going east on Kaiserstrasse."

"Roger, Blue. Take the next left."

"Roger."

"Kaiserstrasse coming up," called Sandra.

Dayan accelerated through an amber light, turning east. Within two hundred and fifty metres he caught sight of the target car, and relaxed, hanging back. "Blue, we're east on Kaiser. Where are you?"

"Also going east, Red. Dunno what the road is, but we'll get onto Kaiser ASAP."

"There's a roundabout coming up, Dayan," warned Sandra. "Don' lose him."

Dayan speeded up in time to see the Focus go straight through the roundabout. On their left, they were passing the ancient red brick ruins of the Roman baths.

"Where the fuck is he going?" he muttered. They were driving uphill now through a residential neighbourhood, getting further away from the river and the city centre. "Target east on Olewiger Strasse."

"The Roman amphitheatre is up ahead on the left," Sandra told him.

"Shit, he's stopping." Dayan caught a flash of the Focus pulling off the road, and swung the Golf off Kaiserstrasse into a hard left turn that took him north. He hadn't had time to hit his turn indicator, and horns blasted behind him. "Blue, target stat three hundred east of the roundabout. We're headed north. Do a drive by."

"Roger."

Dayan took the next turn on the right and started to circle around the amphitheatre in an attempt to get back onto their original route. He was sure Kumaradeven hadn't spotted them, so this must be the meeting point.

"Red, confirm target stat and on foot into the arena," Sumith reported. "We're approaching a junction."

"Roger, Blue. Do a U and go back to where you can see the entrance."

"Do we follow on foot?"

"No, just watch the entrance. If they have any brains they'll be watching the entrance from inside."

Dayan slowed the Golf to a crawl as he looked up a wooded slope on his right. The trees were firs and hadn't lost their foliage in winter, so he couldn't see very far. He knew he was somewhere behind the amphitheatre, and heading back towards Olewiger Strasse, the road that ran past the front of the arena, which had to lie beyond the hill.

He parked on the grass verge and pulled a tourist map of Trier out of the glove compartment, one that he had picked up in the Cologne tourist information office, and quickly scanned it, hoping to get an idea of the amphitheatre's layout. But the map wasn't detailed enough.

"Red on foot into the arena," he informed Sumith and Bandara. "C'mon, Sandra."

Leaving the Golf, they scrambled up the steep slope, the damp pine needles deadening the sound of their progress, but making the going unsteady. Soon they came to a chain link fence, and they went to the right, hoping to get around it. Beyond was a vineyard. It was quickly apparent that the fence stretched the length of the ridge, and so they crossed it, Dayan hoisting Sandra over before following. They worked their way up the muddy slope, between the posts that were still bare of grapevines. At the far end they got over another fence, and the top of the ridge was just ten metres ahead.

Raising a finger to his lips, Dayan moved up in a crouch. Sandra followed till he dropped flat in the pale grass at the top. Together, they inched their way forward and looked over the spine. Beyond and below them lay the ancient Roman amphitheatre. The slope that they'd just climbed formed part of the amphitheatre's walls, and they were now looking down over the grass-covered stands that had once sat thousands of cheering spectators, to the hard-packed oval of the arena in the centre.

The amphitheatre was dotted with tourists, in spite of the time of year, strolling around and taking photographs. Halfway up the arena's stands, several stone park benches had been placed, in a linked ellipse that let tourists relax and observe the man-made bowl from every angle. Directly below Dayan and Sandra was one of these benches. Its position commanded an excellent view of the amphitheatre's entrance, and three people were sitting on it. One of the trio was Kumaradeven, and of the two he was intently talking to, one was obviously a woman.

"Target has made contact," Dayan informed Blue Team. "One male, one female."

"Rog."

They were too far away to make out conversation, but they seemed to be discussing several papers and pictures. Dayan carefully took out his binos and focussed them on the trio, struggling to sharpen the image at such a short range. He could just make out some maps over the trio's shoulders.

After about ten minutes, Kumaradeven abruptly rose and said his farewells, shaking the couple by the hand in turn. Lighting a cigarette, he quickly made his way down the grassy tiers towards the entrance of the amphitheatre. The other two remained where they were.

"Target on foot back out," Dayan advised the others. "Tail him. We'll stay with the new pair."

"Roger that."

As soon as Blue Team had announced that they had Kumaradeven in sight, and that they were following him west, back towards the Mosel, Dayan and Sandra raced back to the Golf.

"What the hell were they looking at?" Sandra panted as they got to the car.

"Some maps," replied Dayan. "And photos. Couldn' be sure, but they looked like shots of the Rhine. Must have been the snaps he took from the bridge."

"This mus' be the ERA team, then."

"Some of them, at least."

They got to the amphitheatre entrance in time to see the couple drive off west in a midnight blue BMW 523i station wagon.

As Dayan and Sandra tailed the car at a discreet distance, Sumith reported that they were following Kumaradeven north along the river in the direction of the *autobahn*.

"Stay with him," ordered Dayan. "You'll have to cover him in Cologne. We'll have to stick with this bunch."

He couldn't be sure if there'd be any further contact between the two groups, and if this was an assault team, they couldn't risk losing them.

They followed the BMW to the Mosel, and then north along the east bank. At first Sandra and Dayan thought the Tamils were headed for the *autobahn* too, but instead of taking the main road north, the BMW continued along a narrow waterfront street that dead-ended close to a cheap youth hostel. Instead of risking a drive by, Dayan swung the Golf east onto a wider street that headed back towards the city. He stopped on the pavement and

Sandra walked back towards the river to check out the hostel. She was back in a few minutes to confirm that the BMW was parked in front of the hostel and there was no sign of activity.

The pair sat in the Golf for an hour, and when the Tamils didn't reappear, they decided that they were using the hostel as a base. Dayan drove Sandra back into the city, dropping her off to book them into a bed-and-breakfast establishment on Dietrichstrasse. He then drove into the city centre to return their car to the rental agency, which had a branch in Trier, and rent a new one. They needed something fast enough to stick with the BMW, but not too conspicuous. He settled for a grey Ford Mondeo. He then drove out to the Mosel once more to check the hostel, noted the BMW still there, and joined Sandra at their bed-and-breakfast.

She had booked them into a double room as Mr and Mrs Singh, using fake Indian passports, and Dayan suggested that they get some sleep in case it was an all-nighter. Sandra said she needed a shower first and disappeared into the bathroom. She had already phoned Sumith and been told that Kumaradeven had gone straight to his apartment in Bickendorf, Cologne, and hadn't left there since. They would continue monitoring his home phone. Sandra and Dayan had both brought overnight bags, and he changed out of his mud-stained clothes. The double room had single beds, and they crashed out for an hour. Sandra had paid in advance for three nights.

They awoke at 6pm and it was already getting dark. Climbing into the Mondeo, they approached the river along Maarstrasse, the street that met the waterfront at right angles. The waterfront street, Zurlaubener Ufer, ran along the Mosel, and dead-ended fifty metres beyond the youth hostel. As they neared the river, the dead end was to their right, and the rest of Zurlaubener Ufer stretched away on the left. Dayan was still driving, as Sandra was more familiar with the map than he was, and he turned left and parked on the riverbank. In the rear-view mirror he could see both the hostel entrance and the BMW.

They waited, hoping that they wouldn't have to do this for days. Around 7pm, the couple came out of the hostel with two other Tamils, both men, and got into the BMW. Sandra and Dayan ducked out of sight as the BMW's headlights panned across their car. The vehicle disappeared down Maarstrasse, in the direction of the city centre.

"Aren't we following them?" Sandra asked as they straightened up.

"I don't think they're leaving Trier yet," Dayan replied. "None of them had any bags or anything. Probably jus' going for dinner." He patted his stomach. "Which reminds me that my stomach thinks somebody has cut my head off. Shall we also go an' get some food?"

Sandra nodded. She was starving, too. "Why don't we get a snack and drive around a bit," she suggested. "Get a feel of the city."

With a grunt Dayan started the Mondeo and they took off. They couldn't find a parking spot in the city centre, so they drove around for half an hour, checking out the city before finding a spot close to the Porta Nigra. They grabbed some *döners* — a sort of huge pita bread roll stuffed with lamb and salad and topped with goat cheese — at a Turkish fast-food joint, Sandra having to yell their order over the pounding beat of *rai* music, and walked around the Porta Nigra, munching.

The city wasn't a very big one, by German standards, with less than a hundred thousand inhabitants, but its colourful history made it a popular tourist destination. Founded by the Romans in 15BC, it had once been the capital of the Western Empire, and was filled with relics from the past.

It was a clear moonlit night, and as Dayan and Sandra walked past the Porta Nigra, its huge black stone arches glistened with frost in the pale light. It was the old city gate, and had once been part of a Roman wall encircling Trier.

When they drove back to Zurlaubener Ufer, they couldn't spot the blue BMW at first, and Dayan had to take the car right down the *cul-de-sac* and past the hostel before they saw it nestled behind a minibus. Dayan did a U-turn at the end of the street, and since it was dark, chose a parking spot where he could see the hostel entrance and the BMW clearly. They decided that if by 11pm there was no more action from the Tamils, Sandra would take a taxi back to the motel and sleep for a few hours. She would then relieve Dayan so that he could get some rest.

By 9:30, Sandra was dozing, and Dayan dreaming of a cigarette. Suddenly he saw a figure leave the hostel and cross the street. He nudged Sandra, who came fully awake with a start. In the light of the hostel porch Dayan had recognized the woman who had met Kumaradeven that afternoon. The BMW was only twenty-five metres away from them as the woman opened its door. They saw the courtesy light come on, and watched the woman rummage around, leaning in through the open door.

She finally straightened up and shut the door, looking into the BMW. Then she glanced down the street straight at the Mondeo. Both Dayan and Sandra stiffened. Their car was in shadow, but could she see them? Suddenly the woman turned and started walking briskly towards them.

"Fuck, we're spotted," hissed Dayan, reaching across to Sandra, and simultaneously drawing the pistol from his waistband and sliding it under his right thigh. "Quick, start kissing me."

The woman was already less than fifteen metres away and closing fast.

"Not enough," muttered Sandra. "She won't believe it."

Before Dayan realized what was happening, she was leaning towards him, her hands fumbling at his groin, unzipping his jeans. He could only stare at the approaching woman with wide eyes as he felt Sandra's fingers draw him out, her lips descending over his limp penis. The Tamil woman seemed to be looking straight at him, and then she was gone, somewhere past the car and down the street. Dayan gasped and stifled a cry as Sandra raised her mouth away from him.

"Where is she?" Dayan felt her breath on the head of his now rapidly stiffening penis, hot and wet with her spit. "Did she spot us?"

"Dunno." He tried to keep his voice steady as he checked the rear-view mirror. In the darkness at the end of the street, he saw movement, shadows shifting, and then the flare of a cigarette lighter. "She's at the cigarette machine." He saw the glow of a cigarette end, and then footsteps. "She's coming back!"

Instantly, Sandra's mouth was on him again. Dayan hunched over her as he heard the footsteps pause at his door, hoping the Tamil woman wouldn't realize they were Sri Lankans. He slipped the safety catch on the 9-mm Browning Hi-Power. Sandra's head bobbed realistically, her lips moving up and down his length, and it took all of his concentration to stop his pelvis thrusting himself up into her. Then the footsteps receded and he raised his head. The woman was crossing the street at a leisurely pace, heading for the hostel.

Dayan forced himself to say, "OK, she's gone," and Sandra straightened up.

He looked at her in amazement, but she was watching the hostel, studiously avoiding his gaze.

"We better split," Dayan whispered. "If someone comes out and sees this car still here, we'll be screwed."

Starting the car, he pulled away, driving quickly past the hostel and turning onto Maarstrasse. He pulled into a car park two-hundred metres up the street and waited for fifteen minutes to see if the suspected terras had been spooked enough to make a getaway. There was no more sign of the Tamils or their car.

＊

When they got to their room, Dayan shut the door and turned towards Sandra. She was looking at him with an expression he couldn't fathom. He started to speak, deciding that he would handle the whole thing in a professional manner. Their cover had almost been blown — no pun intended — and they'd done what was necessary to escape detection. The short wait in the car park and the drive back to their motel had been in silence, Sandra staring out of her window, and Dayan racking his brains for something to say.

But now, before a word came out of his mouth, she stepped up to him and kissed him, pressing against him, pushing him back against the door. She was wearing a grey pullover and a long olive-green thigh-hugging skirt over knee-boots. He could feel her tongue push into his mouth, and the heat of her body as his hands came up her sides, returning her embrace. He stepped towards the beds, still locked together with her, and she didn't resist.

In a moment they were tumbling back onto one of the beds, fumbling blindly with each other's clothes, kissing, panting, fingers scrabbling.

"Quickly," she gasped, her first words since she had taken him in her mouth. "Never mind the clothes."

He bunched her skirt in a fist, pushing it up her long legs to her waist. Looking down their bodies, he could see she was wearing translucent white panties, and the dark triangle of her pubic hair showed through. She lifted her hips, letting him tug the panties down to her ankles, from where she kicked them off. Then he was pushing to his feet struggling with his jeans. He dropped them and his penis throbbed before her, fully erect. He never wore underwear, a habit he had lost in the jungle, and found hard to pick up again now that he was away from it.

Her thighs opened and he looked into her face, almost questioningly. Her eyes were wet, the hazel-green irises glittering.

"Please. . ." she gasped.

He almost dived onto her, entering her in one convulsive thrust. She cried out as he pistoned into her, no skill or technique needed tonight. It was the act itself that they both craved, the joining and not the style of it.

Unlike most women Dayan had fucked, she didn't close or roll her eyes as he glided in and out of her. She just stared back at him, her thighs gripping him. In what seemed like seconds she was coming, her booted legs crossing over his back, ankles locking, and Dayan knew he was on the verge, too. She gave a series of hissing moans, each longer than the other, her teeth gritted together. With each of her gasps Dayan felt her internal muscles contract and relax, gripping him, drawing him over the edge with her.

Her final, long gasp turned into a soft scream, that formed his name, and she climaxed. In the same moment he stiffened over her, tumbling into those green pools that seemed to stare into his soul as he came.

*

The ringing of the phone awoke Sumith, in the team's Bayenthal flat in Cologne. He lunged for it, noting that it was 11pm. Grabbing the receiver, he heard Bandara's excited voice.

"*Ado*, Sumith, our bugger's done a *maru*."

"*What?*" Sumith scrambled out of bed, throwing a shoe across the room to get Kamal out of bed. "Where'd he go?" Bandara was on stag in the van close to Kumaradeven's Bickendorf flat.

"Dunno. He got a call ten minutes ago, and someone spoke to him in German. Couldn' understand everything, but I heard the caller tell him something was ready. Our chap didn't say anything about going anywhere or anything. But about five minutes ago I went round to check and his car was gone."

"Fuck!" Sumith was already dressed and pulling on trainers. "Keep your eyes open. We'll be there in a few minutes."

It was a full fifteen minutes before Sumith and Kamal turned off Venloer Strasse and parked close to the van. They found Bandara with his wiretap headset back on. He pulled it off as they climbed into the van.

"Bugger's back," Bandara announced.

"Already?" muttered Sumith. "Couldn't have gone far."

"I was on the main road having a fag and watching," explained Bandara. "He took two heavy wooden boxes out of the car and went into the building. I think he went into the cellar because I saw a light come on. You can see the ventilation openings just above the pavement from the road, no? The light came on for a few minutes."

"How big were the boxes?" Kamal asked.

" 'Bout three feet by two, I suppose."

"What the hell is he picking up at this time of the night?" voiced Sumith aloud.

"Bet they were weapons," said Bandara. "For whatever job they're planning. Better call Dayan, no?"

"No point calling him 'til we know what it is for sure," pointed out Sumith. "It'll be silly to make a major fuss over a crate of books or something."

"Who goes to pick up books at eleven in the bloody night?" Kamal wanted to know.

"Well, le'ss fucking find out, no?" Sumith grinned at Kamal. "You went in with Dayan las' time, so you know the way. Go in an' have a look in about an hour, after everything's quietened down."

"Thanks."

"I'll cover you from the car. If there's any scene jus' come running out an' we'll hook it. At worst case, we can hit Kumaradeven here, an' Dayan an' Sandra can hit the terras in Trier."

It was almost 1am when Dayan's mobile phone rang. Reaching sleepily across Sandra's still form, he picked up the blinking phone.

"Dayan? It's me." He recognized Sumith's voice. "Putting a hump, or what?"

For a couple of heartbeats Dayan was at a loss for words, caught on the hop by Sumith's almost intuitive wisecrack. "Yah, doggy-style," he finally managed. "Whazzup?"

"Our friend here jus' picked up some new toys." Sumith sounded pleased with himself, and Dayan sat up in bed, fully awake. "Six sixty-sixes, a couple of pistols, and a couple of SMGs."

Sumith explained briefly the night's activities and how Kamal had broken into the cellar and made the discovery. He wanted to know what to do.

Dayan shielded his eyes as Sandra, switched on the bedside lamp. This was the final proof they needed that they weren't imagining the whole thing. The 66-mm M72A2 shoulder-fired rocket launchers meant that it was definitely a hit. And probably not just an attempt on the life of a single individual. They wouldn't need six rockets for that. They knew the possible area of the impending attack, but not the target itself.

"Sit tight," he instructed. "If everything works right, the guys here will be moving up to Cologne one of these days. We'll decide what to do then."

After he had hung up, Dayan explained to Sandra what had happened. She switched off the light and they lay there in the darkness, nestled together in the single bed, in silence. After a full five minutes she spoke.

"Maybe we should tell the cops now. They could pick up Kumaradeven immediately."

"And what about the four here in Trier?" asked Dayan. "They'd be free to plan another attack."

"We could follow them," she argued. "Watch till they try another attack and get the cops onto them, too."

"Follow them for how long, Sandra?" he asked cynically. "We're just five of us. An' these buggers are probably Black Tigers. They'll be sharper than Kumaradeven. They're bound to spot us soon. And if the German cops pick up one Tiger, they'll start putting surveillance on other known ones. Which means we won' be able to get anywhere close. Our orders are to watch the Tigers here in Germany and hit them when needed, not have them arrested." Sandra didn't reply, and he made up his mind. "We have to hit the assault team as soon as they pick up the weapons and we know the exact target."

Sandra leaned her head on his shoulder. "But why wait til' we know the target?"

"Because if we hit them during the attack, they'll be all together," he answered. "And it'll also cover our arses. It'll be obvious to the Germans that we're the good guys who saved the day."

Though he had only had a couple of hours sleep, the sex with Sandra seemed to have relieved the weeks of stress, and Dayan felt more rested than he'd felt in months.

"Maybe they're going to hit somebody driving through that area," Sandra suggested. "On one of the riverbank roads that run under the Severins Bridge."

"Could be. But who? Has to be a Sri Lankan or a Canadian. Unlikely that they'll change strategy just yet."

"I'll call Sunil at the embassy," Sandra said. "Maybe he can check on whatever political activity there's going to be in Cologne over the next few days."

"OK. But don't give him any details. Just tell him we think there could be an attack close to the Severins Bridge." Dayan looked at the luminous dial of his watch. It was almost 1:30am. "Let's get cracking. We better switch cars an' go check on our friends."

But before he could get out from under the blanket, he felt Sandra's smooth thigh slip over his own. As he tried to see her face in the darkness, he felt her teeth nibble at his ear.

"Sandra—"

"I think we can delay another half an hour, no?" she breathed. She slipped down in the bed, her tongue trailing down his neck to his left nipple. Her tongue flicked it, sending an electric jolt down to his penis, making it jump into her waiting hand.

He groaned as her mouth moved down his torso and over his belly. With a sharp intake of breath he felt her tongue glide up the underside of his member, from base to tip. Dayan reached for her head, but with a giggle she pulled away, throwing aside the blanket and mounting him. Still gripping him with one hand, Sandra plunged her hips down on him, impaling herself with a soft cry.

He gasped as the cool air of the room was replaced by her hot wetness, and he reached up in the darkness to cup her outthrust, bouncing breasts.

CHAPTER 13

MONDAY 18th MARCH: "So we know the rough area, Sunil, but not exactly what the target is, nor when." Sandra Koch was talking on her mobile phone as Dayan steered along the A1 *Autobahn* in the direction of Cologne. "But we think it's going to be in less than a week."

The morning after their meeting with Kumaradeven, the terrorists had left Trier. The BMW had maintained a moderate pace, staying with the other late rush hour traffic and enabling Dayan and Sandra to follow without being conspicuous. Although Dayan had switched the Mondeo for a dark Mazda 323 just that morning, he wasn't going to risk it. He had phoned Cologne and got Kamal and Bandara to drive like maniacs down to Blankenheim, where they took the lead car role and allowed the Mazda to drop out of sight.

"Fuck, I think I know what the target is," Sandra heard Major Sunil Jayawardene say on the phone. This was followed by some moments of silence, and she grew impatient.

"Well?" she snapped. "Are you going to tell, or what?"

"Look, Sandra. . ." He hesitated. "It's a bit of a tricky situ."

"We *need to know*, Sunil," she insisted. "Otherwise there's no guarantee that we can stop this in time."

"OK." He seemed to make up his mind. "Our consul general here in Bonn makes a weekly trip to Cologne. . ." Jayawardene hesitated again, then continued quickly. "He visits a particular address on Foller Strasse, close to the Severins Bridge. We think he's having an affair. I followed him several times for security reasons without him knowing. Guess where he always parks?"

"On Holzmarkt Bayenstrasse, no?" she guessed quickly. "The road that runs under the bridge."

"Yup."

"And when does he go for his little undercover operation?"

"Thursday afternoons. He's usually in Cologne just after three." Jayawardene paused. "But if he's a target, I'll have to stop him going for some reason. Hint about a threat."

"Today's only Monday, so that gives us a few days. Don' say anything to him yet. I'll get back to you."

After Sandra had rung off she gave Dayan the good news.

"OK. So now we have time, date, and place," he said. "If we're right, they'll do a CTR today or tomorrow. And some sort of rehearsal. That'll then give us a chance to plan how to hit them."

By now they were driving through Sielsdorf on the outskirts of Cologne. The terras in the BMW followed the A1 as it skirted the western edge of the city.

"Bet they're going straight to Kumaradeven's place," warned Sandra, watching the map once more. "If we're right they'll take the Venloer Strasse turnoff. That'll take them straight through Bickendorf."

"Blue from Red," radioed Dayan. "Anticipate target will take Venloer Strasse turnoff. Lead him in."

"Roger, Red," Bandara answered.

Sure enough, a few minutes later, Bandara warned them that he was turning southeast towards the city and that the BMW was following. As the turnoff came up, Dayan took it as well, slowing down to city speed limits before exiting onto the long straight Venloer Strasse. The surroundings were still pretty deserted and open, but he could see built-up areas looming over the roadside treetops. A rail track, part of Cologne's *U-bahn* or subway system, paralleled the street. Unlike the underground metro networks of most European cities, Germany's 'underground' frequently ran on the surface, only diving into the earth in busier areas of the cities.

Dayan slowed down even further as they got into a more urban area and the rail tracks disappeared off to the right somewhere. They were almost into Bickendorf when the radio crackled with Bandara's voice.

"Red, target stopping at Zulu. We're carrying on an' will stan' by."

"Roger."

When they were three hundred metres from Kumaradeven's apartment block, Dayan pulled over. He got his binos up in time to see two of the terras cross the street and enter the building. He was sure one of them was the woman. Dayan's eyes ached as he lowered the binos, tired from long hours of alertness and driving. He handed the binos to Sandra and leaned back in his seat, closing his eyes.

"Tell me when they come out."

With his eyes shut he was now aware of her perfume, soft and musky. He had a flash of Sunethra suddenly, but couldn't understand where the picture came from. With a start he realized that for the first time on an operation, he could recall his wife's face. He looked across at Sandra, her eyes glued to the binos. Her hair fell in brown waves down to her pullover, and he could see the soft skin beneath her ear. He remembered what her skin tasted like and cursed himself, closing his eyes again. What the fuck was he getting into? They were here on a job. He couldn't let his horniness distract him from their mission. And that was all it was anyway. Horniness. As soon as the job was over, he'd fuck her a couple of times and then they'd go their separate ways. Well, maybe three times.

"Here they come!"

Her voice snapped him back to reality and he reached for the binos, but Sandra slapped his hand away. She kept watching as he switched on the ignition.

"They've got two sports bags with them," she commented. "Did they take them in?"

"No. Mus' be the weapons."

With Blue Team as backup they tailed the BMW south through the city and past the sprawling University of Cologne. The terras were finally traced to an apartment block off Luxemburger Strasse in Sülz, an area popular with students of all races due to its proximity to the campus.

"Wonder how they rented this place without us knowing about it," mused Sandra aloud as they watched from the end of the street. "We were watching Kumaradeven all the time."

"Maybe he got someone else from the WTA to do it," suggested Dayan. "Or it could be a regular safe house."

They had parked in an alley, and were now smoking in the shadow of a railway bridge that crossed above the street. The pavement was littered with discarded food and paper cups and stank of urine. Posters advertising movies and musical events covered the nearby walls and the bridge supports.

A pair of attractive young women swung out of a nearby kiosk and walked towards Sandra and Dayan, lighting up as they approached. In spite of the chill in the air, both women had their jackets open, and Dayan could see the hardness of one woman's nipples poking through her tight pullover. His eyes would have lingered longer, but Dayan was concentrating on the apartment building. The women ignored him, walking quickly past. Dayan had been surprised when he first arrived in Germany to find that few women flirted with their eyes the way they did in Sri Lanka. They barely made eye contact, he realized. It was another disappointing discovery about white women.

A big bearded German in a filthy army jacket and torn jeans attempted to beg from the two young women, but was pointedly ignored. Their camouflage-patterned stretch pants rustled as they quickened their pace.

For a generation that studiously proclaimed its contempt for anything military, Dayan found it odd that young Germans seemed to snap up camouflage as a fashion statement. One more of the country's strange contradictions.

Graffiti crawled across the supports of the railway bridge, and one phrase caught Dayan's eye. *Nazis raus!* Nazis out. While

Dayan was impressed with the quality of life in the country — the safety and efficiency and accessibility that Sri Lankans longed for — he was amazed at a nation that seemed almost schizophrenic in its character, simultaneously both wallowing in and disconnecting itself from its dark and recent history. He wondered whether Sri Lanka would ever have the opportunity to look back on her own dark past with the luxury of viewpoints.

The beggar walked towards Dayan and Sandra and demanded a cigarette. Sandra stepped involuntarily back. They could smell the beer on the man's breath from several feet away.

"*Ich spreche kein Deutsch*," Dayan said with a shrug. I speak no German.

"*Zigaretten*," the man insisted, making a smoking motion with his fingers to his lips. "*Zigaretten*."

"Sorry, don't understand," Dayan shrugged again.

The German finally gave up, and with a glare at the two, swayed off, muttering.

"Why didn't you give him a fag?" asked Sandra with a puzzled look. "He's just a beggar."

"I don' give anything to beggars at home in Sri Lanka, why should I give *him* anything?" Dayan's eyes were cold and dark though they remained on the apartment block the terras had entered even as he spoke. "Children are starving back home. No medicine, no schools, no. . ." His voice trailed off and for a moment he was quiet. "Never expected to see beggars here, though." He glanced at her with a quick smirk. "An' did you see the bugger? Has enough money for booze, but asks me for a smoke. Arsehole probably has more money than I do."

Before Sandra could reply, Dayan turned and headed off down the alley. A glance in the direction of the apartment building showed the four terras crossing the road to their parked car. They hadn't been indoors more than five minutes. Obviously, the terras were in a hurry to get on with the recce phase of their operation.

Kamal and Bandara had gone to switch cars and they now radioed their availability. The BMW was headed east through

Barbarossa Platz in the direction of the Severins Bridge, and
Dayan vectored Blue Team onto them. Five minutes later,
Bandara confirmed that they had the target in sight close to the
Poststrasse *U-bahn* entrance, still headed for the river, and Dayan
dropped back.

As they drove through a maze of side streets, Sandra called
out directions to Dayan, attempting to approach the Rhine from
a different direction. Bandara, in the meantime, was giving a
running commentary on the BMW's progress.

"Target east on Gotering. . . Passing under Severinstrasse
. . .Approaching Severins Bridge. . . Target east across the bridge
now. . . not stopping yet. . ."

"Stay loose, Blue," Dayan warned. "They'll stick close to
the bridge."

By now he had parked in the maze of back streets that
divided the Rhine from the parallel Severinstrasse, and he and
Sandra were now hot-footing it north along Severinstrasse to a
point where it crossed over Gotering, the road that led to the
bridge. From here, Sandra claimed they would have a clear line
of sight down the length of the bridge.

"Target turning left off the main road. . ." said Bandara,
". . .towards the river. . ."

"Don't get spotted, Blue. Hang back, I have the bridge in
sight, and will have the terras as soon as they get back on it."

"I'm losing them in these small side roads, Red." Dayan
and Sandra could hear the frustration in the SF soldier's voice.
"*Ammata hukanda*— I'm on a one-way street. . . Ah've lost them,
Red."

"Stan' by, Blue. Find a spot an' park. I'll take the target."

Dayan trained his binoculars down the length of the Severins
Bridge. There were several sightseers and joggers on the kilometre-
long bridge, but he couldn't spot the terras. It didn't, however,
cause him any worry. He knew the Tigers — and he was sure
that's what they were — had to approach west across the bridge.
Soon he had them, walking in two pairs, looking casual as tourists.

Just before they reached the spot where the bridge crossed the Rheinauhafen pier with the Chocolate Museum at its tip, they stopped. The distance was long, but Dayan was sure they had a pair of binos with them, and were looking and pointing at the western bank.

What Dayan couldn't figure out though, was why they were standing where they were. They were at least a full four hundred metres short of where the Severins Bridge crossed over Holzmarkt Bayenstrasse, the road the Sri Lankan consul general was expected to travel along. Why the hell were they standing out there over the middle of the bloody river?

The rest of the day crawled by, and they stopped the surveillance on Kumaradeven's house and switched their full efforts to the suspected assault team. They would keep an observer in a van close to the apartment building in Sülz twenty-four hours a day. They would use a different van each day.

That afternoon Dayan was sitting in the back of the VW van, its windows tinted, when the terras took off in the direction of the Severins Bridge again. Quickly informing the others of his whereabouts, he followed. When the four Tamils headed over the bridge, he circled round and took up position on the Severinstrasse overpass. After fifteen minutes of waiting, Dayan began to worry that they had spotted him and kept driving into east Cologne. Half an hour later he was sure that something had gone wrong. If they had spotted him, they might call the whole operation off and just disappear. They'd never get near them again. He phoned the others and sent Sumith to check the Sülz apartment. Ten minutes later Sumith informed him that there was no sign of the BMW anywhere.

"Maybe they switched cars, too," suggested Dayan. "Stay there and watch the flat."

"Roger."

After an hour of waiting, Dayan decided it was a lost cause. Cursing himself for being careless, he was about to leave when he spotted the dark blue BMW 523i approaching west across the bridge.

With a sigh of relief he focused on the car as it got closer. Just as it reached the point where the bridge crossed the pier, Dayan saw it pull to the side and onto the pavement. No one got out and Dayan lowered his binos, wondering what was going on. It was then that he saw that a panel van had stopped about two hundred metres further back, at the spot the terras had been reconnoitring that morning. Through the binos he saw two people get out of the van — one was the woman — and walk to the bridge rail. About three hundred metres further east, he made out a third parked vehicle, this time a red Opel Corsa.

This was it, he realized with a rush of excitement. This was the rehearsal. And the BMW was at a spot that overlooked the consul general's route. The other two vehicles would be the backup, and the terras must have picked them up from somewhere across the river. He mentally memorized the three vehicles' positions. Now they could come up with their own counter plan.

That evening, Dayan called a patrol meeting to plan out the hit. Sandra was watching the Sülz apartment while the SF men met in their own flat in Bayenthal. The hit would be carried out by the SF; the decision had been made much earlier. They were trained for this, while Sandra wasn't. It was the reason they'd been sent to Germany. She would be filled in later on the plans.

Surveillance of the terras' flat had confirmed the arrival of the two new vehicles, which had been crowded into a high-walled courtyard next to the building. The BMW had been left out in the street. At first, the Sri Lankans wondered why the van — a brown Renault Espace — and the little Corsa hadn't been left outside as well, ready for a fast getaway. Then they decided that the two new vehicles had probably been stolen on the eastside of the city, and would only be used for the attack.

Sandra had phoned Jayawardene at the Bonn consulate and suggested that they needed a decoy to drive the consul general's car to Cologne. It was possible that the LTTE had someone at the consulate — or watching it — who would initiate the attack only when the consul general's car left Bonn. Jayawardene had been brought up to date on the terras' presumed plan, and he had immediately volunteered to be the decoy himself.

It was a courageous decision, Sandra had thought. He would be in a very dangerous position if the SF interception didn't go smoothly. All the terras needed was one 66-mm rocket to turn the consul general's car — and Sunil Jayawardene — into flaming wreckage.

"So that's the scene," Dayan concluded after he had described the terra rehearsal at the Severins Bridge. "The Beamer mus' be the primary vehicle, parked here. . ." He pointed to a large-scale map of the target area. "The van is the backup, here. . ." He jabbed his finger again. "An' the Corsa is a blocking car. . . here."

"Looks a bit weird to me, though," said Sumith, scratching his head. He was looking at several blown-up satellite photographs of the bridge. "If the van is the backup, why's it parked two hundred metres behind the Beamer? It'll take them too much wasted time to get up to the spot."

"Mm." Kamal nodded in agreement. "At firs' glance it looks to me as if the van is the primary with the two cars as blocks, front an' rear. That's what Ah'd do if I was them."

"But the Beamer's the only car within view of Holzmarkt Bayenstrasse," Dayan pointed out, tapping the photographs. "It *has* to be the primary vehicle."

"Jus' seems a bit of a silly layout to me," went on Sumith, still not convinced. "I don't see why they need both a backup and a block behind them an' nothing in front."

"Well, there's no threat from the front, no?" answered Dayan. "There's a centre barrier along the whole length of the bridge, an' two hundred metres beyond in both directions. So nobody can jump lanes. The only way to approach the target area is from the east. From *behind* the terras. That's why they have the double cover behind."

"Maybe they're going to use a command-detonated claymore on the consul general's route," volunteered Bandara.

"The Beamer gives the signal an' the buggers in the van blow the claymore."

"Nah," said Sumith. "They don' need to use three vehicles an' sit up there in the open on the bridge to do that, no? They could have one bugger positioned on the riverbank to fire the claymore, and a car parked somewhere nearby for a quick *maru*." He shook his head. "Nope. This is definitely a rocket job. We saw the sixty sixes, no?" He chewed his lip for a moment. "But Ah'm still not convinced on the layout of this."

"Well, this is what we have," said Dayan. "So let's work on it 'til we hear anything new." He smoothed out the map. "The terras drive east across the Severins Bridge, circle around an' come back west. They get into position at about 1500, and the consul general's car arrives between 1500 and 1510. The terras in the Beamer hit the target, and they all push off west into the city. They'll dump the vehicles an' get out of Cologne, maybe by train. They probably entered Germany from France via Luxembourg, so the French border will probably be their destination." He looked around at the faces of his patrol. "Any ideas?"

"You said you had a good view down the bridge from your position today on the Severinstrasse overpass, no?" Sumith's tone held more of a statement than a question. "How 'bout a sniper hit from there?" He looked down at the map. "Can't be more than three hundred-odd metres from there to the Beamer."

Dayan grimaced thoughtfully. "Yeah. . ." he said hesitantly, "but Ah'd have to hit with the firs' shot. There'd be no chance if I miss. They'd get the rockets away. And I can't guarantee a firs' round kill because of the wind. I noticed that it was pretty gusty along the river."

"So le'ss keep it simple an' do a drive by hit," suggested Kamal. "Two cars, two of us in each. Car number one drives up to the BMW and bumps the rocket team off, car number two hits the Corsa. Then we take the van from both sides."

"Or le'ss mirror them," ventured Bandara. "Use the same three-car formation as the terras. We drive east, stop on the pavement opposite them, and hit them with rockets ourselves."

Dayan shook his head. "Too chancy. What are you going to do if a bus or truck drives across your line as you fire? You blast a whole bunch of civils, plus maybe even yourself. And even if we hit the terras, sixty sixes or RPGs will cause too much damage. If civils get killed in the crossfire, we'll have the German cops on our necks faster than grease through a fucking goose."

He leaned back and lit another cigarette. The room was thick with smoke, and Kamal crossed to a window and opened it.

"If you buggers keep fagging at this rate we won't have to worry about the bloody terras killing us," he grumbled. "We'll all die of lung cancer before that."

Bandara blew smoke rings in his direction.

"I think the drive by hit is the best idea," Dayan said finally. "Simple, with less things to go wrong." He looked at Sumith for a moment. "But your idea of a sniper on the Severinstrasse overpass may not be a total write-off. Why don't you take that yourself, Sumith? You'll be on your own, and as soon as we hit the Beamer and the Corsa, start putting rounds into the van." Sumith nodded. "It'll keep the buggers static till we can deal with them. Even if they manage to get moving, one of our cars can block 'em. The job will be initiated by the hit on the Beamer. Fit?"

"Fit," replied Bandara. "So who hits who? If Sumith's sniping that leaves three of us. Shall we get Sandra in on this?"

"No," said Dayan emphatically. "First, she doesn' have the training for this sort'f shit. We don't know how she'll react when the bullets start flying. Second, we'll be back off to Sri Lanka when this is all over, whereas she'll be staying. She can't get involved in anything that could be classed as criminal. Plus, most importantly, we need someone to keep an eye on Kumaradeven while the hit is going down. As soon as the bugger realizes there's been a fuckup, he might take off. I want that cunt dead, too, before we wrap this job up."

"So that's two in one car and one in the other," said Sumith.

"Kamal, you and I will hit the Beamer," Dayan suggested. "You drive an' ah'll shoot. The Beamer's bound to have two people in it, so that'll be the crucial one. Banda, you take the Corsa. You'll have to do it on your own, but when we open fire, your fellow might be distracted. OK? Any questions or ideas?"

"What happens if a terra gets away on foot?" Kamal asked.

"Ah'll try'n' pin them down an' direct you buggers onto them," said Sumith.

"Anything else?" Dayan asked. There were no more questions or suggestions. "OK. Sumith, go relieve Sandra. Banda, Kamal, le'ss go return the cars to the agencies an' get three new ones. We need big powerful ones in case we have any dramas on Thursday. I'll double-check the weapons tonight. Kamal, you take the comms and maps. Make sure everyone has maps of the area and of the entire city. Codes will be Alpha for me an' Kamal, Bravo for Banda, Charlie for Sumith. Jayawardene's car will be Delta. The terras' Beamer, van, and Corsa will be X-ray, Yankee, and Zulu, respectively. Emergency rendezvous will be this flat. For twenty-four hours. After that, it'll be Sandra's flat in Marienburg for forty-eight hours. Sumith, drive down to Bonn with Sandra tonight an' pick up a rifle. Jayawardene said he had a G-3SG/1 and an MSG-90. You can take your pick. Le'ss get everything ready before tomorrow morning, then we have a two-day margin for any fuckups."

CHAPTER 14

Sri Lankan Airlines flight UL231 banked steeply, giving its passengers an exhilarating view over its port wing of the blue waters of the South China Sea. As the big Airbus A330 levelled out in the late morning sunlight, on its final approach to Changi Airport, the flight attendants moved down the aisles. The brilliant peacock green of the young women's saris shimmered as they made final checks on their charges, making sure seatbelts were fastened and tables folded up, clearing away the last drink cups.

In his window seat in Economy, Mahesh Balachandran drained the last of his apple juice and handed the plastic cup to the flight attendant. He'd had a couple of beers soon after takeoff from Katunayake, but then had switched off alcohol for the rest of the flight. The young woman smiled, but it was an expression slightly strained after hours in the air. Balachandran clicked his table back into place and switched his in-flight entertainment screen to the forward-looking camera under the Airbus' nose. The screen filled with a hazy image of the sea, with the darker blur of Singapore beginning to creep down from the horizon.

He started to feel the increasing pressure in his ears as the plane descended, rocking slightly in the thermals. As the pressure grew uncomfortable, Balachandran tried swallowing, but knew it wouldn't help. An exploding mortar shell close to Batticaloa in 1995 had damaged the canals of his inner ears and made takeoffs and landings painful. Sometimes it would take days for his ear passages to return to normal.

Soon they were passing over Singapore's northeastern coastline, and off to the left he could see the Changi Ferry Terminal.

Balachandran was the third of his six-man team to arrive in Singapore. They had spread out the arrivals over a week, and the last man would arrive two days before the mission started. He tried to forget about his ears as the Airbus' undercarriage kissed the runway and he pressed himself back in his seat when the pilot threw in the reverse thrusters. The big Pratt & Whitney turbofans screamed like banshees as the plane rapidly decelerated.

For the hundredth time, Mahesh Balachandran ran the steps of the operation through his mind. He still didn't like it. It was far too complex, and had too many separate coordinates. Too much depended on the people in Colombo.

UL231 braked to a gentle stop at Terminal 2, and Balachandran grabbed his shoulder bag and moved with the other passengers to the exit. At the door, he gave a hurried nod in reply to the flight attendant's practiced "*Ayubowan*," and walked quickly down the covered jet way.

Security was tight at Changi, and was another reason why he disliked the airport as an initiation point for the operation. He would have much preferred Katunayake, where they would be comfortable and well supported. But orders were orders. He had argued during the briefing against such a complex plan, but had been told it was a necessary part of covering both their trail and fighting the media war as well.

The security official scanned Balachandran's passport carefully, glancing up repeatedly at his face. It was Balachandran's real passport, but paranoia made him nervous that there would be something wrong. He fought down the irrational fear and looked around the airport, trying to appear calm.

He wore a dark double-breasted business suit, and his hair and moustache had been neatly trimmed. His stylish matching luggage, polished shoes, and frameless glasses made him look like a mid-level banking executive. He was of average height for a South Asian, average weight, average looks.

Balachandran watched the official tap a computer keyboard, comparing his passport with something on the screen. Sri Lankans didn't require a visa for Singapore, and that was one of the reasons the country had been chosen.

"Are you visiting Singapore on business, Mister Balachandran?" the Chinese official asked, his face pleasant but watchful.

"Yes, unfortunately," replied Balachandran with an apologetic shrug.

"And what business would that be, sir?"

Balachandran pretended irritation at the questioning and answered tightly, "Ah'm in imports and exports."

"Ah." The official handed over his passport. "Enjoy your stay in Singapore, Mister Balachandran."

He walked out of the terminal and onto Airport Boulevard, glancing around for a taxi. A rank of cabs was parked at the pavement, and all the drivers were waving at the arriving passengers. He got into the first vehicle in the rank and told the Sikh driver to take him to the hotel in Tagong Pagar.

The driver kept up a running chatter on the places they were passing, the Singaporean economy, his family's health, the boredom of his job, and anything else, it seemed to Balachandran, that came into his mind. He seemed to think his passenger was an Indian, but when he learned he was Sri Lankan, the driver switched to cricket.

"*Pukka* test series your fallows had against the West Indians, no, *la*?" he said, continuing without waiting for Balachandran to answer. "But those black fallows are useless. You just wait, will you, till the Shajar Cup. Sri Lanka versus India in the first match. That will be interesting, *la*. Now that Sachin is back, we are unbeatable. But of course, your fallows. . ."

Balachandran tuned out the man's drivel, watching the surroundings they were driving through. He had never been to Singapore before. In fact, his only trips outside Sri Lanka had been to India and Pakistan. For a moment he recalled his last trip.

The visit to Madras, when he had sat drinking the awful Assam tea in his parents' dingy home in the slums of the refugee camp. Well, maybe soon he would be able to afford a house in the city itself. Even his sister's Indian-accented Tamil had annoyed him at the time, but that was just one more result of living amongst strangers. Once more Balachandran had tried to convince his father to return to Sri Lanka, tried to tell him that it was not like Black July anymore, that he knew people in the right places who could ensure the family would be safe. But the old man had been as stubborn as ever, claiming he had no intention of living in a land that had done what it had to the Tamils. At least here in Tamil Nadu they were Tamils, his father had said, even if they did not know how to speak the language as it was intended. And here they could live as they pleased, he had said, and Balachandran had seen the flash of eyes, heard the veiled contempt the old man felt for the people whose orders his son followed.

They were already in Tagong Pagar, and the streets were crowded with people and traffic. The city seemed as noisy and chaotic as Colombo, but somehow infinitely cleaner, perfectly ordered. Chinese, Malays, and Indians jostled each other on the crowded pavements.

They were on a broad avenue now, and Balachandran noticed, through the trees that lined Eu Tong Street's centre island, a huge fortified complex on his right, on the far side of the avenue. Armed police guarded the entrance and patrolled the perimeter fence.

"What's that place?" he asked the driver, interrupting his description of the nearby Pearl City Park.

"Ah. Police, mister, police," came the answer. "Big police barracks. Narcotics, CID, everything. Very safe area this is. And Damenlou Hotel is just round the corner. Very good, *la*."

Fucking superb, muttered Balachandran to himself as the taxi turned down Smith Street. Who the hell decided on *this* hotel anyway? As if there weren't enough things that could go wrong already, they had to be billeted next to the Pentagon.

The taxi pulled up outside the small budget hotel. In contrast to the concrete canyons of the main road, this street was lined with old colonial era buildings, and the Hotel Damenlou was one of them. In fact the whole area reminded Balachandran of a cleaner version of the Fort in Colombo.

"This is a very good area, mister." The Sikh driver was still talking as he hauled Balachandran's suitcase out of the boot. "Good pubs and nightclubs. Try the Alphabet. Very good. I can take you there." He handed Balachandran a small cheaply printed business card. "There is my mobile number. You call me tonight, *la*? I take you everywhere."

Balachandran made noncommittal sounds as he walked into the hotel with the driver following. He glanced at the card, which proclaimed Jawant Singh to be a *"taxi driver and tour guide"*, and pocketed it.

After he had paid and tipped the driver, he stepped up to the reception and signed in. The room had been booked for him through a travel agent in Colombo. The other members of the team would be scattered through this and other similar hotels in Tagong Pagar. All the bookings had been done separately, through different travel agents.

There was a message from Suresh at the reception, telling Balachandran to call him once he was in his room. The message gave Suresh's room and extension numbers.

*   *   *

2340 LOCAL (1740 GMT): The humidity hit Jennifer Jensen — Jen-Jen, to both friends and colleagues — like a hot dishrag thrown in her face, as she opened the door of the Airbus A340. It never failed to make her gasp, like falling into a bathtub. She smiled automatically at the passengers filing past her and down the gangway, wishing them a pleasant stay in Sri Lanka. But she wasn't really seeing their faces. Jen-Jen sneaked a look over their heads and through the door, at the lights of the arrivals terminal, glowing orange in the distance. She wondered whether Tim would be there to meet her. Maybe he had gotten away from Trinco early.

When the passengers had all disembarked and boarded the low-slung buses that would ferry them to the terminal, the crew secured the aircraft and left it. Even though they were allowed special privileges, as crew members, such as not having to queue through immigration and customs, Jennifer Jensen decided she hated the Bandaranaike International Airport at Katunayake.

It had been almost a year since Air Canada had started flying into Colombo; a year since she had first set foot on the island and fallen in love with its charms and unexpectedness. A year since she'd met Tim Ferguson. But even though she loved this country with its friendly but cynical people, she couldn't bring herself to like its air gateway.

The airport, like many the world over that had been built or hastily expanded in the 1970s, was lit in a cold manner, its tiled floors and stark walls harsh and unforgiving. But at Katunayake the harshness went beyond the lighting. It had an air of desperation; of people struggling to escape; a mood of nervousness and fear that was relieved only when you left its premises, or when the wheels of your plane left the ground. Part of the reason for this atmosphere was the crowds of migrant workers that thronged inside the airport and outside, travelling to or from the Middle East. Many of those departing were obviously poverty-stricken, often the sole bread-winner in a large family, their every possession mortgaged to cover the airfare and the employment agent's fee. For these people the airport authorities held the power of life, able to cancel a booking on the mere suspicion that a passport or a visa was a forgery. Petty officials and security guards went to great lengths to prevent a smooth flow of people, harassing and frightening helpless housemaids on their first trip out of the country.

In arrivals, newly-rich returnees talked in forcibly loud voices, each trying to outdo another in their accounts of the jobs they now held. They were usually flashily but tastelessly dressed.

Loose black leather trousers over orange trainers, leopard-spot dresses and bright eye shadow. They mingled with quiet, tired European tourists, standing in irritated discipline as the returnees argued and pushed and jumped the queue.

The hard-eyed, rifle-toting Air Force sentries that prowled the airport didn't help things either. Their numbers had been doubled since the LTTE attack the previous year, and gave the airport the look of a military base rather than a civilian transport hub.

Every time Jennifer Jensen flew into Colombo, the same thoughts assailed her, and every time they did so, she shook them off by reminding herself how happy she was not to have to fly into Madras anymore.

Walking with the rest of the crew, she breezed through customs and walked into the meeting area. As the doors slid open, half a dozen local men stepped compulsively forward, their bodies acting before their minds told them that Jen-Jen and her companions were crew members with their own transport. These men had a monopoly on the taxis that plied the routes between Katunayake and Colombo city, and they endlessly nagged incoming tourists for business.

She saw a tall figure in the background of excited brown faces and smiled with relief — Tim. Wheeling her carry-on bag behind her, she increased her pace, meeting him at the exit. Jen-Jen was tall, almost five feet eleven, but Tim was easily six inches taller than her, and when she ran into his arms, he swept her off her feet in a bear hug. She ignored the whispering Sri Lankans standing around and kissed him.

Tim Ferguson was a big man as well as tall, and the blonde stubble on his face made her realize he had probably got in straight from the field. He was a hydro-engineer with Agrican, a Canadian agricultural development organization that operated in Sri Lanka. He was attempting to improve and redesign some of the irrigation systems in the country's dry zone.

Jen-Jen had met him on her third stopover in Colombo. She had been sitting on the terrace of the Mount Lavinia Hotel, having a drink with one of the other stews, when a hulking blonde-haired man had walked over and asked whether he could join them. Surprised, but amused, taken in by his obvious good looks, the two had consented. He said he had noticed their Canadian accents, and was dying for lack of company. He had been in Sri Lanka over a year, and it was only his second visit to the capital. He said his work in the Eastern Province took up too much of his time. Though Tim Ferguson had chatted politely to both women, it had been clear that he was captivated by Jen-Jen, by her jet black hair and striking blue eyes.

That chance meeting had been the beginning of an on-and-off relationship that they shared whenever she was in the country. Tim had shown her a side of Sri Lanka she'd never have known without him; a side that was far separated from the polished five-star hotels and nightclubs of Colombo, the speed and glitz, fashion and pollution of the capital; a world separate even from the national parks and model villages frequented by tourists. This was a world of simple pleasures and choking poverty. In this other Sri Lanka, village schools were closed by curfews that were not imposed by government order, but by wild elephants invading a road. It was a world where middle-aged farmers ploughed their fields with water buffalo — a snapshot from another century — while their children hungered for Nike shoes and dreamed of jobs in the big city.

By the time Tim released her from his embrace, the rest of the Air Canada crew had disappeared down the covered walkway to their bus. Tim took her bag and they walked out to the car park. Minutes later, his Agrican Landcruiser was roaring up the airport road.

"Will you have time for Trinco?" he asked her once they were past the Air Force checkpoints and on the Colombo Road.

He worked in Trincomalee, the Eastern Province's largest city. It also neighboured the huge air and naval base of China

Bay. On many of Jen-Jen's previous visits he had taken her to the nearby village of Nilaweli, the beach hotel there a haven of calm in the middle of the war.

"No," she replied with a shrug. "Wish I could, but I'm only here for forty-eight hours this time." Jen-Jen looked at him with a mischievous half-smile. "Any plans?"

Tim grinned back. "Well, I did book us a room at the Mount."

She laughed. Whenever the two stayed together in Colombo, Tim would get them a room at the Mount Lavinia Hotel, their first meeting place. The hotel lay a couple of kilometres south of Colombo, taking its name from the suburb that sprawled around it on a low seaside hill between the city and the Ratmalana Air Force Base. Jen-Jen had no doubt that they'd spend most of the forty-eight hours she had in bed.

Traffic was light in Colombo at this time of night, and within an hour and a half they were driving into the courtyard of the hotel. The view of the Mount Lavinia Hotel as it appeared through the trees of the approach road still had the ability to make her stare, just as it had the first time she'd seen it. It was built in the style of many of Sri Lanka's British-period mansions, spotlights making its white walls and colonnades stark against the night sky. The cobbled courtyard was enclosed on three sides by the high wings of the hotel, and a fountain sparkled in its centre. The hotel had once been the country residence of the British governor.

Tim tossed the Landcruiser's key to a valet, and lifted Jen-Jen's bag and one of his own out of the back, only to have them grabbed by a porter who whisked it away into the reception.

"I've got some papers to send to Johnny in Bangkok," Tim said as the doorman in his quaint spiked topee and knee shorts ushered them in. "If you're flying through there. He can come pick it up from your hotel."

"I'm not on the Bangkok run anymore, Tim," she replied. "I'm going through Singapore, and without a stopover."

*   *   *

The evening after his arrival, Mahesh Balachandran went out for a drink with Suresh. They walked along the sheltered pavements of Tagong Pagar Road, looking for an ATM. The buildings that lined the street overhung the sidewalks, supported on colonnades, and turning the pedestrian area into a long veranda.

The previous afternoon he had reconfirmed his seat on the Air Canada flight to Vancouver, British Colombia. There were still two days more for the commencement of the operation, but he was impatient. He had always hated the waiting, the time when fear gnawed at your stomach like slowly rising cold water.

He used his HSBC MasterCard to withdraw Singaporean dollars from the special account set up for them. Now they could pay cash and not have a credit card fingerprint that could track their movements.

Balachandran had changed out of his suit into a batik shirt and casual cotton trousers. Suresh was similarly dressed. They strolled the streets, occasionally looking at a tourist map until they found the pub.

The place was dim and smoky, crowded even though it was a weekday. Big sofas littered a lounge and bar area, and several pool tables occupied a cleared out space on the right. On the left, was an open dance floor, but it was fairly empty at this early hour.

Balachandran scanned the room, and a flash of colour on a wall caught his eye. Moving shapes glinted on the brown sandstone walls, and as he walked into the pub, he realized that they were goldfish, seemingly swimming up the face of the walls as if they were suspended in the air. But then he realized that every inch of the walls were lined with non-reflective glass. The glass stood about six inches from the sandstone, and the intervening space was filled with water, turning it into a tall, but suffocatingly narrow aquarium. Balachandran wondered at the mind of a person who could put live creatures into such an environment just to create an ambience.

The whole pub had an aquatic look, with blue carpets and ceilings, and lights throwing liquid patterns everywhere. Even the waitresses were dressed as sea nymphs, and the bartender as an oriental Poseidon.

Suresh had spotted Nireuben at the bar, and they walked over. The other three hadn't arrived yet. Balachandran had confirmed that day that the others had arrived in Singapore, and this would be the first meeting of the entire team since they entered the country. Nireuben greeted them and informed Balachandran that Ramesh had gone off to buy a pair of sunglasses, and would join them soon.

Nireuben was drinking a Tiger beer, and Balachandran and Suresh ordered the same. When the beers had been opened, the three of them swung round on their stools and leaned back against the bar, sipping and watching the crowd, chatting softly about the city.

Suresh chuckled at something Nireuben said.

"What?" Balachandran asked, not having heard the conversation due to the music.

"How does a Sri Lanka Army firing squad stand?" asked Nireuben, leaning across Suresh.

"How?" smirked Balachandran.

"In a circle," answered Nireuben, poker-faced.

Suresh laughed again and Balachandran smiled and nodded his appreciation.

Ten minutes later, Ramesh arrived and helped prop up the bar.

The pub was teeming with prostitutes of all ages and races, but most seemed to be Chinese or Malay, and in their late teens. They worked through the crowd, eyes roving, fingers stroking potential customers to life. Two of them now moved across to the four Tamils at the bar. Both were Chinese, not much over sixteen, in tank tops and micro mini skirts that couldn't have been more than six inches from belt to hem. The first girl stepped up between Balachandran's knees. She was short, just over five feet, and her small breasts pushed into Balachandran's crotch as he sat on the high barstool. Her palms stroked his thighs.

"Buy me a drink, mister?" she breathed up into his face.

Balachandran looked down into her almond-shaped eyes. She was incredibly beautiful, and he wouldn't have believed she was a whore if he'd seen her elsewhere. He had never fucked a Chinese woman, and he could feel the beginnings of an erection pushing at her cleavage. She could feel it too, and wiggled her breasts invitingly.

Suresh leaned over from his stool. "I checked one of these out day before," he said in Tamil. "They are hot in bed, brother. Want to have a go?"

By now the second girl had climbed onto a free barstool, and she slowly crossed her pale legs, giving them an eyeful of her transparent black panties.

"Want some friends for the night?" she asked.

"We already have too many friends," Balachandran replied in English, pushing the first girl gently away.

With contemptuous shrugs the girls left. They weren't going to waste time convincing the four men when there were many potentially willing customers in the place. The other three men looked at Balachandran with mock disappointment, but they understood his reasoning. The operation was a mere forty - eight hours away, and this was no time to lose focus.

Balachandran grabbed hold of a sea nymph who was gliding past. He had noticed some cubicles beyond the pool tables and flashing a couple of notes under her nose, he got her to arrange one for them.

They had just sat down when the last two members of the team arrived and crowded into the cubicle. They began to go over the plan once more.

"Any news from Colombo?" Nireuben asked.

"We'll get the final word only after takeoff," replied Balachandran. "We're to go through with it as if it's confirmed. If it's aborted, we'll just have to cancel everything an' fly home."

*   *   *

1945 LOCAL (1345 GMT): The clearing was newly-cut from the scrub jungle and its soil was loose and dry, the dust storm raised by the hovering Mi-17 helicopter horrendous. The DFI superintendent turned his face away, pulling his fatigue cap lower. The landing lights of the chopper cut through the darkness and the swirling dust, and he watched the uniformed figures, faces wrapped in scarves and eyes shielded by goggles, race from the cover of the low bunker to unhook the heavy pallet as it touched down beneath the chopper's belly.

It was about time the radios got here, the superintendent decided, turning to peer into the surrounding jungle. He had already been here for a full two days while the bunker was constructed. Oh, well, he'd had worse billets than the old Anglers' Club with its spectacular view of Clappenberg Bay. He hoped the Special Task Force platoon that had been detached for this security detail was keeping its eyes and ears open. Trincomalee was largely a safe area now, but you never could tell, and the big Russian helicopter would be a tempting target.

It had been a while since the superintendent had commanded a platoon in the jungle, and it had to be something pretty bloody important to have him chewing dust out here. Well, orders were orders.

As the Mi-17 was relieved of its load and pulled away, turning towards the sea, the DFI officer lifted his walkie-talkie to pull the platoon perimeter in tight.

*   *   *

1500 CENTRAL EUROPEAN TIME (1400 GMT): By Tuesday afternoon, all the preparations were complete. Sandra had been briefed, and was back at her post in the van outside the Sülz apartment block. Bandara was on his way to relieve her, and Sumith was napping in the patrol's flat. Kamal had left on foot, to pick up a late lunch for those in the flat from a nearby Vietnamese restaurant. Dayan was watching *CNN*'s broadcast of the continuing war in Afghanistan and the recent heightened tension between India and Pakistan while he stripped down one of the compact MP-5K — *Kurz* or short — submachine-guns for the umpteenth time. His eyes didn't leave the TV screen as his hands smoothly stripped and reassembled the weapon.

The feel of the cool metal and plastic parts of the German-designed SMG eased the tension he had been feeling ever since the previous day's planning session. A niggling thought that he had missed something vital kept bugging him. The others had been right about the terras' attack formation looking wrong. Logic said that the centre vehicle — the van — should be the primary. But it was impossible to hit Holzmarkt Bayenstrasse from there, he told himself for the thousandth time. But what if they had mistaken the target? What if the terras were aiming for something that his team had missed?

The ringing of his mobile phone interrupted his thoughts. Wiping his greasy hands on a rag, he picked up the phone. A glance at the call-back display showed him that it was Sandra.

"Dayan here," he said into the phone.

"Dayan, the terras are off!" Sandra's voice was shrill with suppressed excitement. "It looks like the attack's today."

"What?" he said, trying to stay calm. "Are you sure? It's two days early."

"I'm watching them right *now*, Dayan!" she snapped. "They're getting into all three vehicles in front of my eyes. And they loaded two sports bags into the van. Mus' be the weapons."

"OK, Sandra." Dayan was talking rapidly. "Call Bonn an' find out if the consul general has brought his trip forward unexpectedly. Call me back as soon as you know. And as soon as the terras're out of sight get over to Bickendorf an' watch Kumaradeven. We'll take this."

"Be careful, huh?" he heard her say, but he was already hanging up.

"Sumith!" he yelled as he speed-dialled Bandara's number. What a fuckup this was turning into. "Get up, the hit's today!"

Sumith came stumbling out of the bedroom as Bandara came on line. He was tugging on his jeans unquestioningly, reaching for the ski bag that already contained the MSG-90 rifle.

"Banda, hold on," Dayan said, then looked up at Sumith. "*Machan*, the hit's going down today. Dunno what the fuck is going on, but the terras are mobile with all the vehicles and their weapons. Get your arse over to the Severinstrasse overpass. Keep your phone on you, but we'll come up on comms as soon as we're in the area." He returned his attention to the phone again as Sumith ran for the door. "Banda, did you get all that? Where are you?"

"About two hundred metres from Barbarossa Platz. I heard everything. I'm turning off now and heading for the bridge. Where do we meet?"

"Under the bridge, on the east bank. I'll bring your *Kurz*." Dayan was already scrambling into his boots and jacket. He grabbed the weapons and ran for the door, dialling Kamal.

When Dayan's call came in, the fourth member of the SF patrol was already standing in front of the Vietnamese cashier, about to pay for the food that was waiting in little cardboard cartons. Ever the soldier, Kamal grabbed the food, slapped down enough money to cover the price, and ran out onto Bonner Strasse. Dayan was swinging the big Audi A6 out of its parking spot when Kamal came sprinting up, his mouth stuffed with a spring roll.

"Want one?" he mumbled as Dayan handed over the wheel to him and strapped into the passenger seat.

"Yah, gimme." Dayan grabbed a roll and tossed the carton into the back. He pushed the two black submachine-guns into the foot well as the car screamed down Ubierring towards the Rhine. "Turn left at the river," instructed Dayan, then cursed as the steaming hot spring roll burned his mouth.

Sandra phoned to say that the consul general was happily at his desk in Bonn, and that Jayawardene was checking on any possible alternate target. She herself was on her way north to Bickendorf. Everything was going to shit, decided Dayan. They had no idea what the target was and no one had the terras in sight.

He switched on the radio and did a comms check. "Alpha, comms and status check," he said.

"Charlie in position," Sumith confirmed.

"Bravo going east across the river," announced Bandara.

"Anyone have eyes on the terras?"

"Negative."

"Negative."

By now Kamal was driving across Sionstal and taking a right-curving feeder that would bring them into the eastbound lane over the bridge.

"Alpha, I have you in sight," called out Sumith.

As they reached the centre of the bridge, Sumith came on the air again. "Terras passing below me now. Confirm X-ray, Yankee, and Zulu. They're about five hundred metres behind you, Alpha."

Dayan turned to look over his shoulder, but could see nothing of the terrorists in the traffic.

"Bravo at RV."

"Rog."

Kamal was turning off the main road and back towards the river when Dayan's phone came alive again.

"Dayan, it's Sunil," said Jayawardene's voice. "Listen very carefully."

For an insane moment Dayan was reminded of the female resistance fighter in the British television comedy 'Allo 'Allo, whose regular line was, *Listen very carefully, I will say this only once*, while the other characters constantly asked her to repeat herself. If the situation wasn't so serious, Dayan would have burst out laughing.

"I just saw an internal DFI memo mentioning that there's a Canadian trade delegation in the country," Jayawardene went on. "They're on a sightseeing tour of Cologne today, and one of their stops is the Chocolate Museum. They're supposed to meet the press outside and answer some questions in just ten minutes."

Dayan cursed, asked Jayawardene to try and warn the Canadians, and hung up. Kamal already had them on the riverbank by now and they could see Bandara's VW Passat up ahead. A grassy picnic area stretched down to the water on their right, with students lounging around and soaking up the early spring sunshine. Looking across the Rhine, Dayan could see the flash of the museum's angled glass panes.

Of course. It was a perfect shot from the Severins Bridge to the viewing deck that fronted the museum's riverside.

"All call signs, this is Alpha. Terra target is a Canadian delegation in the Chocolate Museum. Target is three hundred metres north of the bridge on the tip of the west bank pier."

"Roger, Alpha," answered Sumith. "Terras are at the east end of the bridge now."

The three SF soldiers squatted down behind their cars, backs against the bodywork, facing the river, as the van and two cars of the terrorists roared north past them. The terrorists were headed up Siegburger Strasse, and would soon turn inland and circle around to get back into the westbound flow of traffic that would take them across the Rhine.

"Alpha and Bravo at RV," Dayan informed Sumith. "Terras passing now."

"Rog."

Dayan nudged Kamal. "Did you spot the numbers?"

"Two in the van and one in each of the cars," came the answer.

"So the van is the primary, then." Dayan was craning his neck, trying to follow the terras' progress. "OK, all call signs, Yankee is the primary," he said. He was keeping the radio on so that Sumith would get the good news. "Alpha will hit Yankee, Bravo will hit Zulu. Charlie, you take X-ray."

"Rog."

"OK, it's a go!"

The terras had disappeared round a corner, and the Sri Lankans piled into the two cars. Kamal put the Audi into gear and they roared off in pursuit. Behind them, Bandara let them cover three hundred metres before following.

*

Through his binos Sumith watched the blue BMW lead the trio of terra vehicles onto the bridge. They were at the limit of his 25x40 binoculars, but he could still make them out. He would switch to the less powerful rifle scope when the vehicles reached their pre-assigned positions. He had parked the bottle-green Alpha Romeo station wagon on the overpass, and Sumith now crouched by its front passenger door, looking over the stone parapet. The car was illegally parked and he hoped a cop wouldn't arrive just yet. It wouldn't do to have a policeman look into the vehicle and see the big semi-automatic sniping rifle resting against the front seat.

"X-ray, Yankee, and Zulu in sight."

"Roger. Alpha fifty metres from the bridge."

When Sumith saw the BMW's right signal indicator come on, he lowered the binos and picked up the rifle. He rested the bipod on the stone parapet and locked his knees, snuggling his face against the MSG-90's adjustable cheek comb.

The night before, Sumith had stripped the rifle's working parts and re-oiled them. He had left the scope alone until dawn, when he had driven with Dayan out to the Stadtwald, a huge park between Lindenthal and Junkersdorf on the western edge of the city. As soon as there was enough light to see a half-kilometre, Sumith had quick-zeroed the 12-power scope. He had earlier created a bench rest by securely tying and taping the rifle across a sturdy wooden armchair, and he had then pinned a square of white card to a distant tree trunk. Sumith had been tempted to use a homemade suppressor to muffle the single shot, but worried that the device would affect the trajectory of his bullet. In the end he had resigned himself to doing without it, hoping that no one would recognize the shot for what it was. After skewing the rifle and chair round to his satisfaction, Sumith had made sure the chair was well seated into the soil; and taking no chances, he had made Dayan sit in the armchair, adding his weight to it. Crouching down, Sumith had fired a single shot at the target, both soldiers wincing at the report, Dayan in spite of his earplugs.

Through the scope, Sumith had noted that his shot was slightly high and to the right of the crosshairs, showing up as a dark spot on the white card. Using the scope's turrets, he had cranked the crosshairs across till they sat squarely on the bullet hole. The rifle was now quick-zeroed to five hundred and fifty yards, the range he had thought he would be firing at. It wasn't perfect, but they couldn't have risked the multiple shots a proper zero would have needed, and it was good enough for firing at large vehicle targets.

Sumith now quickly clicked in the required minutes of angle for the new range, not trusting himself to hold off the necessary thirty-six inches of elevation required to take the BMW under fire. He had enough to worry about with the gusting crosswind.

Though the scope was not as powerful as the binos, it had better definition, and Sumith now laid the crosshairs on the BMW's windscreen as it pulled off the road and onto the pavement, instinctively dropping his aim slightly to compensate for the downhill trajectory. The driver showed no sign of getting out, and Sumith couldn't see beyond the windscreen's reflections. Nevertheless, he steadied the crosshairs below where he guessed the driver would be.

His field of vision through the scope wasn't wide enough to take in the van, so he would have to wait for the word. Sumith began to exhale slowly, emptying his lungs and steadying his pulse. He ignored the traffic driving past behind him, trusting the car to block him from casual view. It wasn't a pedestrian area, and he was sure the hit would be done in minutes.

"Alpha engaging," Dayan's voice crackled in his earpiece.

"Bravo engaging."

Sumith didn't reply or acknowledge, slowly squeezing the MSG-90's trigger past the kilo and a half pull-weight that would release the firing pin.

*

Dayan saw the brown Renault Espace van's right signal indicator begin to blink as it started to pull to the side of the road less than a hundred metres ahead.

"Follow them in," he said, and Kamal steered the Audi in.

The van rocked and bounced, its body pan screeching against concrete as it mounted the high pavement. Pedestrians turned to stare, then screams rang out and people began to run as two ski-masked figures burst out of the van.

Dayan had released his seatbelt when they had got onto the bridge, and now he cocked the stockless MP-5K as Kamal slowed to a halt alongside the pavement, ten metres behind the Espace.

"Alpha engaging," he snapped, opening the door and diving out.

The van blocked his view of the two terrorists, and he gripped the double pistol grips of the submachine-gun with both hands as he crabbed to the right.

In a second he was clear of the van and had the *Kurz* up and ready to fire. The two terras already had the 66-mm rocket launchers extended and on their shoulders, standing side by side at the railing, aiming downstream. Two open sports bags sat at their feet.

Everything went into slow-motion as Dayan saw the nearer, smaller figure — it had to be the woman — whirl and lower her launcher. She was dropping the 66 now, her eyes bugging through the ski mask, scrabbling at her jacket and screaming to her companion, who lowered his eye to his own launcher's sights once more. Dayan saw the pistol come out of the shoulder holster, sweeping across the woman's chest, and he squeezed off a three-round burst.

The hammering roar of the *Kurz* seemed to slam everything back into normal speed, and Dayan saw the woman pitch back into her partner just as the man fired the 66. The whoosh of the rocket launch made Dayan's heart sink. I've fucked it, he thought. Anger and frustration threatening to cloud his vision, he gritted his teeth and fired a longer burst, fighting to control the jumping SMG. The *Kurz* was less than two feet long, and with no butt stock, was a tough weapon to hold steady on full auto. Ten 9-mm bullets stitched the male terrorist from hip to head and he dropped like a stone.

Before Dayan could look round, he heard Kamal shout, "He missed!" from behind him.

A glance downstream showed him a white column of water settling back into the river a dozen yards to the right of the museum. He could see crowds on the viewing deck of the museum, running like disturbed ants. Still covering the fallen terras, he stepped up to them and put the last two bullets in his fifteen-round magazine into their heads.

He noted that the two open sports bags held the spare rocket launchers. Somewhere inside the van, Dayan could hear the shrill tone of a mobile phone.

"Yankee down," he said into his lip mike, even as he heard automatic gunfire from behind him and the boom of Sumith's MSG-90 from the western end of the bridge.

*

"Bravo engaging," Bandara said as he pulled on the Passat's handbrake. He opened the driver's side door and rolled out. He heard a screech of tires as a Volvo swerved to avoid the open door.

The Opel Corsa was parked on the road, not on the pavement, its hazard lights on. The driver was standing in front of it, leaning against the hood, and he whirled at the sound of tires. Seeing Bandara, he drew an AKSU-74 carbine from his trench coat.

Bandara saw him crouch behind the Corsa to fire, the carbine levelled, and realized he'd never get his own *Kurz* up in time. He dropped flat onto the wet road and heard a burst of gunfire. At first he thought it was the terra, then realized it was further up the road, from the van's position.

Bandara popped up to his knees to fire but found the terra was no longer there. The Corsa's rear windscreen exploded outwards as the Tamil fired a burst of 5.45-mm rounds from the car's interior. Instead of ducking for cover as bullets thumped past him and into the Passat, Bandara put two bursts into the Corsa. The little car's engine gunned to life, and it rocketed into reverse, smashing into the Passat.

Bandara realized that the driver, seeing his westward escape route cut off by Dayan and Kamal, was trying to go in the opposite direction, and the Passat was blocking his path. Traffic whizzed past the two cars, horns blaring in protest at the affront to orderly German roads. The Tamil drew forward a few feet and then reversed again, crunching into the heavier Passat in a vain attempt to break out.

Crouched on the road side of the Passat and, realizing his own position was hopeless, and probably dangerous, Bandara looped around the car's rear and onto the pavement, trying to flank the Corsa and get a killing shot at the driver.

"Yankee down," he heard Dayan announce, and then dropped flat as a burst from the AKSU blew out the Corsa's front passenger window. The little two-door hatchback was falling apart from the volume of fire being directed at it from inside and out.

Finally, the terra gave up on the Passat and reversed directly into the overtaking traffic in a suicidal attempt to get around the obstruction. The Corsa was instantly hit by a Mazda sports car that rammed it forward a dozen yards. More cars piled into the wreckage in a cacophony of screeching tires, rending metal, and shattering glass.

Seeing his chance, Bandara sprang to his feet, reloading as he ran to the Corsa's passenger door. Looking in through the twisted window he met the driver's dazed eyes as he lifted his head from the steering wheel. Blood was soaking into the ski mask. Bandara levelled the *Kurz* and emptied the fifteen-round mag into the man.

"Zulu down," he announced and started to run west along the bridge.

A quick glance at the Passat had shown him that it was irretrievably hemmed in by the piled up traffic.

"X-ray mobile west," came Sumith's frustrated voice over the net.

*

Sumith's first round had punched through the BMW's windshield, leaving a white splash like a thrown egg, and sending the driver diving out of his door. Sumith could now hear bursts of gunfire as Alpha and Bravo took on their targets. The driver of the BMW was crouched by the left rear wheel of the car, scanning the road ahead for a sign of his attacker.

The wind was gusting, as Dayan had warned, and Sumith tried to compensate for it and for the fact that he was firing downhill. He had to aim low and to the left. But even so, his second shot missed as well, raising a puff of concrete from the pavement.

Now no doubt realizing that his comrades' own attack was falling apart and that he was in danger of being pinned down from two sides, the terra started to creep forward, using the car as cover. Sumith traded accuracy for volume of fire, and began pumping bullets into the car and its surroundings, trying to keep the man pinned down until Dayan and Kamal could deal with him. But in spite of the fire, the terra crawled into the car and started to pull away from the pavement.

"X-ray mobile west," Sumith warned the others, still firing at the approaching car. But it was even harder to hit a moving target with the wind as it was.

"Roger, Alpha mobile west," came Dayan's reply.

The BMW closed to two hundred and fifty yards, and more of Sumith's shots began to strike home. If he kept on this track, Sumith knew he would have him for sure. But then the BMW swerved suddenly, taking a right turn into an exit that curved back and down towards the Rhine. Sumith lowered the rifle as the car disappeared down the exit ramp.

"X-ray did a right turn back towards the river."

*

Dayan acknowledged Sumith's warning as the Audi headed across the bridge. He slapped Kamal on the shoulder.

"Faster, you bugger. You're driving like an ol' granny."

With a grin, Kamal shifted gears and stepped on the accelerator. Behind them, they could hear the wail of police sirens.

"Bravo, check."

"Bravo on foot west across the bridge," Bandara panted.

"Get down to Holzmarkt Bayenstrasse an' stan' by."

"Rog."

"Charlie, get down to the river, too," Dayan ordered. "All call signs, X-ray maybe trying to get to the target to finish the job."

Kamal took the car into a screaming right turn off the bridge, tires squealing in protest as they rocketed back towards the river. As they turned onto Holzmarkt Bayenstrasse, the two men saw people streaming down the road, running from the direction of the Chocolate Museum. Panic was on many faces, on others just worry.

"There!" Kamal snapped, swinging the wheel.

Between the road and the river, lay a grassy park - like area, dotted with trees and framed by flowerbeds. On the far side of the park, a paved pedestrian and cycle path ran along the waterfront. The blue BMW was stalled in the grass with white smoke billowing from under the bullet-riddled hood, the driver's door open. The car was empty. Through the trees, Dayan could see the pier and the museum, and the narrow footbridge that connected the bank to the pier. The bridge was choked with people fleeing the museum, and Dayan saw a couple of uniformed policemen trying to control the crowd. There was no sign of the BMW's driver.

"Come on!" Dayan said to Kamal, and they both ran diagonally through the park, trying to get to the bridge before the terra got there. "All call signs, check," he panted as they ran.

"Charlie on foot south along the river. Ah'm fifty metres from the museum."

"Bravo. Ah'm still on the bridge. Can't get down. Cops everywhere."

"Stan' by, Bravo," Dayan answered. "Charlie, can you see X-ray?"

"Negative, Alpha."

A burst of submachine-gun fire up ahead made Dayan raise his *Kurz*. The crowd seemed to ripple like water, people screaming, and he saw a policeman go down. He zeroed in on the running terra, now just short of the footbridge, but there were too many figures in the way.

"Fuckfuckfuck. . ." Dayan muttered, trying to push people out of the way, aiming the *Kurz* one-handed. "Kamal, can you get him?"

The taller man was up on tiptoe, trying to aim his pistol over the heads of the crowd, but it was hopeless. "No shot."

"Charlie has eyes-on," came Sumith's breathless voice. "Fuck, he has a grenade, he's —"

Dayan heard the thudding double-tap of a Browning Hi-Power. The crowd was scattering now, and he sprang across the dead cop. The man's partner, a policewoman, lay belly down on the paving stones, uninjured, wide eyes staring at the blood spreading from her colleague's body.

As the crowd parted, Dayan and Kamal both saw a fallen figure ahead. He wore black jeans, jacket, and a ski mask. The man lay facedown, his hands under his body, and his legs scrabbling feebly for purchase on the wet paving stones. Sumith was fifteen metres beyond the terra, still running, pistol held in both hands.

Dayan and Kamal dropped to their knees to cover Sumith as he reached the fallen man. Bracing his feet shoulder-width, Sumith pointed the Hi-Power at the terra's masked head and shot him twelve more times, emptying the mag.

"X-ray down," he said unnecessarily, looking up at Dayan.

A mobile phone in a holder clipped to the terra's belt began to ring.

"All call signs, ERV, ERV, ERV!" Dayan said into his lip mike as he and Kamal ran back to their car.

"Alpha, Bravo here," came Bandara's whisper. "The cops are all over my car. I had to dump the *Kurz* in the river. Shall I leave the Passat an' fuck off?"

"You'll have to bluff it out, Bravo," Dayan informed him. "If you abandon the car, the cops'll trace it back to the rental place anyway, an' then they'll have us. Get to a supermarket an' buy some strong detergent. And a change of clothes. Wash your hands thoroughly, dump what you're wearing, an' then go back an' talk to them. Say you got scared when the shooting started and ran. Copy?"

"Roger."

The reason for the detergent and the change of outfit was in case the police checked Bandara's hands and clothes for gunpowder residue.

Dayan and Kamal were just getting into the Mercedes when Dayan's phone rang.

"Dayan, it's me," said Sandra's excited voice in his ear. "My boy here is making a move. Ah'll stay with him, no?"

"Is he going by car?"

"No, he's walking to the underground, it looks like, an' Ah'm following. He's got a suitcase with him an' looks pretty nervous. He's bound to spot me if I get on the train with him. Are y'all finished there?"

The last question was as innocuous as a wife asking her husband whether he'd finished the marketing. Dayan grinned and confirmed that the hit had been a success and that there were no friendly casualties.

"Call me as soon as you know where he's headed," he said, "an' we'll cut him off."

"He dialled two numbers a few minutes ago, but didn't get an answer. Not five minutes later he was out'f the house. Don't know who he phoned."

"Our friends by the bridge, I think," Dayan answered. "When he didn't get an answer, he must've realized there was a cock-up. D'you think he's going to the main station to take a train out of the city?"

"If he is, he'll have to switch at Appelhofplatz. Ah'll call you when I know. Where are you now?"

"Couple of minutes from Bayenthal."

"Gotta go," she whispered. "The train's coming. I left the van keys in the exhaust."

* * *

Sandra watched Kumaradeven step onto the train, and got into the carriage behind his. She had already bought a ticket at the machine on the platform, and now she worked her way up to the end of the carriage. Unlike regular trains, the subway had no connections between carriages, but through the glass partition, she could watch Kumaradeven. The man seemed very much on edge, eyes jumping from face to face. He had shaved his beard off at some point that day or the night before, leaving only a moustache, but long hours of watching the man had made it possible for Sandra to have recognized him just from his gait, even if he had been wearing a disguise. She hung onto the overhead handrail with one hand, using that arm to cover her face as she watched him.

A few stops later, at Hans-Böckler-Platz, Kumaradeven left his seat and Sandra thought he was going to get off. The station was used by the *Regional Express* and *Regional Bahn* lines that ran south out of the city, and would be ideal for a quick getaway, but then she realized he was merely giving up his seat to an old woman.

However, at the next stop, Friesenplatz, Kumaradeven did start to edge towards the door. There was no direct connection from here to the Cologne central station, Sandra realized, so he was obviously not going there. This stop was actually a proper station, larger and crowded with rush-hour commuters, and it was easier for Sandra to pass unnoticed. She punched in Dayan's number.

"He's switching trains at Friesenplatz," she said as he answered on the first ring.

"Where to?"

"Dunno yet."

"We're standing by."

Sandra followed him through the mall that was part of the upper level of the station. Kumaradeven stopped frequently to look into shop windows, and she knew he was checking his tail. Although she ducked into doorways or sheltered behind knots of people, she couldn't be sure that he hadn't spotted her. She wished she was armed. She held the provisional rank of an Army lieutenant, but she had never fired a pistol in her life. She wondered whether the Tamil was armed. He was wearing a tan trench coat that he kept buttoned up, and she decided he could have a weapon under it.

When Kumaradeven took the stairs down to the Number 5 *U-bahn* line, she knew she had fucked up. This train would take him direct to the central station, and he wouldn't have to switch at Appelhofplatz.

She got Dayan on the phone and gave him the good news, then jumped aboard the train, a couple of carriages down from Kumaradeven. By now she was sure Kumaradeven had spotted her. There was no reason for him to have switched trains at Friesenplatz unless he wanted to test her. If he saw her again at the *Hauptbahnhof*, he'd be sure.

Sandra prayed Dayan would get to the main station before her, but she knew it was a futile hope. The station was only two stops away.

When she got off the train at the main station, Kumaradeven was already on his way to the escalators, hurrying through the crowd. Maybe she was clear, she thought and, with renewed hope, followed him up to the surface level. He crossed the main central hall of the station, weaving through transit passengers who were standing around smoking or sitting on their bags, and headed for the ticket office.

Sandra glanced through the huge glass-panelled entranceway to the Dom beyond, hoping to spot Dayan striding in, but was disappointed.

"We're at the *Hbf*," she hissed into the phone. "Where *are* you?"

"Stuck in fucking traffic close to Appelhofplatz. We'll be there in a few minutes. What's the situ?"

"He's buying a ticket."

"Where to?"

"He's still in the queue. Ah'll have to go closer. Call you back."

Kumaradeven was one person away from the head of the queue for the *Inter-City Express*. Behind him, a huge Scandinavian with an even bigger backpack, stood patiently. Sandra joined the queue, taking cover behind the backpack. Kumaradeven stepped up to the counter and Sandra heard him ask for a ticket to Paris.

Peeling out of the queue, she walked quickly out of the ticket office. Checking the huge status board in the entrance hall, she noted the platform number for the *ICE* to Paris. It was leaving in twelve minutes. She jogged down a hallway, watching out for the platform number, and when she spotted it, raced up the escalator to the platform. Once out in the open air, she lit a cigarette and stood behind a drinks machine from where she could watch the two escalators.

Five minutes later, Kumaradeven emerged from the further stairwell, but instead of boarding the sleek white train sitting at the platform, he put down his suitcase, lighting up as well. He seemed much calmer to Sandra now, less suspicious. Maybe he had been just dying for a fag, she told herself. But why wasn't he getting on the train? Was he just having a last smoke or was this all a ruse to cover his tracks?

Sandra glanced at her watch. There were four minutes more for departure. Her phone rang.

"Dayan here. We're in the car park. Where are you?"

"Platform Two. Get here fast. He's about to get on the *ICE* to Paris."

She rang off and watched Kumaradeven grind out his cigarette. But instead of boarding the train, he headed back down into the far stairwell. What the fuck was he up to now? He was cutting it really close. There were barely two minutes left.

Passengers on the *ICE* were waving their final goodbyes to friends and relatives on the platform.

Sandra took the nearer stairwell down to the entrance hall level, and as she stepped out of it she realized she could not see Kumaradeven on the other side. Whatever he had in mind, he was moving fast. The escalators and stairs connecting the lower level to the *Inter-Regional* and *Inter-City* platforms led off to left and right from a long tiled hallway, and now as Sandra stepped into the crowded hallway, she felt a hand grab her by the jacket and pull her off balance. The next moment she found herself nose to nose with Kumaradeven. She was staring up into his dark eyes, and could smell the tobacco on his breath. Something cold and hard jabbed into her chest, making her gasp, but before she could catch her breath, she felt a smashing blow and a pain that both burned and chilled her at the same time.

Kumaradeven's eyes began to disappear down a long black tunnel, and as she struggled to breathe, she felt the floor come up and hit her in the back. His eyes were gone, and even the ceiling lights were dimming. Her throat felt coppery and dry.

*

Dayan jogged through the crowded entrance hall, sidestepping people and jumping over small dogs, luggage, and other obstructions, Sumith following him. Kamal was parking the car. If Kumaradeven got on that train, it would mean a long chase, possibly into France and as far as Paris. Dayan preferred they end it right now.

They ran past escalators and spotted the Platform 2 sign up ahead.

"Go left," snapped Dayan, heading for the right stairwell.

A knot of people were clustered around the bottom of the dual stairs and escalator on the right. Dayan pushed through the protesting people and almost tripped over Sandra.

He looked down in shock into her open eyes. Blood speckled her pale lips and swamped her pullover. With a curse he raced up the escalator and out onto the platform. The white *ICE* was already pulling away from the platform, its windows blurring as it gathered speed.

"*Fuck!*" There was no sign of Kumaradeven anywhere.

Sumith shrugged helplessly from further down the platform.

"Sandra's down!" Dayan shouted to Sumith and lunged back down the stairs.

Kamal was already there, bending over Sandra's still form. Several people standing in the crowd were using mobile phones to call for an ambulance. As Dayan and Sumith got there, Kamal looked up, his fingers bloody.

"She's dead, *machan*."

Dayan felt for a pulse at her throat, hoping Kamal was wrong, but there was none. Kamal had ripped up Sandra's pullover to get at the wound. Her white bra was soaked crimson, and two dark-ringed bullet-holes stood out against the pale skin between her breasts. Dayan could only stare, his gaze flicking from her blank hazel-green eyes to her breasts. All he could think off was that last night, when he had looked into those burning eyes, felt those breasts fill his hands, the nipples scraping his palms.

He was snapped out of his daze by Kamal hauling him to his feet.

"It's too late, Dayan," the big SF soldier said, trying to hold Dayan's gaze steady. "We have to get the fuck out of here before the cops come. By the time we finish answering questions, Kumaradeven will be long gone."

Sumith turned back from where he had been looking at a train schedule mounted on the wall. "That train gets to Aachen, on the Dutch border, in thirty-five minutes. If we drive like mad we might jus' get there in time."

Dayan nodded numbly. "OK, le'ss go."

Before they left, he bent and tugged Sandra's pullover back over her breasts. Then they turned and ran for the entrance. Dayan speed-dialled Bandara's number as they ran.

"Banda, where are you?" he asked, when the man answered.

"The cops finally let me go, but they kept the car as evidence. I had to take the underground."

Dayan could hear trains in the background as Bandara spoke. "Where *are* you?" he snarled, in no mood for long conversations.

"Neumarkt. I'm about to change to get to Bayenthal."

"Don't. Keep going to Bickendorf. Sandra left the van outside Kumaradeven's. Key's in the exhaust pipe. Take it and go over to Sandra's flat. Clear out any of our stuff that's there. Then go back to our flat and clear the place. Don't leave anything behind. Once that's done get us another base. Anything. Even just a bed-and-breakfast place. Kumaradeven's on a train headed out of the country. We're going after him by car. Might catch him at the border."

"Fit. Is Sandra coming back to her flat or what?"

Dayan sighed. "No, Banda. She's dead."

CHAPTER 15

The big Audi A6 seemed to hug the surface of the *autobahn*, rocketing along. Kamal had his foot firmly down on the accelerator and they were doing almost a hundred and sixty kilometres per hour, well over the one-thirty recommended by the highway code. Dayan sat in the front seat, map-reading as Kamal skilfully threaded the car through the westbound traffic. Sumith was in the back, eyes peeled for police cars. It was 5pm and dusk was already falling over the countryside. Kamal had the headlights on.

There wasn't much talk except for Dayan's occasional terse instructions. The other two knew how much Sandra's death had affected him and held their silence.

As it got darker, Dayan studied the map by torchlight, trying to concentrate on a route that would shave a couple of minutes off their estimated time to Aachen. The city sat almost astride the borders of Germany, Belgium, and Holland, and whichever way he looked at it, the A4 *autobahn* seemed their best bet. There may have been shorter routes, but the secondary roads would force them to slow down.

He tried to shut his mind to Sandra's death, but the sight of her eyes staring up at the station ceiling haunted him. He cursed. What was the matter with him? She had been an Int officer, she knew the risks involved. But the fact remained, Dayan knew, that she hadn't been trained for this sort of covert operation, and he shouldn't have let her tail Kumaradeven. But, he argued with himself, he had had no choice. They were spread too thin on the ground, operating in unknown territory, and had been trying to cover all the options. But another part of him, a part deep inside, told him that she had been a woman, and he had been her lover, and he should have been there to protect her.

*

Dayan had seen many women killed in his war, on both sides. He had killed many of them himself. The first human being Dayan Premasiri had ever killed had been a woman. It had been on his first major operation, back in 1995. He had finished basic training just in time to join the 4th Singha Rifles on Operation *Riviresa* — sunbeam — the campaign that would ultimately recapture Jaffna from the Tigers after twelve years of being the capital of the rebellion. Their brigade had been advancing on a three-battalion front, and Dayan's Bravo Company had been the lead company of his unit. They had been close to Nirveli, northeast of Jaffna, when they sprang a huge ambush and were cut off. For three days Bravo Company had been pinned against an open expanse of salt marshes, fighting for their lives. The Air Force hadn't had enough choppers to pull them out or reinforce them, and the riflemen had fought in place. On the first day they had captured a platoon of teenaged Tigers. They were raw troops — like Dayan — in their first battle, and when their adult officer had been wounded they had surrendered. The officer had been dispatched by casevac chopper to brigade HQ for interrogation, but there was no room for any more prisoners on the Huey. With not enough rations to feed the prisoners, nor troops who could be spared to guard them, OC Bravo had ordered their execution. The job had fallen to a makeshift squad of replacements who had just joined the regiment, Dayan amongst them. The OC had felt it would be good training for the recruits.

Dayan still remembered the teenaged LTTEers, some no older than fifteen, boys and girls. There had been around twenty of them, filthy and bloody. Male and female, they had all been thoroughly beaten at the time of their capture, frightened and angry riflemen taking out their frustrations on a visible enemy.

But none of them had been raped, not even the older girls. OC Bravo, like most Sri Lankan company-grade officers, would not put up with such an outrage. Many of them veterans of two wars, they easily condoned the torture or execution of women and children, if it served a military purpose, but with a peculiarly slanted sense of honour, wouldn't tolerate rape.

The prisoners had been turned loose on the edge of the salt flats and told to run. Dayan and the other replacements had then been ordered to hold their fire till the prisoners had made a hundred metres. Not a single teenager got beyond two hundred metres, but several had been merely wounded, screaming and crying as they lay in the sun-baked mud. The NCOs had then asked for volunteers to mop up the wounded. Four were picked, Dayan one of them. He had joined the Army to kill Tigers. Well, he might as well find out what it was like, he had told himself at the time. Besides, anyone not volunteering would definitely be picked for any shitty jobs in the near future.

The four volunteers had been detailed to work in pairs, one doing the killing, while the other covered him. The wounded were obviously unarmed, but since it was good training, they would proceed on the grounds that they were mopping up after an actual action. A corporal had been told to accompany each pair to make sure everything was carried out according to orders, and to provide any needed instruction. There had been only three wounded, and Dayan and his partner had been asked to deal with one, while the other team took care of the other two.

The actual job had fallen to Dayan, and the wounded terrorist had been a girl of about sixteen. She had been shot twice, through the small of the back and one leg, and lay face up, crying softly. The NCO with them had shown Dayan how to bayonet the girl under the ribs, searching up for the heart, pointing out the exact spot for the blade, and afterwards how to roll the body over, using it as cover against any hidden grenades. When the corporal hadn't been watching, Dayan had used his bayonet to slice off one of the girl's ears. He had intended to keep it as a souvenir, but threw it away several days later when it began to stink.

The girl's face was the only one of his kills that Dayan ever saw in his dreams.

It had also been soon after that battle that Dayan had decided special operations was where he wanted to be. After the fall of Jaffna, he had been evacuated to the military hospital at Palaly with a bout of malaria. After his release, he had been with a fatigue party loading ammo onto Hueys for resupply flights to frontline infantry units. Nearby had sat a group of men waiting to be airlifted off the peninsula. They had not looked anything like the regular troops that filled the airbase. Their British- and Pakistani-pattern DPM fatigues were sun bleached and mud stained to an almost uniform ochre, their long hair held back by bandanas and headbands. Hard, cold eyes stared out of cammed up, bearded faces, and they carried their assault rifles as if they had come out of the womb with them. Many of their headbands had the word DELTA printed on them with marker pen, and Dayan had discovered later that the men belonged to Delta Group of the 1st Commando Regiment, and that they had been part of the special operations units that had set the stage for the following offensive. Six months later, Dayan had applied for a transfer to the Commandos, only to be told that he would have to wait seven months before he'd be considered for the next intake. He had, however, been offered a chance to take the selection test for the Special Forces, a unit just as hard as or harder than the Commandos. Eight months later, Dayan had been one of fourteen volunteers — all which remained of the eighty who had begun selection — to be badged with the eagle, sword, and crossed arrows of the SF.

*

The Audi had just crossed the Erft Canal, west of Cologne, and was burning through the Kerpen *kreuz* where the A4 crossed over the A61, when Dayan's mobile phone rang. It was Bandara.

"You buggers can turn round an' come back," came Bandara's calm voice. "Guess whose tail Ah'm on?"

"*What?*" Dayan sat bolt upright in his seat, and the other two stared at him. "Are you sure?"

"I had jus' got to Bickendorf when I saw Kumaradeven's wife come out an' get in their car," explained Bandara. "So I followed her. She drove to Barbarossa Platz, and our friend was waiting outside the underground."

"Where are you now?" Obviously, Dayan realized, buying a train ticket to Paris had just been a ruse. And Kumaradeven had killed Sandra to cover his tracks. While they were chasing the train, he was taking a different route.

"Turning east off Luxemburger Strasse in Klettenberg, onto Militärringstrasse. Either he's going to get onto the A4 at Marienburg and keep going east, or south along the A555."

"Hold on." Dayan was peering down at the map. "Take the Blatzheim turnoff," he said to Kamal. "We need to get onto the southbound A61."

"What?" said Bandara on the phone.

"No, not you. I was talking to Kamal. Stay with our friend. My bet is he'll take the A555 if he wants to get out of the country. The A4 will just take him deeper into Germany." Dayan thought for a second. "Can you hit him before he gets on the *autobahn*?"

"No way, *putho*," Bandara replied. "Cologne's crawling with cops. They'll nail me for sure. An' anyway," he added, "I didn' have time to pick up a weapon."

"OK. Keep me posted an' stay with the bugger. We'll take the A61 south and try to cut him off close to Bonn."

"Better hurry up. This bloody van isn' so fast, an' if he spots me I won' be able to stay with him."

"Stay with the fucker if you have to *fly*, Banda. No excuses. We'll get there as fast as we can."

By now, Kamal was taking them back east on a secondary road, past the town of Blatzheim, on a route that would connect them to the A61.

"Where d'you think the bugger's going?" Sumith asked from the back.

Dayan spoke without looking up from the map. "Well, if he's still trying to get to France, he'll stay on the *autobahn* past Bonn, then continue south on a B-road through Trier and Luxembourg, and into France. That's the most obvious route."

"We know he's a sneaky bastard," spoke up Kamal. "Wha'ss the not-so-obvious route?"

"He'll turn onto the A61 *autobahn* south of Bonn, then follow it down past Koblenz to Ludwigshafen, then on to Karlsruhe and across the French border further east. He'll be able to get right into Strasbourg." Dayan pondered the proposed route. "Basically he'll follow the Rhine upstream till it reaches the border."

Sumith leaned over the seatback, looking at the map over Dayan's shoulder as Kamal turned onto the A61.

"Why don't we take this route, then?" asked Sumith after a few minutes, tapping the map. He was indicating a network of *autobahnen* that ran almost due south from Bonn to the French border. "We could go through Saarbrücken, cross into France and cut the fucker off on the French side, before he reaches Strasbourg."

Dayan thought about it for a while, then shook his head. "After the shit hitting the fan in Cologne, the border security might be tight. Ah'd prefer to catch him in Germany. An' we'd be cutting it too fine if we try to get him north of Strasbourg. No margin for error." He ran his finger over the map. "Ideally, we should nail him once he's on the A61, and before he reaches Koblenz."

Bandara phoned in a few minutes later, to confirm that Kumaradeven and wife had filled up with petrol, and were on the A555 to Bonn. Over the next twenty minutes, Bandara would call periodically to give the Tamil couple's location, and it became gradually obvious to Dayan and the other two that they would reach Meckenheim — where the A555 met the A61 — before Kumaradeven. This was an advantage they hadn't counted on. If that were the case, they'd just have to slow down and allow

Kumaradeven and Bandara to catch up. They could bracket the terrorist and hit him.

Dayan forced his mind to remain objective, to fight down the anger that threatened to cloud his judgement. He told himself that he could savour the feeling of revenge against Sandra's killer after the man was dead.

As they passed through the Meckenheim *kreuz*, Dayan checked with Bandara on the target's progress.

"Three klicks away from the Meckenheim *kreuz*," Bandara reported. He also told them that Kumaradeven was keeping his Ford Focus scrupulously to the speed limit, but that he, Bandara, was struggling to stay with him in the heavy van.

"Don' worry, Banda," Dayan assured him. "We're ahead of you now, so we'll jus' let him catch up."

Soon Bandara was calling to say that they were approaching the *kreuz*, and that Kumaradeven had his turn indicator on. He would follow the target through onto the A61.

"Notice the amount of cops around?" Sumith said from the back.

For the first time Dayan noted that he could see several green and silver German *polizei* cars and vans travelling in the same direction as they were. He recalled that he had seen many more since they had left Cologne.

"It'll be a job to hit the bugger an' get away," pointed out Kamal.

"We'll just have to wait for our chance," answered Dayan. He had no plans of giving up the hunt. "We have time, no? Maybe we can't get him before Koblenz, but it's still at least a couple of hours to the French border."

The phone interrupted them. "He's not turning," Bandara said tersely.

"Shit."

"Yup. As soon as I put my signal on, the bugger switched his off and went straight. I had to follow, an' now I'm sure the bugger has spotted me. He's increasing speed, an' I dunno how long Ah'll have him in sight."

"Fuck. Look's like he's going straight through Trier for the Luxembourg border. Do what you can, Banda, we'll have to get off this road and across to you. But by the time we get onto your route, we'll be well behind you."

Dayan cursed himself; he had taken it for granted that Kumaradeven wouldn't take the obvious route. The man was probably panicking and wanting to get out of the country as quickly as possible. Examining the map, he saw that while the A61 ran southeast, the B257 that Bandara and their prey were on ran almost southwest. Another secondary road ran east and west and connected the two routes through the town of Ahrweiler, forming, respectively, the base and two sides of a triangle. If they took this latter road, they would be back on the trail of the terrorist.

"Take the Bad Neunahr turnoff," he told Kamal.

For the next fifteen minutes Kamal pushed the powerful car to its limits, racing along the winding B road. The road took only single lane traffic, and Kamal gave several German drivers near heart attacks as he pulled into the oncoming lane to overtake slower vehicles, suicidally playing chicken with trucks, their closing rate over two hundred and fifty kilometres an hour. The SF soldiers, however, didn't bat an eyelid as they rocketed mere inches away from destruction. For Sri Lankans, this was everyday driving back home.

In spite of all the risks and speeding, Bandara announced that he was passing through the Burg Are intersection of the two routes a full fifteen minutes before the Audi was due to reach it. He still had intermittent sight of Kumaradeven's Focus, but wasn't sure how long this would last.

There was more traffic once the B257 was reached, and Kamal had to slow down, much to Dayan's frustration. He consoled himself with the fact that if they were being delayed, so was Kumaradeven. They were driving through the wooded hills of the Eifel range, fir trees standing like dark giants in the headlights, and the terrain slowed them down further.

Once more, the Sri Lankans were struck by the number of police vehicles that seemed to be patrolling the roads, with no definite intention apparent.

"Target turning east onto B258," reported Bandara.

Dayan bent over the map once more, trying to figure out what the fugitive was trying to do now. The B258 opened into a network of roads between Nurburg and Mayen, and eventually connected back to the southeast-northwest-running A61 *autobahn*. Kumaradeven was apparently trying to shake Bandara off by heading back away from the border. Dayan noted that east of Nurburg, the B258 forked, both roads eventually reaching the *autobahn*, but over a dozen kilometres apart.

"Banda, close up with him," Dayan ordered. "We're about ten minutes behind you. You have a major fork coming up, and we need to know which road he takes."

"No chance, Dayan," came back Bandara's tense voice. "Almos' no traffic, an' the bugger is speeding up. I can't stay with him."

"OK. You take the southern route, we'll take the northern."

They would have to sweep both roads, and hope that Kumaradeven would head for the *autobahn* once he was sure he'd lost Bandara.

By the time their Audi was back on the A61, half an hour later, there was no sign of Kumaradeven. Bandara was approaching the *autobahn*, further southeast, but was having no luck either. For the next hour, the van and the Audi switched positions and speeds, searching desperately for their quarry, but knowing with each passing minute that it was a hopeless quest. Kumaradeven had given them the slip. They didn't even know if he was still on the A61. He could have taken any of the dozens of back roads that crisscrossed the area. Fatigue and disappointment weighed heavily on all of their minds, but especially

Dayan's, as they raced through the hills of the Hunsrück, the *autobahn* paralleling the Rhine, fifteen kilometres distant.

Various options were thrown around the car as they drove. Sumith suggested they tip off the police that an armed terrorist was running for the border. That way, even if they couldn't kill Kumaradeven, they could make sure he was arrested. Dayan pointed out that they didn't even have proof that Kumaradeven was still armed, and there was very little the police could hold him on. Kamal stated that this maybe so, but at least it would put them in contact with the Tamil again.

They were passing Alzey, and would soon be close to Ludwigshafen. From there the French border wouldn't be more than half an hour away. Whatever they decided, it would have to be soon.

Bandara, several kilometres ahead, saved Dayan the trouble of a hard choice by calling in at that moment.

"Got him!" the man shouted over the phone. "Eyes on."

"Where?" demanded everybody in the Audi simultaneously.

"There's a petrol shed about three klicks before the Worms turnoff. I saw the bugger's car outside the restaurant. Didn' see him, but it's his car for sure. I saw that Garfield sticker he has on the back. Didn' want to risk him seeing me so I didn' stop."

"OK," Dayan said. "Slow down, but keep going. We'll pick him up." He could barely control his excitement at this second chance.

When they turned into the petrol shed and rest area, the Ford Focus was sitting exactly where Bandara had described it. It was empty.

"You buggers put some air in our tires," Dayan suggested. "Ah'll go an' get us something to drink an' see where our friend is."

Dayan knew it was possible that Kumaradeven had merely abandoned the Focus, and he needed to confirm that the trail wasn't already cold.

"Don't spook him," warned Sumith in farewell.

Walking towards the restaurant, Dayan saw two police cars parked beyond it. Several policemen and -women were standing around the vehicles, drinking coffee out of plastic cups. He noticed a couple of them watching him, and kept walking. He couldn't believe that this police presence was just because of the Cologne incident. It looked like part of an overall security measure. He finally guessed that the Germans were just wary of any more trouble. Probably didn't want a running urban guerrilla war in their country, he decided.

A babble of German from the adjoining restaurant met Dayan as he stepped into the mini supermarket. Most of the tables were occupied by travellers who had stopped for dinner, and many of them had their attention diverted from their plates by a television mounted on the wall. Dayan wondered idly for a moment what could be so interesting, but then saw Kumaradeven standing in a queue at the cash counter. He had two cans of Sprite cradled in his arms, and some bars of chocolate. Grabbing several Cokes, Dayan joined the line behind the Tamil. Kumaradeven tensed immediately as his eyes fell on Dayan's obviously South Asian features. For an instant, Dayan thought the Tiger would drop everything and run.

"Vhyarabout Indiyar are you from, *yaar*?" Dayan asked, his English thick with a Punjabi accent.

For a moment, Kumaradeven stared blankly back, his eyes narrow with suspicion. Then he visibly relaxed and started to turn away.

"No, no. I'm from Sri Lanka."

"Ahh."

The LTTEer quickly paid and headed for the door as Dayan stepped up to the counter. Paying and collecting his change, Dayan walked out, spotting Kumaradeven standing outside the toilets, smoking. Without a second glance at the man, Dayan walked past. As he was stepping out into the chill night, he saw a Tamil woman come out of the toilet. She was dark and long-haired, her eyes wide with barely controlled fear. Then Dayan was out in the darkness, walking quickly towards the Audi.

The three SF men sat in the car, sipping at their Cokes until they saw Kumaradeven and his wife get into their Focus and leave. Kamal let them make a hundred metres, then followed, Dayan informing Bandara of their progress.

"I still don't get what the fuck all these cops are doing here," grumbled Kamal.

Dayan explained his theory, but decided to phone Major Sunil Jayawardene to check.

The Int officer had already heard about Sandra Koch's death, and in answer to Dayan's query about the police, chuckled. "Don't you fellows listen to the news? Why don't you switch on the radio?"

CHAPTER 16

The long narrow length of Ziegestrasse was crystalline clear in the Schmidt & Bender scope's 12 x 42 sight picture, teeming with morning rush-hour pedestrians and cars. Most of the street was shadowed from the rising sun by the closely-built nineteenth-century architecture of Berlin's Mitte area. The man behind the scope crouched perfectly still, relaxed but focused, the scope eye hardly blinking. He had been in this position for half an hour, waiting. He knew he only had a few more minutes before his target would appear. Walking people filled his vision, crowding beneath the crosshairs like termites. But the man behind the scope ignored them. He was not interested in them. All his concentration was focused on an intersection three hundred and thirty yards west. Specifically on a small corner kiosk that sold Indian and Sri Lankan snacks, cigarettes, newspapers and other odds and ends. The sniper could see the middle-aged man sitting behind his counter, sipping tea and reading a magazine.

The sniper was in his late twenties, with the dark complexion and slim build of most Sri Lankan Sinhalese. He was dressed in a dark pullover and black jeans, with short hair and a neat Vandyke beard that gave him the look of a yuppie executive on holiday. The only features that distinguished him were his eyes and hands. His eyes were large and deep-set, dark, with long curling lashes. They were almost effeminate, but with a cold penetration that made it hard for people to hold his gaze very long. His hands were almost obscenely large for his frame, thickly veined, and with long powerful fingers. At the moment they were wrapped around the L-96AWS 'takedown' rifle that the sniper held snuggled into his cheek and shoulder.

The fourth-floor flat itself was unremarkable. A spartanly furnished room and kitchenette, made somewhat noisy by the window that opened onto the intersection of Ziegestrasse and Monbijoustrasse. What was unusual about the room was the fact that every inch of the walls, floor, and ceiling were lined with mattresses. Only the door and one window remained free. The lights were off in the room, and its interior was gloomy, untouched by the morning sun that was brightening the sky behind it.

A table had been placed against the wall opposite the open window, and a straight-backed chair placed on top of it. The sniper sat on this chair. In front of him, also on the table, stood a small stepladder. The sniper was resting the rifle's bipod on a step of the ladder, elbow on knee, aiming through the window. The mattresses at his back had been untidily daubed with dark floor paint in order to hide his silhouette.

He moved the scope away from the kiosk and let his vision drift further up Ziegestrasse, through the canyon of dark buildings and the red-roofed Friedrichstadtpalast, to the next intersection at Friedrichstrasse.

At precisely 8:12am, a cyclist crossed through the intersection, as he did everyday at the same time, and turned down Ziegestrasse. The cyclist wore a brown bomber jacket and dark suit trousers, a small backpack below his hunched shoulders. He rode with practiced ease, moving fast, on his usual route from the underground station on the other side of the River Spree to the office of the World Council of Churches which had given him and his staff the use of a portion of their premises off Oranienburger Strasse, further north.

The sniper followed his progress, but didn't try to lead him. He knew his moment would come at the next intersection. He watched as the Tamil wheeled to a halt by the corner kiosk. The man behind the counter didn't look up, merely slapping down a newspaper and a breakfast packet of string hoppers before scooping up the proffered money. As the cyclist unfolded the paper and scanned the headlines — a daily habit that the surveillance team had noted — the sniper fired a single shot. The muzzle flash of the rifle was suppressed by the black cylinder screwed onto the muzzle, and what little wasn't, was dulled by the gloom and depth of the room. The report of the 7.62-mm round, also suppressed, was further deadened by the mattresses and was unlikely to have carried even as far as the apartments on either side of this one. However, as a precautionary measure, both had been rented at the same time as the centre one, and were empty. Only a corner of the building could be seen from the intersection to the west, only a single vertical row of windows, and if anyone happened to notice an open window, the dark-painted mattresses at the sniper's back hid any silhouette.

Three hundred and thirty yards away, the head of the LTTE's European arms procurement network tumbled against the kiosk, his bicycle clattering to the pavement, as the bullet punched into his head, blowing away the left side of his skull as it exited.

Everything was still and quiet in the room on Monbijoustrasse. There was a faint smell of cordite in the air. In the scope's field of vision, people ran around while others attempted to help the Tamil, not realizing at first that he had been shot, thinking he had suffered some sort of seizure, mistaking the head wound for an injury he had received while falling off his bicycle. The crosshairs were the only thing that stood steady, like part of the street's architecture, lying on the fallen man as he bucked and thrashed, his spine arching, the dying brain sending chaotic signals through his nervous system. Blood spattered around him in a fanlike arc, and more blood and tissue were stuck to the whitewashed wall of the kiosk.

After a full minute, the man's limbs stilled, and when the sniper was sure the target was dead, he moved. He unloaded the rifle and broke it down to fit into the special briefcase factory-manufactured by Accuracy International for the rifle. Carrying the briefcase, he left the room, taking the ancient elevator.

The old lady who owned the building received a cheerful smile from the nice young photographer as he walked out onto the street. He had told her he was from Bangladesh, and was doing a special project on the city. In an hour, a truck would arrive to remove the mattresses that the sniper had told the landlady were for some special portraits he was doing. At the time the old lady had given him a knowing smile. She didn't care. She considered herself open-minded and was used to her tenants' various vices.

The assassination had taken place the day before Dayan's team hit the ERA terrorists in Cologne, while he and Sandra were preparing to leave Trier.

*

1430 EASTERN STANDARD TIME [1930 GMT]: Just over thirteen hours after the Berlin shooting, while Dayan, Sumith, Kamal, and Bandara had been planning their own hit, PC Danny Staminski and WPC Mary Andrews were chatting softly as they watched the tourists turn off Front Street and go past them. Faces from every conceivable race on earth seemed to file past them, chattering and smiling cheerfully. Toronto's tourist industry, already reeling from the September 11th attacks in the United States had slumped to an all-time low with the March metro bombing. In an attempt to attract tourists from new markets — especially the Far East and Southeast Asia — Canadian airlines had slashed prices and offered free tickets. The last week or two had seen a somewhat revived industry, but still nowhere near the numbers prior to September 2001.

The two police constables scanned the faces and bodies of the tourists headed towards the CN Tower. They were supposed to look for frightened or hateful expressions, nervousness, bulky clothing that could hide weapons or explosives. These individuals were to be singled out for questioning and possible search. It wasn't the most friendly way to treat foreign visitors to one's country, but this was a new world; and if not a brave new one, then an extremely nervous one.

The Ontario Provincial Police took its job very seriously, and didn't hesitate to stop people who looked suspicious. Two more policemen stood at the far end of the pedestrian walkway leading to the CN Tower, and there were more inside. Civilian flights over the city were heavily monitored and controlled.

Danny Staminski was talking about rugby football. He himself played for a small local club, and though the sport didn't have as wide a following in Canada as baseball or hockey, its fans were far more fanatical. He had been trying for days to get Mary Andrews to come to a game with him, but so far had lucked out. All she was interested in was baseball. Staminski was heavily built, with shoulders that strained his blue uniform shirt, his face florid in the afternoon air. Andrews was a contrast to him, with a small-boned face that was a heritage of her mother's Caribbean blood. She wasn't very big, but had a runner's taut, toned body.

Staminski had been talking about the rush he felt when he watched the ball being worked down the back line, but stopped when they noticed a commotion at the Simcoe Street intersection further east.

"Now what?" grumbled Staminski, hitching up his pistol belt. He hated being interrupted when talking rugby.

It looked as if some sort of protest march was trying to turn off Simcoe and onto Front Street, in the direction of the CN Tower. Police were already barricading the Simcoe Street pavement, and Staminski and Andrews could see horse-mounted troopers trying to control the crowd and move them back north.

Andrews was talking into her walkie-talkie, and soon turned back to her partner. "Looks like some Tamil protest group wants to picket the tower," she explained. "The mayor has refused them permission."

Tourists were still moving past, though some had paused to take photographs of the protesters. Staminski and Andrews tore their attention away from the intersection and back onto their job. Staminski watched the lines of people moving towards the base of the CN Tower, annoyed that some had gone through while he had been watching the protesters.

Suddenly he stiffened and nudged his partner. "Shit, look a' that!" As Andrews looked round, he was already moving, up the steps to the walkway.

"What?" she asked.

He grabbed her shoulder and pointed. "Look a' that guy over there, Mary," he said in a harsh whisper. "Look at his pants."

Andrews saw him indicating an Asian man in a thick parka. The man's cotton trousers were clinging to his legs as if they were wet, bunching at the knees and hips. But it wasn't raining.

"Warn the lobby team and back me up." Staminski was already running after the man. "Hey, you! Stop!"

As Andrews keyed her walkie-talkie, she remembered their anti-terrorism training. One of the signs they had been warned to watch out for in suicide bombers was 'sticky pants'. When a suicide bomber armed the explosives strapped to his body prior to detonating them, usually via a switch in his trouser pocket, the static electricity caused by the circuit made his trousers cling to him.

At Staminski's shout, the suspected terrorist half-turned, looking over his shoulder, but instead of stopping, increased his pace. Andrews saw her partner draw his revolver.

"You, in the yellow jacket, stay where you are! Police!"

Andrews could see that the suspect was almost jogging now, with Staminski in pursuit. Putting away her radio she drew her own .38-in Smith & Wesson and joined the chase. She was thirty metres behind Staminski, who had almost caught up with the suspect, and beyond them, she could see two more cops exiting the CN Tower lobby in answer to her warning.

Staminski had just clamped a big hand on the suspect's shoulder when the man blew himself up. The concussion flung bodies in all directions and sent glass from the lobby doors spraying through the interior. Andrews saw Staminski and the terrorist disappear in an orange flash before the blast picked her up and hurled her into the traffic on Front Street.

TUESDAY 19th MARCH 0820 GMT: While Sumith and Dayan had been returning to their flat after zeroing the MSG-90, Gunam Jesudasan was stepping out of the shower and, not having bothered to shave, threw on his clothes and headed for the door. It would take him almost forty-five minutes to get to Barking from his small house in the northwest London suburb of Stanmore. And knowing the traffic, he cursed, it would take him longer. Normally, a half-hour either way would have meant nothing to him. As administrative head of the International Secretariat of Tamil Eelam, he was his own man. But today he needed to go online as early as possible to monitor the media's coverage of the second wave of ERA attacks. They had already begun with the bombing of the CN Tower the previous day, and more attacks were planned for Tuesday, but not in the concerted manner of the first wave. Like a squad of infantrymen firing at will, the different cells would get uncoordinated after the first volley.

The secretariat's offices on Katherine Road had once been known as the International Secretariat of the Liberation Tigers of Tamil Eelam, but proscription by Her Majesty's Government had meant the LTTE moving underground in the United Kingdom.

A sigh from the bed made Gunam Jesudasan pause at the door and remember why he was late.

"Already?" she mumbled sleepily, tousled dirty blonde hair appearing over the covers.

Jesudasan's English girlfriend was an insatiable lover, and her lips and tongue had awoken him at dawn. She had spent the next half-hour in animal pleasure, straddling him, locked into a chain of orgasms that merely left him exhausted. The result had been him not hearing the alarm clock and oversleeping.

"Yeah, Ah'm late," he muttered, slamming the door behind him and taking the stairs three at a time.

Joggers were already out on the street, and people were walking their dogs or taking the kids to the nursery. There were flowers in the roadside hedges, and the street almost had a rustic charm to it. A large step away, both in distance and looks, from his old neighbourhood of Brixton.

Jesudasan unlocked the garage and walked around his VW Polo. Taking a small flashlight off a nearby shelf, he dropped to his knees to aim it up into the mud-encrusted wheel wells. He then spread an old blanket on the floor and lay flat, checking the car's underside. Ever since his meeting with Major Sundari, this had been a daily routine of Jesudasan's. He knew that London was the safest possible place he could be, but when the LTTE had decided to make this war an international one, Jesudasan had realized he couldn't be too careful. The fact that he was late wouldn't keep him from this precaution.

Once he had finished checking the car's exterior, he shone the flashlight's beam through the windows, checking the foot wells and dashboard. A quick inspection of the interior light close to the rear-view mirror showed it intact. No telltale wires to trigger a detonator as a door was opened. It was safe. He could check the ignition once he was inside.

Jesudasan unlocked the driver's side door and checked under the seat for a pressure mat. It was too easy for a common shop door mat to be used to trigger a bomb. Instead of ringing a bell to announce the arrival of a customer, it would detonate the explosives that would ring out the departure of another careless idiot.

The LTTEer climbed into the Polo's driving seat, and bent to examine the ignition mechanism. The rocking motion of the car on its suspension, caused by his entry, tripped the mercury tilt switch in the glove compartment, which in turn detonated the three kilos of Semtex hidden in the seatback. The explosives went off with a thunderous crack that snapped Jesudasan's spine like a twig and hurled his decapitated head through the windscreen. The Polo's roof had peaked upwards like a tent.

:

1315 CENTRAL EUROPEAN TIME (1415 GMT): As Dayan and his team had been racing through Cologne to the Severins Bridge, miles away in France, two men were evidently enjoying their *chapattis* and devilled potatoes. Though the Rani was a Tamil restaurant, the table was set with traditional European cutlery. This was, after all, still Paris. The two men ignored the knives and forks, however, tearing the *ghee*-fried *chapattis* into small pieces with their fingers before using the scraps to scoop up the semi-mashed potatoes.

The Rani was fairly crowded for lunchtime. The Hôpital Saint Lazare district, east of the Canal de Saint-Martin was really a bit too far from the city centre to attract the usual maul of yuppies. There was, however, amongst the South Indians and Sri Lankans, a fair smattering of Europeans who were experienced enough in southern Indian food to recognize a good restaurant.

The entire restaurant was furnished in cane, even the tables, though these had been topped with dark green glass. Dried and varnished palmyrah fronds, imported from Jaffna, covered the walls, and coir rugs softened the floor. Behind the cash counter sat the owner, a dark middle-aged Tamil in a suit, and recessed into the wall above and behind him, was a small shrine to the Hindu god Ganesh, the owner's namesake, blue elephantine features staring vacantly over the diners' heads. Sticks of incense standing before the shrine perfumed the room, and soft Tamil music played in the background. On the opposite wall from Ganesh, smiling across at this lesser god, was a larger-than-life portrait of Velupillai Prabakharan in a crisp white tunic, his grin framed by the Tamil film star moustache he had affected in the 1980s.

The two men ate quickly, not talking much, except for a few appreciative comments about the food. Two bottles of cold French beer sat at their elbows, moisture dripping down to soak into the cork coasters. When they had finished the *chapattis*, one of them waved to the waiter, and when the man came over, ordered *gulab jamun* for dessert. His companion didn't stop him, instead leaning back and lighting a Gauloise. They could afford it. The restaurant owner knew who they were, and would not charge them. It was one of the reasons the old man was guaranteed his wife and daughter would be joining him in Paris next month.

The man with the cigarette was named Tony Thevarajan, and at twenty-nine was a couple of years older than his companion. He sipped at his beer and enjoyed his smoke as the dessert was served — small deep-fried balls of flour and coconut in sugar syrup. They might as well enjoy this, as it would be their last proper Tamil meal in some time. If everything went well that afternoon, after the target was hit, the two of them would have to go into hiding. They would have to stay away from the country's Tamil community and its restaurants.

Tony Thevarajan continued to smoke and sip his beer, his own *gulab jamun* untouched while his companion ate with gusto. His eyes wandered over to the next table, where two dark-haired French women were seated. They were both young, pretty, with firm bodies, and one of them held his gaze for a moment, the tip of her tongue catching a drop of *lassi* that clung to the corner of her mouth. Thevarajan had seen them here before, and the Rani's owner had told him they were both *Médecins Sans Frontières* nurses who had served in Sri Lanka. Eelam, Thevarajan had corrected the owner at the time, and now he regretted that he'd have no time to get to know them better.

He was still smoking when three Asians — all men — entered the Rani. What drew Thevarajan's attention to them, was that instead of hanging up their coats and requesting a table, they quickly crossed the room. One of the three peeled away and walked over to the cash counter, where he seemed to be whispering something to Mr Ganesh. Thevarajan frowned as he realized the other two were making their way through the tables towards his own. Something in the two men's eyes made Thevarajan put down his beer and start to warn his companion.

But before the two Tamils could move, they realized that they were looking down the barrels of two Browning Hi-Powers that had miraculously appeared from under the jackets of the newcomers.

An instant later, the two men opened fire, emptying their pistols into the two seated Tamils. Thevarajan's companion fell sideways out of his chair, hit repeatedly in the back, his convulsively scrabbling fingers dragging the tablecloth and the remains of their meal down with him. Thevarajan's body remained upright, however, head slumped back, shot fourteen times in the chest. His cigarette still hung from his lips, and his killer reached over and withdrew it. The man took a long drag on the Gauloise, then with a look of distaste on his face, dropped the butt onto Thevarajan's lap, where it hissed out in the blood soaking his shirt and trousers.

When the shooting started, diners and waiters alike had dived screaming to the floor, and now lay huddled on the coir rug. Only the three newcomers and the Rani's owner remained standing, Mr Ganesh only because he was held up by the man who had come over to the counter. The people on the floor were smart enough to stay where they were, and the three men stepped over the prone figures of the MSF nurses and walked quickly to the door. In seconds they had stepped out onto Rue de Maubeuge and were gone.

The sharp smell of cordite swamped out the incense. Only the music still played.

*

2355 AUSTRALIAN CENTRAL STANDARD TIME (1425 GMT): As Dayan and his SF team had been about to open fire on the ERA terras, on the other side of the world, Madhavan Subaramaniam was giving Darling Harbour a final glance as he turned the grey Lexus off Highway 40. He headed east along Park Street, deeper into the city of Sydney. It was already past midnight in New South Wales, but in a couple of hours he would be back on board the freighter he served on as an electrician, ready to sail. He had, earlier in the day, heard the news on the car radio of the attempted bombing of the CN Tower in Toronto. Though he had heard that the ERA had claimed responsibility for the attack, the Canadian police were full of praise for the heroic cops who had foiled the bomber before he could gain entrance to the tower.

Madhavan Subaramaniam snorted in annoyance. What did they know of heroism? What was heroism except to willingly sacrifice one's life for freedom? For a cause one believed in. To willingly give your life for any small portion that would make that cause a reality. That was heroism. Not the weak attempts of paid men who defended corrupt ideologies.

And, he reasoned, as he saw Hyde Park looming up ahead, hadn't the broadcasters themselves stated that there had been more than a dozen deaths, and many more injuries. At least four of the deaths had been cops, so it could not be called a failure. One didn't have to succeed to terrify. It wouldn't be long before the Canadian people forced their government to see sense, in turn forcing the Sri Lankans to a ceasefire.

Subaramaniam wiped all thoughts of Toronto out of his mind now as he reached Hyde Park and turned north, into Elizabeth Street. He started peering out, checking building numbers as he drove. He had never been to the Sri Lankan Consulate before, but had been given specific instructions.

The car he was driving belonged to the consulate, and its Tamil driver, complaining of a leaking oil sump, had told its owner, the consulate's chief of staff, that it needed repairs. That had been three days ago. Instead of a garage, the Lexus had been handed over to Subaramaniam's ERA cell. The deliberately damaged oil sump had been fixed, and a little surprise had been installed in the boot. A hundred and twenty kilos of ANS fertilizer mix, with a two-kilo Semtex booster charge, the whole thing timed to go off at 9am the next morning. If the car was placed in exactly the right spot in the consulate's underground garage, the resulting explosion would bring down the four-storey building.

The chief of staff was impatient to have the car back, and had been told by his driver that the garage would work through the night to have the Lexus at the consulate first thing. The driver had told Subaramaniam that the civilian security guards at the gate would be expecting him. They were both retired policemen, and were more interested in a quiet night than anything else. There would be no trouble.

Finally locating the consulate just beyond the King Street intersection, Subaramaniam turned in and stopped before the garage's padlocked gate. He flashed his headlights and saw a uniformed security guard leave the guardhouse next to the consulate's main doors.

As the man approached the car, Subaramaniam realized with a sense of unease that he was no middle-aged pensioner, but a young guy in his twenties. He also looked alert and unfriendly, annoyed by this late night visitor. Subaramaniam hated when things didn't go scrupulously to plan, but then they rarely did. He'd have to bluff it out.

"What d'you want, mate?" the guard asked gruffly as Subaramaniam rolled down the window.

"I'm from the garage, here to return the car," replied Subaramaniam.

"Never told me nothin'," said the man suspiciously. "Whose motor is it, then?"

"Dunno. Jus' told me to drive it here."

The guard turned back to the cubicle, where a second man in uniform could be seen standing in the doorway. This guard was portly and middle-aged, scratching his head sleepily.

"You know anythin' about this Fred?" called out the younger guard.

"Yeah, yeah." The older man was ambling over now. "It's just the chief of staff's motor. It's been sent away for repairs. Let 'im in, Joey."

"Bleedin' strange time to deliver a car," muttered Joey, turning back to Subaramaniam. "Got any ID?"

Subaramaniam was sweating now, but handed over the company identification card — the name was a fake — that stated he was an apprentice mechanic.

"I'd better search the car," Joey decided, and Subaramaniam's heart began to pound.

The bulb of the courtesy light in the boot had been removed, and a separate wire run to the Semtex booster charge's detonator. If the boot was opened, an electric charge would bypass the timing and power unit and blow everything sky-high. It was a precaution against the bomb being discovered.

"Let 'im in, Joey," grumbled the older man. "It's just routine."

"Nothin' routine about a car being delivered at midnight, is there?" Joey retorted. "An' what with all this terrorism going on, and all."

"You're watching too much *CNN*."

However, Joey was insistent that Subaramaniam open the boot. But instead of popping the boot, the Tamil got out of the Lexus.

"Look, I don' have time for this," he told Joey. "I was jus' told to drive the car here. If you wan' to search the car, be my guest. I'm off."

He started to walk away, north to the next intersection that was just twenty-five metres away. If he could get round the corner before they opened the boot, he just might escape the blast.

"Just a minute, you!" yelled the older guard, Fred, but Subaramaniam kept walking.

"Ah, let 'im go," muttered Joey, pulling the keys that were still in the ignition. "We'll drive it in ourselves. After we search it." He walked round to the back of the Lexus.

But Fred suddenly felt a twinge of anxiety. Instincts that had got him through thirty years as a Sydney copper were suddenly making his hair stand on end. "Look, maybe we should call for the police to come check it out."

"Bollocks," said Joey, fiddling with the boot lock. "We'll do it ourselves. That guy was just some darkie wanker."

Subaramaniam was already running west towards the waterfront when he felt the tremendous blast and almost stumbled to his knees. He regained his footing and kept running.

The explosion destroyed the entire front of the consulate, and caused structural damage to neighbouring buildings up and down Elizabeth Street, including the Japanese Embassy on the far side of the street. Windows were shattered as far as Bridge Street to the north and Liverpool Street at the southern edge of Hyde Park. The sound of the blast carried even to the far side of the harbour.

*

1700 LOCAL [1500 GMT]: While Dayan had been trying to accept Sandra's death at the Cologne main station, Francis Oakland was smiling with anticipation as he heard the guide speak, his Afrikaans casual, as if he were pointing out an interesting butterfly to his clients.

"*Haai op de aas.*" Shark on the bait.

The forty-foot cabin cruiser bobbed in the gentle swells eight kilometres off the rocky coast of Gansbaai. The water was a deep aquamarine blue in the afternoon sun. Gansbaai was two thirds of the way from Cape Town to Hotagterklip on the very tip of the Cape of Good Hope. The coast around the cape, with its ample populations of fur seals, was a year-round hunting ground for the creature the Canadian military attaché to Pretoria had come in search of — the great white shark.

Admiral Oakland had first become curious about sharks — and the great white in particular — on a visit to Italy during his Navy days. Scuba diving off Sicily, he had rounded an outcrop of reef and come practically nose to nose with a great white. It had been hard to judge at the time who was the more surprised, but Oakland had felt hot urine flooding his swimming trunks as the shark flicked on its side and dived into the blue depths. That experience had triggered a curiosity that had sent the sailor diving and boating in known shark areas whenever he had the opportunity. Though Canada wasn't as popular with great whites as the United States, he had once spotted one off Nova Scotia. When Oakland had, a year and a half ago, been posted to South Africa, he had immediately seen the opportunity to follow his aquatic hobby.

At every chance, the sailor would hire a boat and guide, load his personal dive gear, and be off into the waters where the Indian and Atlantic oceans met.

For the last year or so, Dion Terreblanche had been his regular guide. Oakland had been out shark watching with many experienced South African guides; however, no one but Terreblanche had ever brought him within touching distance of a great white. The Afrikaaner was tall and lean, with blonde hair bleached almost white by the sun and salt, and he owned a shark watching operation at Kleinmond, between Gansbaai and Simon's Town. Terreblanche had shown the grey-bearded sailor how to stroke a great white in just the right spot to avoid being bitten. Both men had done it repeatedly, from a boat as a shark rose out of the nearby water, and from the nerve-wracking safety of a dive cage.

This was the first occasion on which Francis Oakland had brought his wife along. Though his seventeen-year-old younger son John shared his interests in diving and sharks, and often joined him on his excursions, Oakland's wife did not. Karen didn't even swim very well, and was terrified of being on a boat surrounded by sharks, to say nothing of being in the water with the creatures. It had taken many weeks of persuasion before she had agreed to come along.

Except for the three Oaklands and Terreblanche, the party consisted of a second Afrikaaner — Terreblanche's first mate — and two Canadian bodyguards from the Diplomatic Protection Group.

It had been a relaxed afternoon, with everyone lounging around sipping beer and soft drinks from the icebox, waiting for the chief guests to be brought in by the bloody carcass of the nurse shark being towed astern. Now everyone was tense with anticipation. John grabbed his camera and Karen drew her knees to her chest, raising her feet off the deck and onto her seat, as if the shark might jump aboard and nibble at her toes. Oakland, Terreblanche, and John crowded the stern rail, and the Afrikaaner began to draw in the bait rope.

Soon they could see a tall dorsal fin slicing the blue water a couple of dozen metres behind the boat. A crescent-shaped tailfin swept from side to side a full eight feet behind the dorsal fin. The shark had to be at least twelve feet long, without doubt a great white.

Oakland had his eyes glued to binoculars, and John was already clicking away, squinting through the long telephoto lens. The shark followed the bait right in, and as Terreblanche lifted the dripping body aboard, the great white's snout exploded out of the water an arm's length off the stern. John's Nikon clicked frantically at the gaping mouth with the ragged teeth that gave it its name of *Carchorodon Carcharius*. The shark's cold black eye seemed to stare back at Oakland as it hung there, puzzled at the disappearance of its prey, then with a final frustrated snap, it slid back beneath the surface.

The two men and the boy just stared at each other open-mouthed, hearts pounding. All three of them had seen this before, but being that close to something so big and dangerous, something that hadn't changed much in millions of years, was more than the normal adrenalin output could handle. Not even Terreblanche, who had seen this countless times in his life, could quell the excitement and instinctive fear.

Oakland looked over his shoulder and got a grin and a thumb's up from the first mate at the wheel. He was disappointed to note that Karen hadn't even left her seat, and had missed the whole spectacle. She stared back at him with big terrified eyes, and he smiled tolerantly. But he still could not understand someone who could hang back from the sight they had just witnessed.

The attaché also noticed that the two DPG men were not interested in the shark, but had their binos trained out to sea. Following their gaze he saw another cabin cruiser, similar to their own. It was lying five hundred metres further off the coast.

Turning away from the rail, Oakland walked over to the pair. "What's up?" he asked.

The embassy had received a security warning from Ottawa after the wave of attacks in early March on Canadian and Sri Lankan interests, and the previous day's attack on the CN Tower had made Oakland momentarily consider cancelling his diving trip.

One of the bodyguards lowered his binos. "That boat's been just sitting there for a tad too long," he said. Both policemen had been out boating with the ambassador before, and were accustomed to seeing other shark watchers. "There's no one on deck either."

Oakland raised his own binos and gave the boat in question a cursory inspection. There was no movement.

"Maybe they're having a quickie in the cabin." He grinned and returned to the stern.

The afternoon progressed well, with several more great whites approaching the boat. Oakland managed to coax Karen to the rail, but she shrieked and dived for cover whenever a shark towered out of the swells. The DPG men continued to keep an eye on the other boat, but no movement or threat was visible.

An hour before sunset, Dion Terreblanche and John climbed to the upper deck to ready the big steel diving cage, while Oakland checked the scuba kit. He was making a final check on the demand valves when the sound of a snarling outboard engine made him look up.

A small fast craft was approaching from the northwest, along the coast from the direction of Hermanus. A small-boat buff ever since he had served an exchange tour with the US Navy SEALs' Special Boat Squadrons, Oakland tried to identify the speeding craft as it bounced off the swells, its bow rising clear of the water. It appeared to be about twenty-five feet long and had a fibre-glass hull, but seemed to have some sort of inflatable gunwale. It looked like a civilian version of the military RIB or rigid-hulled inflatable boat. But what was that strange structure mounted forward of the coxswain's position?

He gave up on trying to squint into the sun and was turning to tell the DPG bodyguards to check the craft out when the first

30-mm grenade slammed into the wheelhouse and ripped Terreblanche's first mate apart. The first grenade was followed at a regular rate of three a second.

The AGS-17 automatic grenade launcher mounted on the fast approaching RIB was essentially a machine-gun that fired 30-mm high-explosive rounds. As the RIB slowed to a halt fifty metres away, the man behind the AGS-17 swept the military attaché's cabin cruiser from end to end, then back again, concentrating specifically on the stern. When he stopped to reload a fresh drum, the cabin cruiser was a flaming wreck, beginning to settle lower in the water.

The man standing next to him saw movement near the dive cage slung from an articulated arm amidships, and opened fire with an M-16A1 rifle. A body fell overboard, and he then emptied the thirty-round mag into the lower deck, even though there was no sign of life.

✻

0730 PACIFIC STANDARD TIME (1530 GMT): While Dayan, Kamal, and Sumith had been speeding towards Aachen in a futile attempt to catch up with Kumaradeven, it was still early morning in Los Angeles. Kumar Arasaratnam was already at his desk, checking his email, and replying the more urgent ones. This was part of his daily morning routine, along with a cup of Broken Orange Pekoe Ceylon Tea, and a quick scan of the memos his secretary had left for him the previous evening. Kumar Arasaratnam had been told by fellow members of the *Illankai Tamil Sangam* to abstain from drinking Ceylon Tea as the money from sales helped strengthen the Sinhalese government of Sri Lanka, but he had found it impossible to comply. He felt it was his only treacherous act against the cause of the Tamils, and it was, after all, just a small one. His conscience didn't trouble him.

He still had an hour before his first meeting and, once he had finished with his mail, he went online once more. This quiet period of surf time was one of the reasons why he chose to begin his working day a full hour before the rest of the firm. The media networks were still full of the previous day's CN Tower bombing, but there was nothing new. A few, had begun to pick up on the BBC's coverage of the killing of a Tamil activist in Stanmore, close to London, and one network was even making a connection between it and the shooting of a Tamil aid worker in Berlin almost twenty-four hours previously. Kumar Arasaratnam decided to visit the TamilNet website to see what the international mouthpiece of the LTTE had to say on the matter.

Arasaratnam held deep sympathies for the men and women fighting to free Eelam from its Sinhalese occupiers. Even after he had first arrived in the United States to begin his Harvard studies, he had been a regular follower of the military and political situation in Sri Lanka, though most of his views were darkly coloured by the LTTE's version of events. These views were further reinforced at the *Illankai Tamil Sangam* meetings he attended. Quite natural, since the ITS was one of the LTTE's front organizations.

Kumar Arasaratnam specialized in immigration law, and during his time with Dawson, Primble & Wallace, had already successfully defended several Sri Lankan Tamils in their fight against federal prosecution. When Ottawa's crackdown on Tamil militants in Toronto had begun the previous year, Arasaratnam had even considered offering his services in the defence of these newly oppressed individuals. He had heavily lobbied the senior partners to be allowed to do so, but had been told firmly that if he wanted to defend terrorists, he would have to do it after he had resigned from the law firm of Dawson, Primble & Wallace. Arasaratnam had seriously considered his options, even flying up to Toronto for a weekend in February, but had realized that Toronto's own high-profile defence lawyers were jostling each other for an opportunity to defend the persecuted. Arasaratnam had decided he would bide his time, and returned to Los Angeles.

As he did each day, Arasaratnam logged onto the TamilNet site, but for the first time in six years a message appeared on his screen saying that the site in question was unavailable and currently under modification. Below, were several links to other sites that promised updates on the latest Tamil news and interests.

Frowning, Arasaratnam scrolled down the list of links. They were all familiar to him, sites that all followed the Tamil Eelam military, political and diplomatic war, with various individual leanings. For the past several days, Arasaratnam had found the TamilNet site to be strangely swinging away from its usual blatant worship of the LTTE and its leader, Velupillai Prabakharan. Previously, the site had criticized the brave but misguided attacks of the Eelam Republican Army, but called the attacks a natural result of Canada's persecution of a refugee community. But lately, the site had seemed to be actively encouraging more attacks by the ERA, and even quoted prominent LTTE spokespersons who admitted that the new terrorist group was a newly-established wing of the Tigers. Other pro-LTTE websites had immediately denied the quotations as absolute falsifications and outright lies, claiming the TamilNet site had been hacked into by anti-Tamil elements. But the controversial website continued to function, daily displaying new connections between the LTTE and the ERA. In addition, TamilNet was also openly admitting that the Tigers had sustained heavy losses in their defeats at Elephant Pass and Paranthan. It even showed pictures of surrendering LTTE fighters.

And now this, wondered Kumar Arasaratnam. What was going on? He clicked on the first of the links, and waited as the TEEDOR site began to load. It took longer than usual, but the result made the young lawyer sit back in horror and disgust. A picture filled his monitor screen, showing a stocky Asian man being sodomized by a muscular white man in military fatigues. The smiling face of Velupillai Prabakharan, the LTTE leader, had been skilfully superimposed over the Asian man's face. It was good enough to be mistaken for a genuine photograph.

Grimacing, Arasaratnam returned to the links page and clicked on the next site. The result was the same. Prabakharan smiled cheerfully back at him as he was buggered. Arasaratnam clicked at random on half a dozen of the listed links, but they all served to load up the same graphic. Grimacing and angry, the lawyer started to connect to the host server's helpline in order to lodge a complaint.

1700 CENTRAL EUROPEAN TIME (1600 GMT): As Bandara had been following Kumaradeven and his wife out of Cologne, full darkness was falling in Oslo. Though it was late March, there was still snow on the streets, the weak sunshine during the day doing nothing to melt it. The waters of the Akerselvka River were finally free of ice however, though the shoreline was still frozen.

The Tamil woman walked out of the train station onto Nylandsvelen and walked south. She didn't see the SF soldier who followed at a discreet distance. The man spoke into his jacket lapel as she turned into a supermarket. She walked through the aisles, pretending to examine various products, but checking the angled ceiling mirrors for anyone following her. When she was satisfied that she wasn't being tailed, she left.

The soldier didn't follow her, but whispered into his lapel as he picked up a packet of Marlboros and a carton of milk before joining the queue at the checkout counter.

A Sri Lankan couple examining bridal outfits in a shop window ignored her as she passed, still headed south, letting her go fifty metres before they crossed the road and walked in the same direction.

"Panther here, we've got her," the man said into the mike concealed by his scarf.

The Tamil woman walked south for a further two hundred metres before turning east off Nylandsvelen.

"X-ray's not going south," reported the man as he and his female partner crossed the road once more to maintain contact. "What's going on, Leopard?"

"Dunno, but stay with her," came the terse order in his earpiece.

"Rog."

Soon it became clear that the Tamil was still suspicious. She was leading the trailing couple into a maze of backstreets and alleys, moving steadily away from the Akerselvka River.

"This is Panther," the man said, his arm affectionately round his partner's shoulders. "We'll have to drop off before she spots us."

"Rog. Where is she?"

"Walking into a small square two hundred metres east of Nylandsvelen."

"Are you still following, Panther?"

"Negative, but I still have eyes on. She's going into a small pub on the eastern side of the square."

"Roger that, stay where you are an' watch the door till I get there. Lion claims she didn't have the bomb on the train, so maybe this is where she picks it up."

"Rog."

Three minutes later, Sergeant Kevin Fernando and Corporal Chanaka Siriwardene pulled to a halt in their black Saab at the south-western corner of the square and got out. The square was shaped like a reversed L, the vertical arm running north-south and the horizontal arm east-west. A street ran through the northern tip of the L, and it was from this end that the terrorist had entered. Two more streets met at the juncture of the L, and where the Saab sat was the entrance to yet another street, this one leading towards Nylandsvelen. At the southern end of the square was an art gallery and bookshop, and the two men crossed to it. Sergeant Fernando had already dispatched the couple south to the intersection of Nylandsvelen and Gunnerus Gate.

As they reached the store, Fernando glanced at his watch.

"What the fuck is she doing *here?*" he muttered. "The protest will reach Gunnerus Gate in ten minutes."

"Maybe she'll pick up the suicide kit at that pub and then go down to the protest march," suggested Corporal Siriwardene as they watched the pub door in the reflection of the store window.

"If she waits any longer she won't have time to get there on foot."

There had been rallies and protest marches in Oslo all throughout the day by both Tamil and Sinhalese factions, triggered by the previous day's bombing in Toronto. The culmination was a protest march by Oslo's Sinhalese community which was due to head up Nylandsvelen from the docks and turn onto Gunnerus Gate, from where it would make its way to the Canadian Embassy. The marchers were going to protest the perceived lack of energy on the part of the Canadian government to crack down further on the LTTE in Toronto. The joint SF-Int team in Oslo suspected that the ERA meant to bomb the protest march.

"Here she comes," warned Siriwardene.

The woman walked out onto a small raised terrace that fronted the pub, now empty due to the cold weather, and looked quickly around the square, scanning the parked cars. Fernando and Siriwardene slipped into the store and watched her as they browsed through books. The woman was of average height for a Sri Lankan, with a dark sulky face. The two soldiers watched her cross the square to the cars parked before a museum that formed the inside corner of the L-shaped square. With a final glance around, she unlocked a silver Mazda hatchback and got in.

"Shit, she's got a car," muttered Fernando.

After a minute or so the woman got out again and crossed the square again to a phone booth that stood before the pub. She had left her coat in the car and now wore only a tight pullover and ski pants. It was obvious she had no suicide rig strapped to her torso.

As the soldiers watched the woman in the phone booth, a voice crackled in their earpieces.

"Jaguar, Yankee's just got a call on his cell phone."

"Is he still on Gunnerus Gate?"

"Roger that."

Jaguar was a soldier watching a Tamil parked in a Peugeot 206 close to the protesters' march route. The car had been left untended the previous night, and at first the soldiers had thought this must be the car bomb. But a routine sweep of the area by the Oslo police had turned up nothing. Half an hour earlier, the car's driver had returned to it and spent the intervening time smoking.

The woman was now returning to the Mazda.

"Jaguar, what's he up to?" Fernando asked.

"Nothing. Just sitting there."

"Is he still on the phone?"

"Negative."

"He's a filler," snapped Fernando, realization dawning on him. "X-ray's got a car bomb. All teams, stan' by, stan' by!"

The woman was halfway across the square as Fernando and Siriwardene exited the store. They walked across the horizontal arm of the L-shaped square, chatting casually, headed for the museum entrance close to the Mazda. Fernando glanced at her out of the corner of his eye and saw that she had stopped dead in the middle of the square, staring at him. The next instant she exploded into motion, running towards the Mazda that now lay between her and the soldiers. Fernando swung his coat out of the way and went for the pistol in the waistband of his jeans.

"We're blown," he said into the throat mike as the Browning Hi-Power came free. "All teams, go, go, go!"

The woman was still five paces from the car when Fernando and Siriwardene opened fire together. As the first bullets hit her in the chest and stomach, she fell facedown on the cobblestones, her hands grasping at her wounds. The two men kept moving forward, still firing, the 9-mm rounds making the woman's body shudder and roll onto its side. They only stopped shooting when they could see the woman's hands and see that they held no transmitter that could detonate the car bomb. By then, both their mags were empty, and the terrorist had been shot twenty-eight times.

"X-ray down," announced Siriwardene over the net as they ran for the Saab.

"Yankee down," came the call from Jaguar.

The Saab roared out of the square, heading north. "All teams, ERV, ERV, ERV!" ordered Fernando. An anonymous call to the local police would tip them off to the explosive-laden Mazda sitting by the museum.

*   *   *

Dayan Premasiri switched off the radio and sat back. The other two soldiers were quiet, too, everyone amazed at the extent of the violence, at just how many Special Forces and Int teams were operating worldwide. Some of the SF squadrons must have been stripped bare to provide the personnel for these operations. Then slowly, the three men began to grin as it gradually dawned on them that Sri Lanka had managed to reduce the impact of the second wave of LTTE/ERA attacks. Soon they were whooping and laughing with delight, pounding the steering wheel and dashboard. Dayan phoned Bandara and told him the news as well. Morale had been restored.

But the incidents that had hit the headlines worldwide, were causing special problems for Dayan and his patrol. The high number of police cars on the roads meant that they would have to bide their time. Wait for an opportune moment to hit Kumaradeven.

The police presence also meant that both hunters and prey had to slow their speeds down to comply with restrictions. Bandara was still somewhere ahead, out of sight, but Kamal kept the Audi A6 close to the LTTEer's Ford Focus. They weren't sure if the Tiger knew who they were, but the man was staying with the flow and speed of general traffic, not drawing attention. Kamal hung about half a dozen cars back.

CHAPTER 17

While the SF team, the ERA terrorists, and in fact the entire city of Cologne had been still sleeping, Colin Peters was thanking the waiter for the tall glass of ice cold beer. The man grinned in reply, the white teeth in his round dark face complementing his brilliantly white starched jacket. The brass buttons on his jacket were polished to a dull glow, and his black trousers were neatly pressed. Colin Peters thought the whole effect was quite splendid, but spoiled by the rubber slippers the Tamil wore.

Peters savoured the cold bite of the Lion Lager, and watched the morning sun on the blue waters of the Bay of Bengal. He had had an early morning swim and a breakfast of scrambled eggs, toast, and papaya. He had already noticed the National Aquatic Resources Association driver hovering around the reception area, and knew it would soon be time to leave. One beer, and an uneventful drive would see them in the North Central Province town of Habarana for lunch at the Hotels Corporation rest house opposite the Tourist Police post. Peters had been eager to leave before breakfast, preferring to reach Negombo by midday and allow himself almost thirty-six hours of rest before leaving for the airport at Katunayake, but the NARA driver had dissuaded him. Better, the man had warned, to let the morning Army patrols sweep the road from Nilaweli to Trincomalee thoroughly before they ventured the official Land Cruiser forth.

A faint throbbing at the far edge of the sound spectrum, and a low, fast-moving dark spot on the horizon were the only things to spoil the tranquillity of the Nilaweli Beach Hotel. Peters knew it was a Navy gunboat returning to its base at China Bay from a night patrol further north.

This was a world of contradictions, marvelled Colin Peters. A world in which the only surviving beach hotel in the Northern and Eastern provinces operated in the middle of the war zone in absolute tranquillity, paying off both opposing forces. In a war zone that had left every other hotel a blasted ruin abandoned to the jungle, this one required its clientèle to book months in advance for the April season. While the vegetable fields in the surrounding countryside thirsted for the irrigation waters that held the key to a good crop, the hotel had a fully operational fresh water swimming pool. In a world where refugees displaced by the war suffered malnutrition in their camps, the hotel served one of the best lobster thermidor Peters had ever tasted; and at a mere five hundred rupees per go, around six US dollars.

Colin Peters had breakfasted in the main dining area, open on the seaward side to the ocean breezes, but had moved across to the sea bar, a wood and cadjan structure built between the swimming pool and the beach, to enjoy his beer.

Peters was an Englishman, a marine biologist with the World Wildlife Federation. Forty-five years old, tall and ascetic, with wispy brown hair, he had never been married. Throughout his life, classmates, and later, both pupils and colleagues, had suspected, though never been given proof, that Peters was gay. They were right, though Colin Peters himself at times wondered whether he really deserved the distinction since he could have counted the number of relationships he'd had on the fingers of one hand; and even then he'd have a couple of fingers left over. His passion was whales, particularly blue whales, and they were his reason for visiting Sri Lanka. The deep waters of the Trinco Trench — an underwater canyon, pointing like the finger of Neptune, straight at China Bay — could yield a wealth of marine life. But the blue, the biggest living creature ever to move across the face of the deep, was the reason Colin Peters was there. The very bar where he sat was proof of the blue's existence: the sitting area was fenced off from the beach by the vertebrae of a long-dead whale, the bones dug out of the sand years before to overawe visitors.

It was also the creature that was taking him away, across the Pacific, to Taddousac, in Quebec, at the mouth of the St Lawrence River. The blue whale had taken Peters to many fascinating places across the world, researching, examining, and trying to find a way to make sure the huge mammals would not be reduced to a fossilized memory.

He drained his beer and rose to his feet. The waiter saw him get up and came over quickly, to accept the generous tip he knew the English scientist would leave him. He was moving fast, because he knew that to delay was to lose his well-earned money to the long-tailed langurs that hovered in the nearby trees, watching their human relatives with greedy, mischievous eyes.

Peters nodded in reply to the waiter's thanks and walked around the pool to the dining area. Other waiters smiled their goodbyes as he headed through, moving briskly through reception to the white Land Cruiser parked under the porch. His bags were already loaded, and the bill paid. As they headed up the dusty road between potato and garlic fields, towards the main tarred road, Peters consoled himself that he would be able to have at least one day to relax in Negombo before he caught the flight to Vancouver.

*

1420 LOCAL (0820 GMT): As half a world away, the morning rush hour traffic had begun to fill the streets of Cologne, the usual afternoon school traffic was grid locking Colombo's streets, as it did each day, with drivers blaring horns and cursing each other as they inched along the narrow streets. It was stiflingly hot, the humidity belying the seemingly mild temperature of 27°C, and those without air-conditioned vehicles looked like they were sitting in a mobile sauna. There were many reasons for this daily frustration. One was that the city's narrow streets and avenues, most unchanged from the middle of the twentieth century, just could not handle the sheer volume of new vehicles that were registered each year. Another reason was that rather than trust their children to the crowded and inefficient public transport system, most middle-class parents hired privately owned vans and minibuses to ply the daily routes to Colombo's schools. Many who owned cars simply took their progeny to school themselves each morning, and picked them up again each afternoon. Children whose parents could not afford either, happily trotted through the dusty streets and squeezed into overcrowded buses.

Anyone who hadn't an absolutely urgent reason to be out and about, made sure they remained in their homes or workplaces during these hours.

Devini Sundaralingam, and the man driving the Nissan Sunny she was travelling in had no burning reason for being on the streets. And, in contrast to the frustration and annoyance evident on the faces of the drivers around them, the two LTTEers looked surprisingly relaxed. They could have done the close target reconnaissance at any time of their choosing, but the school time rush provided them the perfect cover.

Devini ignored the blasting horns and running children from the international school further down the road, leaving that to Jegen. At least three quarters of the children were foreigners, belonging to the families of diplomats and expatriate workers. She had her full focus concentrated on the target, though anyone watching her at that time would have noticed nothing beyond a young mother being chauffeured to pick up her child from school. The tree-lined avenue had been photographed and videotaped for her by the surveillance team weeks before, but this CTR was something she insisted on, a way for her to see the target in three dimensions, to ensure that nothing had been mistaken for what it was not, to determine that nothing had changed.

As the car inched past, she took note of the security guards at the entrance, the lack of people at the gate at this time of day. She already knew that the guards used hand-held metal detectors to scan anyone entering the premises, and that there was a telephone in the guardhouse beyond the gate. She could see the plainclothes security man behind the bullet-proof glass. She knew the guards would not admit anyone who hadn't an appointment. She also knew the security guards were unarmed.

Devini also eyed the line of trishaws parked opposite the target, the drivers lounging in their seats, smoking, or clustered together and chatting, eyeing the teenaged female students and the young mothers, on their way to and from the school. Devini estimated for the hundredth time how long it would take one of them to drive to the nearby police station, or the Army checkpoint at the end of the road, and raise the alarm.

*

Four hundred metres further down the road, Daniel Devanayagam bounced with barely concealed excitement as he watched the soldiers in camouflaged fatigues who manned the barricades. The men looked bored but watchful. The school rush-hour was the high point of a boring watch. It gave them a chance to ogle the fresh young schoolgirls from the Colombo International School in their white blouses and short tan skirts. The barricades consisted of sandbags and concrete-filled oil drums, and they almost entirely blocked the avenue in a series of fortified revetments. A narrow opening allowed a single vehicle to zigzag through. Across the front of the barricade was a red and white barrier, similar to one at a rail crossing, which could be raised and lowered. The avenue was closed to everybody but residents, due to the fact that one of its exclusive addresses was occupied by the Foreingn Ministry.

Daniel Devanayagam was interested in neither the soldiers, nor the schoolgirls. They were part of his daily routine of travel to and from his Roman Catholic school in Maradana, one of the city of Colombo's fifteen numbered divisions. At the age of twelve, Daniel was just beginning to realize that the shorter a girl's skirt was, the tighter the feeling was he got "down there". Today, however, this was not the reason for his excitement.

The van that deposited Daniel at his school each morning, and collected him once more each afternoon, was already half full of students from half a dozen different institutes, both male and female. Colombo's state- and church-run schools were both almost exclusively gender-specific. It was a holdover from the British public school system. The van now sat in the traffic jam, facing the military barricade beyond the intersection, waiting to turn into the crawling flow of vehicles moving past the Colombo International School.

Today was the last day of school for Daniel, the end of term before the long April holidays and the Sinhala and Tamil New Year. He knew the international school students had another two weeks of classes, their semesters following the American system, and normally he'd have felt some pity for them, but today his excitement allowed him no room for other emotions. He wondered whether Suzie would be waiting outside the international school for the van.

Suzie was a Canadian, a year younger than Daniel, and his only friend in the van. A shy boy, Daniel had found the girl's big blue eyes and unyielding curiosity about everything bringing him out of his shell. It had been her curiosity that had made her ask him, on the first day they had met, a year ago, about the scar on his knee. He had told her about his fall from the rambuttan tree on his father's Malwana estate. That answer had spurred a series of fresh questions, and the friendship had begun.

However, it wasn't even the prospect of meeting Suzie that was at the core of Daniel's excitement. It was the fact that tomorrow he would be flying to Canada. It was the first time he would ever have been aboard a plane, and it thrilled him to his soul. And better still was the thought that Suzie would be going with him. She had flown many times and had offered to explain everything to him. Daniel had scorned the offer, claiming to know everything there was to know about planes and flying, even if he had never been in the air himself. He had watched *Top Gun* twice on video, and *Air Force One* thrice. It was true that the plane they would be boarding wasn't an F-14 Tomcat, but it wasn't so different from Harrison Ford's 747, was it?

Ever since the news had arrived that *Amamma*, living with Daniel's uncle and aunt in Scarborough, was critically ill, and demanding to see her children and grandchildren, it had been an agony of waiting for the twelve-year-old. It had taken several weeks for the invitation letters and tickets to be got, and even then, there was no guarantee that the embassy would let them go. It had taken a letter from a Toronto doctor, plus *Appa*'s proof of ownership of the Malwana estate, to tip the scales. The visa officer had been reassured that the Devanayagam family would be returning to the island.

Suzie's family was going home on holiday to Calgary, and she would be missing the last two weeks of school. It had been discovered just a week ago, that the two families were booked on the same flight.

The van finally squeezed through the intersection in a flurry of horn tooting and arm waving by the Sinhalese driver, and eased to a halt in front of the school. The rear door had been barely slid open — like a Huey gunship door in *Platoon*, Daniel had always thought — when a ball of blonde energy blasted through the opening and pounced on the seat Daniel had been saving for her.

"What time are you leaving home tomorrow?" began the usual barrage of questions.

* * *

1745 CENTRAL EUROPEAN TIME (1645 GMT): Dayan wondered why Kumaradeven didn't just surrender to the cops and save himself. It was what he would do if the situation was reversed. Maybe the man was under orders to get out of the country no matter what, he speculated. Or maybe he just fancied his chances at dodging his pursuers and escaping.

They were just crossing the Ludwigshafen *kreuz* west of the city, and Dayan realized that Bandara would now be pretty close to the *Kreuz* Mutterstadt. This was where it was assumed Kumaradeven would turn onto the A65 that would take him in a long curve down to Karlsruhe in the south, close to the border.

"Banda, take the A65 turnoff south," Dayan instructed. "Towards Karlsruhe. Are you there yet?"

"Rog, one klick away."

Five minutes later, they saw the Focus start to slow and switch its turn signal on. Kamal followed, as did several other vehicles, but it must have been obvious to Kumaradeven that he had gained a new tail. As they climbed the ramp on to the A65 and joined the stream of traffic, the soldiers realized that the Focus was already out of sight, having obviously made a drastic increase in speed. With a curse, Kamal pulled around a big Scania truck with French plates and slammed on the sauce, cutting across gesticulating European drivers in an effort to get into the left-hand lane. He rapidly took the powerful car up to a hundred and eighty kilometres per hour, and they soon had their quarry in sight. The Tamil was obviously onto them, and was using the fact that there were no cops in sight to zigzag through the traffic.

Dayan had just warned Bandara that the Focus was gaining on him, when the SF soldier radioed in to say that Kumaradeven had just ripped past him like a bat out of hell. He himself was now doing one-thirty and struggling to control the ungainly van. Minutes later the Mercedes passed the van as well, Sumith grinning and waving cheerfully while Bandara gave them all the finger.

They were fifty metres behind the Focus, and Dayan checked that his *Kurz* was loaded and that the mag was properly seated. Behind him he heard Sumith chamber a round into his pistol. But try as he might, Kamal couldn't get alongside the Focus due to the moderately heavy traffic on the *autobahn*, and Dayan didn't want to open fire until he had a clear shot. A protracted gun duel would bring the cops down on them.

Every time they passed under a road or rail overpass, the SF team noted the flash of radar-controlled cameras. They were well over the speed limit, and the police cameras were taking shots of their plates. No matter what the outcome of the chase, Dayan knew that their mission in Germany was over.

Close to Neustadt an der Weinstrasse they passed a red Porsche Turbo, the sports car was doing one-forty, but they passed it like it was standing still. The German driver's expression as they flashed past made Kamal's day.

"Whooo-*hah!*" he yelled, settling lower behind the wheel and Dayan was forced to grin.

His friend and fellow soldier was thoroughly enjoying this drive. He had once done a special driving course with the Presidential Security Division, and was one of the reasons he had been picked for this mission. This was the first time he had actually been able to test his skills in the real world.

As the *autobahn* curved south, Dayan looked into the darkness on the right of the road. Somewhere out there were the Haard Mountains and the Pfälzerwald *Naturpark*. He wondered briefly whether Kumaradeven would be tempted to try and lose them on the narrow mountain roads before sneaking back south and across the border. But then he decided that it was in the terrorist's best interests to stay on the beaten path as long as possible. It would be dangerous enough for Kumaradeven when he had to leave the A65 for the B9 that would take him the final dozen kilometres into France.

Close to Kandel, about two kilometres before the B9 turnoff, they ran into a traffic jam. Leaning out of the car as they slowed to around twenty kilometres per hour, Dayan saw flashing police lights ahead. Soon they could see vehicles that had been pulled to the side of the road, their drivers' credentials being checked by uniformed and heavily armed police officers. Several *Bundesgrenschutz* troops — the German federal border guards — stood around, hefting MP-5s and holding leashed and muzzled dogs.

Dayan and Sumith slid their weapons under the seats and feigned relaxation. Dayan sent a quick word to Bandara, who was catching up rapidly now. They could see that most of the vehicles being checked were occupied by Asians or Middle Easterners.

Dayan saw a black PT Cruiser full of young Turks being searched in spite of vehement protests from the occupants.

Neither their quarry's Focus nor their own car was stopped, and they were soon picking up speed beyond the checkpoint. Within minutes they were approaching the B9 turnoff, and Kumaradeven cut across to the right-hand lane, causing other vehicles to brake and horn in protest as, without checking his speed, he curved into the exit. Kamal had anticipated the move and had already moved into the slower lane. Now he followed. The B9 was deserted of traffic, and they could see Kumaradeven's tail lights disappearing down the road at speed.

"Let's get on the NVGs," snapped Dayan, even before they were off the ramp, and Kamal killed the headlights, pulling onto the soft shoulder of the road just beyond the ramp.

Sumith handed out the night vision goggles headsets and all three men pulled them on and hit the switches. The world turned green and black as they pulled back onto the road, driving totally blacked out. Bandara called in to say he was approaching the turnoff. He didn't have NVGs and would have to rely on his headlights. Dayan instructed him to hang back out of sight, and he replied that it wasn't a problem, as he couldn't go faster even if he wanted to.

Changing gears frequently to keep the RPMs down and avoid giving themselves away due to engine sound, Kamal chased after the terrorist. His tail lights were rapidly getting closer, and Dayan knew that when he checked his rear-view mirror, all he'd see would be darkness.

The road tunnelled through tall fir trees, and on the straight stretches they'd catch glimpses of Bandara's headlights behind them as he rounded a bend. Dayan hoped that if Kumaradeven spotted the lights as well, he would pat himself on the back with the idea that he was well in the lead. They were still moving at close to a hundred and thirty kilometres per hour, too fast for the narrow road, but Kamal's driving was smooth and there was no telltale screech of tires.

Soon they were less than a dozen metres behind the Focus, and Dayan knew they hadn't much more time. The border was just over five minutes away, and they were close enough to the car ahead for Kumaradeven to begin hearing their engine and spot reflections off the Audi's body. The Focus was a sharp silhouette in the NVGs, stark against the pale brightness of the twin pools of light cast by the headlights on the road and trees ahead.

Dayan rolled down his window on the car's right side, and Sumith did the same with the left rear one. Now, whatever manoeuvre was necessary they could cover the Focus. The wind howled in as they readied their weapons. Kamal was just increasing speed to bring them within striking range, when an oncoming minibus rounded a bend ahead.

Dayan had just warned Bandara that they were "Engaging now," when the minibus' headlights swept across both cars, ruining the NVGs.

The minibus swerved as the shocked driver instinctively swung the wheel, glimpsing the dark Audi as it shot out of the blackness just in front of him. As the minibus screamed past, Dayan was aware of the Focus suddenly zigzagging, Kumaradeven suddenly realizing his danger and turning up the speed. Cursing, the three SF men discarded their NVGs, and Kamal switched the headlights onto high beam.

A short burst from the *Kurz* blew away the Focus' rear windscreen, Dayan fighting to hold the submachine-gun steady in the gale-force wind. He was leaning out of the window, firing across their own hood. Sumith added his fire as well, popping away with his Hi-Power. The Focus was rocking on its suspension, bathed in light; its two occupants huddled low in the front seats. Dayan emptied his mag and reloaded in time for Kamal to try and overtake. But Kumaradeven was having none of it and swung his own wheel. The left rear of the Focus crunched into the approaching Audi. Kamal dropped back a fraction, but the collision had more effect on the lighter Focus than on them. The terrorist vehicle swerved, almost missing the next bend before Kumaradeven regained control. Kamal speeded up again and was met by two quick shots from the Focus that punched holes in their own windscreen and narrowly missed Dayan. The SF sergeant answered with a full magazine of 9-mm fire, watching sparks and pieces of debris lift off the Focus' body.

Kumaradeven missed the next left-hand bend and the Focus leaped the roadside ditch and piled into the trees beyond at over a hundred and twenty kilometres per hour.

Kamal took the bend with skill, using the gears and brakes to bring the car to a halt two hundred metres beyond. Slamming the Audi into reverse, he sent it careening back along the soft shoulder, sending clouds of dust and gravel billowing in the beams from the headlights. Not a word had been spoken by the trio since they had opened fire, and now when the crumpled Focus came into view, Kamal pulled on the handbrake and got out to cover the other two as they trotted back on foot to inspect the damage.

The Focus had wrapped itself dead centre around a huge fir tree, the chassis of the car accordioned into a third of its original length. Kumaradeven hadn't been wearing his seatbelt — presumably he had released it in order to turn and fire at his pursuers — and had been flung clean through the windscreen. The car's steering wheel was still grasped in his clenched hands, as he lay folded against the tree trunk, his legs sprawled across the buckled hood. White steam was billowing around him from the car's engine. There was a strong smell of burned wiring and petrol. Stepping up gingerly, Dayan noted that the Tiger had been hit at least thrice in the back, which was obviously the reason he'd lost control of the car. His face had been slashed to ribbons by the windscreen glass and was covered with blood. Dayan could find no pulse when he touched his throat, but nevertheless put two more bullets into the man's head.

Dayan felt neither remorse nor satisfaction as he looked down at Sandra's killer. It had all happened too quickly for him to feel anything but excitement and fear during the brief fire fight, and now his emotions seemed cold and drained.

"Always wear your seatbelt," Sumith advised Kumaradeven's lifeless form as he stepped round to the passenger's side of the car to peer in.

The airbags had deployed, and through the compressed mess of steel, plastic, and glass, Sumith could see blood and long black hair splashed across the passenger side airbag's white surface. Over the sharp tang of petrol he could smell the stink of excrement, and he knew the warm liquid soaking into his trainers was blood. He couldn't even find a free opening to check for a pulse, and just turned away.

That was the moment when they got the yell for help from Bandara.

*

Bandara's van had just passed the Büchelberg intersection, halfway between the A65 and the border, when the dark Citroen Xantia came screeching out of the side road, headlights flicking to life. It had obviously been waiting for him. He yelled a warning into the radio just as two pistols opened fire from the Xantia. Bandara was unarmed since he had chucked his *Kurz* into the Rhine and hadn't had time to pick up another weapon since. He just ducked low behind the wheel and jammed his foot down on the accelerator.

But the van was no match for the Xantia, and the car was soon alongside. Bullets smashed into the side of the van, spraying glass into Bandara's face and almost blinding him. Given little choice, he quickly braked, his head almost below the level of the dashboard. The Xantia shot past, and he had a glimpse of a face in the back seat. Shifting gears he slammed the van into the back of the car with a sickening crunch, busting one of his headlights and the Xantia's tail-lights in the process. With a rending of metal, the car increased speed, pulling away and letting its rear bumper clang to the road to be run over by Bandara.

Peering over the dash, he called desperately for help.

"Under attack by a Citroen Xantia with French number plates!" he transmitted. "*Ado*, boys, I need assistance here, I don' have a fucking weapon even!"

꙳

Kamal was already swinging the Audi into a U-turn as Dayan and Sumith sprinted back. They had all three heard Bandara's call for help, punctuated by the gunshots.

"Banda, location?" Kamal asked, but there was no answer.

"Banda, we're coming," Dayan said as they covered the last few metres, "but where are you?"

But Bandara was silent. Either he was hit or had lost comms for some reason.

Before Dayan or Sumith could get into their car, a vehicle came speeding down the road from the north and braked when it saw the wreck of the Focus. Then the driver saw the Audi and changed his mind. A volley of gunshots opened up from the moving car, sending Dayan and Sumith into cover in the ditch, Sumith having to clear the Audi's boot in a headlong dive.

Bullets punched into the Audi and shattered glass as the other car moved past. Dayan popped up to his knees and put a burst into the car, realizing it was the Xantia that Bandara had described. He saw faces in the other car lit up by the strobing flash of the *Kurz*, and saw them duck or fall as the Xantia rocketed off south towards the border. Sumith sent a few more shots after it, and then both he and Dayan leaped back into the Audi.

Kamal had been hit in the left thigh, and was fumbling and cursing as he tried to use his belt as a tourniquet. Dayan got back out and ran round to the driver's door.

"Get him in the back," he snapped to Sumith as he hauled Kamal out. "Ah'll drive."

As they roared off back north, Sumith looked up from Kamal's wound. "Who the fuck were those buggers, d'you think?"

"Must have come across the border after a call from Kumaradeven," replied Dayan. "Must have missed us somehow and got onto Banda." Even as he speeded north, Dayan didn't feel too good about finding Bandara unhurt. If he was mobile he would have followed the Xantia. Oh, well, he hoped, maybe he's just wounded and sitting by the road, having a fag.

That hope was shattered when they rounded the next bend to find the van on its side in the middle of the road. In the headlights they could see that the cab was riddled with bullet holes. A passing car had arrived on the scene, and having parked fifty metres north, a young couple was staring into the van. Dayan and Sumith got out of the Audi and ran over.

"*Polizei, Polizei!*" Dayan yelled, waving them off, but the couple just stared suspiciously at his Asian features. In the excitement and tension of the moment, Dayan couldn't remember any of his German, and instead he waved his *Kurz* threateningly until the couple fled back to their car.

Sumith was trying to unstrap Bandara from his seat, but it was obvious the SF soldier was dead. He had been hit several times, and one bullet had entered below his left eye. Most of his brains had been smeared around the cab in the subsequent roll.

"Leave him," ordered Dayan, "we have to burn the van."

He walked back to the car and saw Kamal struggling to get out. Dayan shook his head, waving his hand dismissively, and Kamal collapsed back in his seat.

"He's *dead?*" he asked in disbelief.

"On the spot."

Dayan rummaged around in the back, and when he found what he was looking for, trotted back to the van. Sending Sumith back to move the car further away, Dayan pulled the pins on two thermite grenades and lobbed them into the diesel-soaked cab. He sprinted away, hearing the twin thumps as the grenades blew, and then a roar as the diesel caught.

Bitterly, they watched Bandara's funeral pyre. Dayan realized that while they had avenged Sandra's death, it had been at the cost of another comrade. He dialled Jayawardene's mobile number and explained the situation.

"Can we proceed to the border?"

"Negative," replied the military attaché tensely. "The Germans have closed the border crossing and moved in a GSG9 detachment. An' we *don't* want you tangling with them."

Dayan knew that *Grenschutzgruppe 9*, the German border guards' special anti-terrorist unit was a bunch on the same scale as the British SAS. These were the big boys. And anyway, the Sri Lankans had no quarrel with the Germans.

"What do we do, then?" Dayan asked. "We can't stay in the country, no?"

"That's for sure. We're monitoring the police frequencies, an' they've dispatched armed police units to cut you off already. Drive back north to the Büchelberg intersection an' turn *right*."

"OK." A final glance confirmed that the van and Bandara's body would take a long while to be identified, and Dayan got into the car. "What then?"

"Four hundred metres along the road you'll find a clearing on the right. Some trees screen it from the road, so it might be hard to find, but get there fast. Ah'll have someone pick you up an' take you across the border."

"One of our's?"

"Sort of," said Jayawardene cryptically.

*   *   *

2345 LOCAL (1845 GMT): The big four-engine Airbus A340 sat on the tarmac at the Bandaranaike International Airport north of Colombo city. An unseasonable rain shower made the long white fuselage reflect the powerful tungsten lighting. The rain that puddled on the tarmac and matted down the fur of the dogs, also made sure that there were no idle airport workers hanging around. Not that there would have been many. Since the August 2001 attack on the airport and the neighbouring Air Force base, security had been tightened drastically. All tarmac personnel were subjected to an extensive Airport Security and a DII vetting process, which extended all the way back to their childhood.

A result of the security tighten up had been that the Airport Security explosive search teams had been totally reorganized, its members reabsorbed into regular duties, and their posts taken over by former Army Ordnance Corps personnel. These teams swept every arriving and departing aircraft; the incoming ones as soon as passengers and crew had disembarked and before any hidden explosives could be collected by cleanup teams; and the outgoing flights just after whatever necessary maintenance had been completed and before Sri Lankan Airlines catering brought in the food. The loading of the food itself was stringently supervised by Airport Security.

A Sri Lankan Airlines aircraft maintenance man opened the A340's rear left door for the first dog handler and his big German shepherd. The Sri Lankan Airlines staffer grimaced in exasperation as the dog shook itself, spattering the red-white-blue-liveried interior with raindrops. As was the practice in such weather, each entering security man left his raincoat in the rear galley to avoid dripping water in the cabin area. The exception this time was the team's senior man, who stood at the back of economy class, watching his men sweep the plane while he dripped rainwater onto the freshly cleaned carpet. When the airline staffer pointed out the patches of moisture soaking into the pile, he was pointedly told to man the door and mind his own business.

The men and dogs swept through to the cockpit, checking seats, lavatories, galleys, and luggage storage space thoroughly. Once they were finished, the senior man would do a walk-through of the long-haul Airbus' two-class configuration of business and economy, hoping to pick up something so obvious it might have missed the eyes or noses of the rest of the team.

The maintenance man stood aside to let the returning men and dogs file off the aircraft. When he stepped back into the cabin, he could see the team commander strolling off up the aisle towards business class, eyeballing his surroundings and stopping randomly to peer into overhead luggage storage space or glance into lavatories. He still wore his dark blue raincoat, and the Sri Lankan Airlines staffer cursed the ex-soldier's arrogance.

Derek de Alwis, the explosive search team's head passed the lavatories just behind the wings, and into the next section of economy. Once he was sure he was out of sight of the Sri Lankan Airlines man, he took the first of the packages from under his raincoat, and following exact instructions, taped it to the underside of the starboard outboard aisle seat two rows forward of the lavatories. He then crossed quickly to the port side and taped another of the packages under the corresponding seat on that side. Walking on, he repeated the procedure, two rows behind the amidships galley. He then passed through the galley and placed the last two packets in business class.

Once that was done, he continued his walk-through inspection all the way to the cockpit. On the way back, he checked that the packets were firmly in place, ignored the cold look on the maintenance man's face, and watched as he closed and sealed the door with security tape. The commander of the explosive search team affixed a UV-scannable sticker to the tape before joining his men and their dogs on the tarmac. The plane would remain secured for the next twenty four hours until an external sweep was done just prior to takeoff.

*   *   *

2000 CENTRAL EUROPEAN TIME (1900 GMT): The three SF men were huddled under the trees at the edge of the clearing, watching through their NVGs as an Aerospatiale Gazelle light helicopter in the markings of the French *Gendarmerie* hovered over the clearing. The chopper was fully blacked out, with no lights showing, and came in to land without the benefit of landing lights.

Dayan watched as the co-pilot's door opened and an armed figure dismounted. The man was dressed in jeans and a dark parka,

and was carrying an Uzi submachine-gun. Dayan couldn't be sure, but the man looked south Asian. The figure stood by the Gazelle, peering into the darkness, as the pilot shut down the rotors, then he started to trot towards the road. Dayan let him close to within twenty metres, then stopped him with a shout. The man stood staring into the shadows, the submachine-gun held casually in one hand, alongside his leg, neither casual nor threatening. He was close enough for Dayan to now confirm that he was an Asian.

"*Chandra!*" challenged Dayan in Sinhalese.

There was a pause of several beats before the man shouted back the answer. "*Kirana!*"

Dayan nodded to Sumith to lead out, and hoisted Kamal across his shoulder in a fireman's carry. *Chandra Kirana*, or moonbeam, was the code word for an emergency extraction, and it had been suggested by Dayan. Only the team, Jayawardene, and SF Ops at Maduru Oya knew what it was.

As they moved into the open and towards the chopper, its pilot started the rotors turning. The man with the Uzi waved a greeting and then turned back to the chopper, leading the way at a trot. He opened the rear door for them, and Dayan and Sumith lifted Kamal's big frame into the cabin. The pilot was a European wearing NVGs, like the three SF men, and now he said something over his shoulder in French to the man with the Uzi.

"We better get going," he translated. "We spotted German police cars leaving the highway just before we came in to land. The French don't have as many scruples as the Germans when it comes to these things, but to hang around any longer will be stupid."

Dayan had been staring at the unidentified Sri Lankan, sure he had met him somewhere before, and now when the man spoke he remembered.

The guy was a DFI man named Amarasuriya, and had done the SF escape and evasion course at Maduru Oya a year or so ago. Dayan had been one of the instructors. The course was essentially for potential SF troopers and non-badged outsiders. There were people from the Air Force, Navy, police, and various other Army units, and they were put through a very realistic and brutal regimen of training which would prepare them for survival behind enemy lines as well as capture and interrogation. The first part of the course was exclusively for the non-SF troops, and was actually a rigorous selection programme to judge whether the potential trainees were fit enough for the actual course. The instructors were all jump-qualified Special Forces NCOs, and harassed the trainees at every opportunity.

"What are you?" they would scream in the recruits' ears as they did pushups before breakfast. "*WHAT are you?*"

Everybody else on the course would answer, "I'm a shit hat, sir!" but Amarasuriya would yell "I'm James Bond, sergeant!" The instructors ran him till he was vomiting bile, but he never cracked, successfully finishing the course.

Amarasuriya had already recognized Dayan, in spite of the NVGs that made him look like an alien, and he now grinned and passed a lit cigarette back to his former DI.

"Fit?" he asked.

"Fit," Dayan replied, accepting the smoke. "Can I ask who owns this chopper and where we're going?"

"The chopper belongs to GIGN," Amarasuriya answered. GIGN was the *Groupement d'Intervention de la Gendarmerie Nationale*, the French police anti-terrorism unit. "And we're taking your man to the French Army hospital outside Paris. You two will be dropped at the Sri Lankan embassy for the moment."

CHAPTER 18

The young Sinhalese man strolled through the Bandaranaike International Airport's duty-free area, smoking and looking at the displayed goods, trying not to appear nervous. Even though he had already made it through check-in and immigration without raising any suspicions, he expected at any moment that Airport Security would drop a heavy hand onto his shoulder, and he would be locked up forever.

At a lean and wiry twenty-two years of age, Vijitha Dhampahana was dressed exactly as he had been instructed by the man in Pettah in a respectably priced pullover and jeans. He didn't want to go to prison, but neither did he want to stay free in Sri Lanka anymore. A job as a trishaw driver in Colombo barely made him enough money to feed himself and his elderly parents. Girlfriends were many, but marriage was out of the question. The trishaw had been bought with the money he had saved, working on a two-year contract as a gardener's assistant in Saudi Arabia. Vijitha Dhampahana had no wish to return to the Middle East. He had hated the time spent there, in a country of hypocritically puritanical laws, a place where Asians were spat at and looked on as nothing more than paid slaves. But for him, and people like him, with no money, contacts, or fluency in English, Sri Lanka held no comforting future either.

For a year, he had tried to get a tourist visa to a western European country, knowing that once he was there, he would be able to disappear, pick up the language, and find a job — however menial — that would let him send back money to his parents. And then, soon, he could return, and marry a beautiful wife. But unfortunately, the visa officers at the respective embassies had seen many like Dhampahana. He fitted the perfect profile of the illegal immigrant — young, single, poor and disenfranchised. They had turned him down without even the benefit of an interview.

It had been the chance meeting with a former school classmate that had given Dhampahana his opportunity. The classmate had been well-dressed and obviously affluent, and in answer to Dhampahana's questions, confided that he had just returned from Italy for his sister's wedding. He had explained to Dhampahana about his illegal entry into Europe, his first jobs as a janitor, waiter, petrol shed attendant. Until after years of waiting he had been granted legal immigrant status. He had told of his current job, guiding British and American tourists around the sights of Rome. He had told Dhampahana of his car, and his apartment, and his Italian wife. He had offered to introduce Dhampahana to people who could help him, get him into Europe.

Dhampahana had gone with the classmate, been told that it would cost him three hundred thousand rupees. Dhampahana had been ready to turn away. Even if he sold his trishaw, he could not raise a third of that money. He had been told that if could pay half the money, however, the rest could be paid once he found a job.

He had sold the trishaw, and his father had mortgaged their small two-room house, and between them they had raised a hundred and twenty thousand rupees. The contact — a Tamil in Pettah — had agreed. But he had been told they couldn't get him into Europe. It would have to be Canada, take it or leave it. He had taken it. Even then, Vijitha Dhampahana had to wait almost six months. Even after he had been given the doctored passport with the Canadian visa, the passport that held old visas to Europe and Canada, he had had to wait. His own face had replaced the former owner's, though the old name — Dhampahana's new name — remained. Dhampahana hadn't known what the delay was, but he was sure that there were many prospective Tamil illegal immigrants who were being given first jump. Dhampahana had blocked out

the thought that he knew who the Tamil man in Pettah was, or rather *what* he was, and who he represented. He did not want to know. If the man could get him to Canada, that was all that mattered.

He had arrived at the Bandaranaike International Airport three hours before the scheduled departure, allowing himself ample time to get through check-in and immigration. Ample time to get caught. But customs had searched his two suitcases and small knapsack perfunctorily, his smile at the young female officer helping him on his way. Then there had been check-in. When the staffer behind the counter had run his passport under an ultra-violet light scanner, Dhampahana's heart had been pounding in his throat, and when the man had handed the passport to a woman in a sari to check once more, Dhampahana was sure that he had been caught. He had worried about how his father would repay the mortgage when Dhampahana was in jail. He had tried to tell himself that this was normal, that every Sri Lankan had his passport thoroughly checked, and that they had done the same when he had left for Saudi. But he hadn't been able to recall such a careful check. Finally, his passport had been returned to him, along with the return ticket — the ticket he would not need again once he was in Toronto — and a boarding pass. Dhampahana had originally intended to ask for a window seat, but he was so eager to be away from the check-in counter that he hadn't bothered. The gruff immigration official had just stamped the passport with a cursory glance at its owner.

Butting his Gold Leaf in an ashtray, Dhampahana knew that there was still a long way to go before he could relax. There was still the final check at the boarding gate. He was glad he wouldn't have to switch flights in Singapore. He had heard of illegals being turned back from Singapore, Hong Kong, or Dubai, because officials there suspected a passport. Vancouver would be the final hurdle before he took the last leg of his journey to Toronto.

He glanced at his watch, and then took the escalator back down to ground level. Boarding would begin in a few minutes.

Although the man in Pettah had insisted that his clothes would lessen suspicion, Vijitha felt like a fraud in them. The pullover was too big for his narrow shoulders, the jeans too tight.

* * *

THURSDAY 21st MARCH 0042 LOCAL (1842 GMT): Soon after the seatbelt warnings had been switched off, Jennifer Jensen started the first drinks service, pushing the trolley down the aisle. The Air Canada A340 had been scheduled to leave Katunayake at 2350 on Wednesday night, but it was more than half an hour past midnight when they finally took off. The airport baggage handlers were on a "go slow" campaign, they were told, demanding a five-percent increase in salary while claiming that patriotism prevented them from an outright walkout.

In spite of the fact that, true to rule, she and Tim Ferguson had got very little sleep in the last forty eight hours, Jen-Jen felt rejuvenated and relaxed. Sex agreed with her, she decided for the umpteenth time. She felt a tingle run down from her nipples to the juncture of her thighs as she recalled the passion of the preceding one and a half days, only getting out of bed to eat or swim in the terrace pool.

It would be a three and a half-hour flight to Singapore, most of it in darkness, and if she was lucky she could get an hour's sleep. Provided the passengers all had a stiff nightcap and settled down to the movie. She was already dreading the long haul from Singapore to Vancouver.

She continued handing out drinks as she moved down the aisle. Then she saw him. A new one, not one of the two who had flown into Colombo with them. Even the sight of him filled her with a sense of unease rather than the confidence his presence was meant to inspire. He was dressed in a dark business suit and conservative tie, of average height, short hair and clean shaven, a grey figure that no one would notice or remember. Not unless the event which haunted every flyer since September 11th 2001 occurred. The man was getting an overnight bag from one of the overhead lockers, and when he realized he was blocking her path, he turned with a quick smile.

"Sorry," he said, returning to his seat.

"Something to drink, sir?" she asked, forcing a smile and pretending she didn't know what he was.

"A Coke, please."

As he reached up to take the plastic cup from her, his coat fell open and she got a glimpse of the small black pistol in its horizontal spider rig. Jen-Jen quickly turned away, pouring a shot of Red Label for the Englishman in the window seat.

Air Canada had resisted government suggestions after the September 11th attacks to carry armed sky marshals on all flights, resolving only to have them aboard flights into the United States. Since February 2002, however, the Canadian aviation authorities had made it mandatory that all domestic and international commercial flights carry sky marshals, and crews had got used to the quiet, armed men who casually boarded and disembarked with the rest of the passengers.

Jen-Jen, however, just could not get used to knowing there were firearms on board her plane. It seemed to go against everything that they were trained in. She knew there would be at least one other marshal somewhere on board, probably up in business class.

*

Captain Johnny Burnett began a climbing turn that would put AC634 onto an east-southeasterly heading. By the end of the turn, the Airbus was at twenty-five thousand feet and still climbing steadily, heading back across the southern half of Sri Lanka. First Officer Mike Harrap logged them out of the Katunayake pattern, and prepared to take over from Burnett.

The co-pilot had just finished his task when they saw a small green light at the top of the control panel begin to blink steadily. Burnett turned on a small display screen on the centre console, and colour video footage of the forward galley behind the cockpit appeared. A stew stood at the cockpit door with a tray of coffee. After checking on the screen that the stew was relaxed and smiling, and that no passengers were in the background, Burnett pressed a button below the screen, and the first door unlocked. Once the door had thudded shut, he pressed a second button, thus unlocking the inner door, the one that opened into the cockpit itself. Unless the master override switch had been hit, unlocking both doors simultaneously — an act that would automatically transmit a distress message over the airwaves — the second door could not be unlocked until the first had been shut. The two doors, with the claustrophobic space in between, had meant the forward galley being moved several metres aft and, therefore, reduced passenger seating. The loss in revenue was one of the prices of increased safety.

Like the closed circuit television camera in the forward galley, half a dozen more were spread through the Airbus A340's cabin, monitoring the movements and temperament of the passengers and crew. As with the security doors to the cockpit, they had been a result of the September hijacks the previous year. In January 2002, the United States Federal Aviation Authority had made it law that all flights into and out of the country, as well as all domestic flights, had to have bullet-proof doors and cameras in operation. Several NATO countries had already followed the US lead, beginning with Britain, and more — including Canada — were expected to do the same. Airbus had been forced to work at breakneck speed to modify its existing fleet, and all future aircraft coming off the production lines would carry the safety features as standard. AC634, earlier on the Vancouver to Los Angeles run, was one of the Air Canada planes fitted with the doors and cameras.

The stew entered the cockpit and served the pilots their coffee, staying to chat for a few minutes. Through the cockpit windows was a spectacular night time view of the curving southern coastline of Sri Lanka, the lighted towns glowing through scattered clouds. To the right, further south, was the inky blackness of the

Indian Ocean, stretching unbroken for ten thousand kilometres to the frozen shores of the Antarctic.

*

As soon as the seatbelt warnings had been switched off, Suzie Kopleck raced back into economy, looking for Daniel Devanayagam. Her father, as CEO of a multinational milk-food manufacturer's Sri Lankan operation, could well enjoy expense-account business class seats for his family. Not so the Devanayagams. They'd had to budget very carefully to make this trip possible.

Daniel and Suzie had exchanged seat numbers prior to takeoff, and so she knew exactly where to look for him. She found him polishing off his first Coke, and happily plumped herself into the seat Daniel's father offered her. Robin Devanayagam told his wife he was going up to chat to the Koplecks for awhile. He had met them several times when their children had some mutual interest that a parent was expected to ferry them to. Leaving his wife with the kids, he moved up the aisle towards business class. Maybe the whisky was better up front.

*

Colin Peters had resigned himself to his Johnnie Walker Red Label as he looked out into the darkness and tried to find an easy-listening music channel. He would have preferred a Famous Grouse, but there was none available. Next time he would fly Sri Lankan Airlines, he decided. He was sure there was Famous Grouse up in business class, but the WWF didn't think its marine biologists warranted anything higher than economy.

*

Vijitha Dhampahana smiled nervously at the stewardess, and asked for an orange juice. He had decided to stay off alcohol for the duration of the flight. He would need all his senses razor sharp when he faced the officials at Vancouver. A cigarette would help right now, he knew, but there was no chance of that for the next fourteen hours. Dhampahana watched out of the corner of his eye the white passenger in the seat next to him, and hoped he would not embarrass himself when the in-flight meal came around. Knives and forks weren't the most natural of things to Sri Lankans raised from childhood to eat with their fingers, and the restrictive elbow room in economy didn't help things at all. It had been bad enough several years ago, enduring the contemptuous stares of the haughty Sri Lankan lady sitting next to him on the flight to Saudi, but this *suddha* would be much worse.

* * *

0600 CHINA COASTAL TIME (2215 GMT): The light breakfast in the Damenlou Hotel's small restaurant was very good. Mahesh Balachandran opted for a cheese omelette, toast, orange juice, and tea. The restaurant was virtually empty at this early hour. Even Suresh hadn't made an appearance. But Balachandran wasn't concerned. A glance at his watch told him there was still a full hour before they needed to be at Changi. The six of them would arrive at the airport separately, check-in and board as if they had never set eyes on each other before.

He had slept well, going to bed early — by 8pm — the previous evening, knowing he would need the rest in the long sleepless days ahead. He had been awakened at 3:30am by the call from Colombo, confirming that AC634 had taken off, and that it was half an hour late. It was expected that the pilot would make up the delay, landing on schedule at Changi at 0705, China Coastal Time. After the phone call, Mahesh Balachandran had not returned to bed. He had spent the next two hours sitting at the window, watching the city come to life, running the operation through his mind once more. At 5:30am he had finished packing, used the toilet, and had a shower. When he had come out of the bathroom an hour later, Balachandran had popped a couple of Imodium capsules. Like the packets of speed he carried in his jacket pocket, the Imodium was one more drug he would need for the operation. Once it began, he would have no time for sleep or bodily functions.

Finishing the last of the toast, he forced himself not to rush, to pour himself another cup of tea. He still had another ten minutes before he needed to catch a taxi to Changi. Balachandran didn't want to spend any more time than was necessary at the airport. The longer he was under the eyes of the security officials, the longer they'd have to notice something special about him. Balachandran knew there was nothing special about him, but long experience had taught him to leave nothing to chance.

*   *   *

The stewardess woke Colin Peters from his light doze and politely asked him to stow his table and bring his seat back to the upright position. Air Canada AC634 would soon be arriving at Singapore Changi International Airport.

Peters slid up the blind on his window and squinted in the morning glare. All he could see was scattered cloud, and the hazy blue of the Straits of Singapore. He quickly slipped on a pair of sunglasses. There was a faint throbbing in his head, a combination of the vibration from the big Pratt & Whitney engines, and the two whiskies he had downed. He silently debated the idea of swearing off alcohol for the rest of the journey.

On the left side off the Airbus, opposite Peters, and several rows back, Vijitha Dhampahana leaned forward in his aisle seat and looked past his neighbour, trying to catch a glimpse of the sea. When the Canadian next to Dhampahana glanced at him, he quickly settled back in his seat, not wanting to seem rude.

Further forward, just behind the partition dividing economy from business, Robin Devanayagam had shown Daniel how to switch back and forth between the Airbus' two belly cameras, one pointing forward under the nose, the other straight down. The twelve-year-old was now engrossed in alternately watching the coast of Singapore scroll down his screen as they neared shore, picking out the tiny fishing vessels they were passing over, and excitedly pressing his nose to the window perspex to confirm that it was all real.

Sitting on the far side of the aisle from her husband, Rajkumari Devanayagam watched her son's antics in amusement, flinching in exasperation as he jammed a finger onto the entertainment monitor's interactive menu, almost bending the screen.

*

"Six three four, switch to Singapore Control on two three four decimal two. You are cleared below nine thousand."

Captain Johnny Burnett pushed the A340's nose gently forward, dropping below nine thousand feet. Next to him, the co-pilot switched frequencies to bring up the local air traffic control. The morning sun's reflection was dazzling as it bounced off the water between the Southern Islands, turning them into cardboard cut-outs. AC634 was flying a direct path towards Telok Blangah on the southern coast of Singapore.

"Air Canada six three four from Singapore Control. You are cleared to six thousand. Turn right to one zero degrees. Switch to Changi Director on three four zero decimal five."

Burnett began the turn when he could make out the oil refinery on the island of Bukum. The sun seemed to slide across the sky until it was blazing into his eyes. Bukum swung out of sight beneath the left wing as the nose pointed down the Straits of Singapore towards the open waters of the South China Sea. They were flying along the heavily populated southern coast of Singapore, still descending.

"AC six three four, this is Changi Director, cleared two thousand five hundred. Turn left onto zero three degrees. QNH eight seven five decimal five."

Burnett banked the Airbus, as the co-pilot reset the altimeter, watching the coastline pivot round till Changi was sitting square on their nose. They had made up for the half an hour delay at

Katunayake, thanks to a slight tail wind. In fact, Burnett realized, they were a few minutes early.

"Six three four, cleared to lock on ILS for runway two right."

The pilots could see the runway now, blue-green water bracketing both ends.

"AC six three four, call the outer marker. Reduce speed to final approach."

Burnett extended the flaps, reducing speed and feeling the thump and vibration as Mike Harrap dropped the undercart.

"Cabin crew, prepare for landing."

They were low over the water now, seemingly skimming the wave tops, though Burnett knew this was just an illusion created by the size of the A340.

"Six three four, you are cleared to land on runway two right. Contact Tower on five four decimal six."

*

Flashing her practiced smile, Jen-Jen wished the two dozen or so disembarking passengers a pleasant stay in Singapore. The bulk of the three hundred and thirty five seats on board AC634 were filled with passengers flying on to Canada.

She waited at the door for the Changi cleaning staff to come on board and do their thing. She could already see the refuelling teams scuttling around the undercarriage of the aircraft, connecting the long hoses. Minutes later, the cleaners filed past her, spreading down the aisles and through the plane. They were all of Indian descent, Jen-Jen knew, descendents of low-caste labourers imported by the British to do most of the island's menial work. Tim had told her the same was true of the tea plantation workers in the Central Highlands of Sri Lanka. She watched as the cleaners stooped to pick up scraps of discarded paper and food wrappings from between the seats, and cleared out the galley waste disposal.

Jen-Jen's lips tightened as she watched a westerner in business class get to his feet and stretch, flexing his long limbs.

What made her notice him were his eyes. They were bright and sharp, like a sheepdog's, watching the cleaners' movements. She now knew he was the second sky marshal.

* * *

1010 AUSTRALIAN WESTERN STANDARD TIME (0010 GMT): Even the spectacular view of Lake Burley Griffin didn't take Patricia Fenster's mind off the attaché case. She had decided to go into Canberra's city centre on a shopping trip while her husband was cloistered in the Ministry of Trade on Capital Hill. But even the shopping expedition provided only temporary distraction from the nagging fear.

The fear had begun a week before the Fensters' official visit to Australia. It had begun even before she had been handed the attaché case. The case was innocent enough, fashionably conservative, in dark leather, hinting at femininity. It was an attaché case a high-flying female attorney might carry, or a young tech industry CEO. Even its contents, when she had disobeyed instructions and looked inside, had seemed to hint at no danger or evil.

The fear had begun, however, when Patricia received the big brown envelope in the mail, addressed to her personally at the club. Hand delivered. The envelope had arrived a day before the attaché case. The envelope with the glossy colour photographs of her and Ian McEdwards in Sri Lanka. The fear had seemed to leap off the desk where the pictures had fallen and clutch at her throat. A fear that wondered, with evil whispers, if copies of the pictures had been sent to her husband.

The writing on the back of one of the pictures had instructed her to visit a particular beauty salon the next day. The salon was a very exclusive one, with an elite clientele that booked well in advance. Patricia had found that an appointment for her had already been made.

She had cursed herself, still did, for the mistake she had made that hot November afternoon in Teldeniya. But the heat had been oppressive, the cool water of the swimming pool making her nipples rigid. The water, and the sight of Ian McEdwards in a tight black pair of swimming trunks.

Donald Fenster's bedroom skills were never enough to keep Patricia satisfied. Never had, not even when she had first met him. But she had fooled herself, told herself that she could do without passionate sex. That his affection and money would be enough. Her first extramarital affairs had been discreet, few and far between, but as time moved on they had become more daring, more desperate. But only once previously had she ever slept with anyone assigned to Donald's staff. The parliamentary personal secretary hadn't been very much better than her husband in bed, and the encounter was never repeated. The civil servant had soon transferred to another department and the matter had been forgotten. She had always flirted with the bodyguards, and some had even made it clear that all Patricia Fenster had to do was ask prettily. But she never had. She had decided that extramarital affairs were best kept far from home.

Until that afternoon with Ian.

Patricia wished he was still on the SPG team assigned to Donald. Just so that she could discuss this with him, ask his advice. He would never have panicked the way she had done, given way to blind fear. He would never have lost all dignity the way she had, begged the anonymous man who had called her at the salon that day. Begged the man not to publicize the pictures of her mistake, while he had laughed coldly. Patricia had made it clear that she would do anything to keep the incident quiet, *anything*. When the man had stated that there was something he wanted, she had been ready to write an immediate cheque, or jump into bed with him if it were necessary. The man seemed amused, had told her, in his American accent, to be at a restaurant in Hull that night. Alone.

By sneaking out of the back of the club and cutting through several back alleys, she had managed to avoid having her bodyguard and driver accompany her. She had taken a cab across the river to Hull. At the restaurant, she had introduced herself by name, as instructed, and asked for a table for two. Along with the menu, the waiter had brought her a narrow white envelope. The envelope had contained two keys, each with its own triple-digit plastic tag, and a handwritten note, telling her to order dinner. Half an hour later, the waiter had brought a phone to her table. There was, apparently, a call for her.

It was the man who had phoned her at the salon. She had been told that one key was for a left luggage locker at the Ottawa Central Station. She would find an attaché case in it, and was to carry the case with her on her journey with her husband to Australia. She was not to open the case, and was to keep it with her at all times. She had been told that when she landed in Canberra, she would find that the second key fitted a left luggage locker at the airport. She had been told to leave the attaché case in it. Also in the locker, she had been told, she would find a second attaché case, which she was to carry to Sri Lanka. The key to the Canberra locker was to be left in a white envelope at the hotel reception for a Mr Harris to collect. The man on the phone had been very insistent that Patricia accompany her husband on the next leg of his trip, which would be to Colombo. She would receive further instructions there about the handover of the second case.

The blackmailer had warned her that if she didn't carry out his instructions to the letter, she would return to Ottawa to find the very entertaining pictures of her and Mr McEdwards on the cover of every tabloid from British Columbia to Newfoundland. If she obeyed orders, she would never see or hear from him again.

She had abandoned her dinner half-eaten and headed immediately for the railway station, where she had found the attaché case waiting for her. It was brand new, and she had explained it away to Donald as a whim she had ordered online.

It had taken Patricia Fenster two days to summon the courage to disobey the blackmailer and check the contents of the case. It had been packed solid with envelopes of varying sizes and shapes. They had all been sealed and addressed to people in

various Australian cities. The names on the envelopes had all sounded Anglo-European to her. She hadn't dared to open the envelopes, and had repacked the attaché case once more.

On the very same day that Patricia had opened the case, Ian McEdwards had asked for emergency leave to visit his sick mother.

Patricia had left the case at the Canberra airport, picked up the second attaché case, and had handed the key, in its envelope, to the Hilton receptionist, as ordered. Within hours the key had been collected by the shadowy Mr Harris, and hadn't been returned since. The second case was identical in every way to the first, and contained just two small buff envelopes, neither of them addressed. That had been over two days ago. The only thing that had puzzled Patricia, and still did, was the fact that Donald showed no indication of planning a trip to Sri Lanka, either officially or personally.

As the car stopped in front of the Hilton, Patricia wished that she could discuss the whole thing with McEdwards. Embarrassing though it would be, it would make her feel less alone with her fear — fear that she was doing something not just illegal, but dangerous. For the thousandth time she wished she had broached the subject with McEdwards before he'd gone on leave. If she had his number, she could call, but she didn't.

Tomorrow, she decided, she would get on the internet and check the Calgary online white pages for his phone number.

*

By the time Air Canada AC634 was being refuelled at Changi airport in Singapore, Donald Fenster and his delegation were breaking for midmorning tea on the third day of trade talks at Capital Hill in Canberra. Instead of joining the others for a bit of networking, Fenster was due to meet the Canadian ambassador at the High Commission itself.

It would give Fenster an opportunity to update himself with any further terrorist incidents in Canada or elsewhere. He had already arrived in Australia when what seemed to be the second wave of attacks had been reported, and if the talks were not so crucial for trade in the southern Pacific, Fenster would have been tempted to fly back to Ottawa immediately. He could only imagine the chaos on Parliament Hill with recriminations and counter-recriminations. Fortunately, his minister of state was holding the fort against some cabinet ministers and members of the Commons who were calling for Canada to ease its hard stand against the LTTE. These individuals were suggesting that a relaxation of the efforts against the Tigers would enable the militant group to clean up its own house, and stop the attacks on Canadian interests.

But Fenster was adamant that Canada should not relinquish its responsibility to fight terrorism in exchange for short-term gains. His previous month's meeting with the Sri Lankan foreign minister had convinced him that the Sri Lankans could help prevent a second wave of attacks, and the haphazard and uncoordinated method in which the second wave had been carried out itself was proof that the Sri Lankans were hitting back. Only the killing of Francis Oakland in South Africa had been a hundred-percent success. Both the bombs at the CN Tower in Toronto and the Sri Lankan embassy in Sydney had detonated prematurely, and while both had resulted in heavy damage and some loss of civilian life, it was nowhere near the disasters of the first wave of attacks. The ERA had again hacked into the Canadian government website and claimed responsibility for Oakland's assassination, as well as the CN Tower and Sydney bombings.

While the Sri Lankan government was publicly claiming to have had no hand in the assassination of known Tigers in Berlin, London, Paris, and on the Franco-German border, there had been strong speculation within the Canadian Security Intelligence Service that all three had been hits by undercover Sri Lankan operatives. Fenster preferred not to have an opinion on the subject, as Ottawa's policy was to condemn extra-judicial killings in all forms. The shooting deaths of the two Tamils in Oslo, and the four in Cologne were obviously preventive strikes, both of which had saved Canadian and Sri Lankan lives. Again, the Sri Lankan government was shrugging their shoulders and commenting on the weather. At least for the moment.

Neither the ERA nor the LTTE were identifying the dead terrorists in Cologne and Oslo as their own, and it was still hard to establish a solid link between the two groups, even though the French GIGN was claiming that investigations into the two dead LTTEers in the Paris restaurant had uncovered explosives in their apartment with which GIGN had said they were planning to bomb a Canadian student delegation. The LTTE was accusing the French of planting evidence.

Everyone was remaining mum about the hacking of the TamilNet website. Even the media networks had passed it over. Only a few of the tabloids had gleefully pounced on it, and Fenster had seen a Sri Lankan rag that gleefully proclaimed *Prabha Gets the Bum's Rush* in three-inch-tall banner headlines, along with a discreetly censored picture of the screen image.

With a wail of sirens, the two Canberra police outriders took off, leaving Fenster's limousine and two escort cars to follow. Fenster's security had been tightened and beefed up further following the Sydney bombing, as it was obvious the ERA was widening its geographical field of attack.

As he settled back in his seat, Fenster decided he would cut short his time in Australia. He needed to be back in Ottawa, where he could coordinate things and have the ear of the Prime Minister. This was no time for government to go soft and cave in.

* * *

0830 CHINA COASTAL TIME [0030 GMT]: Reading a copy of *The Strait Times*, Mahesh Balachandran hid his rising impatience as he sat in Terminal 2's Sakura Lounge, waiting for the boarding call. There was no reason for him to be impatient or nervous; everything was going perfectly to plan. It was just the anticipation that was making him tense, the urge to get it over with. But he controlled his feelings, to even an expert observer, he was nothing more than one more South Asian businessman. It was one of the reasons he had been chosen for this operation.

Balachandran had passed through all the security checks at Changi with no problem. There was nothing in his luggage or on his person to be given a second look. This was the easy part. He could see Ramesh sipping fruit juice on the far side of the lounge, not showing any sign of having recognized him. Balachandran wondered idly whether the other four had made it through all the airport security checks. Even if one of them had been stopped, they could still carry out the mission with only five; even with four, in the unlikely event of two of the team being stopped. And if the operation was blown, they'd soon know when they tried to get through the boarding gate. That was the final security check.

At 8:45am, he heard the call to begin boarding for Air Canada Flight AC634 to Vancouver, and stood up, leaving the newspaper folded on the couch. Ramesh lit a cigarette, showing no hurry to leave the lounge. Balachandran took the escalator down to Level 2F and walked east towards Gate 32. The long hallway was thronged with travellers, and he noted that there were more people coming through immigration from luggage check-in.

He could see none of the others, and didn't look for them, walking at a brisk but unhurried pace, eyeing with unseeing eyes the advertising light boxes that lined the hallway at regular intervals.

As he turned the corner at the end and walked north towards the boarding gate, he spotted Alagaran sitting in one of the small smoking areas, having a last puff. Balachandran shook his head in wonder, walking on. A non-smoker himself, he couldn't understand how someone could remain in those little smoky cubicles for long, for even a few seconds.

*   *   *

0645 LOCAL (0045 GMT): The sun was still rising over the city of Colombo, touching its buildings and trees with gold, cutting through the dawn mists that softened its streets. Colombo could not be called one of Asia's more beautiful cities, but early mornings seemed to soften the city's harsh lines, make her tree-lined avenues look timeless, its stifling closeness charming.

Devini Sundaralingam hated cities, all cities. She had hated Madras, and Toronto. She had even hated London and Paris. As she watched the sun rise over this city that she hated above all others, Devini longed for the open sandiness of the Jaffna Peninsula, its low scrub jungle and tall palmyrah trees; she wished that the glass sitting on the window sill held, instead of dark, golden tea, the milky opacity of *pathaneer*. She remembered her father sneaking her a mouthful of the cool, sweet liquid early in the morning, when they had been holidaying with an uncle on the peninsula. Later in the day, the pale nectar of the palmyrah flower would grow heavy and sour with fermentation, its alcohol content rising, slices of onions and green chillies spicing the pre-lunch toddy. By evening it would be strong enough to be used as the base for arrack, distilled and bottled and sold.

But *Appa* was dead, cremated in a foreign land, and her uncle and his family were in a Batticaloa refugee camp, and in two days time she would bring fear to the city of hate. Fear for the Sinhalese and hope for her people. Fear of defeat in the moment of their victory, for the murderers of her parents, and hope for the Tamils when all hope of victory had been wiped out beneath the boots of the enemy soldiers and the blades of their helicopters.

* * *

0923 CHINA COASTAL TIME [0123 GMT]: As Air Canada AC634 turned off taxiway-A and onto runway 1-Left, Mahesh Balachandran was buckled into his business class aisle seat, and lost sight of the South End Reservoir as the Airbus turned. The four big Pratt & Whitney engines rose to a screaming crescendo, and Balachandran had to consciously stop himself from bouncing in his seat with excitement. He loved this moment, when the pilot would release the brakes and the aircraft would leap forward like a spurred horse, pressing him back into his seat. Balachandran could see traffic on the West Perimeter Road as the A340 rotated back on its undercart, the nose-wheel rising into the air. In seconds, the runway was dropping away and they were airborne.

Balachandran focused his attention on the overhead seatbelt warning, waiting for it to switch off. That would be the signal. Suddenly he realized how calm he was, now that all the anticipation, and worrying was over. The moment would be ten minutes after the seatbelt warning switched off.

*   *   *

0730 LOCAL (0130 GMT): The road was slick with morning dew, the roadside grass and foliage heavy with moisture, the air still cool as he sucked it in, breathing steadily. Eric Christofelsz's breathing hadn't changed much after three kilometres, his body moving with what seemed an easy rhythm as he ran. A smoker, it took iron control for him to keep his breathing down, and he had grown accustomed to the painful constriction in his chest. He wore sweat-stained maroon track pants and an old black T-shirt. The six-kilometre run was the way he started every morning, had done so ever since Delta Group had taken over as the hostage-rescue group.

Commando, airborne, maroon beret. . . This is the way we start the day! He remembered the chants of the bastard PTIs as they never even broke a sweat on the long runs.

Although he ran every morning, Eric Christofelsz made sure he varied the routes of his runs. Ganemulle was a safe town, situated northeast of Colombo, and had been so ever since the Commandos had set up camp nearby, back in the early 1980s, but it never paid to be careless. The town was proud of its elite troops, of their disproportionately large contribution to the war. Even in the bad days of the late '80s, when the communist insurgency had turned every small town and village into a killing ground, Ganemulle had remained safe territory. At a time when soldiers had gone home on leave armed and ready, preferring the relative safety of a military base to their own homes, Ganemulle had been a place the commandos could walk alone and unafraid. While in other parts of Sri Lanka soldiers had looked over their shoulders while taking the wife shopping, while some had returned home to dead kids and raped wives, commandos had openly dated the local girls in Ganemulle.

But old habits died hard in the Commandos, or *you* did, the instructors had been happy to tell Christofelsz when he had first joined the regiment. That had been back in 1990, the regiment's first direct civilian intake. Before that, both the Commandos and Special Forces had relied heavily on volunteers from regular Army units, but battalion COs, tired of seeing their best men siphoned off to *prima donna* elite units, had ensured the number of volunteers dried out to a trickle. Forced to expand to cover the demands of an ever intensifying war, the Commandos and SF had started to directly recruit civilians.

Christofelsz remembered the first interview board at the age of eighteen, two Commando officers and a warrant officer. He remembered ogling the para wings and sharpshooter badges and gallantry ribbons that had stared back at him from the chests of the interviewers. He remembered asking himself whether he had what it took to achieve what these men had, understanding that in their questions about his schooling and hobbies and sports, they had been asking him the same thing.

He remembered having felt unnerved by the warrant officer's cold, uninterested stare, remembered the dead eyes and the scarred face, had left the interview convinced he had been rejected. There had been over a thousand hopeful boys there that day, and eighty had been chosen to attempt selection for the Commandos. Of that eighty, twenty-one of them had been badged eight months later, Christofelsz among them, receiving from the CO the maroon beret and crossed-swords badge of the Commando Regiment.

Commando, airborne, all the way. . . Earn my pay blowing Tamils away!

He still wondered what it was that the selection board had seen in him. Wondered whether if, one day, sitting on a board himself, he'd be able to pick a winner.

Raising his hands as he ran, Christofelsz examined for the umpteenth time the two ragged scars on his hands. They were almost identical: circular scar tissue in the centre of his palms, replicated on the backs of his hands. His very own stigmata, he thought bitterly. Thinner, longer scars ran out from the circles in his hands to a point between his second and ring fingers. He still remembered the pain, the shocking blows as the nails were hammered in, blows that he had felt in every bone in his body. Captured by black Tigers in 1993, while on a recce patrol, he had been nailed to a makeshift cross and left to die. Fortunately, the Tamils hadn't had the experience of Roman legionaries and had driven the nails through his palms and feet, and not his wrists and ankles. It had taken Christofelsz four hours to work up the courage and determination to make his first attempt at pulling himself free of the nails. It had taken him a further three hours to accomplish his escape, fainting from the pain and loss of blood each time he tore a limb free. He had wondered at the time if it was this determination that the recruitment board had seen in his eyes when they selected him. He had wondered again, over the next two days, as he staggered, naked and delirious, through the scrub, if the board had been wrong, if all his training was to be wasted with his death. Christofelsz had been almost dead when an Air Force chopper had spotted and rescued him, and it had taken him almost a full year to recover physically.

The one thing he knew the board had been interested in was his knowledge of Tamil. At a time when the rest of the Army was requiring its recruits to have completed the eighth grade, the Commandos asked for at least O-Level qualifications. It was a sign of the regiment's recruitment criteria not only on the physical, but mental levels as well.

Eric Christofelsz wasn't a very big man, only about five feet eight, but with a hundred and seventy pounds packed tightly onto his frame. Like the grey eyes set in his light-skinned angular face, his body was more European than Asian in its lines, with thick wrists and ankles and powerful limbs. In contrast, his hair was as black as a crow's wing. Eric Christofelsz had been born for war. A Burgher, the son of a Nuwara Eliya tea planter, English was his mother tongue, while he studied all of his twelve years at Trinity College, Kandy, in Sinhalese. Growing up surrounded by Tamil cooks, gardeners, and plantation workers, he spoke Tamil fluently, though he had some trouble reading and writing it.

As a boy, Eric could never remember having ever been told a fairy tale or the other bedtime stories most children his age were told. Eric and his younger brother had gone to bed to dream of the Desert Rats in North Africa and the Marines at Iwo Jima. Instead of Red Riding Hood and the big bad wolf, Eric and his brother recreated the Battle of Little Big Horn.

Christofelsz wondered whether his father ever regretted having told his oldest son those second-hand war stories. He had certainly seen the fear, held behind his father's eyes with rigid self-control, the day Eric had left home for the Army; a self-control the old man had passed on to his sons.

And the Christofelsz family itself had a history that seemed to trace the wars of Britain and its Commonwealth. Two brothers had been the first to set foot on the island in the 1750s — Swiss mercenary soldiers serving under the Dutch. Liking the country, they had stayed, marrying local Portuguese girls. Later generations of the Christofelszes would fight for Holland and later Britain, helping put down the Sinhalese rebellions. Three Christofelszes were at the capture of Kandy in the mid-nineteenth century, and there was one at the Siege of Ladysmith during the Boer War. Two Christofelszes gave their lives on the Western Front for their adopted country, Ceylon, and the empire that ruled it, and another would be listed "missing, believed killed" at Dunkirk two decades later. Eric's own grandfather had fought his way from Libya to Palestine in the Second World War, helping Britain kill Germans, Italians, and Arabs alike. A great uncle had been the regimental sergeant major of the 1st Ceylon Light Infantry. Eric had even heard, during one of his father's few drunken moments, of a cousin on his grandmother's side who had served in the

German SS, dying in place with the rest of the *Florian Geyer* Division
at the Battle of Budapest.

Eric Christofelsz had often wondered why his father and
his uncles had never followed the family tradition and served,
choosing instead the plantation and shipping industries. Christofelsz
had never asked, and his father had never volunteered the reason.
The old man had never thought it necessary to defend or explain
himself, least of all to his sons, and went through life with a quiet,
closed determination. His stories to his sons had never been about
his own boyhood experiences, but always of his own father's. Now,
Eric Christofelsz realized that he knew so very little of his father,
more about his mother, but still very little of them both, not even
how they had met.

Christofelsz promised himself, as he had done countless
times before, that the next time he was home on leave, he would
take the old guy out for a drink and ask him all the questions he
never had before. Why had he never joined the Army, and how
had he met Mum; what was it like to grow up without a mother in
1940s Ceylon, and why had Uncle Graham shot himself.

But he knew, even though he didn't admit it, that it would
never happen. His father rarely drank anymore, and it was the
old guy who asked the questions, mostly about the war. And Eric
now found the roles reversed, with him telling the war stories.
The public version anyway, the clean ones. He wondered whether
Grandpa had ever told the true stories about North Africa, about
what it had been really like to go in against the Afrika Korps with
bayonets fixed.

Christofelsz slowed down as he approached the camp's gate.
He checked that his pager was still in place, clipped to the waistband
of his jogging pants. He was on one-hour alert, here at Ganemulle,
the ten-minute team was at the airport. The four S's — shit,
smoke, shower, and shave — and he'd be ready for breakfast.
Then the Killing House with the others for a quick run-through.

* * *

0945 CHINA COASTAL TIME (0145 GMT): As the seatbelt warning winked off, Mahesh Balachandran rose calmly to his feet and headed forward. On the far side of the cabin, he could see Nireuben also moving up the right-hand aisle. Balachandran stopped two rows from the front of business class and dropped to his knees. He smiled apologetically at the middle-aged business man's affronted stare as he groped beneath his seat. His hands closed around the rectangular package, and in one quick movement he ripped it free of the tape that held it to the underside of the stored life jacket. Getting back to his feet, he continued forward to the toilets. Beyond, he could see the flight attendants in the galley behind the cockpit, getting the drink trolleys ready.

Once inside the toilet, Balachandran split open the heat-contoured rigifoam box and stuffed the pieces into the waste disposal. He then tore open the sealed plastic packet that had been inside the rigifoam. Sealed, in case of an unforeseen sweep by explosive-sniffing dogs at Changi. He dropped all but one grenade into his jacket pockets, placed the little 9-mm Micro-Uzi in the sink, and checked his watch. A few minutes more. He then took the chance to have a quick piss.

Exactly ten minutes after the seatbelt warning had been switched off, Balachandran stepped out of the toilet and into the forward galley. Simultaneously, Nireuben entered the confined space from the far end, and the cabin crew's eyes went wide as they saw the submachine-guns and grenades. They stared in horror, but did not scream. Too well trained for that, Balachandran realized.

He looked up into the CCTV camera mounted in the galley, and knew the pilots would be staring unbelievingly at the cockpit screen. The emergency call would be already going out to Changi. The Singaporean Air Force and the air arms of the neighbouring countries would be scrambling their alert patrols into the sky. After September 2001, there was zero tolerance for hijackings. Fighter planes would be ordered to shoot down a hijacked airliner rather than risk another New York or Washington DC.

Balachandran taped a grenade to the perspex of the galley's right-side window, in plain sight of the camera. From further down the cabin, there were screams and yells of fear as the rest of the team went into action, shouting at the passengers, using the threat of the SMGs and grenades to reinforce the shock, to keep people in their seats. The team was snapping orders in English, controlling the passengers.

Over the background voices came a yell from business class. "Freeze, marshals! Put your—"

The shout was cut off by four quick gunshots, Nireuben firing his Micro-Uzi on semi-auto. Balachandran grabbed the nearest stewardess and dragged her back past the toilet. The sky marshal was already down, in the right aisle, having been knocked back through the curtain that separated business from economy. The curtain had been ripped off its rail and was clenched in the dying man's left fist. His right held a pistol. Balachandran saw Nireuben stoop over the man and disarm him.

Balachandran had spotted the marshal the moment he had boarded. The man had been standing by the forward toilets, as if he had been waiting for it to come free. Balachandran had, however, noted at the time that the toilet wasn't occupied, and that the marshal's eyes never left the embarking passengers. He had also noticed that the man was still wearing his suit jacket, even though all the other male passengers who had spent the last few hours on board had taken off theirs. Evidently Nireuben had spotted the man, too.

Blank terror wiped all rational thought from Jennifer Jensen's mind as she stood petrified in the hijacker's grip, staring at the last twitches of the sky marshal's foot. Much as she had hated having the marshals on board, the death of this one made her realize how helpless they now were. She stifled a scream as an arm with muscles strong as steel bands pulled her against the hijacker's body. Oh, God, not this. Not this. It had been every crew member's recurring nightmare ever since the previous September. But something, some rational whisper, had always told her it would never happen to her. Now it was, now she was going to die. And she knew what they wanted, what they were going to do, how they were all going to die. The Petronas Towers. They were going to fly to Kuala Lumpur, and crash into the Petronas Towers, the world's tallest buildings.

The gun was pointing over her shoulder, covering Brian Stolz, the chief purser, as he took an involuntary step forward. A grenade hung by its pin from the little finger of the hijacker's right hand, the one holding the square, ugly gun.

"Into your seats!" the hijacker holding her snapped. "All of you. Seatbelts on. If you get up, we'll kill you."

Balachandran pushed Jen-Jen towards the armoured cockpit door, and pressed the intercom button, looking up into the camera. He knew the pilots would be flipping their fingers across the screen menus, bringing up the different views from the cameras in business and economy, seeing the armed men and the cowed passengers and crew.

"Open the door, captain," he said into the intercom, "or everybody dies."

The pilots would already be relaying descriptions of the hijackers to Changi, he knew. The number of hijackers, what weapons they were carrying, whether they were male or female. But Balachandran knew it wouldn't matter what they told the people on the ground. The assault teams would never get the chance to storm Air Canada AC634.

The cockpit door stayed shut, and there was no answer from the intercom. Balachandran knew he could start shooting the passengers and crew. He knew that no pilot could take that for very long. But Balachandran knew he didn't have to bother. They had an easier way. He looked over his shoulder and nodded to Nireuben, who was standing at the head of the right aisle, covering business class. Nireuben stepped back into the galley and pulled the pin on the grenade taped to the window.

"Captain, my colleague has just pulled the pin on the grenade you can see," Balachandran said, his voice calm and faintly amused, hiding the tension he felt. "A rubber band is still holding down the striker lever. When my colleague removes that, we will all have five seconds before the grenade blows open the side of the fuselage." He nodded again at Nireuben, and without hesitation the man reached for the grenade.

There was a beep as the cockpit door was unlocked. Nireuben paused, hand still holding the grenade.

"Both doors, captain," Balachandran insisted.

As the manual override was tripped, opening the second door and alerting ground control that cockpit security had been breached, Nireuben and Ramesh began to move the business class passengers back into economy, silencing any protests with well-aimed kicks and shoves. The dead sky marshal was dragged to the front of business class and strapped into a front row seat.

CHAPTER 19

At the Katunayake Air Force Base, next to the Bandaranaike International Airport, Red Team of the 1st Commando Regiment's Delta Group went to red alert as the news of the Air Canada hijack came in. AC634 had originated in Colombo, so it was highly likely that the hijackers had boarded there, too. If that was the case, they would most probably be Tamil terrorists. And if that was true, the Commandos wanted to have first bite. An air hijack was a rarity these days, and it was what hostage-rescue unit commanders had wet dreams over. The one-hour alert teams were choppered out to the airbase and brought up to a half-hour standby. A C-130 Hercules sat fuelled up and ready in the shade of a hangar.

It all depended where AC634 landed. Colombo and the —Commandos would have their chance. Changi was a seventy-five-percent possibility, if the Singaporeans didn't want a mess on their hands. Anywhere else in Southeast Asia was definitely a no-no. Those countries' own hostage rescue units would be drooling for a real-life chance to storm an airliner. If AC634 headed back to South Asia — and they certainly had the fuel — it would bring a whole new set of possibilities into play. If the hijackers landed in India, the Commandos could forget about being involved; India would never let foreign troops onto its soil. If the hijackers went to the Maldives, it was a fifty-fifty chance, depending on the Maldivian government. India had a full Para-Commando in the Maldives, but no Special Action Group hostage-rescue units. If the plane went to Pakistan, given that country's special relationship with Sri Lanka, the Commandos could get in. But it all depended on any number of variables, ranging from the hijackers nationalities to their demands.

Daniel Devanayagam watched the hijacker from under his baseball cap, wondering what Harrison Ford would do in this situation. Maybe he'd wait till the man's back was turned and then hit him fast and hard, then disappear down into the cargo hold. But even Daniel realized that a twelve-year-old would be no match for a grown man. Besides, the hijacker never seemed to turn his back, and there was a second armed man standing behind Daniel, by the amidships toilets. And he had no idea how one got into the cargo hold. *Air Force One* had been a bit vague on the subject. Why didn't airlines let everybody carry guns, like in the wild-west? Then when the hijackers tried something like this, they'd get blasted from all sides, like stagecoach robbers. Daniel had seen only these two hijackers, but Suzie had told him there were more up front.

Besides, the Canadian cop had had a gun, and that hadn't helped much. When the man had been shot, Daniel had tried to stand up on his seat to get a better view, but his father had held him down. Suzie, however, had seen the body, and said there was more blood than there had been even in *Reservoir Dogs*.

Suzie and her parents had been moved back into economy with the other business class passengers. It hadn't been a fully booked flight, and there had been enough room in economy for everybody. Suzie and her mother were seated next to Daniel's mother, John Kopleck, Suzie's father, was seated somewhere further back, where he had found a free seat.

Daniel nudged his father and asked him whether he thought they could knock the hijackers out together, but his father just told him to sit quietly until reinforcements arrived.

When the hijackers had first made their move, Robin Devanayagam had tried to use his credit card to activate the combination entertainment system control and cellular phone plugged into the seat armrest, but the hijackers had been too fast, moving down the aisles and disabling the phones.

Further back, in the rear third of the cabin, Francois Gerard, the second sky marshal watched in horror as the two hijackers who were covering this section moved down the aisles, disabling the entertainment system controls and confiscating personal mobile phones. Gerard's training screamed at him to draw his pistol and open fire. He could still pull it off before the hijackers settled down. But he had heard Steve's shouted order from the front of the plane, and the burst of fire that had cut it off. Passengers whispered that someone had been shot and killed in business class.

Gerard's heart pounded as the hijacker came closer, the Micro-Uzi covering the passengers while he ripped out the remote controls, rummaging through hand- and shoulder-bags, and patting down men and women for phones. If he didn't act now they would find his pistol and then the game would be up. But his legs were paralysed, and all he could do was stare. Do it now, it's easy, just draw the pistol and slip the safety, cock it as you're getting up do it now before he gets any closer, but oh shit that Uzi's already cocked and locked and the other guy's watching me and I don't wanna die, but oh God if I don't do it now it'll be too late, just do it do it do it—

The hijacker was standing over Gerard. The man pulled the entertainment system control handset free and jerked the wire loose from the armrest. The muzzle of the submachine-gun was in Gerard's face. The hijacker tossed the remote to his comrade who dropped it into a plastic bag with the others. He flipped open Gerard's jacket and saw the pistol in the spider rig. With a warning yell, the man stepped back, gripping the SMG with both hands.

"Put your hands up!" the man shouted in English. "Now, or you die!"

The young German tourist sitting next to Gerard screamed and cowered, and the Canadian raised his hands.

"OK, man, OK. No problems—"

Tossing his SMG into his left hand, the hijacker punched Gerard in the face with his right, moving with such blinding speed that the marshal didn't even have time to blink. He rocked back, eyes tearing, pain shooting into his brain from his broken nose. Not daring to lower his hands, Gerard felt his pistol removed. He was pulled out of his seat and thrown face down on the floor and searched carefully. He was then dragged to his feet and pushed roughly along into business class. By now he had blinked the tears from his eyes, and was able to watch as another hijacker handcuffed his ankles to the seat legs with cuffs that he took from a stewardess. Gerard knew that all flights carried these to restrain unruly passengers. When the tears returned to Gerard's eyes, they weren't caused by physical pain, but by the sight of his partner Steve Brown sitting slumped in the seat at the far end of the row. His face was as pale as paper, and his chest swamped with blood.

Colin Peters swallowed to relieve the dryness in his throat, but it didn't help much. He had been about to ask the stewardess for a beer when the armed gunmen had taken over. As he watched the hijackers taping over the lenses of the security cameras in the cabin, Peters wondered who the men were, what they wanted, whether this was another terrorist suicide mission, and whether they were all going to die. He also wondered whether the hijackers would let the cabin crew continue serving drinks.

Further down the cabin, towards the rear of the plane, Vijitha Dhampahana fought down the rising horror he was feeling as he stared at the hijackers. Tigers, they had to be Tigers, he told himself. But why now, when he was almost free, about to begin his new life? Dhampahana had lived in Colombo almost all of his life, and had never seen a live terrorist before, though he had once seen the dismembered corpse of a suicide bomber. Although he had on several occasions seen the results of LTTE attacks on the capital, he had never seen the attackers themselves. As Dhampahana furtively watched the hijacker standing by the amidships toilets, he wondered what the man was thinking, whether he felt any fear for his own life, remorse for the people he was going to kill.

Within minutes of Air Canada AC634 declaring a hijack emergency, the Singaporean Air Force scrambled a pair of Tornado interceptors from Tengah, in the northwest of the island. The two aircraft lit their afterburners and climbed quickly to twenty thousand feet, settling into an elliptical patrol pattern northeast of Singapore. AC634 was already out of Singaporean sovereign territory, fast approaching Anambas Island, already inside Indonesian airspace. The Tornados were a precaution, in case the Airbus turned back towards Singapore. After the suicide attacks on New York and Washington DC the previous year, no one was taking any chances.

A pair of Indonesian Air Force F-16s from Squadron 3 based at Ishwahyudi Air Base on Java, had been already airborne at the time, and they now screamed north over the Straits of Karimata. The pilots had orders to intercept the Air Canada plane if it turned south towards Jakarta. The F-16s carried a full supplement of AIM-9F Sidewinder air-to-air missiles, but had no orders to open fire just yet.

At Sukarno-Hatta International Airport, close to Jakarta, the *Satgas Atbara* went on ten-minute alert. Loosely translated as Counter-Terrorist Task Force, the unit was part of the Indonesian Air Force, and was responsible for hostage-rescue situations.

By the time the Indonesian F-16s had arrived over the South China Sea and were reporting the fact that AC634 was headed north, the Airbus was already being painted by the radar of a Royal Malaysian Air Force AWACS aircraft.

As soon as the airliner entered Malaysian airspace, east of Bunguran Island, the AWACS diverted a pair of MiG-29s from Sultan Ahmed Shah Airbase at Kuntan, on the east coast of mainland Malaysia.

So far there had been no radio contact between the Airbus and the ground since the cockpit had been breached.

*   *   *

1300 LOCAL [0700 GMT]: By now the hijack was all over the networks across Asia. In Colombo, Devini Sundaralingam and her team watched the breaking news on *CNN*, *BBC*, and *Sky*. The anchors at the various stations hadn't much information, and journalists at Changi knew nothing beyond the fact that an Air Canada flight bound from Singapore to Vancouver had been hijacked. News had leaked out that the hijackers were thought to be South Asian — either Indian, Pakistani, Bangladeshi, or Sri Lankan. Recent events worldwide made sure the Sri Lankan Tamil terrorists were the most likely suspects.

Devini looked at her team, wondering what the hell was going on. She had known which countries were being targeted, what the timetable was. She was the only one, except for the Leader, who knew. But she hadn't known about this. Hadn't been told. If this was a Tiger operation, it had to have been a direct order from the Leader. But the timing would screw up her own operation. If the hijack wasn't resolved this same day, security would clamp tight in Colombo.

"Part of the plan?" asked Jegen, Devini's second-in-command, noting her puzzled expression. His face was narrow and bony, with a jutting chin below a thick moustache, and the whole thing topped by an explosion of curly hair.

Devini shrugged. "Must be. But it's the first Ah've heard of it." She stared unseeing at the television screen, idly flipping between the news channels. "We'll have to push our timetable forward. Before they tighten all security." Devini looked at Jegen. "Tomorrow morning?"

"But we planned for the afternoon because of a reason," Jegen pointed out. "We know which security guards are on duty. An' the afternoon's the only time there won' be a crowd of applicants in the place."

The rest of the team of Black Tigers were silent, watching the debate.

"We have to take the risk," Devini replied. "We didn' plan for this hijack, no? What if that plane lands at Katunayake an' they clamp down a curfew? What if they start house-to-house searches in Colombo? This place may be safe," she waved a vague thumb around, indicating the small Cinnamon Gardens annex, "but it's not *that* safe." She looked around at the faces of the four men and one other woman who made up her team. "We have to begin the operation while we still can!"

* * *

The two Royal Malaysian Air Force MiG-29s were at forty thousand feet over the South China Sea, heading east, when they spotted the Airbus in the red and white colours of Air Canada. AC634 had dropped down to thirty thousand feet, and was beginning a left turn to the northwest; a turn that would point it roughly towards the Malaccan Peninsula, the southern third of which constituted mainland Malaysia, with the city of Kuala Lumpur on its western coast. One of Kuala Lumpur's proudest landmarks was the one thousand four hundred and eighty three feet tall Petronas Towers, the tallest man-made structure in history.

Calling to his wingman, Major Mohammed Riyaz Al-Hadj Khan rolled his MiG-29 Fulcrum Alpha one hundred and eighty degrees, onto its back, and pulled the stick back into his stomach. The G-forces jammed him deep into his seat as the two fighter planes went into a screaming split-S. With his vision greying and tunnelling out, Major Khan pulled out of the dive at thirty-five thousand feet, headed back west. Slamming the stick over, he did a tight right-hand turn to the northeast, then still descending, a second turn, this time to the left. He rolled out on a north-westerly heading, the turns having also served to slow his MiG down to the Airbus A340's speed of eight hundred kilometres per hour. Switching on their navigation lights, Khan and his wingman did a series of desperate S-turns to stay with the slow-moving airliner. While Khan's wingman stayed behind and a thousand feet above AC634, Khan hung off the Airbus' port wing.

"Alpha Charlie six three four, this is the Royal Malaysian Air Force, do you copy?" Khan radioed. He looked across to the

Airbus' cockpit, but could not make out any faces. There was no answer from AC634. "Alpha Charlie six three four, this is the Royal Malaysian Air Force," he repeated. "You are in violation of Malaysian air security. What is your destination?" No answer. "Alpha Charlie six three four, if you do not acknowledge or change your present course to leave Malaysian airspace, I have orders to shoot you down. Do you copy, Air Canada?"

※

As if to reinforce the threat, Captain Johnny Burnett saw a second MiG do an overhead afterburner pass, climbing away to the right once it was several kilometres ahead of the Airbus.

"What do I do?" Burnett asked, his voice tight as he tried to control the panic. He could see the air-to-air missiles mounted under the first fighter's wings. He could see the MiG pilot in silhouette, gesturing at him. Burnett wondered whether a democratic government would really order its air force to bring down a civilian airliner if they thought it threatened a major city. There were rumours that, following September 11th, many air forces had just such standing orders. And an Asian nation was the most likely to do so. Burnett glanced across at Mike Harrap, and saw the co-pilot's face was pale with fear.

"Stay off the radio." instructed Balachandran, strapped into a jump seat behind the pilots.

"Look," Burnett snapped, irritated that the hijack leader didn't seem to get the gravity of the situation, "if he fires a missile, we're screwed. And you won't get a chance to voice your demands to—"

"Stop talking and *fly*," growled Balachandran. "I won't tell you again. I don't want to kill you just yet. But if you don't follow orders exactly, I'll do it. Your co-pilot will cooperate better once you're dead." Then he added, "The MiG won' fire."

Watching the MiG-29 on their wing, Balachandran hoped he was right in calling the Malaysian's bluff. They still had a long way to go. But he doubted that the MiGs had orders to fire unless there was a direct threat. The Airbus' present course would take them over Kota Bahru, on the Malay-Thai border, and he knew the Malaysians must know this too. They would much rather hand the problem over to Thailand than have a messy confrontation in which world opinion might not look favourably on a civilian airliner with over three hundred passengers and crew being brought down into the sea. Nevertheless, Balachandran wondered idly what the reaction from the MiG pilots would be if he were to change course for Kuala Lumpur.

The MiG-29 on their wing pulled up and away in a tight left-hand climbing turn. They could see neither of the Malaysian fighters now, but soon the radio was crackling again.

"Alpha Charlie six three four, this is the pilot of Royal Malaysian Air Force MiG-29 callsign Cobra Lead. If you do not change course in two minutes, I *will* open fire. Acknowledge."

Burnett had to clench his left fist on the little computer game-style joystick of the Airbus to keep his hand from shaking. "Look, man," he said, not bothering to try and hide the fear, "I will *not* endanger my aircraft, or these passengers."

In an instant, Balachandran had unbuckled his seatbelt and was crouching behind Burnett's seat. The muzzle of the Micro-Uzi jammed into the side of the pilot's suntanned neck.

"It isn't *your* aircraft anymore, it's *mine*," he snarled into the Canadian's ear. "An' if you don't do *exactly* as I say, I will shoot both you and your co-pilot on the spot, an' we will all go straight down into the sea. *Before* the MiG has a chance to shoot. So *stay on this course*."

The seconds flickered away on the instrument panel-mounted clock in Major Riyaz Khan's MiG-29. He was one thousand five hundred metres behind the Airbus, both the interlocking circle and rectangle over the airliner in his head-up display and the whine in his headset confirming the infra-red lock of an AA-6 Acrid missile. With a glance at the clock, he wondered what the hijackers would do There were supposed to be over three hundred passengers or board the Air Canada plane. Khan had read about the Korean Air Lines 747 that had been shot down by the Soviet Union in 1983. He wondered what the Russian pilot had thought as he triggered his air-to-air missiles.

"Cobra Lead to Nest," he transmitted. "Alpha Charlie is maintaining course. I have an IR lock. Permission to fire."

"Stand by, Cobra Lead."

"Cobra Lead to Nest, be aware I am close to stall-out."

"Stand by, Cobra Lead."

Khan and his wingman had their flaps extended in an effort to stay in position, and he could already feel the controls getting soggy at this low speed.

"Cobra Lead from Cobra Nest, hold your fire until further orders. Stay with Alpha Charlie. He seems to be headed for Thailand."

Flipping down the arming switch on his missile button, Khan increased speed and climbed away, his wingman staying with him. He wasn't sure whether he felt relief or disappointment. Three hundred lives were a lot to have on your conscience, but he was a warrior, sworn to follow orders and defend his country. If he thought the Airbus was a threat to Malaysia, he wouldn't hesitate to shoot it down.

*   *   *

The Canadian Forces CC-144 Challenger was at thirty five thousand feet, travelling in its high-speed cruise mode of nine hundred kilometres per hour, just short of the speed of sound. Sitting in one of the comfortable cabin seats, Lieutenant Jan Conway tried to relax and get some rest. They had a long flight ahead. The rest of his platoon was doing what most long-distance travellers always did — a few were watching the in-flight movie or listening to music, but most were already asleep. The CC-144 Challenger belonged to 412 Squadron, based at Ottawa, and was usually used for VIP transport. The cabin was fitted out accordingly, in first class luxury. There was even a steward, who had a range of impressive alcoholic and non-alcoholic beverages, ready to hand. Jan Conway hadn't needed to warn his men to stick to the soft drinks.

Within half an hour of Singapore alerting Ottawa to the AC634 hijack, Joint Task Force 2 had got a platoon into the air. Singapore had agreed to let JTF2 handle any assault on the plane that was deemed necessary. Provided of course, that AC634 returned to Changi. Conway's had been the ready platoon, based at Canadian Forces Base Kingston, in Ontario, for any hijack situations, and had been immediately airlifted by CC-130 Hercules to Ottawa. A second platoon would follow them to Singapore in a CC-150 Polaris heavy jet transport — essentially a converted Airbus A320 — as soon as they were ready.

The news on the hijack was still sketchy. Conway and his men knew that there were six hijackers, armed with submachine-guns and grenades. The pilot of the Airbus had managed to report that much before the hijackers got into the cockpit. The in-flight cameras had been disabled just minutes after the pilots had started the emergency video feed back to Changi. There was no continuous routine monitoring of the cabins of in-flight airliners; only in the case of a perceived emergency would a pilot broadcast video footage to the ground. And, in spite of all the media hype on the new security measures, the armed men had got into the cockpit just as easily as ever. There were still many things JTF2 didn't know, like whether the hijackers had plastic explosives, whether the hijackers had any females among them, or where they had come aboard. And, how, wondered Conway, had they got the firearms and grenades on board? Colombo, and especially Changi, would have rigorous security checks. The other option was that the weapons had been hidden aboard the airliner in Colombo, by cleaners or caterers. But Conway knew that almost all airports did security sweeps of aircraft prior to passengers coming aboard. He had first thought it most likely that the hijackers had boarded at Colombo — especially as they had been identified as South Asians — but if that was so, why had they waited so long to trigger the operation? Were the hijackers after someone special who had boarded at Changi? A passenger list would soon confirm or deny that. If the hijackers had boarded at Changi, they could check for possible identification by airport authorities.

There were so many questions that Conway needed the answers to, but none of them seemed available just yet. Maybe by the time they reached Singapore, they'd have them. Two hours out of Changi, they would start going over the plan for the assault and the immediate action drills. Of course, it could all be for nothing if the hijackers didn't return to Changi. But Ottawa would try to negotiate a role for JTF2 no matter which airport the plane landed at.

*   *   *

1150 CHINA COASTAL TIME (0350 GMT): "Ladies and gentlemen, this is Major Mahesh, the commander of the Black Tiger Seelan Special Detachment of the Liberation Tigers of Tamil Eelam," Mahesh Balachandran's voice boomed over the cabin speakers, making the passengers look up nervously. "My men and I now have control of this plane and everyone on it. We don't want to hurt anyone on board, and we have no intention of crashing this plane into any buildings or cities. So please stay calm and quiet if you wish to survive this flight. Having said that, please be assured that my men will not hesitate to kill anybody who tries to resist. We don't hold any grudge against individuals, and our battle is against the tyrannical Sinhalese government of Sri Lanka and its racist friends in Ottawa. Your lives are in *their* hands, and if they do not accede to our demands we will blow up this plane.

"I have instructed the cabin crew to provide you with whatever food and drink you want. Please remember to ask them for any duty-free goods you wish to purchase, and enjoy the in-flight movie. Thank you for flying Air Canada."

Johnny Burnett watched Major Mahesh hand back the tannoy mike with a smirk and strap himself back into the jump seat. Cool as ice, and with a weird sense of humour to boot.

Nothing like the way the Canadian military had predicted terrorist hijackers would behave in their training films and exercises. No screaming or rhetoric, no beatings. Just the cold eyes and the calm voice. Burnett had been stunned by the ease with which the two sky marshals had been overpowered. These bastards were obviously well trained.

It was two hours since the hijackers had gotten into the cockpit, and there had been no communication with the ground or the escorting fighter planes in all that time. No demands, no threats. The Airbus was flying over low mountains that were blanketed in dense jungle, flying an east-northeasterly course that followed the Malay-Thai border as it bisected the Malaccan Peninsula. If he looked out of the portside cockpit windows, Burnett could, if he craned his neck, just make out the two Malaysian MiG-29s, still holding station, half a kilometre away. Mike Harrap had reported a pair of Royal Thai Air Force F/A-18 Hornets that had been with them ever since they had reached the border half an hour ago. The Hornets were also loaded for bear, and had tried to make contact with the Airbus, but to no avail. Major Mahesh had insisted that they maintain radio silence.

Both Thai and Malay patrols had kept their distance, not venturing closer than half a kilometre to AC634. Neither patrol wanted a misunderstanding with their trigger-happy counterparts this close to the border.

Balachandran handed over control of the cockpit to Nireuben and headed aft to inspect the plane. The whole team had trained specifically for the Airbus A340, and Nireuben would know what to watch for in the cockpit.

He ignored the second sky marshal, who was still cuffed to his business class seat, and headed through into economy. The passengers followed him with their eyes, knowing instinctively that he was the commander. There was fear in all the eyes, he noted, though in some cases mixed with anger or curiosity, but fear was the dominating expression. And one could smell it, he realized, as he walked down the aisle, stopping to exchange a word or two with the other members of the team, even up here in the sterile air-conditioned atmosphere of the cabin it could be smelled. Balachandran had smelled it many times before, mixed with the stink of high explosive, blood, and shit, as the mortars and machine-guns poured fire at them in an ambush in the jungle; almost hidden by the sharp tang of salt and gun oil as they rowed up to a beach at night. And he had no doubt that the smell of fear on the Airbus would soon be underlined by other, equally unpleasant odours, of sweat, and blocked toilets.

*   *   *

1600 AUSTRALIAN WESTERN STANDARD TIME (0600 GMT):
"Where are they now?" Donald Fenster asked. The trade talks had broken up for tea, and though he had been informed of the hijack earlier, he wanted the latest update.

"Last reported over the Andaman Sea, east of the Nicobars," the parliamentary private secretary replied. "Still headed west."

"And we still have no idea who they are, or what they want?"

"Nothing concrete, sir, but the pilot managed to get out the fact that they looked South Asian, and that there were four or five of them. Given the course of the plane, I think it's safe to assume they're ERA. Looks like they might be headed for Sri Lanka or India."

"Keep me posted on any further developments."

*   *   *

1500 LOCAL (0900 GMT): "Where are they now?"

The Sri Lankan who had spoken wore no unit badges or signs of rank on his fatigues. The only distinguishing item was metal parachute wings pinned to the right breast of his Pakistani Bhutto-pattern camouflage smock. The trousers he wore were British DPMs, bloused into battered jungle boots. His bandido moustache drooped down on both sides of his chin, and his hair was long and unruly. Captain Saliya Dayananda was 2/ic Delta

Group of the 1st Commando Regiment, and the officer commanding Red Team for the duration of the hostage-rescue tour. He and the lieutenant who was normally Delta's int officer, but currently Red Team's 2/ic, had taken over the Air Force operations room at Katunayake.

"Five hundred kilometres east of Madras, and getting closer to India all the time," answered the wing commander who ran the ops room. He knew the Commando officers only by their first names, but understood that the one with the moustache was commanding the black-clad killers who were now billeted in the Air Force NCO's mess. "Indian MiG-21s from the Nicobars tracked them out over the Bay of Bengal, but had to turn back when they were short of juice. MiG-29s from Cochin will pick them up soon. They're still refusing to answer radio calls, an' we don't know what the Indians will do if they try to cross the coast. Buggers have been a bit touchy about terrorism lately."

In December 2001, Muslim Kashmiri terrorists had launched a suicidal attack on the Indian parliament in New Delhi, almost succeeding in wiping out the entire Indian cabinet. The resulting sabre-rattling had almost ended in outright war between India and Pakistan. While India had ruthlessly promoted terrorism against its neighbours during the latter half of the twentieth century in an attempt to destabilize them and emerge the dominant power in the region, it was vociferous and self-righteous in its condemnation of terrorism within its own borders, especially in the new era of the US War on Terror. Many direct parallels could be drawn between India and the United States.

*   *   *

1010 CENTRAL EUROPEAN TIME (0910 GMT): The French immigration official in departures at Charles de Gaulle inspected the three black Sri Lankan diplomatic passports, glancing up at the faces of their owners. Though the photographs in the documents matched the faces, they matched them a little too perfectly. The passports were obviously new and had never been used before. There weren't even visas in them for France or the Schengen States, not even a date of entry for Europe. When the official queried this obvious irregularity, the three Sri Lankans — one in a wheelchair — shrugged and said in English that they spoke no French.

The official decided he would have to get his superior, diplomatic immunity or not. The senior immigration man spoke English, and was told by the apparent leader of the Sri Lankan trio that, as the passports stated, they were Sri Lankan civil servants, and had just completed a defence-related training course on the island of Corsica.

Captain Paul Toussainte couldn't decide whether the colour of the three Asians might be the result of the Mediterranean sun, or just their natural heritage.

"But these passports have no entry stamp for France, nor any visas," the Frenchman pointed out. "There is not even a stamp showing you have left Colombo." He glared into the cold brown eyes of the Sri Lankan, eyes that stared back out of an impassive face. "These passports have — according to the entries here—" he pointed to a page— "been issued by your Paris embassy just a few days ago. Where are your old passports, and when did you enter France, Mister. . . Fernando?"

Dayan Premasiri held the Frenchman's gaze as he answered. "I can't tell you that because it's a classified matter. Our old passports were stolen while we were at the beach in Corsica. If you have any problems you may phone the Sri Lankan embassy in Paris. But I suggest you stamp our passports *now* and let us be on our way. If we miss this flight, I can promise you that the shit will come down on you from *very* high up."

Toussainte's jaw clenched. He had never met civil servants who talked quite like this one did, but this one didn't look like a civil servant either, none of them did, in spite of the dark business suits — and even those didn't seem to fit perfectly. It had something to do with the hard faces and the watchful eyes.

Toussainte had seen that look before, occasionally passing through immigration, and they invariably belonged to men of GIGN, *les Paras*, or *la Légion Etrangère*. Professional killers, they had always made Toussainte want to stand back.

He glanced at his watch. The Sri Lankan Airlines flight to Kuwait was due to take off in fifteen minutes. "If what you say is true, then your names will be in our immigration records as having entered France," he said in a last attempt to preserve authority, knowing that he had already lost. "It will take only a matter of minutes to check the computer."

Dayan smiled patiently, as if talking to a retarded child. "You will not find our names on your computer. I already told you, it's a classified matter."

"*Where* did you say you were doing your training?" Toussainte was desperately trying to save face. "I will have to check."

"Calvi, in Corsica."

The Frenchman blinked. Calvi. *2ème Régiment Etranger de Parachutistes*. The Foreign Legion's paras. Toussainte nodded at his subordinate, indicating that the passports should be stamped, and retreated into his office. Dayan didn't bother thanking him.

The Sri Lankans were already on board their flight before Toussainte was able to get hold of someone at the Sri Lankan embassy who would answer his questions. Yes, he was told, the three men were Sri Lankan Ministry of Defence officials on a training course, and yes, the training had been conducted at Calvi, and no, there was no name or phone number they could refer him to on the island of Corsica. By the time Toussainte got through to the personnel officer of 2REP at Calvi, the Sri Lankan Airlines flight was already airborne, but he persisted in his inquiries in an attempt to salvage his professional pride at having to disobey the regulations.

The Foreign Legion personnel officer told him he was quite sure that he had no such names on his records, and there were certainly no Sri Lankans among the non-Legion foreign personnel doing specialist courses. He promised to check further and call Toussainte back.

The captain hung up and wondered whether he should call
the police immediately or wait until he was sure there was something
illegal going on. Five minutes later, the phone rang and Toussainte
grabbed it.

Instead of the Legion officer from Calvi, the new caller
identified himself as a GIGN colonel, and then proceeded to tell
Toussainte, in no uncertain terms, that he should forget all about
the three Sri Lankans, and cease any further inquiries if he valued
his career. Toussainte was informed that it was a GIGN
affair and involved national security. The caller hung up without
further ceremony.

* * *

1515 LOCAL (0945 GMT): "Air Canada six three four, this is
Madras Control, you are refused permission to land. I repeat,
you are refused permission to land."

Johnny Burnett's jaw clenched, looking back over his
shoulder at Major Mahesh. He knew this was all a game, that
both the authorities on the ground and the terrorists would jockey
for position, trying to establish who was boss. Burnett knew that
the authorities would give in first, that was what they were trained
to do, to calm down the situation until the hijackers could be
talked into surrender or hostage-rescue forces could get aboard.
But even with his knowledge of the rules of the game being played
out, Burnett had to fight to still the anger he felt against the unseen
man in the Madras tower. Didn't he know that the hijackers weren't
playing games? Or that if they were, it was for much higher stakes.
Stakes that Johnny Burnett and the other crew members and
passengers couldn't afford.

"Tell him you're short of fuel, that you're declaring an
emergency," instructed Balachandran calmly. "Tell him that if you
cannot land, you will crash."

"Control, this is six three four. I am short of fuel and
declaring an emergency. We *must* land."

"AC six three four, this is Madras Control. Negative, repeat, negative. We know you have enough fuel to have reached Vancouver, and surely have enough remaining to make Male or Colombo. All airports in India are closed to you, I repeat, closed. You have permission to overfly Indian territory, but if you lower below fifteen thousand you will be shot down. Madras out."

Balachandran stared out the starboard side, his face expressionless. An Indian Air Force Mirage 2000H was holding station off the starboard wing, and he knew that a second Mirage would be trailing them, missiles ready. Madras was imperative. The blame had to be placed on the proper shoulders. Madras' refusal to let them land was an expected ploy, something that would crack under the right pressure.

"Vent the wing tanks," Balachandran said.

"*What?*" both pilots asked almost simultaneously.

"I said, vent the wing tanks," Balachandran snapped.

"Look, you can't be serious," protested Burnett. "They won't let us land. Why don't we try some other country?"

"I can shoot you both without getting out of my seat," pointed out Balachandran. "Don't make me. Just vent the tanks. *Now.*"

"How much?"

"All of it. Leave just enough for a straight-in approach to Madras International."

*

Back in the cabin, Daniel Devanayagam tugged excitedly at his father's jacket sleeve. "*Appa*, look! Look at the smoke from the wing!"

Robin Devanayagam followed his son's pointing finger to where two thin white streams of vapour trailed back from the port wing, close to the big engines.

"Why're they doing that, *Appa*?" Daniel asked. "Are the pilots trying to signal the fighter planes?"

"Dunno, son," replied his father. "I think it maybe part of the landing procedure."

"Are we landing?" hissed Suzie from across the aisle in a fierce whisper. "Where are we landing?"

"They're emptying the fuel tanks!" a Sri Lankan passenger further down the cabin cried, his face pressed to the plexiglass of the window. "They're going to crash us into the sea!"

More passengers screamed with fear, other pleaded with the hijackers, who were yelling for everybody to shut up and stay calm. A middle-aged man on the far side of the plane struggled to his feet, his mouth open in an O of protest.

"Please, we're only innocent—"

A gunshot cracked through the babble of voices as a hijacker standing by the amidships galley fired his Micro-Uzi on semi-auto. There were even louder screams and then abrupt silence as the passenger dived back into his seat.

The tannoy crackled to life with the familiar voice of Major Mahesh. "Ladies an' gentlemen, please remain calm. There's no need to panic. We will be soon landing in Madras, and the white vapour you can see from the wings is just extra fuel being dumped in order to lighten the plane."

Strapped into her rearward-facing jump seat, Jennifer Jensen straightened up from where she had ducked, hands over her ears, when the hijacker had stepped down the aisle and fired the single shot. When she heard the report, she had known they were all going to die. The bullet would penetrate the pressurized fuselage causing explosive decompression. The tiny bullet hole would become a gaping opening and then rip away half the fuselage. She had been trained for such an eventuality, and knew that disaster could be averted if the hole could be plugged before it widened. She wondered whether the hijackers would shoot her if she got to her feet. But as she looked down the aisle, Jen-Jen couldn't make out a hole in the cabin wall, just a small grey smear on the cream-coloured plastic above the windows. She guessed that the angle of the shot had been acute enough to cause a ricochet, saving them. There was no other explanation for it.

*

"Tell Madras you're beginning approach," Balachandran ordered Burnett.

The captain swung the Airbus in a lazy turn until they were headed for land on a westward heading. "Madras Control, Air Canada six three four. I am coming in to land. Reducing altitude now."

"AC six three four, this is Madras Control." There was an audible tone of resignation in the controller's voice. "You cannot land. We have barricaded the runways."

"Madras, this is six three four. I have vented my fuel tanks and have only twenty minutes of flying time left." Burnett's voice was tight with fear. "We're landing whether the runway is clear or not so—"

"Alpha Charlie six three four, this is Sabre Lead," a new voice cut in, and everybody in the cockpit knew it was the voice of the Mirage flight commander. "I am an Indian Air Force interceptor. Return to fifteen thousand feet or I will open fire."

Balachandran was now kneeling behind the pilots' seats, SMG held loosely in one hand. The grenade was nowhere to be seen.

"Ignore that," he said softly. "Keep going. They won' fire. You know that. And they'll clear the runway."

"What if they don't?" The voice of Harrap, the co-pilot, quavered. "Just one piece of debris on the runway could mean disaster."

"Then we die," Balachandran said in his ear. "But relax, they'll clear it. D'you think Ah'm an idiot? We have trained for this a long time. This is my business," he laughed, "and business is good."

The plane was descending steeply now, passing through ten thousand feet as they approached the coast. The Mirages were out of sight, somewhere behind and above.

"AC six three four, switch to Madras Director on eight seven decimal four."

Balachandran grinned. It had worked. Permission to land hadn't been verbally granted, but the order to switch frequencies was a tacit admission of defeat. The pilots' faces hadn't lost their tension, though. They had no fuel to spare, and it would be a dangerous exercise, barricades or no.

"Madras Director, this is Air Canada six three four at nine thousand."

"AC six three four, this is Madras Director, you are cleared down to six thousand. Turn left onto two four zero degrees."

"Madras Director, six three four, I have fuel for one straight-in approach. I cannot go around, so make it good."

*   *   *

"Madras is letting them land," the Sri Lanka Air Force wing commander reported to Captain Saliya Dayananda as the radio transmission came in.

The Commando captain turned to the officer from Brigade Int, who was still with him in the Air Force ops room.

"Will the Indians let us in?"

"MoD is on the line with the buggers, but they're stalling," Lieutenant 'Bullet' Fonseka replied. His nickname came from his prematurely bald head, the remaining hair of which he kept meticulously shaved. "Kept saying they wouldn' let the plane land so there was no reason for us to come. We'll see what they say now."

"OK, now that we know the plane's at Madras, I'll move the team up to Palaly." This was a reference to Palaly AFB on the Jaffna Peninsula. "We can work on our DA drills while we wait. The Black Cats mus' be rubbing their hands at this chance. Fire a call to Major Anil Prakash, if you can? His squadron's the HR team at Indira Gandhi in New Delhi. See whether they're willing to work with us."

"Roger that."

The Black Cats were the Indian National Security Guard, the country's combined forces anti-terrorist unit — the nickname taken from its shoulder patch — and one of its Special Action Groups constantly kept a squadron on alert for hijack situations.

Balasuriya trotted out of the room to get his Red Team airborne. He still had a large doubt about whether the Indians would allow Sri Lankan troops on their soil, but he had to be ready to move if they did.

* * *

"Six three four, you are cleared to two thousand. QNH nine nine seven."

The A340 was on a west-southwest heading, lined up with Madras International Airport's two main runways.

"Six three four, lock on ILS for runway twenty-five right."

The terrain below was a dusty green, with brown rivers carving their way through the landscape. Balachandran could just make out the outlines of the airport through the haze close to the horizon.

"AC six three four, call the outer marker. Reduce speed for final approach."

Sitting strapped into her seat, Jen-Jen felt the thud and increased drag as the undercarriage locked into place. The plane rocked in some turbulence, and through the windows she saw the horizon dip and sway, a glimpse of treetops. Somewhere further down the aisle she heard a woman crying softly.

"Cabin crew, prepare for landing."

Jen-Jen almost smiled at how normal the words sounded, so routine that she would have barely registered it if not for the fact that it was spoken by the hijack leader and not Captain Burnett.

The jump seat next to her was empty, the steward who would normally have sat in it having been ordered to sit with the passengers. Jen-Jen had wondered about this at the time, but now realized the reasoning behind it as the hijacker who had fired the shot at the middle-aged passenger sat down next to her. The man put the hand grenade away and strapped himself in, giving her a quick cold smile when he had finished. The chunky submachine-gun was still cradled in his hands. Jen-Jen saw the other hijackers sit down for the landing as well.

"AC six three four, you are cleared to land on runway twenty five right. Contact Tower on one two zero decimal three. Out."

Sitting in the jump seat behind the pilots, Balachandran watched the two parallel runways float up towards them. He scanned the terrain ahead, confirming the landmarks with the chart he had open in his lap. He knew enough about the A340's controls and about aerial navigation to know this was Madras, but experience made him double check. He had no intention of letting himself be flown to the wrong place. The airport layout was familiar to him from his previous visits, plus the aerial photographs, air charts, and intelligence reports. In the far distance, beyond the two four thousand-metre northern and southern runways, he could see the western runway, angling away to the south. The approach lights of the northern and southern runways began just beyond the north-south coastal highway, and further south, in the angle formed by the highway and the runway axis was a sprawling shanty town. To the north of the northern runway, and stretching down its length — on which they were about to make their landing — were the terminals, hangars, fuel tanks, and other miscellaneous buildings and structures that made up any international airport, even one in the Third World. Ready or not, Madras, here we are.

Both runways were lined with light and heavy vehicles, both civilian and military. It was obvious that they had been recently used to barricade the runways, and had only just been removed.

At 1345 hours local time, with a jolt and a screech of tires, six and a half hours after it had taken off from Singapore Changi, Air Canada AC634 touched down on runway 25 Right at Madras International Airport.

"Six three four, please proceed via taxiways Juliet and Alpha to stand Victor one two six."

Balachandran felt himself pressed forward in his seat, and looked up from the chart, keeping a finger on the route they were following as Burnett reversed the Pratt & Whitneys. He scanned the rows of parked aircraft on the ramp between the runway and the buildings. Most of these were short-haul airliners and cargo planes, being refuelled or having minor maintenance done to them. The A340 had already passed the big international passenger terminals where the long-haul aircraft were parked. He looked back down at the chart.

"Tell them we want stand Victor one six three," he said.

"Tower, this is six three four," Burnett spoke over the radio, his voice more professional now that the danger was past. "I have been instructed that we will require stand Victor one six three."

"Air Canada six three four, you are clear to occupy stand Victor one six three. Please proceed via taxiways Juliet and Alpha."

Burnett had handed over the controls to Harrap, who turned right, off the runway. Soon they were moving back the way they had come, paralleling the runway until Harrap swung the big Airbus left off taxiway-A and parked neatly at stand V163. Both the neighbouring stands were free of aircraft, and in fact, the nearest plane was a full five hundred metres away. Less than a hundred metres in front of them, huge aviation fuel storage tanks squatted in the blazing afternoon sun.

CHAPTER 20

The Sri Lankan Cabinet Crisis Group was modelled on Britain's COBRA — the Cabinet Office Briefing Room — and had been formed by the new government soon after winning the general elections, in order to handle individual terrorist incidents which threatened national security on a strategic level. The CCG was chaired by the State Minister for Defence, and consisted of the head of the Joint Operations Command, the heads of the Directorate of Internal Intelligence and the Directorate of Military Intelligence, the Inspector General of Police, and the Director of Special Forces.

The meeting on Friday morning was held at the new MoD offices in Colombo's Old Parliament, facing the Indian Ocean and sitting across the mouth of the Beira Lake from Army HQ. The British colonial-era building had originally housed the country's post-independence parliament until that institution was moved to its more "culturally acceptable" new home that had been architectured by Geoffrey Bawa and, situated on its own little islet in Sri Jayawardenepura's Diyawanna Oya.

The reason for the CCG meeting was that the LTTE hijackers of Air Canada AC634 had finally made a statement at 11pm Indian time — 11:30pm Sri Lankan time — the previous night, a little over nine hours after landing at Madras. They had also demanded food and drink for themselves and the passengers, and the Indian authorities had provided it. An hour later the hijackers had asked the Airbus to be refuelled, and had then taken off once more. The airliner had last been reported to be circling off the coast of Madras, closely watched by Indian Air Force patrols.

"OK, y'all have the transcript of the hijackers demands," Defence Minister John Jayavickrama began without preamble. A parliamentary secretary had handed these out to the members of the CCG. "They claim to be the Black Tiger Seelan Special Detachment of the LTTE, and all they want is the release of Tamil political prisoners in Canadian jails and the removal of the Canadian Foreign Minister."

"That's all?" muttered IGP Vimal Warnasuriya. He was fifty-seven, with a thick head of slicked-back hair that, by its perfect black sheen, confirmed everyone's suspicions that it was dyed; except, that was, for an Indira Gandhi-like streak of silver that shot back from the policeman's left temple, and which he naively thought everyone took for a natural feature.

"Mm," grimaced the minister. "They also claim to be well-armed and have enough explosives to blow up the plane if any attempt is made to storm it. They have given the Canadians twenty four hours to remove Donald Fenster from his post, after which they will kill the hostages. The Foreign Ministry is in touch with the Indian Home Ministry, and we have been informed that India will handle all aspects of the situation. What they're saying is, no Sri Lankan commandos.

"Our ambassador in New Delhi has been in contact with us, and in answer to our questions of yesterday on what the Indian HR team was doing for nine hours, the ambassador claims that no approval had been given by the Indian Home Ministry for a storming of the plane. His view is that this was partly due to indecision on the part of the Indian politicians, and partly due to lack of Canadian approval for an assault. The Canadians apparently wanted information on the hijackers' identity and demands before any decision was made.

"In the meantime, as I said last evening, the Indians have already appointed a negotiator, and I have just been informed that they might be open to having a Sri Lankan negotiator on site as well." Jayavickrama looked across at DIG Mike Salgado, the DII head. "I think that'll be one of your boys, Mike, since they're the best qualified for the job." Several DII superintendents had been trained in the United States as hostage negotiators by the FBI. "Get him across to Madras. Can he leave immediately?"

"Actually, Mister Minister," cut in DIG Jaliya de Silva, the DFI head, who had been asked to sit in on the Cabinet Crisis Group meeting for the obvious reason that the hijack was taking place outside Sri Lanka's borders, "my head of station in New Delhi is a trained negotiator, and as soon as the plane landed in Madras, I briefed him in anticipation of this situation. He's already in Madras. It'll just take a phone call and he can contact the Indians."

"OK, good show. Get it done. Give his name to my chaps and they'll make sure the Indians are expecting him." The minister scanned the faces of the others seated at the table. "OK, first of all, do we know who these men are, and where they got on board?"

"Ah've seen the tapes from the onboard cameras, Mister Minister," Mike Salgado said. "Changi provided us with what little there was before the terras blacked out the cameras. There are six terras, all male, armed with SMGs and han' grenades, but no sign of explosives. Very professional. No screaming and dancing, just went about the business of taking over."

"Definitely very well trained," Major General Sarath Perera, the Director of Special Forces added. He was absently fingering his shaven scalp, as if looking for any hairs he had missed.

"What about air marshals?" the minister asked. "I presume all Air Canada flights carry several?"

"AC six three four had two on board," Sarath Perera confirmed. "There was firing seconds after the hijacking began, and it looks on the film as if at least one of the air marshals was shot. Whether he was killed, we don't know. We also don't know about the second air marshal."

"Changi has compared the faces of the hijackers with passports of the passenger list," Salgado added. "All six boarded in Singapore. Their names mean nothing, but two of the faces appear in old NIB files. Both are known Champion Black Tigers."

"Do they know how they got the weapons on board?" Jayavickrama asked.

"Not yet," answered Salgado. "They're examining the tapes of the luggage X-rays, but nothing so far. Very unlikely that the hijackers brought the weapons on board themselves. Security's too tight at airports these days."

"What are you saying?" the minister asked. "That the weapons were put on board here at Katunayake?"

"It's possible, Mister Minister," pointed out Major General Perera. "Commando Brigade has set up an ops HQ at Katu, and they'll be working closely with Airport Security to look into the possibility."

"Have your chaps been given access to all the tapes and int?" the minister asked Perera.

"Yes, they've seen it and are already planning out an assault. Red Team is at Palaly, and can be on the ground in Madras in two hours, if needed. But it's all out of our hands if the Indians won' let us in, no?"

*   *   *

"How long have you been monitoring this?" asked the new watch officer, standing at the shoulder of the radio operator.

"Since I took over at oh-six-hundred, sir," the man replied. "It's in the log of the earlier watch, and the one before that. Prabath — the signaller I took over from — warned me to watch for it. They started monitoring it soon after takeoff with the first signal for today being logged at—" he checked the page— "zero-zero-thirty."

The watch officer in charge of this particular signals intelligence section picked up the log and flipped through the pages. They were in the second-level basement below the huge headquarters complex of India's Research and Analysis Wing in the city of New Delhi.

"It looks like they detected it as soon as AC634 entered Indian airspace," the watch officer said. "Our fighter planes didn't pick it up?"

"Apparently not, sir. It's on a separate satellite frequency."

"And always the same word?"

"Yes, sir, the same. Transmitted every hour — Zulu, as you can see, not Indian time — on the hour."

"But no reply?"

"Nothing. It's as if the hijackers are maintaining an authenticity code. It's the same system used with undercover teams or special forces."

"If there's any reply, inform me immediately," the watch officer said, "and try DF'ing the reply."

*   *   *

Checking over her shoulder, Devini Sundaralingam noted that the blue Mitsubishi Lancer was still behind them, two vehicles back. The streets of Colombo were already jammed with early rush-hour traffic. The Lancer and her own Toyota Corolla were threading their way through the backstreets of Cinnamon Gardens, trying to avoid the bulk of the traffic on the main roads, but the rest of the working population of the city seemed to have the same idea.

Devini was wearing a cream skirt suit and sitting in the back of the car, Angelo playing the part of the driver. Banu was in the front passenger seat. The other three were in the trailing Lancer, Jegen at the wheel. They too were dressed neatly to look like young executives.

Part of the reason Cinnamon Gardens had been picked as a base for the operation was that it was less than ten minutes to the target, and also their route would not involve having to pass through any Army or police vehicle checkpoints. The entire team had meticulously forged national identity cards that proclaimed them to be Colombo-born Muslims — to explain away any detectable accent — and company IDs that identified them as executives of advertising agencies located in Cinnamon Gardens and Bambalapitiya. However, it would only take a suspicious cop or soldier to have the vehicles searched, and the hidden submachine-guns and explosives would soon be found.

The weapons and explosives had been among a huge quantity that had been smuggled into Colombo during the Christmas 2001 truce, and later, in January, during the goodwill relaxation of security measures in the city by the new government.

The two cars drove past the Otters' Aquatic Club and onto Bullers Road, avoiding the heavily fortified five hundred-metre length of road at the eastern end of Wijerama Mawatha. They detoured around the checkpoints and crawled up Gregory's Road, past the vehicles disgorging hordes of chattering pupils outside the Colombo International School.

Three hundred metres further up the road, the two cars parked by the curb just short of the target. Devini and Banu got out of the Corolla and waited for the other two — a man and a woman — from the Lancer to join them. They all carried slim official-looking briefcases. Angelo and Jegen stayed behind the wheels of the cars.

It was only 7:30am, and the place opened to the public only at 9am, but Devini noted that a queue of hopefuls was already waiting outside the wrought-iron gates. They looked a cross-section of Colombo's working and middle classes — smart young men in white shirts and ties, others in jeans and sports shirts, middle-aged ladies in saris, old men in either suits or sarongs, and young women in dresses. They all looked nervous and hopeful at the same time, and they all carried files of documents. Some discussed tactics and wondered aloud about their chances of success. Others kept their hopes and fears to themselves, waiting with ill-concealed impatience to be let into the premises at the posted time of 9am. Some, a very few, looked totally at ease, having done this many times before, taking success for granted.

Ignoring the curious and annoyed stares of the people in the queue, Devini and the others walked straight up to the gates. The middle-aged and uniformed security guard standing outside the guardhouse beyond the gates pretended not to notice her until she called to him in an authoritative voice.

At her sharp "Excuse me!" he sauntered slowly over, making sure she knew he was in charge. The blue uniform he wore was crumpled and the yellow badge of the private security firm was faded from hours in the sun.

"Please wait in the queue," he said in Sinhalese. "Applicants cannot enter until nine."

"I'm not here for a visa," she told him in English. "I have an appointment with the Cultural Attaché." Devini showed the guard her Canadian passport.

"You are too early. The gentleman is not here yet."

"My colleagues and I have an appointment with the attaché at eight. We're fifteen minutes early, but we'll wait *inside*. In the lobby."

Devini noted that conversation in the queue had quietened. She could see that the plainclothes security man behind the plexiglas in the guardhouse was peering at her, having seen the Canadian passport.

The guard at the gate had known he was defeated when the passport appeared and now looked back to his superior for instructions. The man behind the plexiglas gestured for Devini to be let in, and the gate buzzed as an electronic lock was deactivated from the guardhouse. The security guard popped open the small doorlike pedestrian sub-gate and waved Devini in.

"Onlyyou," he said to her. "Speak to that gentleman there." He jabbed a thumb in the direction of the guardhouse. "The others wait here."

With a glare that made the guard decide to forget about trying to bodyscan her with his hand-held metal detector, Devini strode purposefully towards the guardhouse. The man behind the plexiglas was younger, in his late twenties, and smiled politely at her as she placed her briefcase on the counter, leaning towards the plexiglas in anticipation of her request. His eyebrows first raised in surprise then plunged into a puzzled frown as she walked past the counter and round the guardhouse. As expected, the door was unlocked, and she yanked it open, drawing the 9-mm Makarov pistol from under her suit jacket. Eyes staring in shock, the man fumbled for the phone.

"Don' touch that," she snapped.

*   *   *

"Mister Minister, can you comment on the hijackers' demand that you be removed from your post before negotiations can begin?"

Standing on the steps of Canberra's Capital Hill in the warm Australian sun, Donald Fenster looked over the heads of the gathered reporters as he weighed the Australian Broadcasting Corporation man's question.

"All I can say is that I am not surprised at the LTTE's demands," he finally ventured. "Our policies in Canada have been hurting them and it looks like they have finally revealed their true characteristics."

Fenster was, in fact, on his way to the Canadian embassy where he was due to join a video conference call with Department of Defence officials in Ottawa in order to discuss options. The Canadian Minister of Foreign Affairs and International Trade had no doubt that if he wanted to try and maintain control of the hijack situation, he would have to hand over the trade talks to a subordinate and return immediately to Canada.

"Mister Fenster, would you be willing to step down from your government position in order to save the lives of the hostages?"

Fenster recognized *CNN*'s senior Australian bureau chief, and fixed the man with a steady eye. "Both myself and the Canadian government intend to do whatever is necessary to resolve the hostage situation in a satisfactory manner. At the moment I don't think it would be appropriate to engage in an exchange of speculation that could very well endanger the very hostages we're trying to save." Fenster started to move down the steps. "Please excuse me."

"One more question, Mister Minister," said a journalist at Fenster's elbow, and recognizing the rolled 'R's of a Canadian accent, the minister paused. "When you said 'whatever is necessary', did that include sending Canadian hostage-rescue teams to India? We have already heard that the Indian Government is refusing to allow foreign troops into—"

"The Indian authorities are currently negotiating with the hijackers, and I can see no reason for any military personnel to be involved right now. Canadian or otherwise." Fenster turned away. "That'll be all for now, folks."

*   *   *

The Bravo Squadron sergeant major was standing on the tarmac, wearing jeans and a Lacoste polo shirt, as the passengers exited the Sri Lankan Airlines flight from Kuwait into the blazing morning sunshine of Katunayake. Dayan Premasiri spotted him immediately and grinned from behind his sunglasses. He felt sharp and alert in spite of the long journey from Europe. The five-hour stopover in Kuwait City had given them the chance of some proper sleep. Dayan had taken the opportunity, resisting Sumith's insistence that he join him for a sightseeing tour of the city

He shook hands with the big warrant officer, who gave him a crooked smile in return.

"Heard the hunting was good," SSM Yatiyawela growled.

Dayan shrugged and lit a cigarette, waiting for the other two members of his patrol. "Looks like no duty-free for us, uh?"

"Tough shit. I have a chopper waiting to take y'all straight to Maduru Oya for debriefing. Gunatilake goes to the hospital. We'll drop him on the way."

Dayan had hoped he would be able to look in on Sunethra for an hour or two before reporting back to SFHQ, but it couldn't be helped. At least they could get straight onto the Huey and be off. He didn't think he could take much more of airports.

Sumith greeted the SSM as he got off the plane. He for one was quite pleased to be foregoing customs. He had several litre-bottles of whisky and vodka that he had picked up in Paris.

Kamal's wheelchair was escorted by two pretty but tired stews. With a pat on the buttocks of the nearest girl — an act that made her stare daggers at him — Kamal said his goodbyes. Without a word, the stews left him in the care of his comrades and walked stonily away. Apparently the big SF soldier hadn't been a well-behaved passenger.

Sumith pushed Kamal's wheelchair along, dumping his hand luggage, along with Dayan's, in the wounded man's lap, ignoring his loud protests on the seriousness of his wound. Since most of their kit had been abandoned in Cologne or lost with Bandara's van, they had no checked luggage. As they walked towards the Air Force perimeter, the SSM filled Dayan in about the recent hijack. They didn't discuss the European operations, though there were a few moments of awkward silence after the sergeant major said he was sorry about Bandara's death. Dayan just nodded, but didn't say anymore on the subject.

Dayan decided that it was good to sweat once more, after the chill of Europe. He inhaled the near hundred-percent humidity in the air. He had removed his suit jacket and his shirt was already sticking to his skin. Entering the Air Force base, they were forced to shelter behind the guardhouse as a gale of dust blew at them from the turning props of a C-130 transport taxiing towards the runways.

Welcome home.

* * *

In the Ministry of Defence building in Colombo, John Jayavickrama was wondering aloud whether he should fly up to Palaly to see first hand the Commandos' direct-action drills, but was being quietly persuaded against it by Major General Perera. The Director Special Forces was pointing out that the captain commanding Red Team was highly competent, and that the unit was at a high state of readiness.

He had just succeeded in convincing Jayavickrama to stay well away from Palaly, when Brigadier Arjuna Devendra noticed a police aide enter the room and speak quietly to the IGP. Vimal Warnasuriya asked a couple of whispered questions and then dismissed the man with a nod. The IGP's face remained calm, but

Devendra saw his eyes narrow almost imperceptibly, and watched long fingers drum a nervous tattoo on the polished Burma teak tabletop.

Devendra wondered what could be important enough to disturb the country's top cop in the middle of a CCG meeting. For an irrational moment he wondered whether it was something to do with the hijack, but then realized that if it were he would have been the first to know. It didn't matter anyway, he decided, as he saw Warnasuriya lean forward and clear his throat. It looked as if they were about to find out.

The IGP's next words cut through the babble of muted conversation and left behind it a swathe of stunned silence.

"Mister Minister, I have just heard that there seem to be armed men in the premises of the Canadian High Commission."

For several heartbeats the quiet hung in the room, then everybody started talking at once.

"*What?*" from Major General Sujeeva Fernando.

"Wha'd'you mean there *seem* to be?" the minister asked testily.

"When did this happen?" asked Devendra.

"Are they Tigers?" queried Perera.

"How d'you know?" came from Jaliya de Silva.

Finally, Jayavickrama raised a hand to quiet the others. "Quiet, gentlemen! Let the man speak." Voices died away and everybody fixed Warnasuriya in a crossfire of curious looks. "What exactly has happened, Vimal?"

"Well, sir," the IGP began hesitantly, "fifteen minutes ago, a trishaw driver arrived at the Cinnamon Gardens Police Station and reported that he had seen several armed men and women run into the Canadian High Commission and attack the security guards at the gate. The duty inspector sent a couple of constables to check on it, and when they tried to enter the high commission premises, they were shot at."

Cellular phones around the table began ringing as various civilian and military outfits began reporting the incident to their respective bosses. The Colombo National Guard battalion had already dispatched a patrol to Gregory's Road to cordon off the area, but the police were still technically in charge. Blue Team, Delta Group's Colombo HR team went to full alert in anticipation of being called out. The police were trying to establish a phone link into the embassy, but no one was answering their calls.

∻

The insistent buzzing of the phones was an irritant Devini Sundaralingam was happy to put an end to as she finally picked up the receiver in the Canadian ambassador's plush office. For half an hour she had ignored the phone calls as her team took up positions in the three-storey building and herded the embassy staff into a banquet room where they were guarded by one of her men. If the alarm hadn't been given before, the shots Preethi had fired at the two cops would certainly have done it.

Due to the early hour, they had only a few staff members as hostage, most of them secretarial or administrative personnel. The only senior Canadians in the building were the ambassador himself and the senior visa officer, both of whom had a reputation of trying to get over the bulk of their paperwork early in the day. If Devini had stuck to the original timetable they would have had at least four times the number of hostages present, but she consoled herself with the thought that the smaller number would be easier to control and guard.

"Yes," she said curtly into the handset, settling into the ambassador's high-backed chair.

She had been on her way to check the teams' positions and had decided it was as good a time as any to open communications with the enemy. The ambassador's direct line was the only one that had continued to ring for the past half-hour. There were direct lines to both the big communications room in the corner of the top floor, currently being used by Devini as a headquarters, as well as to the various attachés' offices, but those phones had ceased to ring long ago.

For a moment there was silence at the other end of the line, as if the caller was startled to have actually got through.

"Just a minute," he finally managed, and Devini heard him call someone else to the phone.

"Good morning," a gruff new voice boomed in Devini's ear. "This is the Cinnamon Gardens Police OIC. May I know whom Ah'm speaking to, please?"

Devini pictured an overweight superintendent, used to getting his way with just the mention of his designation. "Good morning," replied Devini blandly. "Whom d'you wish to speak *to?*"

"Is the ambassador or his secretary there? We have received reports of firearms in use on the embassy premises." There was a pause and then the policeman spoke more sharply. "Who did you say you were?"

"This is Colonel Sundari of the Eelam Republican Army, and Ah'm in command of the unit occupying the embassy of the racist Canadian government." Though Devini's rank within the LTTE was that of a major, it had been decided that she would use the rank of colonel in all negotiations, giving the unspoken impression that her team was larger than it was. "You will stop phoning the embassy until we contact you. This will happen only when the ERA is ready to issue a statement and not before. Until then I advise you to keep any policemen or soldiers in the area away from the embassy grounds, both for their own safety as well as that of the prisoners. I can assure you that we're well armed and able to defend ourselves, and we'll execute the prisoners if our instructions are not followed to the letter."

Devini hung up before the cop could say anything more and rose to her feet. The ambassador's office, on the first floor of the building, was deeply carpeted and furnished in heavy south Sri Lankan style. French windows with dark tinted glass opened out onto a balcony that overlooked the driveway. The room made a good vantage point from which to dominate the front gate, but Devini knew that the senior visa officer's room at the far end of the building was even better for the purpose, and had stationed a man there already.

She stuck her head into the banquet room where the dozen hostages were sitting against the wall under the watchful eye of Preethi. Devini nodded at the woman and noted that the heavy drapes had been drawn across the French windows.

She continued her inspection of the building, making sure that Jegen had positioned everybody correctly to cover all possible entry points, as well as dominate the grounds. Devini was especially concerned about the perimeter behind the embassy, where the boundary wall was particularly close to the building.

She would let another hour pass before she made contact with the police. Let them sweat awhile.

"OK, they've definitely identified themselves as ERA," IGP Warnasuriya said. "But so far no demands or statements. We aren't sure yet how many of the terras there are, even though Cinnamon Gardens CID is interviewing the visa applicants who were standing outside the embassy at the time." The cop shrugged. "When the guns appeared everybody panicked and ran. Witness statements put the terras somewhere between four and ten, very cool and professional, and at least one woman amongst them." Warnasuriya looked across at Mike Salgado. "They said they'd call back when they have a statement, so maybe you can send one of your negotiators over to the Cinnamon Gardens station?"

"Yah, OK," nodded the DII chief. He rose to his feet, continuing, "Actually, gentlemen, I think it'll be better if you excuse me for the moment. I better get over to HQ and see what we can find out about the situ. I'll stay in touch." With that Salgado left the room.

"What about your chaps?" asked the Defence Minister of Major General Perera.

"Blue Team is on stand-by at Bullers Road, an' can be at the scene in five minutes," replied Perera. "They already have a man over at the police station, observing."

"Can we have an assessment of the situation, gentlemen?" Jayavickrama asked, suddenly looking weary. "Is this the coordinated operation between the Tigers an' the ERA that it looks like?"

"Hard to sayyet, sir." De Silva was the first to speak. "We'll have to wait till they issue some demands, but it looks like it."

"But if it's a coordinated effort," commented General Fernando, "both operations being planned by the Tiger high command, why're they still keeping up with this ERA nonsense?"

"Rather, why are the Air Canada hijackers operating as LTTE instead of ERA?" asked Devendra. "The Tigers have gone to such pains to distance themselves from the ERA, why are they now throwing it all away by hijacking a plane?"

"There have been several denials of LTTE involvement in the hijacking posted on certain Tamil-interest websites," Jayavickrama said, "but the media hasn't picked up on it."

"It's been mentioned in a couple of European and Canadian newspapers," corrected Devendra, "but not on TV."

"But what does this mean?" pressed the minister impatiently. "Why would the Tigers claim responsibility only to deny it later? Is this claim by the hijackers genuine?"

"It could be an attempt by the ERA to draw the Tigers in," suggested Perera, "force them to join the fight."

"But that would mean the LTTE and the ERA are two different organizations," disagreed de Silva, "but everything we know up to now points to the fact that the ERA is just a deception operation by the Tigers."

Various arguments flitted back and forth across the table for the next quarter of an hour as the CCG waited for more news. Jaliya de Silva suggested that both the embassy terrorists and the hijackers were LTTE members, but from different wings. He speculated that the hijack was probably part of a new phase in the Tigers strategy now that it was obvious the ERA attacks were not having the desired effect on the Canadian government. Devendra questioned the logic of this, stating that the capture of the embassy was obviously the climax of the past waves of ERA attacks, and if the LTTE had a new strategy, they would hardly jump the gun like this without waiting for the results of the embassy attack. Fernando then put forward the opinion that maybe there had been a bit of a bugger-up on the part of the Tigers, and that someone somewhere had got the timings wrong. He pointed out that they had just been told by Warnasuriya that Special Branch was trying to track down all of the embassy staff still on their way to work in order to determine just how many hostages were actually in the embassy. It was obvious that the ERA had struck too early, not waiting till all the staff had reported to work, usually around 8:30am.

* * *

The Canberra Hilton's air conditioning was having overwhelming success in defeating the dry heat of the afternoon. In fact, it was so successful that Patricia Fenster gave an involuntary shiver as she stepped out of the controlled humidity of the hotel's gym, where she had just finished her thrice-a-week schedule.

She had let her exercise routine slip in the days before and since her arrival in Australia. Nervous tension caused by the blackmailer's demands had made it impossible for her to summon the energy to do anything constructive. But there had been no further contact with the blackmailer, and since she had deposited the attaché case at the airport left luggage, picked up the replacement, and had the key collected by the anonymous Mr Harris, Patricia had felt the tension begin to ebb away. Maybe it would soon be over, she told herself irrationally, maybe there would be a change of plan and she would be told she didn't have to ferry the case to Colombo.

When the news of the Air Canada hijack had hit Canberra, her fears had slammed home with a jolt. She had speculated that it was all some terrorist plot, but then had argued with herself, and finally decided that the LTTE wouldn't be interested in her sexual adventures.

When she had discovered that Ian McEdwards' Calgary phone number was not listed, she had given up hope of discussing things with him. But anyway, she thought as she walked through the hotel lobby to the elevators, she and Donald would soon be returning to Ottawa. The blackmailer had made a mistake about the trip to Sri Lanka, and soon she could forget about all this and return to a normal life.

"Mrs Fenster!" She looked round to see the concierge hurrying across the lobby towards her with a cheerful smile. Patricia stood there in her leotards, enjoying the man's appraising glance down her body as he walked up to her. "Excuse me, madam, but this was left for you at Reception by a gentleman named Harris."

Trying to keep her hands from shaking, Patricia took the plain white envelope that the concierge handed over. She knew without looking that it contained a luggage locker key. She could feel it sliding around.

"Thank you," she managed, forcing a smile. "How long ago was this?" She wanted to ask what Mr Harris had looked like, but knew that it would raise the concierge's suspicions.

"Around twenty minutes ago, madam," the man explained. "I knew you were in the gym and decided it was better not to have disturbed you. I hope I was right."

"Yes, of course, thanks a lot." Patricia left the concierge standing there and headed off to the elevators, forcing herself to walk calmly.

In the lift, she tore open the envelope, and a single key dropped into her palm. The small plastic tag had a three-digit number on it. The same locker she had first deposited the attaché case in. With the key was a note saying that there had been a change of plan, but unlike the reprieve Patricia had been hoping for, it said that she was to exchange attaché cases again, but only on the day she was leaving Canberra.

She was glad that Donald was still away at Capital Hill and would not be back for a while. Walking into the penthouse suite on trembling legs, she knew she wouldn't have been able to put up any semblance of normalcy.

She poured herself three fingers of Smirnov, dropped in a couple of ice cubes, and took a big gulp, gasping at the icy fire that raced down her throat. Patricia slumped on the sofa before the huge plate glass windows that opened onto a view of downtown Canberra, but she couldn't calm down or relax. Her pulse, already racing from the hour in the gym and the arrival of the envelope, would not respond to the alcohol and slow down.

Finishing her drink in three gagging swallows, she headed for the bathroom. She opted for a shower instead of a bath, knowing that she was too wound up to lie still, and turned her face into the jets of warm water. After a few minutes of that, she felt her nerves losing their edge, the alcohol doing its work. Leaning back against the marble-tiled wall, Patricia masturbated quickly, playing the water from the hand-held showerhead over her breasts as she used her other hand to touch herself, up between her thighs. She climaxed in minutes, sobbing with released tension, seeing a flash of Ian's contorted face as it had looked that afternoon in Sri Lanka, pumping himself into her. As her orgasm ebbed, her knees finally buckled and she slid down to sit under the falling water. Her forehead rested on her crossed arms, elbows on her knees, her tears mingling with the warm water.

*   *   *

As it always was in late March, the Palaly airbase, situated on the northern edge of the Jaffna Peninsula, was hot and dusty. The northeast monsoon, which blew across the peninsula in December and January, was now nothing but a distant memory. The low scrub and few trees that still remained within the huge military base were dark green or dried brown, both powdered with the chalky dust that seemed to work its way into every crevice, natural or man-made.

Mi-17 transports, Huey gunships, and Hind attack helicopters seemed to be constantly moving in and out of the airbase, part of the grinding machine that constantly fed the war its ration of flesh and steel. The beating rotors of the choppers raised mini-tornadoes of dust, and landing Hercules and Antonov transport planes sent hurricanes of grit that cloaked everything in sight.

Eric Christofelsz, as the sixteen-man No 2 Patrol Team's sergeant, had been put in charge of the direct-action drills, while No 1 Patrol Team, OC Red, and some Brigade staff types started on a more concerted plan to assault the hijacked airliner. While Christofelsz's patrol team officially had an officer — a second lieutenant — in command, he was still considered too inexperienced to handle the job properly, and so it had fallen into Christofelsz's able hands, leaving the subaltern as just another patrol commander — a job usually handled by a corporal. The DA drills were the emergency plans for use in the event that Red Team had to go in immediately, before a proper assault plan could be formed, and they would be constantly modified to the latest available intelligence.

A section of Palaly AFB, part of the special operations compound, had been cordoned off and handed over to Red Team to practice the DA drills. A large area had been measured from aerial photos of Madras airport and marked out with wood and canvas, to represent AC634 and the nearby buildings. Everything had been modelled with the idea that the Air Canada plane would return to the same stand it had occupied the previous evening.

Some years previously, the burned-out fuselage of an Avro turboprop transport had been salvaged by the Commandos and fitted out to represent the interior of an airliner. It had been a bit of a stretch of the imagination to picture the inside of a disused military transport as a modern airliner, but it had been all the Commandos could manage until the providential August 2001 terrorist attack had gifted them a Tri-Star to train on. The old Avro fuselage had been dumped at Palaly, and was now put into use to practice the DA drills.

Christofelsz had been running the men through the drills since first light, but with regular rest breaks in between. It wouldn't do to have the troops exhausted when the "Go" was given, nor to have their edge dulled by too much training.

A disused barracks was being used to billet the commandos, and they had unrolled their sleeping bags on the mouldy mattresses, their kit scattered around in an organized chaos. Taking a break from the drills, they were smoking, drinking tea, and looking at maps and photos. Singapore had emailed copies of the suspected hijackers' passports, and the mug shots had been blown up to life-size. Photocopies of the mug shots had been taped to the Hun's-head targets in the Avro fuselage so that the assaulters could memorize the hijackers' faces.

* * *

0845 LOCAL (0245 GMT): "The news team *must* be from the *BBC*," Devini said sharply over the phone. "An' don' try any funny pranks. I know the faces of all the *BBC* newscasters in Sri Lanka. If you send in anyone from another organization, there'll be trouble. They have half an hour to get here. If they aren't already outside."

Devini didn't mention that she had the television sets in the comms centre on, and had already seen that almost all the leading Sri Lankan TV stations had news teams outside the embassy grounds, being kept at the two ends of Gregory's Road by the police. *CNN* already had a team in place as well, and she had seen a breaking news announcement on that channel claiming the Canadian embassy in Colombo had been taken over by unknown persons. But there was still no *BBC* team on the scene.

The reason she had asked for the *BBC*, was that in the past they had seemed to have a vague sympathy for the Sri Lankan Tamil cause, and were less likely to cooperate with the Sri Lankan authorities.

"We want to make our demands live on *BBC World*," Devini continued. "But the *BBC* team must have a digicam and not video. They can plug into the embassy's satellite uplink. I don't wan' to see them coming in here trailing a whole load of cables."

The reasoning behind this was that the quality of the broadcast picture would be poorer than a conventional taped broadcast, and would therefore reveal less of her team's defences to the watching special forces that Devini had no doubt were waiting in the wings.

"Colonel, we'll speak to the *BBC* bureau chief immediately, but we can't guarantee that they'll be willing to come in there."

The speaker at the other end of the line wasn't the superintendent she'd spoken to earlier that morning. This man had claimed to be from the CID, but Devini had no doubt that he was a trained DII hostage negotiator.

"They'll come," she replied confidently. The *BBC* bureau chief would be wetting his pants with anticipation.

"OK, we'll speak to them," agreed the negotiator. "Colonel, we need to reassure the families of the embassy staffers. We would like to know the names of the people you're holding, please."

Devini knew the game. Everything would have to be an exchange. She would have to make concessions in return for everything she wanted. Fine, she thought, let them think everything's going according to the rules. For now.

"We have fourteen prisoners," she said, "since that is what you want to know. Their names will be released once the *BBC* team is here."

                                                    ✳

Twenty minutes later, the negotiator phoned to say that the *BBC* was at the embassy gate. Devini Sundaralingam had already moved down to the ambassador's office, where she intended to make the broadcast from. She sent a man to the gate to let them in, and from the window she watched two European men enter. Both wore jeans and button-down shirts, and she noted that the man with the camera was already taking shots of the masked and armed figure who led them in. Devini saw Sujeevan tell the cameraman to stop filming, and then both Europeans were blindfolded before he guided them to the embassy's front door.

Devini stood behind the ambassador's big desk, waiting for the news team. There was no one else in the room. The rest of the team would be on high alert, as this would be a prime moment for an assault team to try and spring a surprise. Jegen was in the comms centre, and would monitor the *BBC World* channel once the broadcast began. In fact, he had reported that the *BBC* anchor had already announced that there would soon be a live statement by the terrorists in the Canadian embassy.

Sujeevan led the two newsmen into the room and stood them in front of the desk. He then walked around behind Devini and stood with his MP-5K submachine-gun at port arms. It was all designed to look professional and intimidating on television. For a moment, she watched the two Brits standing there nervously, probably wondering if they were going to join the other hostages.

"You may take your blindfolds off now," she said finally, and the two newsmen tugged away the strips of cloth, blinking around at their surroundings.

They both stared at Devini for a few moments, and then the cameraman began to fiddle with the digicam.

"I'm Mark Turner," the one who seemed to be the journalist said, then gestured to his colleague, "and this is Johnny Flinders." He hesitated. "You must be Colonel Sundari." He pronounced her name phonetically, with a hard 'D'. "How would you like me to conduct this interview?"

"Sit down," Devini waved at two chairs in front of the desk, settling back into the ambassador's chair. "Before we begin, let me make a few things clear." Both Brits sat and watched her expectantly. The cameraman had stopped fiddling. "First of all, this is *not* an interview. You will ask no questions. You may do the usual introduction, but after that I'll give a statement that will explain our acts and end with our demands. After this you'll be allowed to leave. The *BBC* is just a voice for us."

"I'm not sure my programme director will go for that," Mark Turner said. "I'll have to phone him. What's in it for us?"

"I'm sure your programme director will agree. The *BBC* gets this scoop. Take it or leave it. If you refuse, I'll jus' get *CNN* in here. Ah'm sure they'd jump at the chance."

In the next ten minutes the journalist sorted things out with his studios in Hong Kong, and the cameraman plugged into the fibre optics cable that had been run down the stairs from the comms centre. He then did a few test takes of Turner. Finally, everything was ready, and with the heavy curtains drawn against the daylight, the cameraman switched off all the room's lights, except for the desk lamp, creating a rather dramatic setting.

Turner spoke into the camera, beginning his introduction, and Devini phoned Jegen in the comms centre and got confirmation that it was on the air, albeit with a three-second distance-induced delay.

Finally, the camera swung towards Devini, and at a nod from Flinders she began to speak.

"My name is Colonel Sundari, and Ah'm the commander of the Eelam Republican Army unit holding the Colombo embassy of the Canadian government. We have resorted to this drastic measure in desperation, caused by the tyrannical, brutal, and repressive measures instituted by the Canadian and Sri Lankan governments. The world is ignoring the plight of the Tamil people and their right to self determination."

Johnny Flinders watched her through the viewfinder as she continued her political spiel. She was talking naturally, not reading from a pre-prepared paper, and her eyes projected genuine emotions rather than fanaticism. This one is good, he decided cynically, not fooled by her charisma. He had seen fanaticism before, from one end of the map to the other, from right-wing American militias to the Al Aqsa Martyrs Brigades to John Walker Lynn.

"In return for the freedom of the prisoners in this embassy, we have several demands we wish to be carried out," Devini continued. "Number one is the release of all Tamil political prisoners held in Canada on trumped up criminal charges. Number two is the cessation of all US military aid to the racist Sri Lankan government. Number three is an immediate cessation of hostilities by the Sinhalese army against the Tamil population in Tamil Eelam — what the Sinhalese call their Northern and Eastern provinces — and the immediate dispatch of United Nations peacekeeping troops to enforce the ceasefire." She paused to let that sink in. "There will be a non-adjustable deadline set for all these demands, at the end of which, if the demands have not been met, our prisoners will be regrettably executed. The deadline will be set only after the arrival of a negotiator we will now designate. This negotiator must arrive here in Colombo within eighteen hours of this broadcast. As before, if this demand is not met, the prisoners will be executed." Devini paused, then as if as an afterthought, she added, "The negotiator we want is Donald Fenster, the Canadian Minister of Foreign Affairs and International Trade."

※

"What the fuck is this nonsense?" asked General Sujeeva Fernando, watching the *BBC World* live telecast on the big television in the Cabinet Crisis Group meeting. "One lot wants Fenster sacked, the other lot want him as a negotiator!"

"Shh!" John Jayavickrama waved a hand at the JOC head. "Let's hear what else she has to say."

Brigadier Arjuna Devendra watched the slightly pixelated scene on the screen. It showed a gloomy room, melodramatically lit by a single desk lamp, giving it the look of an old black-and-white spy movie. The self-proclaimed Colonel Sundari's face was unmasked and well lit by the lamp, and he studied it, trying to see beyond the projected aura. She seemed to have an attractive face, with good bone structure, but beyond that it was hard to tell due to the bad quality of the satellite link. Not beautiful, Devendra thought, not even pretty, but certainly not unattractive either. A dark figure loomed behind her, hard to make out in the sharply flung shadows. The figure in the background, obviously a man, was armed with an SMG and wearing a Balaclava hood. When the report had begun, Devendra had phoned Int HQ to make sure it was being taped. By now someone would already be going through the computer files, trying to match her face. Devendra could faintly make out what looked like a heavily framed painting or photograph on the wall behind the terrorists. They were probably using the office of one of the senior embassy staffers, maybe even the ambassador's office itself. The chair Colonel Sundari was sitting in certainly looked comfortable enough.

"Before this broadcast ends," the terrorist leader was saying, "we're going to give you a demonstration of just how serious we are about our threats and demands." She turned and nodded to the figure behind her and the man moved out of the picture briefly, then back in as the camera followed him jerkily. A rectangle of light appeared in the darkness as a door was opened and then shut. The camera swung back to the woman, and Devendra noted she was wearing some sort of a business suit.

There was a ripple through the CCG members as there was momentary silence from the TV.

"I hope they aren't going to kill a hostage as a demonstration," muttered Jayavickrama.

"Unlikely," said Major General Perera. "Killing a hostage now will make further negotiations with us difficult."

"They're not trying to negotiate with *us*," de Silva pointed out. "If you notice, we've been quietly left out of the equation. "All the demands are being made from the Canadians, Americans, and—"

"Quiet, he's saying something!" snapped Jayavickrama.

The *BBC* man was talking, but it was soon obvious that he was just outlining what had taken place up to now for the benefit of viewers who had missed it. He soon broke off however, as the camera swung back to the opening door.

Two dark figures entered the room, and it was possible to make out that they held a woman between them. The camera followed the trio as the woman was marched round behind the desk and into the pool of light. She was a white woman, in her early to mid-thirties, obviously one of the hostages. She looked tense and badly frightened as she looked into the camera. Colonel Sundari got to her feet and moved out of the way, and it looked to the CCG as if the Canadian woman was going to be asked to speak.

"Is that the ambassador?" asked Fernando.

"No, the ambassador's a man," Jayavickrama said. "Besides, she's too young."

But instead of being questioned or forced to speak, the Canadian woman was bent roughly over the desk until she was facedown on its surface. A couple of sets of handcuffs were produced by one of the men, and she was handcuffed to the desk legs nearest the camera, her legs on the far side, her body bent over and held fast, like a sacrifice on the altar. Colonel Sundari then drew a pistol and pointed it at the woman's head. Even with the bad picture quality, Devendra could see that the Canadian woman's body was shaking with fear.

"Shit, they *are* going to shoot her." Jayavickrama said in wonder. "And on live TV!"

But what followed was even more brutal and shocking than a live murder.

"This is Francine Carter," announced Colonel Sundari to the camera. "She's the senior visa officer. Or so she says. But she's actually an agent of the Canadian Security Intelligence Service, the organization responsible for many attacks against Tamils in Toronto."

"Is this true?" asked Jayavickrama, turning to de Silva. "Is she CSIS?"

De Silva nodded once. "Chief of station."

"Let this be a lesson as well as a demonstration to the hawks in Ottawa," Colonel Sundari said, holstering her pistol and moving out of the frame.

One of the terrorists who had brought Francine Carter into the room stepped up to her and drew a combat knife, using it to cut away the skirt of the woman's business suit. He then did the same with her underwear. Pale buttocks were silhouetted against the background darkness beyond the handcuffed woman's dark blonde hair.

The CCG members stared in shock, and the senior visa officer suddenly realized what was happening and started to wrench at the handcuffs. The second male terrorist held her against the desk as the first man unzipped his trousers. The camera wavered but stayed on the spectacle, the cameraman obviously fighting off his shock.

"Look, please, you can't allow this to—" the *BBC* journalist could be heard off camera, however he was cut off by a calm but sharp command from the female terrorist.

"Quiet! You, keep filming."

There was a scream of horror and disgust from Francine Carter, and around the world, stunned viewers watched the terrorist lunge up between her buttocks, impaling her. The senior visa officer was pleading for help, struggling, but was pinned down by the combined weight of the two terrorists as the rape continued.

CHAPTER 21

It had been a frustrating twenty-four hours for Lieutenant Jan Conway. With all the refuelling stops, it had been almost midnight on Thursday before the Canadian Forces CC-144 Challenger had been able to land at Katunayake. The frustrations had begun even earlier, when satellite communications with JTF2 headquarters at Dwyer Hill in Ottawa had informed them that New Delhi was refusing to allow armed foreign troops on its soil.

Colombo had been more than willing to let the JTF2 platoon land, and had promised that they could liase fully with the country's hostage-rescue unit, apparently known as Red Team. Conway had never heard of this Red Team, and by the time they had disembarked at Katunayake AFB, been met by a captain from that unit, and learned that it was part of the 1st Commando Regiment, the jetlag had set in.

At first Conway had been told by the Commando captain that they had an operations centre at the airbase, monitoring the situation in Madras, and that after some sleep, the Canadians would be fully briefed. He had also been told that someone from the Canadian embassy would arrive in the morning to meet them. In the meantime he and his men would be billeted in the SLAF Officers' Mess — even though, it was pointed out, not all of them were actually officers.

Conway had woken up at 4am, his body clock out of sync, and decided that he would have a look at the Commando operations centre. The captain who had spoken to him the night before and given him directions to the op centre, wasn't there, and the Air Force Police sergeant at the door told him, in broken

English, that he had orders not to let any unauthorized personnel in. And foreigners were definitely unauthorized.

The JTF2 platoon had an excellent English breakfast at 7am, and were kicking their heels an hour and a half later, when Conway got a call from the Canadian military attaché. The man — a Canadian Forces brigadier — sounded tense and worried, and with good reason. He informed Conway that the embassy in Colombo had been taken over by terrorists, and that he was trying his best to find out what the situation was. In the meantime, the JTF2 platoon was to sit tight and watch the TV news for information.

The Canadians had trooped off to the Officers' Mess lounge in the hope of finding an English news channel, but had found the place full of SLAF officers watching the news in Sinhalese. There had been lots of footage of tree-lined avenues and a long shot of what one flight lieutenant claimed was the Canadian embassy, but not much else. None of the Sri Lankans seemed to know what was going on except that the embassy had been taken over by "fucking Tamil terrorists".

Finally, Conway remembered that their CC-144 transport had satellite television, and they got hold of the flight crew who in turn got the plane's electrical systems going. They were just in time for the *BBC* live telecast, and Conway felt anger and disgust take control of him as he watched the terrorists start to rape the visa officer. The JTF2 platoon was going nuts, cursing and shouting in frustration. Some of them turned away in shock, but no one switched off the TV.

Mercifully, after the terrorist had made a few frenzied thrusts into the struggling woman, the picture broke up and was replaced by the horrified face of the *BBC* anchor in Hong Kong.

"I apologize for that. We seem to be having some satellite problems with our connection to Colombo," the man mumbled, trying to compose himself. "But we'll get back to that story later. Just to remind our viewers, the Canadian embassy in Colombo has been taken over by ERA terrorists, who are in the middle of giving a. . . what was supposed to be. . . a news conference right now. The ERA has claimed responsibility for the recent waves of violence that have hit Canada and other countries worldwide—"

Conway stormed off the plane and took a deep breath of air. What the fuck was going on? Was that really what they thought they were seeing? Could it have been a trick? What sort of people would rape a helpless woman and broadcast it live to the world? He headed back into the plane to start making some calls.

*

The senior visa officer's struggles had knocked the phone off the ambassador's desk, and it wasn't until Sujeevan had climaxed and withdrawn that Devini picked it up and replaced it. By the time Banu stepped up to Francine Carter and entered her, she had stopped struggling, and just lay there, sobbing. Standing this close to the table, Devini could smell the musk of sexuality as Banu grunted with each thrust. She looked at the two Brits. When the woman had first been thrown across the desk they had both scrambled to their feet and backed off slightly. Now the journalist was looking at the floor, his face pale, not wanting to watch, but the cameraman was still shooting, seemingly shielded from the reality by the filter of his viewfinder.

Suddenly the phone buzzed and, distracted by the tableau in front of her, Devini didn't notice it at first, but then snatched the receiver up.

"Yah?" she said hoarsely.

It was Jegen. "Wha'ss going on down there?" he demanded. "Ah've been trying to get through to you for how long now."

"What's the matter?"

"They've stopped showing the assault on the woman."

"*What?*"

"As soon as it started the *BBC* said they were having communication problems and stopped showing it."

Still holding the receiver, Devini drew her pistol and pointed it at the journalist.

"Get your director on the line," she ordered. "Tell him that if we're not on air in a minute, a hostage dies."

The journalist punched in the speed dial on his mobile phone with a shaking hand, and spoke tersely to the person at the other end.

"Tell me when the programme is on again," Devini said to Jegen over the ambassador's phone. "Ah'll hold on." Cradling the receiver between her neck and shoulder, she cocked the pistol and placed it against the senior visa officer's head.

Banu had already spent himself, and now left the room to return to his post, his duty to the cause done for the moment.

"We're on air again," the journalist reported, putting away his phone. "My director apologizes and—"

Devini cut him off with a wave of the pistol, getting Jegen to confirm the man's words. When he did, she hung up and looked back into the camera. She considered whether to order Sujeevan to rape the Canadian again for the benefit of her international audience, but then wondered absently whether he had the stamina for a second round. She could always get another male member of her team into the room if he could not, she mused, but finally decided against it. The alternative would be more meaningful, and would serve to drive home the point that she wasn't fooling around.

"Welcome back, ladies an' gentlemen," Devini said. "I apologize for that interruption. Since our orders were not carried out, Ah'll now demonstrate the result of that foolishness. The authorities — and that included the media — were warned that if our demands were not met to the letter, a prisoner would be executed. That will now be done."

. Devini then shot the half-naked senior visa officer twice in the side of the head. The shots boomed in the room, making everybody jump, even the cameraman. The journalist looked on the verge of collapse. After the first jerk when the bullets hit, Francine Carter's body lay very still, one handcuffed hand twitching spasmodically, wrenching at the handcuffs, as if trying to free itself even in death.

"Look, they've just raped and murdered a defenceless Canadian woman, for God's sake! What more do you want?" Jan Conway fought to keep his voice down on the satellite link to Dwyer Hill. He had already given up trying to convince the military attaché to let his men storm the embassy. "Colombo's just an hour or so away, at least lemme take a small team down there to do a recon of the target."

"Negative," said the officer at the other end. "If there's gonna be any assault on the building, it'll be done by the Sri Lankans. And the politicians at this end are quite happy to keep it that way."

"But what's the point in my platoon being down here?" protested Conway. "I thought we were gonna work alongside the Sri Lankan hostage-rescue unit?"

"Affirmative, but only on the hijack scenario. The embassy's totally a different matter. I know it's stupid, but it's not a Forces decision. The military attaché's trying to OK it so that you can join the Sri Lankan team training for the hijack. So stand by. It could take awhile. The Sri Lankan authorities in Colombo are running around like headless chickens over the embassy scene."

"Look, the chances of us going into Madras to storm the jet are lower than zero." Conway continued to argue, even though he knew it was a lost cause. It was more an outlet for his frustrations rather than the hope of winning the argument. "We'll just be stuck out in the middle of nowhere with our thumbs up our butts."

"Tough shit, that's the way it is, so sit tight."

*

Blood had pooled on the table's dark surface, and was still dripping off the edge to soak the carpet. The senior visa officer's body had been sent out of the embassy in the care of the two shocked *BBC* men, who had been forced to carry the dead woman to the gate, but flecks of bone and brain matter was still strewn across the room.

Devini watched the blood drip as she waited for the phone to ring. She knew it would ring, but she wondered how long it would be before the police negotiator could summon the presence of mind to make the call. The next hour would be the decider. Either the authorities would cave in and hand the problem over to the Canadians, or decide to send in their Army killers. Whatever the decision, watching the blood, Devini knew there would be a lot more of the liquid shed before the planned drama could end.

The stink of cordite, blood and excrement hung heavily in the room, clinging to the thick drapes and the carpeting, and erasing the previously faintly discernable odour of sex that had made Devini's nipples come erect during the rape. Now she wondered what the Canadian woman had been thinking during that assault.

Devini's only real experience with sex were the two rapes she herself had undergone in her teens, and now she wondered whether the senior visa officer had had similar thoughts to hers. Her own first rape — by her LTTE instructor — had been painful and confusing rather than frightening, unlike the second experience. She still had to quell the trembling in her limbs when she recalled the bearded Sikh soldiers. She had been terrified that they would kill her when they were finished, and the relay of grunting sweating bodies had gone by in a blur.

The phone began to ring, and after thirty seconds Devini picked it up and heard the police negotiator's voice in her ear.

*

1000 LOCAL [0400 GMT]: "I think we should go in immediately, before there are anymore killings," Major General Perera said.

There was a subdued note amongst the CCG members, even an hour after the *BBC* broadcast. Official control of the siege had been handed over to the Army soon after the killing of the senior visa officer, but the embassy and its grounds were officially Canadian crown territory, and the Sri Lankan Ministry of Foreign Affairs needed to sanction any military action.

Soon after the killing of the visa officer, the Cabinet Crisis Group had gone into a half-hour recess in order for its members to confer with their respective staffs. Now they were back with the latest information and briefs. The only person absent was Mike Salgado, who was personally overseeing the DII's investigation of the depth of the ERA's Colombo operation.

"Blue Team is already onsite and conducting a recce of the target area," Perera continued. "They're still waiting for Municipal Council plans of the embassy building, but the direct-action drills can be used 'til then."

"What percentage guarantees can Blue Team's commander give us of success?" John Jayavickrama asked, worried, as all politicians were, of risk.

"With the DA drills, sixty-percent," answered Perera. "If we have more time with the building plans, we can make it ninety-percent."

"At the moment, sixty-percent is too risky," decided Jayavickrama. "If we go in now, it'll be without Canadian approval, and the only way we can justify that is as a life-saving last resort. If we fail, the shit will hit the fan, and the Canadians will hold us responsible for any deaths amongst the embassy staff."

"But if we wait, we have no guarantee that they won't kill more hostages." Perera was well aware of the Canadian Joint Task Force 2 team sitting on its hands at Katunayake. He knew that the longer the CCG held off on ordering an assault, the more likely it was that Canada would request any action being taken to be carried out by JTF2. Perera had full confidence in Blue Team, and wanted them to carry out the assault as soon as was safely possible. He had no doubt that the Canadians would be good at their jobs too, but they were still an unknown quantity to him.

"As long as we do as the terras ask, there's no reason for them to kill anymore hostages," pointed out the minister. "They want Donald Fenster to negotiate with them directly, an' they'll get that. He has already indicated that he'll be leaving for Sri Lanka as soon as is practically possible."

Perera sat back, defeated, and Jayavickrama turned to the police chief.

"What is the DII negotiator saying about the situation?" he asked. "Is there any chance of extending the deadline?"

"He doesn't even want to attempt that," the IGP said. "He feels the woman — Colonel Sundari — is too far on edge, possibly a psycho. He thinks any try at real negotiation might make her explode and kill another hostage. The deadline expires four hours and fifteen minutes after the hijackers' deadline."

"Shit." Jayavickrama pinched the bridge of his nose, squeezing his eyes shut. "What's the situ there?"

"The plane landed at oh-eight-hundred," Perera reported, "refuelled, and took off again an hour later. They obviously don' want to stay on the ground long enough for the Black Cats to assault."

"An' no contact with the hijackers, except for instructions to refuel," added Jaliya de Silva. "My chap's sitting next to the Indian negotiator at the moment, an' he says the hijackers aren't answering any radio calls."

"I think, at the moment, that's the more urgent problem," Arjuna Devendra chipped in. "It's obvious that Canada isn't going to sack Fenster, especially now that he's needed here in Colombo."

"The jet took on enough fuel to last them as long as the deadline," said de Silva, "but not much more."

"What are the Indians saying?" Perera asked.

"They're aware of the situation here in Colombo — obviously — and I think if the plane gets on the ground they'll try to storm it. The Black Cat team at Indira Gandhi in New Delhi has flown to Madras, an' they're probably going through the same drills as your chaps."

"What's the story with Red Team?" cut in the minister.

"They're working on several options, depending on which stand the plane parks at," said Perera. "We're getting regular satellite shots of the airport from the Americans, so we know which stands are free."

"How regularly?"

"Every two hours. They've had a military satellite on permanent station over the subcontinent since last year. The thing is, it'll all mean nothing if the hijackers stay in the air till the deadline."

Devendra's cell phone vibrated discreetly in his shirt pocket and he glanced quickly at the caller-ID before answering. He listened for several minutes to the staff officer at Int HQ before hanging up. Catching the minister's eye, he cleared his throat.

"The Americans have just sent across some air recce shots from Diego Garcia," he said calmly. "The *Vikrant* carrier group just did a hundred an' eighty degree turn and is heading towards Sri Lanka. They'll be off our western coast in less than twenty four hours."

"What is the *Vikrant* carrier group?" Jayavickrama asked.

"The INS *Vikrant* is an Indian aircraft carrier with a squadron of Sea Harriers and another of Sea King transport helicopters on board. They've also got an Army battalion on board, and are being escorted by a missile frigate plus several destroyers. The whole lot was off as part of the UN peacekeeping mission to Madagascar, but now they're heading back."

There was silence for a moment or two, and then John Jayavickrama spoke. "Half an hour ago, soon after the BBC broadcast, the Indian ambassador to the UN spoke to the Security Council. He has volunteered, in the event of UN peacekeepers being sent here, to have Indian troops form the large part of the contingent. The ambassador has also told the Security Council that there will be a four-day delay before India can begin operations in Africa, due to increased tensions with Pakistan. I guess they must be wanting to show the UN that they have the muscle ready to do the job."

"Well, the *Vikrant* certainly isn't sailing towards the Arabian Sea," pointed out Devendra.

"Don't want anybody else in their back garden, looks like," Sujeeva Fernando commented.

*   *   *

1215 LOCAL (0645 GMT): The smell inside the A340's cabin was steadily growing worse. The toilets were beginning to give up on the effort of trying to cope with demands beyond regulations. Popping another Dexedrine capsule, Mahesh Balachandran returned to the cockpit and relieved Nireuben. The pilots had AC634 on autopilot, but were taking turns monitoring the controls in the mind-numbing boredom of flying a vast triangular path over the Bay of Bengal, each leg five hundred kilometres long, with its western apex being the city of Madras. Johnny Burnett was back on watch while his co-pilot dozed.

Balachandran handed Nireuben the cup of black coffee, and the man headed back to his regular post.

Using the aircraft radios, Balachandran had been monitoring the news stations for information on what the Indian, Sri Lankan, and Canadian governments were planning to do about the hijack. Because of this, they had all heard the reports on the ERA capture of the Canadian embassy. Balachandran was slightly irritated by this unforeseen event, one that seemed to be taking the focus away from the hijack.

Watching the Indian MiGs that were still holding station, he wondered what he could do to refocus world attention on AC634. In the end, he knew, it would make no difference. At the final curtain of the act, the result would be the same. But he also knew that its impact would be defused by the media vying to cover two stories.

If he were to take AC634 back down to Madras, he knew the attention would be back. But that was a change of procedure he didn't like. Deviating from the original plan of staying airborne until the deadline expired, would cause new dangers. By now, the Indian and Sri Lankan militaries would have drawn up plans to storm the airliner, and landing would present them just the opportunity. It was the primary reason for not landing in the first place. It had been a balance between public attention and a secure defence.

Making up his mind, he started to give Burnett his orders. The danger would come in the dark, like a creature of the night, but Balachandran knew that they would be long gone before night fell.

*

Colin Peters felt his stomach lurch and came fully awake. He hadn't really been sleeping, his stomach wouldn't let him. He had given up on alcohol, as it just seemed to make his bowels looser than they already were, and he had no intention of visiting one of the overflowing lavatories if he could help it. Grimacing in discomfort, he now watched the horizon tilt as the Airbus banked. They were descending, and he wondered if by some chance the ordeal was finally over.

Vijitha Dhampahana also hoped fervently that they would land and that everybody would be released. But would they send him back to Colombo, he wondered. Would he have to plan his escape and run the gauntlet all over again? Surely they would let everybody continue on their journeys?

Daniel Devanayagam was blissfully asleep, unaware that the plane was heading back down towards the Indian coast. He had tired long ago of trying to keep track of their progress on his map screen. All they were doing was flying in a triangle.

Jennifer Jensen's thoughts were filled with images of Tim Ferguson and their last hours together. Normally, she'd be walking the aisles, checking the passengers, preparing for touchdown, but there seemed no point to that. All the passengers were buckled up, and who gave a fuck anyway if their seats weren't in the upright position? She returned her thoughts to Tim and, as she felt her ears pop, wondered idly if she'd be seeing him anytime soon.

* * *

The JTF2 platoon had been sitting in the sun by the runway for half an hour, waiting for the pilots. An hour before, Jan Conway had been called by the military attaché and informed that the Sri Lankans had agreed to let him and his men join the team training for the hijack job. There was no clear indication as to what extent the two units would cooperate, or whether they would be operating as one or separate entities. Conway's platoon was to get its collective butt up to Palaly post haste and play it by ear from then on.

At Air Force Ops, Conway had been told a resupply flight was headed for Palaly in ten minutes, and they could take that. The JTF2 soldiers had grabbed their gear and headed for the runway to find the C-130 in question sitting in the sun, deserted. That had been half an hour ago.

Fifty metres away, about eighty Sri Lankan replacement troops were also waiting to board the transport, most of them heavily laden with kitbags and packs. The soldiers were watching the white men curiously, but Conway didn't want his men getting chatty with the infantry just yet, and ordered them to stay put.

Eventually, the aircrew arrived, strolling unconcernedly along, smoking, wearing snappy Rayban aviator glasses and tailored US-woodland-pattern camouflage fatigues. They started to turn and burn, and an Air Force loadywaved the waiting troops aboard.

The centre cargo area was taken up by huge pallets of rations and ammo and other supplies. A single bench ran the length of the hold on both sides of the fuselage, and this was already occupied by the forty or fifty young Sri Lankan soldiers who had been first to board. But as soon as the Canadians boarded, some of the Sri Lankans gave up their seats to them, opting to sit on the steel deck. The Canadians tried to protest, but the soldiers — most of them teenagers — just grinned and wagged their heads. The engines were too loud for conversation, so the Canadians just shrugged and took the proffered seats.

The ramp came up as the plane started to roll, and soon they were airborne. With nothing to do, Conway watched the Sri Lankan soldiers. It was obvious that most of them were fresh out of training and were going into the war zone for the first time, their American woodland-pattern fatigues still creased from the packing, and their jungle boots shiny. It also seemed that none of them had ever flown before, for as soon as the plane was in the air, they pressed themselves to the tiny windows for a glimpse of the earth below.

The Sri Lankan troops all wore helmets and carried Kalashnikov assault rifles that never seemed to leave their hands. But in spite of all the trappings of war, the soldiers looked like children to Conway; like all Asian teenagers, seemingly younger than their years to western eyes. He wondered what their fighting calibre would be like. At the moment they seemed like they would be more comfortable following a buffalo through a paddy field or trying to steal a kiss from a local Lolita, rather than be out hunting terrorists.

Conway hoped that the much-vaunted Red Team would be more experienced than these boys, with older, veteran soldiers.

It was at this point that he felt cold eyes scanning him, and turned. At the far end of the hold, sitting jammed into a corner was a man who was noticeably older than the teenagers around him. His fatigues were British DPMs, faded and stained, and he wore a bush hat instead of a helmet. Even at this distance, Conway could see the big scarred hands that held an old wooden-stocked T56 with a folding cruciform bayonet. The man held Conway's gaze for a heartbeat, before looking away, but in that time the Canadian felt as if he had caught a glimpse into an old disused well: dark, cold, and unfathomable, with strange thoughts crawling like dim creatures across the bottom.

Conway wondered at those eyes, and tried to remember if he had seen anything like them before. A career soldier with twenty years of service, Jan Conway had been to many parts of the world, both on Canadian, NATO, and UN operations, but he had never seen eyes quite like these. As a sergeant in the Airborne Regiment's 2nd Airborne Commando, he had been into Kuwait with the Coalition Forces during Desert Storm, but hadn't been in the fighting. In 1995, soon after he had received his commission, Conway had met some of the members of the 3rd Airborne Commando on their return from the disaster of Mogadishu, and he had looked into their eyes, tried to read the pain and horror that they had witnessed in that African land. While he had seen both these things in their gaze, they were not the eyes he stared into now on the C-130 Hercules, flying towards the Jaffna Peninsula. But then, Conway told himself, Canada hadn't been at war for twenty years.

The Sri Lankan never met Conway's eyes again, but for the rest of the forty five-minute flight, the Canadian soldier felt his skin seared as if by a blowtorch. Even though the JTF2 platoon's weapons were stowed out of sight in black padded sports bags, their black fatigues and boots — into which they had changed before the flight — gave no doubt as to what they were. There was no way they were going to be mistaken for engineers or aid workers.

Conway's thoughts drifted back to the year of his commissioning; it had been a scandal-ridden one for the Canadian Forces. The 3rd Airborne Commando's deployment to Somalia on peacekeeping operations had been a public relations catastrophe — torture of prisoners and brutality towards its own recruits being just two of the accusations splashed in the media. Ottawa had folded before the public outcry and ordered the Airborne Regiment disbanded. Jan Conway, a thirty-two-year-old second lieutenant, had been about to be cast adrift in a faceless military. Two years previously, however, the Canadian Forces had formed a new strategic anti-terrorist unit, Joint Task Force 2, which had taken over the national hostage-rescue mission from the Mounties' soon to be defunct Emergency Response Teams. With his parent regiment breaking up, Conway had applied to join JTF2.

The C-130 descended steeply over the sea north of the Jaffna Peninsula and rocketed in at low altitude, bouncing hard onto the runway. Conway tried to get his first glimpse of the infamous peninsula through the windows, but all he could make out was swirling clouds of dust.

The ramp lowered and everybody stared out into an ochre world, unmoving, as if they had just landed on Mars. Then the loady yelled something and the young replacements were galvanized into action, quickly jogging off the plane. The last Conway saw of the dead-eyed soldier was of the man strolling unhurriedly through the dust towards a stripped-down Land Rover that sat on the edge of the runway with a long 105-mm recoilless rifle mounted on its back. He could just make out several figures crouched next to the vehicle, shielding their eyes and cigarettes from the prop wash.

Conway and his men walked quickly away from the C-130 and the dust, but by now their black fatigues were well powdered with ochre. Conway saw a soldier walking towards them, hatless, longer than regulation hair ruffling in the wind. The man had an MP-5 slung across his chest. Maybe this was the reception committee.

"Hi!" Conway said to the man, noting that he was scanning the white faces for a sign that someone was in charge of them. "Are you here to meet us? I'm Lieutenant Jan Conway."

"Morning," the Sri Lankan said. "My name's Christofelsz." He shook Conway's proffered hand. "Ah've got a truck over here to take us to the FOB."

Eric Christofelsz appraised Conway from the corner of his eye as they walked. The Canadian was big, well over six feet with the weight to match. His face was lined by a life spent outdoors, and was capped by blonde hair that was just a shade short of white; a slash of blonde moustache lay beneath a slightly too-large nose, all of which was gradually turning ochre from the surrounding dust.

"Is it always this dry out here?" Conway asked as they stopped by a canvas-topped Tata 1210 truck parked next to a hangar.

"Except in December an' January," came the reply. "Then you drown." They arrived at the truck and Christofelsz jabbed a thumb at the back. "Your guys can chuck their kit in the back. You can join me up front with the driver if you like. Not so comfortable, but we don' have to go far."

Once everyone was on board, the driver floored the accelerator and the truck lurched along the dusty road. Conway tried to make some sort of mental map out of the vast grid of roads, tin sheds, and converted civilian buildings they were driving through, but to no avail. There didn't seem to be any real structure to it beyond the airbase. One moment the truck might be hurtling between rows of sheds, and around the next corner it would pass alongside a wall of impenetrable scrub jungle with no sign of proper defences. The only uniformity seemed to be the barbed wire and the palmyrah trees on the horizon. And the dust.

*   *   *

The big Airbus stood in the burning sun, one thousand seven hundred and fifty metres from the control tower in which Superintendent Chula Abenayake of the DFI was sitting. The hijackers on board AC634 had asked for the same stand that they had used more than four hours previously, on their second landing at Madras. It was also the same stand they had used on their first landing, twenty four hours before. Probably, they felt comfortable in that spot, and Abenayake could see why. With the huge fuel storage area in such close proximity to the plane, the authorities wouldn't want to risk a fire fight.

This time, like the previous time, there had been no refusal on the part of the Indian authorities at the hijackers' demand to land. India was already committed.

Abenayake listened to the Indian negotiator talk to the pilot. There had still been no direct voice contact between the terrorist leader and the authorities. All his requests and demands had been made via the pilot, even the statement the previous night. At the moment they were discussing a practical method in which airport sanitation personnel could replace the plane's lavatories.

So far, Abenayake had not had any direct involvement in the drama, beyond being an interested observer. However, the same rules applied, and like the Indian next to him, he had been cut off from all outside news beyond what was being fed to the hijackers. This was in order that a negotiator's voice would not betray the fact that he knew an assault team was in position. Since Abenayake might have to take over the negotiations if the circumstances changed, he was being kept in the dark, too. This went very much against the grain of his training and experience as a Sri Lankan DFI operative, but he had no choice. His training with the FBI had taught him the value of the tactic.

*

Inside the Airbus, the temperature was mounting steadily. The engines, and with them the air conditioning, had been shut down for just half an hour, but the outside temperature of 42°C was rapidly ensuring the cabin turned into an oven. Children cried fretfully, and adults discarded pullovers and unbuttoned shirts and blouses. Everybody was kept in their seats until the lavatories had been switched, but once that operation was complete, the cabin crew were allowed to serve the diminishing store of soft drinks and fruit juices.

Ignoring the sweat trickling down his face and neck, Balachandran was scanning their surroundings. Like before, there were no other airliners parked in the neighbouring stands, and there seemed to be very little human activity in this quarter of the airport. In the distance, Balachandran could see the control tower shimmering in the heat like a mirage. He wondered who else was in there with the negotiators. The airport had been closed to all civilian flights, so there wouldn't be the usual number of air and ground traffic controllers. But Balachandran also knew that if there was a hostage rescue unit at Madras, its commander would be up there as well.

He had not requested for their fuel to be topped up, nor for their food to be replenished. They would need neither once the deadline was reached. As foreseen by his superiors, he knew the Canadians would never cave in to the threats of hijackers, and the inevitable conclusion would soon be upon them. And at that time, Balachandran had no intention of letting AC634 be anywhere near Madras.

*   *   *

1845 AUSTRALIAN WESTERN STANDARD TIME (0845 GMT): Her
hands trembling, Patricia Fenster packed her bags quickly, trying
to hide her nervousness from her husband, who was on the other
side of the big bed, packing his own bags. With the capture of the
embassy in Colombo and the horrible broadcast by the *BBC*, it
was becoming abundantly clear to her just who her blackmailers
were. These were not people to disobey, and she had decided that
she would follow instructions to the letter, deliver the bag to
Colombo, and hope that she would never hear from the man with
the American accent ever again.

They were due at the airport in half an hour, and if the pilot
of the Lear Jet went flat out, they would make the deadline in Colombo
easily. Patricia was sure that in all the confusion she'd be able to slip
off to the left luggage lockers and exchange attaché cases.

She hadn't been told where to dispose of the case in
Colombo, and she hoped it wouldn't be a complicated matter; she
didn't want to be faced with an awkward situation that would
require explanation to Donald. Oh, well, she had no doubt her
blackmailer would contact her soon enough. Patricia wondered
whether someone would personally pick up the attaché case. She
wondered what the person would be like, whether he would have
the mark of evil on his face. Or would he look — like the embassy
terrorist — just one more obscure Asian?

"You really must hurry, honey. We can't afford any delays."

Donald's sharp reminder made Patricia realize that with
her thoughts elsewhere, her packing had slowed.

"Sorry," she said, quickly finishing the suitcase and zipping it up.

Minutes later, they were in the limousine with the
bodyguards, racing out of the Hilton grounds and onto the
Canberra streets. An escort car followed, and ahead, police
motorcycles with sirens howling cleared the traffic.

The drive to the airport took a full twenty minutes, and Donald Fenster seethed with impatience. He told himself to calm down, that nothing he could do would make things move faster, and that anyway there was plenty of time, but it didn't work.

The shock and anger that had followed the *BBC* broadcast had faded slowly, being replaced by a cold determination to make sure that the Tamil bitch in the embassy got what she deserved. He knew he would have to use all his political and diplomatic skills to make sure none of the other hostages were murdered, and he also knew that this might very well result in the terrorists going scot free. Fenster told himself, however, that if that happened, he would do whatever it took to make sure that they were eventually brought to justice. Or justice brought to them, as George Bush had said. Hell, countries like the US, Israel, and Sri Lanka, had proved in the past that international justice didn't always mean the court system. Maybe it was time that Canada took an overt role in the fight against international terror outside its own borders.

Well, Fenster told himself, if he could resolve both the embassy siege and the Air Canada hijack satisfactorily, he could just as well write his own anti-terror cheque. If it meant dedicating the rest of his life to this new war, then that was what he would do. And who knew what the future could hold. A successful war could very well pave the road to the prime minister's office.

It was a pity he wouldn't be able to go to Madras to overlook the negotiations with the hijackers personally. The hijackers would hardly be pleased to know that the man they wanted sacked was in fact on the scene himself. No, Frank Vitucci would have to take care of that.

Vitucci, one of Fenster's senior staffers was already waiting at the airport, and would fly on to Madras from Colombo. That was if the hijackers were willing to extend their deadline. If not, Vitucci would get to the party too late.

CHAPTER 22

1500 LOCAL (0900 GMT): The room smelled of cigarette smoke, sweat, and nervous tension. The functional, glass-paned windows were open, but what little breeze entered the room did nothing to dissipate the atmosphere, sluggishly moved by a rust-blistered three-bladed ceiling fan. A glance around the room would show it to be nothing more than just one more clerical pool on a third world military base. The desks were of scarred brown wood topped with ancient vinyl blotters, the chairs were of wood and rotting rattan. A few long unused Remington typewriters had been moved onto one desk, and the world's oldest PC gathered dust on top of a rusting filing cabinet in one corner. Everything, floor, furniture, typewriters, window sills, were covered with a layer of dust, and thick cobwebs clung to the ceiling's corners. It was obvious the room had not been in use for many months, if not years.

The only items free of dust were the former chief clerk's desk at the front of the room, and the three chairs that were pulled up to it. The two facing into the room were wheeled executive chairs in black plastic and mock-leather, and stood out in stark contrast to the rest of the room.

Seated in them were two men, each as different from the other as the chairs were from the room. The one doing most of the talking was short and round, though his stockiness was more muscle than fat. His moon face matched his body, with a pencil-thin moustache under a bulbous nose, and the whole thing topped by thinning, but slicked-back, hair. He wore dark dress trousers, polished black shoes, a sweat-damp short-sleeved white shirt, and a conservatively striped dark tie, loose at the throat in concession to Sri Lanka's heat and humidity. The man next to him was clean-shaven, with hair that was neither too long nor of military regulation length. His faded British DPM fatigues, badgeless except for the stars of a full lieutenant, were bloused into well-worn brown jump boots. His sleeves were rolled up over tanned and muscled arms, and his whole body, though slim, gave of the aura of a big cat at rest. A maroon beret with the Commando cap badge was neatly pushed beneath an epaulette.

Sitting opposite them in an uncomfortable wooden chair was a man in the grey shirt-and-shorts uniform of the airport maintenance staff. The man was thin, dark, approaching forty, and painfully nervous. He constantly wrung his hands and smiled ingratiatingly as he stammered out answers to the stocky man's questions.

The interviews had been going on non-stop since the hijack news had come in, and everybody was tired. The interviewers took it in shifts, but that didn't help much. The interviewees were red-eyed with fatigue, most not having been allowed to go home, or having done so, been called back to the airport at all hours. The interviews had begun with the bomb-detection team that had swept AC634 before takeoff for Changi, and had then moved on to maintenance and sanitation workers, then onto catering staff, and finally to other airport personnel. The interviewers were nearing the end of the line without a single clue as to how the weapons had been taken aboard the aircraft at Katunayake. *If* they had been taken aboard at Katunayake.

Inspector Susantha Jayaweera had serious doubts that this was so. Security at Katu was just too tight these days. He was the head of the DII team conducting the airport end of the investigation into the hijacking. The Commando lieutenant sitting next to him was one of two men from that unit's Brigade int shop who were there as observers, taking no part in the interviews, but making occasional notes. Jayaweera knew that if the interviews turned up a zero, his superiors would order him to start again at the top with the bomb-detection team. He tried to keep the frustration out of his voice now as he questioned the man in front of him.

The man was a ramp baggage handler, and the interview, like most of those conducted, was in Sinhalese. The baggage handler was obviously uneducated and terrified by the presence of the soldiers and DII men, and in their interest in him. It was also obvious that he knew of nothing unusual that could be connected to the hijack. His fear was nothing to take note of either. More than two decades of dirty war had created this fear amongst the civilian population of Sri Lanka. The armed forces were something to take pride in, but, especially since the communist uprising in the late 1980s, also something to fear. Too many young sons had disappeared in the dark hours — bundled into Land Rovers by masked and uniformed men — for it to be any different.

Inspector Jayaweera was about to conclude the interview when the door opened. A soldier stuck his head into the room and caught the Commando officer's eye. The lieutenant excused himself and left the room. Jayaweera wound down the interview, warned the baggage handler that he might be needed for further questioning, and dismissed the man.

The baggage handler was leaving the room when the commando re-entered. Jayaweera saw the lieutenant pause at the door and tell the sentry outside not to let any more interviewees in just yet. He then came over and sat down.

"What's up, Amal?" Jayaweera asked, eyeing the soldier curiously.

The inspector was trying not to resent the Army's presence in this investigation. It was all well and good to have the Rambo characters around when a plane had to be stormed, but until then, Jayaweera felt, police work should be left to cops like him. It was bad enough having Military Intelligence playing James Bond without the Commandos getting in on the act. Thankfully the DMI had not shown up yet, but they were probably prowling around the airport in false beards and wigs. It was all a bit too much like the *Spy vs. Spy* comics for Jayaweera's liking.

Lieutenant Amal Paranagama leaned back in his wheeled executive chair and lit up a Bristol, offering the crushed pack to Jayaweera, who shook his head in thanks, preferring his own Benson & Hedges, one of which he now lit. Both men took several drags before Paranagama spoke.

"The locker search has turned up something."

"What has been found?"

Most of the Bandaranaike International Airport's maintenance and technical personnel had their own lockers in which uniforms and personal equipment was stored. These had been sealed when the investigation began, and were in the process of being searched for any clues to the hijack.

"This." Paranagama reached into a breast pocket and took out something. Opening his hand he let a bullet roll onto the desktop. It lay there for a few moments, its brass casing glinting dully.

"Whose locker was it in?" Jayaweera asked, his tone revealing a hint of exasperation at Paranagama's melodramatic attitude.

"In Lieutenant Derek De Alwis' locker," explained Paranagama. "The head of the explosive search team that swept the plane."

"I know who he is." Jayaweera's ears were pricking up at the first hint of something unusual, but he kept his voice challenging. He was bloody well not going to let this soldier be smug about things. "So what's the big deal? Airport Security carries weapons, no? An' they're on the ranges regularly. The bugger probably kept a round as a souvenir."

"He's ex-Army," said Paranagama, his voice a bit too condescending for the DII man's liking. "Normal bullets are nothing special to him." Paranagama inclined his head towards the bullet on the table. "But tha'ss no normal bullet. Put a closer look at it."

Jayaweera picked up the 9-mm Parabellum round. He immediately realized that it felt slightly lighter than a regular pistol-calibre round. On the base of the cartridge, along with the indicated manufacturing lot number, were etched the two letters '*BM*'.

"What does BM mean?" asked Jayaweera. He took out his own Glock and unloaded it, comparing one of its Parabellum rounds with the one Paranagama had just given him. "They look exactly the same, but this one is a bit lighter."

"BM stands for Bismuth, a company that makes bullets." Paranagama took the round back and examined it. "Very special bullets."

* * *

The Canberra Airport came into view as the convoy turned off Fairbairn Avenue and onto Pialligo Avenue. While sirens of the outriders made pedestrians turn and stare at the black limousine with the tinted windows and the Canadian flag, its passengers ignored the racket.

In the back of the limo, Patricia Fenster watched CI Graham Zewelczy, the head of the bodyguard team, sitting next to the driver, use his mobile phone to warn the pilot that they were almost there. It looked like they were going to be rushed straight through the airport without the formalities of customs and immigration. Patricia hoped she would be able to get away from her husband and the bodyguards long enough to exchange the attaché case with the one in the luggage locker. She had decided she would claim she needed to use the restrooms. Her period had begun the previous night, and the genuine cramps she was suffering from would be the perfect cover.

The convoy swung off the road and raced into the airport premises without much reduction in speed. With a jolt of alarm, Patricia realized that they weren't even going to enter the airport buildings but drive straight up to the jet. Gripping the attaché case with white-knuckled intensity, she doubled over in her seat, giving vent to a soft moan.

"What is it, honey?" Donald Fenster snapped out of his thoughts on the Sri Lankan situation and looked down at his wife.

"It's the cramps again," Patricia gasped. "I really need to use the restroom before we takeoff."

Fenster grimaced, torn between concern for her and the need to be on their way. "Can't you use the one on the jet?"

"No," she said through clenched teeth, "I need to take care of this now."

Fenster spoke quickly to the driver, and Zewelczy spoke to the escort over his Motorola comms system. The limo detoured towards the airport buildings, drawing up at a side entrance where Patricia started to get out, still holding the attaché case. The BG team boss started to detail a man to accompany her, and Patricia glared at him.

"I can manage without help, *if* you don't mind," she snapped at him and strode off.

The SPG officer looked at Fenster in exasperation, but only got an amused and helpless shrug in reply. Giving up, Zewelczy turned away, muttering about PMS to the smirking driver. Fenster frowned but returned to his thoughts.

In the distance he could see the CC-144 Challenger in the markings of the Canadian Forces. From the disturbance caused to the heat waves rising off the tarmac behind the aircraft, he knew that the pilot already had the engines turning and burning.

As soon as she was out of sight of the sliding glass doors, Patricia turned away from her original route to the restrooms and headed for the long-term luggage lockers. Racing against time, hoping the SPG officer wouldn't change his mind and send a bodyguard after her, she searched down the rows of wall lockers. Finding the right one, she unlocked it and retrieved the attaché case that was sitting inside. Whether it was the same one she had brought across from Canada or a new one, she had no idea. It looked identical to the one she'd carried around Canberra with her for the past few days: almost brand new. She pulled the case out of the locker, noting that it was much heavier than the one she was replacing it with.

Not bothering to open the case, she quickly locked the storage space and, still following instructions, bent down and ran her hand along the bottom of the row of lockers directly below the one she had opened. Her hand found a small cylinder and she tore it free of the Velcro tabs that held it in place. What she found herself holding was a cardboard Smarties tube. Opening it, she dropped in the locker key, and pressed the tube back into place. She then raced back towards the restrooms.

There was no bodyguard outside the women's restroom and she hurried in. Nervousness had made her bladder feel like it was bursting. Selecting a cubicle, she pulled her panties down and sat. Taking the opportunity, she examined the attaché case. The combination lock marked it as being different from the ones she had previously carried. Patricia wondered why there was a sudden change to the pattern, and hoped that nobody would notice.

Well, it would soon be over, she told herself. This would be the last leg. She would carry the case to Colombo, hand it over, and forget any of this had ever happened.

For the thousandth time in the last week, Patricia told herself that she would be more discreet in her future extramarital affairs. Maybe she would even give them up altogether, have a proper married relationship with Don. Well, she thought as she patted herself dry, for a while, anyway.

* * *

The mid-afternoon sun blazed down on Brigadier Arjuna Devendra as he walked the half-kilometre from the Ministry of Defence into the Army HQ complex and over to the Directorate of Military Intelligence. He was dressed in white shirt, tan trousers, and a brightly patterned tie, and looked like, possibly, the fashionable CEO of an advertising agency or a software company. The sentries at the camp gate knew him on sight, of course, and let him go through with a respectful nod.

Walking into the foyer of his office, he dispatched an orderly to the Officers' Mess to bring him a packet of rice and curry — if there was any left at this late hour. The Cabinet Crisis

Group had finally broken up for lunch, giving its members a chance to update themselves on the latest developments before the afternoon session.

The pretty sergeant who served as his private secretary stood up as he entered the foyer, waving a handful of phone messages.

"Sort through them, Dharshini," he said, walking through into his office, unknotting his tie as he went. "Tell me what's really urgent. The rest can wait."

Stripping off his sweat-damp shirt and undershirt, Devendra walked through into his private bathroom. Using a towel soaked in cold water, he swabbed his upper body down and then splashed on some Old Spice. As he picked a fresh undershirt and a clean shirt off a hanger, he watched in the mirror as Dharshini entered his office room.

While he dressed, she stood at the bathroom door, eyes turned discreetly away, reading him the more urgent messages.

"Captain Mayadunne called several times about the airport investigation. He said there are some developments that he must brief you on, sir."

Knotting a new tie, Devendra stepped out of the bathroom, listening to Dharshini's listing of priorities. Nothing was as important as the Kàtu investigation, though the debrief of the SF team from Cologne would be interesting.

"Tell Mayadunne to come in at once."

"Yessir, but what about your lunch?" Dharshini paused to adjust the knot in Devendra's tie, and he waved his hand impatiently at her as her fingers straightened the silk.

"Ah'll eat while Ah'm talking to Mayadunne." He looked at her face as she clicked her heels in salute. "What news of Lasantha?"

Dharshini was married to a Military Police staff sergeant currently based in Trincomalee, and the long distance relationship had been telling on Devendra's secretary.

"His transfer to SIB Colombo has been approved, sir." She hesitated, not wanting to overstep the mark. "Thank you, sir."

"For what?"

"For. . . your concern, sir."

Devendra waved his hand in dismissal, hiding a smile as he turned to his desk. She flashed him a quick grin and left.

Devendra knew that Dharshini had been considering requesting a transfer to Anuradhapura in the North Central Province in order to be closer to her husband. As her boss he could have refused the transfer, but it would have been a callous act, he knew. So rather than lose a brilliant secretary, one he knew was wasted on the Army, Devendra had pulled a few strings with his contacts in the Military Police's Special Investigation Branch. In spite of his attempts to cover his tracks, Devendra knew that very few secrets remained so in Sri Lanka.

A few minutes later, Dharshini ushered in Captain Eshan Mayadunne. The younger officer seemed to have intercepted Devendra's orderly *en route*, and now brought in the tray with the lunch packet and bottle of Elephant Ginger Beer himself.

Taking the tray, the brigadier told Mayadunne to have a seat. "You ate already, Mayadunne?" he asked politely, opening the lunch packet's outer wrapping of newspaper and then the inner one of cling film.

"Yessir, thanks. I ate in the mess."

Devendra grunted and without ceremony began to eat, using the fingers of his right hand to pick strips of curried chicken off the drumstick before mixing it in with the *samba* rice, dhal, beetroot, and *seeni sambol*. Like most Sri Lankans, when away from formal situations, he preferred to eat with his fingers rather than cutlery. It was the only way to enjoy good rice and curry, and Army mess cooks served up the best. Shaping the food into a small lump, he paused, hand halfway to his mouth.

"What are you waiting for, man?" he snapped at Mayadunne. "Start talking! As soon as I finish lunch I have to be back at the JOC. Tell me wha'ss the scene at Katu?"

Mayadunne quickly gave him a breakdown on the finding of the Bismuth round in the explosive detection team head's locker, and the subsequent interrogation of the man.

Mayadunne explained that Bismuth rounds were special subsonic ammunition developed by an American company for eco-friendly duck hunters, but had soon found itself a niche in the world of anti-terrorism. The bullets were designed to break down to a powdery residue when coming into contact with anything harder than flesh and bone, and were now routinely issued to air marshals and hostage rescue units. The rounds could be safely fired inside an airborne aircraft without the danger of them penetrating the pressurized fuselage. They were highly specialized kit and not issued to regular military units.

When confronted with the bullet by his interrogators, Lieutenant Derek de Alwis had at first denied all knowledge of it, claiming he'd never seen it before. A severe beating by two beefy commandos had quickly introduced him to the facts of life, and he had admitted the bullet was his. It turned out he had several more at his home in Negombo, a few kilometres north of the airport, and a DII search team had been dispatched to the house, returning with half a dozen more 9-mm Bismuth rounds. For a while the Airport Security officer had tried to make out that he had been given the bullets as a souvenir by a friend in the Special Forces, but another beating, and the threat of even more dire consequences to come had made him cough up the fact that the bullets were part of a consignment of weapons and ammo that he had been ordered to place on Air Canada AC634. He had, at the time, decided to surreptitiously keep some of the extra rounds to test fire on the range at a later date. He had removed them from his locker long before the hijack went into effect, but had somehow overlooked one bullet.

Breaking down completely, de Alwis had spilled the beans on how he had been recruited by the old National Intelligence Bureau — forerunner of both the DII and the DFI — while still in the Army. He had worked closely with NIB operatives while training police Special Task Force troops on booby trap detection several years previously. The orders to place submachine-guns, ammo, and grenades on the Canadian airliner had come, he claimed,

from his former NIB controller, now on the staff of the DFI in
Colombo. The weapons and explosives had come into the airport
on an Air Force Huey, guarded by a DFI team, part of a
consignment of captured terrorist weaponry being brought to
Colombo for cataloguing. De Alwis assumed the chopper had come
in from the Eastern Province.

With the first mention of the DFI connection, Devendra
had stopped eating, and had sat there listening in stunned silence.
Now the food had dried on his fingers, and taking a swallow of
ginger beer, he pushed aside his plate and headed for the bathroom
sink to wash his hands.

"So what about this DFI controller?" he asked over the
sound of running water. "Have you located him?"

"Yessir," Mayadunne replied. "We tracked him down an'
already lifted the bugger. We have him at Nawala. We've started
to work on him, but he won' say a word. Says it's part of a classified
op, an' wants to talk to his superiors."

Nawala was a suburb of Colombo, and housed one of
Int's big comms centres.

Devendra returned to his desk and slurped at his ginger
beer, then lit a cigarette.

"What the hell is going on here?" he said finally, more to
himself than the captain. He looked up sharply at Mayadunne.
"What are the DFI and the DII saying about all this?"

"Dunno, sir. We sealed the whole Katu operation
immediately when the DFI involvement came out. The Commando
guy who was part of the interrogation team contacted us at once
and—"

"What's his name?"

"Amal Paranagama. Lieutenant."

"I know that name," mused Devendra.

"He was attached to us, sir, about a year ago. He was finishing
a tour with one of their groups, and they sent him to us in
preparation for his moving onto their Brigade S-3 staff. Tha'ss
why he called us. He had some commandos onsite to provide

security and he used them to seal the investigation, but the DII man with him, who was heading the investigation, made some calls in the meantime. Now he's standing on his dick, demanding to talk to DII headquarters."

"OK," Devendra said decisively. "Get back to Paranagama ASAP. Tell him to lift the whole operation immediately. Get everybody on choppers to Nawala. Tell him I'll clear it with MoD and his CO, not to worry. Int is taking over this investigation. Ah'll clear it with the CCG when I go there now. When they hear about the DFI connection they'll agree. Tell Paranagama I want everybody — the prisoner, the DII team at Katu — everybody — lifted now. We need to control this an' make sure things don' leak out. The DFI still has too many unofficial connections in the DII. For all we know, buggers from both outfits might be involved in this whole thing." After a moment's thought he said, "Can you trace the Bismuth bullets?"

"Already did, sir," Mayadunne said triumphantly. "We checked the JOC database. Part of a consignment that went to Special Task Force Detachment Five."

"In the Eastern Province."

"In the Eastern Province, sir."

"Everything here seems to connect to the Eastern Province," said Devendra thoughtfully. "Why did the STF need these bullets out there in the jungle?"

"Well, sir, in December there was talk that the STF was going to form its own HR team. They must've requested the rounds for training."

"Hmm." Devendra stubbed out his Gold Leaf and lit another. "I just had a thought. Which STF unit is attached to the DFI for the LRRP ops?"

Mayadunne grinned. "One guess, sir." He was a small, dark-skinned young man, and his sharp eyes glinted now.

"Fuck. Detachment Five?"

"They're still there, sir. We're running the major part of the op, as you know, with the *thambies*, but DFI and the STF are running the Tamil side of it."

"Oh, God."
"Yes, sir."

*

Devendra stood at the tall window that was part of the colonial legacy attached to the building that housed the administrative hub of Military Intelligence. The operational side was more broadly based, scattered through a host of bases throughout the country. The well manicured grounds added to the image of a governor's residence from a 1930s movie set piece rather than the headquarters of the country's leading military intelligence-gathering organization, and looking out over it, Devendra considered the briefing he had just received from Mayadunne.

The Long-Range Reconnaissance Patrols were a top secret project thought up by ultra-hawks in the JOC. Currently the operation was a mish-mash of various security forces units and mercenaries running deep recce and ambush missions, but building up a base of experience for the next two phases.

The first of these was that in the event of an indefinite truce, ceasefire, or protracted period of negotiation between the government and the Tigers, the LRRP operations would be gradually refocused on sourcing a suitably dissatisfied group or groups of individuals within the LTTE, and once sourced, encouraged to break away and oppose the LTTE. The LRRPs would then be used to arm, support, and even fight alongside the dissident factions, thereby destabilizing the LTTE, preventing any consolidation within Tiger-controlled areas, and weakening their position at the negotiating table.

The next phase was to establish long-term stay-behind teams of guerrillas who would, in the unlikely event of the Sri Lankan government deciding to grant Eelam to the LTTE, organize and form the core of a new organization. This new outfit, cadred by Tamils and Muslims opposed to the Tigers, would be used for cross-border hit-and-run raids that would destabilize the new fledgling Tamil state.

The whole set-up was totally independent, commanded by an Army major general — Devendra's predecessor as Director Military Intelligence — who reported directly to the JOC. The operations and planning was by detached Int and special operations staff, while the patrols were commanded by SF and Commando NCOs and made up of Muslims — Malays and Moors native to the Eastern Province. The Muslims had been recruited directly from their villages by Int, and were paid from a special black budget. Int had decided to use Muslims, known for their anti-LTTE feelings, as the safer bet, but the DFI team — attached to the LRRPs for what was envisioned as eventually cross-border ops — had put forth the idea that Tamils should be used as well, claiming — rightly, Devendra thought — that it was the only way of achieving legitimacy with the international community. The Army had been unwilling to go along with this, and the DFI had proposed that the Tamil patrols could be commanded by police Special Task Force NCOs. And that was how the structure had remained, seventy-five percent of the operations run with Army NCOs commanding Muslim patrols, and the rest by STF NCOs commanding Tamil patrols. The operations had been devastatingly successful in the Eastern Province, with many prominent LTTE figures being ambushed and assassinated and valuable intelligence gathered. One of the biggest successes had been the ambush and killing in September 2001 of Colonel Shankar, the commander of the LTTE air-defence forces. A former Air Canada employee who had returned to Sri Lanka in 1983, Shankar had later become a close advisor to the Tiger leader. The whole thing had been kept at the highest classification possible, with the assassinations blamed on internecine rivalries in the Tiger ranks.

Devendra had no doubt that if events proved the interrogators' findings to be true, it would break the reputation of Int's sister, the Directorate of Foreign Intelligence, much the same as events in 1994 had shattered STF Intelligence. In that year, a series of corpses had been discovered scattered throughout southern Sri Lanka, all of them later turning out to be the bodies of suspected Tamil terrorists. The investigation that had followed connected the killings to STF Intelligence. In the resulting scandal and international embarrassment, the politicians had broken the organization and its commanders, ensuring that it was never again a viable force to be reckoned with.

Devendra would shed no tears if the DFI, and its head, were taken down a peg. While he conceded that both the DFI and DII had their uses, and that they contributed valuably to the war effort, the brigadier was proud of the fact that the civilian outfits in no way compared either in efficiency or reputation to their military half-sister. In fact he quite resented the fact that while the DFI got all the glory and acclaim, to say nothing of the fat budgets and plum overseas postings, Int did the real intelligence gathering work both locally and internationally.

Devendra knew, however, that all the petty interservice squabbles would have to take a backseat to the more pressing issue of national security. If indeed there was an element within the DFI's Department E — responsible for the Eastern Province — that had planned and carried out the hijack of Air Canada AC634, and if the facts became public knowledge, the international repercussions would be unimaginable. The Canadian government finding out alone would be a disaster of terrible proportions, one that would undo all the hard work and careful planning that both Int and others in the government had gone to. The fire would spread to the DII, to the LRRP operation, and could even reflect on Int. This cancer would have to be cut out in a decisive manner, no matter what the cost. Devendra had no illusions that everybody even vaguely tainted by the scandal would be burned. It would cripple the DFI but, if handled correctly, could possibly leave in its wake the opportunity for Int to step into the breach.

The question in the brigadier's mind was how far up the DFI's chain did the infection reach? Was the head of Department E involved? Was it a direct order from the man? Did the director himself know of the plan? Devendra doubted that even as ruthless a man as Jaliya de Silva would be foolish enough to give his sanction to an operation as black as this. It was obviously a strategy aimed at discrediting the Tigers at a time when they were looking like the conservative middle path compared to the ERA; but what a horrendous risk, with so much to lose. And it didn't have the look of a hastily planned operation. It would have to have been in place long before the appearance of the ERA.

Devendra knew that Lieutenant de Alwis' DFI controller would soon crack once he was given the good news on what was in store for him if he didn't spill the beans. And then it would just be a matter of time before the flame of guilt burned its way up the DFI's chain of command. Devendra realized that this would mean his being late for the afternoon session of the CCG.

Picking up his mobile phone, Devendra looked up Mike Salgado's number.

*

1700 LOCAL (1100 GMT): By the end of an extremely fruitful two hours, Devendra was walking into the JOC building, and if he wasn't in a jubilant mood, he was at least well satisfied with the progress of things.

When he slipped into the CCG room, John Jayavickrama had already informed the others that Donald Fenster was well on his way from Australia, and the defence minister was now in the process of harrying General Sujeeva Fernando on the abilities of the Joint Operations Command to mobilize troops to counter the threat of an Indian landing.

"How soon can you have a brigade-sized group on the ground at Katunayake?" he was asking Fernando. "An' I don' mean National Guardsmen. Ah'm talking about troops that can stand up to Indian regular forces."

"Well, sir," Fernando blustered, "the Reserve Strike Force is already in the process of embarking from China Bay. We can have 1/SF on the ground at Katu within two hours. If the rest of the units leave their heavy vehicles an' equipment behind, we can have at least one brigade down here in eight hours."

"Eight *hours?*" retorted the Defence Minister. "What am I to tell the Prime Minister? Ah'm supposed to give him a full briefing in a couple of hours, an' I need to tell him that we can defend the capital." Jayavickrama paused for breath. "How long before we can get the armour here?"

"It'll have to come by sea, sir," replied Fernando. "Twelve to eighteen hours."

"What about the Air Assault Division?"

"They're still engaged in operations around Kilinochchi. An' we'll need them to protect Palaly. It's equally likely that the Indians will attempt to put troops onto the Jaffna Peninsula."

Devendra slipped into a seat and looked across at Jaliya de Silva, who seemed to be preoccupied and not really taking any interest in the discussion. Devendra wondered how much the DFI chief knew of the hijack operation and of the now impending disaster.

The seat previously occupied by Mike Salgado was still empty.

"The Navy can detach four Dvoras and a missile corvette for immediate operations," Fernando was continuing. "They'll be able to start harassing the *Vikrant* as soon as it is in range. The Air Force's Number Ten Squadron is already conducting CAPs, and can provide air support."

"I don't think all that will be necessary." The minister waved a disparaging hand. "We just need to reinforce the Colombo garrison, and let the Indians see us doing it. If they know they can't just walk in, they'll think twice."

There was a lull in the discussion and Devendra stepped into the gap.

"Gentlemen, we have a new and equally pressing situation that I need to brief y'all on," he said, and heads turned towards him.

De Silva's face remained impassive.

"What more do we need?" sighed the minister.

Without further ado, Devendra proceeded to outline the development of the Katunayake investigation. There were no interruptions, but the faces around the table gradually began to reflect the stunned incredulity that Devendra himself had felt when he first was briefed by Captain Mayadunne. Devendra studiously avoided looking at de Silva as he talked, waiting till he had ended the narration with the description of the investigation being moved out of DII hands and over to Int. As for the events of the past two hours, he decided to keep them to himself for awhile.

All eyes in the room swung to focus on the DFI head as Devendra concluded his briefing. DIG Jaliya de Silva was too dark complexioned to pale under the weight of these covert accusations, but his suddenly bloodless lips betrayed his feelings. When he finally spoke, Devendra gave him credit for being able to keep his voice steady.

"Look," de Silva began, his eyes darting from Devendra's face to the Defence Minister's, then back again, "Ah'm already aware that there are some irregularities on the DII side in this investigation, but this hardly gives you, Devendra, the right to just take over—"

"Irregularities on the *DII side?*" said Jayavickrama softly, his voice suddenly dangerous. "If what the brigadier says about your *DFI* proves to be even fifty-percent correct, it'll be an unbelievable fiasco."

"Why don' we let Jaliya finish what he's saying?" interjected IGP Warnasuriya, attempting to give his man some breathing space. His expression, as he looked at de Silva, pleaded for some sort of believable explanation.

"You only have the word of one Airport Security chap," continued de Silva. "Whatever has to be looked into can quite competently be done by the DII, thank you very much. An' no matter what the situation is, there's no excuse for the military to start kidnapping DFI officers." De Silva's eyes were blazing now at Devendra. "If you needed additional investigations conducted, Special Branch could see to it." He reached for his mobile phone that was in his shirt pocket. "Ah'm going to check up on this matter right now, Devendra, and I promise you that if I find that your fellows have been hindering this investigation and preventing us from getting to the bottom of this hijack, Ah'll—"

"You'll what?" Devendra's face hid his amusement with a look of deadly intent. "I suggest you put that phone down an' listen to the rest of what I have to say." His voice gave little doubt to de Silva that this was no request.

"There's more?" General Fernando managed.

"Yes, sir," Devendra glanced across. "Not much more, but enough to make things clear." He leaned back in his seat. "The DFI man who gave Lieutenant de Alwis his orders has decided to tell the truth. He's from Department E, and was in Colombo specifically to overlook the placement of the weapons and explosives on the Air Canada flight." De Silva gave a snort of derision, which Devendra ignored. The man's mobile phone now lay on the table before him. "He claims that this was an official Department E operation, sanctioned from the top. At this point, Int contacted Special Branch and explained the situation. They have now placed SSP Mahinda Alahakone, the head of Department E, under arrest. Alahakone has already been flown back to Colombo and is under interrogation right now." Devendra looked back at de Silva, who seemed to now have slumped lower in his seat, staring at his phone, as if willing the device to ring and rescue him from this predicament. "Alahakone is now telling us some very interesting stuff. He claims the operation was carried out against his advice, and he only went along because of pressure from above." Devendra paused for dramatic effect, but de Silva didn't look up. "Pressure from the Director General of the DFI."

"He's lying. . ." muttered de Silva, his voice now shaky.

"Is he? I forgot to tell you that Alahakone's operations chief was arrested with him. The man confirms everything, and there are STF men attached to the LRRP ops who will testify that last year they trained a team of Tamils in hijack operations."

"Look," spoke up de Silva, rallying himself, "I knew nothing about this bullshit. You said yourself that it was a Department E op. D'you think Ah'd be stupid enough to get involved in something like this? An' the STF routinely trains our mercenaries in tactics that might be useful in future LRRP ops. . ."

While de Silva had been talking, Devendra was clicking open his briefcase, and the DFI chief's voice died away as the brigadier held up a sheet of A4 paper.

"I believe this is your signature?" Without waiting for confirmation, Devendra continued. "This is an official letter of recommendation written to the visa officer of the Pakistani embassy here in Colombo. It recommends that tourist visas be granted to six Tamils for a two-week stay in Islamabad last July. The Pakistani ISI has confirmed with Special Branch that these same Tamils did a two-week crash-course on both flight operations and hijack tactics on the Airbus A340. *Hijack* tactics, please note, *not* anti-hijack or hostage-rescue tactics. The Pakis had been told by the DFI that the men were to act as an aggressor team for training of Sri Lankan HR teams and civilian flight crews." Devendra slid the sheet of paper across the polished tabletop. "As we all know — and Sarath will confirm — it isn't Sri Lankan military policy to use dedicated aggressor teams for HR training."

Jaliya de Silva stopped the paper with his hand, but did not bother looking down at it. His eyes locked with Devendra's, weariness beginning to push aside the anger and indignation that had previously blazed there.

"It seems you've had quite a busy afternoon, Devendra," he said.

There was a long silence as the other members of the CCG tried to digest what was happening. After a few moments of eyes darting around, John Jayavickrama managed to find his voice.

"Jaliya, I think you have a lot of explaining to do, so make it fast."

* * *

The afternoon sun blazed down through the shimmering heat waves that rose off the tarmac. In spite of being close to the sea, there was hardly a breath of breeze. The oppressive humidity of the air was stirred each time a Huey came in to land, but the wash of the rotors brought with it a scalding storm of grit that clung to exposed and sweating skin.

Watching the choppers disgorge their cargoes of overburdened infantrymen, Sergeant Dayan Premasiri chuckled scornfully to himself. Reserve Strike Force, hah! What kind of a strike force took hours just to get to the jump-off point? Along with the rest of his troop, Dayan had been sitting in the shade of the bushes for three hours, moving with the patch of shadow as the sun crawled across the sky. There was still no sign of the transport.

Dayan and Sumith Liyanage had barely finished their debrief on the German operation before the alarm had gone up. All leave had been cancelled, much to the two soldiers chagrin. The indignation, however, had disappeared as soon as the reason for the alert became clear. It was rumoured that the Indians were about to attack Colombo, and 1/SF was to be part of the reaction force. No one wanted to go off on leave just as a full-blown war was about to start. Badly depleted by having many of its patrols siphoned off for overseas 'courses', which were actually the combat missions Dayan and Sumith had been on, 1/SF had been struggling to run its incountry missions. They had just been moved back to Maduru Oya to refit when the alert had come in. The unit was able to scrape together enough men to reorganize them into three squadrons, which were then attached to the Reserve Strike Force.

Meant to be used as a strategic reserve, the RSF was based at China Bay, close to Trincomalee, but lacking the air transport necessary to make such a force practical, it was merely used as a conventional force to defend the capital of the Northeast. The RSF consisted of two brigades of light infantry, one mechanized battalion, and attached support elements. The mechanized unit had little air-transportable armour, and the infantry hadn't helicopters directly attached the way the new 51st Air Assault Division had.

Caught on the hop, the RSF had had to hand over its defensive positions to naval infantry units before being airlifted in relays to China Bay. The Armoured Corps battalion would be stripped of their armoured vehicles and sent as light infantry, along with the first infantry brigade.

The Special Forces were detailed with securing the Katunayake Air Force Base before the RSF's arrival, and would be airlifted by C-130s. It was said that the 51st Air Assault had been almost denuded of its choppers, which were being used to get the RSF to China Bay.

A hundred metres away, and almost opposite the SF troops, a couple of companies of riflemen were likewise waiting for their transport. They were all heavily armed and indistinguishable in the dust from Sri Lankan troops anywhere, but Dayan had heard that they were from the 6th Singha Rifles, the sister unit of his own old regiment.

Watching, he could now hear singing, and realized that it was the riflemen, their senior NCOs pacing up and down, waving their arms as if they were conducting a choir. Catching the words, Dayan realized that the lyrics had been altered in a way that the writer of the old 1960s protest song had never intended:

> *We shall fucking co-ome,*
> *We shall fucking co-ome,*
> *We shall fuck-king come! Some! Daaaa-aaay. . .*

Smoking and squinting against the dust, Dayan marvelled at the thought that just over twenty-four hours earlier he had been cursing the early spring chill of France.

> *Deep in our balls, we do believe,*
> *That we shall fucking come some day. . .*

He wondered whether the Indians would really be stupid enough to try a chopper-borne assault on Katunayake. In a way he hoped they would. Katunayake was one of the most heavily defended places in the country, and any attacking force would be cut to pieces. After all the James Bond shit in Europe, and the guerrilla warfare before that, Dayan felt he could do with a properly organized "real" war. It would be good to know who was who and not worry about terrorists disguised as innocent women and children. But even if the Indians decided to send in peace-keepers by force — as they had once threatened to do in 1987 — Dayan decided Katunayake was an unlikely airhead. Palaly was the logical place, close to the Tamils' symbolic capital. But Palaly was now home to the 51st Air Assault, who would already have their cocks up and ready for action.

> *We shall arseholes be-eee,*
> *We shall arseholes be-eee,*
> *We shall arseholes be! Some! Daaaa-aaay. . .*

Dayan turned as Sumith slapped his shoulder. He looked at the corporal, but the man was staring into the distance, along with the two new members of their four-man patrol. Dayan followed their gaze to where he could just make out the first C-130 Hercules lumbering down out of the haze like a huge duck.

The singing ended abruptly as the Singha NCOs roared the men to their feet, getting them into formation and trotting towards the SF troops.

"I can fight!" yelled a sergeant major.

"*SINGHA!*" chorused the troops.

"I can kill!"

"*SINGHA!*"

"*Singha!*"

"*SINGHA! Har, har, HAR!*"

The running men were closer now, and Dayan heard a sergeant major shout the familiar question.

"What do the Singha Rifles *do?*"

"*KILL! KILL! KILL!*"

"What makes the grass grow *green?*"

"*BLOOD! BLOOD! BLOOD!*"
"I can *fight!*"
"*SINGHA!*"
"I can *kill!*"
"*SINGHA. . . !*"

As the riflemen drew alongside, the tough grinning SF troopers jeered and hooted and called them "straight legs", while the battle-hardened teenaged riflemen, unimpressed by even the Long-Haired Devils, hooted back and called them "*khakko*" — crows — a reference to the eagle that was part of the SF cap badge.

"Cock an' lock, *machang*, here we go again," grinned Sumith as the chanting riflemen disappeared into the dust.

"*Airborne, SF, Black Beret. . .*" muttered Dayan, "*This is the way we start the day.*"

Down the line of bushes, Dayan could see the RSM's lean figure striding through the dust, exchanging a few words with patrol commanders and troop sergeants as he walked. All along the line of troops, men rose slowly to their feet, slinging T-56 rifles and shouldering GPMGs and RPGs. Everyone was draped with belted ammo for the GPMGs and spare bandoleers.

The RSM's cold eyes met Dayan's as he drew level. "*Alles klar?*" he said in German without cracking a smile, walking on.

*   *   *

"It was — and is — *vital* that this operation is allowed to go on. The Tigers are beginning to look as respectable as the IRA in international eyes." Jaliya de Silva's gaze flashed across the circle of faces, but lingered the longest on that of the minister of defence. "We all know that the LTTE an' the ERA are one and the same. Anytime now Prabakharan could dissolve the ERA, say that the Tigers have destroyed them, and the LTTE will look like the defenders of democracy."

"Are you *mad?*" Jayavickrama exploded, his face darkening with anger, but also with the fear of what the consequences of the DFI director general's actions could be. "Don't you understan' the predicament Sri Lanka will be in if this insanity of yours comes to light? We have the Indians practically sailing up our front garden, just waiting for an excuse to get involved. Both Canada and the US have been pouring in money and weapons to help fight the Tigers. Can you *imagine* what the American reaction will be to the news that a Sri Lankan intelligence organization has planned and carried out an international hijack? We'll be lucky if they just label it state-sponsored terrorism!"

"But it doesn' have to be made common knowledge, sir," de Silva continued to argue. "The operation has been kept at the highest classification level within the DFI, and totally self-contained by Department E. All the high-level staff will keep quiet because they know what the consequences will be for them, and at field level it'll be handled with the usual operational secrecy."

"This is Sri Lanka, remember," Major General Perera pointed out. "Nothing stays a secret for very long."

"Sarath's right," snapped Jayavickrama. "The risk is far too great. Too many people know. It's now part of a criminal investigation, for God'sake. What are you going to do about that?"

"If we wan' to make sure this really goes deep underground, there are ways," de Silva replied quietly. "People can be removed."

"Removed?" hissed Devendra. "None of *my* people are going to be *removed.*"

"That's enough, Devendra," cut in the minister before turning his eyes back onto de Silva. "Are you going to remove everybody involved in the investigation? Int, Special Branch, DII, the commandos, Department E?" Jayavickrama's eyes narrowed. "The only person who's going to be removed is you, Jaliya. This so-called operation of yours is going to be stopped before anymore damage is done." He pushed a hand through his steel-grey hair and took a moment to gather his thoughts. "How exactly were you planning on ending this little escapade? Were the hijackers jus' supposed to surrender, or what?"

"No, there would be no surrender," said de Silva hesitantly. "We couldn't have anyone being taken alive and interrogated."

"You were going to let the plane be stormed, no?" Sarath Perera said thoughtfully. "The hijackers would die in the assault an' that would be the end of it."

"Of course not," snapped de Silva. "D'you think Ah'd let my own people be sacrificed like that?"

Devendra's smirk went unnoticed. He had no doubt that de Silva would sacrifice anyone to achieve his goals, but it would be difficult to motivate a hijack team to undertake a suicide mission. That was the LTTE's realm.

"The plane will stay in the air until the deadline has passed," de Silva went on. "The hijackers will then kill the pilots and abandon the plane which would then crash into the sea. End of story."

"Are you trying to tell us that you were willing to kill a whole planeload of civilians jus' to discredit the Tigers?" Jayavickrama's voice was barely under control.

"What's a few hundred civilians compared to the tens of thousands the terras have killed already?" De Silva shrugged. "If it'll blacken the image of the Tigers internationally, it'll be worth it. It's a tried an' tested method of counter-terrorism, the Rhodesian Selous Scouts used it very well in the eighties."

"Rhodesia lost the war and is now known as Zimbabwe," pointed out Perera.

"An' what happens to the hijackers when the plane goes down?" asked Devendra.

"They parachute. They're all para-qualified." De Silva looked across at Perera. "They were part of an STF intake that went through the SF para course last year." The jaw of the Director Special Forces tightened. "They will jump from twenty thousand feet so that they won' need oxygen. Their parachutes were part of their hand luggage. An Indian-registered trawler will be at a pre-decided map reference an' will pick them up."

The rest of the CCG was struck dumb by the complexity of the plan, and just stared in amazement. The minister was shaking his head, eyes fixed on the tabletop. The IGP, a non-smoker for years, was fumbling for one of Perera's cigarettes. Careers would be destroyed over this.

"What's the abort drill?" Devendra spoke into the silence. He hadn't taken his eyes off de Silva.

"There isn't one."

"Don' talk cock, there has to be an abort drill."

"What're you talking about?" asked the minister.

"Devendra means there mus' be a plan in case the mission is aborted," Perera explained quickly. "There always is."

"Not in this case," de Silva insisted. "There was to be no turning back."

"He's bullshitting us." Devendra's voice was cold. "He wants the operation to go through."

"Fuck off, Devendra," snarled de Silva. "Ah'm telling you there's no abort."

The head of Int leaned back in his seat and stretched his back. The smile on his face as he lit a cigarette held the whole room silent. "There's one more piece of this puzzle I haven't mentioned yet, gentlemen," he said through a cloud of smoke. "Many of you may not know it, but Int has a long-standing relationship with the DII." At the mention of the DFI's domestic counterpart, de Silva's eyes narrowed in suspicion. "An unofficial relationship that goes back to the old NIB days, and one that is far more trustworthy than that between the DII an' the DFI. And Ah've just been in contact with Mike Salgado. It seems he isn't here in Colombo, helping with the embassy situ, but in Trinco. At a small DFI sigint LP." Out of the corner of his eye Devendra saw de Silva continue to glare at him, but the man's shoulders slumped fractionally. "It seems that an unusually large security detachment from the STF has been assigned to guard this LP, even though it's in a relatively secure sector. Which was the reason it was brought to the DII's attention. The LP has a signaller on twenty-four-hour watch, monitoring a single frequency for a ten-minute period each hour. Every hour, during that ten-minute period, he receives and logs in the same codeword: *Albatross*." Devendra finally turned his gaze back onto de Silva, who was now once more staring at his phone. "You wan' to tell us more about this, de Silva?"

"Look, Jaliya," said Jayavickrama, when the DIG didn't respond immediately, now holding his temper in check with the greatest of effort, "if you wan' to come out of this with any part of your life intact, I suggest you tell us everything. And do it *now*. If that plane goes down into the sea, I guarantee that I will personally ensure that you never see daylight in whatever form ever again."

The DFI head seemed to resign himself to defeat. He began to speak, though his eyes stayed down. "There is a codeword for an abort. The codeword is *Pigeon*. The hourly transmission is from AC634. If they receive the codeword in return, they'll contact Madras and demand to talk to a Sri Lankan negotiator immediately."

"Your man in Madras," interjected Devendra.

De Silva continued as if the Int chief had not spoken. "The DFI head of station — who is also the negotiator — will insist to the Indians that if he's to take over the negotiations, a Sri Lankan HR team must be on stand-by. The Indians will refuse to have a foreign military team in the country, and the negotiator will then suggest a compromise in the form of a Sri Lankan *police* HR team."

"And what makes you think *we* would approve a police HR team," interrupted Major General Perera, "even if we had one?"

"Because firstly, it will be the only way to get a Sri Lankan HR team into Madras, and secondly, because it would be quicker."

"Quicker, how?" asked the minister.

"There are STF troops seconded to the DFI stationed at our New Delhi embassy. Part of the comms set-up. They're trained in aircraft assaults."

"The HR capability planned by the STF last year that never worked out somehow," mused Perera aloud.

"And for whom the Bismuth rounds used by the hijackers were allocated originally," added Devendra.

De Silva gave a single slow nod of confirmation that was almost a theatrical bow. "Negotiations would then continue for a couple of hours to make it look real to the Indians. Once the STF team was in place, most likely at night, and just before the deadline, they would storm the plane. The assaulters would have their weapons loaded with blanks and the hijackers would pretend to be killed. In the chaotic aftermath of a hostage rescue at night, while the Indian authorities were trying to sort out the passengers and crew, the DFI negotiator would insist that the bodies of the hijackers be taken back to Sri Lanka immediately for ID'ing. The Indians of course agree, and a SLAF transport does the hop from Palaly to Madras an' back. At Palaly, the bodies of terras killed in battle would be shown and ID'd as the hijackers and connected unarguably to the LTTE."

CHAPTER 23

1930 LOCAL (1230 GMT): The Canadian Forces CC-144 Challenger carrying Donald Fenster and his retinue was three hours into its flight from Canberra to Colombo when the explosion occurred. The executive jet had landed briefly at Darwin to top up its fuel tanks before beginning the long non-stop leg across the Indian Ocean. That had been just over an hour before, and the Challenger was at forty thousand feet, southeast of Java.

The kilo and a half of Semtex in Patricia Fenster's attaché case was detonated by the three and a half-hour electrical timer that had been set just as the Fensters were leaving the Canberra Hilton. The case was sitting at Patricia's feet, leaning against the starboard wall of the cabin, and the explosion blew a gaping hole in the side of the pressurized fuselage. Just before unconsciousness took hold of her, Patricia had time to see her right leg sail across the cabin, the femur sticking out from the shredded muscles of her thigh, everything messily chopped through by the detonation.

The Challenger went into an uncontrolled dive, the explosion having severed wiring that connected the cockpit to some of the control surfaces, and explosive decompression plus the slipstream proceeded to peel back the aluminium skin of the fuselage like a tin can. Patricia Fenster, however, saw none of this. Her body was the first to be sucked through the hole in the fuselage. Many more followed as the gap widened; any passengers not strapped in were dragged into space, screaming soundlessly in the howling roar of the slipstream, followed by a trail of debris that included things like Donald Fenster's laptop and an assorted array of juice bottles.

The jet was still in a relatively stable, if steep, dive, only rotating along its long axis, and the pilot was able to give a mayday warning and report that there had been an explosion on board. At thirty thousand feet any semblance of stability in the Challenger's dive disappeared as it began to tumble end over end. Air traffic controllers at Darwin heard nothing more coherent from the pilot, but continued to listen to the disjointed and terrified screams of the co-pilot for another thirty seconds. This was how long it took the Challenger to fall to twenty three thousand feet, where the denser atmosphere and the violent tumbling that had already battered the pilot into unconsciousness, tore the jet apart. There was no more radio contact.

At twenty thousand feet the Challenger lost its remaining wing, and at fifteen thousand its tail and left engine. When the aircraft eventually smashed into the surface of the ocean, the resulting explosion left nothing behind that was larger than three feet square.

* * *

1800 LOCAL (1300 GMT): Indian Naval Task Force 5 — known to the Sri Lankans as the *Vikrant* Carrier Group — was two thousand kilometres southwest of Colombo and due south of the Maldives when the new intelligence reports came in. The task force was still steaming northeast towards Sri Lanka at flank speed in good weather

On board INS *Vikrant*, Rear Admiral Sunder Varma, the task force commander, walked into the briefing room. He acknowledged the command master chief's "Atten-hut!" and the crash of feet as men sprang to attention with a nod and a casual "As you were, chaps," before walking up the aisle to take his seat at the front of the room alongside Captain Dev Anand, the *Vikrant's* commanding officer.

Arrayed around the room behind the top brass, in diminishing order of rank, were representatives from the task force's operations, intelligence, and air arm. Also present was the 1st

Maharatta Light Infantry Battalion's commanding officer and his staff, plus the detachment commander of the Marine Commando Force, a lieutenant, along with his 2/ic.

Behind the podium, at the front of the room was a civilian with a military haircut and neat, clipped moustache. He wore white trousers and a pale grey safari jacket. The outfit seemed to be the unofficial uniform of the Research and Analysis Wing, mused Rear Admiral Varma with a touch of amusement.

Once everyone had settled down again, the RAW man started his briefing. "Good afternoon, gentlemen. This won't take long. We just have some new developments in the area of Sri Lankan troop movements. It will directly affect any carrier-borne operations and you need to be aware of it." He used a hand-held remote control device to bring up a series of large black-and-white slides on the screen behind him. They were all satellite images of a large military airbase. "You're looking at the Sri Lanka Air Force Base at China Bay. As can be clearly seen in these pictures, taken at fourteen-thirty Foxtrot — oh-eight-thirty Zulu — there's a lot of air traffic, particularly heavy and medium transport." He used a laser pointer to indicate the silhouettes of what were obviously multi-engine fixed-wing transports as well as helicopters. The positions of the aircraft changed, increased and decreased from frame to frame. "The amount of air traffic has significantly increased since TF5 turned northeast, and we can see here that it's part of a major troop redeployment."

Several of the satellite images clearly revealed lines of troops boarding planes.

The briefer clicked his remote control and another series of images were brought up, this time of a second airbase. Here too there were pictures of troops either boarding or disembarking from transport aircraft. "This is the Katunayake Air Force Base, north of Colombo, and RAW sources on the ground indicate that new troops have been arriving all afternoon."

"Do we know what these troops are, Mister Chatterjee?" Admiral Varma asked.

"From their equipment we think the unit deploying at Katunayake are special operations troops. Either from their Special Forces or Commando units."

"But why are they using Special Forces in a conventional role?" asked the 1/MLI colonel.

"We think it's just a temporary measure to secure the airbase before the arrival of conventional units. After that they'll probably pull the Special Forces back into a strategic reserve to carry out guerrilla attacks on any peacekeeping forces."

"And what do we know about the expected conventional unit?" Varma asked. "Is it their 51st Air Assault Division?"

"No," the RAW man answered. "The Sri Lankan high command seems to realize that any landing in the Colombo area will be just a diversion for the main landing on the Jaffna Peninsula. The 51st is still involved in mopping-up operations in the Kilinochchi area. We think that in a matter of hours, as soon as fresh troops can take over from them, the 51st will be pulled back into the Palaly area."

Varma cursed. There was no way they could be within striking range of Palaly before the 51st redeployed. It could be a full twelve hours, if the weather held, before the *Vikrant*'s Sea King choppers would be in range of the Jaffna Peninsula. That was *if* the diplomats at the UN and the politicians in New Delhi got their fingers out and made the decision to send his task force in. It was still possible that Task Force 5 would be ordered to land in the Colombo area just to jolt the Sri Lankan government. The dual threat of the *Vikrant* and the *Viraat* sailing off the coast of Colombo in 1987 had been part of the persuasion to make President JR Jayawardene sign the Indo-Lanka Accord.

"Getting back to my question," he prompted the briefer, "what can you tell us about the Sri Lankan troops being airlifted from China Bay?"

"We think it's the Reserve Strike Force. Division-sized, mostly airmobile light infantry, with armour and other support attached. They've been in the Trinco area for over a year."

"But I thought that the RSF was incapable of actually carrying out its role," the 1/MLI colonel spoke up. "We were told that they didn't have the necessary choppers to react fast."

"That's what we thought, too," the briefer shrugged apologetically. "And realistically they don't. But by stripping the 51st Air Assault of most of its transport choppers, it looks like they'll be able to have the RSF's 562nd Brigade at Katunayake long before we get anywhere near."

"Any int on the structure of this brigade?" The question was again from the 1/MLI colonel, whose battalion would be the one in the direct line of fire. There was very little doubt that the Sri Lankans would defend their capital with their customary bared teeth and mindless aggression, no matter that the Indians came under a UN peacekeeping flag. "Do they have armour?"

"Yes, the RSF has a tank battalion, but it is unlikely that heavy armour will arrive in Colombo before we're in range."

"Which infantry battalions does the 562nd have?"

"The 1st Sri Lanka Light Infantry and the 6th Singha Rifles. And even stripped of its armour, the 4th Mechanized will be able to fight as light infantry. Both 1/SLLI and 6/SR rotated to the RSF after the capture of Mankulam. They have a reputation of being hard units, and though they took heavy losses in the Mankulam fighting, they've now been refitted and are just below full strength again."

"Isn't 6/SR the unit that clashed with the Ghurkhas in 1990?" It was the first time the Marine Commando Force lieutenant had spoken during the briefing.

During the latter stages of the Indian Peace-Keeping Force's time in northeastern Sri Lanka the previous century, there had been occasional skirmishes between Sri Lankan and Indian units. It had been a time when the new and radically nationalist Sri Lankan president, Ranasinghe Premadasa, had been spewing virulent rhetoric and demanding that the Indian invaders leave immediately. Sri Lankan battalion commanders who had units garrisoned in the Northern and Eastern Provinces had been unofficially urged to push aggressive patrols into Indian-controlled areas, and this had occasionally resulted in small-scale fire fights. The best documented incident was when a platoon of the 6th Singha Rifles on night patrol had bumped into a listening post of the 4th Battalion, 5th Ghurkha Rifles.

"That's right," the 1/MLI colonel replied. "When the Ghurkhas recovered the bodies of their troops, they were all missing their kukris and their ears. Apparently the Sri Lankans like to take souvenirs."

"6/SR was the unit that held Elephant Pass against the LTTE in '91," added Chatterjee, "and before that they were heavily involved in the dirty war that put down the communist rebellion in southern Sri Lanka. They were deployed to Tangalle, in the rebel heartland, and were particularly hated by the communists who referred to them as the SS. The unit is based just outside Trincomalee, so it's likely that it'll be the first of the infantry units into Katunayake."

"And 1/SLLI?" asked the colonel.

"More of the same. One of the Sri Lankans' most experienced units, and has seen a lot of action since the early '80s. The only reason they weren't airlifted south immediately was that they were based a bit further away from Trinco than 6/SR. As for the Special Forces, what can I tell you? I'm sure we've all heard of *their* reputation."

There was a gloomy silence for awhile as the roomful of soldiers, sailors, and airmen digested the good news. Then Varma asked Chatterjee to bring up a map of the Colombo area.

"What about this smaller airbase?" the admiral asked, stepping up to the map. South of Colombo was an airbase marked as Ratmalana AFB. He looked across at Commander Joseph Fernandez, the senior Fleet Air Arm officer. "Joe, can you get our chaps in here?"

Before Commander Fernandez could answer, the 1/MLI colonel spoke up. "Sorry, sir, but I've already explored that possibility. Place is surrounded by roads and impossible to defend.

We'd get the shit kicked out of us. And if what RAW says is true about the Sri Lankan SF unit being pulled back into reserve, that's the most likely place they'll base them. Close enough to Colombo to cover the city and prevent an amphibious attack."

With a thoughtful nod, Varma returned to his seat, still glaring at the map. "Well, let's hope that New Delhi decides on the Jaffna Peninsula as a landing site. That'll give us at least some flexibility."

"Any word on when we'll get the 'go', sir?" asked Captain Dev Anand.

"Well, the decision will have to be on the part of the UN Security Council," Varma replied. "New Delhi just wants us in position so that we'll be obviously the most practical force that the UN can use."

The briefing wrapped up shortly afterwards with a warning from the RAW man that SLAF combat air patrols were now concentrating heavily on Sri Lanka's southern and western coasts and the international airspace beyond.

In a worried frame of mind, Rear Admiral Varma headed for the bridge. He didn't like this situation at all. Most sailors of his age and rank would be drooling at the chance of a real war, especially against a weaker opponent like Sri Lanka. But a peacekeeping mission in an obviously hostile country was something totally different.

The lack of direct air cover was preying on his thoughts as well. INS *Vikrant* had exchanged its squadron of Sea Harrier jets for a second one of Sea Kings from INS *Viraat*, prior to sailing for Africa. It had been deduced by the high command that there would be no use for fighter/bombers in Madagascar, whereas transport choppers were necessary to move the soldiers around in a country where the infrastructure was almost nonexistent. The Sea Harriers were now aboard the *Viraat*, doubling that ship's contingent of jets for sabre-rattling operations against Pakistan in the Arabian Sea. If Task Force 5 was ordered to commence landings in Sri Lanka, they would have no directly available close

air support. Not that Varma thought the Sea Harriers would have
been much use against the Sri Lankans' new MiG-29s, but it was
always comforting to know you had the firepower at hand. He
would not even be able to depend on IAF bases in Tamil Nadu
for air cover. TF5 would be the only Indian Forces operating
under the blue flag of the UN; any action by aircraft based in
India would be legitimately looked on by the world as an act of
aggression.

Returning the salutes of the sailors on the bridge, Varma
walked out onto the starboard wing, away from the noisy flight
deck where a Sea King was landing after a routine anti-submarine
patrol. He could see another one far off in the twilight to the
southeast, paralleling the task force's course.

He let the breeze whip at his thinning hair as he watched
the waves rush past the side of the huge aircraft carrier.
A conventionally powered former Royal Navy ship, the *Vikrant*
could in no way be compared to the big American nuclear-powered
carriers when it came to power projection, but it was still the pride
and joy of the Indian Navy, and quite sufficient to dominate India's
weaker neighbours in the region.

The rest of Task Force 5 was spread out around the carrier,
and Varma absently scanned them with his binoculars as he ran
the different possibilities of the next few days through his mind.
He could see the *Kashin*-class destroyer, INS *Rajput*, holding station
off the starboard beam, and knew that her sister, INS *Rana*, would
be on the port side. If he craned his neck, Varma could just make
out INS *Delhi*, far astern, and out ahead of the whole task force,
the *Godavari*-class missile frigate INS *Ganga*.

Varma cursed the fates that had led the Sri Lankans to
react so fast. There had been nothing of that in the RAW and
naval intelligence projections. It had to be the bastard Americans
and their satellites. Information-sharing, they called it.

A sound from the bridge behind him made Varma turn to
see an ensign come to attention and throw him a snappy salute.
The man held out a piece of paper. "Priority One dispatch from
India, sir."

Returning the salute, Varma took the dispatch and tore it open, trying to keep excitement from showing in his face and hands. INS *India* was Indian Naval HQ in New Delhi. This was it. Either the UN and the politicians had actually got it together, or the mission was being called off. Stepping off the open wing and into the bridge to shelter from the wind, he began to read the decoded transcript.

* * *

1915 LOCAL (1315 GMT): The already tense atmosphere in the Cabinet Crisis Group room turned into an uproar as the word arrived from the Joint Operations Command that air traffic control in Darwin had lost contact with the aircraft carrying the Canadian Minister of Foreign Affairs and International Trade, Donald Fenster. The CC-144 Challenger had disappeared from all radar screens and was believed to be down somewhere south of Java. Terrorism was suspected.

"Is this also your doing, Jaliya?" stormed John Jayavickrama.

"Please, sir," said de Silva coldly, "why should I be interested in getting rid of our strongest ally in the Canadian government?"

"Right now there doesn't seem to be any logic behind your actions!" spluttered the minister. "Next we'll be hearing that the buggers in the embassy are also your gang."

De Silva glowered with impotent rage, and Devendra let the moment drag for a few more delicious seconds before he stepped in.

"This could all be a coordinated effort by the ERA," he said.

"What could be?" asked Perera.

"The embassy is captured, and the terrorists demand Fenster as a negotiator. Seems a bit of a stretch that they would ask for their worst international enemy as a negotiator. But it's looking like it was just a ploy to get Fenster into a position where they could kill him."

"But if the ERA wanted to kill him," argued Jayavickrama, "why go to all the trouble of capturing the embassy? They could have put a bomb on his plane at anytime."

"Well, sir, it would've been the best chance to get him. With such a narrow deadline to meet, they probably realized that the normal security precautions wouldn't have been taken. Fenster wouldn't have wanted to waste any time getting across to Colombo. We won't know exactly until there's a proper investigation into the crash, and security measures at Canberra are checked." Devendra drew a deep breath and continued. "Plus, the Tigers could be playing the same game de Silva here is. Propaganda. Discredit the ERA — the way they have been doing with the international attacks — and present them to the world as the future face of Tamil terrorism. The Tigers know that no one is going to negotiate with the terras in the embassy after this, an' they're left out on a limb. The supposed ERA terras are killed, along with an appropriate number of hostages in a bloody Army assault, and the world community is presented with a few more innocent deaths. The Tigers then play the good guys an' go on their own little witch hunt to get the ERA, which is then conveniently destroyed. The international media are then shown that the Tigers are actually just and decent freedom fighters worthy of being negotiated with. And, as a bonus, the Tigers get rid of a very hawkish Canadian foreign minister."

"Even more reason to allow the hijack to run its course," cut in de Silva. "At leas' that way the Tigers don't have everything their way."

"I think we've heard quite enough on that subject, Jaliya!" snapped Jayavickrama, and the DFI chief slumped back like a scolded child. "Look," the minister said, turning back to the others, "it's damage-control time now. Can we tell the Canadians to use their own hostage-rescue unit to storm the embassy? That way, if anything goes wrong, we won' be to blame. I mean those fellows aren't really needed up there at Palaly, no?"

"I think we'd have a better chance of getting the embassy hostages out alive if we use our chaps," Perera advised. "The Canadian JTF2 doesn't have as much experience in this sort'f thing as we do. They've done some raids in the Toronto area, and they've been used in special forces operations in Afghanistan, but no real assaults of this calibre."

"And I think no matter who actually assaults the embassy, if there are civilian deaths, Ottawa will blame us," Devendra commented. "Besides, if Fenster is dead, the Canadian Department of Foreign Affairs and International Trade must be in chaos. They'll have their hands full trying to find out what has happened, and there might be endless delays before someone can make a decision on JTF2."

A soldier from the CCG signals room next door chose that moment to enter and hand several messages to General Fernando. The JOC head read them quickly, his face lighting up.

"Good news at last!" he beamed, waving the papers. "We've just got the latest American NSA satellite images and their analysis. It seems that the *Vikrant* carrier group has turned back south. They're holding station something like two thousand kilometres southwest of us."

"Wonder why," mused Jayavickrama. "Seems like a sudden change of policy."

"Maybe these communiqués from the Ministry of Foreign Affairs will spell it out," Fernando gloated, shuffling the papers. "One says that the UN Secretary General has made an announcement to the effect that there will be no UN troops sent to Sri Lanka, and that the UN will not be dictated to by armed people holding hostages." A muted cheer went up around the room. "The second message says that the Indian Interior Ministry has agreed to let Sri Lankan troops storm Air Canada AC634, but only if Indian negotiations fail. There's an attached note here from our high commissioner in New Delhi, saying that the crash of Fenster's jet has badly shaken the Indians. Apparently they think that they're being drawn into some sort of international crisis by the LTTE and the ERA, and are suddenly keen to wash their hands of it."

This time the cheer that went up shook the panelled walls of the room. Devendra noted that even Jaliya de Silva had forced out a smile.

*   *   *

1900 LOCAL (1330 GMT): Sunset had brought little relief and the heat in the cockpit was oppressive, like sitting inside a pressure cooker. Captain Johnny Burnett swiped with the back of his forearm at the drop of sweat threatening to trickle down into his right eye, but it just added to the perspiration which slicked the skin of his arms and had already soaked the leather strap of the Breitling Navigator he wore. Major Mahesh, the leader of the hijackers, had refused to let the cockpit windows be opened, and he was suffering the heat along with the pilots, sitting in the jump seat, shirt unbuttoned and undershirt soaked. Burnett thought that the man seemed to be sweating even more than the pilots. It seemed strange to the Canadian. He'd thought that as an Asian, the hijacker would be more tolerant of the temperature.

Turning in his seat, Burnett caught the hijack leader's eye. "I need to use the washroom," he said, "please," he added, forcing out the word.

Major Mahesh nodded, calling over his shoulder to another hijacker, the one called Suresh, who was sitting in business class. Burnett was met at the cockpit door by Suresh, who then stood guard outside the lavatory.

Once he'd finished using the toilet, Burnett splashed water on his face and stared at himself in the mirror. A stocky fifty-year-old, he was still reasonably fit, although he was beginning to lose the battle of the bulge. The cubicle smelled bad, but was still a far cry from the lavatories further down the plane. At least this one was only used by the pilots and the hijackers. Looking at his reflection, Burnett saw that his mahogany-brown eyes were red with fatigue, and that there was a blonde stubble on his jaw and chin. How much longer, he wondered. He wasn't sure if he could take this anymore. The lack of sleep and the constant fear was bringing him close to the breaking point. Pull yourself together, Burnett told himself, hang in there. You're still the captain of this bird, and you're responsible for your people. You have to see this through. But the fear was wearing him down, the idea of not knowing when the hijackers would flip and kill everybody on board. And the deadline that was drawing near with each second and minute. He looked at his watch. 7:02pm. Four hours to go. Would Major Mahesh really take them up over the sea and run them out of fuel? Or would he stay on the ground and extend the deadline, killing a hostage in retaliation for the authorities' failure to meet the demands? And Burnett hoped dearly that his government would do as the hijackers asked. Fire that arrogant hawk of a foreign minister. What the fuck did he know about dealing with terrorists? Why didn't he come here and see what it was like to be dealing with men who wouldn't hesitate to kill? And, oh God, he choked, I'll be the first one they kill. It's always the pilot who's killed first, his body dumped onto the tarmac like a sack of shit. Burnett stuck his head into the sink and ran the water until the shaking stopped.

When he stepped out of the lavatory, Burnett had combed his wet hair back, letting the water run down his face and neck. It would help keep the heat away for a while. Shutting the lavatory door, he felt a draft of cool air touch his face and looked into business class. The hijacker had opened the door on the port side to let in some fresh air.

"Mind if I stand by the door for a minute?" he asked Suresh, who was leaning against the wall opposite the lavatory, hand on his SMG, finger resting on the trigger guard.

"Go back." The hijacker shook his head, and Burnett could see that the man was also sweating heavily, and in the confined space he could actually smell him.

"Look," pleaded the pilot, "I just could use some fresh air, OK? I won't try and escape. You can stand right next to me."

Suresh hesitated, then turned to the cockpit and fired of a stream of Tamil. Major Mahesh replied with a one-word answer, and Burnett knew that it was in the negative.

But then Suresh gestured with the Micro-Uzi towards business class. "OK," he said. "But do exactly as I say. If you disobey, I will kill you."

The doorway was a shimmering rectangle of brightness after the dimness of the lavatory, and Burnett squinted as he walked towards it. At first, the light was so dazzling that he couldn't make out much, but then he could discern a runway stretching into the hazy distance. The sun was almost below the horizon, orange light shining straight through the doorway, and he could make out no human movement.

Two metres from the doorway, the hijacker stopped Burnett and ordered him to put his hands in his pockets. It was probably to stop him signalling to the authorities, Burnett guessed. He was allowed to stand there for five minutes, luxuriating in the breeze that lifted his damp hair off his forehead and ruffled his sweaty clothes.

When he returned to the cockpit, he found Major Mahesh in Burnett's own seat, headphones on, and the pilot, held there at gunpoint by Suresh, could see that the radio was tuned to the previously unknown frequency. Burnett heard, as he had every hour, on the hour, since the hijack had begun, Major Mahesh speak the same word into the mike, repeating it twice.

"*Albatross. Albatross. Albatross.*"

The hijack leader then sat quietly for several more minutes, headphones on, as he had done each hour. He then turned over the seat to Burnett and dismissed Suresh. Major Mahesh's face showed no change in expression.

As he returned to the jump seat, Mahesh Balachandran's face hid the turmoil in his mind very well. His nerves were stretched and his heart racing, the Dexedrine making the sweat pour off him. So that was *it*, he mused. The abort. All that planning, and now it was being called off. Oh, well, that was life. Hurry up and wait, and then it turns out to be a false alarm. Well, it would soon be all out of his hands, he decided. Time for the playacting to begin. He had no doubt that the audience, in the form of the international media, was ready and waiting.

Standing up, he moved over to stand behind the pilots. "Contact the Tower," he ordered.

*   *   *

Turning up the volume, Devini Sundaralingam caught the 7:30pm breaking news bulletin on *Sky News* of an unconfirmed report that the executive jet carrying the Canadian minister of foreign affairs and international trade had gone missing between Darwin and Colombo. The journalist speaking from Darwin stated that the aircraft had dropped off radar screens and had not replied to radio queries since. Aviation authorities had refused to confirm whether the plane had crashed. It was rumoured that Donald Fenster had been on his way to Sri Lanka to personally oversee the hostage situations both at the Canadian embassy in Colombo, and aboard Air Canada AC634, currently on the ground at Madras. Mrs Fenster, as well as several of the minister's aides were accompanying him on the trip.

Other television screens were running *BBC World* and *CNN*, but even though Devini turned up the volume on each of them in turn there was nothing further. Although the respective journalists on the ground speculated that foul play was suspected, they maintained that the authorities were remaining tight-lipped on the subject until a full search and rescue mission could be launched. It was also added that the security surrounding the disappearance of the CC-144 Challenger was due to its possible connection with the hostage situations in India and Sri Lanka.

Switching off the sound, Devini leaned back in the chair, staring unseeing at the bank of screens. She was alone in the embassy's communications centre, taking her turn on watch. The news networks were their extra eyes on the outside, and the televisions in the comms centre were continuously monitoring the local and international news channels. Devini was watching for anything that would indicate an assault on the embassy was imminent. She had no doubt that it would be soon. It would be dark in an hour, and by now the Sri Lankan and Canadian authorities would have realized the trap they had been drawn into. With the death of Fenster following on the heels of the execution of the senior visa officer, it was unlikely that any government would be willing to negotiate with them and maintain its credibility.

Well, Devini told herself, she still had a few surprises on hand for any hostage-rescue team trying to storm the embassy.

*   *   *

The Sri Lanka Air FoMrce C-130 Hercules was flying high enough to catch the last rays of the setting sun which hung in slanting golden beams across the cargo hold, cutting through the haze of dust that still remained after the loading of the long wheel-base Land Rover Defenders. There were two of the black-painted Defenders, parked nose-to-tail and fastened to the pierced-steel planking of the C-130's deck. The special ladder racks on the 4x4s' roofs seemed to make the vehicles look larger, filling the hold. The two rows of men seated along both sides of the fuselage were also black-clad, and would have been virtually indistinguishable from each other at most times. At that moment, however, respirators and anti-flash Balaclava hoods were off, allowing personal features to be recognizable. Primary weapons and body armour, too, were out of sight until they were needed at deployment stage, stored in big high-impact plastic boxes. Only sidearms and personal belt kits were being carried. One smaller group of men, however, stood out from the majority. In spite of their black fatigues, the white skin and bigger frames of the Canadian JTF2 soldiers distinguished them from their new Sri Lankan comrades.

Sitting next to the Canadians, Eric Christofelsz coughed, hoping that the dust would settle soon, or be sucked out by whatever filtration system the aircraft had. They'd probably be landing in Madras before that happened, however, he finally decided.

He closed his eyes, but couldn't sleep for the racket. Christofelsz always hated these airborne or vehicle insertions. Too noisy and uncomfortable for sleep, and endlessly boring when awake. He eased up the volume on his Walkman, but it was a futile hope that Lenny Kravitz could drown out the four howling Allison turboprops.

Without making it too obvious, he studied the Canadian team. They didn't look particularly tense, but not relaxed either. Christofelsz wondered whether they were nervous at the prospect of combat, but then wondered who wouldn't be. He certainly was, and was sure that so were the rest of Red Team. Red Team, however, was a battle-tested unit, and they were all some of the toughest fuckers to ever walk the valley. They had all taken part in ops that ranged from deep-recce patrols into the enemy-occupied Wanni to night time chopper insertions aimed at bumping off a Tiger leader. The Canadians were good at their job, Christofelsz conceded; he had seen that in the few short hours they had trained together. He also knew, from talking to Lieutenant Conway, that they had successfully stormed three Tiger-held buildings in Toronto without losing any of their team. But those were basically police SWAT jobs, and not to be compared with an aircraft hijack. This was the real thing.

In charge of the direct action drills at Palaly, Christofelsz had been told by the OC to use the JTF2 men in whatever way he saw fit. Leaving his platoon to get on with it, Conway had joined Captain Saliya Dayananda and the others working on the long-term plans.

At first Christofelsz thought the best thing was to integrate the Canadians into the Sri Lankan assault teams, so that they could blend into the Commando method of aircraft assault. Two Canadians had been paired with two Sri Lankans in the traditional four-man assault groups. This had quickly proved to be unworkable, with problems ranging from language — the Canadians spoke no Sinhalese, obviously, and many of the commandos spoke little English — to different operational tactics. An aircraft assault was a very complicated affair with timings down to a split-second at times. Little things like differing methods of entry or post-entry tactics could screw it all up.

One example Christofelsz had found was that while the Sri Lankans split the first pair in soon after entry — No 1 went left and No 2 right, No 3 left and No 4 right — the Canadians did it differently — the first pair went one way, the second the other. Another problem was the flash-bangs: in the Sri Lankan case No 1 and No 2 went straight in with No 3 chucking the grenade over their shoulders. They were trained not to flinch at the disorienting explosions. With the Canadians, No 1 threw the flash-bang, then followed the explosion in. It was just a case of operational experience, the Sri Lankans having the benefit of more. The Canadians had also abandoned some tactics as impractical, tactics that were needed to overcome the new security measures on airliners. They had been trained to believe that though the aircraft cockpit could be accessed by an assaulter going through a window, it was too slow and dangerous with body armour and webbing. Therefore the tactic had been discarded. However, if the hijackers had closed the cockpit's armoured double doors, it was the only way in. The Commandos practiced sending the first pair in "clean fatigue", with just respirator and pistol, while the second pair covered them.

Integrating the Canadians and Sri Lankans would take too much time and retraining; time that just didn't exist. So Christofelsz and the other assault group commanders — both Canadian and Sri Lankan — had decided to use JTF2 in their own assault groups. Two of these would hit the business class doors, just behind the cockpit, a couple of seconds before the main Sri Lankan assault. These two seconds, it was hoped, would be long enough to distract the hijackers covering the passengers and allow the commandos the fraction of time needed to kill them before they could open fire on the hostages. This was the DA drill the Sri Lankans and Canadians had been practicing, and it would remain ready to be used until a more concerted assault could be planned.

A figure squeezed past Christofelsz's knees and brought him out of his reverie. It was one of the Defender drivers, checking the ties on his vehicle, even though the Air Force loady would have already done it. It paid to be sure when it came to kit. Everything had to be at a hundred percent when the "Go" was given. Christofelsz watched another man enter the back of one the 4x4s and check on the ladders and weapons boxes, each of the former bearing its own tag. The tag identified the individual ladder, each different from the other. The Commandos had aluminium ladders that had been manufactured to fit the different characteristics of the various doorways on every model of aircraft in the Sri Lankan Airlines fleet, and some that weren't. The lightweight aluminium ladders were designed to fit noiselessly against the fuselages of the planes, and were strong enough to take the weight of four fully-equipped assaulters.

*   *   *

"Any news yet on the crash?" asked John Jayavickrama.

"At the moment, nothing really," answered General Sujeeva Fernando. "There are some media reports that Indonesian fishermen in the area have reported seeing an explosion, but they're not clear whether it was midair or on the surface."

Aides and signallers were constantly entering and leaving the CCG room now, bringing in dispatches and reports from the comms centre next door.

"What about search and rescue, sir?" Major General Perera asked.

"There's a Royal Australian Navy frigate southwest of Java, and it's heading for the area. But it'll still be several hours before its choppers are in range. At the moment it doesn' look good, though. Air traffic control at Darwin reports that they heard screaming soon after the pilot reported an explosion and made a mayday call. Probably one of the crew. Pilots — especially military ones — don' panic easily. I think we can take it for granted that the plane's down and Fenster's dead."

There was silence around the room. Whatever the outcome of the two hostage situations, there would be no doubt that the LTTE had struck their international enemies a hard body blow.

The death of the vehemently anti-Tiger Canadian minister would be a heavy loss to Sri Lankan efforts in North America. As for the inevitable removal of Jaliya de Silva from his post of Director General of Foreign Intelligence and the resulting shake-up of that outfit, while being mostly de Silva's own fault rather than anyone else's, could arguably have been caused by indirect LTTE actions. Looking at the DIG's now empty chair, Devendra still couldn't believe the man's ruthlessness had actually overcome his common sense.

"OK." Jayavickrama was scanning a communiqué that had just come in from the Ministry of Foreign Affairs. "Canada has given us the go-ahead for both Operation *Rama* and Operation *Sita*," he said, using, respectively, the CCG codenames for the assaults on Air Canada AC634 and the Canadian embassy, "but they insist that both should be carried out in concert with their JTF2 team."

"Impossible," Perera said immediately. "The JTF2 chaps are already on their way to Madras with my buggers for *Rama*."

"We'll have to bring half of them back." Jayavickrama shrugged. "Otherwise *Sita* will have to be delayed until JTF2 can finish off there an' get back. We have more time with the embassy deadline, no?"

The Director Special Forces shook his head patiently, trying not to be condescending. The steel-haired politician's highest military achievement was to have once commanded a volunteer battalion of the Rifle Corps.

"Not that easy, minister," he objected. "They've been training bloody intensively with our chaps for *Rama*, and pulling half of them out in the middle of it won' be very good, not to mention the fact that they'd have to slip into the operation planned by Blue Team here in Colombo. Same story if we delay *Sita*. The Canadians will get here exhausted and be faced with a scenario they'd have to adapt to in too short a time. Also, we can't delay *Sita* too much. As soon as *Rama* goes in, it'll be all over the news channels, an' we don' know what the terra reaction will be. They might decide an assault is on the cards and start bumping off the hostages. We have to be ready to go."

"So what d'you suggest we tell the Canadians?" Jayavickrama asked coldly.

"Tell them the truth. Tell them we can't afford to bugger about with civilian lives. If they want their people out alive, they have to give us a free hand."

Jayavickrama nodded curtly. "What is the ERA saying about Fenster's death?"

Perera leaned back in his chair. "With the police negotiator, they're pretending they don' know anything about it. Claiming it's a Canadian ploy to buy time. Insist that if he doesn't show up they'll start shooting the hostages at oh-three-forty-five tomorrow morning."

"Is it possible that they know nothing about this?"

"If I can put my two-cents-worth in," spoke up Devendra, "it *is* possible. It might be a very compartmentalized operation, with the assassination being carried out by a separate LTTE/ERA unit. But whether or not they know makes no difference. I think we can be sure they'll kill the hostages once the deadline passes."

"So we're in agreement then that Operation *Sita* should go ahead?" Jayavickrama looked around the room.

There were nods all around.

"ASAP," Perera said.

* * *

"Those lights are annoying me. Switch them off."

Devini Sundaralingam couldn't see the huge spotlights that bathed the walls and grounds of the Canadian embassy, for the communications room she was in had no windows. The embassy building dated back to the early twentieth century, and was built in the English style of the time, but the windows of the second floor corner room had been bricked up by the Canadians and the walls lined with lead to prevent surveillance. However, Devini had seen the spotlights switched on at dusk, and now that full darkness had fallen, they made the embassy stand out like a shining beacon in the surrounding darkness of Cinnamon Gardens. The dazzling light had made her sentries on the embassy's balconies withdraw into the cover of the building's interior, and precluded their usefulness in detecting the impending assault.

"It's just part of the police cordon," the negotiator explained. "Routine procedure. They need it to isolate the area. You know, we're having a difficult time with journalists trying to slip in and take pictures. This way, they can be kept off. We don't want any unnecessary deaths in a misunderstanding, no?"

Devini knew he was lying. There wouldn't be any journalists within a kilometre in any direction. Gregory's Road in front of the embassy would have been closed to the public, and most likely Maitland Crescent, the avenue at the western end of Gregory's Road, as well. The darkness on the other three sides of the embassy perimeter, beyond the glare of the spotlights, confirmed that those properties had been vacated of their owners.

Gregory's Road formed the northern perimeter of the embassy grounds, and the building itself was separated from the avenue by seventy five metres of flower beds, shrubs, small trees, and clumps of bamboo that surrounded a lawn. A combined generator room and maintenance shed sat in the northwest corner of the grounds, between the embassy and the street. On the eastern side, a fifty-metre wide strip of black-topped courtyard served as a parking area, and divided the embassy from the high perimeter wall and the neighbouring property beyond. On the western and southern sides of the rectangular grounds, the perimeter wall was just five metres away from the side of the building, the width of the driveway that ran right around the embassy. While to east and west the embassy grounds were flanked by palatial residences, on the southern side was the Nondescript Cricket Club, its playing fields providing easily covered fields of fire.

"The only deaths will be from you misunderstanding my instructions," Devini said, her voice flat and devoid of emotion. "I'll give you five minutes, and then another hostage dies."

She hung up.

Within three minutes the spotlights were off, and ten minutes later, Devini left the room, doing her hourly round of the embassy. It was a tour undertaken more to relieve her own boredom than keep her team sharp. They were all trained Black Tigers, physically tough and mentally dedicated to this mission, from which none of them expected to return alive.

Devini smiled bitterly. While every single phase of the embassy mission had been rehearsed and trained for, the one phase no thought had been given to was withdrawal and extraction. As with all their strike missions, members of the Champion Black Tiger units weren't expected to walk away when the smoke had cleared. What a waste of all that training and dedication, she thought. She wished she could have had the chance to change that, to improve it, but she knew she would not. Control of her life had been taken out of her hands when she'd had the cyanide capsule hung around her neck at the end of her training. The capsule that was even now sewn into the lapel of her business jacket.

It was ironic, Devini thought, that the only time the Black Tigers had been humiliated in Colombo had been on occasions when a mission had been aborted midway through or been detected by the Sinhalese. Surrounded and cut off, outnumbered, with no plan for escape, they had been hunted down and killed like crazed wolves, going down fighting or blowing themselves up. In this war, ignored by the world until very recently, there were no Hague or Geneva conventions. Capture, for either side, meant unending pain and horror, and ultimately, if the gods were merciful, death. For herself, Devini would much rather skip the pain and horror bit. She knew that some Black Tiger units tasked for missions in Colombo had, against orders, drawn up their own secret plans for escape if things went wrong. But Devini had never heard of a successful withdrawal after a mission in Colombo.

Walking down the corridor outside the communications room, she checked that the other doors leading off it were locked, and then entered the library at the far end. The heavy drapes were drawn across the French windows, but the lights were on in the book-filled room. Devini crossed the carpeted floor and slipped quickly through the drapes and the one open window. Jegen was at the far end of the balcony, leaning out to peer round the corner of the building into the darkness of the playing fields to the south.

There were no lights from the direction of the Nondescript Cricket Club, and Devini was sure that had been evacuated too. This was the second-most vulnerable side of their perimeter, surpassed only by the western side. Whereas the playing fields provided no cover to the south, the property to the west was dotted with shrubbery and trees that could conceal any attackers. The boundary wall on both sides was a mere five metres away, and provided a perfect avenue of approach for an assault team. It was the reason the first- and second-floor balconies overlooking the danger zones would always be manned, the latter either by Jegen or Devini herself. From the southern end of the balcony that ran most of the length of the building's eastern side, a sentry could cover not only the NCC grounds, but the front car park, the eastern wall, and the front driveway. The balcony's original wrought-iron railing had at some point been replaced by a stone parapet — in the 1970s, from the look of it — and this would provide good cover for a crouching sentry.

Leaning against the fire escape that was bolted to the end of the balcony, Jegen checked his watch as he saw her approach, knowing it was his turn to take over the comms centre.

"How is it looking?" she asked him in Tamil.

"OK. The spotlights are still in position, even though they've switched them off. I can see a lot of movement in the park. I'm not so happy about them being so close to the wall."

"I can tell them to move the lights away, but that will not mean anything. They could have a hundred men behind the walls and we will not know. And anyway, together with Sujeevan and Banu downstairs, whoever is here can kill anybody trying to get through the wire."

A roll of barbed wire fixed to metre-high steel posts atop the wall was, rather than embassy security, a part of the NCC's precautions to ensure non-paying fans didn't sneak in to watch the cricket matches.

"I am not worried about them coming *over* the wall," Jegen replied with a quick shake of the head. "But who knows if they will not try to come *through* it? They could even now be setting up a charge to blow a hole."

"Well, keep your ears as well as your eyes open." Devini ran a hand idly over the painted iron of the fire escape. They had worried at first that it could be used by an assault team to gain access to the balconies, but closer inspection had revealed that each ladder could only be released from above. "Stay here a few minutes longer," she said. "I want to do a quick round before I take over from you."

"OK."

"They should attempt a reconnaissance anytime now," she said over her shoulder as she walked away.

"I know. I will watch for it."

They had foreseen this during the planning stage, Devini knew, and Jegen would know what to look for. An assault force would need to know the locations of both her team and the hostages. Even if they already had snipers in position, the drawn curtains would defeat anything but thermal imaging or powerful x-rays, and she knew the Army did not have those. The soldiers would have to get someone in close to put in microphones and fibre optics.

Going down the stairs to the first floor, Devini first checked on Preethi in the senior visa officer's room. The office was in darkness, and Devini could just make out the young woman seated by the windows. The corner room had a perfect view of the front gate. A few exchanged words and Devini was on her way.

The first floor's layout was almost identical to the one above it and, walking back along the corridor, she checked doors as she went. The locks wouldn't stop an assaulting soldier, but it would certainly slow him down and give her team time to recover.

She entered the banquet room and noted that Banu was still sitting on the big banquet table, covering the hostages with his submachine-gun. The prisoners were all sitting or lying on the floor, crowded together in the far corner, opposite the fireplace on her right. Those at the back had their shoulders pressed against the drapes that covered the French windows opening onto the balcony. Devini spoke softly to Banu, making sure everything was going smoothly. The prisoners were all behaving well, obviously terrified after the killing of the visa officer. Once an hour, anyone who needed to use the toilet was escorted there by either Banu or Sujeevan. It was one of the few chinks in their defence, Devini knew, for in that time, while one guard escorted the group to the toilet, the other had to leave his post on the balcony to watch the remainder of the prisoners. But it couldn't be helped. Better than having the prisoners soil their underwear and turn the room into something that smelled like a sewer. They had considered moving all the prisoners to the toilets each hour, but had finally concluded that it would mean too many prisoners on the move for one guard to watch.

The lights were on, but the drapes drawn. Sticking her head out, taking care not to let more light than was absolutely necessary escape, Devini saw that Sujeevan was patrolling up and down the balcony. It was in the shape of an L, running the length of the southern and western sides of the banquet room. Here, too, the French windows opened directly on to the balcony and were all shut and bolted except for the two at the far ends of the balcony. But even here, the drapes had been nailed to the floor and window frame, making sure they didn't flutter in the breeze and reveal the scene indoors to watchful eyes.

On the ground floor, Angelo was in the drivers' common room, watching from an angle the cars parked in front of the generator building. He was seated far enough back from the glass panel in the door as to be hidden from outside view, even with a night vision device. Devini knew that every half-hour or so he would patrol through the ground floor to the front door on the eastern side of the building, but his orders were to concentrate on the drivers' common room. The door leading from the room to the smaller car park was one of only two giving access to the grounds, and the generator building would be a tempting avenue of approach, providing cover for any attacker who came in from Gregory's Road. The main door was a formidable one, being actually two, an outer and inner one, the former of heavy wood and the latter of glass. Both were heavily reinforced with steel and had locks that were designed to discourage the use of force. It was unlikely that the soldiers would choose this point of entry.

Devini once more checked door locks before heading back up the stairs.

CHAPTER 24

Lenny Kravitz had given way to the Real McKenzies, and full darkness had fallen as the C-130H Hercules came straight into Madras International Airport. Listening to the hammering beat of the heavy metal in his earphones that threatened, but didn't quite overpower the bagpipes in the background, Eric Christofelsz chuckled silently to himself. Here he was, a Burgher, sitting amongst Sinhalese and Canadian troops, about to land in India to kill a planeful of Tamils, and he was listening to a Scottish punk rock band.

> *The world we know is changing fast*
> *The walls are closing in . . .*

Up on the flight deck, standing next to the flight engineer, Captain Saliya Dayananda watched the dark land of Tamil Nadu tilt up towards them. He knew it was a cliché, but the millions of lights did look like jewels on black velvet. But he also knew that it was a beauty better admired from afar. The city of Madras was one of the most overpopulated and poverty-stricken on the face of the earth. Saliya Dayananda knew that he might as well enjoy this moment; once on the ground he'd have precious little time to admire the scenery.

"Better strap in, *machang*," he heard the pilot say over the intercom, and saw the man glance over his shoulder.

"Roger, skipper." Dayananda unplugged his headset from the overhead console and moved aft past the navigator to the bunk at the back of the cockpit and sat on it — there was no seat belt to be found — regretting that he wouldn't see much of the landing from here. Well, there wouldn't be much to see, but that was the whole point.

The flight crew looked barely human with their bulky NVGs on, and the cockpit glowed an eerie red in the subdued lighting from the instrument panels. Even the navigation lights would soon be switched off, just prior to landing. The airport was closed to all civilian air traffic, and they didn't want to alert the hijackers to the arrival of a military transport.

Dayananda plugged his headset into a console at the navigator's desk and listened to the pilots talk to the air traffic control at Madras. The man in the co-pilot's seat on the starboard side of the cockpit was an American, one of the USAF military advisors who had arrived the previous year. This was truly turning out to be an international operation, decided the Commando captain.

The American was from the 1st Special Operations Wing, and a veteran MC-130H pilot. While the aircraft they were in at that moment wasn't one of the high-tech Combat Talons — it was actually a regular C-130H Hercules, bought from the RAF — it had been heavily modified to enhance performance for special operations, with a full load of extra electronics. The pilots from the 1st SOW were part of an effort to train the SLAF's new No 32 Special Warfare Squadron. The unit had just two of the modified aircraft, but more had been promised by the MoD.

"Charlie Romeo eight eight zero from Madras Director. You are cleared through two thousand. Turn right to zero zero five. QNH nine nine seven decimal three."

"Eight eight zero, copy."

The pilot made the small directional changes. The altimeter change between Palaly and Madras was minute.

"Eight eight zero, we have all runway lights and systems switched off. Do you require ILS on Runway eighteen?"

"Negative, Madras. We'll make a visual approach."

"Eight eight zero, reduce speed for final approach."

Sitting behind and between the pilots, the engineer reached forward and wound down the throttles as the undercart came down with a thump. The pilot extended the flaps and the plane began to settle, nose up. The navigation lights were killed now, and the big four-engine transport swooped out of the night sky like a huge owl.

Sitting at the back, Dayananda wasn't wearing NVGs — he wanted his own eyes already adapted to the darkness when they left the plane — and could see nothing beyond the red-etched outlines of the three crewmembers that blocked out most of the forward view.

If he had been able to see what the pilots and engineer could, he would have wished for blindness. The C-130H was at a mere five hundred feet, lower than any civilian aircraft would fly, and totally blacked out, rushing towards the runway. The NVGs flattened depth perception marginally, but they were only a psychological crutch for the pilots anyway. They could have landed the aircraft on instruments, totally blind, if they had so wished. Through the NVGs, the airport appeared a wasteland of green and black, like some Mercurial other world, the runway lights switched off as requested, but the asphalt strips standing out clearly against the grass verges. In the distance to the northeast, the airport buildings glittered and shone, but directly ahead, five kilometres away, at the far end of runway-18, was murky green darkness. That section of the airport was blacked out in anticipation of CR880's arrival.

"Eight eight zero, you are cleared to land. Switch to Tower on one two zero decimal three. Out."

When the jolt of the landing came, it took Dayananda totally by surprise, and he had to fight a momentary feeling of vertigo, having had no point of reference to gauge their altitude. There was a quick screech of brakes, and then the C-130H rolled smoothly onwards, the flight engineer easing the throttles back gradually. There would be no drastic change in speed, with its resultant loud noise signature, Dayananda knew; the Herky's short takeoff and landing distance would be easily accommodated by the four thousand-metre runway.

"Charlie Romeo eight eight zero, this is Tower. Proceed to stand Foxtrot two thirty five via taxiways Nellie and Tango."

There would be no reference over the airwaves that this was a landing military flight; even if the hijackers or anyone else had been listening in, it would sound like a regular passenger aircraft arriving at Madras and being directed to its stand.

While the airports two main parallel runways lay in a northeast to southwest line, the secondary strip the SLAF transport was on ran virtually due north to south; almost, but not quite, bisecting the other two runways at the northwest edge of the airport. Now, as the C-130H trundled towards the end of the runway, Dayananda stood and moved forward to stand behind the pilots. The airport buildings stretched away to his right front, and he could see the dark silhouettes of airliners outlined against the lights. Peering into the darkness, Dayananda attempted to locate the hijacked Air Canada plane, but the distance was too great. From the maps he had studied, he knew that AC634 was parked roughly halfway along, and to the north of, the parallel runways.

Dayananda gave up looking for the Airbus, knowing he would get a much closer look soon enough when he did a CTR, and busied himself resetting his Casio G-Shock to Indian time which was half an hour behind Sri Lankan. He turned and headed aft in anticipation of disembarking. For the moment it was more important that they get off the transport quickly and smoothly. Stand F235 had been picked because it was at the far end of the airport, almost a full two kilometres away from stand V163, where the hijacked aircraft was parked. Once in position, they would be out of direct line of sight, and access roads shielded by the airport buildings would enable them to move quickly and surreptitiously around the terminal area.

*   *   *

OPERATION SITA: It was as close to real human flight as he had ever experienced. Even parachuting was constrained to the demands of gravity. The treetops moved past below his feet no faster than at a brisk walk, and even though he was three hundred feet off the ground and wearing a Balaclava mask, he could get the scent of the flowers that bloomed in the frangipani and flame-of-the-forest trees. Smells seemed to travel much better vertically. The only sounds were the distant throb of traffic on Reid Avenue and Bullers Road, the occasional rustle of the wind in the treetops, and the sleepy cawing of crows as he floated over them. Joggers ran up Independence Avenue, and couples strolled hand in hand, all unaware of him. The breeze tickling his bare feet made him feel like an owl or bat, hunting the darkness for his prey; except that it wasn't darkness to him. The NVGs that strained the muscles of his neck also ensured that the night held no secrets. More like Superman with his x-ray vision, almost believable if not for the faint beat of the chopper. Well, maybe Batman then. He certainly had enough kit strapped to his body.

Very few of the gadgets slung or clipped to Lance-Corporal Errol Seneviratne's torso and legs could be called weapons. Actually, only two of them: the Browning Hi-Power in the low-slung holster on his right thigh, and the parkerized Fairbairn-Skykes fighting knife sheathed on the inside of his left forearm. Both weapons were tried and trusted old comrades, and both had been designed before the Second World War. In spite of the arrival of lighter and newer pistols, like the popular 10-mm Glocks, Sri Lanka's Commando regiments had stuck to the 9-mm Hi-Power. It was faultless in every way, except for its size, which sometimes hindered concealment; and that hadn't been a good enough reason to replace it. Not even the pressure from MoD officials — well paid by commercial firearms companies to push their products — had changed anything. As for knives, the Commandos wanted something that would kill quickly and with the least amount of fuss. Designed by Hong Kong policeman Bruce Fairbairn, its narrow flat blade and razor-sharp double edge had done the job perfectly for the commandos of 1940s Britain, and continued to do so for those of 21st Century Sri Lanka. As for the big utility knives with their serrated twelve-inch blades and hollow handles stocked with exotic things such as piano wire and flint, those were for the Rambos and Arnold Schwarzeneggers. Everything necessary for survival was carried in a commando's beltkit. Knives were for killing.

The rest of Errol's load consisted of more high tech stuff. Miniature cameras, fibre-optic cables, a tiny television monitor, and electronic listening devices. A former Signal Corps technician before he applied for Commando selection, he was now part of the Brigade's permanent anti-terrorist cadre which supported the HR team, and he was here as the assault teams' eyes and ears.

Dangling two metres above Errol in the night sky, clipped to the same rope, was his protection: Private Tony Mendis. Like Errol, he too carried a pistol and knife, but also a backup: a suppressed H&K MP-5K clipped to his chest. Though both men wore black fatigues and Balaclavas identical to the assaulters, they wore no body armour, respirators, boots or gloves. They had all been deemed too bulky or noisy for the stealth that this job would demand.

Their task was to get onto the roof of the Canadian embassy and locate the positions of the terras and their hostages, so that the assault teams could then plan their attack accordingly. To do this, Errol and Tony were using a modified SPIE system. The Special Procedures Insertion and Extraction system was essentially a long rope dangling below a helicopter with varying numbers of men hanging onto it. Developed by the US Navy for use with its SEAL teams in Vietnam, it could be used to insert troops into or extract them out of inaccessible spots by having them clip themselves to the rope, one above the other.

For this particular mission, the commandos were using an extra long rope — three thousand feet — attached to a Huey. The extra length was needed to enable the chopper to stay at altitude and not alarm the terras. Ten minutes previously, the Huey had taken off from the Sports Ministry Grounds, six hundred metres southwest of the embassy, and quickly risen to three thousand feet before lifting Errol and Tony into the air. It had then risen another three hundred feet, this to raise the two commandos above any natural or man-made obstacles in the Cinnamon Gardens area, and also to hide them from the view of the civilians who dotted the streets. To avoid making drastic or sudden changes in direction, something that would cause the two soldiers to swing wildly on their rope, the chopper pilot was forced to fly at something akin to a walking pace, providing Errol Seneviratne with his spectacular view of Colombo at night.

Within five minutes they were crossing the Colombo Cricket Club and approaching the Nondescript Cricket Club, each divided from the other by the narrow width of Maitland Place. This area was even thicker with trees than the rest of Cinnamon Gardens, and Errol spoke into his lip mike.

"This is Echo. Move us up, Pegasus."

High above, the chopper pilot eased his bird higher, gaining another hundred and fifty feet. Flying blacked out, and also equipped with NVGs, he was nevertheless too high up for precise ground navigation. He would have to rely on the men dangling below for guidance.

Errol watched the treetops move slowly past beneath him, like black-green clouds, as he watched for the sloping tiles of the embassy roof. As predicted, the area below was crisscrossed with a tangle of telephone and electricity cables that made any direct helicopter assault on the embassy suicide. Like many things in Colombo, the telecommunications and power systems — particularly the former — had expanded in a haphazard manner in the 1980s and 1990s, with connections being provided to residences as and when they became available, and not in any sort of pre-planned pattern. This had resulted in parts of Colombo looking like some gigantic cat's cradle of wires and cables.

Errol could now see the embassy roof clearly through the treetops, chinks of bright light escaping from the dark building.

"Start sliding us west, Pegasus." He could see part of a balcony on the south side of the embassy, but no movement on it. That would be the southern part of the L-shaped balcony on the first floor. He couldn't see the western part because of the trees. "OK. . . an'. . . now move north. . ."

"Echo from Foxtrot one, Tango one centre on Yellow Zulu."

"Echo from Foxtrot five, Tango three southern end of Blue Zulu two."

These were warnings from snipers positioned to watch the western and eastern sides of the building respectively. Each side of the building was codenamed a colour, and every door and window numbered. Zulus were the balconies. In plain language, the warnings were that there was a terra in the centre of the first floor's western balcony, and another at the southern end of the second floor's balcony, on the eastern side. Because of the code, information could be swapped efficiently between snipers or assaulters with no delays or misunderstandings.

Errol drew his pistol and held it one-handed. It already had a round chambered, and he now slipped off the safety catch. He was directly over the embassy roof, a hundred and fifty metres in the air. Now was the moment of max danger. If the commandos were spotted and the terras switched on the courtyard lights he and Tony would be fucked. And so would the hostages. But that was why they had DA drills. The assault teams would be standing by. A decoy frame charge would blow a hole in the south wall, and that would be followed by a bulldozer smashing through the main gate. Simultaneously, a team would use grenade launchers to fire flash-bangs and CS gas canisters over the west wall into the windows, while another team came in behind the generator room and assaulted in through the side door. It would still be a fuckup of course, since they had no idea where the hostages were being held or which rooms were being occupied by the terras. And if the doors were booby-trapped or barricaded, they'd never get to the hostages in time. Which was why he, Errol Seneviratne — Defender of the True Faith — was dangling from a rope more than a hundred and fifty metres off the ground.

"Pegasus," he whispered, "take us down slowly."

On the long second floor balcony, Devini Sundaralingam turned to walk back towards the library, stretching to relieve her back that had stiffened from long hours of sitting in the comms room. The faint sound of the helicopter made her pause and turn back towards the south. The rotors seemed to be quite some distance away, she decided, at least a kilometre. Looking out over the NCC grounds, she wondered whether it was somewhere out there. It didn't worry her too much, for there had been choppers buzzing around ever since they had captured the embassy, that morning. She raised her head and scanned the sky.

"Echo from Foxtrot five, Tango three may be aware, looking up."
     Watching the terrorist through their KN-250 night sights, the snipers positioned in the grounds to the east of the embassy property, saw her head moving as she peered up at the dark sky. In spite of the hooded pullover and baseball cap, they could tell it was a woman, probably the same one who had been on watch in the afternoon. The BBC team hadn't seen any other women amongst the terras, but it was possible there was at least one other. This, however, had to be the leader; she was the same height and build as the woman they had all seen on the taped BBC World broadcast.
     "Pegasus from Echo, stan' by."
     Errol Seneviratne hung motionless, twenty metres above the embassy roof. He was facing the edge of the tiled roof closest to the eastern balcony, but could see no movement.
     It was a clear starlit night, with no moon; the second-best weather situation for airborne urban night ops. Ideal weather would be heavy rain, but that was too much to hope for. There had been no rain for months. Unlike in rural areas, an overcast sky would provide a cloud base that would be lit up by city lights and silhouette

men and aircraft against it. It would take someone with exceptional night vision, Errol knew, to spot him against the black night, and both sentries on the balconies had taken over their posts less than half an hour previously, coming out of well-lit rooms into darkness. It was why this moment had been chosen. It was also unlikely, because of the tree cover, that the sentries would be able to see much of the sky anyway.

"Echo from Foxtrot five, all clear, Tango three is mobile north, unaware."

"Pegasus from Echo, move us north."

The sloping tiles glided past until Errol was directly over the spot he had chosen. Another whispered command, and the roof came up to meet his bare feet. Digging his toes into the cool dry clay, Errol unclipped himself from the rope and moved quickly aside, making room for Tony Mendis. The roof was a simple one, with a single spine that ran north to south, and four chimneys, two on either side of the spine. As he watched Tony unclip himself, Errol was thankful that the tiles underfoot were of the flat European style; the traditional *Sinhala ulu*, shaped like half-cylinders, would have been impossible to move across silently.

The helicopter moved away, but never beyond earshot, circling as it established its sound signature on the subconscious of the terrorists. With Tony covering him, Errol got to work. Starting with the southeast chimney, he started to lower the microphones down on their cables. Blueprints of the embassy had been obtained from the Town Hall, and meticulous measurements made. The mike wires needed to be long enough to reach the fireplaces in the rooms below, but short enough to keep the mike inside the chimney and out of view of the rooms' occupants. Each mike, along with its wire, was stored in a separate webbing pouch, specifically labelled, and Errol uncoiled the first length of wire. Feeding it into the chimney that led down to the first floor banquet room, he stopped when the strip of fluorescent tape that marked the correct length was level with the chimney top. He then repeated the procedure with each of the rooms that had fireplaces, taping the individual wires in place.

Once that was done, Errol uncoiled the fibre-optic cables. The rubber outer covering on the cables were coloured a two-tone pattern of grey and brown, and were almost invisible. Each cable ended in a ninety-degree hardened elbow beyond which was the attached miniature camera. The process now took longer, because Errol had to plug each cable into the small black-and-white monitor, make sure each unit was working, and rotate the cable until the camera covered as much of the room as was possible.

All of this took a full hour of nervous silence, before Errol moved across the roof to the northwest corner, taping all the wires and cables down as he went. At the corner, he wrapped the dozen wires and cables together securely with the engineering tape and, crouching to keep his balance on the sloping tiles, flung the tentacle over the perimeter wall. A commando on the far side collected the tentacle of wires and cables and walked with it to a telephone pole close to Gregory's Road. Climbing the pole, the man taped the tentacle to the embassy's own telephone cables that stretched from the northwest corner of the building. At his end, Errol did the same, satisfied that anyone looking out of the building would not notice that the embassy had a brand new communications system.

*   *   *

"How many beds are there?" Mahesh Balachandran gestured with his Micro-Uzi, motioning for Jennifer Jensen to move ahead of him into the enclosed space.

"As many as ten, depending on cargo," Jen-Jen replied nervously, moving to the foldable steel stairway. She suppressed an involuntary shudder as the cool metal of the submachine-gun's muzzle brushed her forearm. "But usually we carry just three and take it in turns to sleep on the long-haul flights."

Holding the stewardess in front of him, Balachandran scanned the claustrophobic area quickly, taking in the bunks folded against the fuselage walls. They had been trained in Pakistan to use this space as a last hard defence, a spot from which the plane could be blown up even after it was stormed. With a last look around, he pushed Jen-Jen back to the stairs. Well, he wouldn't need it now, but it was still good to know one's options.

*

OPERATION RAMA: Walking into the control tower, Saliya Dayananda and Jan Conway were met by Chula Abenayake, who looked surprised to see the Canadian there. Balasuriya introduced Conway and himself by first name only, explaining to the DFI negotiator that this would be a joint Sri Lankan-Canadian job.

"I was briefed to expect an STF team," said Abenayake, regaining his composure.

It was Dayananda's turn to look puzzled, and he said, "I don' know anything about that. They must've changed their minds."

The panorama of the airport lay spread before him as he walked over to the sloping plate glass of the tower. He could make out the hijacked plane almost one thousand eight hundred metres away, standing out because of the row of lighted windows down its side, alone, with only empty stands nearby. Dayananda was glad he had chosen the newly constructed cargo centre building on the far side of the airport as his op centre; it had a much better view of AC634, and from just a thousand-metre range. The cargo centre, which had been used by the Indian HR team — 51 Special Action Group of the National Security Guard — as their op centre, had just been vacated when the Sri Lankans and Canadians arrived. 51/SAG's OC, Major Anil Prakash had stayed behind to give the newcomers an informal briefing on the situation. In spite of the recent tension between Sri Lanka and India, the meeting had been friendly enough, all three officers sensing a mutual solidarity in their shared purpose.

Dayananda had met Anil Prakash once before when the tall, rake-thin Black Cat had been part of the Indian premier's bodyguard during a SAARC summit in Colombo several years previously. A former platoon commander in 10 Para-Commando

Battalion, Prakash had served in Sri Lanka with the IPKF in the late 1980s, and had used the SAARC summit as an excuse to get himself on a flight to Jaffna just to see his old hunting grounds. Dayananda had been at Palaly, recovering from a bout of dengue fever, and had been at the Commando Officers' Mess when the Indian had been hosted to lunch.

Dayananda turned back to where Abenayake had retaken his seat and had put on a headset. The top floor of the tower seemed quite crowded: the negotiators — three Indians and two Sri Lankans — a ground traffic controller, and some uniformed Indian police officers who were there to provide security. Luckily, with the airport closed, there was no need for the full complement of ground traffic controllers. Somewhere below, air traffic was still being monitored and diverted to other airports in the region.

"Anything new from the hijackers?" the Commando captain asked.

"As they landed the hijack leader spoke for the firs' time, instead of using the pilot to relay his orders. Wanted to know if the Canadians had made a decision on Fenster yet. They obviously think that Ottawa will try to stall when the deadline is close."

Dayananda and Conway exchanged glances but didn't say anything on the subject. It was obvious that Abenayake knew nothing of Donald Fenster's death. In fact, he wouldn't know if the Commandos and JTF2 were there as a stand by option or as a determined effort to end the hijack by force. It was quite normal for the negotiator to be in an information bubble, being fed only bits and pieces of news relevant to the negotiations.

"What can you tell us about his personality?" Conway asked.

The DII profiles on the hijackers that Sri Lankan Military Intelligence had passed on for Red Team and JTF2 to study had been surprisingly thorough, giving combat experience, character analysis, and suspected specialist training. It had convinced Conway that the Sri Lankan intelligence network was highly professional. The profiles had even given the lengths of time the hijackers had served in LTTE recon units. Conway wondered how they had got that info. Now he was just hedging his bets, since it wouldn't hurt to get some on-the-spot intel.

"He calls himself Major Mahesh," said Abenayake in reply to Conway, "an' Ah've been chatting with him on and off for the past hour. Very general stuff, mostly about the war. He seems very relaxed and happy to talk. He definitely spouts the usual LTTE line about oppression of the Tamil minority, equal opportunity, a traditional homeland, etcetera." The negotiator paused and shrugged, looking somewhat puzzled. "But I feel it's as if that's all it is: a line. He sounds very cynical, hardened. A professional killer, doing a job he's sick of."

"But they've threatened to blow themselves up with the aircraft," Conway pointed out. "He must believe in his cause very much if he's ready to die for it."

Abenayake shrugged again.

"You're here, ready to risk your life, Jan," Dayananda said with a half-smile. "What cause do *you* believe in?"

Conway flashed a smile. "I believe in the cause that lets me walk over to McDonalds and get myself a burger whenever I want it." The smile faded. "The passengers on that plane can't do that right now. That's why I'm here."

"Whatever works for you." Dayananda inclined his head in a slow nod and turned back to the negotiator. "Has he asked for anything more, food an' drink, fuel?"

"No, nothing."

"Kinda strange, don't you think?" Conway mused. "I'd have thought he'd wanna be airborne when the deadline expires. Perfect way to avoid being stormed."

Dayananda shrugged. "He's got another two and a half hours left. Besides, it'll look more spectacular if the plane blows up right here." He turned to the Indian police chief superintendent who was nearby. "Which brings me to my next question: superintendent, what about the media fellows? Where are they? I don' want news of our arrival or movements being broadcast live." To avoid being spotted by curious media types, both

Dayananda and Conway had changed into jeans and polo shirts soon after landing.

The cop hoisted his Sam Browne belt in a futile attempt to move it higher over his ample belly. "Well, we have an information centre in the main terminal with a media liaison team there. They're releasing only select information to the press. But to be honest, most of the reporter-chappies — and their cameras — are scattered round the perimeter of the airport, trying to get shots of the plane. Now that it's dark, most would've come inside, but there are still some from the big networks near gate thirty-one." He turned and pointed southwest, across the main runways. "It's about three kilometres from here, and the closest they can get to stand V-one-sixty-three. Obviously, we're not allowing reporters to run about all over the place."

"How far is gate thirty-one from the plane?" asked Dayananda.

"Two kilometres or so. I doubt they can see much."

Dayananda decided the cop was probably right. Even if the cameramen from the international news networks had night vision devices, it was unlikely they'd be able to make out much beyond five hundred metres. With luck, they would not have even spotted the landing of the C-130H. It was ironic, he thought, that the media seemed sometimes to be better equipped, technologically, than some armies.

*

Sitting in the first-floor cargo-handling area, Eric Christofelsz watched the sniper team commander talking to his guys. They were in a corner of the huge room, huddled around maps of the airport, shooters cradling the long rifles and spotters the backup weapons, gesturing and talking softly about ranges and angles, wind speed and direction, humidity and bullet-drop. They would soon be off, each pair on its long lonely walk, to get into positions from where they could relay the latest int on the hijackers and, ultimately support the impending assault.

A few minutes later, Christofelsz saw the boss come in

with Conway, both men going over to join the snipers. They would probably move in with them for a CTR.

He checked his watch. 2045. Two hours and fifteen minutes to the deadline. Christofelsz and the DA teams were in full kit, sweating in spite of the air-conditioning, respirators ready to be donned. If the negotiations fell apart, they could hit the plane in minutes. Decoy number one would be the Herky with landing lights blazing and engines howling. Decoy number two would be the sniper shots into the cockpit and open port side door. Then the lights would go and the assault teams would hit the Airbus from the dark starboard side.

While this was the assault plan that they had already practiced, it could change marginally or drastically, depending on what the CTR and the sniper team revealed. Until the details could be worked out and the assault plan finalized, the DA drills would remain in place.

Somewhere off to the left, two of Christofelsz's patrol team were talking — like soldiers everywhere — about women and sex, and particularly about the recently declared — and highly publicized — law that raised the age of consent in Sri Lanka to sixteen years for all races.

"How can you tell when a bit is old enough to jump?" one commando asked.

"How?" came the bored query.

"You take her an' get her to sit on a proper lat," explained the first soldier. "A proper one, like the officers have — an' Christo over there has at home—"

"Didn' know y'all *have* latrines in Kudaweva or wherever your village is," cracked back Christofelsz with a grin. "Thought y'all went an' did it in the nearest river."

"Kaduwela," the first commando corrected. "An' we do have lats. Proper Army-issue squatting pans. I bought a surplus one from the Service Corps when I was building my house."

"So how can you tell when she's old enough?" interrupted the second commando, interested in spite of himself.

"Yah, you get her to sit on a lat — a *commode* — and if her feet touch the floor on both sides, she's old enough."

Christofelsz chuckled and settled back to wait.

Commando, airborne all the way, he muttered to himself, *This is the way we end the day.*

❊

Colin Peters stared stuporously out of his window with unseeing eyes. He was exhausted. It was almost forty eight hours since he'd left Colombo, and in that time they had been through several time zones. The arrival of darkness had brought no respite from the heat and humidity, and he could smell his own body odour, to say nothing of the enclosed stink of almost three hundred other human beings. His throat was dry, but he knew that there was nothing left to drink on the plane. When was it going to end? He wanted to get up and scream, run down the aisle and jump through the open doorway, soar into the air and across the oceans to England. He wanted to smash his head, or better still, the head of one of the hijackers, against the cabin wall. He wanted to do *some*thing, *any*thing; anything but sit here quietly on this fucking plane in the middle of fucking India.

Vijitha Dhampahana was dreaming of Canada, a land he was losing more and more hope of seeing with each passing hour. He wished they were already at Vancouver. Then he would have been strong, chanced his luck at overpowering the Tigers and making a run for it, braving the bullets if it meant he could stay in Canada. And even if he had to stay a captive for a while, it would be bearable. At least there, in Canada, it wouldn't be so hot. He had been told that it was always cool and comfortable in Canada, like the hill country. And in winter there would be snow! Vijitha wondered what snow would feel like. Cold and frosty, like ice cream that had melted during the power cuts and then been refrozen. He dreamed of all the things he could buy once he had a job in Toronto. Once he had finished paying off the price of his journey, he would send back money to his father so that the old man could redeem the house. And enough money so that his mother could buy the washing machine she always had wanted. Vijitha decided he would rent a small flat — a cheap one — so that he could save up money. Just one room with a little kitchen and bathroom. But a bathroom with running water, so that he wouldn't have to use toilet paper like the *suddho*. Vijitha admired many things about westerners, but the disgusting habit of wiping one's self instead of washing, was beyond him.

Daniel Devanayagam was bored. He had read all five of his Lara Croft and Spawn comics several times over, plus all the in-flight magazines and safety manuals. The personal entertainment systems were no longer working, so there was nothing to watch except for the empty airport outside his window. He wondered how long it would take Delta Force to get there, and though he knew they wouldn't be led by Chuck Norris, he was sure it would be someone equally impressive. The fact that this was a Canadian plane, that he himself was Sri Lankan, and that the Delta Force was American, didn't deter Daniel. Those were just minor details. He was sure they would come. Ever since they had landed, his father had been urging him to try and sleep, like Suzie, but he resisted. Just like a girl to fall asleep just when things were going to get exciting, he thought with disdain.

The cockpit lights were off, probably so that they could see out better, realized Dayananda. Through the binoculars, he could see movement on the flight deck, but no real details of people. Night vision aides were of no use since they were all virtually whitened out by the bright lights that bathed the apron and AC634, parked two hundred and fifty metres away from his position. If he wanted a sniper to take a shot into the cockpit from here, he would have to wait till the lights were switched off.

Lying on Dayananda's right was Jan Conway, and on his left one of the sniper-spotter teams. All four of them were stretched out on the flat top of a huge aviation fuel tank in the south-western corner of the fuel depot. The three men were twenty metres off the ground, hidden in the pocket of darkness created by the lights that lit up the storage area, and with a view of the Airbus's port side and nose.

After a few minutes of observation, Dayananda tapped the Canadian on the arm, and they both wriggled backwards towards the access ladder.

*   *   *

OPERATION SITA: The black-and-white picture was grainy and lacked proper definition, but served its purpose, revealing the position of the single armed man and the cowed civilians beyond.

"X-ray to Echo, can you clock cam five one-five degrees?" OC Blue said into the radio.

A hundred metres away, on the roof of the Canadian embassy, Errol Seneviratne reached down the chimney in question and rotated the cable carefully in a clockwise motion. In the ops centre next door, the watchers saw the picture swivel to reveal the rest of the room.

On the monitor screen, a dark curved slab cut across the top right of the picture, with the legs of a seated man bisecting the screen. What was obviously a submachine-gun rested across his thighs. Beyond was the expanse of the banquet room's floor, looking as big as a football field in the tiny camera's distorted fisheye image. In the far corner was a grey mottled huddle. The hostages. The picture was too indistinct to be able to tell individuals, or even the number of prisoners, but it looked roughly as if they were all there, and there was no reason to imagine any would have been separated. Some sort of flower arrangement had been placed in the unused fireplace, and though this hampered the view somewhat, it also provided cover for the camera.

"What's that?" someone asked, pointing to the black slab.

"That'll be the banquet table," answered the embassy's military attaché, the only Canadian in the room. "They seem to have moved it."

Other than OC Blue and the military attaché, there were twenty-five other men crowded into the living room of the sprawling manor house that had been commandeered as an ops centre. Two were dressed in civil kit and were from the brigade int shop, a third was the HQI of the nearby police station, a fourth was the Air Force liaison officer, and a fifth was the sniper team commander. The remaining twenty were the four-man assault teams. The buzz of static from the adjoining dining room announced that it had been converted into a comms centre.

Wires and cables snaked across the dining room floor, and a row of six monitors were ranged across the dining table, each with a label that indicated the room it pictured on its screen. Next to each monitor was a small speaker similar to the ones attachable to desktop computers, transmitting the sounds picked up from the embassy rooms. Everyone was huddled around the table as if a cricket test was on, each team watching the room they would be assaulting.

"OK," OC Blue said, his voice formal, "for the record, Operation *Sita*: to free the hostages and prevent the terras from causing any further damage." He repeated this, as was operational procedure, before letting his tone revert to its chatty routine. "Ah'll quickly go through it again in sequence. Timings Ah'll leave out for the moment, because that'll depend on *Rama*. We need to go as soon as they're committed." It had been explained to the military attaché earlier that this was because word of Operation *Rama* might hit the TV news channels almost immediately and cause the embassy terrorists to panic.

"First, terra and hostage positions:

"On the second floor, we know for sure that Tango Three or Four are always manning balcony Blue Zulu Two. The embassy comms centre is here in the southwest corner, but we don't know how many terras are in there. It hasn't a chimney or window, so we can't get a look in. The library in the northeast corner is empty, so probably whoever isn't on watch on Blue Zulu Two will be in the comms centre. Other than the library, there are offices right along the east side of the floor belonging to the military and cultural attachés and their staffs. Again, no way of looking inside, but because they have windows opening onto balcony Blue Zulu Two, where there is a sentry, it is unlikely they're occupied. This admin area in the northwest corner is empty.

"On the first floor, we have the hostages here in the southwest corner banquet room — directly below the comms centre — with either Tango one or two on guard, and the other mobile between balconies Yellow Zulu and Green Zulu. The French windows here and here—" the major pointed at the plan of the embassy floors— "are open, but the curtains are drawn. Both the ambassador's office room here in the southeast corner, and this pantry over here in the northwest corner, are empty. Next to the pantry are staff toilets. Stretching up the east side, between the ambassador's office and the northeast corner are a row of rooms belonging to the trade attaché and his staff, and the visa section. No way of looking in there.

"On the ground floor, the staff dining room in the southwest corner is empty, but the mike has picked up sounds of movement, so it's possible that there is a terra mobile on the ground floor, probably patrolling this corridor from the stairs to the front door. There are waiting rooms in the southeast and northeast corners, a drivers' common room in the northwest corner, and next to it, an office area from where visas are issued. That gives us five terras. There are probably more, possibly as many as eight altogether, so that leaves us three unaccounted for. Most likely there will be one here on the second floor, either static at the stairs or mobile in these corridors." He pointed to the main north-south-running corridor and the narrow hallway that led away at right angles to the west. The landing was at their junction. "Two more will probably be in the same position on the first floor, or in the rooms overlooking the front garden.

"Delta Team jump-off is Gregory's Road, insertion on foot. Alpha, Bravo, and Charlie teams jump-off is the embassy roof, insertion by STABO. Echo Team will remain in place to provide cover, as will Foxtrot.

"Once every hour, the Tango on guard outside the banquet room leaves his post for about five to ten minutes. We now know that he does this to escort hostages to the toilet. However, it'll be easier to hit him when he's on the balcony, so 'Go' will have to be when he's outside. The operation will be initiated by power to the embassy being cut, which will — we hope — bring someone out to the generator room, probably the terra on the ground floor. The terra's appearance will be the 'Go'.

"Expect all outer and inner doors to be locked, barricaded, and booby trapped.

"When the power goes, Delta Team will scale the north perimeter wall and flank both sides of the generator room here in the northwest corner of the grounds. When the terra makes an appearance, they will hit him and assault through the side door into the drivers' common room. Delta Team will then clear the ground floor and secure the foot of the stairs.

"At 'Go', Foxtrot Three will hit the Tango on Blue Zulu Two. Foxtrot One and/or Foxtrot Two will hit the Tango outside the banquet room – depending on whether he's on the Yellow or Green side of the building.

"Echo Team will drop CS and flashbangs down the chimneys, beginning with the banquet room.

"Bravo Team will rope down to Blue Zulu Two on the second floor and assault through the windows of the library and the cultural attaché's office, using frame charges if necessary. Bravo will then clear the second floor and secure the comms centre and the head of the stairs.

"Alpha Team will rope down to Yellow and Green Zulu on the first floor, and assault through the open French windows. If these are unexpectedly closed, axes will be used for entry. Explosive entry is out because of the danger to the hostages, who are grouped together in the corner of the room, against the French windows. Alpha will then hit the Tango in the room and clear and secure the hostages.

"Charlie Team will rope down to Blue Zulu One on the first floor and assault through the windows of the ambassador's office, using frame charges. Charlie will then clear the first floor and secure the corridors and landing.

"Once the embassy is secure, a human chain will be formed, and the hostages will be passed from Alpha Team to Charlie and then to Delta and out into the side car park in front of the generator room. While this is happening, a hostage handling team will then enter through the main gate and re-secure the hostages and make sure there are no more Tangos with them."

OC Blue looked around at the faces of his men. "OK. Any questions? Let's tear this up an' start looking at the problems."

* * *

OPERATION RAMA: "Excuse me, boss, this jus' came in from Gane."

Saliya Dayananda and Jan Conway had been going through the assault plan with the teams when the signaller interrupted. With a nod, OC Red took the paper. It would have been burst transmitted from Commando Brigade HQ at Ganemulle, under the control of which the HR team operated and, looking at it, Dayananda saw that it was in fact from the S-3.

The message was a personal dispatch from the brigade int officer, a lieutenant colonel and was, in effect, passing on a tip-off from Military Intelligence. Int suspected that when the lavatories on AC634 had been changed earlier in the day by Madras sanitation staff, explosives may have been brought aboard for the hijackers, including suicide vests. Red Team was advised that the hijackers might attempt to surrender during the assault, but this should be taken as a ruse. The terrorists were likely to blow themselves up if given the opportunity, and the assaulters were advised to take no chances.

Dayananda handed the message to Conway, and told the others the gist of it. The Sri Lankan was doubly puzzled by the message. First of all, he found it hard to believe that the Indian authorities hadn't supervised the sanitation crews more thoroughly, and he wondered why Anil Prakash — the Indian HR team commander — hadn't mentioned the suspicion; and on the second count, it was as if, he mused, someone back in Sri Lanka was worried. They didn't need to reinforce his boys' killer instinct, he reasoned. His commandos weren't going in there to take prisoners, and he doubted that the JTF2 guys had any intention of doing so either. Dayananda had heard that the reason the Canadian HR role had been passed from the police to the military had been just that: hijackers rarely, if ever, survived an assault by a military HR team, and this was usually because the assaulters went in to save the lives of the hostages and not to make arrests. This meant, obviously, the neutralization of the terrorists as quickly as possible, and the most efficient way of doing that was to kill them. The Mounties, like many police forces, had a problem with that.

Dayananda finally pushed the thoughts out of his mind and got on with the work of coordinating the assault sequence. He was just being paranoid, he told himself. HQ was probably just passing on info so that he would have the best picture of the situation.

He himself had no such qualms about killing terrorists, hijackers, or any other kind of hostage-takers. In short, Captain Saliya Dayananda had no scruples about killing. A career officer with eight years service, he had killed many times, both in battle and in situations considered not to fall neatly into the rules dictated by the Geneva Conventions. An officer with the 4th Vijayabahu Light Infantry for three years, he'd had all his heroic adolescent fantasies of war — gained as the well-read but only son of a university professor of literature — wiped out in the heavy fighting of the mid-1990s. Along with those fantasies had disappeared the guilt and nausea he had first experienced at the sight of violent death, destroyed in the cauldron that had also once destroyed half his platoon before his eyes in a single ambush. By the time he had transferred to the Commandos in 1997, he had become a highly rated infantry officer, decorated twice for individual courage. After serving eighteen months with the Commandos, he had returned to his parent regiment for two more years — during which he had commanded a company, served on the brigade staff, married, and fathered a baby daughter — before being recalled to the Commandos.

Dayananda remembered now that when he had taken part in the assault on Lake House — the Colombo building which houses the offices and printing press of the state dailies and weeklies — in October 1997, during his first stint with the Commandos, the Tiger terrorists who had taken some of the newspaper staff hostage had worn suicide kits, and two of them had blown themselves up.

The first floor of the cargo centre was awash with kit that had been strewn around, and maps were everywhere. Everyone had photocopied blowups of their sector of the airport, and were studying gates and taxiways, working out approach routes and angles.

Along one wall was taped the row of six enlarged colour photographs that had earlier been used on the Hun's-head targets, all showing mug shots of the six hijackers. In the shots, they were all dressed respectably and had their hair combed neatly, giving the impression that they had been blown up from passport photos.

Dayananda looked at his watch and saw that it was 2130. An hour and a half to the deadline. Air India had agreed to move an Airbus A330 to this end of the airport, and he wanted his assault teams to do a couple of rehearsals on it before the real thing.

Instinctively, he looked up at the east-facing windows of the cargo centre, but the Venetian blinds were closed and he couldn't see the hijacked plane that he knew was a thousand metres beyond.

*   *   *

Brigadier Arjuna Devendra took his coffee out onto the colonnaded southern walkway of the Ministry of Defence in Colombo. Leaning against one of the tall, fluted columns, he cradled the monogrammed coffee cup and saucer, and lit a cigarette. The night was warm in spite of the sea breeze that blew across the Galle Road and ruffled the dark surface of the Beira Lake.

Exhaling smoke, Devendra took a tentative sniff. Obviously, the recent cleanup of the notoriously polluted lake had worked. He could hardly smell it.

Finishing his coffee, he placed the cup and saucer at his feet and straightened up, stretching his back and yawning. Had it been just thirty six hours since this all started? It felt like weeks. Well, not much longer, if they were lucky. Both Red and Blue Teams were almost ready to go.

The sound of footfalls made him turn to see a uniformed figure approaching. As the man drew nearer, alternately moving through the light of the spotlights in the grounds below and the shadows of the columns on the walkway, Devendra recognized the head of the Colombo Sigint Section. Clicking his heels, the man held out an A4-sized buff envelope.

"'Evening, sir," Captain Palliyaguru said. "These jus' came in by email a few minutes ago. I thought Ah'd better bring you the printouts immediately. It's from the British Security Service, but the shots were taken by their Special Branch. There's a printout of the mail itself also in the envelope."

Devendra thanked the man and headed for the well-lit vestibule, the captain following. Inside, he opened the envelope and extracted five large colour photographs. The pictures were all grainy, as if taken through a telephoto lens with fast film. Two showed a man in his mid- to late-twenties entering and leaving what looked like a pub somewhere in Britain. The next picture showed a young woman entering the same pub. The last two shots were of the same woman crossing the street with the pub in the background.

The brigadier recognized Colonel Sundari immediately from the *BBC World* broadcast, and unfolded the email printout. It was from a Mr Hammond, and Devendra noted that the email had been addressed primarily to the DII.

FROM: Aliens Desk, Security Service, Gordon St., London.
TO: Directorate of Internal Intelligence, Colombo.
CC: Directorate of Military Intelligence, Colombo.

Pictures taken at Katherine Rd., London, as routine during unconnected operation by Special Branch, dated 21 December 2001. Forwarded to self by Northern Irish Section.

Subject, female, identified as SKANDARAJAN, SAROJINI (Canadian passport holder, resident of Scarborough, Ontario; no known history of terrorism), employed by THE CANADIAN RELIEF ORGANIZATION FOR PEACE IN SRI LANKA (pro-LTTE non-governmental organization engaged in fundraising), Toronto, Ontario.

Subject, male, identified as JESUDASAN, GUNAM (British national, resident of Stanmore, London; entered UK in 1988 under refugee status; suspected member of LIBERATION TIGERS OF TAMIL EELAM), employed at time of death (in bombing outside residence, February 2002) as Administrative Manager by INTERNATIONAL SECRETARIAT OF TAMIL EELAM, Katherine Rd., London.

Both subjects entered and left pub (THE BLARNEY) within five (05) minutes of each other, and were only known Asians in establishment at time. You may draw your own conclusions.

Best regards,
TM Hammond,
Assistant Chief, Aliens Desk

Devendra smiled and refolded the printout. Perfect. This was just what he needed to conclude the embassy situation.

"Send a set of the woman's pictures immediately to this address on Gregory's Road, Palle," he instructed. "There is a Commando operation in progress at the moment. Tell the OC that this is the terra leader, the same woman who came on TV. Give him her name also, it might help." The captain started to turn away, but Devendra stopped him. "Wait, man, I haven' finished. Send a full set of pictures — the man *and* the woman — to the Military Spokesman's office tonight. Tell the duty sergeant to start putting a press kit together. The usual smear type, connecting the woman to this known LTTEer. Tell him I will call him in an hour and give him the exact details of names, places, dates, etcetera, and that I will clear it with Brigadier Jinadasa."

CHAPTER 25

2210 LOCAL (1640 GMT) OPERATION RAMA: The lights around AC634 shone like a beacon fire that would hold back the lions. But not for long, Mahesh Balachandran told himself, not for long. They were probably out there somewhere in the darkness beyond the circle of light, getting into position. Fortunately these were trained lions, their claws sheathed. The cockpit was still in darkness, the pilots just dark silhouettes against the brightness outside, as still as statues, but Balachandran knew they were not asleep. They, too, knew there was now less than an hour to the deadline. The lions were cutting it rather fine, hanging on for a dramatic finish.

Easing the spare headset on, Balachandran spoke into it. "Tower, this is Air Canada."

"Tower receiving you, Major Mahesh."

"It is now 2210, Abenayake. Ah've been monitoring the *BBC World Service*, and there's still no word from Ottawa. What d'you have for me?"

There was a momentary hesitation at the other end before the negotiator replied. "Ah'm in the same boat as you, Major Mahesh. We're also still waiting. The Canadian embassy in New Delhi tells us that they'll have news for us soon."

Liar, smiled Balachandran to himself. There would be no word from Ottawa. But they all had parts to play, he supposed. He wondered if the negotiator was in on the operation. Probably not, he decided. The man's tone held too much tension. If he knew what the conclusion of the drama would be, he would be as relaxed as Balachandran himself was. Either that, or the negotiator knew something he and his team did not. Something that was making him nervous. But what could have gone wrong? So far there was nothing that could trigger any warning bells. It was just his own paranoia, he knew, but nevertheless he would remain vigilant.

Balachandran turned as Alagaran stuck his head in from business class, his eyebrows raised in silent query. Balachandran shrugged in a very vocal reply.

"Shall I close the business class door?" Alagaran asked in Tamil, referring to the one door that had been left open as a concession to the heat.

"No. Better if we leave it open. It will make things easier when the assault comes. They are bound to use it. I suggest you sit in the doorway and keep an eye out for them. It should happen anytime now. I would rather not be taken completely by surprise. And tell the others to safe their weapons. No need for accidents, no?"

"Foxtrot from X-ray, check?"

"Foxtrot one has some movement behind the pilots. Cockpit lights still out."

"Foxtrot two, nothing here."

"Foxtrot three has a partial in Papa Red."

"Foxtrot four has movement in the cockpit."

Foxtrot 3, the Commando sniper positioned two hundred and fifty metres to the southwest of AC634, in the Airbus's eight o' clock position, studied the open doorway through his 12-power scope. At this range, the optics made the door to business class look close enough to step through. At first it had looked like the occasional movement he had been seeing for the past half-hour, usually a hijacker moving past the doorway; but now, as he concentrated, Foxtrot 3 could make out what he realized was a leg and shoulder. The lights were on in business class, and Foxtrot 3's spotter, peering through his own 20-power spotting scope, confirmed that it seemed to be that of a man standing by the forward galley, looking into the cockpit.

"Stan' by, Foxtrot."

Foxtrot 3 held his breath for a couple of seconds, settling the crosshairs on the hijacker's thigh. He held them there for several heartbeats, then held off slightly to the left. It was not a sure shot by any means, but it was the only one offered to him, and he accepted it, the characteristic patience of the born hunter telling him that a better one might soon make itself available.

"Wind?" he queried softly, his jaw not moving.

"Same," answered the spotter, lying a couple of metres to the sniper's left and just behind his shoulder. "Ten miles per hour from seven o' clock."

The wind had held steady, blowing over the sniper's left shoulder for the past half an hour, and he considered making the necessary adjustment to the scope's windage turret. He had already guessed that it would only be a single minute of angle — one sixtieth of a degree — and the formula he had just keyed into the pocket calculator lying on the tarmac at his left elbow confirmed it — 2.735 multiplied by 10, and the whole divided by 15 before the total was divided once more by 2. Snipers the world over stuck to the imperial system, and so the two hundred and fifty-metre range became two hundred and seventy-three point five yards, and this was counted in the equation in hundreds of yards and multiplied by the wind velocity. The number fifteen was a constant that varied only according to the range. The final number in the equation was because the ten miles per hour wind was blowing at almost forty-five degrees to the bullet's line of flight and was therefore only a half-value wind, halving the total.

The wind had been gusting all evening, and the sniper didn't want to keep fiddling with the scope every time the wind changed. He finally decided to leave it alone, preferring to compensate by holding off.

Inching carefully to his left, he pivoted on the L-96AWP rifle's bipod, scanning down the length of the airliner's fuselage. Foxtrot 3 and his spotter were lying in dry grass, the muzzle of the rifle jutting out over the asphalt surface of taxiway-A, and the sniper's movement rustled the blades of grass, raising dust that threatened to make him cough. Not taking his eye from the scope, he raised the open carton of orange juice and took a long drag through the plastic straw sticking out of it. He would have preferred a Coke, but he knew fizzy drinks made him belch, and that could spoil his breathing and thus his aim. Nothing seemed to have changed along the length of AC634. Most of the windows were blank eyes, the blinds pulled down, but behind some of the plexiglas rectangles he could see occasional faces, either looking out or slumped in weariness.

Wanting to be ready for the "Go", he moved his aim back along the fuselage of the hijacked plane towards the nose. The windows were streaming through the circle of his scope as he tracked left, but then something made Foxtrot 3 stop, and then swing back to the right. Years of training and experience had made his subconscious notice something discordant, a change in the regular pattern.

Steadying his aim, he saw that the anomaly was at one of the economy class windows, just forward of the port wing and its adjacent closed door. Foxtrot 3 could see a face at the window, a face that was distorted because its owner was pressing it against the plexiglas. A child's face. The boy had a hand pressed to the plexiglas as well, seemingly shielding the lights behind him so that he could see out. But what had caught Foxtrot 3's attention was something the boy held in his hand. What seemed to be a strip of cloth or paper in the boy's palm was being flattened against the window.

Holding his breath to keep the scope absolutely still, Foxtrot 3 unblinkingly gazed at the window. The pale strip was a number one, meticulously cut out of what seemed to be paper; even down to the serifs. Obviously this small chap didn't want any misunderstanding.

"Tilak," he said to his partner, "What have you got at Papa Eleven?"

There were a few seconds pause as the spotter located the correct window. The sniper knew the more powerful spotting scope would make sure there was no doubt.

"Small bugger holding up a fucking number one," came the confirmation.

"X-ray from Foxtrot Three," the sniper said softly into his throat mike, depressing, with his right thumb, the transmit button attached to the rifle's olive-green reinforced plastic composite stock, trying not to jiggle the scope image, "there's a passenger — a small boy — signalling from Papa Eleven." He described what he was seeing, and got an acknowledgement from the boss. Then another voice cut in on the net.

"Foxtrot Four, Tango in Papa Red. I have a partial."

Foxtrot 3 swung his rifle, aiming in on the open doorway. An armed figure was standing in the opening, looking out. The sniper laid the crosshairs on the target's right shoulder.

"Foxtrot Three, I have a shot at the Tango in Papa Red."

At the same time, his right thumb depressed the tiny tit above the rifle's pistol grip. Eight hundred metres away, in the cargo centre, on a panel of four red lights that sat in front of Saliya Dayananda, the one designated Foxtrot 3 switched to green.

The sniper watched the hijacker drop into a crouch before swinging his legs out over the edge of the doorway.

"Foxtrot Three, Tango in Papa Red is sitting down. Armed with an Uzi. Looks like a sentry."

"Foxtrot Four, I have a shot."

In the cargo centre, another of the lights on the panel switched from red to green.

"Foxtrot Three an' Four from X-ray. ID?"

Moving the crosshairs to the dark V where the hijacker's white shirt was unbuttoned, Foxtrot 3 studied the man's face. It was shielded from the light behind him, and the airport lights were hitting him at an angle, creating strange shadows, but the faces of all the hijackers had been memorized by both the assaulters and the snipers.

"Foxtrot Three, it's Tango Five."

Dayananda glanced across at the wall to confirm what he already knew. Tango 5 was Alagaran Krishnaraja.

"Foxtrot, stan' by, stan' by."

He wondered what the passenger's signal meant. The number one could mean that there was just one hijacker in sight. Did that include the hijacker in the doorway? No, impossible. If the boy was in economy, the doorway would be out of sight. Maybe it meant nothing. He was just a little kid after all. Maybe he was just buggering around. Dayananda looked down at a diagram of the Airbus's interior.

"If there's a terra in this section of economy, as the boy is signalling," he said to Bullet Fonseka, pointing at the plan, "an' one bugger at this door, that leaves four more. One in the cockpit for sure — Tango One, the leader — an' three more further back in economy. Probably one in the amidships section, one in the aft section, and maybe one here at this partition dividing the two sections."

"Well, that doesn' really tell us anything new," Fonseka shrugged. "At the moment we can only guess at the exact positions."

Dayananda cursed silently. Normal procedure called for mikes or minicams to be attached to the target aircraft well in advance of an assault so that all the hijackers' locations could be noted. But there had been no time, and there was precious little left now.

The radio crackled to life at that moment. "Golf at Checkpoint Victor."

The others were jammed up against Eric Christofelsz's knees as he sat huddled in the bed of the orange Nissan 4x4 pickup truck belonging to the Madras airport services. The back of the pickup was packed with the twelve bulky figures of Charlie, Delta, and Echo teams, all of them in full assault kit with Balaclavas and respirators in place. The three ladders were lying across the cab at an angle, held in place by three standing men.

As the pickup moved the assault teams to their jump-off point, Christofelsz listened as the snipers talked to the boss. He could feel his heart pounding, and his breath rasped loudly in his respirator, making him sound to his own ears like Darth Vader. To keep his hands from trembling, Christofelsz unclipped his folding stock MP-5A3 from his chest and checked first the magazine, and then the powerful torch mounted over the receiver, making sure they were both firmly in place. Slipping off the safety in the darkness, he checked the chamber with a gloved finger before resafing the submachine-gun. Still working blind, he then ran his hands over his own body, searching for anything that could jingle, or even worse, catch on something during the assault and slow him down. He had done all of this earlier, before leaving the cargo centre, but he did it again out of habit.

Job done, Christofelsz leaned back from his uncomfortable perch on the pickup's side to look ahead past the cab. They were still on taxiway-R, skirting around the southwest end of the northern runway, but fast approaching taxiway-C.

Teams Charlie, Delta, and Echo had a jump-off point a hundred metres from AC634, and directly in its six o' clock. To reach the jump-off, the pickup would parallel the northern runway, along taxiway-C. Roughly midway along the runway, they would be dropped off, walking the five hundred or so remaining metres, and crossing the runway in the process, until they were in position.

This area of the airport was in total darkness, and the driver of the pickup truck had its headlights off, following the luminous green cat's eyes that glowed dully down the centre of the taxiways. Far off to the south, almost a kilometre away, Christofelsz could see the lights of traffic on the airport perimeter road. A few minutes later, the pickup turned left onto taxiway-C, the driver increasing speed on the dead straight strip of asphalt.

"Golf at Checkpoint Victor," Christofelsz heard him say into his radio.

None of the black-clad troops were talking. Everyone was quiet and engrossed in their own thoughts; mentally walking themselves through the op plan, rehearsing their own individual parts for the umpteenth time.

Christofelsz, as the commander of Charlie Team, would be the first through his doorway, and in his mind's eye he saw the strip charge blow and the door roll open. The flashbang would go in as he reached the top, and then he'd be in, turning left, back to the lavatory wall. . .

*

"Alpha and Bravo in position," Jan Conway said into his mike. It was installed inside his respirator, a wire running down his sleeve to a button that he could palm.

He and Alpha Team were crouching on the roof rack of the black Land Rover Defender that was parked in the lee of the cargo centre, its petrol V8 engine idling. Behind it was the second Defender, with Bravo Team on its roof. JTF2 had borrowed two drivers from the Commandos to handle the right-hand drive Defenders. While Conway had been confident in the abilities of his men to manage left-handed with the stick shifts, he had thought it safer to have drivers who were more familiar with them. Conway didn't want a stalled vehicle jeopardizing the entire operation.

Jan Conway could feel his entire body vibrating with tension and anticipation. He pulled his gloves tighter and patted the MP-5A3 slung under his arm. Looking over his shoulder, the rest of his team were a mass of shapeless black. This was *it*. This was what the hostage rescue textbook had been written for: an aircraft assault, the most dangerous hostage situation conceivable.

Listening to the snipers giving their terse reports, Conway had a flashback of the first Scarborough job, the raid on the LTTE offices above the restaurant on Kentin Avenue. He hoped they could get through this operation without any casualties. It was something you trained for, mentally and physically, but there was nothing that could really prepare you for it.

By rights, Conway should have been sitting next to Dayananda in the op centre, directing the operation, but the

Canadian had ducked out of it, preferring to lead Alpha Team. OC Red would be calling the shots anyway, Conway had decided, and he himself would be a passive observer most of the time. He'd rather be in amongst the shooting, and if all went well, he'd be the first man into the plane.

"Golf at Checkpoint Kilo," Conway heard in his earpiece.

※

Knowing that Golf had another thousand metres to go before he dropped off Bravo, Charlie, and Delta Teams, Dayananda glanced at his watch: twenty-two minutes to the deadline.

"Call the embassy."

Pulling out his mobile phone, the Canadian lieutenant who was on the military attaché's staff, pressed the speed dial button, calling up the embassy in New Delhi. The number was his boss's direct line, and he was at his desk, waiting for just this call.

"Sir, this is Coleman. It's time." He got an acknowledgement, and then hung up. "On the way," he said to Dayananda.

OC Red was dead calm now that things were ticking. The nerves and tension he had felt on the flight from Palaly were gone, replaced by a visual image of the whole operation. The airport map in front of him seemed to come alive, like a virtual reality chessboard, moving with all the separate sub-operations.

※

One by one, the four big Allison turboprops came to life, sending a cloud of dust roaring across the tarmac and turning the heads of Alpha and Bravo Teams. Conway could see the C-130H Hercules sitting five hundred metres away, its lights still off. He checked his watch, and saw that it was eighteen minutes to the deadline.

※

The two lights designating Foxtrot 3 and 4 still showed green on the panel in front of Dayananda, and he didn't bother raising his night binoculars to confirm the fact that Tango 5 was still in the Airbus's open doorway. Instead, he spoke to the Herky pilot.

"India from X-ray. Check?"

"Turning and burning, X-ray."

"Golf at Checkpoint Hotel."

As the pickup truck slowed to a halt at the intersection of taxiways-C and -H, the assault teams vaulted quickly over the side. There was still no talk, and within seconds everyone had formed up into their teams and were off the taxiway and into the dry hip-high grass. The pickup truck continued on its way, job complete.

Unclipping his SMG, Christofelsz led Charlie Team off at an angle, staying parallel to taxiway-H, instinctively using the raised asphalt as potential cover. There was no dramatic moment before he moved off, no eyeball contact with the others, no pep talk or brave words. Everybody just hitched up their kit and set off.

For Christofelsz's part, he whispered a quick barely articulate prayer, first to God, and then for good measure, to Michael the Archangel, the patron saint of the paratroops, hoping it would be understood.

Defend me as I defend my country. . .

He was followed by Charlie 3, carrying the ladder, then Charlie 4, with Charlie 2 bringing up the rear. The other two teams followed in identical formation with fifteen metres between teams.

"Charlie mobile," Christofelsz announced.

A minute later he heard, "Delta mobile," and then another minute later, "Echo mobile," as the other teams moved out.

The dry grass rustled deafeningly as they waded through it, dust rising around the black-clad figures before being whipped away by the breeze; and Christofelsz was thankful for his respirator.

Looking ahead, he could see Air Canada AC634 five hundred metres to the north, bathed in the orange-tinted airport lights, sharply outlined against the shadowed aviation fuel tanks beyond. Sliding the cocking handle of his MP-5A3 halfway back, Christofelsz checked the chamber again.

*

"Sir, the call is for you."

Chula Abenayake turned away from where he had been observing the hijacked plane through binoculars, and saw that the young Indian constable who had answered the phone was holding out the receiver to him.

"It is the Canadian embassy."

Abenayake grabbed the phone. "Hello?"

"Good evening, this is Brigadier Steve Tolson from the Canadian embassy in New Delhi. Is that the Sri Lankan hostage negotiator?"

"Yes, my name's Abenayake. Assistant Superintendent Chula Abenayake." The DFI negotiator tried to keep his tone calm, but he knew time was running out. This would be Ottawa's final decision.

"Superintendent, I have been authorized to inform you that Donald Fenster, our Minister of Foreign Affairs and International Trade, has agreed to resign. There will be a press conference in an hour, when the news will be released to the media. If the hijackers want confirmation, they'll have to extend the deadline until the news networks go on air with it—"

"Yes, colonel, thank you very much." Abenayake was talking fast now, knowing he needed to reopen negotiations with the hijack leader. "Excuse me, and good night."

Hanging up, he grabbed the headset and pulled it on, adjusting the lip mike. "Tower to Air Canada six three four, come in."

*

"Charlie at Checkpoint Nellie," Christofelsz reported in. He paused for a moment, then crouching low, raced across the sixty-metre wide main runway, his team following him.

Crossing open ground was always a tense moment, even though he knew that the darkness shielded them from the hijackers. It was an instinctive thing and, like all predators, he knew that as much as possible, a stalk must be carried out through cover. The fact that the sniper teams surrounding the plane would give him ample warning of any terrorist reaction was small comfort.

Leaving the other two teams to cross the runway, Charlie Team continued forward. There were fifteen minutes to the deadline.

*

Taking his eye away from the scope, and leaving the big rifle sitting on its bipod and butt spike, Foxtrot 3 rolled onto his left side and looked back towards the main runway. Raising the Sopolem OB44 night sight, his eye was drawn by the small dust cloud the assaulters had raised while approaching through the grass. They were now two hundred and fifty metres away, rushing across the runway in teams. It was lucky, he commented to his spotter, that the hijackers hadn't any night vision devices, though he doubted they'd be of any use in the bright lights that bathed the plane.

Getting back on the scope he saw that Tango 5 was still in the doorway designated Papa Red. The hijacker looked alert enough, but there was no sign that he was aware of the killers creeping up on him.

*

"Look, we have told you people, there will be no extension of the deadline," the negotiator heard Major Mahesh say. Abenayake had just told him of Ottawa's decision, but there had been a puzzling silence at the other end rather than jubilation. Now the hijack leader's voice dripped suspicion. "We must have some sort of proof before we can make any concessions."

"But you *will* have proof in an hour," argued Abenayake. "It's just a slight extension. It'll be on the news as soon as the press conference starts. Probably live. Why don't we use the time to discuss how you will hand over the hostages, and what I can do to help. Do you want to leave Madras by air or what?"

*

"Charlie at Checkpoint Alpha."

Dayananda was watching the Airbus through his binoculars, in particular the cockpit area. It was still dark. By now, he knew, the tower should be giving Tango 1 the good news. The next step in the negotiations would be the hostage handover and the hijackers' getaway. Hopefully, the discussions would be one more thing to occupy the hijack leader.

"All teams from X-ray. Comms check."

"Alpha."

"Bravo."

"Charlie."

"Delta."

"Echo."

"Foxtrot One."

"Foxtrot Two."

"Foxtrot Three."

"Foxtrot Four."

"Hotel."

"India."

"X-ray to all teams, stan' by, stan' by." Without lowering his binos, Balasuriya said, "Diversion one!"

*

In the cockpit of AC634, Balachandran had got to his feet, talking to the negotiator, knowing the man was lying. There were ten minutes to the deadline, and this would be just a distraction to divert the hijackers' attention from the assaulters. It was all out of the textbook. Now there would be two diversions from one direction followed by the actual assault from the other direction. Mahesh Balachandran had been trained from the same textbook.

He almost wished that this was real, that it could all end in an actual climatic firefight. He could teach those arrogant STF cops a thing or two.

The distant roar of aircraft engines made him walk forward to stand behind the pilots. He could see the lights of a plane moving in the darkness at the far western end of the airport. He could not make out much because there was a three-storey building in the way, but he was sure that this was diversion number one.

"Alagaran," he called out without turning from the cockpit window, "can you make out what that is?"

He pressed the Micro-Uzi into Captain Burnett's shoulder. The last thing he needed right now was for the pilots to get any heroic ideas and fuck up the story.

"Military plane moving towards the runway," answered Alagaran from the open doorway. "Some sort of transport."

Ignoring the negotiator's jabbering over the headphones, Balachandran started to answer Alagaran, telling him to keep his eyes open; but the next moment he saw blazing headlights round the corner of the three-storey building between him and the military aircraft. His brain registered two vehicles moving at high speed along the road that would take them across the Airbus' nose, between it and the fuel dump. Aha, diversion number two! Both were on the left, so that would mean the assault would come from. . .

*

"Foxtrot Three, Tango Five is on his feet and aware of India," said the Commando sniper as he watched Alagaran standing in the doorway with a pair of binoculars to his eyes. "I have a shot."

"Foxtrot Four has a partial on Tango Five."

"X-ray, all teams, stan' by, stan' by."

*

Still crouched atop their Defenders, Alpha and Bravo Teams watched the C-130H as it moved clear of its stand and onto taxiway-N. The pilot was holding down the brakes from time to time while simultaneously opening the throttle. The resulting cacophony was known as "blipping", and along with the Herky's landing lights, was causing a spectacular distraction.

"Diversion two!" Jan Conway heard in his earpiece, and just had time enough to tighten his grip on the roof rack before the driver gunned the Defender's engine and the vehicle shot forward with spinning tyres.

They had trained for this, but it was still frightening, and it took all of Conway's strength to hang on as the Defender rounded the cargo centre like a bat out of hell. Darting a glance over his shoulder, he noted with relief that the rest of his team were still in place, albeit clinging to the rack for dear life. Beyond, he had a momentary glimpse of the second Defender, headlights blazing on high beam.

Conway gritted his teeth, thankful for his gloves. Falling from a Land Rover and breaking his neck was not the way he wanted to go out.

*

Crouched in the grass at the edge of the tarmac wasteland, Eric Christofelsz watched Alpha and Bravo Teams racing down the road at breakneck speed. He grinned behind his respirator and Balaclava, estimating that the Defenders must already be touching a hundred and twenty kilometres per hour on the straightaway. They would reach the Airbus faster than anticipated.

"All teams, stan' by, stan' by."

Christofelsz placed a gloved palm on the gritty tarmac of the ramp, boots digging into the dusty earth between the grass blades. He trembled, wishing so much to be up and off, the waiting done. Looking over his shoulder, he got a terse nod from Charlie 3, the aluminium ladder tucked under an arm.

"Alpha at Checkpoint Oliver." Conway's voice was breathless, jarring with the Defender he was clinging to.

"Bravo at Checkpoint Oliver," said another Canadian accent almost simultaneously.

"All teams, stan' by, stan' by."

*

Conway was trying to keep an eye on the Airbus and also watch for the upcoming intersection at the southwest corner of the fuel storage area, but finally gave up on the plane, concentrating on holding on and gathering enough breath to make his radio calls.

The intersection was coming up fast, and Conway tightened his grip, already making the call. "Alpha at Checkpoint Mary."

He had barely got the words out of his mouth when the Defender heeled over on its suspension, sixteen-inch tires screeching, taking the ninety-degree turn towards the Airbus with no perceptible reduction in speed. Conway felt as if his shoulders were being torn from their sockets.

"Bravo at Check—"

"Diversion three!" he heard X-ray's voice crackle in his earpiece a second before everything went black.

*

Foxtrot 3 kept his scope steady on the open business class door. Strangely, Tango 5 wasn't watching the fast approaching Defenders. The hijacker was leaning out of the door, looking back along the plane's fuselage at the darkness beyond the tail. Towards the assault teams. Almost as if he knew, mused the sniper.

"Alpha at Checkpoint Mary," he heard the Canadian commander say, and the sniper was already reaching up over his scope.

"Bravo at Check—"

"Diversion three!"

Even as the entire airport winked into darkness, turned off by a commando standing by at the main power station, Foxtrot 3 was switching to night vision. The Simrad Optronics KN250 night sight mounted over his regular scope, gave the sniper's 12-power Schmidt & Bender a day/night capability, and the hijacker was now a dark green silhouette against the yellow-green light from behind him. The man was still leaning out of the door, peering into the darkness, and Foxtrot 3 exhaled slowly, settling the crosshairs on the terrorist's right pectoral muscle.

"X-ray to all teams, *Rama, Rama, Rama!*"

Foxtrot 3 squeezed the trigger, and the recoil and muzzle gases erased the scope image.

※

In his position atop one of the aviation fuel tanks, the Foxtrot 4 sniper fired simultaneously at the hijacker in the doorway. The man was hit by both bullets and crumpled sideways into the plane, his Micro-Uzi clattering to the tarmac.

Two hundred and fifty metres to Foxtrot 4's left, atop another tank, Foxtrot 1 – the sniper team commander – began firing into the cockpit. Ejecting the empty casing and slamming another home, Foxtrot 4 joined in, remembering to keep his aim high.

※

Balachandran yelled to Alagaran to clear the doorway, still watching the rapidly approaching vehicles. In the lights from the fuel storage area, he could see that the vehicles were Land Rovers, painted black, and there seemed to be dark shapes huddled on the roofs. *It's a diversion*, he told himself, *they'll go straight across our nose and the assault will come in from the right side.* He had better warn the team to get away from the starboard side doors. But he hesitated, watching the speeding Defenders.

As the two vehicles reached the corner of the fuel storage area, on Balachandran's left front, the world seemed to go black. For an irrational moment, Balachandran thought he'd gone blind, but then saw the glow of the instrument panel and realized what had happened.

The headlights of the Defenders were off too, and he imagined them racing on past in the darkness. But if they were a diversion, why had they switched off their headlights. Peering out of the cockpit windows, there was still enough ambient light outside for him to see two dark chunky shapes headed straight towards the plane, cutting diagonally across the tarmac. Eyes widening in instinctive fear, Balachandran realized that these were the assault teams, and not diversions. Not bad, he mused, admiring their plan in spite of himself, amused that they had actually gone to the trouble of a full assault plan. Oh well, a good training opportunity, he decided, turning away from the cockpit windows. Better get the team into cover before—

Then Balachandran heard Alagaran stumble and fall back into the forward galley. Excitement, he deduced, but it could be dangerous.

"Everyone down!" he yelled in Tamil, stepping through the cockpit door into the forward galley. "Assault coming in!"

Looking past the lavatory and down the empty business class, Balachandran slipped in Alagaran's blood. Dumbfounded he looked down at the body lying against the lavatory wall. There was blood everywhere; soaking into the carpet, trickling across the linoleum floor of the galley, painting the walls. Alagaran had been shot at least once in the throat, and it was a very messy wound.

What was going on? he screamed to himself. Had Alagaran shot himself accidentally when he fell? But there were no shots and the guns should have been safed and anyway Alagaran was very very good with guns so how could this—?

Beyond the doorway, the darkness seemed to swarm with movement, and Balachandran's eyes fought to adjust themselves. They were coming, the lions were here. He saw the glint of a ladder.

There was a snapping thud and something smashed into the door jamb, ricocheting past the hijacker's shoulder and long experience told Balachandran's unbelieving brain that it was a bullet even before he heard the echoes of the shot. And now he could

hear more shots from somewhere in the direction of the airport
buildings, and he realized that his ear canals, damaged years
previously, had been further traumatized by the constant landings
and takeoffs, and had now dimmed his hearing so much that he
had missed the shots that had killed Alagaran. It was some sort of
a trick, he told himself, stumbling backwards; they have betrayed
us. The fucking Sinhalese are trying to kill us and I should never
have trusted them but what do we do now—?

The door, the cockpit door, there was still a chance.
A chance to delay them, to get help, to explain. But something at
the back of Balachandran's mind told him that there would be no
time for explanations.

Diving back into the cockpit, he started to drag the
armoured outer door behind him, but was met by a hail of gunfire
from the front of the flight deck. Pressing himself to the floor,
halfway into the cockpit, he swung his Micro-Uzi to cover the
pilots. Where had they got guns from? Hadn't they been searched
and anyway pilots weren't authorized to carry guns at least not yet
anyway but maybe—

Then Balachandran realized that the pilots were huddled in
the foot wells beneath the instrument panel, and that the bullets
were punching through the windscreen. Snipers. Then even before
he could recognize that the fire had ceased, he heard the portside
window ripped away, and something came sailing in to bounce
onto the floor.

Grenade! Wrapping his arms around his head, eyes clenched
tight, Balachandran hurled himself back out of the cockpit. A
thunderous explosion and a concussive wave helped him on his
way, white light searing through his eyelids. He stumbled blindly
over Alagaran's body and into business class. There was just one
chance now, one chance to buy a few seconds of time.

*

Conway unclipped a flash-bang, running shakily after Alpha 4,
who was carrying the ladder. All thoughts of the harrowing ride

on the roof of the Land Rover replaced by the burning determination to be up the ladder and into the Airbus. On his left, he could see the shadowy shapes of Bravo Team heading for the plane's nose.

As the ladder was placed against the fuselage, Conway saw movement in the doorway above him and swung the MP-5A3 up but the target ducked out of sight. The Canadian could hear the echo of rifle shots rolling across the airport as the snipers went into action.

Clambering up the ladder, he felt it flex from the weight of the men behind him. Conway heard a flash-bang go off in the cockpit and knew that fast as he had been, Bravo Team had been faster. Tossing his own grenade over the lip of the doorway, he counted the seconds, going in right behind the explosion, almost falling over the body in the doorway, hearing Alpha 2 put a burst into the man. Conway pivoted right immediately, around the lavatory, knowing Bravo Team would clear the cockpit.

*

As the airport lights went off, Christofelsz rose to his feet in the darkness, his team and the others behind rising with him. He was already off and running before X-ray's command came over the net. Off to his left he heard the boom of a rifle and the screech of tires ahead. They could all hear the shots from the fuel dump now.

Christofelsz covered the hundred and twenty metres to the Airbus at a dead sprint, submachine-gun across his chest, the others following, running silently in their rubber-soled Danner boots. The plane loomed up like a huge monstrous bird in the darkness, cutting off the sky that glowed with the lights of Madras. The adrenalin pumping through his veins made the entire run seem like it was in slow motion to Christofelsz, the plane not getting any nearer no matter how hard he ran.

Finally he was in the gloom under the wings, no pausing now, past the main under-carriage, halting below the second door on the starboard side. He dropped to a crouch, covering Charlie 3 as he quickly placed the ladder against the fuselage. Charlie 4 raced up it unhesitatingly, and a subconscious part of Christofelsz's mind registered the loud detonations of flash-bangs from the cockpit. There was a second's pause as Charlie 4 put the strip charge in place and dropped down several rungs. Christofelsz pressed himself tight against the commando's back, feeling the weight of Charlie 2 against his own shoulders.

Go go go go go. . .

There was a loud crack as the strip charge blew, and Charlie 4 bolted up the ladder, giving Christofelsz a kick in the face for good luck. The burly commando grabbed the handle and wrenched the door open, the shattered lock giving way; and he swung clear of the ladder, hanging in midair from the door.

Bright light poured from the open doorway. *Go go go go. . .*

Christofelsz went up the ladder like a cat, his momentum letting him use just his legs, his hands grasping the shouldered MP-5A3, the mounted torch already on. As Christofelsz's shoulders came level with the bottom of the doorframe, Charlie 2 tossed the Haley & Weller E182 stun grenade over him and into the plane

Counting the seconds, Christofelsz went in, squeezing his eyes shut and pressing the side of his head into his hunched right shoulder to minimize the effects of the explosion. He was trained to overcome the massive disorientation caused by the flash-bangs, but the hijackers obviously weren't. Diving through the residual smoke, Christofelsz saw a hijacker on his knees in the amidships galley, hands pressed to his ears. The commando's submachine-gun was set to three-round burst, and he let the kneeling hijacker have the first one in the head. The massive hydrostatic force of the Bismuth rounds disintegrating inside the man's cranium made his skull balloon grotesquely before he keeled over.

"Down, down, down!" Christofelsz yelled in English, pivoting left and moving down the aisle towards the rear of the Airbus. "Stay in your seats!"

All around him, passengers were screaming, huddling in their seats, stunned by the explosions and the paralysing speed of the assault.

From his window seat, Colin Peters had watched in shock as Charlie Team stormed up the ladder to the door three rows in front of him, and had wisely ducked in time to avoid the effects of the explosion on his eyes. However, he still felt confused and disoriented by the horrendous decibel level of the detonations and, frozen in his seat, he now saw what looked like a scuba diver rush through the smoke, carrying a black submachine-gun and shouting at everybody to stay seated.

Ahead of him, Christofelsz could see Delta Team pouring into the plane, firing as they covered their angles. Concentrating on the aisle he was moving down, he saw an armed man break free of the smoke on the port side of the cabin, close to Delta Team's entry, stumbling blindly, shouting something.

"*Vedithiyand' epa! Vedithiyand' epa!*" the man screamed in Sinhalese. Don't shoot.

Christofelsz swùng his weapon unhesitatingly to cover the hijacker but didn't fire; not because the man was shouting in Sinhalese — Tamil terrorists often used the language to distract Sinhalese soldiers — but because it was a risky shot with panicky passengers in front of and behind the hijacker. From the corner of his eye he could see Charlie 3 moving down the opposite aisle, weapon levelled.

His bladder threatening to rebel against his control, Vijitha Dhampahana huddled lower in his seat, watching the frightening shape stalk down the aisle, gun pointing straight at him. Why was this man trying to shoot him? Hunching over, he looked back down the aisle in the opposite direction, and saw a hijacker approaching, also waving a gun. *Buddhu ammo*, quaked Vijitha, they'll shoot at each other and I'm in the middle. I don't want to die here. Maybe, he decided, if he could get across the aisle to the other side of the plane he would be safe. His knees shaking, he rose to his feet.

Christofelsz saw the passenger get up, blocking Charlie 3's shot, and cursed. The hijacker was still advancing, Micro-Uzi in one hand.

"*Indhaganing!*" Charlie 3 shouted in Sinhalese, pushing the passenger down, but Christofelsz knew there was no time.

He crouched to get a slight upward angle on the hijacker that would spare the passengers behind him, but before he could fire, the hijacker went face down, shot from behind by one of Delta Team. Another Delta Team member was advancing up the aisle on Christofelsz's side.

Christofelsz nodded and pointed his weapon straight up, and the other commando did the same.

"Blue clear," Christofelsz reported, turning to move back up the aisle, heading for the cockpit.

"Green clear," he heard someone say.

Temporarily deaf, dizzy from the massive shock to her ear canals, her eyesight only just returning to normal, Jennifer Jensen saw the black-clad man step over her and continue on his way. She was barely conscious, her left arm and side numb, and she could feel the blood soaking into her uniform. Jen-Jen had been in her jump seat on the starboard side, facing back down the aircraft, her back against the forward economy lavatory, and there had been no warning of the impending assault. She had heard explosions from the front of the plane and had been getting to her feet when the door next to her had been shattered. The explosion had blown Jen-Jen into the first row of passengers, and she now lay at their feet, fighting to stay conscious.

Christofelsz saw that the front end of economy as well as most of business seemed to have been cleared; but the Canadians of Alpha Team were clustered around the front of business class, guns pointed at the floor, looking as if they were about to open fire at someone on the ground, someone hidden by the seats.

As he got closer, Christofelsz saw that at some point, the twin seats in the centre of the front row had been removed. In its place was a rectangular opening in the floor, a steel access ladder leading down into the darkness. The Canadians were covering the opening with their weapons. He saw Conway take a CS gas canister from a pouch.

"What's going on?" Christofelsz asked.

"There's a hijacker down there in the hold," Conway replied. "Probably the leader. I'm gonna smoke him out."

"No, wait!" snapped Christofelsz. "If the bugger gets gassed he might blow himself up. We'll have to go in ourselves."

Conway looked at the Sri Lankan sceptically. Beyond the grenade taped to the business class galley window, they had found no explosives in place. Certainly nothing that could blow up the plane. But before he could argue, Christofelsz had tossed a flash-bang down the stairs, following it in himself.

The explosion still echoing in his ears, Christofelsz landed in the hold and, rolling badly to the right, came up in a crouch against the bulkhead, unbalanced, half kneeling and half sitting. The torch on his MP-5A3 cut through the smoke and pinned the shape of a man in its beam on the far side of the crew rest area. The man was crouched in a corner, his face scorched by the proximity of the flash-bang's detonation, and he was bleeding from his nose and ears, his bloodshot eyes staring blearily into the torch's light. He held his hands up in front of him, one clutching a Micro-Uzi, the other a grenade. In another corner, the twin seats from up above had been left leaning against the bulkhead.

"Waitaminute!" the man cried in Tamil-accented Sinhalese before Christofelsz could fire, and the commando now recognized the face of Tango 1, the hijack leader. "Grenade!"

Christofelsz could see that the pin had been pulled on the grenade. Could he kill him and get up the stairs before the grenade went off? He doubted it, and even if he did, there was no telling what else the explosion would set off. But why hadn't the terra thrown the grenade immediately, or opened fire? Was he trying to surrender? This was a Black Tiger, Christofelsz knew, and they didn't surrender.

"Do not shoot," Balachandran continued. "This is a black op and I am—"

Conway came diving headfirst through the opening, his big body coming down between the commando and the hijacker in what was intended to be a parachute landing fall, and Christofelsz saw Balachandran's staring eyes jump to the new threat, the Micro-Uzi following. The burst from the SMG hit Conway in midair and slammed him into the bulkhead.

Everything switched back to slow motion for Christofelsz, as he heard the air driven from Conway's lungs, the big Canadian tumbling limply to the floor. But Christofelsz was already coming up onto his knees, the submachine-gun aimed by instinct, the torch beam spearing the terrorist as he screamed inarticulately. Aiming over Balachandran's extended arms, he put a burst into the man's face, seeing his head snap back and hit the bulkhead, then as the arms dropped and cleared the body, two more bursts into the chest. The hijacker, still on his knees, slumped forward until the top of his ruined head touched the floor, and Christofelsz saw the grenade roll across the floor, stopping against the far bulkhead, caught in the angle between it and the seats.

Like a man in a nightmare, fleeing from some unseen horror but not quite escaping, Christofelsz hauled himself to his feet, mind racing. Dropping his weapon, he reached for Conway's still form, but gave up on it immediately. Christofelsz was a strong man, but he knew the Canadian soldier weighed over two hundred pounds, even without his assault kit, and there was no way he'd be able to get him up the stairs before the grenade went off.

Moving on autopilot now, the commando crossed the rest space in two bounding strides and grabbed the hijacker's body, pulling him upright. Holding the nerveless body in front of him as a shield, he dived headlong at the grenade.

The explosion hit him while he was still airborne, and he felt his body tumble through the air, shrapnel ripping through him. Everything began to go dark. He had lost his respirator, and could feel the floor against his cheek. His ears were ringing and he could taste blood. Christofelsz wondered how his parents would take the news. His only regret was that he wouldn't have the chance to buy the old man that beer.

CHAPTER 26

2315 LOCAL (1715 GMT) OPERATION SITA: Errol Seneviratne watched the dark shapes materialize like ghosts out of the darkness overhead. Crouched on the roof of the Canadian embassy, he had just been told that Operation *Rama* was already in progress, and he knew that Operation *Sita* would soon be underway as well. Errol held his breath as Alpha Team — the first of the assault teams — touched down together; smoothly. Unlike the SPIE rig that Errol Seneviratne and Tony Mendis had been hooked up to, Alpha was in STABO rig. The Stabilized Tactical Airborne Body Operations harness allowed the men to dangle four abreast instead of one above the other. While this meant that they needed a larger opening in jungle canopies or other vertical obstacles, it let a four-man team land together as a fighting unit and get into action faster than with the SPIE rig.

Alpha Team landed on the western slope of the roof and began to get into position quickly and quietly at the south-western corner, deploying their abseiling ropes.

Errol could hear the faint throb of the helicopter rotors as it moved away and was replaced by a second, bringing in Bravo Team. The sound of rotor blades didn't, however, seem to be causing any anxiety with the terras, and the snipers reported no unusual activity.

As Bravo Team touched down on the roof's east slope, Errol slipped quietly across to help them get into position. On the opposite slope, he knew, Tony would be doing the same with Alpha.

The four assaulters of Bravo were slipping out of the STABO harnesses as Errol made his way to the team commander.

"Anything new?" asked Bravo 1 — 2nd Lieutenant Ranjith Welgama — an anonymous dark shape, his face concealed behind a Balaclava and respirator, his query a whisper in Errol's earpiece.

Errol shook his head.

Donning their Danner boots, the team started to attach their abseiling ropes to the anchor cables Errol and Tony had stretched between the chimneys and the roof's corners. Normally, for such an assault, the roof tiles would have been removed in places where the abseiling ropes could be tied to the rafters, but with the terrorists occupying the floor below, there was too much risk of noise.

With a rustle of clothing, Charlie Team arrived.

*

"Alpha in position," came the call over the radio.

Major Sumindha Soysa, OC Blue, acknowledged the report and looked across at the group ops officer, now acting as 2/ic Blue. "Power?"

"Ready," the lieutenant replied. "We'll cut power to the whole street so that it'll look like a normal failure."

Soysa was already turning away, talking to his snipers, knowing that if the terras were as good as they seemed, they wouldn't be fooled.

"Foxtrot Three has Tango Four on Blue Zulu Two, unaware."

"Foxtrot Two has Tango Two on Green Zulu, unaware."

"Foxtrot One has no movement."

Soysa leaned back. Things were going like clockwork, and it had him worried. All journalists were being kept well back by the cops so that there would be no early warning of the assault. There had been no mechanical problems with the choppers, and the assault teams were almost in position. A perfectionist himself, Sumindha Soysa sometimes hated the uncertainties of combat, knowing from experience that not everything could be controlled.

Thirty years old and a Commando veteran of many years, Sumindha Soysa had served throughout the Northeast both in special operations and as a conventional infantryman. Commissioned a second lieutenant in the Gajabas in 1990, he had first gone into the Commandos three years later as a patrol team commander, losing twenty of his one-hundred and forty-five pounds during the gruelling selection process. Being a patrol team boss had given him little responsibility beyond the paperwork. For most of his time with the unit he had stood back and, showing a wisdom beyond his twenty-two years, had let his veteran NCOs run the team. Returning to the Gajabas two years later, to take over an infantry company, he had done well, using the practical leadership skills he had learned in the Commandos to good effect, and putting special forces behind him in the drudgery, frustration, and occasional terror of regular combat operations. Three years in various postings, a bullet in the stomach, and a slot in an int course later, he was surprised to be invited back to 2/CR as an assistant int officer. A year later, in 1999, Soysa had left the Commandos once more to take a staff course before joining the operations staff of the 551st Brigade. Another year had passed before the now senior captain returned to special operations, this time as the 2/ic of 1/CR's Bravo Group. Desperate to get out of staff and orderly room duties, Soysa had applied in 2000 for a six-month exchange posting to the British SAS. To his astonishment, he had been picked out of sixty three applicants and sent off to Hereford, the base of the legendary Special Air Service. In early 2001 Soysa had returned, after an exhilarating six months spent in Britain, Kuwait, and Belize, to take over the command of Delta Group, his predecessor having been killed when the Elephant Pass base was overrun. Soysa had been OC Delta since. Never married in spite of his dark good looks, he was absolutely dedicated to the Commandos, determined now to stay with them even if his career suffered, as he knew it inevitably would.

In spite of all his training and combat experience, Soysa had never participated in a real hostage-rescue mission before. Nevertheless he knew that things shouldn't be going this smoothly.

"Any changes on the bugs?" he asked the cluster of men monitoring the minicams and microphones hidden in the embassy's fireplaces.

Soysa got a series of headshakes in return.

"All teams, stan' by, stan' by."

*

Placing the soles of his boots firmly against the sloping roof tiles, Alpha 1 leaned back towards the rain gutter at the western edge of the embassy roof. He was still a metre up the slope so that the terra on the first-floor balcony would not glimpse him; his gloved left hand on the abseiling rope, the figure-of-eight descender attached to the front of his harness closed, locking him in place. A flick of his wrist would send him sliding over the edge. Unconsciously, the commando flexed his knees, bobbing with anticipation. *Stand by, stand by.* Leaning over, he checked that the abseiling rope was coiled smoothly into the canvas bag attached to his right leg, below the knee. This was so that the first assaulter on each rope could hurl himself over the edge without worry that a rope dropping down to the balcony ahead of him would alert a sentry. Next to Alpha 1, on his right, Alpha 3 was in an almost identical stance, his MP-5A3 held one-handed. Beyond the south-eastern corner, Alpha 2 and 4 were also poised and ready on the southern edge of the roof.

"Delta in position," the commando heard a voice say.

Alpha 1 was Staff Sergeant Wasantha Basnayake, and he was the oldest of the assaulters. At thirty four, 3 Patrol Team's sergeant, he was constantly fending off the old-age jokes of his comrades. A qualified close-quarter battle instructor, his team had been picked for the most crucial part of the operation, the securing of the banquet room and the hostages being held there. A fourteen-year veteran of the Commandos, Wasantha had seen action in every part of Sri Lanka, and been shot twice for his troubles while fighting both the Tamil terrorists and the communists.

It was warm beneath the Balaclava hood and the respirator, and Wasantha blinked savagely and cursed as sweat trickled into his eyes. Why the fuck couldn't they design a respirator that would allow a sweatband to be worn without breaking the seal? The Balaclava was supposed to soak up sweat from the brow, but the thin fireproof Neoprene seemed to absorb nothing.

Wasantha had worn the hood and respirator uncountable times in training, but the anticipation of action seemed to change everything. He thought momentarily of the first time he had worn a hood in combat. Then, like now, it had been both a shield and a mask, a psychological weapon as well as a defensive one. Wasantha wondered whether he'd always associate heat and sweat with combat. It had been back in 1988, just before he'd taken selection for the Commandos. A private in the Gemunu Watch, his unit had been based at Boossa on the southwest coast, close to the tourist beach town of Hikkaduwa.

Wasantha remembered sitting in the back of the Land Rover, sweating in his hood and OG overalls, the vehicle's headlights cutting through the blackness that lay over the paddies. Of course, he hadn't been sweating as much as the two guys lying at his feet. The two teenagers had been stripped to their underwear, their hands tied behind them with their own sarongs. They were blindfolded and pleading their innocence. Trembling, crying. Wasantha and the other soldiers had largely ignored them, smoking and chatting as they headed back to base. Only when the begging and pleading got too noisy had the occasional boot lashed out at the JVPers. Wasantha had tried not to look at them too closely, for he knew what their fate would be. There had been several rubber tyres stacked in the back of the Land Rover as well, and the prisoners could feel the treads pressing into their skin. They had thought the tires were for them, and had pleaded to be spared. Wasantha knew their pleas were useless, but there would be a time ahead of them when they would wish they had been killed tonight.

Wasantha now remembered how the communist prisoners had been handed over to the int team for interrogation; the way the warrant officer dressed in jeans and a T-shirt had casually stubbed out a cigarette on the shoulder of one of the prisoners, like an unspoken welcome to the terrors ahead. There had been a shriek, but then Wasantha's attention had been taken up with dragging the three prisoners that the int team had handed over in exchange for the two teenagers. These men had to be dragged because they could no longer walk. They had been in Army custody for awhile and had served their purpose.

Later, standing by the roadside, seeing the lights of the small town a few hundred metres away, Wasantha felt no pity for the three men. He felt no hate for the terrorists, but he felt no remorse either. They were merely the enemy, and though they were Sinhalese just like him — the only distinction their race won them being that they were officially documented as "subversives" and not "terrorists" — it didn't matter. Back then Wasantha had had no experience of the Tigers, and the JVP was the only enemy he had known.

After the prisoners had been shot, the soldiers had stood at a distance and smoked, waiting to make sure the tires were burning well, and that no one tried to remove the bodies. Wasantha remembered now that he had been happy the wind hadn't been blowing in their direction.

"Bravo in position."

Wasantha looked up to the roof's spine and could dimly make out Tony's silhouette as he checked the anchor ropes.

"Charlie in position."

"All teams, stan' by, stan' by!"

Tony was now moving over between the chimneys, getting the grenades ready.

"Foxtrots from Charlie One," Wasantha whispered into his mike, "where's Tango Two?"

"Between Green Zulu Alpha and Bravo, static."

That meant that the terra on the southern leg of the L-shaped balcony, outside the banquet room, was standing between the second and third French windows. Alpha 2 and 4 would drop down on either side of the sentry, and Wasantha hoped the man would be dead before then.

"Stan' by, stan' by!"

*

On the opposite side of the roof, Lieutenant Ranjith Welgama — Bravo 1 — rocked on his rope, looking back over his shoulder. He was the 3 Patrol Team boss, though that was unimportant on this operation as he was doing the job of a corporal, commanding a four-man assault group. The patrol teams, each with twenty-four men, were largely irrelevant during the HR tour, except for administrative or disciplinary purposes, the entire hundred-man Delta Group having been split into Red and Blue Teams.

Ranjith wondered if it would be a trap, every assaulter's nightmare; the terras waiting with weapons cocked. He heard a soft cough from below, and then a sniff. Ranjith heard the rustle of movement from the sentry, and didn't want to even whisper to the snipers for fear of being heard.

"Foxtrot Three to Bravo," a member of the sniper team on the east side of the embassy said into his ear. "Tango Four mobile north. Still unaware."

The sniper must be psychic, decided Ranjith, smirking behind his hood.

He tried to relax, leaning into the rope to take the pressure off his knees. Every muscle and sinew in his body trembled, like a thoroughbred racing horse at the gate. *Stand by, stand by.* There couldn't be more than a couple of minutes more till the electricity was cut. He wanted to look at his wristwatch but didn't want to take his hand off the rope in case he missed the 'Go'. His gloved right thumb checked to make sure the submachine-gun's safety was on. The last thing they needed now was a negligent discharge.

On Ranjith's left and right, assault troops hung poised along the edge of the roof, like perched crows. Right next to him was Bravo 3, a frame charge slung over a shoulder; further away, on his right, Charlie 1 and 3; and further still, close to the northeastern corner of the roof were Bravo 2 and 4. Directly in front of Ranjith, above him, but close enough to touch, were the backs of Charlie 2 and 4, ready to go the moment Bravo cleared the edge. Ranjith was reminded of a team of formation skydivers waiting to exit their aircraft, and as with skydivers, the Commando assaulters needed to have their timings down to fractions of seconds.

There was no crosstalk between the assaulters, and the only voices on the radio net were those of the snipers and spotters monitoring the sentries.

Ranjith bobbed quickly like a boxer, making sure no part of his kit rattled. *Stand by. . . stand by, stand by.*

Then X-ray's voice boomed across the net, crackling in thirty earpieces. "Stand by, all teams. . . Decoy one, Decoy one! All teams, stand by, stand by!"

*

In the communications centre directly below Alpha Team, Devini Sundaralingam was sprawled on the carpet in front of the bank of television sets, each of the half-dozen screens tuned to a different channel showing local and international news. She was watching the programmes more out of boredom than any interest.

The search for Donald Fenster's plane was continuing but had only turned up some scattered debris. So far no bodies had been discovered. While the Australian and Indonesian authorities were still reluctant to speculate on terrorism being the cause of the jet's disappearance, the news anchors and various military and terrorism "experts" being interviewed seemed eager to suggest either a hijacking or a bomb. With producers keen to see action that would keep viewers glued to their screens, anchors and journalists pressed politicians and diplomats both in Canada and Sri Lanka for details of planned crackdowns on the LTTE and ERA. News networks that had previously criticized the two countries for their heavy-handed tactics, now seemed to smell blood, gleefully suggesting that immediate action was imminent against both the hijackers of AC634 and the occupiers of the embassy. Devini knew, however, that the rape and execution of the Canadian spy had a lot to do with this change of attitude. The media, fickle and contradictory as ever, while seemingly shocked and horrified at the rape and killing of a westerner, continued to voice the demands of interviewed talking heads that the UN Security Council intervene in Sri Lanka for the sake of Tamil human rights. At the same time, most of the western electronic media was also criticizing India for what was termed "an escalation of tension" in the region.

They were also running endless interviews with members of the public — especially Canadians and Americans — who had watched the now infamous *BBC World* broadcast, itself destined for the television journalism hall of infamy, alongside with the Rodney King tape. Some of those interviewed had said that they were considering suing *BBC* for airing unsuitable materiel that had caused viewers psychological trauma.

The idea that an overweight Canadian, sitting in front of a TV with a beer and a bag of chips, could be psychologically traumatized amused Devini.

She was trying to relax her body totally, even though her brain stayed alert. She had taken the first of the Dexedrine an hour previously, along with some espresso she'd discovered in the pantry, and this ensured she kept sharp. She knew she would have to continue taking the speed at regular intervals until the assault came. She also knew that boredom rather than fatigue would be her greatest enemy.

There had been regular phone calls from the police, asking for Devini to name a new negotiator, pointing out that Donald Fenster was no longer available. Devini had continued to claim it was all a Canadian trick, and she had put up a front in spite of the fact that she knew the authorities were not fooled. They would have woken up to the fact by now that the embassy was only bait to lure the Canadian minister to his death. Nevertheless, the game had continued, with the police trying to strike a deal with her, offering free passage in exchange for the hostages. Devini had refused, reiterating that the prisoners would be executed when the deadline was reached. Each phone call had been progressively more tense and, for the police, increasingly frustrating.

Devini knew that it wouldn't be long before the limit of patience was reached and the operation turned over to the Army; if that hadn't been done already. She wondered whether she should kill another hostage just to move things along, but then decided that she was in no hurry. Though she had already accepted her impending martyrdom, there was no rush. When the time came she wouldn't hesitate, but for now every moment of what was left of her life was to be savoured.

A breaking news item on *CNN* brought her attention back to the TV screens, and she turned up the volume on that particular set. A journalist at the Madras airport was claiming that gunshots could be heard from the direction of the hijacked Air Canada plane. The screen filled with a grainy green picture, and Devini could just make out the jutting shapes of several aircraft against the sky, but not much else.

At that moment the communications room was plunged into darkness, and Devini scrambled to her feet. This was it! She scrabbled on the nearby table for the mobile phone and the NVGs.

*

The commandos were already in position, backs hunched and heads bowed, their hands cupped in readiness. As the electricity to Gregory's Road was cut off at the Electricity Board substation, Delta Team used the bowed backs of several national guardsmen as springboards, clambering up and over the four-metre-high wall that fronted the embassy grounds. This section of the wall was shielded from the embassy itself by the generator shed, and in the preceding hours the outward-curving spiked steel railing and tangled razor wire atop the wall had been quietly removed. There was a two-metre-wide alley between the generator shed and the wall, overgrown with grass and small bushes, and the four assaulters of Delta dropped quietly into it; or rather, they tried to do it quietly.

Delta 1 and 2 were the first to hit the ground, and it was one of them who tripped the transparent monofilament wire strung across the alley, six inches above the ground and hidden by the long grass. It was never discovered which one of them made the fatal error, but what was certain was that the trip wire was hooked around a bent nail that had been hammered into the boundary wall, the wire running vertically for another ten inches to an empty fruit tin that had been nailed upside down to the wall. The tin was hidden by creepers that covered most of the wall's surface, and inside it was a smooth, round HE grenade, its pin removed, the grenade precariously held in position by the pressure of its striker lever pressing against the inside of the tin. The tug of the trip wire that was tied to it, pulled the grenade free of the tin and released the striker lever.

The snap and fizz of the shortened fuse igniting was so unexpected that the commandos didn't react for those crucial two seconds. The explosion, confined to the narrow space killed Delta 3 instantly and sent shrapnel ripping into Delta 4 legs. The entire team was knocked flat by the thunderous crack.

"Delta is down, Delta is down," managed the team commander, shakily trying to gather his wits, staring in shock at the black splashes of blood on the walls of the shed and in the grass as he tried to report over the net. "We have casualties

*

"Golf from X-ray," OC Blue snarled into his mike, his mind racing, strangely relieved that his earlier pessimism and paranoia had proved correct, and now hoping that there were no more unpleasant welcomes waiting for his men, "go go go go!"

There was no chance of surprise now. The hope that a terra would come out to switch on the generator could now be tossed away. There would be no easy entry, and he hoped the reserve Golf Team could get in to secure the ground floor in time.

"All teams," Major Soysa commanded, "*Sita, Sita, Sita!*"

*

Fuckfuckfuck. Foxtrot 3, the sniper on the eastern side of the embassy building saw Tango 4, on the second floor balcony, whirl and duck at the sound of the explosion, and he knew that something had gone tits up in the Delta assault. The exchange over the radio confirmed it, and the sniper didn't even flinch as he heard the roar of a diesel engine and then the crash as the big yellow Mitsubishi excavator smashed down the main gates.

"Fox Three Bravo has movement at Blue One One," the spotter snapped.

A corner of the sniper's brain registered that his partner was referring to the corner window on the first floor, overlooking the driveway.

"All teams, *Sita, Sita, Sita!*" screamed his earpiece.

There was a burst of submachine-gun fire from the embassy, but he didn't move.

"Tango at Blue One One," said the spotter unnecessarily. "Ah'm taking him."

There was a loud crack from the spotter's G-3SG/1, but Foxtrot 3 ignored it, still trying to get a bead on his designated terra, who by now had disappeared behind the balcony parapet. The commando saw a flash of movement at the edge of his scope image and knew it was Bravo and Charlie teams coming off the roof. He also knew that he had buggered up his task.

But even now he was still trying to decipher what he had seen in the instant the terra had dived for cover, like a photoflash image registered on his brain in the green underwater picture of the night sight. The hood of Tango 4's sweater falling back, a glimpse of projecting alien-like eyes beneath the bill of the baseball cap.

"Fox Three to all," he shouted into his mike, trying to get through the chatter of all the teams and the command staff on the net, "the Tangos have NVGs! I repeat, the Tangos have NVGs!"

*

Covering his lip mike with one hand, Soysa turned to yell for his 2/ic to get the cops to turn the searchlights on, but the younger officer was already on the air, giving him a thumbs-up as he talked.

*

Like all the other assaulters, Bravo 1, Lieutenant Ranjith Welgama, who was on the east side of the roof, heard the explosion that followed the blackout, and like the others he cursed when he heard Delta 1 say his team was down. That could mean deaths, or at the very least serious injuries.

Ranjith bounced on his toes, slipping off the safety catch on his submachine-gun. *Stand by, stand by. . .* All around him, the others were rocking and swaying rhythmically, waiting for the word. *Stand by, stand by. . .*

"All teams, *Sita, Sita, Sita*!"

Go go go go go. . .

Without conscious thought he bounced down the slope and over the edge of the roof, beginning the four-metre descent that was more of a controlled fall down to the balcony below. The four men of Charlie Team followed Bravo, kicking hard, arcing out into space to clear the second floor balcony and reach the one on the first floor.

In the second he was airborne, the rope hissing through his gloved left hand, Ranjith's eyes and submachine-gun were already questing downwards to cover Tango 4, who should have been dead by now. But instead of a corpse, Ranjith glimpsed a crouching figure wearing NVGs. *Fucking ambush!* his mind screamed at him, hearing the ripping chatter as Tango 4 triggered his MP-5K. Bullets cracked past Ranjith and then he thudded onto the balcony, falling into a crouch and bringing up his own submachine-gun, knowing it was too late, hearing voices yelling and chattering in his earpiece. Then the world turned dazzling white and the night seemed burn away in high-watt revelation. Ranjith saw Tango 4 raise a hand to his now blind NVGs, firing the *Kurz* one-handed and sending bullets tearing into the windows on the commando's left. Squeezing down on the trigger, Ranjith sent a three-round burst into the terra's chest, knocking him over backwards, his legs tangled under him. Standing up, Ranjith put two more bursts into the man's head, sending a fan of blood and bone matter spraying across the balcony, then turned to see Bravo 3 tape the frame charge over one of the windows leading into the cultural attaché's office.

At the far end of the balcony, Bravo 2 and 4 had found one of the French windows opening into the library ajar, and were already piling in. The thunderous detonations of flash-bangs that had been dropped down the chimneys rent the night.

Hearing the explosions ring through the building, Devini Sundaralingam dropped her phone — the rest of her team would have their hands full — and cocked her MP-5K. Heading for the comms room door that led out onto the main corridor, she stopped short as she heard more explosions — and this time, breaking glass — from across the corridor. The soldiers were coming in from the eastside windows, over the balcony. But how, she wondered. There had been no warning from Jegen and Preethi who were covering the front yard. And there had been no sound of the helicopters that would have betrayed a roof assault.

Opening the door cautiously, she looked out into the dark corridor that glowed green in her NVGs. She could see smoke creeping under the locked library door at the far end. Smoke or tear gas she told herself, or maybe both. She could hear movement in the cultural attaché's office directly opposite, and she took out a grenade.

Then there was the boom of a shotgun and she saw the library door open, a dark figure stepping through. Raising the *Kurz* she fired a short burst and dived back into the comms room, unsure whether she had hit anything.

She considered moving through the far door into the hallway that led to the landing. She could get down the stairs and hold it against all attackers. Long enough for Sujeevan and Banu to kill the prisoners. But not against these soldiers, she finally decided, they would be too fast and well trained. They'd catch her in a pincer movement, cut her off and kill her. No, better to pin down one of the attacking groups and make a last stand in this room.

Crossing quickly to the far door, she made sure it was locked, and then ran back to her post in time to hear another shotgun blast, very close now. Slinging her *Kurz* around her neck, she took out a fragmentation grenade and pulled the pin, holding it in her right hand as she flung open the door with her left.

She was confronted by a demonic sight that would have shocked someone untrained to expect it. The door to the cultural attaché's office was hanging on its hinges, its lock blown away by a solid steel Hatton round, and a black alien-like figure was framed in the doorway, revealed to her in the green light of her NVGs, its huge oval eyes flat and dark, black gloved hands pointing a black gun at her. From behind the figure, CS gas — Devini felt it sting her eyes and burn at her throat — billowed out into the corridor. A torch mounted over the figure's weapon sent its beam cutting through the smoke.

Devini flung the grenade at the soldier and saw it strike him in the chest and fall to the floor. As if it was all in slow motion, she saw the figure throw itself backwards, even as she was swinging the comms room door shut, a burst from the man's SMG punching through the heavy wood and insulation of the door as she dropped to the carpet. The grenade went off, and she knew it was too close even before she felt its fragments rip through the door and hit her in the leg and left side.

*

The reserve Golf Team clung like maniacs to the big Mitsubishi excavator as it ploughed through the embassy gates, the steel dozer blade it had been fitted with held high. The gate buckled and gave under the diesel monster, and they roared up the driveway. The red and white striped barrier outside the guardhouse snapped like a toothpick, and Golf almost cheered. This was like a bad action movie.

Golf 4 was in the driving seat, and increasing speed, he sent the excavator into a lumbering turn towards the generator shed, cutting the corner and destroying a low hedge of bougainvillea with its huge tyres.

A burst of SMG fire came towards them from one of the upper floors of the embassy, and a couple of bullets spattered the Mitsubishi's cab roof but did no further harm.

There were several cars parked outside the generator shed, and Golf 4 was showing no signs of slowing down as he bore down on them.

"*Stop!*" bellowed Golf 1, crouching behind the cab with the other two members of his team and hanging on for dear life. But there was so much chatter on the net that he wasn't sure if Golf 4 could hear him.

It didn't matter much either way, because the excavator didn't stop until the dozer blade crunched into the first car, lifting it up and smashing it into the next one. The Mitsubishi's huge cleated tyres bit into the wreckage and finally ground to a halt.

Jumping to the ground, Golf 1 ran past the excavator, giving Golf 4 the finger as the commando dragged himself out of the cab. SMG up and ready, Golf 1 ran in a half-crouch, staying close to the embassy and ducking under a window, approaching the door to the driver's common room at an oblique angle. A burst of fire from his right, beyond the cars, brought him to an abrupt stop and he levelled the MP-5A3. But the bullets had been fired into the embassy door, and he relaxed as he saw a commando peer around the generator shed and wave.

From the size of the guy's shoulders, Golf 1 knew that it was Delta 1. He didn't seem to be injured, and from the way his head was slightly moving, Golf 1 knew the man was talking to him. But the chaos on the net was still too bad for him to understand anything.

Giving up, Golf 1 tugged off his respirator, relieved at the gush of cool night air.

"*What?*" he yelled to Delta 1, flattening his back against the side of the embassy, staying away from the door in case a grenade was tossed out.

Delta 1 also pulled off his respirator, and Golf 1 could now see that there was blood on the commando's face.

"There's a bugger in there!" Delta 1 shouted. "An' they have NVGs!"

Golf 1 turned and nodded at his team, pulling his respirator back into place. Golf 4 moved away from the building, covering the square opening in the door where the single pane of glass had been shattered by gunfire. Golf 3 crept up and placed a frame charge against the door. He pulled the fuse and everyone scurried back. The explosion blew the door in and Golf 2 chucked a flashbang in and followed it with a CS canister.

Golf 1 went straight through the doorway, torch cutting through the pale smoke, and moved right, while Golf 2 went left. The torch beams triangulated the room and revealed it was empty. A closed door stood tauntingly on the other side of the room.

Golf 3 came in and put three Hatton rounds into the door's lock and hinges, the boom of the shotgun deafening in the room. Golf 1 pulled the door off its frame and there was a yell of "*Grenade!*" in his earpiece, somehow cutting through the chatter.

Golf 1 propelled himself backwards, still holding the door, using it as a shield, and felt the blast knock him off his feet. Sliding the pitted and smoking door aside, he sat up, thankful that the door connecting the driver's common room to the hallway beyond was one that opened towards them. An assaulter crashing through the door would have had the booby-trap go off at his feet.

More flashbangs and Golf 2 and 4 went piling through the doorway. Up on his knees, still shaky, Golf 1 heard automatic fire and saw Golf 2 go down.

As he got to his feet, Golf 1 heard the rumble of an explosion from the floor above, more powerful than a frame charge or flash-bang, and dust drifted down from the ceiling to mingle with the CS gas and the smoke from smouldering carpet and curtains that had been set alight by the stun grenades.

Fuck, they've blasted the hostages, he cursed.

*

Up above, Charlie Team had dropped past the second floor balcony where Bravo Team was killing Jegen, swinging through the glare of the spotlights and onto the first floor balcony outside the ambassador's office. They had been told it would be unoccupied, but were taking no chances; they'd all heard the warning that there was a terra in the corner room. While Charlie knew that X-ray had a view of the ambassador's office through the minicam and, theoretically could warn them of any terras entering the room, the increasing chatter on the net was blocking any clear transmissions. A frame charge was used on one of the French windows, sending broken glass scything across the room. Flash-bangs were tossed in and then the team went straight in, weapons ready. Nothing.

The ambassador's private bathroom, opening off the office, was duly checked and, like the main room itself, was found to be empty. CS gas was billowing out of the fireplace, the result of the canisters that Echo Team had chucked down the chimneys. The door leading into the rest of the building proved, however, a temporary obstacle as it was locked. Hatton rounds were used to demolish the lock and hinges and Charlie 1 — Corporal Gamini Suraweera, a recent arrival in the Commandos — remembered many deadly years clearing Tiger booby-traps in the Northeast and ordered rope to be attached to the door, yanking it free of the frame from a relatively safe distance.

There were no booby-traps, and Charlie 2 stuck his head into the corridor, only to pull it hastily back as a submachine-gun sent rounds blazing down from the doorway at the far end. Apparently the snipers had not hit the terra in the corner room — the one belonging to the murdered senior visa officer, Gamini Suraweera remembered.

Charlie Team rolled two CS canisters down the length of the corridor, and under cover of the smoke, leapfrogged to the landing where a hallway led off to the left. Two commandos fired short bursts while the other two moved past the closed doors on the main corridor's right side. The door to the visa officer's room — from where the gunfire had come — was now shut, and Charlie was about to clear the other rooms leading off the corridor, when a massive explosion almost knocked them off their feet. It had come from the banquet room, and they all realized, with a sinking feeling, that the mission had gone badly wrong.

*

There had been a few heartbeats of silence on the net as the teams jumped off, and then the chatter had begun as they broke in and made contact with the Tangos. OC Blue was trying to make sense of it all, staying quiet, knowing the team commanders would have their hands full. Even without the radio Sumindha Soysa could hear the thunder of flash-bangs and the chatter of automatic fire from the next building. But then a loud explosion drowned out the other sounds and left a momentary silence on the net. They had lost both audio and visual links to the banquet room. Soysa forgot his earlier determination to stay quiet and shouted into the mike, demanding to know what was happening. There was no clear answer as the crosstalk began again with vengeance, strained voices snapping back and forth, gasping, panting, cursing.

Giving up, Soysa turned to his 2/ic. "I can't make out a ball an' no one can hear me. Get on the bloody phone and' tell Decoy One to put the embassy lights back on."

"The spots are already on, no?" pointed out the lieutenant.

"Not the bloody spots, the *inside* lights!"

*

On the second floor, up above, Ranjith Welgama also heard the explosion, but was too busy cursing and checking his wounds to give a fuck. He had only just got the door shut on the terra bitch's grenade when it had gone off. Not fast enough, though. Some of the shrapnel had penetrated the door and hit him in the lower body. Luckily, the body armour had saved his stomach and — thank Jesus, Allah, Buddha, and all the other fucking gods — his balls, but his legs had been spattered and were oozing blood.

Bravo 3 had the door open again and was lying flat, putting single rounds through the comms centre door.

Ranjith tried to get Bravo 2 and 4 — who should have cleared the library by then — on the radio to find out if they could flank the comms centre, but X-ray and the command group were yelling blue murder, trying to find out what the explosion was and what had happened to the hostages.

Ranjith gave up and got to his knees, knowing they had to get out of this room. A second grenade could come sailing across the corridor at any moment. Scrambling to his feet, he dived headfirst over Bravo 3, clearing the corridor and slamming his full bodyweight against the comms centre door, hoping fervently that the terra hadn't had time to barricade it. And that she wasn't waiting on the other side, SMG levelled.

The door wasn't barricaded and crashed open, sending Ranjith tumbling awkwardly into the comms centre. He rolled frantically, trying to get away from the doorway that would be an instant target for anyone in the room. He quartered the comms centre, his torch picking out shattered radio equipment, computers and television screens.

Ranjith saw movement on the far side of the room and a muzzle flash. He fired instinctively, pushing the MP-5A3 out in front of him, holding it double-handed in a modified Weaver stance, heard bullets thud into the carpet in front of his face.

Behind him, Bravo 3 came piling in.

*

Devini had only just managed to roll away from the door, her leg and side burning, when the semi-automatic fire began to punch through the already riddled wood. One round severed the sling of her MP-5K, and she had no time to retrieve the weapon as it fell. She drew her Makarov pistol as she back-pedalled for the door opening onto the hallway, hoping she could get out before the soldiers stormed the comms centre.

Hands shaking, she had just unlocked the door when the one on the opposite side of the room exploded inwards, a black shape hurtling in and rolling across the carpet.

Pointing the pistol, Devini blazed off four rounds before the world seemed to explode with white fire.

CHAPTER 27

Like all the other commandos, Staff Sergeant Wasantha Basnayake — Alpha 1 — had mentally flinched at the sound of Delta Team tripping the booby-trap. He heard the team commander's shaky voice and the yelled order for Golf Team to go, but he shut it all out, his eyes scanning his men as they waited on their lines on both sides of the roof's southwest corner.

Wasantha took a step back, knees bent, ready to push off, and the others followed his lead. *Stand by, stand by. . .* He was looking over his shoulder now, down into the blackness, the balcony still out of sight, hoping the Foxes would take care of the sentry.

"All teams, *Sita, Sita, Sita!*"

The four commandos kicked off the roof together, falling backwards through the darkness, their ropes keeping them upright and stable.

Still in the air, they didn't see Sujeevan drop to a crouch, swinging his *Kurz* upwards. But this balcony had a wrought iron railing instead of a stone parapet, and provided no cover. The terrorist was hit between the shoulder blades by Foxtrot 3 and went down like a sack of rice.

Wasantha heard flash-bangs go off inside the banquet room, and then he was slowing his descent, landing on the balcony in a crouch. The concussions of the stun grenades set the drapes in the room flapping, confirming to Wasantha what the snipers and the cameras had revealed, that one of the French windows facing him — the one on the far left — was open. Leaving the fire axe he was carrying where it was, clipped to his belt, he slipped off the safety on his MP-5A3, jabbing a gloved finger at the open window for Alpha 3's benefit.

Alpha 3 ripped the curtain aside, Wasantha covering him, and tossed in a flash-bang. The detonation and Wasantha's entry were simultaneous.

*

Banu had been daydreaming of the senior visa officer's buttocks when the electricity to the embassy was cut. He had been remembering how hot she had felt when he had entered her. Sitting on the big banquet table, he had squirmed, feeling the beginnings of an erection, imagining he could still feel a faint stickiness on his penis. He had heard that many white women had AIDS and he hoped he hadn't caught it from the visa officer. Well, he told himself, he'd never get the chance to find out.

Banu was twenty-seven years old, and had been a Tiger since he was fifteen. He had killed more people than he could remember, mostly Sinhalese and some Muslims, but also Tamils. It didn't bother him as to who they were, knowing they were all enemies of Tamil Eelam, enemies of the Leader.

Banu had never really had sex with a woman. What they had done to the Canadian woman couldn't be called that. Rather than enjoying it, he had been fearful of being unable to perform under the scrutiny of the camera. He had been involved in a rape once before, when he was seventeen and his unit had attacked a Sinhalese border settlement. Though it had been ten years ago, he still remembered it in detail, the smell of sweat and fear, the screaming teenage girl being held down as his squad took turns.

But that wasn't sex either. Even with Rachel it hadn't really been sex. Not *really*, he told himself. It wasn't real unless the woman was willing and you were able to put it inside. Rachel may have been willing, but she hadn't let him enter her, prizing her virginity far too highly, like most Tamil girls, and Banu had had to be satisfied with climaxing between her dark, pressed-together thighs.

He shook his head at the folly of it. Rachel, a Black Tiger like Banu, had been governed by the hypocritical Puritanism imposed on the LTTE by its leaders. Leaders who seemed to exercise their right to pleasure without criticism. Forbidden to marry or have sexual relationships without higher authority — authority seldom given — most Tigers stole what pleasures they could while the big shots turned a blind eye. His only sexual encounter with Rachel had been that once, the night she left for the reconnaissance mission to Trinco. Even years later, Banu wondered whether at the moment of her death she had ever regretted not having slept with him.

Already unnerved by his thoughts, the sudden darkness caused by the loss of electricity, made Banu jump to his feet and toss the half-smoked cigarette into the fireplace. He was reaching for the NVGs he had left within reach on the banquet table, when the explosion of a grenade in the front yard made him twitch nervously. He instantly knew that someone had tripped a booby-trap, and that someone had to be an attacker.

Finding the NVGs, he pulled them closer and switched them on, the battery-operated hum indicating it was warming up. He slipped the MP-5K's fire selector to semi-automatic, bracing the end of the stockless submachine-gun's receiver against his hip as he drew back the cocking handle with his left hand, checking the chamber by feel with his right forefinger. When Banu released the handle, letting the return spring slam the bolt back home, the smoothly metallic clickCLICK brought a whimper of fear from the prisoners. He heard the rustle of movement and pointed the weapon at the dark mass of huddled hostages.

"Quiet!" he snapped in English. "Don' move!"

The clunk of the first flash-bang landing in the fireplace made him whirl, scrabbling for the NVGs. Banu was facing the stun grenade at a distance of just a metre when it went off. The concussion and the blast of light knocked him flat, and it was only iron discipline and long training that brought him back to his knees, almost totally blind, both eardrums ruptured.

What little vision he had left was defeated by the blackness that plunged back into the room and by the CS gas that made his eyes stream and his stomach retch. Vomiting, he didn't hear the screams of the terrified and stunned hostages, or Sujeevan dying on the balcony outside, never saw the dark shapes that descended alongside the still kicking body of the sentry.

Fighting the effects of the gas, his submachine-gun lost somewhere in the confusion, Banu turned instinctively towards the hostages, climbing to his feet and lunging forward, pulling the lanyard at his waist, setting the fuse on the explosive-packed vest he was wearing.

His senses already overwhelmed by the first barrage of explosions and CS gas, Banu barely felt the concussions of the flash-bangs that came hurtling in from the two ends of the balcony.

*

Wasantha came through the French window with his submachine-gun up and ready to fire, eyes squinting, and shoulders hunched to protect his ears from the flash-bangs. Through the disorienting explosions and the swirling smoke, he saw a figure moving diagonally across the room and he instinctively knew what was happening.

Wasantha Basnayake had seen that posture before. In 1996, he had been part of the CO's bodyguard during a visit to Jaffna of the then Minister of Housing and Construction, Nimal Siripala de Silva. Escorting the CO out of the Jaffna town hall to the minister's waiting motorcade, Wasantha had had a grandstand view of a racing Tiger suicide bomber. The man had only been stopped from throwing himself at the waiting vehicles by the equally suicidal intervention of a military policeman. Gunning his dirt bike, the corporal had ridden the bomber down, dying in the explosion that had sprayed shrapnel across the VIPs. The minister had walked away with enough scratches to give a heroic battlefield interview on the evening news, but that single glimpse of the suicide bomber had stayed imprinted on Wasantha's mind: the scurrying legs, the crouching body — like a rugby player moving in to tackle an opponent.

Aiming instinctively, knowing he was going to die, but not caring, adrenalin pounding through his veins, Wasantha squeezed the trigger repeatedly, sending three-round bursts across the banquet room.

The charging terrorist staggered and tottered to his left as the 9-mm bullets hammered into him, but still kept moving forward.

Wasantha's vision was like a tunnel, the respirator's eyepieces preventing peripheral vision, but he saw a second torch beam cut through the smoke on his right as Alpha 2 came in firing.

Hit from two sides, the terra pulled up short, his body riddled, and Wasantha saw the man's knees start to buckle. Knowing it didn't matter, but doing it anyway, the commando bent his knees and raised his aim fractionally as he had been trained, sending bullets into the suicide bomber's neck and face. The man started to fall backwards and was driven back by bursts from Alpha 2 that hit him in the upper chest. Slamming into the banquet table at hip height, he tumbled over and into the fireplace.

By now, both Wasantha and Alpha 2 had emptied their thirty-round mags, and as one they tugged the Hi-Power pistols free of the low-slung gunfighter holsters. At that instant Banu's explosive vest detonated with enough force to hurl the banquet table across the room.

*

Diving straight through the doorway leading from the driver's common room to the hallway, Golf 1 went right through the hail of fire, miraculously being missed by 9-mm rounds that shredded the doorframe. He rolled across the cursing form of Golf 2, who had taken a bullet in the left shoulder, and lying flat, looked over his SMG sights in time to see the terra huddled at the foot of the stairs get hit by Golf 3. The man went face down into the carpet, but Golf 3 was on his feet, still firing as he moved forward, emptying his magazine as Golf 1 moved up to cover him.

Dropping his now empty MP-5A3, Golf 3 unleashed the tremendous footballer's kick that had once secured the Clifford

Cup for the Army rugby team. The terra flipped clean over onto his back. He then drew his pistol and put a double-tap into the already dead man's forehead.

They had been warned that the Tangos might be wearing suicide bomb kits, and anti-terrorist training dictated that the commandos keep firing until the suspected bomber's hands could be seen to be clear of any detonator; or until the terrorist was very obviously dead and unable to set off his explosives. This one was certainly dead, having been shot twenty-six times. He was wearing an explosive vest.

Leaving Golf 2 to look after himself and cover the stairs, the rest of the team spread out to clear the ground floor. But before they could move off there was another explosion from above, and debris, smoke, and body parts came raining down the stairwell.

*

On the first floor, Corporal Gamini Suraweera ignored the explosion that had come from the banquet room and proceeded to carry out his job of clearing the floor. Leaving Charlie 4 to watch the senior visa officer's door, the rest of the team cleared the other rooms leading off the corridors and landing. Doors were demolished with Hatton rounds and flash-bangs tossed in before each room was stormed in pairs. All the rooms were empty, including the staff toilets across the corridor from the senior visa officer's room.

*

Inside the senior visa officer's room, Preethi had barricaded the door with the heavy desk and was crouched in the corner by the east windows, MP-5K levelled at the door she knew the soldiers would come through. The lights were off and she had her NVGs on. She wondered whether she could get the window open and jump down to the ground. But she hadn't even dared look out since the sniper bullet had smashed through the glass. She considered crawling to the north window but worried that she'd be caught between the sniper and the soldiers at the door.

The loud explosion that had dropped framed pictures from the walls had told Preethi that the prisoners had been killed, but she had no time to feel satisfaction. It also reminded her that her own explosive vest lay on the floor, discarded out of discomfort. By some oversight, they had been issued with men's vests, and these pressed uncomfortably against her breasts. Unlike Devini, Preethi was more generously endowed, and she had unlaced the vest, deciding there'd be time enough to put it on later. Now she didn't dare lower the *Kurz* even for the few seconds it would take her to shrug into the vest.

She could hear the detonations of stun grenades in the neighbouring rooms, and knew it wouldn't be long before the soldiers came through the doorway. Her eyes jumped nervously from the door to the nearby vest, wondering if she could kill more soldiers with it than with the *Kurz*. There was a louder *BOOM*, this time from the floor above, bringing slabs of plaster raining down around her, and Preethi realized another of her comrades had made the ultimate sacrifice. Making her decision, she lowered the *Kurz* and made a lunge for the vest. Before she could touch it, the door hinges and lock were shattered by shotgun fire. Then Preethi heard a body slam into the outside of the door and she raised the submachine-gun and put a burst through the wood at waist height before grabbing the vest.

*

Gamini Suraweera wasn't sure what damage the second explosion — this one from the second floor — had caused, but he told Charlie 2 and 4 to secure the landing while he broke into the senior visa officer's room with Charlie 3. The stainless steel Hatton rounds had done their work and Gamini hurled himself at the door. He should be playing it safe, he told himself, kick in the door and spray the room. But he didn't want to be framed in the doorway like Mona Lisa when the terra inside opened up. The decision saved his life.

He bounced off the door, falling back on his arse, and it would have almost been funny except for the half-dozen 9-mm bullets that came hammering through to bury themselves in the opposite wall.

Gamini realized that the door was probably bolted on the far side, and possibly barricaded as well. The team had no more frame charges, so he used the fire axe on his belt to chop at the edge of the door, standing at an oblique angle while his partner put shotgun fire through. Fierce return fire punched back at them. As soon as there was a large enough hole, Gamini tossed in a flash-bang and a CS canister, turning to nod at the other commando. Charlie 3, dropping the now empty shotgun and drawing his pistol, hit the door at a run, and it practically fell apart, the sections of wood moving back far enough for both men to push through.

Halfway into her vest, submachine-gun in one hand, Preethi was driven back into her corner by the loud detonation, her NVGs whiting out under the flash, deafened, firing blindly on full auto. Gasping with shock, she took in a lungful of CS gas and choking and crying, dropped the *Kurz* and held up her hands.

Gamini ducked as the MP-5K fired into the ceiling, his torch raking the smoke, bringing his aim onto the crouching figure in the corner. He and Charlie 3 fired together, the deadly streams of bullets meeting and crossing in Preethi's body. Both commandos kept firing until their weapons were empty.

*

The lights seemed to blaze in the comms room as the power was switched back on, burning out the sensitive NVG optics. Ripping off the goggles, half blind, Devini stumbled through the door into the hallway beyond, followed by a hail of gunfire. Evidently she hadn't hit anything either. The stairs. If she could get to the landing before they cut her off . . . There was no guarantee the earlier explosion had killed the prisoners.

With her left hand she pulled the safety on the explosive vest she was wearing under her jacket.

Devini heard a door crash open behind her, and knew she had failed. The soldiers seemed to have crossed the comms room with superhuman speed. Not wanting to waste time in turning to shoot, she concentrated on lengthening her stride, feeling the cotton business suit skirt rip up the back.

She was alongside the balustrade that protected the stairwell now, almost daring to believe she had made it, dropping the pistol so that her right hand would be free to pull the fuse, she reached out her left to vault the wooden rail, willing to risk a fall down the stairs in an effort to get to the next floor. Then the solid shot Hatton round fired by Bravo 4 hit her between the shoulder blades.

Bravo 2 and 4 had moved through the library and cleared the administrative rooms in the floor's northwest corner in time to step into the hallway opposite the doorway Devini had just exited. Bravo 4, in the lead had raised his Mossberg 500 ATP8 shotgun and fired instinctively.

The cry that escaped Devini's lips was one of frustration rather than shock or pain. The stainless steel rifled slug snapped her spine and destroyed her heart and she felt herself propelled clean over the wooden balustrade and into the space of the stairwell. As the dimming world turned upside down she yanked on the fuse.

The fact that Devini was already in the stairwell and facing down saved Bravo Team from death or serious injury. The explosion tore her body apart, sending most of the pieces, like shot from a cannon, straight down the stairs.

*

In the banquet room, Sergeant Wasantha Basnayake sat up groggily, his throat burning and head spinning. The room was full of choking smoke, and his whole body ached. He remembered then that Tango 1 had blown himself up, practically in their faces. The explosion had knocked his respirator askew, and now Wasantha tore it and his Balaclava away, rolling over and vomiting onto the charred carpet. His hearing was coming back and he could hear the hostages screaming and crying all around him. He pulled himself towards the French windows, still holding his pistol, the MP-5A3 dragged along by its sling. Sharp fingers of pain jabbed into his side and he knew ribs were broken. The carpet was littered with debris, some of it the remains of the banquet table, and Wasantha realized this was the cause of the broken ribs.

Crawling out onto the balcony on all fours, he took huge gulps of air, trying to clear his lungs of the CS gas. He could feel blood trickling down into his boots and, looking down, he saw that his fatigue legs were in shreds. Fortunately for Wasantha, the banquet table seemed to have taken the brunt of the explosion, and the wounds to his legs were mostly from flying wood splinters.

There was another loud explosion, this time from the floor above and, pulling his respirator on again, Wasantha waded back into the smoke, cursing and still coughing. The lights had come back on and this made it easier to make out the chaos in the room.

"Come in, Alpha!" Wasantha managed to make out the OC's voice over the background chatter. "Alpha from X-ray, respond! Wha'ss going on?"

Looking around, Wasantha could see the body of Alpha 2 lying against the far wall, where he had been flung by the explosion. He was not moving.

"X-ray from Alpha!" he yelled. "Tango one blew himself up. We have casualties. Room clear. Wait."

He could see casualties amongst the hostages as well, some unmoving, while others were screaming and crying. Ignoring their injuries, Alpha 3 was rolling them over and snapping plasticuffs onto their wrists while Alpha 4, who was covering him, motioned with his SMG for the hostages to stay down. Thoroughly shocked and disoriented by first the flashbangs, then the assault, and finally by the explosion, the civilians were now totally cowed by the masked gunmen threatening them. People were coughing, crying, vomiting, but Alpha 3 was reinforcing the shock, showing no sign of gentleness as he kicked legs apart and roughly frisked people for explosives before restraining them.

This was standard procedure, Wasantha knew — there could be terras who had hidden themselves amongst the hostages. It had been a lesson learned by the Israeli Sayaret Matkal at Entebbe and the British SAS at Prince's Gate, and hostage-rescue units the world over had taken careful note.

Wasantha moved across to Alpha 2, searching for a pulse at the throat. The commando was alive but out cold, bleeding from the arms and legs, though like Wasantha, his torso had been protected by his body armour.

The chaos on the radio net was winding down, and Wasantha couldn't hear any more gunfire or explosions. He shouted for Charlie Team to get into the banquet room ASAP, but got no immediate response.

More blood could be seen escaping from under Alpha 2's respirator, and fighting off his own pain, Wasantha started to drag him towards the balcony. Before he could take more than a couple of steps, however, both doors crashed open and three members of Charlie came crashing in ready to rock.

"You're a bit late for the party," commented Wasantha, handing over the unconscious commando to Charlie 2 and 4, who carried him out onto the balcony.

"Looks like you bought too many crackers, but," pointed out Gamini Suraweera, jabbing a finger towards the blackened remains of the fireplace as he crossed the room to give Alpha 3 a hand with the hostages.

Wasantha heard calls of "Bravo clear," and "Golf clear," and then the command from X-ray that would send in the hostage handling team.

"Charlie clear," Gamini said, as he and Alpha 3 stepped away from the now cuffed hostages.

"Alpha clear," Wasantha added.

He could hear feet pounding up the stairs from below, and more coming down from the second floor. Time to clear out and let the cops clean up the mess. The still unconscious form of

Alpha 2 was being lowered over the balcony by his abseiling rope to waiting medics below. The rest of the commandos formed a line and began passing the former hostages from man to man. The hostage handling team had to actually enter the building and help because it seemed as if almost all the assault teams had taken casualties.

Outside, the sniper teams shouldered their long rifles and faded away into the darkness, while Errol Seneviratne and Tony Mendis pulled the minicams and mikes out of the chimneys before abseiling down to join their comrades in the front yard.

In the banquet room, Wasantha limped over to have a last look at the terra who had almost succeeded in killing him. There wasn't much left of Banu. The biggest piece Wasantha could make out was a lower leg lying on the far side of the room. The fireplace, now a blackened rectangle half filled with bricks that had come crashing down from the chimney, was what had probably saved Wasantha and Alpha 2. Most of the blast had been channelled upwards from Banu's chest into the chimney as he fell backwards. The banquet table had absorbed the rest of it.

Within minutes, the hostage handling team had made sure that there were no more terrorists amongst the former hostages, and they had been whisked away in police ambulances. Delta 3 had been killed by the booby-trap behind the generator shed, and Delta 4 had been critically injured. Both men had been already choppered out of the SSC grounds. The rest of Delta Team, with lesser injuries, plus the wounded from Alpha, Bravo, and Golf, were taken in the Commando Land Rovers to the Military Hospital at Galle Face.

Within ten minutes of the "clear" being sounded, the embassy premises had been evacuated and the police moved in, scratching their heads at the carnage. The media was allowed past the barricades and swarmed down Gregory's Road to be stopped at the embassy gates from where they took suitably jumpy and grainy footage of the embassy's broken windows, to which sound effects would be later added for the "live" coverage of the assault already breaking on the world's TV screens.

SMOKE
& DUST

Truth can never be told so as to be understood,
and not be believed.
— William Blake

Dhanno dhanithi. Only those who know can know.
— Sinhalese saying

CHAPTER 28

SUNDAY 24th MARCH: For a few moments, there seemed to be several suns, and they seemed to have strange elongated shapes, seeming to whirl dizzily as Eric Christofelsz blinked up at them. He tried to sit up, and it felt as if the side of his skull was being torn off. Squeezing his eyes shut, he lay back, fighting the nausea.

"Welcome back," said a voice that Christofelsz knew he should recognize.

He opened his eyes again and tried to focus on the ceiling lights that had now stopped their spin. There seemed to be something wrong with his vision, however, making him see double, and he closed an eye in an effort to focus, but it didn't help.

A figure blocked out the overhead light, bending towards Christofelsz.

"Fit *dher*?" the man asked with a grin.

It wasn't the earlier voice, and Christofelsz managed to fit the blurred face to someone in Delta Group that he knew. Welgama.

"Airborne fit," he croaked.

There was laughter from somewhere on his right and Christofelsz managed to roll his head without too much pain. He was in what looked like a small hospital ward with a dozen beds. Almost all the beds were occupied with men in the silly tan-and-brown striped pyjamas that the Sri Lanka Army Medical Corps insisted all its patients wore. His vision seemed to focus somewhat as Ranjith Welgama helped him into a sitting position, propping a pillow at his back.

Christofelsz noted that the lieutenant was limping as he made his way back to his own bed, reknotting his sarong.

There were seven other men in the room, beside himself, all of them from Blue Team. The embassy assault must have been a major fuckup, he decided, if they took this many wounded. Then he noticed the big white man in the bed next to him, grinning and nursing a bandaged and splinted arm. Conway.

"Are we in Sri Lanka?" Christofelsz managed.

"Yeah," drawled Jan Conway. "Military Hospital, Galle Face."

"Already?"

"Wha'ddaya mean 'already'? It's tomorrow." The Canadian picked up a wristwatch from the bedside table and looked at it. "Actually, it's the goddamned day *after* tomorrow. You've been out more than thirty-six fucking hours."

Dragging aside the blanket, Christofelsz examined himself. His whole body ached and his arms and legs were covered with bandages. Couldn't be so bad, he told himself. They were small bandages.

"You were lucky," Conway commented. "You've got severe concussion, but the Tiger's body took most of the blast, and our body armour covered our more juicy parts. But that burst from the Uzi didn't help me much."

For a moment Christofelsz stared blankly at Conway, and then it all came washing back; Tango 1 in the hold, the grenade, the Canadian diving in.

"By the way, thanks," muttered Conway, then smiled broadly to cover his embarrassment. "Anytime you wanna come visit Canada, pick up the phone. You won't have to bring a dollar with you. I mean it." He tapped his chest. "Thanks to you, the worst thing I got were these cracked ribs and this fractured shoulder. The rest are all just scratches. That fucking flak vest stopped those bullets. Thank Christ for Bismuth. But it still felt like a kick from a moose."

Christofelsz waved away the thanks and looked around. "Anyone has a fag?"

There was more laughter and Conway said, "I don't think the nurses will like that."

"What're they gon' to do, sen' me to Jaffna?"

"Tha'ss what they said." Wasantha Basnayake spoke painfully from across the ward. He, too, had his ribs taped.

A packet of Gold Leaf came sailing in from somewhere, followed by a box of matches, and Christofelsz lit up gratefully.

"What happened?" he asked Conway, exhaling a long plume of smoke.

"You mean, after you did your John Wayne act?" chuckled the Canadian. "Nothing much. We hauled the passengers and crew outside and handed the whole circus over to the Indian cops. Some of the civilians are being treated apparently for shock and minor burns, and one of the stews was injured by the strip charge on one of the doors. All the Tangos were wasted. You and I were the only casualties on our sides."

"What about you buggers?" Christofelsz nodded at the other commandos. "Fucked up or what?"

"Bullshit," said Ranjith Welgama, drifting back across to sit on Christofelsz's bed. "We kicked their fucking arses back to Jaffna."

"Ah? Then what're all'f y'all doing here?"

The lieutenant was silent for a moment, lighting a cigarette from the pack lying on the bed. "It was a tough one. Booby-trap, suicide bombers, the works. One team didn' even get in. We lost Asela, an' Senadheera had to get a leg taken off." He glanced across the ward to where the remaining two members of Delta Team were lying. The team commander was staring blankly at the ceiling while the other commando tried to talk to him.

Christofelsz grunted and dragged on his cigarette. What was there to say? So many now. How many more? Oh well, would he have exchanged the assault on the Airbus for all the wasted years as a civilian? He knew the answer to that, and looking around at Conway and Welgama and Basnayake and all the others, he knew what their answers would be.

"So when do those sexy nurses bring me something to eat?" Christofelsz demanded. "And don't we get any visitors?"

"Well the visitors are being kept back till you an' Jan here are debriefed," Ranjith said. "So the rest'f us are bloody thrilled that you needed your forty winks." He got to his feet. "As for the nurses, Christo, Ah'll jus' go nex' door an' get one. There's a two hundred-pound cutie who's been eyeballing you since you were brought in."

Christofelsz laughed but quickly stopped when it brought pain shooting through his head. He turned back to Conway.

"Where're the rest'f your chaps anyway?"

"Bastards are down in Unawatuna, working on their tans while I'm stuck in this dump!"

*

The Sunday morning papers were filled with reports on the two hostage situations that had recently been brought to an explosive conclusion by Sri Lankan and Canadian commandos. Taking a tentative sip of his piping hot tea, Brigadier Arjuna Devendra scanned the pages with satisfaction, not bothering to read in detail. He would do that after lunch.

The two boys were chattering about the upcoming visit of a British pop band, their teenage animation prompting Nelun to advise them that they had better eat their breakfast of string hoppers before the *kiri hodhi* got cold.

Devendra wasn't listening to the banter of his family as he put aside *The Sunday Observer* and picked up *The Sunday Leader*. The papers were filled with "in-depth analysis" and "exclusives", a follow-up to Saturday's huge headline type and dramatic prose. All the newspapers had been competing for attention and claiming to have the true story; and now, more sober language gave the impression that real research had been carried out.

Devendra saw that the passport photos of the hijackers had been released to the media, along with the men's false LTTE records. It read particularly well, he decided, and was quite convincing. Just enough detail to sound realistic without being expansive. Psy Ops seemed to have outdone itself. He must remind Nelun that it had been a while since Brigadier Jinadasa and his wife had been over for dinner. It was true that Devendra hadn't been very happy about the Directorate of Psychological Operations stalling on the release of the news that Sarojini Skandarajah — alias Colonel Sundari — was a senior member of the LTTE, but maybe the week's delay would have a better impact. The Director Psy Ops had promised that the Military Spokesman's Office would release the communiqué in time for the following Sunday's papers, along with the pictures from London and still frames taken off the BBC footage. Jinadasa had explained that the week's delay would allow the hungry news hounds to pounce on the new item once the drama of Operations *Rama* and *Sita* had been exhausted. The direct link between the ERA and the LTTE, plus the hinted at "intelligence reports" of Sarojini Skandarajah having had the "martyr's meal" with the Tiger supremo, would be the nail in the terrorists' coffin. Horrified Canadians, already screaming for ERA blood after the live BBC broadcast, would force world opinion firmly against the LTTE. Devendra smiled, visualizing the LTTE merchant fleet being seized in their home harbours of Thailand, Burma, and Columbia; financial assets, already frozen in Britain, Canada, and the United States, would be confiscated worldwide. This was the beginning of the end.

With a mixture of amusement and annoyance, Devendra noticed that the traditionally anarchist *Sunday Leader*, had filed an article under the heading, *"Human Rights Group Claims Excessive Force Used by Army During Embassy Assault"*. The Red Cross, tasked with handing over the bodies of the dead ERA/LTTE terrorists to their families, had released the fact that one of the dead men had been shot twenty-six times, while a woman had as many as forty-four bullets dug out of her body at last count. Some had also been shot multiple times in the head at close range, and the reporter speculated that they had been captured alive and then executed. The article claimed that an Army spokesman had refuted the accusation of executions having being carried out, saying that since the terrorists were wearing explosive vests, the commandos had taken no chances with the hostages' lives. The reporter scoffed at this, pointing out that two suicide bombers — including the terrorist leader — had managed to blow themselves up in spite of Army efforts; and anyway, how many times did a person have to be shot before death was established?

Devendra turned the page, happy that most of the press coverage praised the military's quick and deadly response, suggesting that the co-operation between the Sri Lankan and Canadian hostage-rescue units was a benchmark for the future.

Finally, Devendra found the piece he was looking for. At the bottom of one of the inside pages was a headline that said, *"Sudden Removal of DFI Boss"*. The report simply stated that the Director General of Foreign Intelligence had been abruptly removed from his post on Friday, and would soon be taking over as Deputy Inspector General in charge of the Eastern Province. *The Sunday Leader* sources claimed that Jaliya de Silva had been removed due to the DFI's apparent failure to give sufficient warning of international ERA attacks. DIG de Silva had been unavailable for comment. Talk in intelligence circles was that both the DFI and DII were to be brought under an umbrella organization which would coordinate all non-military intelligence activities. It was predicted that DIG Michael Salgado, currently the head of the DII, was to be promoted in order to take over the newly created post of National Intelligence Director. The article also went on to say that Inspector General of Police Vimal Warnasuriya would be applying for early retirement that year.

Devendra gave a grunt of satisfaction and put the newspaper aside. At least they had got the last bit right, he thought. He himself had given the Prime Minister and the outgoing Inspector General the strong recommendation that Salgado was the best man for the job.

The other papers had run no articles on the subject.

* * *

It was a drizzly early spring day as the replacement Air Canada flight broke through the low clouds west of the Sea Island Indian Reserve on its final approach to Vancouver International Airport in British Columbia. Passengers seated at the windows — especially the Canadians amongst them — sighed with relief as they caught a glimpse of the shore.

In the cockpit, Captain Johnny Burnett and his co-pilot Mike Harrap were seated in the jump seats behind the flight crew. As the airport appeared out of the murk below, Burnett felt tears prickle dangerously at his eyes. There had been times during the two-day ordeal when he had doubted he would ever see Canada again.

"Looks good, huh, Johnny?" Harrap said, wiping at his own eyes.

"That it is, Mike that it is."

In spite of the long flight, the tension, fear and fatigue of the hijack, the former passengers and crew of Air Canada AC634 gave a thunderous round of applause as the tires touched the runway.

Vijitha Dhampahana clapped along with others just to fit in. His heart was pounding and he was dreading the grilling that he knew was awaiting him. The hours following their rescue had been agony for him as he was questioned by Indian policemen on what had happened during the hijack. Even though they hadn't examined his forged passport too closely, he was sure they were onto him. Even when they had been all put up at the five-star Taj Samudra hotel in Madras to await the arrival of their replacement flight, Vijitha had been unable to relax or enjoy the good food. He had constantly been on edge, waiting for the knock on his room door that would signal the game was up.

As the plane docked at the International Terminal, he got to his feet with all the other passengers, trying to appear cheerful. Relax, he told himself, you know all the answers. You've practiced this a hundred times. Shit, the doors were opening. . .

Jennifer Jensen was one of the first to leave the plane, being pushed along in a wheelchair. Dressed in a fresh uniform

that covered most of her bandages, she composed her face for
the banks of photographers she knew would be waiting for them.
Except for her bandaged leg and a cut above her left eyebrow
that had needed suturing, she knew she looked fairly OK. But she
didn't kid herself as to the psychological injuries that she knew
would take longer to heal. Her parents would be waiting outside,
but what Jen-Jen really wished for was that Tim could be here.
He had promised to get a furlough as soon as possible, and she
knew that his presence was what she really needed.

Once he was through immigration and customs, the latter
having been largely waived for the now famous hostages, Colin
Peters dodged the waiting journalists as he headed off to find the
nearest bar. He had half an hour to kill before his connecting
flight to Montreal departed, and he intended to spend it with a
very large whisky. He was looking forward to the cool bleakness
of north-eastern Quebec, hoping to wipe the whole scary episode
away by submerging himself in his work with the whales.

The Devanayagams finally said goodbye to the Koplecks
at Vancouver; while the Sri Lankan family was flying on to Toronto,
the Canadians were catching a flight home to Calgary. The two
families had grown close over the long hours of the hijack and
the wind-down period in Madras. While the fathers gruffly shook
hands and slapped backs and promised to laugh about it all over a
stiff drink before the Devanayagams returned to Sri Lanka, the
mothers hugged tearfully. Unnoticed for a moment, Daniel and
Suzie made surreptitious plans.

* * *

TUESDAY 26th MARCH: The grey Toyota Corolla turned down a
dusty side road in the sprawling refugee camp south of Madras.
It was four days since the conclusion of Operations *Rama* and
Sita. While the driver stayed with the car, the other two men crossed
to a low-roofed shack made of crumbling brick and tin sheets.
The two men, both moustachioed and wearing casual shirts, dark
slacks, and sturdy shoes, stopped outside the rickety plywood door

and knocked. They were both relaxed, not expecting to have any trouble. Sri Lankan Tamil teenagers loitered around, staring at the strange car and then drifted off. Only children continued to watch the proceedings with open curiosity.

An old man dragged the door open and peered out with reddened eyes. "Yes?" he asked, looking the men up and down, sensing their authority.

"Are you Balachandran Mahesh?" one of the men asked, his voice neither polite nor rude.

"Yes," the old man answered, and now a woman appeared behind him, her old eyes red and swollen with weeping.

"And Mahesh Balachandran was your son?"

The old man straightened up, his face tightening with anger. "Yes, he was my son. What do you want?"

"Did you give an interview to a reporter of *The Hindu* concerning your son?"

"Yes, I told him that my son was not a terrorist."

"My name is Inspector Vishvanath, Special Branch. You are under arrest."

* * *

THURSDAY 28th MARCH: Ian McEdwards was driving fast, well over the limit of a hundred kilometres per hour, the big Jeep Cherokee roaring along Canadian highway-11 as he headed for the Banff National Park. He was nearing Nordegg, and the snow-capped Rocky Mountains were looming on the horizon. Driving skilfully, his mind nevertheless was in chaos, whirling its way through random trains of thought.

Though his reason for taking compassionate leave had been that his mother was seriously ill, McEdwards knew none of his colleagues in the Special Protection Group were going to follow it up. His mother would turn away any callers and his own mobile phone was switched off after the rash of condolence calls he had received following the loss of the rest of his BG team, killed along with Donald Fenster.

The guilt had been overwhelming, and once it had been established that there were no survivors from the executive jet, McEdwards just knew he had to get away and clear his mind. Glad to have her younger son home, Sarah McEdwards, a widow, had nevertheless, been understanding, sensitive to his pain, and had made no comment when he said he was going camping in the Rockies. Hiring the Jeep in Edmonton, McEdwards had piled his tent and sleeping bag aboard and taken off.

For a full irrational day, following the announcement of Fenster's plane going missing, McEdwards had thought of going to his superiors and coming clean on the whole blackmail issue. He had plotted on how he would hunt down the man with the American accent. He had even kidded himself that if he was thrown out of the Mounties he'd go after the blackmailer on his own. Yeah, right, he told himself now, in your dreams, kiddo. He had nothing to go on. No name, no location, nothing. All he'd succeed in doing was ruining his career.

His career. What a joke. A bodyguard who wasn't around when he was needed. But he wondered what he could have done even if he had been with Fenster. Die like the rest. But he also knew that there had been a reason the blackmailer hadn't wanted him with Fenster; they had been worried that he would notice something. He wondered what it had been and whether he'd ever know, and decided he would not.

McEdwards wondered what Patricia had felt at the moment of her death, wondered whether it had been quick. Another question that would stay unanswered.

He glanced across at the newspaper lying on the seat next to him, which he had bought in Red Deer where he'd stopped for lunch. It was almost a week since the storming of the Air Canada jet and the Colombo embassy, but the papers were still full of it. The front page had a large colour night time picture, grainy with distance, of ominous masked figures moving away from the backdrop of the hijacked plane. Black rectangles of censorship masked their eyes, but it was obvious, nevertheless, that some of them were white.

The media, long critical of the Canadian Forces and police paramilitary units, were now enthusiastically worshipping at the altar of strength.

The display in India, along with the reports of Canadian infantry units fighting in the mountains of Afghanistan — in combat for the first time since the Korean War, the media was saying — had established the country's ability to carry the War on Terror to global dimensions. In spite of this, the death of Fenster had brought certain changes in Ottawa's attitudes. Frank Vitucci, one of Fenster's senior staffers and as virulent an opponent of the Tigers as his boss, had been killed along with the minister, and this had left a void within the Department of Foreign Affairs and International Trade. The department's minister of state was inexperienced and lacked the skills Fenster had in countering the many doves in Ottawa. It looked as if there might be certain amendments to the new Anti-Terrorism Bill before it was actually passed as law. The majority of the powers that be didn't seem to be totally convinced of the connection between the LTTE and the ERA. There was talk that while Ottawa might approve continued military and monetary aid to Sri Lanka and the arrest of Tamil militants in Canada, it was unlikely that the extradition treaty would come into being.

Whatever the outcome of Ottawa's political fencing, Ian McEdwards decided that he'd had enough of being a bodyguard. Maybe he could get a transfer to CFSEU when he returned from his week in the mountains, or Criminal Intelligence, do some real detective work for a change.

*   *   *

SUNDAY 31st MARCH: "Look, Jinay, what the Hell is going on?" Devendra's voice was tight with anger as he spoke into the phone. He was sitting at the small desk in his book-lined study at home. "My people went to a lot of trouble to get that int, and I had your word."

A full week had passed since Devendra had been promised by the Director of Psy Ops that Sarojini Skandarajah's membership in the LTTE would be in the media; but the Sunday papers had nothing on the subject. While there were now personal accounts and in-depth interviews with some of the former hostages, the headlines now screamed out the news of the ceasefire declared by the government just a day ago, and the announcement by the Prime Minister that talks with the Tigers were in the offing.

"It's out of my hands, Arjuna," Brigadier Jinadasa replied, his own voice tense. "I repeat, there's not a bloody thing I can do. This came direct from MoD, a personal order from Jayavickrama, apparently, an' I got the feeling that this came down from even higher. Probably the PM's office."

"An' you don't know anything further?" asked Devendra bitterly, knowing that even if Jinadasa did, he wouldn't be passing anything unauthorized on, friendship or no.

"Jus' that it's something to do with the talks."

Devendra already knew that. "OK, Jinay, thanks. What to do? That's life. Dinner is still on, nex' Friday, no?"

"Of course. Renuka jus' reminded me las' night."

Devendra hung up and cursed in frustration. The talks, the fucking talks. Why was the government throwing away this golden opportunity to kick the LTTE when it was down? A kick in the balls that would paralyse the organization's international support. The ceasefire was just what those bastards up there wanted. They had their arses to the fire with the Security Forces gradually hemming them in. Though Devendra knew it was true that the ERA terror attacks had taken the international focus off the LTTE, and that Canadian resolve was now faltering after the death of Donald Fenster, the momentum gained in the early months of the year could be sufficient to see the Tigers destroyed as a military force. And with that they could be brought to the negotiating table with no preconditions; or at least none that demanded the government lifting of the ban on the Tigers, or the withdrawal of security forces from the Northeast. This newly-announced ceasefire was just what the LTTE needed to regroup and resupply.

Was the government using the proof of the LTTE-ERA link as a threat, or some sort of bargaining chip?

Picking up his electronic diary, Devendra began to search his memory for favours owed to him by people in the Defence Secretariat that could now be called in.

* * *

Dayan Premasiri blew cigarette smoke out into the night as he stood at the bedroom window and let the sea breeze cool his body. Though he had welcomed the humid heat of Sri Lanka after his months in Europe, he had now had just about enough. Thank God the power cuts were down to just an hour each day now. The Electricity Board had promised that with a few more weeks of rain they could be done away with altogether.

With the winding down of the crisis in the country and the threat of an Indian landing averted, his squadron had been withdrawn from Katunayake and sent back to the Northeast. He and Sumith Liyanage had both been granted two weeks leave, however, with immediate effect. Sumith had returned to Maduru Oya with the squadron to pick up some of his personal stuff before heading off to his hometown of Matale in the Central Highlands. Dayan hadn't wasted time, however, and had headed straight home to Colombo, stopping off at the Military Hospital to look in on Kamal Gunatilake, whose leg wound was coming along nicely. The big soldier had been offered a slot as a heavy weapons instructor at the Special Forces Training Centre that he would take over as soon as his medical leave was completed.

Dayan had already decided that he would visit Bandara's family before he returned to his unit. He knew he wouldn't be able to offer them much comfort or enlighten them on where their son and brother had died, but he could tell them something more about Bandara's last moments than the bland official letter had offered. The letter stated that Corporal JL Bandara had drowned during an amphibious training exercise off Batticaloa, his body having been lost at sea.

A soft sigh from the bed behind him made Dayan look over his shoulder. Sunethra rolled fitfully on to her stomach, unconsciously pushing the tangled bed sheet away, her long black hair spread over the pillow, concealing her face. A gleam of sweat from their recent lovemaking traced the curve of her spine and Dayan found himself fighting off an image of Sandra on the bed in Trier, eyes burning into his as he entered her. For a moment the image threatened to overwhelm him and he took a long drag at the cigarette until his lungs burned, then the picture was gone, leaving him with an impression of greenish-hazel eyes, tangled hair and long legs that he pushed into that special part of his brain reserved for old and cherished remembrances, memories of former comrades like Bandara. It was a long line of men now dead, their bodies burned or buried, or lying in some long-forgotten jungle grave; or crippled, living out their bitter lives in a world full of memories and people who didn't want to know. Sandra Koch was now placed in that crypt, a beautiful abstraction, to be taken out and examined at the right moments. It was a soldier's survival mechanism and it served Sergeant Dayan Premasiri very well.

He had tried to keep the painful memories of Sandra away since his return from Europe, and had largely succeeded. At least he had until yesterday. His mind flipped back to the previous day, to his visit to the Koch home in Wattala on the outskirts of the city of Colombo. While Sandra's parents knew she had been shot by a terrorist in Germany, the letter from the Army's Directorate of Welfare informing them that their daughter was a Volunteer Force lieutenant serving with the Military Intelligence Corps had come as a complete shock. The visit by an Int captain soon after her death had not shed any light on what their daughter had been doing in Germany, only that the Army would be very appreciative if the Kochs did not give Sandra's story to the media. The captain had informed them that Sandra's body would be flown back to Sri Lanka for a military funeral, adding that while as a Volunteer Force officer she'd had no claim to a permanent salary or pension — her next-of-kin receiving only her life insurance money — the salary would be paid to her parents until Sandra's never-to-be-reached retirement age, after which her pension would be paid until her parents death. The captain had informed them that this was being done as recognition of Lieutenant Sandra Koch's loyalty and bravery. He had never alluded to the fact that this might be a payment for their guaranteed silence.

Sipping at his tea, Dayan had told Sandra's parents as much as he could, telling them that she had suffered no pain, that her death had been quick; telling them how much Sandra had helped in the success of their mission, that she had never shown fear. He didn't tell them of the night in Trier, or the way Sandra's voice had trembled when she told him that Kumaradeven had spotted her. He never told them how her green eyes had captivated him, eyes he now saw framed by her father's wrinkled eyelids. There had been no tears, just the numbed shock still there in the old couple's faces days after the funeral. And the bitter line of Elroy Koch's mouth, the bitterness of a man who had given both his children to a war he had no interest in and an enemy he had never met, bitterness towards a war that was now reflected in the hard-eyed young man who sat sipping tea in his living room.

Flicking the cigarette through the bars of the window, Dayan realized there would be no sleep tonight, and he dressed silently, slipping out of the house in the hope of finding an open bar somewhere and the peace of mind he now craved; an end to the guilt he had never felt before in all his years as a soldier, years once protected by the loss of conscience that is a vital part of military training.

* * *

APRIL: The banks of photographers faced each other down the length of the converted classroom. The school itself had long been out of use as a place of education, last having been used as a temporary holding centre for Security Forces and police prisoners captured by the LTTE. Before that it had been a refugee camp for various ethnic communities driven from their homes by the terror of war. None of the refugees had lingered very long due to air strikes by the Sri Lanka Air Force and shelling by Tiger gunners that had targeted the nearby town of Kilinochchi. The entire school had been given a fresh lick of paint that looked as ludicrous as makeup on a half-rotten corpse. The classroom in question, however, had had its scars filled up and floor repainted and waxed. The wall at the front of the room, still displaying a pitted and faded blackboard, had been hung with thick, pale green drapes. Ceiling fans powered by generators stirred the air.

The two rows of photographers looked as different from each other as it was possible, in clothing, physical characteristics, and manner. While the men arrayed opposite the drapes looked like correspondents in a war zone anywhere — faded and well-worn clothes and shoes, slightly overweight, with bad nicotine habits — the other group looked fit and smart, their tigerstripe fatigues having been tailored and pressed. While the civilians looked nervous and slightly ill at ease in this last bastion of the Tigers, the LTTE photographers projected the confidence they felt on their home turf.

Both groups, however, took pictures of each other with abandon, the civilians wondering why the Tigers wished to record their likenesses.

The area between the two lines of clicking and flashing cameras were taken up by rows of folding steel chairs, and each had a journalist's arse perched on its edge. The reason the said arses were on edge was that the persons scheduled to take their place behind the long table on the dais at the head of the room had not appeared as yet. The table itself was of polished jak set with bowls of frangipani and jasmine flowers and little flagpoles hung with LTTE flags.

Finally, there was a stir of movement at the door and the first of the bodyguards entered, a Black Tiger of the Imran Pandiyan Regiment's VIP protection detail, wearing dark aviator glasses and a short-sleeved white shirt that hung over dark trousers, the whole effect carefully modelled on the Sri Lankan police VIP protection divisions.

The photographers' flashes intensified their popping as a line of people moved into the room and over to the long table. The undercover Int and DII men amongst the media mentally identified each of the newcomers as they entered, taking their pictures for the files. They had already snapped shots of all the LTTE photographers, plus the video camera crew outside, and now they snapped the bodyguards as well as the VIPs. They identified the Tiger military chiefs of the Northern and Eastern Provinces, the heads of the political and intelligence wings, and the senior media advisor.

The next man in made the strobing of the cameras turn the room into a light show. Like the others, he was dressed semi-formally in white shirt and dark trousers, but was much older. His alcohol-reddened eyes peered dully through thick lenses at the gathered media as he crossed to the table. The LTTE's middle-aged "ideologue" was followed closely by his Australian wife. Edward Manoharan, based in London for over a decade, had been the presentable political face of the LTTE before the ban on the group by the west had come into place. His hands seemingly clean of blood, he would be a political possibility as a future head of state, another Yasir Arafat, impotently following the orders of the real power.

There was no doubting the fact that the last of the VIPs to enter, the man who brought the camera flashes to a dazzling climax, was the true leader — The Leader, as he was called — of the Liberation Tigers of Tamil Eelam. Dressed in what would later be described by a *BBC* journalist as "North Korean-chic", he smiled savvily at the banks of lenses as he moved stiffly in the heavy ballistic vest he wore under his tunic. Unlike Manoharan, with his dour features, bad teeth, and shifty eyes, the Leader was a man with a round cheerful face and an infectious grin.

This press conference, announced just a week previously, a full month after the conclusion of Operations *Rama* and *Sita*, was the first time in almost fifteen years that the Leader had appeared before the media. What followed left the journalists clinging to their seats to ensure they were still on earth, and would later make both political and military analysts drop their jaws when they saw the reports.

While the press conference would drag on for a full two and a half hours, the bombshell broke in the first minutes with Edward Manoharan speaking as "the voice of the Leader". The man himself sat back for the moment, waiting for the storm of questions he knew was coming.

"We have brought you here to the heart of our homeland," began Manoharan, speaking to the room, "to prove to the world that we are sincerely and seriously committed to peace. This is why we declared a unilateral ceasefire months back. This was not, however, reciprocated by the new Sinhalese government, which went on a new military offensive, both locally and internationally. In spite of this, the LTTE is willing to build bridges, and therefore we have decided to declare another ceasefire in reply to the new government ceasefire. We have also begun cracking down on other dissident Tamil groups, misguided in their beliefs that carrying out international acts of terror would help our cause. We also accept the United National Party government's invitation to enter into talks that will discuss an interim administration until the core issues can be focused on at a later date. We are, therefore, ready to set a date for the proposed talks in Thailand, as suggested by the government." Manoharan paused and took a sip of water. "We will now take questions."

There was a tumult of shouted voices as it dawned on the journalists just what the LTTE had announced, and the Tiger media advisor, sitting next to Manoharan, raised his hands for quiet.

"Please," he said, "one at a time. I will point to individuals and you can then ask." Looking over the lake of raised hands and hopeful faces, he selected one. "Why don't we start with you in the second row, yes, you, in the blue shirt."

"Brian Fernando, *Sunday Times*, thank you. I would like to ask if this means that the LTTE is willing to drop the earlier conditions that it wanted met before it would sit down for talks."

"Yes," answered Manoharan, "in the interests of peace, we have decided to engage in unconditional talks."

"Mohan Almeida, *Island*. Does this mean that *all* conditions have been dropped, such as the raising of the government ban on the Tigers, and the withdrawal of the security forces?" The incredulity in his tone voiced the feelings of all the gathered journalists.

"As I have already said, there will be no conditions."

"John Nagasingham, *Times of India*. Several members of your organization have been indicted for the murder of former Indian Prime Minister Rajiv Gandhi, including your leader. What is your position on this?"

The Leader spoke for the first time leaning forward towards his mike. "Four of the accused have already been sentenced to death by Indian courts, but we are seeking an amnesty from India for the rest of our organization." A faint smile played at the corners of his lips. "As the legal proceedings are still going on, we are unable to comment on it."

"Are you denying your involvement in the Rajiv Gandhi murder?" the Indian reporter asked.

The Leader seemed to sigh, his face hiding any irritation he might have felt at the journalist's persistence. "This is a tragic incident that happened ten years ago, and I would rather not comment on it."

"Don't stick too much to the past," Manoharan advised. "Next question?"

"Richard Goodman, *BBC*. The Sri Lankan Prime Minister has stated that he is willing to discuss everything short of Tamil Eelam. Is the LTTE willing to drop its claim to a separate state, and its demand that the need for a separate state must be recognized before it will begin negotiations? Thank you."

Once more it was the Leader who took the question. "The conditions are not yet right for us to abandon our political struggle for a separate state. We hope that in the future, these conditions will make themselves apparent. However, these talks are concerning an interim administration, and not the core issues. Therefore, as we said before, the talks will be unconditional."

* * *

The crowd roared with delight as the flank forward came charging across to intercept the opposing winger as he flashed down the touchline. Arjuna Devendra winced at the smack of body against body as the wing-threequarter was tackled into touch. The referee blew for a line-out and the crowd howled its approval. Rugby wasn't really Devendra's game, though he was Colombo-educated and had attended one of the city's leading Buddhist schools. He much preferred football and, of course, cricket, the country's unofficial religion.

Devendra was not there however as one of the spectators; he was edging past them towards the members' stand in front of the club house. His bodyguard stayed close, the man's eyes jumping around the crowd, watching faces, but the brigadier himself was relaxed, as always preferring anonymity to a show of strength. The man he was here to meet, was a rugby fanatic, having played it both as a schoolboy and during his time as a tea planter in the hill country. A devoted member of the Colombo Rugby and Football Club, he would not have missed this match easily. The club was playing its arch rival and comparative neighbour, the Colombo Hockey and Football Club.

The club official at the entrance to the members' enclosure had been told to expect Devendra, and he let the brigadier and his bodyguard through with a respectful nod. The glass-fronted façade of the air-conditioned clubhouse was on Devendra's right, but he knew his host would not be in there. The man would be as close to the touchline as he could get, and Devendra scanned the rows of seated spectators until he spotted the iron-grey head.

Not wanting to disturb the older man's game, Devendra stood watching idly as the match went on for another ten minutes, concluding with the home team being beaten by a single penalty goal. The crowd started to disperse, headed off to their cars or buses, the club members either moving into the cooler confines of the clubhouse or lingering in their seats, gulping beer and grumbling. Devendra watched the man he had come to meet shake the hand of the home team's captain in consolation. As his host turned away from the field, Devendra started to make his way down to him. The sharp eyes of the older man's nearest bodyguard latched onto Devendra as he advanced, then relaxed as he recognized the brigadier.

"Ah, Arjuna, how are you?" State Minister for Defence John Jayavickrama raised his hand in greeting. "How long have you been here? Should have come down and joined me, no?"

"Not really a rugby fan myself, sir." Devendra shrugged apologetically at the blasphemy in this temple dedicated to the sport.

"No? Never mind, it was a bloody disappointing match in the end. I wouldn't have minded losing to Kandy, but to CH&FC. . . ?" The minister sighed and took Devendra's arm. "Take a walk with me, Arjuna. I have something to explain to you."

Leaving the stands, the two men walked along the touchline, two of the minister's bodyguards, plus Devendra's, trailing at a discreet distance. Devendra quickly scanned the stands and the old trees beyond that surrounded the club's property. Dusk was falling fast, but it was still light enough to snipe by. He forced himself to relax even though he knew John Jayavickrama wasn't a man to waste too much time on personal security. Devendra had yet to see a cabinet member without a dozen Ministerial Security men around, and he had never heard of a defence minister sitting in the stands at a rugby match. It was another sign that the new conservative United National Party government seemed to — at least on the face of it — want to trust the Tigers. Devendra wondered at the folly of it. Two heads of state of two countries

— Ranasinghe Premadasa and Rajiv Gandhi — had tried to make a deal with the LTTE. Both were now dead in identical situations, blown up by suicide bombers at public events. A third — Chandrika Kumaratunge — had narrowly missed death, losing one of her eyes in the process.

There were other signs of the peace initiative. Devendra had seen almost no checkpoints on the streets of Colombo during his drive to the club. He wondered how many more suicide bombers were entering the city after having travelled down the newly-opened Jaffna-Kandy highway.

"I heard you had been making inquiries about the Ministry's decision to withhold the Sarojini Skandarajah profile from the media," Jayavickrama finally said once he had finished filling his pipe and lighting it, "or rather, the Devini Sundaralingam profile, I should say."

Intelligence reports had indicated that a new grave, with the marker bearing the name of Devini Sundaralingam, had appeared in an LTTE cemetery in Kilinochchi. Interrogation of a prisoner had revealed the rumour that the body in the grave was that of Colonel Sundari — alias Sarojini Skandarajah, alias Jezina Fawaz — which had been handed over, via the Red Cross, to relatives in Batticaloa ten days after Operation *Sita*.

"Your inquiries are understandable," he continued, cutting off Devendra's protest. "The London surveillance was proof enough of the Tigers' connection to the ERA. Never mind whether it would have stood up in court or not, it would have been accepted by the media and therefore, the international community. It would have finished any standing the LTTE had overseas."

"Isn't that what we want, sir?"

"Yes and no. Sun Tzu said that one should always leave an enemy a way out."

"And the upcoming talks are the terras' way out?" Devendra asked bitterly.

"Of course. You must have seen the transcripts and the video of yesterday's press conference?"

Devendra nodded. He had seen them within hours of the end of the conference, and today it had hit the headlines.

"But why are we letting our guard down like this?" he asked. "No checkpoints in Colombo, freedom of movement between the Northern Province and the south. The terras *can't* be trusted. How many times must they spit in our faces, how many young men must we cremate before the lesson is learned? The Tigers are jus' buying time 'til they're ready to fight again."

There was silence for a minute as they walked past the goalposts.

"There has to be trust, Arjuna, however frightening it is," the minister said with a sigh. "Without trust, there is no future." He turned to look Devendra in the face. "What d'you think would have happened if we hadn't ordered this ceasefire, offered the option of talks?" Jayavickrama asked, turning to resume his walk, blowing out a plume of fragrant smoke. "We would have continued the military offensive, eventually brought the entire North and East under our control. Do you then think this government — and successive ones — would have the political will to deal with the Tamil issue, to prevent it smouldering on and breaking out into violence again? I think not. The JVP and the Buddhist priests in the bloody *Mahasanga* are already screaming blue murder, accusing us of betraying the Sinhalese people. *If* we succeed in taking over the whole North and East — an' that's still a big if — they'll never let us give the Tamils self-determination. No, negotiations have to be done now, when the Tigers are on their knees but still threatening enough to scare the shit out'f both the far right and the far left."

"Bullshit, sir," Devendra said calmly, and the minister raised an amused eyebrow. "Are you trying to tell me that all that long-term wisdom came from the PM?"

"Not quite," Jayavickrama said. He sighed. "India had a lot to do with us declaring a ceasefire and acceding to talks." He enjoyed the brigadier's puzzlement for a moment before continuing. "RAW had been monitoring radio transmissions from AC634, and they heard the codeword being transmitted hourly. They also heard the abort signal, and without knowing what it was, got a satellite fix on its source. Not an exact trace — OK? — but close enough to know that it came from south of Trinco. They knew that there was no way that the Tigers could have a powerful transmitter that close to the China Bay complex without having it detected. So they suspected it was someone other than the Tigers. Someone sanctioned by us. But the kicker was that soon after the plane was stormed and the hijackers' faces and stories spread all over the newspapers, a man claiming to be the father of the hijack leader surfaced in a Madras refugee camp. Gave an interview to an Indian reporter fellow that claimed his son was no terrorist, but working for the Sri Lankan government. It was lucky that RAW had somebody in that paper and the article was suppressed. The father was arrested immediately and paid off to stay silent."

"How had we missed the parents?" Devendra asked.

"Another cock-up at DFI. The families of the other five had been located and paid off, but this bugger — Balachandran — was supposed to be an orphan. His family was supposed to have been killed in the fighting, but apparently had fled to India in '83.

"Anyway," the minister continued, "the Indian government told us that if we did not declare a ceasefire, meet the Tiger conditions for talks, and begin negotiations, they would let the real story of the hijack leak. We knew it would be impossible for us to meet those conditions if we wanted to have any negotiating power at the talks, so we used the stuff we had on the Sundaralingam woman as a similar lever to what the Indians were using on us. Told the Tigers that the talks would have to be unconditional if they wanted their link to the ERA to be kept quiet."

"So both parties, basically, are being forced to the table," Devendra mused aloud. "But can they be forced to eat?"

"That remains to be seen."

"What I don't understand, sir, is what the Indians want out of all this. They have no love for the Tigers after the Rajiv Gandhi assassination, and have always been trying to get hold of the LTTE boss. So what has changed now?"

"My guess is, it is — as it has always been — the Tamil vote in south India. When things begin to look really bad for the Tigers, the Tamil Nadu population starts to kick up a fuss. But *you* tell *me*, Arjuna. *You're* the spymaster, not like me, a humble servant of the people." Grinning, Jayavickrama turned back to the clubhouse. "I hope you'll join me for a drink . . ." The minister paused and looked back at Devendra. "Ah'm told you and your boys are very good at finding just the right bits of evidence to convince our rather reluctant allies in the west."

Curious as to just what the older man was getting at, Devendra caught up with him and they crossed the rugby field once more.

After what seemed to be some moments of thought, Jayavickrama said, "You know, Arjuna, we have no idea of whether these peace talks will end satisfactorily. However much trust the PM is prepared to place publicly in the Tigers, there are some of us who must prepare for what might be the inevitable."

Devendra watched the minister out of the corner of his eye, but the man continued to puff contentedly at his pipe.

"If the PM were to concede too much to the Tigers in Thailand," Jayavickrama went on, "it might be necessary for new 'evidence' to be found of Tiger connections to international terror. The connection to Al Qaeda last year was very good, Arjuna, very good. Very convincing, too. A definite link to the drug trade might be what is needed next, such as in Columbia. The closer the connection to an area of American interest the better. Alternately, a link to a US-targeted terrorist group might also be useful. We already know that the Tigers used their shipping network to transport Al Qaeda weapons to the Muslim groups in the Philippines. The last reported instance was in early 2001, but if proof of *recent* activity were to somehow fall into American hands. . ."

EPILOGUE

"Look!" Daniel Devanayagam yelled, making everybody in the minivan jump. "A moose! A moose! There!" He was squirming against the restriction of his seatbelt, trying to turn his head through a hundred and eighty degrees to look over the seat back.

"*Where?*" everybody shouted back in unison, heads swivelling in all directions to scan the surrounding woodland and marsh.

"There, there!" Both Daniel and Suzie were bouncing excitedly.

"Behind us. Stop!"

John Kopleck pulled the minivan over to the side of Highway 60 and leaned out of the window, looking back along the road in the dimness of dusk.

"I think you're right, kid. Come on."

Switching off the engine, he got out, and the others all followed suite, the mothers sharply telling the children to stay on the soft shoulder. In the gloom on the far side of the highway, a massive shape could now be seen, cropping peacefully at the tall marsh reeds.

It was the Devanayagams' last ten days in Canada, and both Daniel and Suzie had conspired to get their respective parents to take them camping. So the Koplecks had flown down to Toronto and hired the minivan, for a week in the Algonquin Provincial Park and along the shores of Georgian Bay. Robin Devanayagam had frantically done a tour of his relatives homes in an effort to gather the necessary tents, sleeping bags, and other outdoor gear, and off they had gone, covering the three hundred kilometres north in half a day. Daniel had been thrilled at the prospect of all the bears and wolves he was going to see and take photographs of, but the four days in the park had been disappointingly empty of interesting wildlife. Suzie had told Daniel all about the moose she had once seen on a previous trip, but he wasn't interested at first. He wanted to see something *dangerous*. An oversized deer couldn't compare to a real live bear, not to a boy from a country where elephants were commonplace. But after days of seeing nothing more interesting than geese and a loon that Suzie's mother had been very excited about, Daniel was willing to settle even for a moose.

With the mothers keeping a tight hold on Daniel and Suzie, and with John and Robin leading the way, they quickly crossed the highway. The moose, an eight hundred-pound bull, regarded the intruders thoughtfully for a few moments, then continued its munching. Everybody goggled at the huge antlers now a suddenly unnerving ten metres away, and talked in whispers.

After a few minutes, as the dusk deepened, Daniel tugged at his father's arm and asked him whether it would be safe to take a picture. Would the moose run away, or worse, attack? Robin Devanayagam nodded his approval, and the boy raised his camera and peered through the viewfinder. He could barely make out the silhouette of the animal, and he fretted that he wouldn't have any proof to show off back in Sri Lanka.

He pressed the button and the flash went off, turning everything silver-black for a blinding instant. The moose looked up for a moment, then began to drift off, apparently offended by the rudeness of these visitors. The next instant the bull jolted into startled motion as a scream split the evening.

As the animal crashed off into the brush, everybody stared at Suzie who had dropped to her knees, still screaming, her eyes squeezed shut and her hands clamped over her ears. Her parents, horrified, tried to calm her while the Devanayagams stood by in helpless shock. Daniel hugged his father's leg. He had never seen Suzie act like this. It took a minute or two, but he finally made out what she was screaming.

"*Don't shoot me! Don't shoot me! Don't shoot me!*"

It was a month and a half since the soldiers' flash-bangs had announced the storming of the plane.

❊

Two months after landing in Canada, Vijitha Dhampahana finally got steady employment in a motorcycle repair centre, working illegally for what seemed to him good money. The repair centre's owner had recognized the immigrant's talent with two-stroke engines, and had been only too happy to hire it on the cheap. He kept Vijitha in the back, beyond the curious eyes of the Immigrant Task Force. A hard worker now that he was at last in the land of his dreams, Vijitha began to save what money he could spare after he had paid the monthly instalment to the human traffickers. There wasn't much left when he had paid the rent for his flat — which had an attached bathroom and toilet — and bought his food, but he knew that soon he would have enough to plan his future. He never mentioned his experiences during the hijack, but carefully noted down all the recurring nightmares. He had heard that psychological trauma might be a useful thing if the law ever caught up with him and he was threatened with deportation.

❊

Two months after the crash of Donald Fenster's jet, the Australian and Canadian authorities confirmed that the aircraft had been brought down by an explosive device in the cabin, suspected to have been in a piece of hand luggage.

A week later, Inspector Ian McEdwards, now attached to the Toronto Combined Forces Special Enforcement Unit, shot a Tamil drug dealer dead during a stakeout. While both he and his partner claimed that they had suspected the dead man to be armed, no weapon was found. McEdwards was spared prosecution, but was sent on enforced leave. A psychological evaluation is pending.

❊

Colin Peters would spend the six months following the hijack studying his beloved whales at the mouth of Quebec's St Lawrence River. He used a converted shrimp boat as a research vessel for his daily and nightly observations of the huge mammals, and its captain got used to the constant smell of whisky on Peters' breath. While the captain knew that the quiet marine biologist had been a hostage on flight AC634 — now synonymous with Canada's growing involvement in anti-terror operations — in all their long hours together Peters never once mentioned the hijack.

*

Air Canada was very considerate to Jennifer Jensen. The physiotherapy and skin grafts to her leg would take months, and they also recommended she take whatever psychiatric therapy she needed. When she asked for additional leave that too was granted. They understood when she said she didn't think she could fly anymore. She was promoted and given a suitable slot in the ground operations of the airline.

While cosmetic surgery would eventually remove almost all of the scars on her body, the string of psychiatrists she went to couldn't quite get rid of the nightmares. They recommended a loving environment, somebody that Jen-Jen could talk to at night when the flash-bangs lit up her bedroom and she saw the black-clad men coming in through the smoke. But there was no one she could really talk to.

Maybe if Tim had stayed on, Jen-Jen sometimes thought idly. But though Tim Ferguson had returned to Canada on furlough two weeks after the hijack, things hadn't really worked out between them. Accustomed to their intensive, passionate, weekend affairs, they hadn't been able to get into the routine of a regular relationship. A month later he had gone back to his work in Sri Lanka.

An insomniac, she now became a workaholic, throwing herself into her work, trying to fill her hours with things to do.

*

Captain Johnny Burnett continued to fly for Air Canada, as did AC634's co-pilot, Mike Harrap; both men regularly flying into Sri Lanka. They also are regularly invited by police, military, and aviation organizations, both in Canada and the United States, to give lectures on aircraft security and hijack situations.

*

Two months after Operation *Rama*, Sergeant Jan Conway broke his pelvis rappelling from a helicopter during a building assault exercise in Ottawa. Taking early retirement from the Canadian Forces he joined a French private military company training police and military hostage-rescue teams in the Middle East.

*

Once his leave was over, Dayan Premasiri returned to Bravo Squadron of 1/SF for a month before being posted to the LRRP operations in the Eastern Province. Soon after Operations *Rama* and *Sita*, the whole Long-Range Reconnaissance Patrol operation had been restructured, the Sri Lanka Army taking over total control of it. The Tamil patrols were disbanded and reorganized into special teams run by Military Intelligence while the Malays and Moors continued to operate as recce patrols, commanded by Special Forces and Commando NCOs. LRRP operations were significantly increased following the declaration of the ceasefire.

Dayan and an SF officer were given the job of forming a special training cadre that would instruct the Muslim auxiliaries in sniping, demolitions, and other forms of guerrilla warfare.

Eric Christofelsz, when he got out of hospital, rejoined Delta Group for the remainder of their tour as the HR group in Colombo. Though he was granted a few days leave to return to his family, he never managed to convince his father to go out for a beer.

* * *

Deputy Inspector General Jaliya de Silva fumed as he sat next to his driver. While he had retained the official car and driver, the former DFI director general's bodyguard complement had been cut down to almost nothing. Now he had to be content with a couple of uniformed policemen outside his garden gate in addition to the driver. Didn't they know he was a marked man, that he was high on the terras' hit list? No, the bastards didn't give a fuck. They were too busy kissing that Tamil motherfucker's arse.

De Silva had accepted his posting to the Eastern Province with the promise to himself that he would bide his time. He wasn't foolish enough to voice objections to the posting. That would have done him no good. Too many big mouths had disappeared too easily for him to underestimate the government's will to keep the hijack under wraps. Besides, it was just like the government to allow him to be extradited to Canada to appease the world in the event that the dirty secret became public. No, de Silva was willing to wait. He would soon be in the East, and there were still many people out there who would remain loyal to him. He just needed to lie low for a while, gather his resources. Then they would know just what they were dealing with.

As he always did, the driver headed inland from de Silva's Bambalapitiya residence and turned onto the Galle Road, pulling up in front of the dingy Hotel Al Muzammil. Despite the name, the Hotel Al Muzammil, like many of its kind in Sri Lanka, wasn't a hotel but a cheap eating house.

"Cigarettes, sir?"

"Yah, one packet."

It was a regular feature of their trips together that the driver would always stop at the top of the Bambalapitiya street de Silva lived down and pop out quickly to buy the boss his usual Benson & Hedges.

It was now two months since the hijack had ended, and this was de Silva's last week in Colombo. He glowered at the evening traffic that was flowing past, and had no illusions that the farewell

party being thrown for him at the Otters Aquatic Club by some
of his friends and colleagues would improve his mood.

A movement at the driver's window made de Silva look up,
expecting a beggar. Instead, he saw a distorted image of himself
reflected in the black visor of the motorcycle helmet. The helmet
was on the head of the bike's pillion rider, his feet, like those of
the rider, braced on the road where the bike had stopped next to
the Mazda.

De Silva was practically looking down the barrel of the
Stechkin automatic pistol as the first two rounds punched through
the glass and hit him in the chest. The gunman then switched the
Russian 9-mm pistol to its unique full-auto capability and, steadying
the weapon, put the remaining eighteen rounds into de Silva's
head and chest in a one and a half-second burst.

The motorcycle had disappeared into the traffic before de
Silva's stunned driver could even get out of the restaurant.

*

That same night, a small office block on Duplication Road in
Colombo's Colpetty area was burned practically to the ground,
the fire spreading incredibly fast. A delay in the Air Force-controlled
fire brigade's arrival meant that there was very little the fire fighters
could do to save the building. Later investigation revealed that the
fire seemed to have originated in the offices of a law firm on the
ground floor; a firm which had, as one of its clients, the former
director general of the DFI. Investigations also showed that a
wall safe containing — according to the firm's senior partner —
several wills and testaments had been opened prior to the fire.
Needless to say, the contents of the safe were now a pile of
ashes, and arson was obvious.

In the chaos that followed the fire, it was several days before
de Silva's lawyer remembered the duplicate set of envelopes his
client had given him. De Silva had warned him that the contents

of the envelopes were of the utmost importance, and so the lawyer had kept the duplicate set at his alarm-protected home in the suburb of Nugegoda.

Although the media was quoting police sources as accusing the LTTE of the assassination of DIG Jaliya de Silva, the lawyer didn't know if the killers of the former DFI director general were in fact Tigers or not, and he didn't really care; he had very specific instructions. In his study, he took the three envelopes out of the safe — this one hidden behind a sliding bookshelf — and looked at the addresses. The envelopes were A4-sized and thickly padded. One was addressed to the editor of the local *Sunday Leader* newspaper, while another was addressed to *CNN*'s Colombo correspondent. The third was addressed to the Canadian ambassador.

Part of the instructions the lawyer had received from de Silva were that in the event of the man's untimely death, the envelopes were to be sent to the addresses. The lawyer stared at the envelopes for a full five minutes, as if trying to make up his mind, then ripped open the first envelope. It contained a sheaf of papers — some were computer printouts, and others photocopies of documents — and an audio cassette. Locking his study door, the lawyer put the cassette into a Walkman and put on the earphones. Pressing the 'play' button, he carefully read through the papers as he listened. When he was finished, he opened the other envelopes and removed identical papers and cassettes; the papers went into his shredder, along with the envelopes. The shredded strips of paper were then put in a cardboard carton, and the cassettes were dismantled and the magnetic tape spooled out before also going into the carton.

The lawyer then took the carton out to the rubbish heap at the end of the garden where the dead leaves and weeds were burned once a week. Taking a bottle of kerosene with him, de Silva's lawyer doused the carton and set it alight. He then stood and watched till the contents of the three envelopes had been destroyed.

*   *   *

The helicopters were black silhouettes in the thermal imager's viewfinder, their engines glowing white-hot, the sky a grainy grey behind them, lit up by the night lights of Bangkok. The American in the top floor penthouse suite of the Laksi Plaza didn't have to be told they were Royal Thai Air Force. The menacing shape of the Cobra gunship that trailed the two Bell 412 transports was evidence enough even if he hadn't been in this same position the previous day. He had been on the same terrace when the Boeing 767 provided by the government of Norway had landed. The American hadn't seen the delegation as they transferred quickly to the helicopters. The terminal buildings of the airport on the far side of Vipavadi Road had blocked his view, and that was one of the reasons why the security wasn't as tight at the Laksi Plaza as it was in buildings with a direct view of the airport. But now, as then, the American didn't need to see the faces. He knew the Leader would be there.

"They're landing," the American said, not turning away from the scope as the two Hueys vanished behind the airport buildings, leaving the Cobra to circle like a nervous hawk.

Behind the American and beyond the open terrace windows, a young Indian woman sat before a low coffee table, an open briefcase facing her. The case was actually a disguise for the powerful burst-transmission satlink radio. She now began to type a short one-line message on the integral keypad.

The burst transmission bounced off a military communications satellite and down to the USS *Peleliu* in the Andaman Sea, two hundred kilometres off Ranong on Thailand's west coast. The forty thousand-ton *Tarawa*-class amphibious warfare ship was the floating headquarters for this mission, and the codeword was instantly relayed to the helicopters.

Fifty kilometres south of Bangkok and five hundred and fifty kilometres northeast of the *Peleliu*, the four choppers were already airborne, skimming the waters of the Gulf of Thailand as they approached the city. There were four aircraft — two UH-60 Night Hawk transports escorted by two MH-5 scouts — and they were painted overall in flat black. None of them had any markings or navigation lights on. Jumping off from the Royal Thai Navy Air Base at U-Tapao, down the coast from Bangkok, the choppers had taken off as soon as word was received that the delegation had left the heavily guarded hotel north of the city.

The American pilot of the lead Night Hawk acknowledged the signal from the *Peleliu* and glanced over his shoulder into the troop compartment. A thumbs-up from the commander of the Black Cats told him that he had been listening in on the net.

"Seven minutes," the pilot said.

"Roger," the Indian captain replied.

It was the same throughout the rest of the choppers: while the aircrews were American — from the 1st Special Operations Squadron — the troops that would do the actual snatch were all Indians of 52 Special Action Group. Not that anyone could have told them apart; the aircrews had their faces covered by NVGs and the Black Cats had any exposed skin streaked with green and black cam cream.

They could see the lights of Bangkok ahead, and the scout choppers spread out slightly and began to gain altitude. The delegation would be well on its way by now, hurrying in convoy down the expressway that would take them into the city and towards the Hilton where the talks were scheduled to begin tomorrow morning.

After the snatch, the choppers would head west, crossing low over the Malaccan Peninsula. They would cut through Burma, between Palauk and the mountain of Myinmoletkat, trusting in surprise to get through before the communists could scramble any interceptors. They would rendezvous with the *Peleliu*, now steaming north at flank speed, and head for the Andaman Islands

The prisoners would then be handed over to the Indians for transport on to the subcontinent.

"Five minutes. . ."

The Black Cat captain spoke into his own lip mike. "Red One to all teams, stand by, stand by!"

AUTHOR'S NOTE

In concluding this tale, I would like to state that what you have just read is very obviously a work of fiction, and is not intended to speculate on clandestine operations that may or may not have been conducted by the Sri Lankan government or the LTTE.

Certain events, such as the September 11th tragedy and the LTTE press conference have been well documented, but again, they have been adapted by me to fit the plot. The characters as well as the events aboard American Airlines Flight 11 are fictitious and should not be taken as a narration of actual events. In fact, except for historical and other documented figures, all the characters are works of my imagination and do not represent anyone living or dead.

While the battle scenes in chapters 5 and 9, are loosely based, respectively, on the battles for Hamburger Hill and the Ia Drang Valley during the Vietnam War, similar battles have been fought between the Sri Lankan security forces and the LTTE for over twenty years.

It is possible that bodies such as the Joint Intelligence Committee and the Cabinet Crisis Group do exist within the Sri Lankan military/governmental framework, but their actual makeup may vary widely from what I have depicted.

The descriptions and layout of the Madras airport and the Canadian embassy are imaginary, and in the former instance is a generic amalgamation of several international airports.

I must also point out that this story is not intended to incite violence, racial or otherwise, nor is it a recommendation that any of the events described should be carried out. The opinions of the characters, however biased or racist they may be, remain just that.

It might seem to the reader that I have sometimes been generic in my descriptions of certain groups, labelling them 'Tamils' or 'Sinhalese', and this is because the groups are, in my opinion, best described as such. It is not meant to be a racist slur on any particular community.

Finally, I would like to mention a few people who have helped during the writing of this story, and without whom it would have been a lot harder and probably less fun: Barbara Roth, for her help with civilian air operations and terminology; Arjuna Gunawardene, for help with the structure and operations of the Black Tigers and other LTTE field units; Heinz Tiedemann, who was kind enough to read the manuscript and make several helpful comments; my wife, Antje, my most ardent fan and virulent critic, without whom this book might not have happened. And finally, my publishers, Sam Perera and Ameena Hussein, for all their advice and help in the sometimes painful editing process.

David Blacker,
Dehiwela, October 2005.

GLOSSARY

AGS-17	:	Soviet 30-mm crew-served automatic grenade launcher, often mounted on helicopters, armoured vehicles, and light naval craft.
AK-47	:	Kalashnikov AK-47. Soviet 7.62-mm assault rifle.
AKSU-74	:	Kalashnikov AKSU-74. Soviet 5.45-mm carbine.
AWACS	:	Airborne Warning and Command System.
Ayubowan	:	Sinhalese greeting, also used in farewell.
Bangalore torpedo	:	Long tubular explosive charge used to blow paths through barbed wire defenses.
CAP	:	Combat air patrol.
CASEVAC	:	Casualty evacuation.
CCG	:	Cabinet Crisis Group. Sri Lankan governmental crisis management team similar to the British Cabinet Office Briefing Room (COBRA).
CCIS	:	Canadian Criminal Intelligence Service. Federal police unit.
CFSEU	:	Combined Forces Special Enforcement Unit. Canadian police organized crime squad.
CLAYMORE	:	Type of directional antipersonnel mine that fires hundreds of steel pellets.
CO	:	Commanding officer, usually of a battalion or larger-sized unit.

COLT COMMANDO	:	Civilian version of the US 5.56-mm M-4 carbine, which in turn is a shortened M-16A1 automatic rifle.
CP	:	Command post.
CR	:	Commando Regiment. Sri Lanka Army special operations unit.
CSIS	:	Canadian Security Intelligence Service. Civilian intelligence-gathering organization.
CTR	:	Close target reconnaissance.
CVR	:	Cockpit voice recorder.
DA	:	Direct action.
DFI	:	Directorate of Foreign Intelligence. Sri Lankan organization responsible for intelligence gathering. Administratively subordinate to the police.
DII	:	Directorate of Internal Intelligence. Sri Lankan counterintelligence organization. Administratively subordinate to the police.
DMI	:	Directorate of Military Intelligence. The administrative headquarters that controls the Sri Lanka Army Military Intelligence Corps.
DPG	:	Diplomatic Protection Group. Police unit providing bodyguard services to Canadian diplomats.
DPM	:	Disruptive pattern material. British camouflage fatigues.
ERA	:	Eelam Republican Army. Sri Lankan Tamil terrorist splinter group.
ERV	:	Emergency rendezvous.

FAA	:	Federal Aviation Authority. US government agency responsible for civil aviation.
FOB	:	Forward operating base.
G-3SG/1	:	Heckler & Koch G-3SG/1. German 7.62-mm automatic sniping rifle.
GIGN	:	*Groupement d'Intervention de la Gendarmerie Nationale.* French national police anti-terrorism unit.
GLOCK	:	Austrian firearms company, but usually refers to the Glock 17, a 9-mm semi-automatic pistol.
GMT	:	Greenwich Mean Time, also known as Universal Calculated Time.
GPMG	:	General-purpose machine-gun.
GSG9	:	*Grenschutzgruppe 9.* Anti-terrorism unit of the German federal border guards.
GW	:	Gemunu Watch. Sri Lanka Army infantry regiment.
HE	:	High explosive.
HI-POWER	:	Fabrique Nationale Herstal Browning High Power. A Belgian 9-mm semi-automatic pistol
HQI	:	Headquarters inspector. Usually the second-in-command of a police station.
HR	:	Hostage rescue.
HUEY	:	Bell UH-1 series of utility helicopters. Derived from the original US Army 'HU' designation.
2/ic	:	Second-in-command

IPKF	:	Indian Peace-Keeping Force. Combined-arms corps sent to north-eastern Sri Lanka in 1987, following the Indo-Lanka Accord.
ISI	:	Inter-Services Intelligence. Pakistani military intelligence unit.
ITF	:	Immigration Task Force. Canadian federal police unit.
IGP	:	Inspector General of Police.
JIC	:	Joint Intelligence Committee. Sri Lankan military intelligence coordinating committee.
JTF2	:	Joint Task Force 2. Canadian Forces special operations unit.
JOC	:	Joint Operations Command. Sri Lankan security forces HQ.
JVP	:	*Janatha Vimukthi Peramuna* (People's Liberation Front). Ultra-nationalist left-wing Sri Lankan Sinhalese terrorist group that re-entered mainstream politics in the mid-1990s.
KUKRI	:	Traditional utility knife of the Himalayan tribes, now a symbol of the Ghurkhas.
KURZ	:	German for 'short'. See also MP-5.
L-96	:	British bolt action sniping rifle. The Accuracy International L-96AWP is the 7.62-mm special forces model; the L-96AWS is of the same calibre, but is a suppressed weapon; and the L-96SM comes in 8.6-mm Lapua Magnum.
LOADY	:	The person in charge of the cargo pallettes on board a cargo aircraft. Usually a senior Air Force NCO or WO.

LP	:	Listening post.
LRRP	:	Long-range reconnaissance patrol.
LTTE	:	Liberation Tigers of Tamil Eelam. Sri Lankan Tamil terrorist group.
M-16A1	:	US 5.56-mm automatic rifle.
M-72A2	:	US 66-mm shoulder-fired disposable rocket launcher, also known as a LAW or light anti-tank weapon.
MAHASANGA	:	Ruling council of Sri Lankan Buddhist priests.
MAKAROV	:	Soviet 9-mm semi-automatic pistol, generally thought to be a copy of the German Walther PPK.
MICRO-UZI	:	Smaller version of the Israeli 9-mm Uzi submachine-gun.
MLI	:	Maharatta Light Infantry. Indian Army infantry regiment.
MOSSBERG 500 ATP8	:	US 12-bore pump-action shotgun.
MP-5	:	Heckler & Koch MP-5. German 9-mm submachine-gun. While the MP-5A3 is the most widely used version, the shortned MP-5K or Kurz is also popular.
MSG-90	:	Heckler & Koch MSG-90. Military version of the German 7.62-mm PSG-1 semi-automatic sniping rifle.
NARA	:	National Aquatic Research Association. Sri Lankan marine conservation organization.

NIB	:	National Intelligence Bureau. Sri Lankan civilian intelligence organization, placed under the police force for administrative purposes. Later replaced by the DFI and the DII.
NSA	:	National Security Agency. US electronic intelligence-gathering organization.
NVGs	:	Night-vision goggles.
OC	:	Officer commanding, usually of a unit or detachment smaller than a battalion.
OIC	:	Officer-in-charge, usually a police designation, and often referring to the senior officer of a police station.
PMSD	:	Prime Ministerial Security Division. Sri Lankan police unit tasked with protecting the prime minister.
PNV	:	Passive night vision.
POL SAMBOL	:	Relish made of coconut and chillies.
PSD	:	Presidential Security Division. Sri Lankan police unit tasked with protecting the president.
PTI	:	Physical training instructor.
RAW	:	Research and Analysis Wing. Indian civilian intelligence organization.
RCMP	:	Royal Canadian Mounted Police. Canadian federal police force.
2REP	:	*2ème Régiment Etranger de Parachutistes.* The 2nd Parachute Regiment of the French Foreign Legion
RIB	:	Rigid inflatable boat.

RPG-7	:	Soviet 40-mm shoulder-fired rocket launcher that fires a projectile with a 120-mm warhead.
RSF	:	Reserve Strike Force. Sri Lanka Army division-sized combined arms force.
RSM	:	Regimental sergeant major. The ranking non-commissioned or warrant officer within a battalion or regiment, usually a warrant officer first class.
RTU	:	Return to unit.
RV	:	Rendezvous.
S-3	:	Usually the intelligence officer of a battalion or brigade, but also refers to his staff.
SAARC	:	South Asian Association for Regional Cooperation.
SAG	:	Special Action Group. Indian Army special operations unit, a part of the National Security Guard (NSG).
SAS	:	22nd Special Air Service Regiment. British Army special operations unit.
SEALs	:	BUD/SEAL (Basic Underwater Demolition/Sea Air Land) teams, are US Navy special operations units.
SF	:	Special Forces. Sri Lanka Army special operations unit.
SIB	:	Special Investigation Branch. Plainclothes unit within the Sri Lanka Army Corps of Military Police that investigates crimes committed by soldiers, as well as hunting down deserters.

SiG	:	Usually refers to the range of compact 9-mm semi-automatic pistols manufactured by the Swiss company SiG-Sauer.
SIGINT	:	Signal intelligence.
SLLI	:	Sri Lanka Light Infantry. Sri Lanka Army infantry regiment.
SPG	:	Special Protection Group. Canadian federal police unit tasked with protecting cabinet ministers and other high-ranking members of the government.
SPIE	:	Special Procedures, Insertion/Extraction.
SR	:	Singha Rifles. Sri Lanka Army infantry regiment.
SSG	:	Special Service Group. Pakistani Army special operations unit.
SSM	:	Squadron sergeant major. The ranking non-commissioned or warrant officer within an Army squadron, and like a company sergeant major, is usually a warrant officer second class.
STABO	:	Stabilized, Tactical, Airborne Body Operations.
STECHKIN	:	Soviet 9-mm machine-pistol.
STF	:	Special Task Force. Sri Lankan police paramilitary special operations unit.
STRING HOPPERS	:	Small steamed noodle cake made of rice flour.
SWAT	:	Special Weapons and Tactics.
T-56	:	Chinese-made version of the 7.62-mm AK-47 assault rifle.